SHANNON'S CHOICE

SHANNON'S CHOICE

·Root of All Evil
·Mark of Murder
·The Death-Bringers
·Coffin Corner

by Dell Shannon

William Morrow and Company
New York, New York

CONTENTS

SHANNON'S CHOICE

ROOT OF ALL EVIL

How pleasant it is to have money,
    heigh-ho!
How pleasant it is to have money.

—Arthur Hugh Clough, *Dipsychus*

ONE

Master John Luis Mendoza and Miss Teresa Ann Mendoza yelled. Collectively and loudly they howled into the night, and their joint volume was astonishing.

After a long moment, Alison sat up and said sleepily, "Damn." She slid her legs over the side of the bed and groped for her slippers. Mendoza mumbled something indistinctly profane.

"All right, I'm *coming*," said Alison crossly, fumbling for her robe.

"—Senseless," said Mendoza.

The collective howls redoubled from the next room. "I'm beginning to think you're right," said Alison, yawning. She felt her way over to the door and put on the hall light. He heard her soothing voice reassuring the twins.

He shut his eyes again and tried to close his ears, but it was hopeless. After three minutes he got up, switched on the bedside lamp, put on his robe, and joined Alison. "It is simply not common sense," he said. "At this age, they don't know or care who comes running when they yell. We've got enough money, God knows, to hire a nursemaid. Let *her* stay up all night—in the back bedroom. With the door shut." He took Miss Teresa Ann from Alison and looked down at her screwed-up small face without, at the moment, much affection. Miss Teresa Ann had a good deal of curly black hair and a pair of large brown eyes framed in long black lashes, but right now the eyes were squeezed tight shut, the rosebud mouth was open, and she was emitting regular bellows. Resignedly Mendoza walked up and down joggling her.

"Ridiculous," he said. "If anybody had told me a couple of years ago I'd be walking the floor with a baby at 2:30 A.M. just like any ordinary domesticated male—!"

Alison passed him, going the opposite direction, joggling Master John Luis. "Not exactly your forte," she agreed with somewhat malicious amusement.

"And all so unnecessary! But no, you remember all those tear-jerking Victorian novels about the poor little rich child whose mama and daddy left her to the servants— *Caray*, how can one five-month-old infant make such a racket? Do they *all* do this?"

"Most of them," said Alison. They had to raise their voices over the formidable noise. She sat down in the nursery chair and joggled Master John automatically, shutting her eyes. "I'm beginning to think you have something, Luis."

"Of course I've got something. My God, I can sympathize with Art now —'like a time-bomb,' he said. How right he was. How the hell do people stand it who can't afford—"

"Surprising what you can get used to," said Alison through a yawn, joggling Master John grimly.

"Well, I'm too old to change my habits," said Mendoza. "I'm used to sleeping at night. I've got a job to do all day. Right now, specifically, this burglar-rapist." He peered down at Miss Teresa's red face. "Though from one point of view, I can sympathize with him—slaughtering females." He yawned too. "*Te estás engañando a ti misma*—you're just fooling yourself. At five months, they don't know whether it's Mama or a nice kind hired nurse. Later on you can be the loving parent. When they've learned to sleep at night."

"Think I agree with you," said Alison, nodding sleepily over the yelling Master John. "But the back bedroom isn't decorated for a nursery."

"*¡Eso basta!*" said Mendoza. "So, get the painters back—put up the pretty circus animals on the walls! And make this a nice neutral spare room. But the first thing to do is to acquire the nursemaid, *¿es verdad?*" He joggled Miss Teresa violently.

"Yes," said Alison. "You're perfectly right. I'll go looking tomorrow, if I've got the strength."

"Today. It's nearly three o'clock. Where the hell do *they* get the strength?"

"Babies," said Alison sleepily, "have a lot of energy. If they're healthy babies."

"These two must be the damnedest healthiest babies in Los Angeles County," said Mendoza bitterly. "If anybody had told me I'd be— Do you think it'd be any good singing lullabies?"

"We've tried that," Alison reminded him. "They don't seem to be very musical— I think I sing reasonably well, but it just makes them yell harder. Maybe I don't know the right lullabies." She shifted Master John to the opposite arm.

"There must be hundreds of nice experienced nursemaids available."

"Well, I couldn't say. I'll go and look."

"Today," said Mendoza. "This is undermining my morale, *cara*. I used to think I was a fairly tough fellow, when I was getting eight hours of sleep every night. But with these two time-bombs going off regular at 2:30 A.M., I'm feeling my age."

"I will," said Alison meekly. "I promise. Of course we don't want just anybody, but a good employment agency ought to—"

"I'll tell you one thing," said Mendoza. "It's very damned lucky we haven't any near neighbors, or they'd be complaining to the police. A nice thing, veteran officer like me getting reported for disturbing the peace." Miss Teresa let out a particularly rousing bellow, and he looked at her small person even more bitterly. "I amend the statement," he said. "The damnedest healthiest babies in the state of California!"

As usual, the twins drifted off into beautiful quiet slumber at 5 A.M. Mendoza was prodded awake by a sleepy and sympathetic Alison at eight o'clock; by the time he'd shaved and dressed and had two cups of coffee he felt slightly more human.

"You go and look for that nursemaid," he admonished her.

"I said I promised. I back down," said Alison. "You're quite right, it's senseless when we can afford to pay somebody else."

When he came into the office at a quarter to nine, Hackett surveyed him and grinned. "I told you so, didn't I? You live through it, but you wonder how." He spoke from the mature viewpoint of a parent whose offspring had achieved its first birthday and was creating different kinds of disturbances than sleepless nights.

Mendoza sat down at his desk. "You needn't sound so damn smug. I've got Alison to back down—she's going to hire a nurse. Senseless damn thing, these sentimental notions— After all, as I pointed out, what about me? Valuable public servant, nerves all shot to hell. And why in God's name I ever got involved in all these domesticities in the first place— If anybody had told me a few years ago I'd be—"

Hackett laughed. "We mostly get caught up with sooner or later. . . . We've got a possible ident on that Garey Street corpse. Fellow called in just a few minutes ago—he's coming down. One James Ellis, sounds very ordinary and level."

"Oh? That'd be a step forward."

"I thought you could see him. I want to go over what we've got on this rapist with Palliser."

"All right," said Mendoza, yawning. The rapist was being a tough one; that kind of thing always was. The burglar-killer had, so far as they knew now, entered seven houses—very crudely, in broad daylight—and finding women at home, had assaulted four (raping two of them), and in the course of assault killed the other three, burglarizing five of the houses afterward. The four survivors had been seriously beaten and mauled, but had been able to give the police a good description: it added up to the same man, but that didn't help much in pointing out the right fellow. A Negro, said the survivors, medium dark, a big fellow over six feet and broad, with a pock-marked complexion. They all said, shabby work clothes, dark pants, a tan shirt; one woman said, a tan billed cap. One of those women and two of the neighbors of others had seen him get away, and said he was driving a battered, middle-aged, light-blue pickup truck, a Ford or Chevy. The fourth woman, one of those he'd raped, was under psychiatric treatment and not very coherent or helpful.

And that might sound as if they had quite a lot on him; but it wasn't too much, actually. Los Angeles County had a very large Negro population; a certain proportion of it, of course—larger than you might expect—was made up of professional people, educated people, a good many of whom had very respectable incomes and lived in upper-class residential areas. But there was a larger proportion left over. A lot of men both white and black wore tan shirts and dark pants. And there were a lot of middle-aged, light-blue pickup trucks around.

Right now they were going through the list, gleaned from the D.M.V. records in Sacramento, of all such trucks registered in L.A. County. No guarantee that the right one was on the list, no guarantee that the right one was registered in L.A. County. But it was quite a list and was taking time and manpower to go through. If it didn't turn up anything interesting, then they'd ask Sacramento for wider coverage and start over again. Meanwhile hoping that Lover Boy wouldn't get the urge again before they got a line on him.

That was the kind very tough to crack.

Mendoza yawned and thought about the Garey Street corpse. He was interested in the Garey Street corpse because it looked like an offbeat sort of thing.

It had turned up on Monday morning; this was Wednesday. A very shocked and upset Father Michael Aloysius O'Callaghan had reported that it had been found by some kids at the far end of the playground of a big parochial school. A homicide crew had gone down to look at it, and at the first casual glance it had looked like a fairly run-of-the-mill thing. The body of a young woman, between, say, twenty and twenty-four, a middling good-looking young woman when she'd been alive, blonde; no handbag, no observable exterior injuries, and no clues on the scene at all.

Hackett had said then, grimly, "Another dope party, probably. Or third-rail stuff. Girl passes out on them and they ditch the body the handiest place." Mendoza had agreed. That wasn't the classiest section of town, Garey Street. That kind of thing had happened before: a party of young people experimenting with heroin, or homemade liquor, one of them getting a little too much, the others dumping the corpse in a panic.

The only reservation in his mind was because of the place she was dumped. The parochial school was a large one and, like the public schools, had a twenty-five-foot-high chain-link fence around its playground. The several gates were, of course, locked overnight. It wouldn't have been the easiest job in the world to hoist a body over that fence; and there were all sorts of other places where the body could have been abandoned without any trouble at all: dark alleys, side streets, empty lots.

Still, it had looked fairly run-of-the-mill, until Dr. Bainbridge sent up the autopsy report. The middling good-looking young blonde hadn't died of an overdose of heroin or straight alcohol. She had died from an overdose of codeine; and Bainbridge had pinpointed it as a rather common opiate prescription, even named the firm which manufactured it.

Which aroused Mendoza's curiosity in the blonde. A lot of people committed suicide by taking sleeping-tablets, but suicides didn't confuse things by removing their bodies to unexpected places. This had been, in all probability, a deliberately planned murder; and contrary to all the fiction, a big-city homicide bureau didn't run into that sort of thing very often.

"This Ellis seem very positive?" he asked Hackett now.

"Kind of cautious," said Hackett. "Said when he and his wife saw the cut in the paper this morning they both thought it could be—but of course a corpse doesn't always look very much the way it did alive. They were coming right down." He looked at his watch. "I've got a date with Palliser, see you later." He went out, and a minute later Sergeant Lake put his head in the door and said a Mr. and Mrs. Ellis were here.

James Ellis was a stocky, short man in the fifties, very neatly and conventionally dressed: thinning gray hair, honest blue eyes, a square jaw. Mrs. Ellis was his counterpart: a plain middle-aged woman, just now look-

ing distressed but also very conventional, obviously in her best clothes—
printed silk dress, navy-blue coat and hat. Ellis was a bank teller: a very
respectable fellow.

He was now sitting in Mendoza's office, still looking a bit pale and
shaken even twenty minutes after his visit to the morgue, and taking long
breaths, mopping his forehead agitatedly.

"Just a terrible thing," he said. "A terrible tragedy. Poor little Val."

Mrs. Ellis was crying gently. "We did try to help, Jamie, you know that.
I'll never believe she was really *bad*. It was just it all came at a bad time
for her—she couldn't— Only twenty-three, it doesn't seem hardly fair. Poor
child."

"Valerie Ellis," Mendoza prompted gently. "What can you tell me
about her, Mr. Ellis? She was your niece, you said."

"Yes, sir, that's right. I just can't figure who'd have done such an awful
thing to her. But I've got to say we didn't know just so much about—well,
how she was living, who she went around with—lately. Now, Mabel, don't
you carry on. You know we *tried*. But she—" He mopped his forehead
again, looked at Mendoza earnestly. "It was like she turned against everybody she knew, when it happened, see. Of course we told her right off,
come and live with us—only relations left, and she was only nineteen then
—and our own two both off and married, you see. It wasn't right, a young
girl like that on her own. But she wouldn't. I'm bound to say she talked
kind of wild—"

"Oh, but, Jamie, she wouldn't have done anything wrong! Fred's girl—"

"Well, I dunno," said Ellis slowly. "Kids that age, they go off the rails
sometimes, get into bad company. It was a damn shame, but in a kind of
way all Fred's own fault. I told him often enough—"

"Mr. Ellis. If you'd just give me what information you have, in order? I
realize you're upset, but—"

"Oh, sure—sure. I'm sorry, sir, I see you don't know what I'm talking
about." Ellis tucked his crumpled handkerchief away, brought out a second immaculate folded one, and blew his nose. "Damn shame," he said.
"Little Val. She was an awful cute youngster . . . I dunno whether you'll
be interested in all this, Lieutenant, you just say if you're not. First off, I
guess you want to know where she was living. Far as we know, up to last
week anyway, it was a place on Mariposa Street in Hollywood." He added
the address. "We'd offered to take her in, way I say, and maybe we
should've checked up on her more—her only relatives, and she was so
young. But it was—"

"We *should* have," said his wife. "Just because she was maybe a little bit wild, all the more reason—" She wept gently.

"Well, maybe so, but it was—difficult," said Ellis. "I'll tell you how it was, Lieutenant." His steady blue eyes were troubled. "See, Fred—my brother—he was a go-getter. Not like me," and he smiled briefly. "He was a moneymaker—top salesman with DeMarco and Spann last fifteen years, big engineering firm, maybe you know. He made a pretty high income, ever since little Val'd be old enough to remember—*and* he spent it. Time and again I told him, Fred, you ought to sock some away, just in case—you know? Buy some stock, bonds, invest in real estate. Sensible thing to do. But Fred, he couldn't see it—he never did." Ellis shook his head disapprovingly. "They lived right up to the hilt of what he made—house in Bel-Air, two Caddys, a maid— He wasn't ever a snob, not Fred, nor Amy either, they used to invite us to their parties and all, but— Well, you see what I mean. Excuse me, I get to talking—you want to hear all this? I don't know——" He was an earnest, unhappy, conventional little man.

"Everything you can tell me," said Mendoza.

"Time and again I tried to tell him, it's just not sense to run charges, the interest— And he never would take out insurance either, it was like he was superstitious about it, it'd be bad luck. Excuse me, you don't want to hear— Poor little Val. Maybe we *should* have tried harder, I dunno, even when she acted rude and— But what's done's done. Mabel, don't take on so . . . It was four years back Fred and Amy got killed, in a car accident. The other fellow's fault, it was, drunk driver—but that didn't help Fred or Amy. These damn drunks. Fred only just turned forty-nine—tragedy, it was. Well, just as I could've predicted, there wasn't anything left, see. A lot of debts—the house wasn't paid off—car was a wreck, of course—no insurance. Time everything was settled, the equity he had in the house just about paid off the debts, and little Val didn't get anything. She was nineteen, just in her first term up at Berkeley—just joined some swanky sorority up there. And she'd always had, well, everything—you know what I mean. Clothes, her own car since she got out of high school, anything she wanted. And she—kind of—went to pieces, I'd guess you could say, when she was left like that." He cast a side glance at his wife, unhappy.

"I suppose it was only natural," she said. "A girl that age, and they'd spoiled her. Having to quit college, find a job and earn her living." She wiped her eyes. "We couldn't have afforded to pay her college fees, you see, but we told her she should come right to us for a home—only right thing to do. But she wouldn't. She—"

"She was resentful?" Mendoza filled in as she hesitated. "Bitter at being left with nothing, when she'd been, you might say, brought up in luxury?"

"Yes, it was like that," said Ellis. "She said some pretty sharp things about taking charity. Well, she was some spoiled, way Mabel says. She went off on her own, and—well, we tried to keep in touch with her, we'd ask her over for dinner now and then, like that. But then again, you know, Lieutenant, as I said to Mabel at the time, it doesn't do any harm to young people to be on their own, have to support themselves, learn the value of money. Just the opposite. I thought maybe she'd straighten out, start to get some sense, being all on her own like that . . . She worked at Robinson's first, as a sales clerk. I said to her, she ought to take a business course, nights, get to be a secretary. But she didn't—" He stopped, looking miserable.

"What other jobs did she hold, do you know?" Mendoza was taking notes. "Know any of her current friends?"

"No, sir, I'm afraid we don't. We hadn't seen her just so often this last year. I do recall her mentioning a Paul, but not what his last name was or what he did, anything like that. She worked at The Broadway after Robinson's, and then since about six months ago she was working as a hostess at a restaurant—The Black Cat out on La Cienega. But I don't know—" He broke off nervously.

"She was still working there, as far as you know?"

"Well," said Ellis, "that's just it. I—I suppose we've got to tell you. Damn it, Fred's girl—little Val—"

"I'll never believe she was *bad*," said Mrs. Ellis. "Maybe she got into the wrong company, but— Of course we've got to tell them, Jamie."

"Yes. Well, thing is," said Ellis, "the way I say, we tried to keep in touch with Val. Asked her to dinner once in a while and so on. Sometimes she'd come, but the last—oh, couple of years or so, more often she'd make some excuse. She always acted kind of bored when she did come, didn't stay long. Well—middle-aged people, and she was young." He blinked apologetically. "Thing is—she never said, about quitting her job at the restaurant, but then we hadn't seen her for a few months. It was about a week ago, wasn't it, hon, you stopped off at her place—"

Mabel Ellis nodded solemnly. "We've been worried about it ever since, you can see, Lieutenant. It was a week ago Tuesday—yesterday. I happened to be passing, and I thought I'd leave her a note, ask her to come to dinner on Sunday. Alice and Jimmy were both coming, with the kids, and I thought— Well, it was about three o'clock, naturally I didn't expect she'd be home. But she was. She—acted queer. She wanted to get rid of me, I could tell—as if she was expecting somebody she didn't want me to meet. And when I asked her about her job, if she'd quit, she said—she said, sounding sort of wild and—well, *queer*—she said, oh, she wasn't a sucker to slave at an eight-hour job . . . She wouldn't say any more—she sounded— But I can't believe she was really *bad*," said Mrs. Ellis tearfully. "Such a pretty little girl she was— Oh, Jamie, she wasn't really *bad*, was she?"

TWO

Mendoza collected Dwyer and drove up to Mariposa Street in Hollywood. It was a quarter past ten; he trusted that Alison was just setting forth on her quest for a nursemaid. That jolly domestic, Bertha, was due at ten and could keep an eye on the peacefully slumbering twins, and feed the cats . . . Of all the damned senseless things, putting up with that pair when they could afford to pay somebody else—

The apartment house on Mariposa was an old one, and not very big; all of forty years old, about twelve units in two stories. It was scabrous yellow stucco outside, dark and smelling of dust inside. Six apartments downstairs, six up. Locked mailboxes set into the left-hand wall, and the first door to the right bore a brass plate with *Manageress* on it. "'S hope she's not out marketing," said Mendoza, yawning as he pressed the bell.

She was not. She opened the door almost at once and faced them, a scraggly middle-aged woman, black hair turning gray, pinned back in a plain bun: old-fashioned rimless glasses, sharp blue eyes. "Yay-ess?" Borderline southern.

Mendoza explained, produced identification. The woman took a step back. "Murdered!" she exclaimed. "Well, don't that beat all!" She sounded curiously pleased. "Guess that shows I wasn't woolgatherin' after all, about that young woman. I was figurin' on askin' her to get out. Some funny goings-on."

"Oh? We'd like to hear anything you can tell us, but also we want to see her apartment."

"Sure you do. Tell you the truth, I been kinda curious myself, 'n' I figured it was my right—bein' responsible for the place, so to speak—an' I slipped in to look it over, t'other night. Just to see. I reckon you'll be pretty int'rested in some things, gennelmen." Her sharp little eyes almost sparkled; she was avidly interested. "Yessir, I was goin' to tell her to get out. I don't want no immorality on the premises. Mr. Bennington upstairs is bad enough, but there's plenty o' men like one big spree regular o' Saturday nights, 'n' it just makes him want to sing and like that. All the same—" She had moved to an ancient desk beside the door, rummaged for a bunch of keys; she came out to them, selecting a key. "That's her door right across there. See, bein' right opposite, I could sort of check up on her. She allus was kind of a queer one."

"How long had she lived here?" asked Mendoza.

"Roundabout a year and a half. I don't interfere with tenants so long as they behave themselves, but I allus did wonder about Miss Ellis. Not having no regular job, see. It was funny—young single girl. I'm bound to say, I kept an eye out for men, but I can't tell you I ever saw anything like that. Says to me, she's a commercial artist, see, works at home. Well"—the woman uttered a high whinnying laugh—"time I looked around in here, I sure didn't see no artist's paints. There was a few goings-on—"

"Let's hear about that," said Mendoza. It was an apartment typical of its age and kind: a fairly good-sized living-room, with very tired furniture sitting around haphazardly: an old round-armed couch, chair to match, in faded green frieze; a couple of straight chairs, a 1920 version of a lady's writing-table; a shabby flowered rug. Through a door at the left he glimpsed a corner of white-tiled kitchen drainboard; the door on the other side of the room would lead to the bedroom, with the bath off that.

"Well! Guess I oughta say, by the way, my name's Montague. Miz Montague. If she really was murdered, I reckon 'twas something to do with it, that fella on Sunday night, so I better tell you 'bout that first. See—"

"Sunday night?" The autopsy report put the time of death between noon and midnight on Sunday.

Mrs. Montague nodded portentously. "I'd seen her—the Ellis girl—go out about ten that morning, see. I'd been figurin' on it, 'n' I said to myself, I'll catch her when she comes back, tell her to get out. It bein' near enough the end o' the month. So I was kinda listening for her to come back, see what I mean. And roundabout eight-thirty that night, I hear somebody come in the front door 'n' go to this here door, so I just steps out —and it wasn't Miss Ellis atall, 'twas a man. Stranger to me . . . Well, I don't know as I would know him again, hall's awful dark, you know, 'n' I just had a glimpse at him. But he had a key—that I saw. Hangin' on a bunch. And it was the right key, because he'd got the door open."

"Very interesting." So it was. The murderer? He'd presumably had Valeric Ellis's handbag, and contents.

"Well, I started to ask him what he thought he was doing and where's Miss Ellis, but I never had a chance. Way he acted, I guess I scared him out of a year's growth—had his back to me, see, he'd just got the door open when I spoke. I hadn't hardly said three words before he took off like a scalded cat. I guess now, afraid I'd seen him good and could say what he looked like, maybe. Anyway, he bolted straight out the front door—and he dropped the keys. These are them, not mine. You reckon, Miss Ellis's keys?"

"Very possible." Mendoza was pleased. That was luck. X coming to look through her apartment, find out whether there was anything incriminating on him there, and being prevented. X a nervous type, to bolt like that? How he must have cursed himself for dropping those keys . . . So if there was any lead, it would probably still be here. He stared absently at the glistening new TV in one corner. Quite a large screen. "Go on talking," he said to the woman, "I'm listening." He walked over and switched the TV on, keeping the volume down.

"Well! You understand, Miss Ellis bein' how she was, I wasn't too surprised . . . Why didn't I do anything about it? I didn't know then she was murdered. When I said goings-on, well, nothing I could really put a finger on, just funny. Her not having a regular job and all. Commercial artist, my foot. Nor I didn't like the looks o' some o' the people come to see her. Couple o' men, and that other girl—Maureen, I heard Miss Ellis call her—by the looks of her, no better 'n she should be, all tarted up." Dwyer had vanished into the bedroom. Mendoza stared at the TV, and Mrs. Montague uttered a ladylike snort. "For all she was supposed to be workin' at home, Miss Ellis went out most days, stayed out—but no regular times, see. She was out most evenings unless she had people in. I could hear her coming and going, you know. And then she'd go away."

"Go away?" It was a color TV, a very expensive model. Say around seven hundred bucks, thought Mendoza. He switched it off.

"Sure. She'd go out one day 'n' I wouldn't see hide nor hair of her for maybe two days or so. That happened a lot of times. Nothing regular about it, no, sir."

"You don't say. Ever ask her about it?"

"That I did. Only natural I would, wasn't it? But she flared up, called me an old snoop and told me to mind my own business." Mrs. Montague snorted again. "Real snippy little thing, she was . . . I guess one o' those men came was a regular boy friend, I couldn't say for sure. A lot of times, these two come to see her together. Which was one of the funny things. I wouldn't know their names, but once I just happened to be goin' out when they come, 'n' I heard her say, Hello, Paul. One of 'em"—she stared at Mendoza reflectively—"matter o' fact, looks a little bit like you, sir. T'other one's bigger 'n' kind of blond. And then there was another girl besides that Maureen—Maureen came a lot—the other one's a real platinum blonde, looks about the same kind as that Maureen though. Sometimes there'd be parties and a lot of noise when they got to drinking. I had to go 'n' knock on the door a couple of times. Well, like I say, it all looked kinda funny, and after that strange fella came on Sunday night I thought 'twas my right have a look around. And after *that* I figured all the more, I'd get her out—"

She'd have said it all over again, but Mendoza eased her out. She gave him a malicious smile on the threshold and said, "I reckon you'll be awful int'rested in a couple of things here."

"I just reckon we will be, Lieutenant," said Dwyer from the bedroom door, as the outer door closed. "However she was earning a living, it was a damn good one. Come in here."

In the bedroom the furniture was as shabby and aged as that in the living-room; the kind of furniture you always got in these places—cheap veneer double bed with a sagging mattress, an old painted bureau with the paint chipped; a straight painted chair, a worn carpet too small for the room. Dwyer hooked the stem of his cold pipe round the closet door, which had swung to again on sagging hinges, and pulled it open. "As you might put it, Lieutenant, *considerar.*"

"Are you taking night courses too? Yes, I do see what you mean." In this shabby room, the closet was packed with clothes. Not—he lifted down the nearest hanger—the kind of clothes a former sales clerk could afford. (And, *de paso,* apparently she'd lied to the Ellises about that hostess job, at least: she hadn't worked regularly, so far as Mrs. Montague knew, for about a year and a half.) The label on this evening gown, a frothy affair of blue chiffon, was that of Robinson's most expensive Little Shoppe. He recognized it, having once (somewhat staggered but ashamed to show it) paid forty-nine fifty (plus tax) for a simple little house robe for Alison at the same place.

There were suits, daytime dresses, a jumble of shoes. In the wide drawers of the old bureau, piles of expensive lingerie. On the vanity table, in the bathroom, a miscellaneous assortment of expensive cosmetics, lotions, creams, bath salts.

"You figure maybe," said Dwyer gravely, "she had one of these fairy godmothers? Quite a trick, without a regular pay check. Or should I say a fairy godfather?"

"Could be," said Mendoza. "Could be . . . The boys from Prints ought to be here soon. Interesting to see what they pick up. But—" He considered, conjuring up the dead girl's face. Alive and animate, she'd have been a good-looker—not pretty. In a Scandinavian sort of way—high cheekbones, a wide mouth, winging brows. Tawny blond, not bleached. He visualized that face alive, and saw that it was a reckless face. "Wild," James Ellis and his wife had said.

He said absently, "Isn't it the truth, *dineros son calidad*—money talks." She had grown up with money—money thrown around. "Anything she wanted," the Ellises said. And "spoiled." Then, all of a sudden, no money —on her own—working as a sales clerk. Seeing other women—women without her youth or looks—buying all the pretty things she couldn't have any more. Four years ago. Look up the record, but apparently she hadn't turned crooked—as without much doubt she had, some way—until about a year and a half ago. Was that a valid deduction? Had she ever held that job at The Black Cat?

He wandered back to the living-room. Ill-gotten gains spent on the ephemeral things. She hadn't been interested in her surroundings: not very domestic. Maybe that would have come next, the classy apartment.

"You have an idea?" asked Dwyer, watching him.

"A small one," said Mendoza meditatively. "People who get themselves murdered, generally speaking their inward characters have something to do with it . . . All those clothes jumbled together. All that underwear just tossed in the drawers, not folded. No trees in the shoes—"

"I don't get you," said Dwyer.

Mendoza contemplated the garish lithograph hanging on the long wall, and with an effort refrained from reaching to straighten it. Himself, he was the kind rendered acutely unhappy by the wrinkle in the rug, the coat sprawled over a chair instead of hung up tidily; he'd have been more likely to draw to an inside straight than to neglect putting trees in his shoes or hanging up his suits properly . . . "She was grabbing," he said absently. "Greedy for all the things she'd once had and lost. Buying everything in sight—once she could. Once she had them, not taking care of them. Just liking the satisfaction of having them. She was careless—impulsive. A year and a half . . . Yes, maybe the classy apartment would have come next. And—damnation, I should have asked the Montague woman about garages—probably are some in back, this old a place— I wonder what Valerie was driving? And where the hell are Marx and Horder? I want to have a thorough look here, and I can't until— You go and look for the garage, Bert, find out which was hers and if her car is there. If not, see if the Montague woman knows what she was driving."

He went out to the Ferrari at the curb and used the phone in it to call his office. "They'll be there," said Sergeant Lake soothingly. "I think they just left, Lieutenant."

He walked around the building—driveway down the left side—to find Dwyer, with the bunch of borrowed keys, struggling with the padlock on the first of a row of ramshackle old frame garages across the rear of the lot. "I suppose there could be a chance that there was a print left on one of those," he said mildly.

"All accounts, they've had a lot of handling," said Dwyer defensively. "Montague says—sharp old biddy, isn't she?—the Ellis girl had a '59 Dodge convertible, two-door, white. Damn this thing." But the key turned finally and the old double doors swung open. They looked at the white Dodge convertible.

"Naturally," said Mendoza, "the padlock being fastened. And we're both experienced enough to know better, damn it—all the fault of those damned twins, I'm not operating on all cylinders. X's prints just might have been on that padlock. Because, considering the fact that the body was dumped away from here, I think she died somewhere else. That he brought the car home to tidy it out of the way . . . What else can we say? Did he know which garage was hers, or just have the luck to pick the right one? I think X was nervous— I also think he's a very cautious man. Or—wait a minute—yes. Yes. If he'd brought her home, put an empty pill bottle beside her, ten to one we'd have put it down as suicide or accidental death. Was that what he was starting to do Sunday night when Mrs. Montague caught him? It could be. And then, having dropped the keys, he couldn't come back for another try. He probably had heard from Valerie about her snoopy landlady . . . Mmh, yes, I do wonder if he left any prints around."

"They're mostly smart enough these days to wear gloves," said Dwyer glumly.

"Nevertheless, we'll print the car." Mendoza went back to the apartment and wandered through all the rooms, waiting for Marx and Horder.

Again he pulled open the closet door, contemplated the jumble of expensive clothes crushed together. Shoes haphazard on the floor, not paired, half lying on their sides. There was a cheap fiber suitcase resting half on the shoes. He looked around, hooked the chair over to prop the door open, and pulled the suitcase out. It was not latched; he lifted the lid with his fountain pen. "¡Qué interesante!" he murmured to himself.

"Something?" asked Dwyer behind him.

"Something." Mendoza moved aside; Dwyer looked and said he'd be damned.

"Just loose like that—made-up reefers—my God, must be hundreds of 'em. So, no fairy godfather? I will be damned. But, Lieutenant, it's not often a woman takes to—you think maybe the boy friend?"

"Could be," said Mendoza. He yawned again; he wondered what success Alison was meeting in her hunt for a nice kind nursemaid.

Marx and Horder arrived. Mendoza stood around some more while they went to work printing every surface. They hooked open drawers and lifted out printable objects with tongs or tweezers. They wouldn't be hurried.

In the kitchen, a very basic supply of staples: a few cans, the refrigerator nearly empty. She hadn't done much cooking at home. In the first of the two cupboards, along with a scattering of a few staple items (breakfast cereal, crackers, packaged soups), a half-empty fifth of a popular brand of Scotch, a full bottle of vodka, and a bottle of wine.

Mendoza looked at the bottle of wine twice. A very moderate drinker himself, he wasn't familiar with the liquor trade; but there was something rather unusual-looking about that bottle of wine. When Marx had thoroughly dusted it and lifted what prints were on it, he inspected it closer.

A black-and-white label looking old-fashioned, if that was the word for it. *Rutherford and Miles*, and a dignified-sounding London address. Below that in large ornate lettering, *Madeira*, and below that, *Malvasias*—in parentheses, *malmsey. Alcoholic content 20%*. The wine was a dark amber-red color, looking thick.

Mendoza straightened and stared at the cupboard door. *Malmsey.* There had been some British duke—a long time back—"drowned in a butt of malmsey." Unusual, you could say, if this was the same stuff. He'd heard of a wine called Madeira, but it was vaguely associated in his mind with bygone times—seventeenth, eighteenth century? Evidently it was still produced. But it couldn't be a very popular wine? Something not much called for, maybe. Maybe a lead? Valerie Ellis had kept it on hand—for the boy friend?

"O.K., I guess we've covered everything, Lieutenant," said Horder. "It's all yours. Found an address book in the desk, here it is. You want the car printed? O.K."

"Thanks very much, boys." Mendoza pounced on the address book eagerly.

Looking through it, he sighed. It was going to be quite a job to locate all these names. These damned untidy females with the disorganized minds! Valerie Ellis had written a wild scrawl of a hand, scarcely legible; and in only a few places had she put down addresses—mostly just phone numbers. The scribbles were in a variety of mediums, pencil, ballpoint pens in blue, green, and red, a broad-nibbed fountain pen. Moreover, she hadn't listed names alphabetically. On the same page as *Paul Manton, NO-1-6494*, was *Gloria, CR-3-2894*, and an illegible scrawl which might be either *Frank* or *Fred.*

The little book was very full. Somebody—Sergeant Lake—would be contacting the telephone company to get matching addresses for all these numbers.

Here was *Maureen*, and a Hollywood number. *Ricardo. Bob.* Then, *Glessner*, and a dash, and *meet Rikki's 5 p.m., get $5000.* Well, well. *Paul Manton.*

She had used this little book, evidently, as a current reminder, half desk diary. Some of the notations—no telling how recent any of them were—were extremely interesting. There was that one about Glessner, and later on, *Hoess—meet 8:30 Cat, no double talk.* And, later on, *Monteux, Cat, 8 p.m., $$$.* Altogether, fourteen similar notations.

Somebody—presumably Valerie Ellis—had been collecting under-the-counter money from other somebodies, for something. Did that say? Or had she been working the racket—whatever the racket was—with somebody else?

The reefers? But the one amount mentioned, five thousand bucks, was too high for a reefer-peddling business. Current price, about two bits apiece, here. Of course reefer peddlers frequently graduated into pushing the big H.

Some other racket, the reefers on the side? Obligingly storing the reefers for the boy friend?

And that *Paul Manton* rang a very faint bell in his mind.

"Paul Manton," he said. "Does it hit you any way, Bert? I seem to remember the name, but I can't connect it with anything."

"New one to me. We can ask Records."

"Yes." Mendoza was still leafing through the address book, pausing to decipher hasty scrawls. "I think we will. Just in case."

Here was an intriguing one. *Wilanowski, s.o.b.!!!!* Did that say, maybe, that Wilanowski had failed to pay up? For what? Mendoza grinned at the exclamation points, bitten deep into the page. He turned that page and paused again.

Call P., R.'s bar 8 p.m. Marion, and a phone number. *Meet Vardas 8, Cat, $$.* Psychological point—so interested in money, she couldn't resist adding that symbol. But, *caray,* the untidy, disorganized way she'd jotted all this down, she'd have had to consult every page to find what she was looking for—

There were nine pages blank at the end of the little book. He studied the last filled-in page. *Imarosa, 10 p.m. R's $$$. Call P. home.* In a different ink, *Maureen, new no., 015-4965.* And far below that, scrawled with a blue ballpoint, in letters twice as large as she normally wrote, the legend *Farlow, 1566 Willoughby, Hlywd!!!!!!!!*

Well. Quite a little to puzzle over there. Quite a little of interest.

Mendoza found himself yawning again. He wondered what Hackett and Palliser were getting on Lover Boy the rapist. Lover Boy concentrating on obviously wealthy areas: West Hollywood, two of the victims in Beverly Hills, so that force was in on it too. He'd taken some nice loot in most of the places . . . Sooner or later the D.M.V. list ought to yield results.

He glanced at his watch; it was a bit after noon. Have lunch somewhere, start Lake on getting addresses for all these numbers. What the hell kind of racket had it been that Valerie Ellis was running?

The Black Cat restaurant on La Cienega. By the address book, maybe used for some of the pay-offs? But the personnel there might be quite innocent. Look, of course.

He yawned again. He said, "O.K., Bert, you get back downtown, you and Jimmy can get busy matching up these phone numbers with addresses. But copy them down, will you? I want to study this little book more thoroughly. Oh, and check with the Ellises for all her former addresses, will you? I'll poke around here a little more . . ."

THREE

"Well, I don't know, I suppose she's all right," said Alison in a slightly dissatisfied tone. "She's got scads of references praising her to the skies—she certainly seems experienced."

"So what more do you want? What's her name?"

"Jane Freeman. Miss. I suppose she'll be fine, it's just that she rather reeks of antiseptic, if you know what I mean. She's coming tomorrow. I'll get Bertha to help me move the cribs and so on. I thought the Freeman can have the room next to the back—"

"Yes, fine," said Mendoza absently. He was leafing through Valerie Ellis's address book again, and thinking about several puzzles—small and large—that he wished he knew the answers to. He raised his eyes and stared abstractedly at Master John Luis, who was prone on a blanket on the floor making vigorous swimming motions in the direction of Sheba, curled under the coffee table.

Ramifications, he thought. Going to be a tough one to unravel, all right. Some very unlikely and mystifying little things had come to light, besides the reefers . . .

There was also Lover Boy. Mendoza sighed. Lover Boy was important not only for the obvious reasons but because the irresponsible section of the press and a committee of muddleheaded citizens were using him as an excuse for another campaign against the incompetent police. Over a period of nearly three months this dangerous and brutal criminal has—et cetera, leading to: obviously the police are not trying hard enough, or are simply incompetent. The average citizen just didn't realize how tough one like that could be. They hadn't got the word about the light-blue truck until a week ago, from his last but one victim, the next confirming that. They were working that as hard as they knew how . . .

They'd had an hour's excitement this afternoon, when the patient routine check of light-blue trucks had turned up one registered to an address down on Washington Boulevard, one of the Negro sections. The owner was the proprietor of a garage, and seemed like a very upright citizen; nothing against him, no record. But he employed two mechanics, both of whom sometimes drove the truck. Dave Roberts and Jerry Byrd. He said indignantly, did Mr. John Wilkinson, that Dave and Jerry were good respectable boys, they wouldn't do anything like that . . . But it presented a little problem, which Hackett had laid before Mendoza when he came in from more poking around in Valerie's apartment.

"We don't want to jump the gun, Luis. You see what I mean. There they are, we've got to check. Neither of 'em has any record, they're both regular churchgoers and so on. But—" He didn't have to explain the problem to Mendoza. "How'll we handle it?"

On their rough physical descriptions—size and age—either could have been Lover Boy. But Hackett didn't think either of them was, because neither of them was pock-marked. Also, they had good records, and both were educated boys, high-school graduates. He didn't think Lover Boy was that type, and Mendoza agreed with him. However, a good many white people didn't trouble to distinguish one Negro from another; and a woman who has been forcibly and brutally assaulted might easily make an unconscious mistake.

Mendoza said after thought, "Let Mrs. Gunnarson look at them." Mrs. Gunnarson was the older of the two women who had managed to get away from him. She'd have a little less emotional involvement, and also she was a stable, sensible woman of forty.

And of course she had looked and said, "No, it wasn't either of these young men. He was badly pock-marked, and bigger than either of them."

Hackett had thanked her with emphatic sincerity. With these Black Muslims kicking up all the trouble they could, the last thing they needed was a wrongful identification of an innocent Negro. Shaken, Dave and Jerry had gone back to work with a little story to tell. Hackett and Mendoza and every other man on the force could hope, a little story which would include the fact that the police had leaned over backward to be fair to them. But of course it wasn't the Daves and Jerrys they needed to convince of that: the Daves and Jerrys were already honest citizens. It was the distrustful ones, the insecure ones, the ones on the borderline . . .

Mendoza jumped and opened his eyes at sudden uproar. Master John, doggedly propelling himself with churning motions across the floor, had reached Sheba and started chewing her tail. Sheba shrieked, spat, and fled. Master John roared. El Señor, who had been brooding darkly to himself on top of the credenza, jumped to his self-appointed job and began washing Master John's tearful face.

"No, Señor!" said Alison. "Heavens, you'll have all the skin off—" She made a dive for the baby. El Señor gave her a cold look and stalked out of the room. The whole episode amused Miss Teresa highly; she crowed with delight. "That cat!" said Alison. "It's very nice of him to want to help, but he doesn't realize how rough his tongue is."

"After tomorrow—" said Mendoza.

"Yes. I only wish I liked her better," said Alison. "Oh, well, we'll see how she works out. And I'd better get these two into bed and to sleep."

"For exactly five hours and a half," said Mendoza, looking at his watch. He watched her out, leaned back and shut his eyes, and meditated on what else had turned up today on Valerie Ellis.

Aunt and Uncle Ellis had been nice trusting relatives, never suspecting anything about Valerie, all right. It turned out that she'd held that job at Robinson's just five months, and then been fired for shoplifting. Naturally, no reference given. The store hadn't prosecuted because it was a first offense and it had got most of the loot back.

She'd never worked at The Broadway at all. Nor as a hostess at The Black Cat. So, call it three and a half years she'd been on the bent somehow, alone or with ditto pals. In this racket or that . . . They knew her at The Black Cat. She came in fairly often, sometimes alone, more often with men. Different men, but the same one several times also. Looking interestedly at Mendoza, the head barman had said, "That one looks a little bit like you, sir. About your size too."

Well, he was not unique, reflected Mendoza. Especially in Los Angeles, there were probably some hundreds of men walking around who were about five-ten, slim and dark, with narrow black mustaches.

They now had about three quarters of the list of matching addresses. She'd known a lot of people. And probably they'd find that a large number of them had been purely casual acquaintances. Or, of course, would say so. Anybody who'd been in a racket with her—if anyone had been—wasn't going to speak up about it.

As he looked at the first few full names and addresses Sergeant Lake had laid in front of him, Mendoza had suddenly remembered who Paul Manton was and why the name was familiar. So he hadn't asked Records about him.

A small two-paragraph story on the third page of the *Times* a couple of days ago. An amateur flier, in his own small Cessna, making a successful if dangerous emergency landing along a section of freeway mercifully free of cars . . . He got Jimmy to call the *Times* to check it. Paul Manton, all right, and he was described as a mechanic employed by InterState Airways, Inc.

So he'd been a friend of Valerie's. It didn't say much, yet. Not until they knew more about him—and everybody else mentioned in that little book.

Requestioned, Mrs. Montague had said that Valerie had been away from Wednesday to Friday, getting home on Friday evening. Mrs. Montague had been keeping tabs on Valerie, lately at least; she said Valerie had come in about eight in the evening, and there was a man with her. No, she hadn't seen his face; as with the Sunday evening stranger, he'd had his back to her.

As the names and addresses turned up, automatically they were relayed to Records. So far, not one had any pedigree . . .

After he'd advised Hackett about Dave and Jerry, Mendoza had driven up to Willoughby Street in Hollywood. That last entry in the book, with its row of triumphant exclamation points, interested him.

Willoughby Street was a street of older, dignified homes: very solid wealth. The address Valerie had scribbled down turned out to be a handsome French Provincial house, very neatly maintained, fresh-painted gray and white; ivy in the parking, trim beds of ivy geraniums. Mendoza pressed the bell and presently faced an equally neat, pleasant-faced woman of middle age.

"Mrs. Farlow?"

"Who shall I say it is, sir?"

He gave her his name; she looked surprised and curious, but just asked him to wait. A few moments later she came back and ushered him into a cavernous dim living-room. Another woman was standing by the hearth.

"Lieutenant—Mendoza?" she said in a warm contralto voice. "I'm Mrs. Farlow. I must say I'm curious as to what the police want with me! But do sit down, won't you?"

She was in her late forties, he thought, and not looking it: blond by request, but a subtle job, not obvious. Poise and manner: she spent money on herself and the result was worth it. She'd kept a very good figure. The china-blue eyes were perhaps a little small, the arch of the rather long nose a little too high, the mouth a trifle narrow; but a nice-looking woman, with pride in herself and her home.

Mendoza sat down. "I believe you knew a Miss Valerie Ellis, Mrs. Farlow?"

She was in the act of lighting a cigarette; she had sat down on a long, low, gray-upholstered couch opposite the large gray-upholstered chair he had chosen. She looked at him over the lighter flame. She said, with an upward inflection, "Knew? I—we do know a Valerie Ellis, yes, why?"

Mendoza told her, watching her. She reacted with apparently genuine astonishment and horror. "My God, I saw that in the paper about a body found, but I never— How horrible! Who on earth could have—"

"Did you know her well, Mrs. Farlow?" This was an atmosphere far removed from either Mariposa Street or that of pro crooks.

"I—no," she said slowly. "My God, what a horrible thing to happen. Poor Valerie. What did you—? Why, no, it was rather odd actually, it was only a few days ago I ran across her again. I hadn't seen her for, oh, it must be all of six years—more. She was just a high-school kid then. So I'm afraid I can't help you much, Lieutenant—I wouldn't know who her friends were now, or what she'd been doing. Excuse me, but how did you know I knew her? Because, as I say—"

"Your name was in her address book," said Mendoza, not mentioning those very interesting exclamation points.

"Oh," said Mrs. Farlow, enlightened. "Well, that was the only time I'd seen her in a good six years—last Saturday—so I couldn't tell you anything useful, I'm afraid."

"Mind telling me how you happened to know her, how you happened to run across her again?"

"Why, of course, but I don't see how it'd help— Well, perhaps you know that she used to live down in Bel-Air. Before the Ellises were killed in that awful accident— I saw the newspaper stories about it, we'd moved by then, but you see, they'd been neighbors of ours there. Two houses down, on Bellaggio Road. That was in 1958, Valerie'd have been—oh, sixteen, seventeen, I suppose. We knew her as you would a girl that age, living in the same block. No, we didn't know the Ellises well, actually we only lived there about a year."

"I see. When did you move?"

"Sometime that year—March, I think. And I never laid eyes on the girl again until last Saturday." She spoke a little impatiently now. "It was just one of those coincidences—you know how things happen. She'd been calling on the people next door. I just happened to be coming home when she came out, and she—we recognized each other. We said hello, and so on, and that was about all there was to it. I never knew her well."

Mendoza studied her. If it was an act, it was a damn good one: sounded very genuine. Then why the row of exclamation points after her name?

Well, no clue as to what Valerie's racket had been. There was money here, obviously; and Valerie had liked money. Maybe she'd figured Mrs. Farlow as a mark, having an in with her because Mrs. Farlow had known her as an innocent child?

"Did you ask her in?"

"No, actually I was rather tired and—well, as I say, I'd never known her well, it was just a—chance encounter." Now she sounded a little bored. "I did say I'd been sorry to hear about her parents, I think, and she thanked me—we only talked a few minutes, and then she went off and I came in."

"I see." He was silent a moment; it all sounded very likely and genuine. "Did she—"

The front door banged and a boy's voice announced, "I'm home! Anybody here?" He poked his head round the door, a nice-looking boy about nine or ten, well grown for his age.

"Hi, Johnny. I'll be with you in a minute," said Mrs. Farlow. "Mrs. Bennett's been making fresh cookies, maybe she'll let you have some."

"Oh, boy!"

"And—Johnny! You've still got that extra piano practice to make up, don't forget!"

"O.K., Aunt Grace, I will." He vanished down the hall.

She smiled at Mendoza. "Kids," she said. "Sometimes it seems like more trouble than— But Johnny's a good boy."

"He sounds it." He returned her smile. "Did Miss Ellis say why she'd been calling on the people next door? Which house, by the way? 1568, thanks. Do you know them?"

"Not at all. They haven't been here too long. I suppose she just knew them. No, I couldn't tell you the name, it's a foreign-sounding one, Polish or something. They only came here about six months ago. I think he's a professor of some kind. No, Valerie didn't say anything about them . . . I'm afraid I'm no help to you at all."

Those exclamation points. But very probably that was the answer: Valerie had seen Mrs. Farlow as an easy mark for some racket, had been feeling triumphant at running across her again, a woman who'd automatically believe in her honesty. A woman who didn't know that she'd been left penniless after her parents' death.

The people next door—

That house was Mediterranean, with a little balcony above the front door, a red tile roof. It was a man who opened the door, a grave-faced dignified man in the fifties, with strong aquiline features. Mendoza produced identification, asked his question, and the man listened gravely.

"You had best come in, sir. My name is Dvorzhak, Jan Dvorzhak. I do not think we can be of much aid, but we shall see. Anya!" He spoke heavily accented English.

A quick high young voice answered him from somewhere upstairs, in another tongue, and high heels clattered on the stairs. But before the owner of the voice appeared, another woman materialized from the shadows at the far end of the hall—a dumpy little woman in dowdy black clothes, skirt too long. She asked him a question in the same tongue, sounding frightened.

He said in English, "It is nothing, Marya—nothing. Do not be foolish, you know that the police here are not as the police *there*. The gentleman wants only a little information . . . Ah, Anya. Now—you have said, it is Lieutenant? What is all this asking about Miss Ellis? You will please tell us why you ask?"

Mendoza told them why. The older woman chattered in a frightened high voice, in her own language—Polish, Russian? Dvorzhak soothed her in English. "But what a terrible thing to happen! Now, Marya, be quiet, this is nothing to do with us. Come, control your nerves, my dear. You must forgive my wife, sir, you comprehend we are not safe here a long time, she is—nervous."

"Yes. You knew Miss Ellis well?"

"But how horrible!" said the girl called Anya. "What a dreadful thing to happen! You are—quite sure—it was Valerie? Oh—" She might be twenty; she was slim, dark-haired, fair-skinned, with feathery-lashed dark eyes. Apart from her accent, she was more Americanized than her parents, dressed smartly.

"We're quite sure—it is Miss Dvorzhak?"

"Yes, yes," she said impatiently. "I can hardly believe it—such a way to die. Who would—? Yes, she is a—an acquaintance of mine, sir. An acquaintance only, I have only a little while ago met her. How do you know?"

He explained about Mrs. Farlow briefly. "Oh—" said Anya, a finger to her lip. "I did not know—" Her mother babbled again and was soothed.

"Where did you meet Miss Ellis and when?"

"Oh, one talks to everyone here, sir. It was a few weeks ago, I am in a shop—a very nice little shop on Wilshire Boulevard, I am shopping for a dress, and Valerie was there also. We began talking—she was pleasant, we liked one another, so then we went to lunch together. This is how I met her, but I did not know her well, not at all. Last Saturday afternoon—we had exchanged our addresses, you see—she said she was driving past near here and stopped to see me, a few minutes only. That was how it was."

Of course the name hadn't been in Valerie's address book.

"I see," said Mendoza. "So you didn't know any of her friends—anything about her private life?"

"But nothing, I am sorry." She flung her hands wide in expressive gesture. Her father stood watching gravely. "How should I? I have only met her twice, three times. She seemed a nice person, I am so very sorry to hear of this dreadful thing, but—"

And, a very small something—that the name hadn't been in the book. Possibly Valerie hadn't had the book with her, had copied down the address on a scrap of paper and omitted recopying it. Nothing said Anya Dvorzhak wasn't telling gospel truth. And as for Valerie deliberately (could you say?) making up to her—well, she might have guessed, money, when Anya chose the "nice little shop" on Wilshire, and maybe pick her as an easy mark too . . . What the hell had her racket been?

And then, just as he got back to the office at five-forty, the bombshell had exploded.

They'd nearly reached the end of the D.M.V. list on the trucks, and he was listening to Hackett and agreeing tiredly that they'd better ask Sacramento for lists on Orange and Ventura counties, when a shaken-looking Sergeant Lake looked in and said, "It's the FBI, Lieutenant—" and a tall excited man pushed past him.

"What the hell is all this?" he demanded of Mendoza. "Where—what the hell—"

"Just what I might ask you. Credentials, please?"

"For God's sake!" said the other man, and produced them as if absentmindedly. "Sorry, but we're all on the jump over this one. You wired some prints to Washington about eleven this morning—" Mendoza nodded; it was second nature: prints not in their own files, they asked Washington, and the Feds were so quick off the mark. "So I get a wire fifteen minutes ago chasing me over here. Where the hell did you pick up the prints and when?"

"I couldn't say until you tell me which prints they were."

"Oh, Lord—sorry—but this one's really got us worried." The Federal man mopped his brow. "They're Osgar Thorwald's prints—that's why, friend. I—"

"That Thorwald?" asked Hackett incredulously.

"That Thorwald," said the Fed. "The Thorwald that passed top secrets on to Moscow six years back and got clean away from us. At least we knew—we thought we knew—he was somewhere behind the Iron Curtain, all nice and cozy. We don't want him back in our midst, but my God, if he is we'd like to know where. Where'd you pick up the prints?"

"¡Porvida!" said Mendoza blankly. "¿Como dice? Esto es otro cantar—what the hell is this? The only prints we sent—"

When they came to sort it out, Thorwald's prints had come off that bottle of Madeira wine in Valerie's kitchen cupboard.

The Federal agent said sadly that it figured. "One of Thorwald's foibles—he never drinks anything but Madeira. It was the way we picked him up, before he got away from us—not many places carry it."

So now the Feds were buzzing around, going over that apartment for themselves and demanding hourly bulletins about Valerie. Damned annoying. Talk about surprises. Just try to link any of that up. It didn't make sense.

Tomorrow, see a lot of the other people she'd known. Ask questions. Poke around.

Osgar Thorwald, for God's sake . . .

Talk about an anonymous one like Lover Boy being tough. Once in a long while you got a complex business like this that was twice as tough. He tried to take his mind off it; he needed all the sleep he could get. Must get to sleep. As long as he'd be allowed . . .

"Hmm?" he said sleepily.

"I just said, I wish she didn't look so—so starched," said Alison in the darkness, snuggling closer.

"Probably a very efficient nurse. Just think, tomorrow night we can sleep all night."

"You are feeling your age," said Alison wickedly.

"¡Zorra roja! Lawful wives have no business being so impudent. Come here . . ."

Some two hours later, Master John Luis commenced to yell. His sister joined him.

Alison stirred. Sleepily she sat up. She said, "Damn." She groped for her slippers. As she fumbled her way into her robe, she added crossly, "I don't care how starched and stiff the woman is. As long as she'll deal with them. Little monsters. All right, I'm coming!"

Mendoza tried to close his ears. It was no use. He sat up, switched on the light, lit a cigarette, and thought exasperatedly about Valerie Ellis.

Sooner or later routine would lead them to Lover Boy; but Valerie Ellis . . .

FOUR

And he wondered overnight whether the Feds would take over the case
because of the political angle. Well, a funny twist, but he didn't think
this murder had been political.

They fell on him like ravening bloodhounds when he came into the
office, screaming for the address book. They hadn't known about the book
until he'd left last night. They chased one of their minions off to have
it photostated, every page of it; everybody mentioned in it would get a
thorough screening.

They'd flown a man in from Washington who'd been on the Thorwald
case before—a big genial fellow, Waltham. They crowded into Mendoza's
office, listened raptly to him repeat what they'd heard last night, for
Waltham's benefit—the very little they knew about this case so far. They'd
taken the key to Valerie's apartment last night, and evidently spent most
of the night going over it, but hadn't come up with anything Mendoza's
crew hadn't already come across. As he could have told them.

"I don't know what organizations she belonged to, if any," he said patiently to that question. "Nothing else political shows at all. And it doesn't
smell that way to me. Naturally you're welcome to all we've got, the other
prints and so on. Are you taking over?"

"Well, I tell you, it's like this," said Waltham in his quiet voice. "We
can't tell one way or the other whether the Ellis murder is political. I
agree it doesn't look that way—not the professional taking-off. We're naturally interested in Thorwald, and in her because there was evidently a
link there. But we do know that Thorwald himself was on the run from
the Reds."

"Oh? Thieves falling out?"

Waltham grinned. "Something like that. The news was that he gave them the slip and got as far as East Berlin. That was about seven months ago. No trace of him since. Well, now we know he got here. It's easy enough to get in illegally if you can't legally, and he may have a forged passport or something. But—"

"Excuse me, sir," said one of the other agents, "but could that be a double bluff? The word spread that he's in bad with them, so he can—"

Waltham shook his head. "We don't think so, and neither does the C.I.A. where we got the tip. It looks pretty straight. So you can see that tells us Thorwald himself may not be—er—political any more. Just a stateless citizen making tracks for home, to go to ground. So whatever his connection was with the Ellis girl, it could be a private thing entirely."

"Yes," said Mendoza thoughtfully. "And what the hell was the connection?"

"Well, you don't know much about her yet, do you? Just that she had some racket. Could be plain and simple hustling? Thorwald was always a man for the ladies."

"No. For about ninety-nine per cent sure. She had a suspicious landlady who'd have spotted that. The landlady says a man came home with her Friday night but he didn't stay long. She didn't get a good look at him—just his back—as per the Sunday night intruder. She heard him leave about an hour later. But she doesn't think she'd ever seen him before. Which says nothing, of course."

"Well," said Waltham, "I think we'll handle it like this, Lieutenant. We'll take over the Thorwald investigation, and leave you to sort out the murder. Something may show up to prove the two are unconnected—or vice versa, of course—let's just keep both possibilities in mind, shall we? Tally"—he looked at one of his colleagues—"let's really get press coverage on it. The scare headlines—appeal for public help, all the trimmings. O.K.? Run big cuts of our Osgar—of course, no guarantee he still looks like that, after six years, but—" He shrugged. "I want every place in L.A. County that sells liquor alerted for any customer asking for Madeira wine. Though he may be smart enough to lay off that. Although he evidently bought a bottle on—" He broke off, and said, "My God, but how do we know? The day, I mean. He could have left his prints on that bottle months ago, damn it. Look—Adler, you set it up on the liquor retailers. We've got to start looking somewhere, after all. Anybody asking for Madeira, have 'em say they'll make inquiries about ordering it, and ask for the customer's address. And let's get the Madeira into the press releases too, for nationwide coverage."

"Do you know how many places like that there *are* here?" Adler groaned. "O.K., O.K. And at the same time try to find out where he got that bottle, if it was at all recently."

"Yes. How much was gone out of it?"

"About two glassfuls," said Mendoza.

"Oh. And the press furor should make the job a little easier—a lot of the retailers will pick up the detail about the Madeira. If it *was* recently bought— Yes, and that's another thing, damn it. He may have got the girl to buy it for him."

"A little idea on that," said Mendoza. "Without wanting to interrupt, Mr. Waltham. Thorwald, under an alias, could have been a casual acquaintance of Valerie's. Overnight we've turned up the fact that Valerie knew a couple of people at least with little pedigrees—couple of girls charged with soliciting. She may have known other people in that category, who knows? If it was like that, maybe Thorwald just bought that Madeira as his contribution to a pleasant evening. If it was Thorwald with her on Friday evening, Mrs. Montague doesn't think he'd ever been there before. We don't know that it was, of course. And we don't know how long Thorwald's been here—"

"He's had seven months to get here from Berlin," agreed Waltham gloomily.

"Yes. Well, the fact that he left the bottle—or, of course, gave it to her elsewhere, because we don't know that he's ever been in her apartment— makes me think that he knows where he can buy a further supply."

Waltham thought that out. "All up in the air," he said. "There's another thing, damn it. We don't know how long that bottle's been sitting there. You see, we know quite a lot about Thorwald, from the caper six years back. One of his habits is trying to convert people to this Madeira. A lot of times we know about, he'd given one of his friends a bottle, urged them to try it. And it's not a wine everybody likes. Heavier and sweeter than port—like a liqueur, you know. While we were looking into him before, I ran across half a dozen people who had bottles of Madeira hanging around with a couple of glassfuls gone."

There was a gloomy silence. "Well, I guess that's it," said Waltham, getting up heavily. "We'll hope nationwide publicity will turn up something—because, though we'll take a damn good look around here, he might be anywhere, damn it."

"And," said Mendoza meditatively, "another interesting little thought occurs to me. Just an idea, maybe farfetched. You said Thorwald isn't working for his former bosses any more. Just a stateless citizen. Well, wherever he is, or was, he couldn't live on air. People running from the

Reds don't often manage to carry fortunes away with them. And I seem to recall that he had several engineering degrees which were, of course, canceled or destroyed or whatever happens to such things when a man's defrocked from the brotherhood. So he couldn't get work at his old regular job. We don't know what Valerie's latest racket was—could he have been in on it?"

"That's reaching," said Waltham. "I suppose it could be. But you said she's probably been on the bent for about three and a half years."

"Well"—Mendoza emptied the ash tray absently, brushed ash off the desk—"I've got another guess to make about Valerie. *Perdido por una, perdido por todo*—in for a penny, in for a pound. She'd been brought up to be honest—until she was nineteen, she associated with only nice upright people. When she succumbed to temptation and started shoplifting, her first venture off the rails, she was caught almost right away. Nobody turns into a successful pro crook overnight. I think since she decided to live by her wits, she's drifted into several different capers, maybe steadily downhill. Maybe, teaming up with different people in that line she'd got to know. Maybe she did do a little hustling at some time or other—we'll ask her former landladies—she wasn't, by the autopsy, the nice innocent child she'd been."

"Well, that's up to you," said Waltham. "We'll get busy on our end of it."

"I trust any relevant leads to the murder will be passed on."

"Oh, sure, if we come across anything——" They left him en masse, leaving the office with extra chairs at odd angles, ashes on the floor, and reminiscent of a cheap cigar.

Mendoza reminded Sergeant Lake to remind Waltham that he'd like either the address book itself or a photostat of it back, and started for International Airport to see Paul Manton.

Miss Jane Freeman—forty-three, thin and ramrod-straight as a Grenadier Guard, with a no-nonsense face scrubbed with green soap twice a day and unenlivened by cosmetics—faced Alison frowning just a trifle.

"I'm afraid, Mrs. Mendoza, that psychological opinion does not bear that out, you know. You should simply leave them alone. Naturally, if they are given your whole attention every time they demand it, they will go from bad to worse. Babies are natural tyrants"—a wintry smile flickered across her pale lips briefly—"and one must be *firm* from the first."

"But I'd defy anybody to ignore them!" said Alison. "Do you mean you're simply going to let them yell?"

"Not at all, Mrs. Mendoza, not at all. One must always be thorough. Whenever a baby cries, one must check to see if there is valid reason. If he needs a diaper change, or has hurt himself in some way—you understand. But if he is simply anticipating his next feeding time, or asking for attention, no valid reason exists for spending time with him. The tendency must be checked at once, *or*," said Miss Freeman ominously, "one is asking for trouble later on. When the baby discovers that mere noise does not always get him the attention he wants, he soon stops. I'm sure you see what I mean."

Alison said reluctantly, "Well, yes, in a way. But—" That was all very well, she thought, for small children whom you could communicate with. Could discipline, try to reason with. But quite simply, what she felt was that babies who cried were unhappy, and needed comforting. You couldn't reason with a baby, say, look, you've got no reason to feel unhappy. Heavens, sometimes grown-up people couldn't explain why they felt unhappy. They just did. And she couldn't see why it was wrong to give a baby a little extra cuddling and loving.

"And another thing, Mrs. Mendoza—" Miss Freeman was definitely frowning now.

"Yes?" said Alison uneasily.

"I really am afraid we shall have to keep the nursery door shut at *all* times. Those cats keep coming in." If Miss Freeman had said *king cobras* she couldn't have sounded more portentous.

"Yes, Bast's taken a notion to sleep in one of the cribs, and— They're quite friendly cats, really, they're not doing any harm."

"*Harm!*" ejaculated Miss Freeman. "Why, not ten minutes ago I turned my back for a moment and when I looked, that big black creature was actually licking the little girl's face!"

"That's El Señor," said Alison. "I know, he has a sort of compulsion about washing, he likes to—"

"Most insanitary!" said Miss Freeman severely. "One never knows what germs a pet animal is harboring."

"Well, that's nonsense," said Alison. "They don't. Actually, as Dr. Stocking says—our vet—cats and dogs catch more diseases from people than vice versa. They're perfectly clean cats—"

"I must disagree there, really. Personally I disapprove of keeping pets at all, any animal is bound to be insanitary. But I realize that some people will behave sentimentally. I'm afraid we must at least keep them out of the nursery," said Miss Freeman firmly.

At this point both twins began to yell. "They're hungry," said Alison, glancing at the clock. "I'll just—" She started for the kitchen.

"Now, now, Mrs. Mendoza!" said Miss Freeman archly. "What am I here for, after all? And it's half an hour before their regular time, there's no hurry. Leave it to me, I'll see to it."

"Well, I haven't been keeping to any regular schedule—" After all, thought Alison, even a baby knows when it's hungry!

"A regular routine is always best," said Miss Freeman. "Of course babies differ, some have slower digestions. We'll try a six-hour schedule at first, and see how it works out. Now don't you worry about a thing," and she bustled off kitchenwards.

Alison sighed. She wished she could have nursed them longer; if she still were, she could simply walk into the nursery, whatever Miss Freeman said.

Well, after all she'd hired the woman; let her try her way and see how it worked out.

Bertha had been a silent witness to all this, vigorously polishing the big coffee table in the L of the sectional. "I don't figure," she said now, shaking her tight gray sausage-curls at Alison, "that it's just so natural for a born old maid to know what's best for children. Not that I ever had any myself, but I did bring up my niece Mabel. Just listen to them two yell! Hungry, all right. Well, personally speakin', Mis' Mendoza, the way I figure is, like the saying goes, catch more flies with honey than vinegar."

"How right you are," said Alison moodily.

"She was *what?*" said Paul Manton blankly. He stared at Mendoza incredulously.

Mendoza had located him without much trouble; InterState Airways occupied one of the smaller hangars scattered round the huge International Airport's perimeter. It wasn't a big outfit: ferried small cargo up and down the state. A busy general manager had pointed out Manton, working on a twin-engined plane at the far end of the hangar.

Manton was in his early thirties, tall and broad-shouldered, a good-looking young man in a rugged way; he had tawny blond hair, the same coloring as Valerie Ellis. He wore a once-white overall, oil-stained, and his big, well-shaped hands were dirty too.

"In some sort of crooked business," said Mendoza again. "No regular job. You didn't suspect that, Mr. Manton?"

"My God, no, of course not!" He had been, apparently, genuinely astonished at the news of Valerie's murder. And, intriguingly, for just a flash Mendoza thought his eyes had held fear. News of her identification had been in last night's papers, but only a couple of paragraphs; he could have missed it. (After today it'd make headlines.) Now he was surprised all over again at this further news. His eyes narrowed a little on Mendoza. "For God's sake, are you sure? I mean—I thought—she told me she worked at some department store. Robinson's, I think it was. But, of course, I didn't know her very well. We'd had a few dates, but I wasn't the steady boy friend, like that. She went out with Cardenas more than with me."

"That's Ricardo Cardenas?"

"That's right. I met him at Val's, matter of fact. My God, are you sure about this? Ricardo'd have had seven fits if he'd known—Civil Service is kind of touchy about who employees associate with. What—what was she doing, anyway? She always seemed like an ordinary girl—" Unheeding of the dirt on his hand, he drove fingers through his crest of hair. "This really shakes me."

"Where'd you meet her, Mr. Manton, and when?" Mendoza dropped his cigarette and stepped on it carefully.

"It was about, oh, three-four months ago—another girl I know introduced us at a party. Maureen Moskovitch." He smiled briefly, showing very white teeth. "Sounds funny, but her maiden name was Kelly, she says. I don't know how she knew Val, or how long. But, my God—seemed an ordinary girl—"

"Her landlady tells us," said Mendoza, "that on several occasions two men came together to see her. By the descriptions, I'd make a guess that one was you and the other may have been—"

"Cardenas," said Manton. He blinked and disarranged his hair some more. "Sure. See, I—" He hesitated and looked a little embarrassed. "I guess this is going to sound kind of funny, Lieutenant. I mean, a guy like me—just a mechanic. But, see, I'm interested in folk music. I don't mean like hillbilly stuff, the American stuff, but—you know—the older foreign kind. The really old stuff. And Ricardo, he is too, he's got quite a collection of records—speaks six languages, bright guy—a lot more than I have. Well, I met him at a party Val had—"

"When?"

"Oh, call it a couple of months ago, bit more. And we got to talking, and found out we were both interested in this kind of thing, see? So one thing led to another, and about, oh, maybe three times we met there at Val's place and he brought along some of his records—he's got some really offbeat stuff—"

"And a phonograph?" There'd been no phonograph in the apartment.

"Sure, a portable. But—" Manton lit another cigarette nervously. "Look—"

"Why did you meet there? Why not your place or his?"

"Well—" said Manton. "Oh, hell, even if she is dead—even if she was a crook of some kind, like you say——God, I can't take that one in yet!—hell of a thing to say, but there it was. Way I told you, I had a few dates with her but it wasn't anything serious, see? I was just somebody she knew. Like she knew Maureen and Bob and Linda Hausner—other people. But, first time I met Ricardo there, I could see—anybody could see—she'd really fallen for him. She was crazy about him, the big deal it was. And—well, it wasn't vice versa, see? He liked her O.K., but *she* was just a girl *he* knew, if you get me. Well, that first time we met—Ricardo and I, I mean—and got to talking, Val—sort of dealt herself in. Claimed to be real interested too, wanted to hear his records, and so on. She wasn't really—she was just trying to impress Ricardo, get closer with him. See?"

Mendoza said he saw.

"Well, that was it. We met there a couple of times, but she was bored to death, you could see. He's got some great stuff," said Manton enthusiastically. "Really unusual—but I've got a couple of things he hadn't heard too. And lately we've been getting together at his place mostly, just the two of us." He dropped his cigarette, stepped on it, and said awkwardly, "Like I say, I guess it sounds funny, a guy like me interested in— But that was how it was."

"I see," said Mendoza. "Well, I understand a lot of people are interested in folk music."

"I guess so," agreed Manton.

"What does Mr. Cardenas do? You say he's in Civil Service?"

"Oh, he's a chief accountant in the Welfare office—pensions and so on."

"Mhmm. Would you mind telling me where you were on Sunday?"

"Last Sunday? That's when she—" Manton had an expressive face; it showed surprise, anger, nervousness in succession. "Hey," he said, "I didn't have any—what the hell, you think—Well, anyway, thank God, I've got an alibi." He laughed, suddenly relaxing. "I had Monday off, so I flew over to Vegas early on Sunday—came back Monday night."

"Yes? Where did you stay?"

"Oh, I didn't bother to check in anywhere—when I get in a hot game, what's a little sleep lost? Did myself some good, too."

"Mhmm. Names of anybody you played with? Friends?"

"Well, I guess not—I—you know how you pick up with people, casual—

But, listen, I didn't have anything to do with—" He was uneasy again. "I didn't even know her very well! She was just—"

"A casual acquaintance, yes, I know," said Mendoza. "That was quite a dangerous little spot you got yourself out of, a few days ago. That emergency landing. I read about it in the *Times*."

Suddenly a totally different man looked out of Paul Manton's steady blue eyes. A wholly adult, competent man, mature and sophisticated. A—what was the word? Something teasingly familiar about that expression . . . "Aren't you so right," he said. "I was saying to myself, Well, boy, here it is and don't you wish you'd said your prayers oftener, when I spotted that stretch of freeway. Damn tank springing a leak— It was God's grace there wasn't any traffic, that time of night. They do say, if you're born to be hanged you'll never be drowned."

"You do much private flying?"

"As much as I can." He gave Mendoza a rather shy smile; he was the awkward young mechanic again. "I just got in on the Korea thing—Air Force. So I got trained free, you might say. If I can ever get the capital together—which is about as likely as the Commies lifting the Iron Curtain —I'd like to start my own line, cargo hauling like this outfit I'm working for . . . Well, I'm sorry I can't tell you anything more about Val. The hell of a thing. Seemed like such an ordinary girl, you know—never crossed my mind that she was anything else. And Ricardo will go straight up in the air. But then, neither of us really knew her very well."

Nobody, Mendoza reflected, starting back downtown, had known Valerie well. According to them. After the fact.

He saw the amber flick on on the signal ahead, jammed his foot down and made it across, illegally. And quite suddenly he knew what that expression had been on Manton's face. The look of the gambler saying, Let's take a long chance . . . It was—as Valerie's had been—a reckless face.

Yes?

But all that sounded straightforward. Very likely it was, but what proved it? In a way, his lack of corroboration over at Las Vegas was natural, if he was that kind of gambler.

Mrs. Farlow sounded genuine too (well, she very probably was), and the Dvorzhaks. But no proof.

There were, of course, Maureen Kelly Moskovitch and Gloria Litvak. . . .

Valerie Ellis—mixed up with the underground political thing, for God's sake? Thorwald . . . But the Feds said, Thorwald probably no longer involved with the Commies; on the run from them. Was this, could this be the complex spy story?

Just possibly? Thieves falling out. Thorwald, possibly, turning his coat again—and, having valuable information to pass on to, say, the C.I.A.? So the conspiracy here warned, and setting up a trap for him? Valerie one of the conspirators? And Thorwald getting wise, and—

Because, look at it from that angle—Valerie, spoiled, used to having money, and only nineteen—a lot of mixed-up kids that age got caught by the ideals of Communism. The impossible ideals. Communism, Socialism —two sides of the same coin. Sounding just fine, a wonderful idea—only the catch was, neither remotely workable until human nature got entirely changed around.

Could it be that—

No, he thought. Let the Feds work that angle all they pleased, it wasn't so. Thorwald be damned, this had been a private kill. A personal kill.

He got nuances from people—even from corpses. Valerie had been too much interested in Valerie to possess any ideals. What Valerie had been interested in was cold cash.

He left the Ferrari in the nearest public lot and walked half a block down to the Hall of Justice. After consulting the board in the lobby he rode the elevator up to the ninth floor and told the receptionist he'd like to see Mr. Cardenas.

"Oh, well, I don't know—" She cast him a doubtful look. "Mr. Cardenas in Accounting? Well, I'll see. Excuse me, what name did you—oh, yes." She went away, still looking doubtful. This was an old rabbit warren of an office, corridors leading in three directions from the main room. It seemed to be a busy office, people going and coming, clerks bustling by clutching armfuls of papers.

The receptionist came back and said Mr. Cardenas could see him now. Mendoza followed her down a dusty hall to a door with a frosted-glass panel that bore the simple legend, *Accounting*.

Inside, a large square room had been divided into a number of units by shoulder-high partitions. His guide led him to the one farthest on the left, opened the door set in the partition, and turned away with the air of washing her hands of him. Mendoza went in.

The cubicle was some ten feet square, and held a desk, two chairs and a couple of file cases. The man sitting at the desk looked up at him. "And what can I do for you, sir?" he asked in a pleasant baritone voice. "You're a *police* lieutenant? I haven't even had a traffic ticket that I can recall in— What's it all about?"

FIVE

Cardenas was obviously the boy friend described as "a little bit like you, sir." He was somewhat broader than Mendoza, and his face was rounder; he was in the process of losing his hair. Mendoza put him down as around forty.

He was pleasant and co-operative. As Manton had predicted, he was visibly shocked at the news that Valerie had been in some racket. "Good God, if the chief had found out!" he said. "What was it, anyway? I can't take it in—"

For the rest, he told exactly the same story that Manton had. Even down to confirming the fact—looking suitably embarrassed—that, yes, Valerie had, well, maybe been more interested in him than the other way round. "Not to sound conceited—and I don't deny that I was a little flattered." He laughed. "And also surprised! After all, I was a good deal older—" He'd known her only casually, and not long.

Naturally, naturally, thought Mendoza. And ask Mrs. Montague if she'd seen him, or Manton, calling there longer ago than a couple of months back—probably she couldn't be sure, she would just see their backs going in.

"Where did you meet her, Mr. Cardenas?"

"Through a mutual friend," said Cardenas easily. "A Mrs. Mandelbaum." He gave the address when asked, but looked rather shaken. "Lieutenant, I hope there won't be too much publicity over this—you know in my position, well, my chief— After all, I was a mere acquaintance, I hadn't anything to do with her death—"

"We have to check on everyone, you know," said Mendoza. When the Feds' press releases got out, there'd be publicity—like wildfire running loose there'd be publicity. "It doesn't necessarily mean we suspect you—or anyone else, Mr. Cardenas."

"Well, naturally not," said Cardenas a little stiffly. As if he found the mere suggestion that he could be suspected in bad taste.

"So I hope you won't take offense when I ask you where you were on Sunday from ten o'clock on."

"Where I— Well, I suppose you have to ask." Cardenas looked undecided whether to be angry or not. "Of course. And as far as that goes, I think you'll find it all—er—in order, Lieutenant. From ten, did you say? Yes, well, I was at home then, but I went out to eleven o'clock Mass at St. Mark's. I met a friend there, Dr. Gardner—he asked me to play golf with him that afternoon. Well, it was a nice day and I hadn't had a game in quite a while. We played a round and then had a drink at the clubhouse— that would be, let me see, about four o'clock . . . Yes, we'd gone straight from the church—that is, I stopped by to pick up my clubs, of course. And then we played another nine holes. He said his wife was away and he was going to have dinner at the clubhouse, asked me to join him. Which I did, and later on we both played bridge with a couple of other fellows there, until nearly eleven. I got home about midnight." He gave the names readily. "So you see—" He tucked his round chin into his collar severely. "As if I could be remotely connected anyway—"

If it checked out, Cardenas was pretty definitely in the clear. Mendoza felt a little exasperated. No leads at all. "Thanks very much. As I said, we have to check."

"I just can't imagine who'd want to murder the girl. But of course, if she was involved with crooks of some kind—"

"Yes." Mendoza decided that Cardenas was a bore. The shirt well stuffed. And if that alibi checked, he was out of the picture. He thanked him politely and came away.

He drove up North Broadway to Federico's, and met Hackett and John Palliser just going in. They sat down together, and he brought them up to date on Valerie. "All up in the air, damn it. And what's worse, I'm beginning to have a hunch that it was a private kill in the sense that the motive hadn't any connection with whatever racket it was. So even when we do ferret that out— Well, how are you doing on Lover Boy?"

"We're waiting for Sacramento to send us another list," said Palliser resignedly. Palliser was the newest sergeant in Mendoza's office and a rather bright boy: promising. "I know it's the only way to get at it, but it takes time, and meanwhile all this mud thrown at us by the press—"

"I know. But it's an ill wind, et cetera. When this news breaks on

Thorwald"—some of the afternoon papers already had it—"he and Valerie will probably occupy the headlines for a while and sidetrack the viewers-with-alarm . . . Small steak as usual, Adam, and coffee."

"Yes, sir." The tall waiter looked inquiringly at Hackett.

"Oh, hell," said Hackett unhappily. "I guess the same."

Palliser ordered and asked Hackett with respectful sympathy whether he'd lost any weight. "Three pounds," said Hackett gloomily. "The doctor says at least fifteen more."

Mendoza and Palliser looked at him with the conscious superiority of men not inclined to take on weight. Mendoza said, "You aren't firm enough with her, Art. After all, she did swear to obey you, didn't she? So she's a good cook—and she tells you you're a big man, you need a lot of food. She's heard what the doctor says and she's got a normal I.Q."

"It's not Angel, damn it, it's me. I mean it's not exactly Angel," said Hackett. "Sure, she gives me the high-protein diet, and I'm still trying to learn to drink coffee without sugar—but I can't expect her to go on a diet with me, can I? And, damn it, she's just like you two—eat anything and never gain a pound. Well, so she makes these things for herself, you know, like this special sour-cream dressing, and that wild-rice casserole with mushrooms and bacon, and last night"—a fond reminiscent gleam came into his eyes—"a really extra-special cheesecake—and, well, I get hungry, damn it. After all, I *am* six-three and a half, and only fifteen pounds—"

"No self-discipline," said Mendoza. "Deplorable. Keep the mind firmly fixed on your next physical."

"Thanks for the advice," said Hackett irritably. "The doctor's nuts. According to insurance statistics, I could go another five pounds and be inside the limit. He says they're way off base. But—"

"Never mind," said Mendoza soothingly. "Take your mind off food for a minute, and listen to me. I've had a small brainwave about Lover Boy." They both looked at him alertly. "That pock-marked complexion. All of the women said very definitely, pock-marked. Now, we hadn't thought too hard about it, except as another point of identification. But there's a couple of ways to acquire a pock-marked complexion. One, a bad case of adolescent acne sometimes leaves scars. But that's a little different than actual pockmarks, ¿no es verdad? And they were all quite definite—pockmarks. Well, smallpox is practically unheard-of in this country."

"So?" said Hackett.

"So," said Mendoza, "I suggest that you ask the Immigration people for a list of Negroes coming in from Mexico within the last—call it fifteen years. Calm down, it wouldn't be that long a list—ask them to do the screening. We know his approximate age."

"Well, it's an idea," agreed Palliser.

Mendoza had left instructions with Sergeant Lake that morning; when he came into the office after lunch, Maureen Kelly Moskovitch and her husband were waiting for him.

This kind, always a better chance of getting anything out of them if you brought them in to question. Their own familiar surroundings gave them a little confidence; but their past experience with cops and police stations turned them nervous in the proximity of either.

Overnight, as he'd told the Feds, routine had turned up Maureen—and Gloria—and a few interesting facts.

Maureen was twenty-eight, older than Valerie. She'd been picked up first as a juvenile, at seventeen, for soliciting. Ward of the court until she was of age. By that time she was married to Mike Moskovitch, who had been clean of any record then. The year after that Moskovitch had been dropped on as the very successful daylight burglar who had for six months been taking nice parcels of loot from empty apartments. First offense, and he'd got a three-to-five; he'd served four and had been out for nearly four years. Rather certainly he was at some crook caper, holding no regular job, but they hadn't any evidence on him as of now.

Meanwhile, since about six years ago, Maureen had been picked up for soliciting three times, had served minimal sentences.

They were there waiting for him, brought in unwillingly, nervous and scared. And stubborn. He had them ushered into his office, asked Sergeant Lake to take notes. He started in on Maureen . . .

"All right, all right, so I got a little pedigree! That don't say—you're just nuts, trying to— Listen, Val was my *friend!* We were pals—I just cried buckets when I heard she was dead like that, didn't I, Mike? Honest, you got to believe me—" Maureen was little and dark, and if she'd left herself more or less as nature made her, would have been pretty. But she'd plucked out most of her eyebrows, and substituted outdated thin curves painted on, and exaggerated a small mouth with too dark a shade of lipstick; to a naturally buxom figure she'd added a much-padded bra. Her nails were long and mostly magenta, the polish chipped here and there; and her cherry-colored sweater was too tight. "Listen, we were pals from way back, Val and me! I didn't—"

"That's what I want to talk about," said Mendoza. "I'm not accusing you of anything, Mrs. Moskovitch. I just want all you know about her.

Where'd you meet her, when, what was she doing then? Who did she know?"

"Oh," she said blankly. "You mean—you mean, like if I might know something that'd help you find out? But I don't! Gee, I'd tell you right off if I did, honest—Val was a good friend o' mine—" She looked at her husband. "You can say that, can't you, Mike? I never—"

He scowled at Mendoza, a big hefty young man, very dark, blue stubble of beard showing, dark eyes sullen under heavy brows. "We got nothing to hide," he said. "We're both clean, copper."

"You did know," asked Mendoza of private curiosity, "that your wife did a little time for prostitution while you were inside?"

"What the hell's it to you, bloodhound? So she did. I'm broad-minded, so what?"

"Nothing at all," said Mendoza equably. "So, let's hear what you know, Mrs. Moskovitch. When and where did you first meet Miss Ellis?"

She had calmed down a little. She said reluctantly, " 'Bout three years back. She was living same place I did, on Masefield Avenue."

"What were you doing then?" And as she didn't reply, "You were earning a scratch living hustling, weren't you? I've seen the landlady at that place, she's damn easygoing. Weren't you?"

"You know all the answers," she said sullenly. "All right."

"How was Valerie Ellis living? She didn't have a regular job either. Was she in the same game? And you two got acquainted over—mhmm—mutual interests?"

"That's right," she said shortly. "Sure. She was kinda new at it, I give her some tips."

Mendoza looked at her, but he was seeing Valerie. Valerie, coming from the house in Bel-Air, a sorority up at Berkeley, to that. Within a year. Grant that she'd been spoiled, shocked to be left with nothing. Some fatal weakness of character there too, to slide so easily downhill. The go-getting Fred Ellis—yes, maybe she'd just naturally acquired the idea that money was all-important. Maybe some man getting hold of her, but— And the complacent honest Ellises, only relatives, believing whatever she said, because naturally Fred's girl couldn't do anything bad.

"Was she working alone?"

"I dunno what you mean."

"Let's not waste time, Maureen," he said, sharp and cold. "Was there somebody running her?"

"Not—then."

"All right. When and who?"

"I—she wasn't—she didn't take so good to it. It wasn't awful long she kept at it, see. I'm *trying* to tell you, give me a chance—"

Mike Moskovitch just sat and glowered.

"Who?" asked Mendoza patiently.

"Eddy Warren," said Maureen sulkily. "I didn't—don't know much about him. She sort of turned up with him about six months after I met her, an' after that she moved 'n' I didn't see so much of her."

"But you know what capers they were up to? The same thing, or something else? Did he run any other girls?"

"I dunno."

"Come on, come on—you knew, you kept up with her, she'd have said something. Out with it."

"I—guess it was mostly just the usual old game. You know. They'd hit— like conventions, and like that. Vegas, San Diego, all over."

"The tired old badger game? Shakedown. All right. Who's Eddy Warren, what do you know about him?"

"I don't know nothing about him. Honest I don't. He was just a guy. When I ran across Val again, she didn't say nothing about him, he wasn't around no more. Honest."

"What was she doing lately? Since dropping Eddy?"

"I don't know."

"You'll stay here until I get all the answers I want, you know," said Mendoza gently. "Don't make it so hard on yourself, Maureen. What was Valerie's latest racket?"

"I don't *know!*" she half screamed at him. "I'm not telling you no lies, copper— Jesus, I knew who took her off I'd tell you quick—she was a pal— but I just don't *know.* I saw she was really in the chips, clothes she had 'n' all—an' time goes on, even more—that color TV—I *asked* her—Jesus, wouldn't I ask her? But she'd just laugh an' say she was like a cat, always fell on her feet. I swear to God I don't know—it wasn't nothing like the other, I know that, but she wouldn't say!"

"Take it easy," said Moskovitch coldly. "He hasn't got a thing on you. He can't hold you, make you talk."

"Oh, don't be silly, Mike! I'd talk enough if I knew anything'd help 'em find whoever killed her! It don't seem it could be, somebody killing Val— But I just don't know, honest, Lieutenant. I asked her a lot of times, naturally. But she'd just pass it off."

"How?" he asked softly.

"Oh, any way. Like I remember once she said, Ask no questions, get told no lies. Kind of laughing. An' then, 'nother time, she said—she was serious about it then—she said, let me think back, she said, It's a swell caper, Maureen, a real offbeat one but it sure pays off. An' she said, But I can't talk about it. Be too dangerous. She said a funny thing—she said, about a old proverb—that three can keep a secret if two of them are dead —but she was sure about these other two. It was funny."

Mendoza regarded her in silence. He thought she was coming clean. One like this—no, Valerie wouldn't have confided in her. Maureen would have told the interesting news of Valerie's profitable caper to anybody she knew, if it occurred to her. And it probably would have . . . So, by inference, two other people in on it with Valerie? Whatever the hell it had been.

Looking at Maureen, where she sat huddled chewing her ragged lipstick off, he felt tired. Not for the first time he wondered why he stayed on this job, when he didn't have to. Sense of guilt, reneging on the oath once he had all that money? Not exactly . . . There was an inevitable gulf fixed between the police and the ordinary citizens. All those ordinary citizens clamoring for them to catch Lover Boy and stash him away behind bars . . . The police were the barrier, he thought, between the honest citizenry and the dirt. The incredible muck at the bottom of things. The average honest citizen saw the police in the person of the neat-uniformed traffic officer, white-gloved, his gun neatly sheathed at his hip. The average honest citizen hadn't any remote conception how very dirty the bottom of things was, that police had to probe, getting down in the muck themselves to do so.

They stood outside and complained and jeered. On the rare occasions when some cop got himself entangled in the muck, they rejoiced: knew it all along, corrupt cops. They wrote letters to the editor disapproving of the latest pay hike and telling about overbearing traffic cops.

They didn't know anything at all about the muck that policemen delved into, to keep the honest citizens safe and healthy and happy.

For some five seconds Mendoza succumbed to a prevalent disease among police officers and hated the honest citizenry with a beautiful savagery.

Remembering, say—the latest one—Patrolman Charles Haggerty, beaten and shot to death with his own gun by a gang of juveniles, while a crowd of adults looked on with never a move to help him.

Of course, that had been down on Skid Row.

He forced his mind back to Maureen. He asked, "You remember anything else she said?"

"No. She never told me nothing, for all I asked. Honest, I'd say if she had—I liked Val, she was a swell girl—we were *friends*—"

"All right," said Mendoza abruptly. "That's all. You can go." He didn't watch them out; he swiveled round in his chair and stared out over the panorama of the city, clear and crystal-sharp this February day, smogless. He could see the towers of the new California skyscraper, all of twenty-four stories, at the corner of Wilshire and Western. He could see, blue and sharp, the outlines of the Hollywood hills separating L.A. from the San Fernando Valley.

It was a prettier view than the Moskovitches.

He swiveled back. Sergeant Lake said, "Makes you wonder. But they come all sorts."

Mendoza felt better suddenly. Phlegmatic, comfortable Sergeant Lake comforted him. There wasn't really much difference, he thought, between Sergeant Lake and any other youngish fellow in a white-collar job at six thousand a year, a fellow with a wife and three kids, buying a house on time, worrying about bills, about the kids' report cards. He said, "You're a philosopher, Jimmy. Set up a hunt for this Eddy Warren, will you? Ask Records. Ask Vice."

"Will do," said Sergeant Lake cheerfully. "Like you said, I had this Gloria Litvak fetched in too. She should be here by now, I'll go see. You want her right off?"

Mendoza made a grimace. "I suppose so . . . Why are we here, Jimmy? Deliberately playing in the mud? A lot of other ways to make a living."

Sergeant Lake, on his feet, regarded the question seriously, as he would any question. "Well, that's so, Lieutenant," he agreed. "And if you're not on inside detail, a lot of safer ways too. Like you know, I got shot up three times before I got out of uniform. But of course there's the pension and the hospital benefits. Hadn't been, I'd have had a time finding the cash to pay off the hospital when we had the third one. But, tell you the honest gospel truth, Lieutenant, what sort of tipped the scales for me was a second looie in the Air Force. When I joined up, I mean."

"Oh?"

Sergeant Lake rubbed his jaw, grinning. "He was after Caroline too," he said. "And don't we know, they always like a uniform."

Mendoza laughed "*¡De acuerdo!* You restore my faith in irrational human nature."

Sergeant Lake regarded him benignly and said, "Nor I don't see you've just all that right to look down your nose at Maureen Moskovitch. Seeing that before you got to be a respectable married man—"

"¡*Camarada, simpatía masculino!* I never stooped so low as the Maureens, I assure you!" said Mendoza, laughing. "O.K., go and see if Gloria's waiting." It was three o'clock; he swiveled around and looked out the window again, waiting. He wished he could go home to Alison and the twins and forget all this.

But, even as he thought that, he knew he never could; he wasn't built that way. Given the tangle, the mystery, he had to unravel it for his own satisfaction. Find all the answers, get it all tidily straightened out.

SIX

Lake came back with Gloria Litvak, and Mendoza asked her to sit down. After a sullen moment she did. "I don't know anything about it," she said. "About Val's getting killed. I don't know who'd do a thing like that. I couldn't tell you anything."

"I haven't asked you anything yet," Mendoza pointed out. "I think you can answer the questions I'm going to ask. How long had you known Miss Ellis?"

"I don't see how that helps you on the murder." She was nervous. She fumbled in her bag, got out a cigarette. This one was younger, about Valerie's age. "I didn't have anything to do with that!"

"Nobody's said you did. When and how did you meet her?"

She started to protest again, shrugged, and said, "Cops. All right, I got to know Val about two and a half years ago, around there."

"How?"

She took her time over that one, probably doing some fast figuring as to whether the truth would be dangerous in some way; finally she said, "Oh, well, a guy I knew then introduced us."

"What's his name?"

"I lost touch with him since, I don't know—"

"What's his name?"

"Warren. Eddy Warren."

"Was he running you then?"

"I dunno what— No, for God's sake! I never let a man—" This one was platinum blond, buxom, not very pretty. All the usual accessories, from the dark-red nails to the cheap cologne.

"About that time, Eddy Warren and Val were working the shakedown racket. Were you in on that too?"

Her eyes moved; she had known about that, but she hadn't known that the police knew, by the way her mouth tightened. She'd only been picked up once, and got off with a fine; she wouldn't want to put herself in trouble by making any admissions. She said, "I don't know anything about that. I didn't know Eddy ever did anything wrong. Or Val either."

"Oh, come now," said Mendoza mildly. "Never had any little girlish chats about customers?"

"I'm clean!" she said hurriedly. "I been straight ever since that time your damn college-boy Vice cop tricked me! I never knew Val was—"

"But you'd kept up with her. You saw her fairly often. Don't tell me you just made light conversation about the latest fashions and the current best-sellers. Didn't you ever wonder how she was living, when she hadn't a regular job? Ask her about it? What'd she tell you? What was her racket?"

He didn't really think Gloria would know: another one like Maureen, and Valerie wouldn't have confided. But he saw her eyes move again, before she dropped the lids, and one hand tightened its grasp on her shiny plastic bag. The other hand, holding her cigarette, trembled very slightly. She was scared to death, he saw. And she did know something.

Just scared of the cops? Or maybe, being involved in this just because she'd known Val, being looked at closer and dropped on again? No; she had been nervous, but not really frightened until he'd brought this up. She did know something about Val's racket.

Val and two others. Gloria one of them?

"I don't know what you mean," she was saying mechanically. "I thought she was straight."

"But you knew she hadn't always been. From the time you both knew Eddy Warren."

"No. No." She shook her head blindly. "I never knew that. I never knew her very well." A better education than Maureen; she spoke fairly well. But now her voice was shaking too. "I don't know anything about her getting killed."

"I'm not asking about that. When was the last time you saw her?"

She relaxed just a trifle; she wasn't afraid of that question. "It was a week ago last Tuesday. I just dropped by to ask her to a party. That Thursday it was, week ago today. I didn't stay long because somebody came—I mean, somebody was coming to see her." She'd nearly made a slip there, over something, and had scared herself again. Her eyes slid nervously away from his.

"Somebody came or somebody was coming. Which?"

She was flustered that he'd picked that up. "Somebody was coming, and she said it was private business so I left."

"I see. And you never asked yourself where her money came from, when she hadn't a regular job. Weren't curious enough to ask her about the private business."

"W-why should I? I mind my own business," she said breathlessly. "I thought she had a job at Robinson's, really I did, I thought she was straight. Just like m-me."

"Even when you found her home at—what time—in the afternoon? Well, of course she wouldn't tell you about the private business even if you'd asked. You're sure you never heard her drop any hints as to where the money came from?"

"Why sh-should I? No."

"Well, if you don't know, you don't," he said with a shrug. "At that, I don't suppose she'd talk about it." He let Gloria see that he'd accepted her denial, believed her all along the line. "And especially if you didn't know her very well, as you said. Pity you can't tell me any more, but thanks very much for coming in anyway." He stood up. She got to her feet in a hurry, anxious for release, open relief showing in her eyes. She'd put it across; he believed her, he didn't suspect anything.

"That's O.K.," she said almost happily, and turned to the door. He let her take a step, and then spoke quite casually.

"By the way, did she come to the party?"

"No, she had to be over at Vic's—" Gloria stopped dead still. In her sudden tremendous relief, her hurry to be gone, she'd forgotten to guard her tongue. She'd let out something else, and now she was terrified. Too terrified to open her mouth, try to cover up that slip, which was a pity—because if she did she'd probably tell several stupid lies and give him some lead.

She knew that what she'd just said was a slip; but it didn't mean one damned thing to Mendoza. *She had to be over at Vic's.* Vic who? No Vic had shown up in this case so far.

"Oh," he said, coming out from behind his desk and moving to face Gloria. "That's very interesting, Miss Litvak. So she had to be over at Vic's." He held her frightened eyes. "Vic who?"

Suddenly he thought she was going to faint. A greenish pallor spread over her complexion; she shut her eyes for a moment. He took her arm, but she shook him off. "I'm—all—right," she muttered. "Just kind of dizzy a minute, I got up too quick. Doctor says I need glasses."

"Vic who?"

"I don't know," she said. She was breathing rapidly, shallowly. "That's all Val said, just that she had to be at Vic's that night. I don't know any Vic. And, way I say, she was expecting somebody, so I just left then. And that's all I know."

She wasn't to be moved from that. He had to let her go. He went back to his desk and called Waltham. At least, on this one they were getting quite a lot of their work done for them. The Federal boys were taking a long close look at every individual mentioned in that book, and at their backgrounds and relatives too. Where only one name was mentioned, as was the case with those fourteen names embellished with dollar signs, they were taking a look at everybody in this territory who wore those names. It would take time and men, but they had the organization, and they were good. They would pass their information on, so there was no sense wasting his own men on that.

"I know it's early to ask," he said to Waltham, "but have you got around to Gloria Litvak yet?"

"Let's see," said Waltham. Mendoza heard papers rattle. "We're sending you a daily report, as we cover the list. Take a little time, of course. There's not much here yet. You know about her being picked up, naturally. She's twenty-four, never been married. Graduated from high school. Family looks respectable, nothing against any of 'em. Father's a book-keeper at a manufacturing plant."

"Really? Well, the well-brought-up girls do go off the rails sometimes," said Mendoza, thinking of that case last year.

"So they do. Family consists of parents, one older and one younger brother, uncle—father's brother. Father emigrated from Poland when he was twenty. He's fifty-three now. Mother was born here, but is also Polish."

"You said not much? I'd call that plenty."

"Well, we're still looking at them for any political funny business. Father's a registered Democrat but that doesn't really say anything. Fellow who saw them says, by the way, that the family was terribly ashamed when he mentioned Gloria's little lapse. She doesn't live with them. Place where she does live, well, it's not very fancy, she could be still a subject for your Vice boys. That's about it, so far."

"Well, thanks very much. By the way, I saw Paul Manton and that Cardenas myself," and he told Waltham what they'd said. "You just might have a look to check on it. Just for fun. And I've got a new name for you. Eddy Warren." Sergeant Lake came in and laid a file card before him silently. Glancing at it, he told Waltham how Eddy Warren had turned up. "And I've just got his record. He's thirty-six—skip the description, rather ordinary type—two juvenile counts, dope, and three pickups as an adult. Procuring and resorting. He got a year on the second procuring charge. He's still on probation right now. I'll see his probation officer. Now I do wonder," he added suddenly.

"About what?"

"Those reefers. She might have been storing them for him. If her racket wasn't dope—which we don't know it wasn't, of course. How are you getting on with your end?"

Waltham sounded tired. "Not so hot. You sure run a lot of liquor stores out here. Of course it's a big town. We've been in touch with Interpol—nobody seems to have had a smell of Thorwald since he was seen in East Berlin last June. But he wouldn't have stayed there any longer than he had to, you know. It's not very likely he got into Britain, they keep a damn close check. Of course it's easier—an island. When I think of the thousands of miles of U.S. border right out in the howling wilderness—But my guess is that our Osgar got homesick, wasn't willing to settle for a quite anonymous life in Switzerland or somewhere. Also, there's another thing. We don't know whether they're still after him. Maybe he doesn't know. It could be they just got mad at him for some—er—indiscretion, and once he got away they just said good riddance and stopped chasing him. But maybe not, too. And he might feel a lot safer here at home, where if things got uncomfortably dangerous he could always run not walk to the nearest FBI office and ask asylum for a few Russian secrets."

"Yes, I see that. Well, I know a little more about Valerie now, and I doubt very much that she ever had a political idea in her head. Not a very nice girl, Valerie, but I really can't see her mixed up with a Communist front. Not the type to get idealistically converted—she wasn't given to ideals. And they've got their own experienced agents, why would they offer an outsider hard cash to do a job for them?"

"If," said Waltham, "she was already tied up to Thorwald some way and they saw they could get at him through her?"

"My God, the wild stories you cloak-and-dagger boys think up."

"You'd be surprised at some of the stuff we run into," said Waltham. "Straight out of the paperback spy stories. If she was Thorwald's mistress— Have you got anything on her on that angle?"

Mendoza told him what Maureen had said. "So she'd done a little hustling. Easiest way for a female to earn crooked money. But Maureen said," and he laughed, "she didn't take to it so good. I'll bet. Not just that she was essentially cold—most of that kind are—but she retained, maybe, a little fastidiousness from her expensive upbringing. She found it much more congenial, teaming up with Eddy, to play the old badger game. And it looks as if she graduated from that, and Eddy, to something a little bigger and more profitable. Anything went with Valerie, so long as it brought in the cold cash."

"But if Thorwald—"

"Wait a minute, I'm making a point. By what Maureen said, and by what I know of females, Valerie was essentially sexless. We know she was raking in a pretty good profit from somewhere, so she wouldn't have had to use her sex for money, against her inclinations. I don't think it's at all likely that she was shacking up with anybody."

"Well, by what you say that might be so," said Waltham.

"Anything on Paul Manton yet?"

"No, sorry. We've only really been on it today."

"Yes. Well, I'll get onto Eddy Warren. Good luck." Mendoza put the phone down and got up. "I'll be down in Vice if anybody asks, Jimmy."

Vice was his old stamping-ground; he'd spent nearly eight years there; but it hadn't been in this clean, new, airy office because that had been before the big new headquarters building went up. He drifted down to Lieutenant Percy Andrews' office and asked if he was in.

"Just as of now," said Andrews behind him. "Slumming, Luis?"

"Not exactly. One of your criminal types has showed up in a case of mine." He showed Andrews the file card on Eddy Warren. "Can you tell me anything about him?"

"Sit down. Eddy Warren—" Andrews searched his capacious memory and said, "a smalltimer. Sure, I remember a little. I picked him up that time he got put inside. Remember I was mad as hell because I had to go to court to give evidence on him on my day off . . . He's a little guy, very gentlemanly, and"—he grinned—"by what some of his ladies say, quite a boilermaker. Your type."

"A real Romeo," said Mendoza, translating the pro slang. "Know what he's up to now?"

Andrews shrugged. "He's on probation. Just makes it a little harder for them to carry on business as usual. You know the problem. There just aren't enough men to go round, to keep anything like a thorough check on where probationers live, whom they associate with, and so on. We go through the motions, you could put it. Get them in for the weekly chat, all nice and friendly. You're keeping straight, aren't you, Eddy? Oh, yes, sir, I sure am . . . We can ask his officer, but you won't get much."

"No. I know. The perennial problem."

"But, listen, Luis. This Eddy Warren. Showing up in a homicide? Cross him off your list, boy. He's a rabbit when it comes to the rough stuff. Most pimps are, you know as well as me."

Mendoza grinned. "Well, I never associated so much with you low woman chasers, even when I was down here."

"So you didn't," returned Andrews amiably. "Being halfway a pro card sharp yourself, you got sent into the gambling-dens. You want me to tag along, see Warren with you?"

"Don't think it's necessary. I don't suppose he's involved in the murder, but he might possibly know a few additional facts about Valerie to hand me—if he'd kept up with her at all. Well, thanks very much . . ."

He sent Scarne out to pick up Eddy at his last recorded address. Forty minutes later Scarne called in to say that Eddy wasn't at home, or at a bowling-alley he was known to frequent, or at a bar ditto.

"Well, you wait at the home address, see if he shows by six. If not, I'll put one of the night-duty men on there," said Mendoza.

He spent a little while going over the current cases Sergeants Curraccio, Galeano, and Rolf were working. Nothing yet on that hit-and-run; damn. Probably nothing but an involuntary homicide on Galeano's case.

The new D.M.V. list from Sacramento, covering Orange, Ventura, and San Bernardino counties, arrived by special delivery at five-thirty. Hackett, who had just come in, fell on it eagerly.

"He's just got to be somewhere here," he said. "He's just got to."

"Don't be too sure, Art," said Mendoza. "Seven crimes in ten weeks. He could be a truck driver who lives in San Francisco and hits L.A. once a week."

Hackett swore tiredly. "Don't discourage me. I know that, damn it. But, by God, if I have to go through a list of every light-blue pickup truck registered in all fifty-eight counties of California, I'll get him! I only hope he doesn't kill any more women before I do."

"*Es duro de pelar,*" said Mendoza dryly. "He could also be a truck driver living in Tucson, Arizona, who crosses the border once a week or so with a cargo."

"*Entendámonos,*" said Hackett dangerously, "when you say that, smile! Unless you're asking for an uppercut. Did you see what the *Citizen* said about us today?"

"Don't worry about the press boys. As from about seven hours ago, they're off on this new kick—Thorwald and Valerie. You'll get Lover Boy sooner or later. I wish I was as sure I'd get the X who took Valerie off."

"That's a tough one all right. No leads?"

"Except a hunch," said Mendoza. "And if I'm right, that turns it even tougher . . . a hunch that the motive hadn't one damned thing to do with whatever caper Valerie had been on lately. Damn it. Of course I've only seen a few of the people she knew. But—" He was silent, feeling his jaw. "Well, see what more the Feds turn up tomorrow." He got up and reached for his hat.

El Señor met him at the door, talking loudly. Mendoza caught him as he leaped for his shoulder, and finding the living room empty walked down the hall toward the new nursery, as yet undecorated.

"Alison?"

A tall scraggly gray-haired female bobbed up before him at the door of the room. "Mr. Mendoza? Mrs. Mendoza has gone out to the market, I expect she'll be back soon, sir."

"Oh." Mendoza wandered in. "The little monsters awake? Now, in broad daylight, you don't yell." He grinned down at Master John Luis, who returned the gaze dreamily. Master John, unlike his sister, had inherited his mother's hazel-green eyes, which looked oddly pale in his olive-skinned face. But his black hair grew into an uncanny duplication of his father's sharp widow's peak. "My own fault," said Mendoza severely, admiring him fondly, "such a combination." Master John had contorted his right leg into a comfortable position for sucking his big toe.

"Mr. Mendoza! You must not— The cats are not to be allowed in the nursery, and you must not touch the babies until you have washed—"

He swung around to face her. El Señor swore in his ear, in a bitter voice. "It's Lieutenant," he said. "And I am reasonably clean—is it Miss Freeman?"

"But one cannot be too careful! I beg your pardon, but I cannot have these unsanitary creatures in the nursery. I must ask you—"

"The cats," said Mendoza, "are also reasonably clean. I don't—"

"Oh! Another of them! Get out, you nasty thing!" Miss Freeman clapped her hands at Bast, ambling up to welcome Mendoza. El Señor spat and leaped from Mendoza's shoulder, and Bast shied away down the hall. Master John began to cry.

Mendoza picked him up and patted him. "Miss Freeman, I'm afraid—"

"But you haven't washed!" she said distractedly. "I must ask you, Mr. Mendoza—after all, presumably I know my job—"

Belatedly, he got what Alison had been talking about. He said coldly, "Just whose children are these, Miss Freeman? And the cats have the run of the house. We all take baths at least once a day, I assure you." He heard Alison come in the kitchen door.

"Well, really, I didn't mean to imply—but after all, I am accustomed to having the routine I establish respected—"

Master John stopped crying and started to suck his thumb. Mendoza put him back in his crib. "Routine be damned," he said. "All you're hired for is to walk the floor with them in the middle of the night. I need my sleep." He went out to meet Alison.

"Luis?" She came down the hall.

"*Amada*—I've had the hell of a day, I need a little comforting—"

"*¡Querida, amada!*" She got her arms around him tight as he embraced her.

"*Cariña—*"

"Well, really!" said Miss Freeman pinkly, averting her eyes.

SEVEN

Mendoza was yawning again as he came into his office at a quarter of nine on Friday morning. He'd half waked when the twins went off on schedule, dimly, at two forty-five, but drifted back to sleep again. Miss Freeman might have some peculiar ideas but they could be ignored as long as she stayed up with the little monsters . . . He was awakened again half an hour later by Alison sitting up and lighting a cigarette.

" 'Smatter, they got you into the habit too?"

"I'm sorry, I didn't mean to wake you up," she said worriedly. "That woman and her valid reasons! I know she isn't with them at all, Luis—she's looked for her ridiculous valid reasons and not found any, and she's just letting them cry."

"At least she isn't asleep," said Mendoza. "Not with that next door." The yelling was blessedly dim, forty feet away behind two closed doors, and presently he drifted off again; but he suspected that Alison had stayed awake worrying . . .

He went into the office and found Sergeant Lake looking disgusted. "Women!" said Sergeant Lake.

"What now?"

"That Mrs. Montague. It does make you wonder. She just called up. She says she put it off because she was going on an all-day trip yesterday with her niece and nephew, up to Mount Wilson, and she didn't want us messing around making her miss it. I ask you! So just now she calls to tell us that somebody tried to get into Valerie's apartment again on Wednesday night."

"¡Vaya por Dios! Women, as you say. Details?"

"Some interesting ones," said Lake grimly. "She says about midnight Wednesday she was just going to bed when she heard the front door open. Being the kind she is, she listened at her door and heard somebody fumbling around at the door across the hall. So she looked out, and it's all just the way it was before on Sunday night. A man with a key to Valerie's door, just getting it open—and when he sees her there, he runs for it. Only this time he doesn't drop the key. And she says definitely it wasn't the same man. Smaller. Didn't get much of a look at him otherwise, the light's too dim, but that she'll swear to."

"Well, well. Somebody'd better chase up there sometime today, get a statement on that. I hope she enjoyed her trip to Mount Wilson."

"I almost asked her. And I don't suppose it's even any use to go and print that doorknob, in case he left any, because after he'd bolted, what did the silly old cow do but go across and shut the door!"

Mendoza shut his eyes resignedly in comment. "Can't be helped now— we'd better have a try all the same. Brief Marx, will you?" He looked at his watch. "I trust somebody's sitting on Eddy Warren's doorstep?" Warren hadn't shown up at home last night at all: home being a cheap hotel room on Figueroa.

"Sure, Bert went out on it. The Feds are getting their full press coverage all right, aren't they?"

Mendoza agreed. Thorwald and Valerie were spread all over the front pages, since last night's editions. There were rehashes on the Thorwald case six years ago, a good many cuts. Not much detail on Valerie, but they'd gone to town with what they had. Even cuts of the James Ellises— horrified relatives deny niece could have been involved in crime of any sort. And they'd got onto Maureen and Gloria; there was a bad cut of the latter—*close friend of murdered girl, Miss Gloria Litvak, 1196-A Cherokee Drive.* And the news that both had been picked up for soliciting. The sly inference that maybe Valerie had been on the same lay. Big cuts of Thorwald, with HAVE YOU SEEN THIS MAN? in scare headlines below.

All that brought him, presently, James Ellis. A James Ellis looking sick and bewildered, and apologizing, "I know you're a busy man, Lieutenant, I don't want to waste your time. But what the papers are all saying—I've just got to ask you, have you found out for sure she—she was—like that? It doesn't seem possible—when she was brought up decent and honest—"

"Well, young people go off the rails rather easily sometimes," said Mendoza. "I know how you're feeling about it, Mr. Ellis. But by what we know of her, I think it's very possible that she'd have gone off the rails anyway, even without—"

"My wife's upset, no wonder. Keeps saying if we'd only kept closer touch, tried to check on who she was running around with—"

"If it's any comfort to you, Mr. Ellis, I don't think you could have—changed her, just by that. You'd just have found out about her a little sooner. I don't know whether you agree with me, but I think we come equipped with our essential personalities. There was some flaw in her from the beginning . . ." Which wasn't very useful philosophy to Ellis right now, who might always feel partly responsible for Valerie's downfall. Not much to say to Ellis.

He got some interesting confirmation of his deductions about Valerie when Dwyer brought in Eddy Warren, who'd come wandering home about nine-thirty after a night out. Warren was a dapper little fellow not over five-four, good-looking, self-confident, and not at all worried.

"You've got nothing on me—Mr. Wayne knows that." His probation officer. "I'm being a good boy, I am."

"Staying out all night?" asked Mendoza.

Warren grinned. "Hell, Lieutenant, I'm not *that* good! I suppose you found out from somebody I used to know Valerie Ellis. Well, I don't know one blessed thing about how she came to get took off, but anything else you want to ask, go ahead." He lit a cigarette.

Since they'd never been dropped on for it at the time, he categorically denied the shakedown caper in collaboration with Valerie; she was "just a girl I knew, you know." Sure, he'd known she was a setup then; so what? After pressure he admitted that he'd scouted for her a little—just a while. He was quite frank on that. "Turnabout's fair play, gentlemen," he said cheerfully. "I like my clients to get value for their money."

"I had a hunch she was one like that," said Mendoza.

"Oh, yes, indeed," said Warren thoughtfully. He looked at his cigarette. "I'll tell you no lie, gentlemen, that one was bad medicine. There was a streak in her kind of scared me, you want to know. A wild streak—real wild. Especially when she was lit up a little. I remember once she was telling me how a guy passed out on her, and she laughed and said all of a sudden she wondered how it'd feel to stick the bread knife into him. That kind of wild . . . And one day I said to myself, I said, Eddy, boy, you get shut of that female or she's gonna take you smack into bad trouble. She was Trouble in a big way." That came straight from the heart. He stabbed out his cigarette and cocked his head at Mendoza. "But you boys didn't know her. How come you decide right off it was murder? Sleeping-pills—it could've been suicide or accident and a boy friend or somebody got scared and dumped the body."

"Well," said Mendoza absently, "she got it all in one dose—bang. And there wasn't any codeine prescription in her apartment. And— Never mind. She wasn't a suicidal type?"

"Brother," said Warren in sole comment. "She was too interested in the long green . . . . I hadn't seen her in a good long time, no."

"Is that so? Are you doing any business in reefers lately?"

"Who, me? On probation? Hell, are you kidding, Lieutenant?" His surprised dismay was exaggerated.

"Sure you hadn't kept in touch with Val? Maybe, since you're on probation, you were taking extra precautions—your own place apt to be searched at any time—and were maybe paying her a little rent to stash away your merchandise at her place?"

A muscle jerked in Warren's cheek. "You got one hell of an imagination, Lieutenant. That's crazy."

"Bert," said Mendoza, "let's just see what keys he has on him, shall we?"

Warren was on his feet like a cat, but he knew he hadn't a chance; sullenly he stood still while Dwyer went over him and produced a fat bunch of keys. Mendoza looked at them one by one. "This," he said, looking at the seventh one he came to, "looks very similar to me. Of course the Feds have got her key, but we can always take a little ride up to Mariposa Street and try it. Shall we?"

Warren sat down again. "All right," he said. "But about any reefers I don't know one blessed thing and you can't prove I ever did."

"You admit that this is a key to Valerie Ellis's apartment?" asked Mendoza formally.

"Yeah. Naturally I wasn't going to come out with this, gentlemen, especially as it hasn't anything to do with her getting killed. But as long as you've found out—" He shrugged and lit another cigarette. "It was like this, see. One of my lady friends has a jealous-type husband, and right now he's out of a job and sitting around their place all day. And my hotel mightn't be very fancy, but they stick to the ground rules, she can't come there. So I had this little arrangement with Val—oh, sure, I wasn't in close touch with her any more but I saw her around—you see what I mean, use her place. For a little extra change—it was anything to make a fast buck with that one." He faced them calmly.

He was an old hand. He knew they couldn't prove anything on him at all. They might be a hundred per cent sure that those reefers were his, that he'd paid Valerie to store them for him while he was on probation; there was no proof. None of his prints in the apartment. They could get

Mrs. Montague down, ask her if he was the Wednesday night intruder; she wouldn't be able to say.

"Yes, the first press stories about the identification of the body came out Wednesday night, didn't they?" said Mendoza. "That shook you, and you decided to take a chance that we hadn't looked at her apartment yet—try to rescue your stock in trade. But you didn't quite manage it, did you, Mr. Warren? You got scared off. Just like X on Sunday night. I don't know but what Mrs. Montague's been of some help to us, at that . . . And you underestimate us, we'd been over the apartment thoroughly by then."

"I don't know what you're talking about," said Warren indifferently. "I told you how it was."

"What's your lady friend's name?"

Warren grinned at him. "Why, hell, Lieutenant, I'm a gentleman, I am. You don't expect me to give her away, do you?"

Mendoza suppressed a grin. "O.K.," he said. "Out. Off the merry-go-round, Eddy. We could waste all day asking and answering, but I know when I'm beaten. I may be seeing you again."

"Any time at all, Lieutenant," said Warren, rising unhurriedly. He straightened his tie. "Nice to've met you."

Dwyer scowled after him. "What the hell do you do with the smart-aleck ones like that?"

But Mendoza leaned back in his chair and laughed. "'I'm a gentleman, I am!' ¡Eso es hermoso sin pero!—beautiful. We'll never get him on those reefers, Bert. But at least we've deprived him of them. And damn it, I forgot to get that key—"

"I'll catch him," said Dwyer, and vanished, still looking angry.

A thinnish Manila envelope arrived by special messenger from the FBI. It contained the report on the Litvaks which Mendoza had already heard about, others on Robert and Linda Hausner, Cardenas, and a Marion Keller.

The Hausners were a young couple looking quite ordinary. Said they'd met Valerie by getting talking, casually, in the bar of The Black Cat about six months ago. Linda Hausner was German-born, had met her husband while he was doing his army service in Germany seven years ago. Both her parents were dead. They'd had no idea that Valerie was anything but respectable, but then they hadn't known her well (that phrase was beginning to ring in Mendoza's ears). Bob Hausner had a good job as an electrical engineer at a big manufacturing outfit in North Hollywood, made seven hundred a month. They sounded like honest citizens: buying a house, one kid four, another two, both boys; according to the neighbors no wild parties or fights. The Hausners said they'd been to a few parties at

Valerie's place, that was all. Had met a couple of her friends casually, but not to *know* them.

They looked all right, but there was that little item: the wife was foreign-born.

Marion Keller was something else again. She dated from Valerie's Bel-Air days: a girl Valerie had gone to school with. Her father was a well-known TV director. Marion Keller, now happily married to a wealthy young businessman, said of course she'd always felt sorry for Val—they'd been friends for a long time, and she'd tried to keep in touch with her, to let her know "it hadn't made any difference." She said Val had changed; sometimes she'd be almost rude, say she didn't want any charity—"not that I ever offered her any, of course." And then again she'd be eager to have Marion come in and talk, reminiscing about old days. "To tell you the truth," Marion Keller had said, "we hadn't anything in common any more, it was more a guilt complex than anything else that made me keep in touch with her, especially since I've been married. But I did feel sorry for her, and I used to call her up—go to see her occasionally. Just for that reason."

Of course Marion had never suspected, et cetera.

Mendoza yawned and lit a cigarette.

Cardenas also looked like a very respectable civil servant. He was well thought of by his superiors, got on well with his juniors, was "very conscientious." He certainly was interested in folk music; his apartment living-room bore ample evidence in the form of an expensive stereo outfit and some hundreds of L.P. records. He lived with his sister Maria, also unmarried, also employed in Civil Service, as an accountant.

He had been employed by the Welfare Department for seventeen years. He had been married; his wife had died in childbirth, with the baby. He lived within his means, attended church regularly, was not known to run around with women or overdrink. He had no close relatives except the sister. He was a native Californian.

It was all very depressingly respectable. So unproductive of any suggestive lead. Mendoza yawned again.

They had not found a single Vardas in the county. They had found over a hundred Glessners, sixty-four Imarosas, over two hundred Monteux', and a dismaying number of Hoesses, while the figure on the Wilanowskis—Mendoza could imagine Waltham clutching his brow and groaning. Like the L.A.P.D., they had only so many men . . . If Hackett had not stripped the office bare on his hunt for Lover Boy, Mendoza would have offered to take over part of that list. On the other hand, he knew the

Feds: they never felt a job was well done unless they'd done it themselves. He sympathized; he felt the same way himself.

He was curious as to what they'd turn up on Paul Manton.

But so far, absolutely nothing to suggest a lead to X. Absolutely nothing to point to what Valerie's latest racket had been.

She had to be over at Vic's. He shook his head. It might have some significance, but not for him. He made a note to pass it on to Waltham.

Another messenger dropped by with his requested photostat of Valerie's address book, and he studied it earnestly all over again.

Glessner—meet Rikki's 5 p.m., get $5000.

Five thousand dollars. Split three ways? A nice little take, but nothing spectacular. What did that say?

He thought, say those fourteen mentioned names were marks they had taken. (They?) Glessner was the first. All right. Was five thousand the average take? That made it—he scribbled figures—seventy thousand, a very nice piece of change indeed, even split three ways. It was all supposition, however, because that was the only time a figure was mentioned. And, by the comment in the address book, maybe "s.o.b." meant Wilanowski hadn't paid up.

Another thing the book said to him now was, it hadn't been used as an address book. It had been in use as a daily diary, where she'd jotted down reminders to herself. There wasn't a date noted throughout. How long had it been in use? Anybody's guess—three months, six months, a year.

Possibly, other little address books might have got filled up with her scrawls, and been tossed away? No reason to keep them; she'd leaf through for any phone numbers she'd want, recopy them in the new book.

So, in those other books (maybe other books), how many other little jottings embellished with dollar signs? He sighed. Just no clue at all as to the racket, how often they'd taken a mark, or how, or for what.

Could he pinpoint anything at all definite about Valerie's murder yet? Not much. She hadn't thought she was in any danger, could you say that? Dr. Bainbridge said she'd got the whole massive dose of codeine at once, he was pretty sure, and probably in a drink of some kind. There was alcohol in her stomach: not much. Call it about as much as in a Martini. And not much else: she hadn't had a solid meal in about twenty hours. That was odd, or was it? Not necessarily: a good many young women conscious of their figures didn't eat much breakfast or lunch. She'd died probably before dinnertime on Sunday. Bainbridge had put the outside limit at midnight to be on the safe side.

Why the hell had she been left where she was? And how?

He thought he'd go and look at that Garey Street school.

It was a quarter of twelve. He wondered how Alison was getting on with Miss Freeman. Damned fool of a woman, calling the cats insanitary. Oh, well, so long as she was the one to get up and walk the floor with the twins—

He took up his hat and went out. "Jimmy, I'm going down to—"

The outside phone rang and Lake picked it up. "Headquarters, Homicide," he said mechanically. And then, "I beg your pardon, I don't—" A variety of expressions chased over his face; he said sharply, "Who is this speaking, please?" and began to scribble on his memo pad.

Even Mendoza beside him heard the violent click as the other phone was banged down.

"I will be damned," said Lake blankly. "Probably just a nut, but—"

"What'd she say? I could hear it was a woman's voice."

"Yes. Must have been a nut of some kind. First off she said, 'You tell whoever's investigating the Valerie Ellis murder, it wasn't nothing to do with this Thorwald, see?' That's when I interrupted her. She said, kind of sharp, 'You just listen! I would so tell them! I know why she was killed, she was killed because they murdered that woman six years ago—' And then you heard the phone banged down. Just a crank, you always get them calling in, but it's—"

"¡Parece mentira!" said Mendoza. "That's a funny one, all right. 'Because they murdered that woman six years ago.' They."

"You think it means anything?"

"¿Quién sabe? ¡Sabe Dios! It's just damned funny . . . It's so damned funny, Jimmy, that I'm going to ask you to go and collect the files for me on every first- and second-degree homicide of a female that's still pending, for—what year'd that be?—1958. A nice afternoon's occupation for you."

"Thanks very much," said Sergeant Lake gloomily. "I remember one offhand, Lieutenant. That Overton woman was murdered in 1958—January. We never could pin it to the husband. He married his secretary afterward."

"Maybe a starting-point. Go and look out the files, just for fun," said Mendoza; and, thinking hard, went out to take a look along Garey Street.

At five-twenty that afternoon, just as Hackett plodded wearily into the office after yet another abortive day's routine checking on light-blue pickup trucks, a new homicide was reported. The call came from the Wilcox Street precinct; the sergeant there said, "After a first look, we figured for pretty sure it's one of your colored boy friend's jobs. Looks like the same set-up. So we thought we'd pass it on—with sympathy and all that. How near are you getting? Oh, well, bound to get him sooner or later, routine'll turn him up . . . Yeah . . . Mrs. Gertrude Dasher, 1114 Sierra Bonita in Hollywood. Friend of hers was invited to dinner, knew she'd be there, so when she couldn't raise her she made a fuss and called us. No, not raped, but killed the same way, and stuff missing—so the friend says . . . You're welcome to it."

Hackett put the phone down and passed a hand across his eyes; broke the news to Palliser.

"I've got all these damn reports to make up," he said. "Will you go out on it, John? Start to get the details anyway. God, who is there to take with you? All the damn paper work—"

"All right, don't worry, I'll get on it," said Palliser. "I think Higgins is on night tour now." Sergeant Hackett had been putting in long hours on this one, he thought: so had they all; they were all feeling the needling from the press, and were savagely anxious to catch up to their boy. "You take a break," he said, "have a good dinner, relax. I'm on it."

"I wish to God I could go home," said Hackett heavily. Palliser, on the way out, heard him on the phone, saying, "I know, Angel, but—for the love of God don't tell me what you're having for dinner, darling, I'll break the oath and come home anyway—"

Hackett's wife was one of those inspired cooks. Palliser grinned to himself sympathetically.

He didn't mind the overtime; he kind of had his teeth in this thing now. And he hadn't had a date with Roberta tonight; she was involved with beginning-of-term exams for her fourth-grade pupils.

EIGHT

"I knew there was something wrong, I just felt it in my bones!" exclaimed Mrs. Powell dramatically.

Since Mrs. Dasher had expected her to dinner at five-thirty and would normally have been there to let her in, Palliser reflected that common sense rather than second sight might have led her to suspect something wrong. But he'd met a lot of Mrs. Powells, and he just made a polite murmur. Higgins was poking around the room. They had just come for the body, and the Hollywood boys had left with it, wishing them luck.

"I just don't know why you can't catch this awful fiend! A nigger, too," said Mrs. Powell, as if that logically made it easier.

"Well, we're working on it," said Palliser. The Hollywood boys said that it certainly looked like Lover Boy again. Same setup; back door lock broken in by force, the woman attacked when she saw him, and afterwards the house ransacked. The only discrepancy, of course, was the house itself. This Hollywood street was in a middle-class but not wealthy part of town; the houses were modest, most of them neatly maintained, but not affluent by any means.

Mrs. Dasher's house was an old bastard-Spanish stucco painted cream, with a red tile roof. Two bedrooms, very modest furniture.

He'd taken a look at the back door; the screen door had a piece cut out with a sharp knife, so the hook could be lifted, and the old-fashioned forward lock on the wooden door had been forced with crude violence. Across the driveway, there was a thick, tall privet hedge a good ten feet high, which successfully hid any view of Mrs. Dasher's back door from that other house so close there; Palliser couldn't see its windows, only the upper third of it. It had a nearly flat pseudo-shingle roof. He glanced down the drive. It was a longish drive; these were old-fashioned deep lots and Mrs. Dasher's house was built farther back from the street than either of her neighbors'. If anyone had been passing on the sidewalk, or casually watching from across the street, about all he'd have seen would have been a man fumbling at the door, maybe over a stiff lock. The screen-slashing wouldn't have taken five seconds.

"Well," said Palliser to himself now. And to Mrs. Powell, "Now let's go over this again. We want to be as exact as we can. I realize you can't be sure of every single item." That was a lie; he'd take a bet that she could rattle off an inventory of the place. She and Gertrude Dasher had been close friends for over twenty years, and Mrs. Dasher had lived here for almost that long—since before she'd been left a widow. ("And good riddance," Mrs. Powell had said with a sniff. "He Drank.") Mrs. Dasher had obviously not been the kind who redecorated every few years, or spent much on the house at any time. The furniture was well cared for but old —just old, not antique. The rugs were worn. The refrigerator and stove were clean, but far from new. The clothes in the closet of the front bedroom—or rather scattered on the floor and about the room, now—were the typical clothes of an elderly woman with enough money but not a surplus.

"Better write it down so you won't forget it!" snapped Mrs. Powell. "Policemen! This fiend in human form running around killing helpless women, and you just dawdle around asking silly questions!"

"We're working on it," said Palliser patiently. "Now, you said there was an antique silver tea service—"

"On the sideboard in the dining room, where it always stayed. It belonged to Gertrude's grandmother. Real English silver, teapot and sugar 'n' creamer. And a set of a dozen German silver teaspoons, in the top right-hand drawer of the buffet. Don't you be silly, young man, since we were both left widows I knew this house almost like my own, and I've been through it—with those other policemen practically ready to put handcuffs on me, saying don't touch anything! Impudence. I know what's missing. Her fur coat—a beaver coat it was, three-quarter, and only ten years old, perfectly good, she paid three hundred for it on sale. And her jewelry. She didn't have an awful lot but what she had was good. Her grandmother's cameo brooch and a set of garnets—sunburst pin and a ring and a pair of drop earrings and a pendant—and her mother's engagement ring, and one of those old-fashioned wide hoop bracelets, real gold, and her own engagement ring, and an onyx ring with a diamond set in it, and an amethyst ring that was her twenty-first birthday present because it's her birthstone. *All* gone!" said Mrs. Powell. "*And* her wrist watch!"

"Yes," said Palliser. He thought about the loot Lover Boy had got away with in other instances. A new mink coat, a diamond necklace valued at ten thousand dollars; at another place, miscellaneous jewelry to the value of fifteen thousand: expensive clothes, a diamond wrist watch, another mink coat. Small doubt rose in his mind; he looked around Gertrude Dasher's living-room. *Sunburst pin and a ring and—* He remembered his mother turning over his grandmother's jewelry after the funeral, and talking about garnets. ("Never worth much, they're inexpensive stones, but I always liked them all the same.")

He also thought about his and Hackett's joint deduction about Lover Boy. Obviously, he was a wild one, maybe a little or a lot unhinged; leave that to the head-doctors. But Hackett thought the burglaries were just afterthoughts—just wild snatching at whatever he easily found lying around, and not anything systematic. Because at that place he'd got away with the diamond necklace, there'd been a good deal more valuable jewelry untouched; and at another place, one of those in Beverly Hills, he'd taken a fourteen-carat cigarette case from one bedroom—the owner was positive as to where it had been—and left it in another room where he ransacked a jewel case, taking a lot of costume jewelry as well as real stuff. Just grabbing wildly, said Hackett, and maybe—if he was unhinged—not even attempting to profit by it.

My God, *had* they worked this one. They'd even drawn up solemn maps, with little dotted lines drawn between the addresses of jobs he'd pulled. West Hollywood, Beverly Hills. Palliser thought about that now. Like any cop, he knew the city; and visualizing the map, he saw that the distance between here and West Hollywood was about the same as between West Hollywood and Beverly Hills, only in the opposite direction. There was nothing impossible about all this: if Lover Boy was as unhinged as Hackett thought, he might just have happened to be driving his light-blue pickup truck down Sierra Bonita when the urge hit him, and he— Yes, thought Palliser, there was that. Those places in West Hollywood and Beverly Hills, wealthy homes: larger lots, and any curious neighbors farther away. Here, where houses were set close—Lover Boy retained some natural caution, maybe?—he'd chosen a house very well protected by that tall hedge, by being set back farther from the street. Was that logical?

"Well, thank you very much," he said to Mrs. Powell; and had a little time getting rid of her. The boys from Prints arrived, and he left them to it while he questioned the neighbors.

The people next door, where there was no hedge between, gave him a little surprise but not much help. The householder was one of the sheriff's boys, Deputy Harry Lee. He offered Palliser sympathy—"This is the tough kind, don't we know!"—and nothing else. He hadn't come home until after Mrs. Dasher had been found. Mrs. Lee had been out to market. Home alone had been Davy Lee, out of school with a cold. And Davy Lee, aged eleven, said importantly, "I saw the man who must've been the one. I did too, Dad, I'm *not* making it up! Honest, mister, I did!"

"You saw him come down the drive? Saw his car?"

"Naw, he went to the front door. He came walkin' up the street and he went up and rung the front doorbell."

"That was the salesman, honey," said pretty Mrs. Lee. "The one the Flesches told about." The Flesches lived on the other side of Mrs. Dasher.

"It wasn't either! I saw him 'n' I saw the salesman, didn't I? I answered the door when the salesman rang an' said you wasn't—weren't home an' he gave me the catalogue to give you."

"That was the same man, Dave, because it was about the same time the Flesches said he came." Lee nodded and winked at Palliser, and shrugged.

"It was *not!* I *saw* him! He wasn't as old as the one rang Mrs. Dasher's bell first—it was afterward the salesman came! Honest, I—"

Lee took Palliser's arm and led him out to the entrance hall. "Don't get confused by all that," he said. "I'm afraid the boy's at that stage—not only wanting in on the act, to look important, but we've caught him out in a couple of—call it exaggerations—lately." He grinned. "You know. They all go through it."

"Sure," said Palliser. He didn't know much about kids; without much doubt Lee knew more about his son than Palliser did.

The people beyond the hedge couldn't tell him anything helpful either. They were people in their sixties, Flesch retired, and they'd been having lunch in the kitchen between about twelve and twelve-thirty, not in sight of Mrs. Dasher's house. The Fuller Brush man had come by, they said, at about noon, maybe a few minutes before.

The surgeon said she had died between eleven and one. Technically of strangulation, though she'd been beaten too—head banged in (probably against furniture, the floor) and so on.

The Fuller Brush man—they left brochures, didn't they? No brochure in Mrs. Dasher's house. So—had she been dead when the man rang the bell? And her killer holding his breath, until the salesman went away?

Palliser sat down on Mrs. Dasher's tapestry-upholstered couch and stared earnestly at the picture on the opposite wall. It was a brightly colored print of a young woman in a long red dress, playing a piano, and it was in an ornate gilded frame.

"Dreaming of the girl friend?" asked Higgins.

"Well—" said Palliser. Actually he was thinking about Mendoza. Mendoza and his reputation. They joked about it: Luis and his crystal ball. And the hunches didn't always work out, of course. But sometimes— surprisingly often—they did.

He thought about Mendoza saying, "Routine—sure, we have to go by routine. Facts. But don't ever ignore your feelings, John. This I say to you personally. There are a lot of good cops on this force—any force—I wouldn't say it to. Good men, but not men who have enough empathy to get the nuances, if you know what I mean. You have. So any time you have a feeling about something, follow it up. It might mean something."

Palliser was naturally a rather diffident man; he didn't lack self-confidence or strength of character, but he'd risen rather rapidly from uniform, to be the associate of men like Art Hackett who'd had a lot more experience. When he offered some idea of his own, it was usually hesitantly.

But in the last six months or so he'd found Hackett and Mendoza to be easy, reasonable fellows to deal with. He thought he'd bare his feelings to Hackett on this one, see what Hackett thought.

There wasn't much of Garey Street, Mendoza had found. Two blocks of it along here, between Third and First, and it picked up again a couple of blocks on, to run for another three blocks between Turner and Commercial. It was a rather dreary little street, interspersing old houses with small businesses. The parochial school was an old one, shabby and showing its age: not as large a playground as a public school would have.

Why the hell had X gone to some trouble to leave the body in such a funny spot? Or, come to think, had he gone to much trouble? Maybe somebody who'd once worked as a janitor or night watchman here, still had a key to the gate? Farfetched, but—

Nowhere to park along here, not only because it was a narrow street and parking was allowed on only one side, but because at the moment half this block was filled with workmen and large yellow-painted machines doing something about either the water or the gas mains. They had a deep trench dug along the curb opposite the school fence, lengths of pipe stood about waiting—by their diameter, it was the water, not the gas— mounds of earth made the street a one-way maze for a car. He negotiated it carefully, turned the corner onto Third Street and found that solidly lined with parked cars. Well, a little exercise wouldn't hurt him; a lieutenant's job was too sedentary. He went on up to Santa Fe, and nearly down to the corner of Second Street he found a slot. He maneuvered the Ferrari in, fished for small change, discovered he had no pennies or nickels, swore mildly, and—a solecism big-city dwellers are learning to commit without shame—accosted the first passer-by for change for a quarter. He put a nickel in the parking-meter; nothing happened; he shook it severely, and a little reluctantly the red *Violation* sign disappeared and the needle slid over to 60 *min*. On second thought he locked the Ferrari, and started back down Santa Fe.

Ten minutes later he was staring through the schoolyard fence at the place where Valerie Ellis's body had been found last Monday morning.

This was the side of the school, which faced on Third Street. The body had been close inside the fence, behind a small bleachers erected for the baseball diamond there. He had seen the photographs: body awkwardly sprawled out. As if dropped, say, from the top of the fence? He had asked Dr. Bainbridge, who had shrugged. "What with the post-mortem cyanosis, you know, difficult to say. A dead body would fall like an unconscious person, of course—limp—unless rigor had set in—and probably wouldn't sustain the injuries a conscious person would from any considerable fall. There weren't any bones broken, anyway."

The fence—now he looked at it—wouldn't be as high as most public-schoolyard fences. Call it fifteen feet. It was a very solid chain-link fence, probably newer than the school buildings, supported by very solid steel posts at intervals.

Mendoza sighed to himself. Generally speaking, anybody with a corpse on his hands to get rid of got rid of it in the handiest dark place. Which there were plenty of in any big city . . . Had he brought along his own ladder?

He turned around and looked thoughtfully at the men and machines working in the street. He strolled down to where the trench was; sure enough, a ladder propped in the hole. A deep hole. So, a long ladder.

Most of the men were working stripped to the waist: even in February, in California, the sun was hot. They were deeply tanned; there were several Negroes among them. Lover Boy flitted across his mind and he sighed again. He waited until a man came nearer the curb, and called, "Excuse me, who's the foreman on this job?"

Everybody in hearing stared at him. The man approaching looked him up and down and said, "I am, and what's it to you, bud?" He was a big hefty fellow about forty, burned almost as brown as the grinning milk-chocolate Negro peering at them out of the hole. The foreman stared at Mendoza's exquisitely cut Italian silk suit with contempt.

Mendoza produced identification. "You remember that body found inside the school fence on Monday?"

"Well, I didn't put it there, anyway. Sure, some excitement, cops all around. What about it? . . . Sure we were working here then. Ever since last week, why?"

"You see, it's a peculiar place to dump a body. Not so easy a place to get a body into. And I was just wondering—what do you do with all this at night?" He gestured at the machines. "Take them all back to your—er—headquarters, or park them here?"

"You think the company's crazy, mister, waste time trundling these things back to the garage every night? They come on a job, they stay until the job's finished. Left parked up against the curb, sure."

"Yes." Irrelevantly Mendoza thought that the machines looked like Martian monsters. There was one that had a great iron claw with sharp teeth, at the end of a cranelike jointed arm: the thing had a sinister expression, he thought. "That ladder down the hole—is it left there overnight?"

The foreman laughed. "Mister, you think we're crazy? Anything you leave out loose, neighborhood like this, you don't expect to find it there next morning! All that sort of thing gets locked into one o' the trucks." There were a couple of ordinary trucks there too, with closed bodies, probably for transporting and storing the smaller tools.

"Well, I'd just like to be sure," said Mendoza. "Who's the one responsible for seeing to that? Was the ladder definitely locked in a truck over last weekend?"

"Oh, hell," said the foreman. "Sure it was! You cops! Hey, Tony?"

"What's up?"

"Come here a minute." A lithe young Negro climbed out of the hole, his bare chest glistening with sweat, and came over. "Look, when we quit work Saturday noon, you pulled up that ladder and put her in No. 2 truck, didn't you?"

"That I did," said Tony. "Why? We always do."

"Like I said. This cop here asking. On account of that body they found in the schoolyard, see? You're sure you locked up the ladder?"

"Sure," said Tony absently. "You a cop, sir? Looking into that, like? I don't want to butt in, Mr. Davies, but you reckon maybe the cop oughta hear what Barney says? I mean, nobody ever asked us anything, but if he's right it might have something to do—"

"Oh, for God's sakes," said the foreman disgustedly. "Barney had his mind on a Saturday night spree and that blonde of his—he don't know what he's talking about! How *could* his rig get moved around? It's—"

"Well, but he's pretty sure, Mr. Davies—we never thought as how it might have something to do with that body, but you know, it could be—"

Mendoza said, "I think I'd like very much to hear what Barney says. Please, Mr. Davies."

"For God's *sakes!*" said the foreman. "Wasting time! *Barney! Come here!* Taking men off the job! Listen, mister, all the time we hear nothing but complaints—the damn public—city men take forever on a job, leaning on their shovels—good union wages an' they work about half the time, loaf the rest. Let me tell *you,* mister, we get damn sick 'n' tired of hearing complaints. We work, God knows. Job like this got to be done, we *do* it. You think we *like* tying up traffic, just to make things hard for people? We earn our money, mister, and we earn it honest! I tell you—" It was automatic complaint, uncalled for.

Maybe every trade, thought Mendoza, has its grievances against the rest of humanity.

"I'm not doubting you," he said. Barney was the operator of the sinister-looking machine with the single claw. He left the claw suspended in mid-air, clambered down from the cab, and joined them.

"What's up?"

"All right, all right," said Davies angrily. "So tell your fairy story about last Monday morning to the cop. About the rig."

"You a cop? What about? . . . That body! Jesus, I never thought of that body! But now I *do* think, I bet you—I just bet you that was *it!*" Barney, squat and broad, didn't look as if he thought much about anything. Now he was suddenly excited. "I just bet you! So O.K., I'm imagining things—my God, *I* know how I left the rig, don't I? She isn't exactly the easiest rig made to maneuver, and ain't we got strict orders, don't block traffic no more'n we can help? Well? Listen," he said to Mendoza fiercely, "*I* know how I left her on Saturday noon, I can show you! Right bang up against that right-hand curb I left her"—he pointed—"about the legal distance from the fire hydrant. I checked, on accounta the hydrant. Wouldn't I check? I ask you! And you can say I'm as crazy as the boss here thinks, it makes no never mind, on Mond'y morning that rig was a good ten feet, maybe fifteen, further back from that hydrant 'n I'd left her! I got *eyes,* ain't I? I got—"

"Now that's very interesting indeed," said Mendoza. The foreman made a disgusted sound in his throat. "Tell me—those things aren't so easy to operate, you say—the ordinary citizen couldn't climb right into one and start it up?"

"Jesus, no. You got to know where everything is—all the levers and so on. *You* believe me, mister? I'd swear it on a stack o' Bibles—rest of 'em say I'm just imagining, because how the hell *could* she've been moved? I mean, the ignition was locked, naturally."

"There's an ignition, like that on a car? Yes." And almost any man with a very little know-how, even if he hadn't started out a pro career by borrowing cars, might know how to start a locked ignition—those two little wires— "And once the engine's on," he said, "the power's available to work that claw thing? I don't know your technical terms—"

"That's right, sure, only like I say you'd hafta know which levers—there's one to bend her down, and open her, and close her, and raise her up—"

Eso si está bueno, thought Mendoza irritably. What a setup! It got more and more complicated—and no leads at all! *Was* Barney right? It seemed too big a coincidence if he wasn't. Had that Martian monster been the convenient means of hoisting the body over the fence? Grant that X knew how to operate it, of course, a very easy means. That great claw was a good eight to ten feet long. Open it at ground level: lift the body in: close it, and swing the crane over the fence—within easy reach of the twenty-foot-long arm: open it, and there you were.

But who that they knew of in this case (so far) might possess that knowledge?

A man who didn't know how to work the machine, but had sufficient mechanical ability to figure it out by trial and error? Why go to the trouble?

And—he looked across the street—a good many of the old houses used as business offices: a chiropractor, a dentist, an herb-doctor—maybe nobody there at night—but down the block a few houses still used as residences. Wouldn't the protracted noise of this heavy engine, the creak and groan of that crane, have aroused some curiosity, say, at nine o'clock on Sunday night?

And how had X known this convenient means was waiting here for him? That was easy enough: if he had by chance passed this way recently—

And—hell and damnation—if this astonishing and curious thing was true, there'd be absolutely no traces left inside that monstrous claw, to prove it—after five days of use in between.

And—once again—why the hell had X gone to the bother?

NINE

Mendoza went home, after a brief return to the office, in an exasperated frame of mind. Lover Boy pulling another one, God, that one they had to catch up with—and this very funny new development on Valerie . . . He garaged the Ferrari, kissed Alison at the back door.

"Well, happier with the sanitary Miss Freeman, *amada?*"

"No," said Alison. "She's gone."

"Gone? *¿Como dice—qué se yo?*"

"What else could I do?" she demanded. "That woman! Her and her established routines! I didn't like her, but I *had* hired her, I was willing to try her out a few days, but then she kicked Bast, and I—"

"*¡Porvida!* She's not hurt? *Mi cariña—*" He let Alison go and went to pick up Bast, who was limping pathetically across the kitchen telling him all about it at the top of her voice. "*¡Mi gatita cara! ¡Queridita!* That scraggly old bitch—"

Bast, always pleased for a chance to be the center of attention, uttered a satisfied *Nyeouh* and lay back in his arms with closed eyes. "No, she's not hurt," said Alison, "she's just being a hypochondriac because she's feeling sorry for herself. The limp's all put on. I had her over to Dr. Stocking, she's perfectly all right. But—"

"*Nyah!*" said Bast indignantly.

"She was just innocently walking into the room—that woman had been acting worse all the time, Luis, the most impossible ideas—I think she's got a neurosis about hygiene—and then she tripped over El Señor and he spat at her— Well, it may strike you funny now, but at the time—! I know some people just don't like cats, but after all— All of a sudden she started saying 'you nasty creature' and so on, and I turned round just in time to see her kick Bast—a good hard kick too. Naturally I blew up—"

"*¡Pobrecita!* I should think so indeed!" He fondled Bast. "These neu-
rotic females. You're sure—?"

"I said I took her to the hospital to be sure. She's just feeling sorry for
herself, and I can't say I blame her," said Alison, still angry. "Ask me, all
that woman's funny ideas, she'd have ended up giving the twins a trauma
or something. But they can't all be like that, surely there must be at least
one kind motherly nursemaid available, among seven million people! I
thought I'd try another agency tomorrow."

"By all means. But meanwhile, we're stuck with them tonight," said
Mendoza. "I suppose they're asleep now. Of course. *Naturalmente.*"

"Yes, well, I thought," said Alison, "that just for tonight—I'm sure to
find somebody else tomorrow, you know—I could sleep in there next to
them. To be handy when they start. And then—"

"*¡Valgáme Dios—es el colmo!* What's all this? I forbid it, *absolutamente!*
I've put up with these twin monsters so far, but enough is enough! When
it comes to you moving out on me—"

"Don't be silly, *querido,* if you weren't so self-conscious about it you'd
be acting as sentimental and boastful as any other parent. And it's only for
one night—I'm bound to find somebody else—and besides, it's ridiculous to
move the nursery furniture back just for one—"

"*Nyaouh,*" said Bast plaintively, aware that attention had shifted from
her.

"*Gata hermosa,*" said Mendoza absently, patting her. "I will not allow it.
We can, God knows, hear them plain enough anywhere in the house. As
a lawful obedient wife, your first duty is to your husband—"

"If you remember," said Alison, "it was a civil ceremony at the Hall of
Justice and I never said one word about obeying you."

"*Impudente.* I still say—"

"Of course," she added, "I shouldn't expect a man of your advanced
years to change your habits, and you never have taken kindly to sleeping
alone—I gather, though I've only known you, what, four years—"

"*¡Qué pronto pasa el tiempo*—how fast the time goes!" said Mendoza.
"You will stay where you belong, no argument. Now go and see to
dinner."

"I'm going, I'm going. Autocrat," said Alison. He opened the cupboard
over the sink, poured himself a small drink; and El Señor materialized
from nowhere, demanding his share. "There you are, setting bad examples
—he's turning into a drunkard."

"Nonsense," said Mendoza, pouring El Señor an ounce of rye in a saucer. "He needs it after putting up with that woman for twenty-four

hours." El Señor, licking his chops, uttered a sound of distinct agreement and leaped down to find Sheba or Nefertiti to cuff, that being how alcohol affected him . . .

Alison stayed where she belonged, in the king-size bed in the master bedroom. But inevitably she got out of it, with a sleepy muttered "damn" at 2:45 A.M.

Fumbling into her slippers and robe, she said crossly, "I'm *coming!*" And added to Mendoza, "You go back to sleep, I'll see to them."

He pulled the blanket over his head and tried to go back to sleep. It was, of course, useless. He sat up and smoked a cigarette, ruminating sleepily about Valerie—this curious new twist, that machine—and Lover Boy—and what Valerie's profitable racket might have been—

Until his conscience got to bothering him. After all, he was fifty per cent responsible for the existence of that pair of little monsters down the hall.

He got up resignedly, put on his robe and slippers, and went to join Alison and the twins.

Somewhere there must be a nice motherly experienced nursemaid—like all those nannies in the British novels—for present hire?

"Tomorrow—" he said to Alison. He joggled Miss Teresa determinedly. "Tomorrow," said Alison somnolently, patting Master John.

He sat at his desk next morning and studied all those files Lake had turned up for him—homicides from six years back, of females: cases still labeled *Pending*. Was this woolgathering? That phone call: "Because they murdered that woman six years ago—" . . . They.

There weren't too many of them. This was a crack force, but also, the average homicide didn't present much of a mystery in the crime-fiction sense. When X wasn't pretty obvious on the known facts—and he usually was—the mystery arose because of his anonymity: the casual mugger, the casual rapist, the lunatic. In most of these cases, that was the reason the case was still pending: there just hadn't been enough evidence at the scene or elsewhere to point to anybody.

The Overton woman, first of all. Rose Overton. Husband Gerald vice-president of a small company that manufactured cardboard boxes of all kinds. Reasonably affluent: Mrs. Overton had a little jewelry, her own car, spent her time playing bridge, shopping, entertaining. She was forty-three, he was a year older. No children, They'd been married for nineteen years. Nobody had ever suspected any trouble between them: no public arguments. They had seemed, to everyone who knew them, to be an ordinary couple. And then, one cold January evening, while Mr. Overton was detained in his office, dictating to his secretary Miss Norma Walsh, somebody had forced the back door of the Overton home in Bel-Air and bashed Mrs. Overton's head in with a blunt instrument. It had looked at first glance like a burglary—burglar seen by Mrs. Overton, he hit her to shut her up. But several little things said no. A burglar would know someone was home from the lights; it happened between eight and nine, and that was the wrong time for a burglar to pick. And the burglar hadn't acted like a burglar, dumping whole drawers on the floor to get at the contents in a hurry, tearing clothes off hangers at random. He'd left a few drawers open, that was all, and he had missed an expensive set of golf clubs and other valuables—all belonging to Overton.

Overton, of course, was openly shocked and grieved. He'd been in his office from seven to nine-thirty, and the secretary backed him up. It was a big office-building with a night watchman, who'd seen them both come in at seven, and said Overton didn't leave until they both left at nine-thirty. But he couldn't watch all the exits at once, and there was a fire escape.

Mrs. Overton had been a devout Catholic. Overton wasn't. And a discreet eight months after the murder, Overton had married Miss Walsh.

So, you could spot him as X—there just wasn't any evidence at all. Weapon never found. If Overton had wanted a divorce, wanted to be rid of his wife, nobody had ever heard either of them say so; there was no evidence of any discord between them.

Mendoza thought about the Overton case again now for two reasons. They had lived in Bel-Air—where Valerie had lived at the time. L.A. Headquarters had come into it by being asked by the Beverly Hills boys to check the downtown alibi. And the anonymous woman on the phone had said "they" killed the woman. And if Overton had killed his wife, the secretary must have been an accomplice.

On the other hand, it could have been a "they" who was responsible for Marion Carlson. Attacked and raped and strangled in an alley off Venice Boulevard, not a very good section of town, as she walked toward home after leaving the bus. Absolutely no clue left on the scene: a very anonymous kill.

There were two others like that, only the women hadn't been raped. Agnes Fletcher, aged fifty-one; Ellen Draper, aged thirty. Far apart: Fletcher in Boyle Heights, Draper in Palms. It had looked like a mugger in both cases, maybe hopped-up on dope and hitting a little too hard, just to get the handbag.

Then, Ruth Ganner. High-school kid living in Hollywood. The Hollywood boys had asked for help on it. Nobody had got anywhere. The Ganner girl hadn't been a very nice girl. Had played around with several boys she knew at school, and got herself in trouble. And that was about all they knew for certain. One dark night somebody had stabbed her several times with a very sharp knife and left her body rather casually on the front lawn of the Ganner house. It might have been one of the boys she'd played with, or it might, of course, have been a couple of them. A "They."

But what possible connection with Valerie, then attending a different high school? Of course, kids got around these days . . .

And that left Dorothy Clark. Who had been divorced from her husband George and was living with a boy friend, Brian Lavalliere. None of them very savory characters. Dorothy had a little pedigree for shoplifting and habitual drunkenness; George had been inside twice for robbery; Lavalliere, despite his aristocratic name, was a pro burglar. Dorothy and Lavalliere had been living in a ramshackle rooming-house a couple of blocks off Skid Row. Other tenants said Clark had come around a couple of times, threatening both of them; and said also that Lavalliere and Dorothy had had a few fights. So, when somebody ambushed and stabbed Dorothy from the mouth of an alley a few doors from the house, as she came home late one night—late, and a little drunk—it might have been either man, or it might have been a mugger. A good many types in that section of town carried knives; a certain proportion of them wouldn't think twice about using a knife on the chance that there was five or ten bucks in the handbag. Nobody knew exactly how much she'd been carrying. Insufficient evidence to show who was guilty.

Mendoza really couldn't see those three having any connection with Valerie Ellis. He couldn't see any of these cases having any connection with Valerie Ellis. Except, just remotely possible, the Overton case. The Overtons living in Bel-Air . . .

Six years ago Valerie Ellis had been seventeen, a high-school student: her parents still alive, she'd been the spoiled darling, with everything she wanted.

The anonymous woman on the telephone hadn't got around to saying what the connection had been between Valerie and the murdered woman, but the implication was that she had known something damaging about the "they" who had allegedly done the murder. Maybe had tried blackmail? Well, the blackmail bit would ring true enough: Valerie had liked money however it came. But how had a still-innocent high-school kid stumbled across a criminal secret? And why had she kept silent about it then?

It didn't make sense. Probably the phone call hadn't one damned thing to do with it: just a crank, a nut. Nothing in this whole peculiar business made sense. The place the body was left. That really wild one, the Martian machine used (maybe) to get the body over the fence . . . He made a note to have somebody ask around there, whether anyone had heard it on Sunday night. The mysteriousness of Valerie's latest racket . . .

She had to be over at Vic's. Vic. No Vic visible.

That Gloria female knew something. Bring her in as a material witness, try to scare her into coming out with it? No, thought Mendoza. There was an old saying, catch more flies with honey— Go to see her, try to coax it out of her.

He put out his cigarette and got up, deciding to do just that. And just as abruptly decided first to go and see this Marion Keller, who'd been Valerie's best friend in high school. In high school, six years ago . . .

But he hadn't got to the door before it opened and Hackett and Palliser came in. "Sit down, Luis," said Hackett. "John's got something to tell you. We need your expert opinion."

"Later on," said Mendoza. "Right now I—"

"Now," said Hackett. "You're the expert on hunches. John has a beautiful hunch to lay before you. Look at it and tell us if there's anything in it, *por favor.*"

Mendoza sat down again resignedly.

"It's just an idea," said Palliser. His long dark face, normally grave, lit up when he smiled, and made him look younger; he smiled apologetically now. "Nothing really to say one way or the other."

"In fact, a hunch," said Mendoza. "About what?"

"That Mrs. Dasher. Sure, it looks like the boy we're chasing—same M.O. House broken into, woman assaulted—he's not particular, he's already assaulted one older than Gertrude Dasher—she was sixty-six—and a few things stolen. He didn't actually rape Mrs. Dasher, but then he didn't rape two others. Only they fought and got away, or he would have. All right. But I've got a hunch it wasn't him. That somebody set it up to look like that. For one thing, the other seven women all lived in West Hollywood or Beverly Hills—wealthier sections of town. Mrs. Dasher was off his beat, so to speak. And I know we all think the burglaries are a kind of afterthought, he just snatches up what he finds on a hurried search. Well, here he took everything of any remote value Mrs. Dasher had—and it didn't amount to very much. Apparently he took a good long look through the house. But after all, a dozen German silver teaspoons, and a handful of old jewelry that never had been worth much—" Palliser gestured. "And then there's the kid. There's this hedge hiding the Dasher house from the next house—those people can't see her front walk or porch. All they do say is that at about twelve o'clock a Fuller Brush man came by. But in the house on the other side, there was a bright kid home alone. And he says he saw two men go up and ring Mrs. Dasher's doorbell, one after the other. Says the first man was older than the Fuller Brush man, who came afterward. His parents—father's one of the sheriff's boys, by the way, nice fellow—think he's imagining it, just to sound important. Say he's given to telling stories. Well, I don't know. For one thing, I should think that Lee, being a conscientious fellow, would have impressed on the boy some—you know—understanding of the job. And wouldn't a kid that age, a boy, be pretty proud of a father who's on the sheriff's squad, and not want to let him down? You can see it's all odds and ends—"

"Yes," said Mendoza, "but they might add up. I see what you mean. Very strong hunch, John?"

"Well, I guess I'd say so. When I get to thinking it over."

"And I don't know but what I go along," said Hackett soberly. "I had a little thought of my own about it." He lit a new cigarette. "We haven't given the press all the details, just some. As per usual. And what the Dasher setup looks like—if it wasn't our boy—is that whoever did it and arranged things to look like one of Lover Boy's jobs, knew what's been in the papers but not a couple of other things we know."

"Details, please?"

"Well, it's been in the papers that he robbed the houses after assaulting the women, but not that he's just snatched up a few things at random, on the run, so to speak. And here, as John says, whoever it was ransacked the house for anything of remote value. Then, it's been in the papers that he's broken in by forcing locks, but not that we're pretty sure he uses a pro burglar's jemmy. And Mrs. Dasher's back door—I've just been taking a look at it—wasn't forced that way. We don't think. Somebody just poked something like a pair of scissors, or a strong knife, in and worried around until the lock broke. Crude violence, you could say. And it *is* a break in the pattern, an entirely different part of town."

"So it is," said Mendoza. "And if you're right, something else on our plates. Another mysterious murder. Of course there's an obvious explanation."

"Yes, I saw that," said Hackett, "but it's no help looking for him."

"What?" asked Palliser blankly.

Mendoza leaned back and shut his eyes. *"Esto es otro cantar,"* he said.

"You get a series of crimes like this—as you'll discover with more experience—and sometimes you get some nut or hophead imitating the original X. You'll remember the Black Dahlia, for instance—" He shuddered. "In a town this size, anything can happen. And on this series, what a nice cover-up for serious burglary. What a nice excuse for some borderline lunatic to let out the repressed violence."

"Oh," said Palliser. "I get you. That could be, I suppose. Well, I just thought—"

"An excellent thing for a smart detective to do," said Mendoza a little sleepily. "And a little maxim it's a good idea to remember is, No stone unturned. Always go on the assumption that the worst is so—from our viewpoint—and look at every possibility. ¿Como no? In this case, the worst that could be so from our viewpoint is that this was a private kill, somebody who had some personal motive for killing Mrs. Dasher. That'd be a tough one to unravel, probably. She doesn't sound a likely victim for that kind of murder. But you've got to consider the possibility. Look into her background—look at her friends. If nothing suggestive shows up—well, it could be an imitator, or of course it could still be Lover Boy on an off day."

"Yes, I see that," said Palliser. "My God, on top of everything else—" He sounded dispirited, with reason.

"What did she do, by the way? Still working?"

"I heard a little bit from that Mrs. Powell— I'll want to see her again. She was retired—Dasher, I mean. She'd been a practical nurse. The last few years she'd worked, she'd taken mostly baby cases."

"Really," said Mendoza. He hoped to God Alison was finding that nice motherly nurse. Or was it a dying breed?

"She got a legacy from one of her former patients and retired. She already owned the house. I'll look into it deeper now. As you say, just in case." Palliser got up, looking tired.

"How are you coming along with your little puzzle?" asked Hackett.

"I'm not," said Mendoza exasperatedly. "Some of the damnedest things showing up—I might even lay a couple of problems before you and ask your opinion. Say Federico's, twelve-thirty? I'll tell you all about it."

"*Déjème tomarle el pulso*," said Hackett in mock astonishment, "let me feel your pulse! The great Mendoza, asking advice?"

"Or maybe," said Mendoza, "it's these damned infants. I'm not operating on all cylinders. Maybe the answer's staring me in the face, only I just don't see it. All right, let's all get busy—see you at lunch."

He looked up the number and called Mrs. Keller. Yes, Mrs. Keller was at home and would be happy to tell Lieutenant Mendoza whatever she could about Valerie. Not that she thought she'd be much help, but— Yes, she'd be expecting him then, in half an hour.

"Another batch of stuff from the Feds," said Sergeant Lake.

"Leave it on my desk—I'll see it later."

TEN

"Looking back, I can see now she was always sort of wild," said Marion Keller thoughtfully. "Well, kids haven't much judgment of people, and then too it's only natural—you make friends among the—the available people. Proximity. The Ellises just lived one house down from us, and Val and I being the same age, we naturally teamed up. And maybe too because we were just opposite in some ways." She smiled at Mendoza a little shyly.

Marion Keller was an ordinarily nice-looking young woman, very smartly dressed; her house, on Maybrook Drive in Bel-Air, was a big one, beautifully decorated by someone of individual taste. Marion? She was dark, with a warmly tanned complexion and steady blue eyes; a good deal more mature for her age than Valerie would have been. She had rather large, capable-looking hands. She looked healthy, happy, and good-tempered; and she had the natural poise, the self-confidence, of someone who has always had plenty of money.

She said, "All this awful row in the papers. On account of the Thorwald man, of course. But awful all the same—do you know they even came here? Hal was furious. I'm awfully sorry for that poor ultra-respectable aunt and uncle of hers . . . I never did suspect about her, really, you know. Of course I didn't see her very often. But all the same, I don't think it was the—the usual sort of—"

"No, she wouldn't have been walking the streets, she'd have had a man out picking up clients for her." Maybe Eddy Warren, for a little while; another, or others, afterward. But he didn't think Valerie had lived on that trade very long; she'd found an easier, more congenial racket in the shakedown. And after that, what? "Mrs. Keller," he said, "I'd like you to cast your mind back six years, to 1958. What was Valerie like then? Do you remember anything special, or unusual, happening that year, to her or about her?"

She looked at him in surprise. "Well, we were both just kids then, in high school. I can't remember anything—I don't know what you mean."

"Well, what was she like then?"

Marion clasped her long fingers together, staring at them, and then abruptly sat up and lit a cigarette. "Yes, looking back, I can see there was always a reckless streak in her," she said abstractedly. "At the time, I suppose, it semed to me like—oh, vivacity, a sort of crazy zest for life I didn't have. I've always been cautious, for one thing, but Val would take any dare. I remember she jumped into the Allens' swimming-pool one night with all her clothes on, just because one of the boys dared her. Like that. And she loved to drive fast. I was always nervous, driving with her."

"Wild," said Mendoza, "meaning also the forbidden drinks and maybe dope?"

"Oh, *no*," said Marion quickly. And then, "I don't think so. Oh, I'm sure not—I'd have known, we were together so much. The Ellises—well, looking back at them, he was one of those hearty men, you know the kind I mean, and Mrs. Ellis was, oh, pretty, and just ordinary. They weren't especially strict with Val, I don't think, but I do know that—like my own parents, well, like most parents—she wasn't allowed to drink or smoke. A lot of the older boys—college boys—we knew did smoke, and we'd take a cigarette sometimes, but not regularly. Then." She regarded the tip of her cigarette a little ruefully. "There wasn't anything like dope, Lieutenant. As teen-agers go nowadays, I think we were fairly moral ones."

"Steady boy friend?"

"No, she never went steady with anyone . . . Well, popular? She wasn't the most popular girl in school, I wouldn't say, but she had dates— with a lot of different boys . . . In some ways she was older than her age, and in others younger. And that's hindsight too," said Marion. "One thing I've just realized, thinking about her—since. She wanted to be grown-up, to do all the grown-up things—very much. She was so anxious to—to get there, if you see what I mean. She argued and complained about her parents being old fogies, even when they weren't terribly strict, because they wouldn't let her do some things, tried to keep some authority over her. Well, maybe that's standard practice for seventeen-year-olds. But she was— intense about it. There was that Pitman woman—looking back," said Marion thoughtfully, "I expect the Ellises were quite right."

"Who was that?"

"Oh, now I can see it was just silly, and very likely they *were* right. At the time, of course, I was all on Val's side." She smiled faintly. "You know how girls that age get crushes on glamorous older women? Well, the Pitmans lived next door to the Ellises until they were divorced, and Val had quite a crush on Nan Pitman. To tell you the truth, I don't remember her too well—tall and blond—anyway, she got the custody of the child and moved away. Maybe the divorce was a particularly nasty one and the Ellises knew it, or maybe they just didn't like her, or approve of Val liking her, anyway they told her she mustn't go to see the woman any more. Val used to go there quite a lot. She got in a temper over that all right, said she was old enough to pick her own friends and so on."

"I see. Tempest in a teacup."

"Sort of. Though I guess maybe the Ellises were right, she wasn't exactly a desirable companion, so to speak. Because some time after that—it was after Val had sort of forgotten her, got over it—it was an awful thing, she got drunk one night and accidentally set the place afire and she and the child were both burned to death. I remember Val being dramatic about it, even though she'd got over the crush . . . No, I don't think she was ever very serious about any of the boys she went with. I—as a matter of fact, I don't think she was—capable of any very deep emotion. She just liked a good time—excitement. All I can say is, when that FBI man told me, I was shocked, but I wasn't surprised. That she'd gone down that far."

"Yes. Six years ago— Do you know the name of Overton?"

"No," said Marion. "No, I don't."

"You don't remember any even slightly unusual incident, connected with Valerie, that happened about then?" He tried to jog her memory. "You'd both have been in—what, the second year of high school. Having dates—doing homework—all the teen-age things . . ." Marion went on shaking her head, looking politely puzzled. "I don't suppose you were in the habit of reading the papers much? Following the latest sensational murder?"

"No, I'm afraid not." She looked more puzzled. "Valerie never read much of anything, it was one of the ways we were opposite. She couldn't understand what anyone got out of it."

"Not a very good student, then?"

"Oh, fair. She wasn't much interested in any of her classes, but she was a good parrot, if you know what I mean. She was only going to college because it was expected of her. She was more interested in—" She hesitated, and finished, "Just living."

"Yes," said Mendoza. He felt frustrated. Every faintly suggestive little lead led him to a blank wall. He got up. "Well, thanks very much anyway, Mrs. Keller."

She ushered him politely to the door. "You can understand why she—went the way she did, when you knew her. Having everything, and then suddenly nothing. Somebody more stable would have—accepted it. But possessions—having things—meant a lot to Valerie. And I suppose, once she had got into a—a crowd of people like that, real criminals that is, well, violence—"

Mendoza didn't tell her that the incidence of homicide among small time pros was practically nil. He thanked her again and left.

That Gloria girl knew something. See her next. She had an apartment on Cherokee Drive in Hollywood. He drove up there, but got no answer to his knock. Out. Feeling more frustrated, he went back to his office to look over the latest FBI report.

He wondered how Alison was doing on her hunt for a nursemaid.

Alison was feeling frustrated too. It appeared that nursemaids were as obsolete as scullery maids. These days, there were women prepared to take care of babies but only during the day. The times when servants lived in had passed. No matter how much money you had, evidently, you were expected to look after your own offspring between midnight and dawn; all very democratic, of course, but all the same—

Bertha, now, would have been just fine; Alison wouldn't in the least mind washing the dishes and doing the dusting and so on, Bertha's normal duties, if stout, kind, competent Bertha would walk the floor with the twins at night. But unfortunately Bertha wasn't available, being tied to her own home by what she called her Germing Shepherd, the ubiquitous Fritz.

"Of course, you could hire a practical nurse," said the employment-agency clerk.

"I don't care what she calls herself," said Alison. "That's fine, if you—"

"But there's hardly ever one free," said the clerk. "A constant demand, you know, and not all of them will take baby cases. I can put your name down." She sounded doubtful.

Alison very nearly lost the temper that accompanies red hair. Instead she thanked the clerk and walked out. After all, she thought, this was a roundabout way to go at it. There were such things as classified ads. No harm in *looking*.

She walked up to the corner and bought a *Times*, to save driving all the way home for the morning paper. She walked down to the public lot where she'd left the Facel-Vega, got in and began to look at the classified ads.

And there, under *Child Care*, she found what sounded like the very ideal nursemaid she was looking for. *Widow, no ties, will care for baby or children, any hrs. your home, exp.* And a phone number. Fired with eager hope, Alison jotted down the number, folded the paper tidily, and walked up to the corner drugstore to call the woman . . .

Now she was sizing her up in person, and feeling thankfully that she looked just the thing—just the kind of nursemaid she'd hoped to find. Mrs. Thelma Cole was English. Not quite Cockney, but a humble accent. She was small and thin, but jolly for all of that. About fifty: very neat and clean and respectable-looking. Salt-and-pepper hair in a tidy bun, old-fashioned rimless spectacles. Her modest apartment was tidy and clean too.

"Oh, yes, mum, they can be trying at that stage, I know," she was saying sympathetically. "Do seem to be a thing you got to teach 'em, like, sleeping at night . . . Yes, mum, I've had a deal of experience with babies. I can give you good references, mum. Not so recent, but you see, 'tisn't since I lost me husband I had to go to work again. I'm sure I'd be real pleased to come to you, they do sound like lovely babies, mum . . . Well, living in like, I thought maybe—a hundred dollars a month, p'raps?"

Quite too good to be true, thought Alison, happily writing a check. Luis would be so pleased . . .

Mendoza read the FBI reports before going out to lunch. If there was anything suggestive in them, he didn't spot it. This was slow work, looking out backgrounds, and this they had so far was just surface—what the subjects themselves said, what neighbors and friends said—lawyers and doctors; in some cases relatives.

The Dvorzhaks looked like just what they said they were. Genuine Hungarian refugees. Jan Dvorzhak had been a professor of languages: they were superior, educated people. Had come here two years ago under the quota, after escaping into Austria. Dvorzhak had known other professional men here through correspondence, and had been accepted as a teacher in a private language school. He earned a fair living at that, but had besides an enviable capital investment in securities. He said quite frankly that for years, anticipating the chance to escape the Communist regime, he had been secretly acquiring unset stones, which he had managed to bring away with him. The transactions had been looked into and were all above-board; he had paid duty on the jewels, and eventually sold them for a tidy sum. He was one of the lucky refugees. His daughter Anya was attending college with the intention of becoming a teacher.

The Moskovitches—other end of the scale—an unsavory family. Mike's record—Maureen's record—Mendoza skimmed through that: nothing.

The Farlows. Even though the connection was so nebulous, the Feds were looking at everybody. Mrs. Farlow had been a Grace Eininger. Her older brother, Thomas Eininger, had been a money-maker: whatever he touched turned prosperous. Oil stock, real-estate investments, mining—he'd amassed quite a fortune while he was still a young man, having started with nothing. He hadn't married until he was forty, and then he had married a wife twenty years younger than himself. There had been a baby—a boy; and Thomas Eininger had made a will. Among many other provisions, it provided that in case of his death and that of his wife, his sister be appointed legal guardian of the boy, and co-trustee with his lawyer of his entire estate, held in trust for the boy, John. The unexpected had come to pass; Eininger was an ardent amateur yachtsman, and he and his wife had drowned together in a sailing accident when the boy was two years old.

Meanwhile, Grace Eininger had married Jack Farlow. He might be an amiable weakling; he seemed to be well liked. He'd held a good many different jobs before he and Grace fell into this soft place. Nothing said he was anything but a good-looking lazy charmer; and she seemed to be a perfectly ordinary straightforward woman, maybe the stronger character of the two. The co-trustee, a busy Los Angeles attorney, said he was quite happy about the home the Farlows made for the boy, and what the hell business was it of the FBI anyway? The neighbors said they were nice quiet neighbors, and good to the boy. Parties sometimes, but nothing wild. They also said that Farlow seemed "good" with the boy: the boy seemed quite happy, looking on them as parents.

Nothing, nothing . . . But Mendoza sat up a little over the report on Paul Manton.

Manton's employers said frankly they were thinking seriously of firing him. Again. He was, said his immediate boss with equal frankness, one hell of a good mechanic, but he wouldn't stand routine. Work a couple of weeks honest and regular as you please, and then all of a sudden he wouldn't show; and when he eventually came back on the job, he'd just say, Oh, he'd taken a notion to drop over to Vegas a couple of days, or, Well, he met up with this blonde. Erratic, in other words . . . Like, his boss went on to say, just this last week, he takes off a couple of days without a word, and just when they were particularly swamped, too.

His Air Force record was excellent; he'd won a couple of medals. He'd only been twenty, twenty-one then. Yes, thought Mendoza, remembering that good-looking, strong, reckless face, he'd be that type. Maybe he should have stayed in the service. But again, in peacetime, not the kind who could live with any discipline.

He didn't seem to have any close friends or a regular girl. "Oh, Paul, hell, he plays the field," his boss had said cynically. Which figured. A man with a face like that, thought Mendoza, wouldn't be an ascetic. He drank very little. People who ought to know said he was a very good pilot.

He lived in a middle-aged Hollywood apartment, nothing fancy, and the manageress said he wasn't there much. Just to sleep, and not always that. He very seldom got any letters. He'd lived there for three years and had always paid the rent regularly. Always been a quiet tenant. Apparently he was interested in folk music: a phonograph and quite a few L.P. records around. He didn't seem to live extravagantly; as a top mechanic, of course, he made good wages.

His previous record was predictable; he'd been fired from several good jobs for taking a few days off whenever he felt like it. But he was good enough so that employers had hired him back several times too, and he always managed to get another job if they didn't.

He hadn't seemed nervous in any way at being questioned; said he realized they had to take a look at everybody, and though he hadn't known her well—

It was interesting, but not altogether surprising. And as for linking Manton any closer to Valerie, useless.

That girl Gloria—

Mendoza swore, and took himself out to lunch. At Federico's he met Hackett gloomily contemplating the Dieters' Special Steak, sat down opposite and presented his problem to him.

"Just a great big blank. Nobody admits to knowing where she was going on Sunday, or to seeing her at all. She didn't come home again after Mrs. Montague saw her leave at ten o'clock. And that damned machine— And what the hell was her racket? None of the usual things is indicated."

"No," agreed Hackett. "Offbeat one all right. Funny way to take her off, too—in a way. Unusual. No inspiration hits me offhand, I'm afraid. And as for your anonymous phone call—these six-year-old murders—"

"Well, of course that's a wild one," agreed Mendoza. "Six years ago Valerie was a giggling seventeen-year-old, never opening a newspaper to hear about the latest murder. Though there's always the radio."

"On the other hand—" Hackett picked up his fork. "We like to think we're pretty good," he said inconsequentially, "and mostly when we get a new homicide, whatever variety, eventually we collect evidence on who's responsible. But once in a while—there was that Burnham—something turns up to make us blush a little."

"Burnham," nodded Mendoza. Another offbeat one. One out of the books. A suspicious neighbor coming to the police, and the body found buried in the back yard; and Burnham calmly confessing that he'd murdered eight wives in the last fifteen years—and the bodies showing up where he said they were. "Burnham?"

"It just occurs to me," said Hackett, "and it's not very likely, but it could be—granting that your anonymous caller wasn't just a crank of some sort—that the murder she mentioned never got into the papers. Never got into our files. Got itself written off as accident, suicide, natural death, or never got noticed at all. In a big city, frightening to think how somebody can drop out of sight and never be missed."

Mendoza stared at him. "That's so," he said slowly. "As you say, not very likely, but— And at this late date, how hopeless to make any check! Where to look? Your bright ideas just confuse the issue some more, damn it."

"Just occurred to me," said Hackett.

When he got back to the office, he called Gloria Litvak's apartment. She answered; when he announced himself, told her to stay in and expect him, he thought at first she'd fainted. "Miss Litvak?"

"A-all right," she said tremulously. "I don't know anything more to tell you—honest, I—"

"I'll see you in half an hour," said Mendoza. "Just routine, Miss Litvak."

As he came out of his office, Sergeant Lake stopped him. "I think you'd like to hear what this young fellow has to say, sir," he said formally. A tall gangling young man, looking nervous, was standing beside his desk. "He's got something to tell us about Miss Ellis."

"Oh, yes?"

What young Mr. Jorgensen had to say wasn't very important. He was a clerk at a Thrifty drugstore on Hollywood Boulevard, and he was pretty sure it had been Valerie Ellis who had come into the store last Sunday and he'd waited on her. About eleven o'clock in the morning. He couldn't remember exactly what she'd bought, but something small, inexpensive—maybe a package of aspirin, something like that. "I guess I shoulda come in before, but I wasn't just *so* sure it was her, I had to study on it, make up my mind—"

"All right, you take a statement, Jimmy." Mendoza cut him short; it wasn't important, but of course you never knew what might turn out to be important, so you took statements. He went on out, and drove up to Hollywood to see Gloria. Try to coax what she knew out of her.

Both he and the Feds thought that Gloria was probably earning a living as a call girl. No proof; they hadn't the manpower to tail all these people. If only some lead would show up to point to somebody definite, use the tails, but so far—Gloria was calling herself a model these days. He'd passed her name on to Perce Andrews; maybe he was taking a look at her . . .

Mendoza put out all his persuasive charm, which was considerable. But, looking as terrified as the proverbial bird hypnotized by a snake, Gloria remained stubborn.

"I've told you all I know—honest I have—it was all just like I told you and I don't know anything more about it."

"I think you do, Miss Litvak. I wish you'd think twice and tell me what it is." He smiled at her. "Did you know what her latest racket was? I think so. Unless you were involved in it, you know, we couldn't do anything to you for—" She went on shaking her head stubbornly. She was green with fright. "Look, Miss Litvak. Just because you've had one brush with the police, you needn't be afraid we'll automatically suspect you, or do any railroading. We've looked up your family, and know that they're all quite respectable people, that you don't belong to—" He stopped. She had fainted now, slumping awkwardly from chair to floor. "Damnation!" said Mendoza, annoyed.

He picked her up and laid her on the couch, propping her feet up. He brought her a glass of water when she came to, asked if she wanted a doctor.

"I'm—all—right," she said weakly, turning her face away into the back of the couch. "If you'll just—stop bothering me, and go away. I *told* you all I know."

He couldn't go on pressing her, by the humane rules.

He walked down the stairs, thinking about Gloria, who knew something. Gloria, possibly in on the racket? Not a very brainy accomplice.

She had to be over at Vic's. The phrase haunted him.

He wondered if he'd turn up anything setting a tail on Gloria.

He came out of the apartment-house door, fishing absently for his car keys; a woman brushed past him, up the steps to the front door. He turned right, up toward where he'd left the Ferrari half a block up the street; and then a belated vague memory touched him, and he turned and looked back.

The woman had stopped, with one hand holding the door open, and he thought she had been looking after him. He had no more than started to turn his head—he saw out of the corner of his eye—when she shoved the door wider and ducked in and was gone.

An impression of youth, smartness, lithe energy.

And he thought that had been Anya Dvorzhak. He wasn't sure. He wasn't sure at all, but— A dark, pretty girl like Anya, anyway. Had it been?

Mendoza went back, rapidly. Nobody in the lobby or on the stairs. When he got to Gloria's apartment, she faced him woodenly, her face tear-stained, and said No, there wasn't anybody there. Why should there be?

And maybe there wasn't, then. Maybe it hadn't been Anya Dvorzhak at all. If it had been, maybe Anya knew somebody else who lived here. Coincidence, but they did happen. And Anya just didn't like cops, didn't care to be recognized and questioned. Anybody who had grown up under a Communist regime might very understandably dislike official police.

And also, reflected Mendoza, anybody like that—who had managed to escape—was probably quite experienced at dodging and evading and telling the plausible lies and covering up in general.

What the hell was all this about? Could the Feds be right after all—did the Communists come into this? But the Dvorzhaks would have been thoroughly screened before they were let in—

Maybe, for God's sake, he was getting old. Losing his touch. Floundering around like a new ranker, with no more idea of what had gone on here, what the case was all about—!

ELEVEN

He went back to his office and called Waltham. Unavoidably, he'd noticed the headlines the last two days; he wasn't surprised that Waltham sounded harassed.

"Surprising how many doubles Thorwald has, isn't it?" he asked.

Waltham didn't laugh. "If that's supposed to be funny—" Thorwald had been seen by excited honest citizens in fifty different places between Honolulu and New York, in the last forty-eight hours. As any one of them might really be Thorwald, all the tips had to be followed up.

"Well, we've had a little of that ourselves," said Mendoza. They had. Half a dozen people had called in to say they'd seen Valerie Ellis at such and such a place on Sunday. They had all been checked out, because any of them might be so; but they'd all been proved duds (by men taking valuable time to check) except one report that she'd been seen at one o'clock buying a ticket to the Hawaii Theater. And he thought they'd find that one had been mistaken identity too. He thought Valerie had had something more profitable to do with her time that afternoon than attend a movie . . . Very probably, of all those reports, young Mr. Jorgensen was the only one they could believe; he'd been so diffident about coming in. And what did that say, that she'd dropped into a drugstore?

"What I called about is something a little funny," he said, and told Waltham about the Martian machine. Waltham grunted. "Say anything to you?"

"Yes, damn it," said Waltham, "or it might. Thorwald is an engineer. I wouldn't doubt he could figure out with no trouble at all how to operate a thing like that. He was right at the top of the class, after all."

"¡Por Dios!" said Mendoza softly. "That I never thought of. What a tangle . . . Are you getting anywhere?"

"Odds and ends. This stage, largely eliminating—you know how it goes. We've got leads on about a dozen people who've bought Madeira wine fairly recently, or habitually buy it. We've got all the liquor retailers briefed to watch for that. Oh"—Mendoza heard papers rattle—"that Mrs. Mandelbaum. Report just came in."

"What Mrs.—oh, yes." Cardenas had said a Mrs. Mandelbaum had introduced him to Valerie. "Yes?"

"Well, it doesn't take us very far." Waltham sighed. "Need a month of Sundays to really check all these people, damn it. She looks perfectly level. Widow, living alone at a nice apartment in Santa Monica. German accent you could cut with a knife. Says she met Valerie at a fashion show at The May Company, they just got to talking. She was such a nice bright girl, says Mrs. Mandelbaum; she likes cheerful young things around, she used to invite her to parties and so on. Very shocked—as isn't everybody!— to hear that Valerie was a bad girl. Fellow who looked at her says she's a nice fat old lady, kind of simple. She's lived there about five years, neighbors say the same thing."

"I can't remember another case I ever worked," said Mendoza, "when *some* lead didn't show up within this length of time. Even when we couldn't get evidence for the D.A. Damn it, what was the girl up to? Of course, come to think, it could have been more than one caper. Here a little, there a little. Yes." He told Waltham about his doubtful identification of Anya Dvorzhak at the apartment where Gloria Litvak lived. "No, I'm not a hundred per cent sure, but—"

"Well, I'm bound to say," said Waltham, "just because they are who they are, I think we can mark the Dvorzhaks off—if it is anything political. People coming in like that are very thoroughly screened, after all."

Mendoza said irritably, "I thought you boys were supposed to be hot shots. As a confirmed capitalist, I get worried sometimes. For God's sake, how long are we going to go on being blind? So it takes two to start a fight, it also takes two or more—of honest intent—to create an atmosphere of brotherly love. Can you tell me that, with all our noble democratic sympathy for the poor downtrodden refugees, one or two or more couldn't slip in who are fakes? Provided with the convincing proofs by the Kremlin?"

"Well, no. Of course we've picked up a few like that," said Waltham mildly. "But I assure you, they are looked at. Just for that reason. And this Professor Dvorzhak seems to be a well-known man. I've seen them myself, and checked. Are you coming round to the idea that the murder was political?"

"I am not. I think it was a very private kill. I can't figure the political tie-up." Mendoza was silent and then asked, "You said you knew a good deal about Thorwald. When he landed back in this country, what do you think he'd do? Where would he go? Just as an intelligent guess? Any old friends he could trust?"

"Not old professional friends, no. I'd say nobody he knew, before, except— It depends on whether his friends from Moscow were chasing him. There was an old girl friend—he was quite the ladies' man, in a discreet way—who stayed by him. In fact, if you recall, she got a year's term for sheltering him. Would have been more, but we couldn't prove she knew he was guilty of treason at the time. Lisa Thorne. She was executive secretary to a big firm of attorneys in town—"

"By town meaning Washington?"

"Sure. They didn't take her back when she got out—she's dropped out of sight. If he could have got a message to her before or after he got here— providing he knew where to reach her—it's in the cards she'd have been ready to team up with him again. But no leads on it . . . What would he do? I'd say, if he knew they weren't chasing him, he'd go to ground—with or without the girl friend—in some big city, take an inconspicuous job, look as inconspicuous as possible. Very probably that's what he'd do if they were after him, too."

"Yes," said Mendoza. "I think so too. Well—wish each other luck." He hung up, swiveled around, and looked at the panorama of the city spread before him.

He thought, Paul Manton. A hell of a good mechanic. Very likely he could have taken a long look at the Martian machine's dashboard or whatever it was called, and seen how to operate it. But why? No close tie-up with Valerie that showed . . . And that was another thing. Introduced to Valerie by Maureen Moskovitch. Could a sophisticated man like Manton not have known what Maureen was? So, would he have been so very surprised to hear that a friend of Maureen's was on the bent? It was a little thing, of course.

He swiveled back and looked at the pile of reports on his desk. Odds and ends were coming in. He had Dwyer, Scarne, Piggott, Glasser on it, asking the questions, poking around. And there were the reports from Prints.

No identifiable prints on the doorknob of Valerie's apartment. But they knew who the intruder on Wednesday night had been—Eddy Warren. After, pretty certainly, his reefers stored with Valerie.

A lot of prints in her white Dodge, inside and outside. Tiresome work eliminating the unimportant ones, the garage-hands and so on. And collecting prints to compare, from her circle of acquaintances, the gas station where she had the tank filled, et cetera. Most of those people raised a fuss, expectably, at being treated like criminals. But two rather interesting little facts had just shown up from that. First, as they'd known since first looking at the car, the steering wheel was virginally clean of any prints at all, even smudged ones, as were the push buttons for the automatic transmission, the light switch, and the directional signal switch. And second, there were a couple of Paul Manton's prints on the dashboard and outside of the car.

That rather canceled itself out, thought Mendoza. That said that Paul Manton wasn't X, who'd so carefully removed his prints—after driving the Dodge.

Yes. Build it up. She had been unsuspectingly fed the doped drink, elsewhere. Most probably in a private residence. And had died there. Dr. Bainbridge had said she'd pass out in about half an hour, and probably be dead within four hours. X had planned, had hoped, to get her back into her own apartment, set up an obvious suicide or accident. The safest way, if he could manage it. It wouldn't matter that she hadn't a prescription for those sleeping-tablets; there were ways things like that could be acquired under the counter. So he had, after dark, got her into her own car, probably rolled in a blanket, and driven to her apartment house.

He could find out which garage was hers, if he didn't already know, by trying the padlocks: which one she had the key to. And then he'd gone to get the apartment door open. Mendoza didn't think X had planned to carry her in openly through the front door. Entirely too dangerous. It was a ground-floor apartment, on the driveway side of the building; the best way to get her in would be to open a window, unhook the screen and prop it open, carry her up the dark driveway and hoist her through the window . . . A little job, carrying a body around like that. X a pretty hefty fellow?

Only Mrs. Montague had startled him as he opened the door . . . Yes, *how* he must have cursed himself for dropping those keys—those invaluable keys!

So then he couldn't stage the fake suicide. And for some reason he had decided to leave her—

Despacio, aguarda un momento—wait a minute here. He'd brought her back home in her own car, and the car had stayed in her garage. Well, he could have driven her down to Garey Street and brought the Dodge back again afterward. But also, he might already have got the car all polished up, removing his prints thoroughly, and not wanted to do the job over again. He might have called an accomplice to bring up another car. "They" again . . .

She had to be over at Vic's. Damn it, it seemed almost to mean something, but he couldn't catch the significance.

Rikki's bar, mentioned in the notebook. Ordinary place out on Vernon Avenue in Huntington Park. Yes, she'd been in; the barman, a waiter, somewhat vaguely recognized her picture. She'd been there at least once with another woman, and they thought several times with men. No remotely useful description of the men, of course. But then, most bars were kept so dark. Influence of Prohibition still holding, thought Mendoza irritably.

The patient Dwyer had rung doorbells all along that block of Garey Street. Had anybody heard one of those big construction machines running on Sunday evening?

He had found people who had been watching TV and really couldn't say. He had found people who had been listening to the radio and couldn't say. He had found people who had been away from home until late and couldn't say. The chiropractor lived in a couple of rooms behind his office; he was an amateur photographer and had been in his makeshift darkroom most of Sunday evening, developing a negative and making some prints—he didn't recall. The herb-doctor, a polite young Chinese, was a devout Methodist and had been at some church affair. The dentist had been at the movies with his wife. And then, down at the corner of Second Street, Dwyer had found ancient Mrs. Modjeska. Mrs. Modjeska, eighty-seven and retaining all her faculties if she had lost most of her teeth, said that indeed there had been one of those machines running that night. Only for a very short time, but it amounted to the same thing—Heathens, she said, shaking a finger under Dwyer's nose, breaking the Sabbath. As if it wasn't bad enough to come tearing up the street, making all this dust and commotion—half-naked men out there in broad daylight—they must come back on the Sabbath! It was an outrage.

Dwyer tried to pin her down to a time, but the best he could get out of her was between nine and ten.

So, the Martian machine had been used to get the body over the fence.

That scrawl in Valerie's address book which might have been either Frank or Fred had turned out, by the phone number, to be one Fran Schwartz. The report said tersely, *Another model, question mark.* Address on Bronson in Hollywood. He had phoned a query down to Vice; maybe they knew something about her.

By what Gloria, and Valerie's Aunt Mabel, said, a week ago Tuesday afternoon Valerie had been expecting a caller. Gloria may have seen the caller, wasn't admitting it. A new mark? Something to do with the racket? Then, on Wednesday, she went off in her car, and didn't come home until Friday evening.

In her car . . . The Dodge convertible was four years and four months old; it had been given to her by her father three months before his fatal accident. And it had nearly forty thousand miles on it. That was a little unusual right there, because a girl like Valerie, using a car for the casual little errands around town, calls on friends, wouldn't as a rule average over a couple of hundred miles a month. Of course in this metropolis even the casual little errands could pile up mileage, but even so—

And the funny thing about it was, it wasn't a struck average. They'd found the garage where she always took the Dodge for servicing. The garage kept a record, of course, of oil changes and so on. What the mileage had been when. And up to about twenty months ago, Valerie hadn't driven the Dodge two hundred miles a month. Twenty months ago or thereabouts, the Dodge had had upwards of eight thousand miles on it, an average figure for its age. She'd piled up all the rest of the mileage since. How and why? Connected with the racket?

Odds and ends, odds and ends. Nothing pointing anywhere . . . He wondered how Hackett and Palliser were doing. No sign of either of them in the office this morning . . .

"Too good to be true," said Alison contentedly. "Tell me how clever I am, darling."

"I knew there must be one somewhere," agreed Mendoza. "She seems eminently satisfactory, but of course it's early to be sure." He leaned back, stroking Bast on his lap. The steak had been done just as he liked it, there had been wild rice and mushrooms to accompany it, Alison's copper head gleamed above a favorite topaz-colored gown, the twins were asleep, Bast purred under his hand, and altogether if he'd had any glimmering of an idea about this damned case he'd feel wholly at peace. As it was—

El Señor was washing Sheba, holding her down with one paw. Nefertiti lay purring on Alison's lap. "They've been neglected lately, poor things, what with the twins . . . She likes cats, Luis. She made friends with El Señor right away, and you know he's usually standoffish. And the babies took to her too, I could tell—she's very good with them." Alison heaved a peaceful sigh. "I really think our worries are over."

"For the moment," said Mendoza lazily. "I ran into Saul Goldberg this afternoon, as I was leaving—he said something that struck me. I was com-

plaining, you know, and he came out with this—old Hebrew proverb—
'*Small children disturb your sleep, big children your life.*' A sobering
thought, and probably true."

"Nonsense," said Alison robustly. She threaded a needle, tongue protruding delicately, and bent over the small blue sweater. He waited for the
inevitable explosion. "Oh, damn! Of *all* the—"

"You do amuse me," he said. "You know you can't sew. It arouses all
your most unladylike instincts when you try. Another thing like the nursemaid business—going all conventional just because you have produced a
couple of very ordinary infants."

"You be quiet," said Alison crossly. "You'd think anybody could sew a
simple appliqué to a sweater. All I'm trying to *do*. It doesn't help for you
to sit there and heckle me—*Oh!*"

"Nothing to do with me. I'm not heckling. I'm just saying you amuse
me, *querida* . . . Put that down for a minute and pay attention. Imagine
that you are a young woman very greedy for money, who has in fact engaged in prostitution for same, and is now involved in a very lucrative
racket of some kind. You are essentially a rather sexless young woman, not
much interested in that sort of thing—"

"Well, I'm trying," said Alison obediently. "Yes?"

"Would you be, could you be, very romantically interested in a balding
civil servant who probably doesn't make over ten thousand a year? Even
if he looked a little like me?"

"This is Valerie? I certainly shouldn't think so," said Alison. "Was
she?"

"I don't think so either. But when you come to that kind of thing, it's a
No Man's Land. Who can say what A sees in B? She could have been,
damn it. The two people who say so look very much on the level . . . And
those other girls, who probably would know, are being so damn cagey—
afraid of being involved—keeping back even innocent information—" He
got up, Bast cradled in his arms, and began to pace restlessly, up and down
Alison's handsome big living room. "And then there's another thing—"

Distantly, one of the twins began to cry, and stopped almost immediately. "A jewel," said Alison. "Now I know what the phrase means. A perfect jewel. Such a nice little woman."

"Is Mrs. Mandelbaum what she seems to be? Did Gloria see whoever
came to see Valerie a week ago Tuesday? Who the hell is Vic?"

Alison took up her needle again. "You sound exactly like the announcer
for a soap opera . . . What fascinates *me*, if there's anything in it at all, is
who the woman was who was murdered six years ago."

"That's a wild card, for God's sake."

"I don't think so . . . Oh, Lord, what have I—oh, I see, it has to go under, not over . . . Suppose—you said they're much the same coloring—this Paul Manton is really Valerie's mother's illegitimate son, and the woman who was killed was a friend of hers who knew all about it, and was going to tell her husband, and—"

"¡Zape—vaya historia! Now who sounds like a soap opera?" Mendoza laughed. "I'll tell you one thing just occurs to me—damn it, this lack of sleep is affecting my mind! That phone call. If it wasn't a crank, if it was the genuine article, it tells us that X is probably being blackmailed. That somebody has guessed he is X, and why."

"Oh. Why?"

Bast leaped lightly down to tumble her big blond son away from Sheba and take over the wash job. El Señor withdrew coldly to sit on the credenza and polish his blond paws and face. "What she said on the phone," said Mendoza. "We should have picked that one up right away. She said at one point, 'I would so tell them!' Meaning us. That call was made as a last dead-serious threat to X that if he didn't pay up she'd pass on what she knew. Without any doubt, X was standing right beside her when she made that call. He'd been dickering with her—or refusing to come across—so she showed him she meant business."

"That's—yes, I see what you mean."

Mendoza wandered out to the kitchen to pour himself a scant jigger of rye. El Señor hurried after hopefully and received his ounce in a saucer. Green eyes shut tight, he lapped happily. "Señor Atroz," said Mendoza. "Talk about bad example." He wandered back to the living room, glass in hand. "And where the hell does Thorwald come in?" he asked.

"She was his mistress," said Alison. "Or, all right, you say she wasn't interested in being anybody's. Then she'd found out about him—who he was. He was paying her to keep quiet about it. That was her racket."

"But there's an implication there were a couple of other people in it."

"Only by what Maureen said," Alison pointed out. "That Valerie had quoted that proverb about three keeping a secret if two of them were dead, and adding that she was sure of these two. Well, I ask you, amado, who could she have been surer of than Thorwald and his old girl friend, who had probably joined him? . . . Oh, damn! This abominable thread—"

Mendoza stopped in his tracks and stared at her. "Now that's an angle I never— That could be so. That could be so indeed. Only if it is so, where did Thorwald get the money? By all appearances, a very substantial sum of money."

"Well," said Alison, her red head bent over the sweater, "I wouldn't know if any of the cloak-and-dagger stories are plausible. But we all know that some fantastic things have happened in the last twenty years—things that sound like Ian Fleming at his wildest. Haven't there? Caches of pre-war gold—stolen hoards tucked away— It could be something like that. And as to how Valerie might have spotted him—you say she wasn't the political animal, as the saying goes—I wouldn't guess, but you've just heard that this old flame of Thorwald's dropped out of sight after she got out of jail. She didn't get her old job back—she'd have no references. Probably she wouldn't stay in Washington. How would a woman like that earn a living? You said yourself, the easiest way— And it could have been here."

Mendoza finished the rye. "You're building a story," he said softly. "So?"

Alison cocked her head at him. "L.A.'s getting to be like that place in Egypt—sooner or later everybody gets here. Isn't it? You know Thorwald was here, wherever he is now. Quite possibly his former girl friend was here, to meet him—or he came here because she was here already. Maybe Valerie knew her, and—they'd be very cautious, wouldn't they?—acted as a messenger, a go-between, some way. And found out about Thorwald—maybe because the girl friend trusted her too far—"

"Un momento," said Mendoza. "Grant that Thorwald came back with a fortune in hand. From somewhere. I don't see him paying out hush-money at that rate over a period of eighteen or twenty months—he can't have been here that long anyway—before finally deciding to get rid of her."

"So the Thorwald business was—extracurricular," said Alison. "Maybe quite recent, only a couple of weeks or a month ago."

"Another thing. That bottle of Madeira in Valerie's kitchen cupboard. So she was putting the bite on him—or them—to keep quiet. It hangs together after a fashion. And that was apart from the regular racket she was working. This I like, because I've had a hunch all along that the motive hadn't a thing to do with her racket. All right. Would Thorwald make her a present of that bottle? 'Do try some of this excellent wine just to please me, my dear.' "

"And I've had a thought about that too," said Alison. She stuck her needle in the sweater and looked at him. "That could have been before she began the blackmail. When she was still being friendly to them. And also— Have you had the Madeira analyzed? To see if there's any codeine in it? Because, say Thorwald had spiked it before he gave it to her—or afterward, when she tried blackmail. Maybe he'd given her a bottle of it before and knew she liked it, would drink it of her own volition, maybe a glass before going to bed. She could have drunk a fatal dose—how melodramatic that sounds—and then gone out somewhere, on Sunday. The doctor says she mightn't feel it for a half-hour or so. She could have gone out somewhere, and collapsed and died in, say, the Moskovitches' apartment or somewhere, so whoever it was was scared of being involved and simply carted the body off, not to be associated—"

Mendoza stared at her. He said absently, "I must be losing my touch, all right. *Porvida*, I never thought of that. An entirely new angle—" He wheeled and made for the telephone, to contact Waltham.

Talk about soap opera. But it was *possible*, damn it. It wouldn't do any harm, to have that bottle of Madeira analyzed . . .

TWELVE

Palliser came into the office after six on Saturday night, feeling low. With reason. He'd taken the rest of the day, after they'd talked to Mendoza about it, looking into this Dasher thing. In one way he hadn't got much, and in another way he'd got too much.

There was this and that in Mrs. Dasher's background that looked odd. It could still be that her killer was an utter stranger, imitating Lover Boy; but at least one thing he'd come across might point to—what was Mendoza's phrase?—a private kill.

He found Hackett drinking black coffee out of a cardboard mug and staring glassy-eyed at a pile of reports. "Anything show up?"

"Not yet. And the hell of a list still to get through. What've you got?" asked Hackett dully.

Palliser sat down and started to tell him what he'd got.

He'd been handicapped by the fact that it was Saturday. Not infrequently, police officers resent the five-day week; it not only delays investigations, but the fact that they often work a couple of weeks or more straight without a day off, all to protect the honest citizenry, makes the idea of the honest citizenry lazing around at home a bitter one.

After talking to Mrs. Powell again, and a few friends and neighbors of Mrs. Dasher's, Palliser had found he wanted urgently to see Mrs. Dasher's bank record . . . She had, everyone who knew her agreed, been one to keep her affairs to herself. She hadn't had any really close friends aside from Mrs. Powell. Oh, several women she knew from church, and other nurses she'd known—Mrs. Dasher had had an address book too, but not very full.

"She never gossiped about her cases," said pleasant-faced Myra Thompson. "That I will say. It was a living to her, was all—she wasn't really interested in people, I don't think . . . Why? I mean, I thought it was this awful colored man who—"

"Well, we like to be thorough, Mrs. Thompson," said Palliser vaguely. "You'd known her long?"

She nodded, eying him curiously: a woman in her fifties, stout and amiable. "We took the practical-nursing course together, that's how we met. That's twenty years ago. I'd just lost my first husband and she'd just lost hers, and we'd both thought that was a sensible sort of job to learn. She was ten years older than me, of course . . . Well, we didn't see each other too often, especially since I remarried. Even if she was retired, she wasn't one for gadding around much, you see. Wish somebody'd leave *me* a legacy! Not that I grudged her the luck—she was a hard worker—but I was a little surprised at that. Because, well, she couldn't help it, poor thing, but she wasn't really very sympathetic—just do the work she was supposed to, but no little personal fussing, know what I mean . . . Oh, I don't know any of the details about that, she was pretty closemouthed."

Gradually a picture built up in Palliser's mind . . . "Well, when I say I knew her, I'm bound to say it was kind of casual. We've both lived on the same block a good many years, and she was friendly enough, but kept herself to herself like they say." And a church friend: "Oh, it was just her way, to be secretive. I guess people who live alone get that way. Nobody expected any different, knowing her." And: "I don't say she was mean about money, but she was careful. She'd had to be, I guess, and got in the habit." A picture of a rather house-proud old woman, conventional and solitary, with no close emotional ties and perhaps not wanting any. Closemouthed, close with money.

Mrs. Powell told him a good deal; she had known more about Gertrude Dasher than anyone else; but she couldn't tell him a few essentials.

"Closemouthed, so she was, and hadn't she learned to be! That husband of hers, tell him anything, he'd go letting out real personal things at the nearest bar! And expecting her to manage on practically nothing. What? Well, he was a plasterer, but they wasn't making the wages they do now, twenty years back, you know . . . Well, Gertrude tried hard enough, the good Lord knows, to stop his drinking. Lifelong member of the W.C.T.U., *as* I am myself . . . Drunk? That's not the point, young man —he didn't exactly get *drunk,* but it's the principle—"

Palliser suppressed a twinge of sympathy for the late Harry Dasher, plasterer, who had liked a couple of beers with the boys after work.

"No, she never had any children, she was alone in the world, poor woman. And had the arthritis coming on bad, the last few years, so it was a mercy she could afford to retire."

He asked about that: the fortunate legacy. "Well, she never said the name, I don't know who it was. Some old patient. Nor I don't know how much. Gertrude liked to keep her affairs private, and I respected that, I do myself. I just know it was enough so she could live pretty well, better than before. She wasn't extravagant, I don't mean that, but I noticed she'd buy things she couldn't afford before. Like frozen vegetables instead of canned, and round steak instead of stewing beef, and she sent her coat to be cleaned instead of doing it herself—"

Palliser's picture grew clearer. A little more than close, Gertrude Dasher. He often did the shopping for his mother on his days off, and he had some idea of prices. Not all that much difference these days between round steak and stewing-beef; call it twenty cents a pound. And one old lady, a pound lasting maybe three days. Fifty cents to have the coat cleaned . . .

"Was she working on a case when she heard about the legacy?"

"I couldn't say," said Mrs. Powell. "She never said much about the people she worked for, but I do know she'd been mostly taking baby cases, about then. Taking care of babies for people could afford to pay a nursemaid. So I don't expect it'd be one of them—"

"But she must have told you something about it," said Palliser. She had been Mrs. Dasher's one relatively close friend; they had, she said, usually had dinner together at least once a week.

"Well, she didn't," snapped Mrs. Powell. "For one thing, I wasn't here when it happened. I was on a visit to my married daughter back in Pennsylvania, from February to April that year, and it was when I got back Gertrude told me about her legacy. She wasn't much of a letter writer and neither am I."

Palliser tapped his ballpoint pen reflectively on his front teeth. Grant that Gertrude Dasher had been a secretive, solitary old woman: surely that was a little unnatural? She'd had to work hard all her life; she'd learned to be very close with money (though maybe that had come natural to her). When out of the blue she got a sufficiently substantial legacy that she could stop working, live a little better than she had before, surely she'd have made a few comments on it to a close friend? That nice old Mr. Smith, fancy him remembering me, or, that lovely old Mrs. Jones, I never thought she'd be so kind . . .

And aside from what Mrs. Thompson said about her lack of sympathy, he definitely got that impression himself at second hand: a rather sour, embittered old woman, not likely to have impressed a patient as so kind a nurse that a legacy was in order.

So he wanted to see what her bank record looked like. Find out where the money had come from, in what form. And it was Saturday, damn it. He asked Mrs. Powell if she knew where Mrs. Dasher banked. The Security-First National, the one nearest on Hollywood Boulevard.

To hell with Saturday. Bankers could be forced to do a little work on Saturday without bringing the world to an end. Palliser used the telephone, got names and phone numbers. Made more calls, patient and polite. After a good deal of delay and argument, bank officialdom finally produced for him an annoyed junior vice-president by the unlikely name of Rumpeldorf, who met him outside the doors of the branch in question.

"I suppose you know what a nuisance you're being—" Mr. Rumpeldorf paused inquiringly.

"Sergeant Palliser. I'm very sorry, but we need the information urgently." Mr. Rumpeldorf was trying keys and swearing.

"At whatever inconvenience. Damn the door. I suppose you realize this meant my running around collecting different keys from several people? And that I shall have to disconnect the alarm while we're inside, and I know very little about it? Damn Scobey—they should have sent Nichols down with me—" He got the door open at last.

It was Palliser who disconnected the alarm system; with Mr. Rumpeldorf dithering around at it, he had visions of bringing the nearest squad car down on them. But when it came to looking up files, Mr. Rumpeldorf seemed to know what he was doing, and produced Gertrude Dasher's records at once. The current file showed all of last year's statements.

"We are in the process of microfilming records for 1963 now," said the junior vice-president stiffly.

"Yes." Early in every month, never later than the fifth, Mrs. Dasher had deposited five hundred dollars cash in a checking account. She didn't write many checks. Some time each month, around the middle, she'd usually written a check for fifty or sixty dollars. Household expenses? The account at present contained seven thousand, three hundred and twenty-one dollars and ninety-four cents.

Mr. Rumpeldorf stood sighing and jangling his keys irritably. "I'd like to see back further than this," said Palliser.

"Oh, my God!" wailed Mr. Rumpeldorf. "The *microfilms?* Listen, damn it, we're giving a party tonight—my wife—"

It was very petty and small of him, Palliser acknowledged, but he couldn't help feeling a little pleased at the thought of somebody besides a police officer maybe having an evening spoiled because duty called. The times he'd had to break a date with Roberta—

"And," he said to Hackett, "all those years, five hundred in cash paid in regular as clockwork every month. Nothing to show how she got it. Never any incoming checks. And she lived on less than half that, letting it mount up. Well, it looks funny. I mean, a legacy might come all in one piece or in the form of a trust or an annuity, but I never heard of a trust or annuity that paid in nice crisp green cash."

Hackett rubbed his sandy unshaven jaw and said neither had he. "So she stashed the legacy away in cash in a safety-deposit box? Or, no, of course not, when she kept a checking account."

"She didn't have a box. Not there anyway. Probably not anywhere else, though we'll have to look."

"And you couldn't get into the Hall of Justice to look up the possible record of the legacy."

"No, not until Monday. But if there was a legacy the record's bound to be there. She'd never been out of the state, hardly out of the county."

Hackett looked even more tired. "Well, you may as well go on doing the looking. It's possible, if she was as secretive as you say, that she kept it in some form at another bank—queer old ladies do that kind of thing. But it's also possible that she got that nice bundle of cash through the mail every month. In which case it looks like—"

"Blackmail money. I know."

"A very nice motive for murder," said Hackett. He looked at the reports. "On top of everything else."

Mendoza went to the office on Sunday morning, but he wondered why. Just to await the latest FBI report? There wasn't much more they could do on this, on Sunday. Waste of time seeing these people over again, hearing the same stories.

He wandered around rereading reports, thinking in circles. Not one smell of a lead—

One thing they'd been using men on was the banks, because that was a little mystery on top of the big mystery: what had Valerie done with the money? If he read those notations right, somebody or a group of somebodies had taken around seventy thousand bucks over an unspecified length of time. Say it had been split three ways, as hinted by Maureen's information. She'd spent a lot, Valerie had, but she couldn't—or could she?—have got through twenty-three thousand in—well, how long a time? Eleven dollars and some odd cents in cash in the apartment. They'd talked to sales clerks at that Little Shoppe in Robinson's, at other places she'd shopped; the clerks said she had always paid in cash—where they remembered. No charge accounts. No bank in town had a checking account, a savings account, for her. Or a safety-deposit box. Surely she'd have had some of it left?

Maybe an account under a false name. A certain basic cold shrewdness in Valerie. So, take her picture around, ask. See if anybody remembered. And it might be a bank anywhere in the county, and the number of them—

And it might look unimportant to find out what she'd done with the money; on a thing like this, you looked everywhere, because you never knew where a lead might show.

Hackett and Palliser came in and gave him the news about Mrs. Dasher. Mendoza all but snarled. What looked like another mysterious murder, and maybe a tough one to untangle. With this other thing still up in the air— "It could be hush-money all right. What was the Dasher woman doing at the time it started coming?"

"Nobody knows," said Palliser. "Or claims they don't. And none of her friends are all that prosperous, I think they're on the level. She was secretive. Didn't write letters. If she ever got any, she didn't keep them. Hadn't any relatives. Never talked about her cases—nobody even remembers her mentioning a name, saying she was taking care of a Mrs. Jones or a Mr. Johnson. And, damn it, we can say, maybe hush-money—we see so much dirt, do we suspect it when it isn't there? For all we know, she had an illegitimate daughter who married a millionaire and was taking care of mama. But—"

Mendoza looked at them. At big broad sandy Hackett, eyes red-rimmed from weeks of poring over reports and lists, and at grave dark Palliser looking tired and doleful. He laughed and said, *"Ora esta, ora est otro*—we've just struck a bad patch. It's a long lane, et cetera. Tell you what, boys—it's only just eleven, but I'll take you out and buy us all a drink. I think we need it."

Alison patted Miss Teresa's small rump under the blanket and glanced at her watch; it was twelve forty-five. "Well, that's fine then," she said. "I won't be back until around five-thirty or six, but you needn't do a thing but look after the babies, Mrs. Cole—we're going out for dinner."

"Yes, mum. Sleeping lovely, aren't they?" Little Mrs. Cole beamed at the twins. "You don't need to worry, mum."

Alison smiled at her. A perfect jewel. She said good-by and went out to the garage. She was on her way to see Angel Hackett, just for a casual chat—what with the twins, somehow, she hadn't had a nice long gossip with Angel in ages—and Roberta Silverman had asked her to drop in for coffee and a chat later on. She had an idea that Roberta, whom she liked very much, wanted to ask her this and that about how it was, married to a police officer. She wondered if Roberta and John Palliser were engaged yet. A nice young man, Palliser, thought Alison, backing out the Facel-Vega.

She found Angel home—as predictable, in the midst of stirring up a brand-new recipe. Alison sat down at the kitchen table and told her all about that perfect jewel, Mrs. Cole. Angel congratulated her warmly, breaking off to dive on sixteen-month-old Mark as he started to clamber up on a chair.

"He always falls off—too much ambition," said Angel. "After all, he's only started to walk. Because he's so big, the doctor says. I expect it's only natural, Art being so outsize, but it's embarrassing—he looks a good three years old, and people expect— Do the twins like her?"

"She's marvelous with them—you've no idea what a wonderful feeling it is, just walk out and know they're being looked after so well."

Angel was going out to a wedding shower for an old school friend, and Alison left when the baby-sitter came. She'd just turned onto York Boulevard, on her way to South Pasadena and Roberta's apartment, when she remembered that recipe. One of Angel's, a rather exotic one, something special to do with lamb. She'd promised to bring it, when Roberta called, and had forgotten. Damn.

Undecided, she pulled over to the curb. She could go back and ask Angel, but she'd be in the middle of dressing for the wedding shower, and besides it was early. Roberta had said, about four, and it was only five to three now. Better not bother Angel. Better go back home and get it. What a bore. She'd put it out, ready, right there on the dressing table, and then just walked off and left it.

Oh, well.

She turned off at the next side street, Avenue 63, and drove around the block to start back on York in the opposite direction. Got onto Eagle Rock Boulevard, and then the Golden State Freeway, and off that onto Los Feliz. Followed Los Feliz on up into Hollywood, down to Franklin, and turned up through the winding little streets north to Rayo Grande Avenue . . . Luis and his absurd fancy to live on a street called Great Thunderbolt. But it had turned out a nice house, after they'd had the lots leveled. Say it though she shouldn't, most of the design being her idea, a very handsome house . . . Twenty past three. Just nice time, to get the recipe and be at Roberta's by four.

As she turned onto Rayo Grande, a taxi passed her, turning fast down Sunset Plaza. She glanced after it because it was going too fast, and her one glimpse of the single passenger—of course that was absurd, just someone who looked a little like neat Mrs. Cole—

She pulled into the drive, duly careful for cats: went in by the kitchen door. Both the twins were yelling their heads off. Alison went down the hall. "Mrs. Cole, it's just me—"

Nobody with the twins. "Mrs. Cole?" She looked into the next bedroom, went down the hall toward the living-room. And stopped dead as she glanced casually into the master bedroom, passing.

Drawers of the dressing-table dumped in the middle of the floor—closet doors open—*her jewel case*—

Hardly hearing the twins, she rushed into the room. Jewel case open, face-down on the bed—*all the emeralds!*—thank God most of the diamonds at the bank, she didn't often—but— She stared in dismay at the havoc in the closet. She hadn't a fur coat, an affectation in this climate, but her newest evening-dress gone, the imported suit, the—

She whirled to the bureau. Drawers dumped on the floor. All Luis' extra links, that fourteen-carat cigarette case he never carried—

"A jewel!" said Alison semi-hysterically to herself. "Just a jewel!" She ran for the phone down the hall . . . . . . And after a calm voice had assured her there'd be an officer there directly, she dialed again . . . "Is the lieutenant there? This is . . . *Luis*, the most *awful* thing—"

"Well, well," said Sergeant Albers of the Wilcox Street precinct, "baby-sitting Betty again. Where'd you say the ad was? The *Times*. Get 'em to cancel it, Ed, huh? Oh, sure we know that one."

"I can describe her exactly—Luis, you can too— Of *all* the— She seemed so nice! Really, Luis—"

"I'm sorry, *amada*—just the last straw—" Mendoza lay back on the couch and laughed. "Your perfect jewel of a nursemaid!"

"All the emeralds!" wailed Alison. And one of Sergeant Albers' minions stepped on El Señor's tail; El Señor wailed too, and spat loudly. Mendoza doubled up in another paroxysm. The twins yelled down the hall.

"Well, she won't be looking much like when you saw her by now," said Albers. "She could've been a star actress in the movies, you know. Quick-change artist, and she can put on any of half a dozen accents and make you believe it. Of course, we're on her a lot sooner than she'd expect. Good chance we'll catch her before she gets rid of the loot, or has a chance to put on the blond wig or whatever. Damn lucky you came home early, and spotted that taxi." He eyed Mendoza a little worriedly. "Excuse me, but—"

Mendoza pulled himself together and sat up. "Don't mind me. Don't fuss, *querida*, they'll get your emeralds back. I was just visualizing tomorrow's little human-interest story, VETERAN OFFICER ROBBED. They will call me a veteran. So you know her? A long-time pro?"

"Sure," said Albers. "Quite a nice little racket. Baby-sitting Betty. Betty Bellew. She's only got dropped on once. I mean arrested, sir. She—"

"You needn't translate," said Mendoza, mopping his eyes. "I graduated from the academy while you were studying algebra, boy. Headquarters, Homicide. As you say, a nice little racket. Get into the house by being hired as the eminently suitable servant—"

"She mostly hires out as a baby nurse. Sometimes as a maid. Sure," said Albers, and added, "sir. Excuse me, I didn't know—er—"

"Lieutenant. Don't fuss, Alison. They'll rescue the emeralds, you getting home early and finding out. It's just"—he started to laugh again—"such a jewel!"

"Excuse me," said Albers, looking a little puzzled and interested, looking around the obviously expensive living-room, "you said—some emeralds? I see you're wearing an emerald ring, Mrs. Mendoza. She'd have gone by that sort of thing, you know. How you were dressed, and the address, and all. Made it look as if it'd be worth her while, get into the house. Oh, yes, she's an old hand, is Betty. Slippery as all hell—she'll be intending to go to ground now, while she gets rid of the loot."

"But how can you be sure you'll—"

"The cab company," said Albers. "We got on it so soon, probably before the cab took her wherever she was going. They'll know where she went—there they are now," and he dived for the phone.

Alison said bitterly, "It isn't as funny as *that!*"

Mendoza straightened and put his handkerchief away. "It was just—on top of everything else—! My darling, I hesitate to mention it, but our offspring are raising the roof. Shouldn't you go and see if there's a valid reason?"

Alison uttered a very rude word in Spanish dialect and marched out.

THIRTEEN

They had Betty spotted in a hotel on Fourth Street half an hour after she'd checked in. She'd made no stops on the way, and had four suitcases with her—two of them Alison's. Being a prudent man, Sergeant Albers waited until she came out, had her tailed, and picked up not only Betty but a mild-looking little fellow who kept a dingy jewelry shop on Main Street and had never been suspected as a fence.

Both Mendoza and Alison went down to Wilcox Street to make a formal identification: redundant, since they had her prints and all the loot intact. All the same, Alison said, she might have been doubtful. Gone was the respectable Mrs. Cole with her neat bun and rimless glasses. Betty Bellew was a much made-up Hollywood blonde; she'd even taken the time to paint her nails.

She was reasonably philosophic, if understandably annoyed. "All in the game, you can't win all the time," she said in a flat middle-western accent evidently native to her. "Best haul I'd made in months, too." And then she looked curiously at Alison and said, "Like to ask you just one thing, dearie —if you don't mind—how come, everything else in your place so new and nice, how come you only got those two old beat-up suitcases?"

Well, maybe it was as funny as Luis thought . . . and thank God they'd got everything back; though all that mess to straighten up at home—

"If I know Bertha," said Mendoza as they walked back to the car, "she's busy straightening it up now." They'd had to call her to come and stay with the twins. "I'll take you out to dinner."

"Luis, we can't! Just wish all that on her—" In the end, to prove it to her, he let her phone home.

"Perfeckly all right, Mis' Mendoza," said Bertha. "Lands' sakes, after an upset like that you need to relax some . . . Not touch anything? Why, Mis' Mendoza, you don't rightly think I could sit 'n' look at such a mess 'n' not do nothing about it? Everything's all straight as pie now, and no harm done, barring one o' your best lace brassieres as that El Saynyor got hold of before I did, I'm that sorry. Just you go on to dinner 'n' don't fuss about me. I'd already fed Fritz, like I say."

Mendoza's forebodings came true; and it wasn't a two-paragraph story on the third page, but a second head on the first, because, of course, he was the officer on the Ellis-Thorwald case.

VETERAN OFFICER INVESTIGATING ELLIS MURDER ROBBED, said the head in the *Times;* they'd even dug out pictures. The most prominent was the candid shot of Alison and him an enterprising press photographer had snapped as they'd emerged from the Hall of Justice the morning they were married. It was one of those chance shots that turn out astonishingly sharp: Mendoza was looking toward the camera in obvious irritation, Alison was looking impossibly demure, and there on the steps behind them loomed Hackett with his Angel, and the Lockharts. VETERAN OFFICER LT. MENDOZA AS HE WEDS RESCUED VICTIM OF RAPIST. Mendoza frowned over that persistent *veteran.* All right, damn it, so he had twenty-one years' service, he wasn't senile yet . . .

Naturally he got needled from the time he stepped in the front door of the headquarters building. "Having servant problems, I see, Lieutenant," said the uniformed sergeant at the main Information desk. Lieutenant Goldberg of Burglary joined him at the elevators and repeated this original sally.

"Very funny," said Mendoza. "How could Alison know? A thing that might happen to anybody."

"One problem we don't have to cope with," said Goldberg, blowing his nose. "Who can afford it?" The elevator came and they got in. Mendoza pressed the button for Goldberg's floor, but the elevator stopped at the second floor and Captain Duvalle of Vice got in.

"Well, Luis, I see you're having a servant problem," he said, eyes twinkling. "You millionaires."

"Just one of those things," said Mendoza. "At least we got it all back. Look, Jack, you've got a couple of grandchildren, haven't you—where do you find a good nursemaid, for God's sake?"

"Ask my daughter," said Duvalle. "She's found a couple of dandy ones —free, too. Elvira and me." He got off, still shaking with laughter.

Mendoza walked down the corridor to his office. Sergeant Lake looked up and said, "Morning. See you had a little excitement yesterday. That's quite a racket that female has, isn't it? What won't they think up next?"

"Isn't it? The Hollywood boys were touchingly grateful to Alison for coming home early, so they could get on it so soon and pick her up again." He went on into his office; Hackett was standing beside the desk looking through some papers.

"I see by the papers you're having servant problems," he said, grinning.

"It wasn't funny the first time," said Mendoza. "Anything new in?"

"Not on Lover Boy. John's down at the Hall of Justice looking to see if Mrs. Dasher really got a legacy. Somehow I don't think she did. They just sent up a report on your bottle of Madeira, from the lab. Here it is. What was that idea?"

Mendoza told him, scanning the report. Negative. Simply an innocent bottle of Madeira wine. Well, it had been a wild idea; and come to think, he should have known it was, because there was the drug clerk saying she'd been walking around normally at about eleven o'clock on Sunday morning, and they knew she'd left the house at ten. If she'd had the dose before she left, she'd have passed out long before eleven.

Hackett went out to get on with processing his lists, and Mendoza started to look over the latest FBI report. Sergeant Lake put his head in the door and said, "That Fed's on the wire, Lieutenant." Mendoza picked up the outside phone and said hello to Waltham.

"And if you mention my servant problem I'll hang up on you."

Waltham laughed. "You made the press boys happy, anyway—they haven't had much new on this for a couple of days . . . Something interesting just showed I thought you'd like to hear. Arrived at by some very smart detective work, all on his own, by one of our local boys, Adler."

"Yes?"

"It was Adler who went to see this Paul Manton, among other people. And he didn't like his smell. Adler's a bright boy, he gets the feelings from people. You know? He said to me, Manton's a wild one—of any of the people Valerie knew, he thinks, the one most likely to be mixed up in something wrong. Well, God knows none of us have had time to spare, but Adler's been sniffing around Manton at odd moments when he could, and he's found out a few things. You went to see Manton last Thursday, and one of the things Adler's found out is that as soon as you left, Manton lost no time getting to a telephone box."

"You don't tell me."

"And then he just walked off the job and drove away from the airport in his car. In a hurry."

"I take it there's no finding out where?"

"Well, Adler thinks he knows one place he went. It's a damn funny thing," said Waltham, "how coincidence does play a part in detective work sometimes. You know we talked to Manton in his apartment. Adler and another local, I should say. And as it happens Adler goes in for stereo and knows something about it. He said Manton was nice and easy, very co-operative, looked very level, but he still didn't like him. And he took a good long look around the room, for anything suggestive. Two things he noticed, and that's what started him looking other places. A good boy, Adler."

"Has this story got a point?"

"I'm getting there. What he noticed was that the phonograph in Manton's apartment is brand-new, and that the L.P. albums visible also looked new. And the top ones in the two racks of 'em both had a label saying they'd come from Delancey's—big music store downtown."

"I know it."

"So he went and asked. Unfortunately he didn't have a photograph— we'll get one now, to clinch this for sure—but Manton's a fairly distinctive guy, not a type. He didn't get anything Saturday, but there was a clerk not on that day, so he went back to ask her this morning. And she says that Manton—or somebody an awful lot like him—came in at about three o'clock Thursday and bought a phonograph and about a hundred bucks' worth of records. All folk-music records. He didn't take much time making up his mind, she said, didn't listen to any of the records—maybe what made her remember him. Just asked to be directed to the folk-music section, and picked out records almost at random. And he didn't bother to try out the phonograph before he bought it, either—test its tone or whaever. Just said, I'll take that one. And paid cash, and took everything away with him. To the tune of two hundred and forty-nine bucks and fifty cents, plus tax."

"¿Para qué es esto?" said Mendoza. "What the hell?" And then he said, "Now don't tell me. I see. I see. How nice. Is this starting to come unraveled at last? I wonder—"

"I'm not just sure what it says, but it looked to me as if it had more to do with your end than ours."

"Hasn't it indeed! Thanks very much. I'll let you know what comes of it, if anything. Tell Adler when he has any spare time I'll be happy to buy him a drink." Mendoza put the phone down and went out fast to the sergeants' room to see who was in.

"Morning," said Dwyer. "I see you're having servant problems, Lieutenant."

"The low humor around here— Chase out to International Airport, Bert. Locate Paul Manton and bring him in for questioning. You needn't be too polite if he objects."

"Right," and Dwyer went out.

Indeed, how nice, thought Mendoza. Things starting to break at last?

There had been discrepancies between what Mrs. Montague said and what Manton said, but Mrs. Montague had been fairly vague and Mendoza hadn't thought much of it. She had said "a lot of times" Manton and Cardenas came to Valerie's apartment. Manton had said maybe three times. And what a nice artistic little tale he'd produced, almost on the spur of the moment (if he had missed that Wednesday night story on the identification of Valerie) to account for it! The mutual interest in folk music. And the minute Mendoza left him, he'd contacted Cardenas and passed on the story to him, and then—anticipating a visit from the police, if not the FBI—dashed out to buy the phonograph and records to back up the story.

Cardenas the one genuinely interested in folk music, with the long-time collection, which Manton had known.

Paul Manton was a very astute young man, in some ways.

But, Cardenas?

Manton and Cardenas in the racket with Valerie? How and why? Neither of them was even on the borderline of pro crime. And what caper would those two fit into, anyway?

In a way, he could see it. Cardenas, in Civil Service—notoriously the sort of job that was underpaid, supposedly making up for it in security of tenure. He thought his guess at ten thousand a year might be an overestimate; more likely six to seven. Cardenas might not be averse to making a little side money, if it looked safe. Very safe. Because he'd be a very cautious man about his own safety.

Manton—it wouldn't have to look like a safe gamble to him. He'd said he'd like to start his own airline; maybe that was so. He was a gambler, he'd take long chances not just for the stakes but for the hell of it.

Did this say definitely that Manton and Cardenas had been in some racket with Valerie? Damn it, thought Mendoza, as Alison had pointed out, he didn't *know* that anybody else had been in on it: that was just implication, from what Valerie had said to Maureen, and Maureen not being the brainiest female alive she might not have heard right, or repeated it right.

What this did say was that Manton and Cardenas were in some caper together. Those two . . . There was an old Spanish proverb, appropriate: *Everyone is as God made him and very often worse.* And money sure as hell talked.

And Eddy Warren. Don't forget Eddy Warren, he thought. Without much doubt, paying Valerie a little fee to store his reefers for him safe. (*De paso,* better pass that on to Pat Callaghan up in Narcotics, because it could be that Eddy had some H. stored away with some other obliging pal.) Could it be that Manton and Cardenas had just used Valerie's apartment as a convenient, semi-secret meeting place? Used Valerie as a convenient excuse for foregathering?

It was a thought, anyway.

And—yes, that was a thought too, by God—maybe Valerie hadn't originally known one damn thing about whatever it was they were up to; maybe they'd underestimated her intelligence—and greed; and, finding out, she'd wanted to cut herself in, so they— Not *they;* Cardenas wouldn't have the guts. If so, that had been Manton. Yes.

(That phone call: "Because they murdered that woman six years ago." All right: a lunatic. Even if it wasn't, he didn't know what Manton and Cardenas had been doing six years ago. Conceivably their caper had been running that long; conceivably they had done a murder in the course of it, and Valerie had found out about it—or the woman on the phone thought she had. All right. Ten to one the phone call hadn't a thing to do with it.)

One thing, Paul Manton could very probably have operated that machine.

Only, why? Why, for God's sake?

He looked at his watch. Quite a drive out to International, through traffic. He hoped Manton would be there, and not off playing hooky somewhere again. It would be another hour at least before Bert got back with him, if he was there . . . Mendoza picked up the FBI report and began to study it, but his mind kept straying back to Manton . . . and Cardenas, of all people . . .

At about the same moment, Mr. William Gunn was reaching the deliberate conclusion that something would have to be done about Number Six. Later on people were to say that Mr. Gunn should have realized there was something wrong and investigated Number Six long before; but as the late Mrs. Gunn could have testified, William Gunn was not a precipitate man. He thought things over thoroughly before reaching any decision.

He had been thinking, off and on, about Number Six ever since last Tuesday, but a little harder since last Thursday.

Mr. Gunn owned and managed a small motel on San Fernando Road in Glendale. He did a fair-to-middling business; if it wasn't one of the classy places with a pool, well, he charged fair rates and everything was kept clean and nice. And no funny business. Mr. Gunn had a very sharp eye for funny business, the nervous teen-age couple, the brash salesman with a chippy he claimed was his wife.

Otherwise, well, you got all sorts, running a motel; one thing he'd learned was, you sure couldn't judge people by their looks. People who looked decent and clean as you please, they'd leave the place in a shambles. There'd been that couple from Oregon: woman looked a nice respectable woman and the husband an ordinary white-collar type. Leaving all those empty whiskey bottles when they left, and a lamp smashed, and all that stuff scrawled on the bathroom wall with lipstick. The hell of a job it had been, cleaning it off. People . . .

Then—Mr. Gunn always smiled faintly when he remembered that—there'd been those hillbillies. He'd been of two minds whether to admit he had a vacancy. Oklahoma plates on the old Model-A Ford, stuff tied on top, three kids in patched-up clothes—but the woman had had nice eyes and was sort of shy. Migratory workers, some kind, with a bit more than usual saved up. Woman about ready to have another baby, and the man had been nice and kind with her, sort of anxious. And in the end Mr. Gunn had rented them Number Eight, hoping they wouldn't leave it in too much of a mess . . . When they'd pulled out next morning, the woman had thanked him and said what a nice place he had, it was the first time they'd ever stayed at a motel and they'd sure liked it. And they hadn't left the place in a mess at all; they'd made up the beds nice and smooth all ready for the next guest, and hung up the towels neatly, and left the tiny used bars of soap handy— Mr. Gunn remembered how he'd laughed, but not really laughing *at* them, as the maid stripped off the used sheets.

So, after twelve years of running a motel, he wasn't really surprised at anything. His present Number Six had showed up, alone and without a car, at about nine o'clock a week ago last Friday evening. A man around forty-five to fifty, ordinary-looking fellow except that he had a little short beard. Couple of suitcases with him. Said he was just moving out to California from Iowa, and he'd left the car with his wife back home, he wanted a place to stay a couple of weeks, maybe longer, until he found a house to rent.

Well, Mr. Gunn sometimes had semi-permanent people like that, and the fellow looked respectable and paid him for a week in advance right off, forty-nine bucks, so he led him down to Number Six and showed him about the lights and so on. Four of the units had kitchenettes, and Number Six was one of them.

He hadn't seen much of Mr. Robertson—that was how he registered, James Robertson, of 112 Elm Street, Cedar Rapids, Iowa—since. Naturally, his own apartment and office being right up front, all the guests passed his place going and coming; he wasn't nosy enough to watch for them, but he could hardly help noticing.

Mr. Robertson had gone out, walking, the next morning; of course they were right in the middle of town, stores all around, and Mr. Robertson had evidently visited the market a couple of blocks away—he came back with two big bags of groceries. And stayed in.

Well, Mr. Gunn thought, he *could* have missed seeing him go out and come back—there were times he was out himself, or in one of the other units, or just not noticing—but he didn't think Mr. Robertson had set foot outside Number Six from that Saturday morning until last Tuesday. Then he'd gone out again, and again come back with a big bag of groceries.

And that bag at least had apparently contained something alcoholic. Because at about half-past eleven that night the people in Number Five, who'd driven all the way from Santa Rosa that day (they'd only checked in an hour before), phoned the office to complain about the singing next door. "I'm as patriotic a man as the next," the man had said dryly, "but when it comes to 'The Star-Spangled Banner' at nearly midnight—and not just once, but over and over—and he can't carry a tune." So Mr. Gunn had pulled on his pants over his pajamas and gone down to Number Six and found Mr. Robertson riding very high indeed.

Mr. Robertson had leaned on the doorpost and apologized with the earnest solemnity of the drunk. "Ver' sorry cause any dis—disturbance," he'd said. "Shelebratin', 's all. *You* know how 'tis. You p-pull off shomethin'—been plannin'—C'me on in, have a drink with me, friend—my friend!"

"No, thank you, sir," Gunn had said. "Now don't you think, sir—"

"Pasht time for thinkin'. Shelebrate," said Mr. Robertson rather wildly. "Great shelebrashun. I made it. I got home." He reached out and clutched Mr. Gunn's pajama top. "Tell you a shecret," he said. "Ivory tower, they shaid—grow up, get wise. I thought I wash sho smart. Idealsh. C'me on in, have a drink. I did it. I made it."

"Now, Mr. Robertson, if you'll just quiet down, please—"

"Tell you—tell you—shecret," said Mr. Robertson. He swayed toward

Mr. Gunn, but caught himself. And for one brief moment he seemed completely sober; he said in a perfectly normal, articulate voice, "Dear God, I
could have kissed the ground. Corny. Laugh at it. You don't know until
you've been there."

"Mr. Robertson—"

The other man blinked and swayed again, and the moment was past.
"Wash gonna tell you a shecret. My friend. You promise me—remember
it. Wanta tell—lotsh 'n' lotsh o' people. Gotta tell. Shee? They're a bunch
of bashtards! Thatsh the shecret—bunch o' bashtards. You remember it,
shee?"

"Sure, I'll remember it," said Gunn patiently. He had been just faintly
surprised, because Mr. Robertson had looked so respectable, so conventional; but of course you never knew. He had finally persuaded him back
into Number Six, and to quiet down. Presumably he'd passed out; there
were no more complaints.

And the next morning, looking about as you'd expect, he had come to
the office and apologized very nicely. "I've been kind of worried," he said,
"having to switch jobs at my age—I don't drink much as a rule. I hope I
didn't say aything—er—?"

Mr. Gunn, reassuring him, had figured to keep an eye on him: if he
pulled that again, toss him out.

But since then, Number Six had been very quiet. Too quiet, since last
Thursday night.

On Thursday morning Robertson had gone out shopping again. It was
about then that Mr. Gunn began seriously wondering about him. Changing jobs; waiting for his wife; looking for a house. Oh, yes? He didn't
seem to be doing any house hunting.

He had come back with a bag of groceries, at about eleven, and stayed
in.

About eight o'clock on Thursday evening, Mr. Gunn and his old friend
Mr. Peters had been playing backgammon over a companionable glass of
beer when Mr. Peters glanced up and said, "What was that? Customers?
Somebody outside—"

Mr. Gunn had opened the door and looked out. Two men were walking down the open court, backs to him—vague in the half shadow, but he
saw them. He called, "Can I help you?" but they just kept on going. He
hadn't thought much about it. Guests coming back from a little walk, or
friends calling on somebody, car left in the street.

A few minutes later, it seemed that among Mr. Robertson's purchases
had been a radio of some kind; the people in both Number Five and

Number Seven called to complain. And no wonder; he could hear it from up in front, it was so loud. He'd gone down and knocked on the door of Number Six, hard, and the radio had been turned down right away.

And since then, he hadn't seen Mr. Robertson at all. Coming or going. He'd expected him to drop in at the office on Friday, to pay another week's rent. When Robertson hadn't showed up by Saturday night, Mr. Gunn had gone down and knocked on the door, but got no answer. He'd tried again on Sunday morning, with the same result.

And now, on Monday morning, he had reached the decision that he must do something about Number Six. He didn't know quite what he felt was wrong, or might be, but he thought it was all a bit funny. And Robertson owed him for three nights.

Mr. Gunn knocked out his pipe, rummaged for his extra keys, and plodded deliberately down the court to Number Six. He knocked and called, "Mr. Robertson?" No answer. No stir from inside. He fitted the key into the lock and opened the door . . .

At first, of course, Mr. Gunn got the Glendale police: a couple of big fellows in tan uniform. He got more and more police. From the minute, about half an hour after he'd first called them, when a wide-shouldered tough in plain-clothes said suddenly, "Hey, take away that beard—and look at his ears— Jesus H. Christ, I'd take my oath that's—" and plunged for the phone.

Mr. Gunn, eventually, got the FBI crowding into Number Six. It was a while before he made out who Mr. Robertson had been. Mr. Robertson, lying wide-eyed with a bullet in his brain, five days dead.

When he understood, Mr. Gunn went back to his own place, shaken, and gave himself a drink. He thought about what that man had said, drunk, last Tuesday night. And he said aloud, soberly, to his jigger of bourbon, "Well, at least he died at home. They couldn't take that away from him."

FOURTEEN

Odds and ends, odds and ends . . . Jack Farlow was a member of something called Americans All. So what? Sounded like one of those ultra-conservative groups. Linda Hausner corresponded with several old friends in Germany. This Fran Schwartz—so Vice said—had the expectable record; you could piece it together, and it was possible that Eddy Warren was the link. Gloria, Fran, Maureen and Valerie, working as call girls and at one time Eddy scouting for them. But Valerie breaking away . . . Another small thing, thought Mendoza; the Hausners honest citizens, so, wouldn't they have spotted something a little funny about a couple of Valerie's friends, if not Valerie herself? Maureen at least looked like what she was, if Gloria didn't, quite. Well, maybe they'd never met Maureen . . .

"Scarne's back with Cardenas," said Sergeant Lake.

"O.K.," said Mendoza. "Keep him on ice. I want Manton first."

He got him fifteen minutes later. He had Manton wait in the outer office, opposite Cardenas under Sergeant Lake's eye, while he talked to Bert and Scarne.

"Never batted an eyelid," said Dwyer. "Said, sure, anything he could do, though he hadn't known much about her. He's a very cool customer."

"Not like the other one," said Scarne. "He raised a little fuss. All pompous and blustering. He'd told you all he knew, et cetera. At that, he sounded natural. I mean, a guy in his job—he'd be nervous, just to be associated. Wouldn't he?"

Which was, of course, true. "Manton first," said Mendoza. He was lighting a cigarette when Manton came in; he took time to get it burning nicely, and smiled at Manton slowly, not asking him to sit down. "You're an impulsive young man, aren't you, Mr. Manton?"

"Am I?" said Manton. "In what way d'you mean?" He was in matching tan shirt and slacks today, cleaner and neater. A ruggedly good-looking man, blue eyes pale in his tanned face, and that reckless tilt to his heavy brows.

"You acquire hobbies so suddenly," said Mendoza. "Such as folk music. After I'd talked to you last Thursday, dashing out to acquire the—mmh—appurtenances of the hobby you'd claimed. The phonograph and all the folk-music records. Down at Delancey's."

"Sorry, don't see what you're driving at," said Manton. "Mind if I sit down?" He dropped into the chair beside the desk, pulled out cigarettes and lit one. His strong mechanic's hands were perfectly steady. "Sure, I bought a new phonograph and a few records lately. What's that got to do with Val getting murdered?"

"You never had a phonograph or any records up to last Thursday, did you? Only you'd told me that pretty little story about you and Cardenas having the mutual interest, and you knew we might be checking—us or the Feds—so you provided the local color."

"I don't get you," said Manton. "I'd been planning on getting a new phonograph for some while, my old one was shot. No good even as a trade-in. What the hell is it to you? I told you all I knew about Val. So I knew her—it was the casual thing, I didn't know she was mixed up with crooks of some sort, and Ricardo sure as hell didn't, or he'd— Look, what do you want with him, anyway? We told you how it was, and you know how the Civil Service is, one little hint of any—"

"It's a nice act, Manton, but I'm not buying it. You and Cardenas are in some caper together. You and Cardenas and Valerie were in it. You—"

Manton said angrily, "I don't have to take this, damn it! I don't know what you think you've found out, but that's just crazy! Ricardo—that stuffed shirt? Risking his job? We've told you all we know about Val—damn all—and I'm wishing to God now I'd never met the female! So I've incriminated myself by buying a new phonograph—maybe they've changed the laws since I went to school?" Impatiently he stabbed out the cigarette.

Mendoza stared at him. No, this one wouldn't scare easy. "Maureen Moskovitch introduced you to Valerie," he said abruptly. "So you said. Not being a schoolboy any more, Manton, you read Maureen?"

Manton smiled at him amusedly. "Hell, how d'you think I met Maureen? Sure. But I figured it was a part-time thing with her—that Val didn't know about it. She seemed ordinary, way I said, nice enough girl. Why the hell you're making a deal of this— I hadn't known her long, or very well, it was all just the way I told you." But that wasn't too emphatic;

he didn't overplay it. He was a little angry, a little surprised, a little indignant.

A very tough boy indeed, Paul Manton.

"Not just a few records," said Mendoza, "added to a collection already existing. All the records you've got, Manton. Bought last Thursday. As a cover. To back up that story you'd told me."

"I'd really like to see you prove that," said Manton. And Mendoza read his mind; he knew they couldn't hold him or Cardenas, and as soon as they got away, he'd figure on somehow transferring some of Cardenas' older records to his apartment, pending another police look. Verisimilitude. "This is all damn silly," he said. "Why the hell aren't you looking in the likely directions? What possible reason would I have to—a girl I hardly knew? And Ricardo, that's just damn nonsense!" He laughed contemptuously. "He hasn't got the guts to swat a fly!"

And all right, say that Manton and Cardenas had been in the caper with her—which he wasn't at all sure of—that was perfectly true, on what showed: they'd have had no reason to want her dead. By the evidence of the notebook, the racket had been yielding handsome profits, and depending on what it was, maybe Valerie had been a vital ingredient. "I thought you and Cardenas were pals," he said.

Manton's little cold smile didn't waver. "For God's sake," he said wearily. "We both happen to be interested in folk music, but that's about all we've got in common. I don't stop seeing people as they are because we share an interest."

Mendoza sat back in his chair. No longer the awkward, ambitious young mechanic: Manton was acting his age, letting a little education show. Otherwise, a tough: a very hard one to crack. Mendoza had seen more details of his record by now. He'd been in Communist hands, in Korea, for several months without breaking. He wasn't at all likely to be faced down by a mere L.A.P.D. officer.

Mendoza buzzed Sergeant Lake and asked for Cardenas. The weaker member of the team.

Cardenas came in blustering. But it was natural-sounding bluster. "Really, I cannot understand—a man in my position—you must realize that my superiors— The publicity so far has been outrageous, but to—"

"Mr. Cardenas." Manton had made no attempt to speak to Cardenas, signal him; he sat smoking, looking angrily bored. "Mr. Cardenas—to your knowledge, has Mr. Manton been intending to buy a new phonograph lately?"

Cardenas stopped short and looked bewildered. "A new— Why, yes, he did mention it. But why on earth are you—" He looked at Manton. "Have you got it yet? Which did you get, the R.C.A. or the Silvertone?"

"The Silvertone," said Manton. "I liked the tone better."

Very nicely fielded, thought Mendoza sardonically. Cardenas was smarter than he looked.

"But you didn't listen to the tone," he said gently. "You just said, I'll take that one, and paid for it. Rather a hasty choice, Manton, wasn't it?"

Manton knocked ash off his new cigarette. "Oh, for God's sake," he said. "Talk about a tempest in a teacup. I'd tried out several models at different times, a few days before, at a couple of other places. Been mulling it over in my mind. I decided that was the one I liked, why bother to test it out again? Very nice tone indeed," he added to Cardenas, "you'll have to come over and hear it."

"I only said I thought the changing mechanism on the R.C.A. is more efficient, I— But why the *police* should be interested—! And really, Lieutenant, I don't think you realize how unfortunate it is for a man in my position, even to seem involved in such a— I scarcely knew the girl, after all! Really—"

Cardenas a good deal smarter than he looked. And maybe more guts than Manton had expected. He was sweating, but he sounded natural, the touchy civil servant— And the whole thing was still sufficiently up in the air that— A lot more evidence needed.

Mendoza stared at them another long moment. Manton returned the stare with almost open impudence. A single drop of sweat rolled down Cardenas' round olive-skinned cheek; but his faintly indignant, pompous expression held stiff.

"All right," said Mendoza tautly. "That's all—out. I'll be seeing both of you."

They went, unhurriedly. He followed them as far as the door to the sergeants' office. Dwyer and Scarne were there, talking idly. Mendoza jerked a thumb. "After them. Call in when you can and we'll set up reliefs."

He went back to his desk feeling savage. Take it easy, he told himself, maybe a tail would turn up something usable. Maybe—

"Waltham on the phone, Lieutenant."

"O.K. . . . Yes?"

"They got him," said Waltham sadly. "Thorwald. We just got a positive ident. The Green Tree Motel, San Fernando Road, Glendale. Dead about four-five days. Shot. A very professional taking-off. You like to come and poke around for anything on your end?"

"You don't say," said Mendoza. "How come he wasn't found sooner?"

Waltham sounded sadder. "Motel owner's not a fellow to rush into things. He had a couple of interesting things to tell us. Not that it's of much importance now, I guess, but by what Mr. Gunn says, it seems that our Osgar had repented his sins and found out the truth about his erstwhile pals."

"Well, I suppose it was important to him," said Mendoza.

"I suppose. I don't expect we'll ever know just exactly what did happen, why they wanted to take him off. It doesn't look as if he meant to run to us with any secrets, he'd been here at least ten days and who knows how much longer? Maybe transferring from motel to motel for months. He'd grown a beard, by the way. And nothing, but nothing, to point to who did the job. Of course. Well, we'll go through the motions—but I don't anticipate catching up with X. I just thought you might like to join the party."

"What's the address? I would indeed," said Mendoza. He scribbled down the number and snatched up his hat.

In the anteroom, Sergeant Lake was on the phone. He said, "It's long distance, Lieutenant—they think—"

"*Vaya*, make a note, I'll see it later," said Mendoza, not pausing.

This morning there'd been an inquest on Valerie Ellis; Mendoza hadn't bothered to go because it would be pure formality, police request for an open verdict. As Galeano's hit-and-run seemed to be dying a natural death on them, he'd sent Galeano over to watch it.

Palliser was still poking around on the Gertrude Dasher thing, and nobody but Hackett was in the office when a tired but triumphant Landers called in to say that he thought he'd caught up to Lover Boy.

"Don't tell me! Who and where? D'you want any help?"

"You're damn right," said Landers frankly. "He's about six-five and built in proportion. I don't want my name in the papers that bad."

"I'll be with you. Where?"

"Little drive," said Landers. "I'm about ten miles this side of Camarillo. Meet you at a place called Joe's Roadside Inn, on the highway."

"O.K.," said Hackett, and got going. He'd hear the whole story when he got there. It was a little drive indeed—sixty miles up the coast, once he got out of traffic. But past Malibu, he should make good time, on a weekday.

He made it in an hour and twenty-five minutes, good going, once out of the slow tangle downtown. As he approached the town he slowed a little, watching for Joe's . . . "So what's the story?" he asked Landers, sliding into the booth beside him.

It had, after all, been the dogged routine that had finally turned up Lover Boy, as Hackett had known it was bound to. The truck. Landers had come to this one on his list, from the new Ventura County list, and cursed at the necessity for the drive, got up here and had, he said, the hell of a time finding the address. Which wasn't an address at all, just a farm back in the hills. Nobody around seemed to know much about it. But he finally found it, and one look at the farmer had been enough. "He's our boy for sure. Pockmarks and all. And he's about one degree above a gorilla, mentally speaking. Just as expected. You can hardly understand him, Deep South accent and maybe a cleft palate or something. It's a run-down old place, hardly big enough to call it a farm, off the highway back in there. Woman there too, about the same type."

"O.K., let's go," said Hackett. They took his car. "What's his name, by the way?"

"Henry Jackson. What beats me," said Landers, "is the truck. When you come to think. Well, these rural areas— But you'd think somebody at the local D.M.V. would take a second look at him, spot him for a moron. And I wonder how come he remembered to register it for this year. Maybe some cop stopped him and reminded him."

The farm, when they came to it, was hardly more than a vegetable garden. There was a ramshackle, unpainted one-room cabin built right on the ground. A couple of thin-looking pigs rooting in the yard, a raw-ribbed mongrel dog that shied away from the car. A baby about a year old sat on the ground near the pigs. The baby was dark brown and quite naked, a girl; she had the distended stomach of starvation, and dull eyes. The light-blue pickup truck, a battered eight-year-old Ford, was parked at the side of the shack.

"But there must be people around who know him, who've seen him," said Hackett. "There's been the hell of a lot of publicity on this. Why hasn't somebody called in?"

"I asked around, before and while I was waiting for you," said Landers. "I said I had a hell of a time locating this place. Nobody does know him much. The fellow at the gas station back there, alongside Joe's, he's sold him gas. Knew vaguely that he had a little land back here in the hills, but he'd never paid much attention to him. Joe, about the same story. Jackson doesn't buy much in any store round here, evidently. Nobody could say how long he'd been here. Well, you see the setup—dirt poor."

"Yes," said Hackett. They got out of the car and went up to the door of the shack, knocked.

The man who opened to them was Jackson, obviously. He topped

Hackett by a good two inches and outweighed him by fifty pounds. Hackett saw at once, irrelevantly, that the pockmarks were old scars of some skin disease.

"Who you?" asked Jackson. He took a step backward, his eyes rolling.

Hackett followed him into the shack. There were pallets on the floor, gray with filth. A woman, thin and black, sat on one nursing a very new baby. Terror leaped briefly in her eyes and she clutched the baby tighter. She was wearing the diamond-and-platinum necklace valued at ten thousand dollars. A mink coat lay across one of the other pallets.

"Henry," said Hackett, "we've come to take you in for those women you killed." Jackson mumbled something and took another step back.

"Cops—you cops?" It was just possible to understand him.

"That's right, Henry. You did kill them, didn't you?"

The woman just sat, still as a frightened animal would be still, and her eyes were dull as the baby's eyes. Irrelevantly Hackett found a phrase running round his mind—the Jukes and the Kallikaks, the Jukes and the Kallikaks.

"White wimmen," said Jackson. He sounded childishly pleased. He grinned amiably at Hackett, showing white teeth. "White wimmen. I show 'em, I do. Hang m' pa, they did—an' he nevah done nothin'— White wimmen! I show 'em. They take 'm to jail an' lynch 'm— I get back at 'm good—"

"All right, Henry," said Hackett, "you sure did." He took out the handcuffs and got them on before Jackson grasped what he was doing. "Let's go, Henry."

"You—you—you—take me to jail—" Jackson started to wrestle with the cuffs, looking scared. And then, just as Hackett was tensing himself to meet attack, ready to yank out the gun to use as a bludgeon, Jackson stopped struggling and asked earnestly, "You—you—you gi' me s'me nice po'k chop 'n jail? Ain't had no nice po'k chop long time—"

"I wouldn't be surprised," said Hackett. "We sure will, Henry." They didn't have any trouble getting him into the car; he was, for the moment, docile as a child. Hackett looked back at the open door of the cabin. The woman hadn't moved or spoken the whole time. The baby still sat, staring with dull eyes. There was, he saw, a heap of human manure on one side of the cabin. The dog sidled around sniffing at it.

Landers got in back with Jackson. Hackett thought he'd have to tell somebody official about the woman back there. County relief. Technically speaking, he should bring her in too; but at the moment Jackson was all he wanted to cope with. Better send a couple of boys right back here, bring her in, search the cabin, retrieve the loot there.

They didn't try to get anything out of him on the ride back. They just hoped he wouldn't suddenly decide he'd rather not go, and break loose. In fact, Hackett got so nervous about that, on the way back down to the highway, on the rutted dirt track, that when they got to Joe's he told Landers to drive and got in back with Jackson himself. Landers might be only thirty to his thirty-five, but Landers was only five-eleven and built thin. If Jackson went berserk, there was a good deal more of Hackett to grapple with him. And damn what the doctors said about the extra poundage.

But they got him back, and up to an interrogation room, with no trouble at all. Hackett, a little surprised and very relieved, set everybody present in the homicide office—only five men, as it chanced—to keep an eye on him, while he briefed Palliser, who had just come in. Everybody was feeling pretty happy about this.

"But, my God, that place," said Hackett. "That woman. And I don't want another ride like that soon. You got a picture of your Mrs. Dasher?"

"I have," said Palliser. "By the way, no record of any legacy."

"No," said Hackett. "We didn't expect it, did we?" He called Landers out to the hall. "Sorry to ask you, Tom, but you're the one knows the way. You and a couple of the boys had better get right back there, for the woman and the loot. And, incidentally, your car," he added, remembering that.

Landers, who had not forgotten it, grinned and said he didn't mind.

"Well, I doubt very much whether we'll get anything coherent out of Henry—not quite moron level, but close. But we'll try. And with these damn Black Muslims stirring up trouble, we're going to lean over backwards on this one, being very scrupulous. Nobody's going to ask him anything until somebody from the Public Defenders' office is here to hold his hand."

"Want me to call them?" asked Palliser.

Hackett said yes, please. He could have used a drink; he had a cardboard mug of black coffee instead, and defiantly he dropped three lumps of sugar in it . . .

The lawyer they sent over from the Public Defenders' office, to protect Jackson's legal rights, was very welcome to Hackett. The Public Defenders' office was as alive to certain situations as were the police, and they sent a young Negro lawyer, Marvin Fox, a thin dapper young man with alert eyes and an unexpected bass voice. He sat in on the questioning.

They didn't get much that was coherent, as Hackett had predicted. Henry didn't deny he'd killed the white women; showed 'em he had, for his dad getting lynched . . . "Nah tha' one," he said to the photograph of Gertrude Dasher. "Nev' seed tha' one—who she?"

Palliser looked pleased and worried at once, about that.

They'd try to trace Jackson back, find out more about him. There were a couple of papers on him; no driver's license, but a Social Security card— that would be a lot of help, tell them eventually what jobs he'd held where—and a hunting license, seven years out of date, issued in Clinch County, Georgia.

They took him out to the county jail, finally, and saw him booked in. Lingering on the steps outside, Hackett offered Fox a cigarette. "I can guess how you'll handle it," he said.

Fox made a small grimace, offering his lighter. "Played down," he said. "Oh, yes. There's been a little tension lately, some hot accusations of you boys, about the persecution bit."

"I hope you know that's damn nonsense," said Hackett. "We're spread out pretty thin in this town. We take surveys, we make up statistics, and we naturally find out the crime rate's higher in certain areas—so we concentrate men there. The Negro slum sections, the Mexican slum sections, the slum sections in general. It's not, for God's sake, higher because those people are Negro or Mexican. It's higher because—"

"You needn't tell me, Sergeant," said Fox sadly. "I know. It's because some of those people figure, what the hell, nine counts on us to start, why try? It's because a lot of people follow the course of least resistance. Most of all—but try to get the do-gooders to admit it—it's because, from the time Eve got Adam chased out of the Garden—if that ever happened—there've been smart people and dumb ones, good ones and bad. And you can't make the undesirables over, not all of 'em, by offering 'em a chance at free education and a flat in a nice clean new building. The louts like that one in there"—he jerked a shoulder at the jail behind them—"they come in all colors and they're walking around in every country. But there'll always be a certain number of people who misread the evidence."

"Isn't it the truth," said Hackett.

"And here," said Fox, looking up North Broadway, "come the press boys. So quick off the mark. I think we'll encourage them to take some pictures, Sergeant. Emphasizing the contrast, you know, between Henry and his smart, snappy young attorney."

Hackett laughed and left him to it, dodging the reporters with some difficulty. It was after six. He had to go back to headquarters to get his car, and he went up to the office to see if Mendoza was in, do a little boasting.

"Boss gone home, Jimmy?" Sergeant Lake was just leaving.

"Oh, Lord knows when we'll see our Luis again," said Lake. "He's on a little jaunt over to Blythe."

"Blythe?" said Hackett blankly. "You don't mean Blythe over by the Arizona border? Why the hell?"

"Well, it was like this—" said Lake.

FIFTEEN

There was nothing at all in the faintly shabby, neat motel unit to give them any clues as to how long Thorwald had been back, how he'd got in, who had caught up and killed him. There were a few groceries in the little kitchenette, and a bottle of bourbon three-quarters empty. There was one ancient cowhide suitcase and a newer aluminum one, both American-made, and a scattering of clothes, American suits and shirts, one ill-tailored topcoat that was probably Russian. No documents of any kind; maybe there had been and the killers had taken them.

No radio in the place. The killers had brought one along—a transistor, probably—to cover the sound of the shot. A single shot, and, said the doctor, probably a .38 or .45. See when they got the bullet out. No gun.

"So we go through the motions," said Waltham. "It's a waste of time but we have to do it."

"You think it was them? Well, of course—"

"Who else would it be? Sure. Maybe they were afraid he was going to run to us, and passed on orders to cool him off just in case. Anyway, at least we know where he is now. And it doesn't look as if this business ties up to your murder, does it? Or does it? If the Ellis girl knew where he was—"

"But they don't generally use sleeping-tablets," said Mendoza.

Waltham agreed. "Besides, what you've found out about her, she'd have told anything she knew for cash in hand. Only, it could be they got a little nervous about her knowing them, then?"

"No," said Mendoza. "Let's not reach. The murder is something else. Granted, it's a wild one—a funny one. That machine— But it wasn't the Communists slipped Valerie a spiked cocktail."

"What the hell *was* the connection?"

"I'm beyond guessing," said Mendoza. "I'm not up to standard lately, missing all this sleep," and he yawned. And at Waltham's inquiring look he added gloomily, "Twins. Five months old."

"Oh," said Waltham, and laughed. "I get you. Thank God our three are well past that stage. What disturbs my sleep these nights is Margaret out until midnight with the current boy friend, and Alan's grades in English. Not to mention Mike's grades in arithmetic."

"You're so encouraging," said Mendoza. "There's nothing for me here. Have fun."

All the same—you took it as it came, and after twenty-one years it didn't reach you as it once had—but, all the same, as he drove back downtown, he thought about Thorwald, who had repented his sins, singing "The Star-Spangled Banner" in a drunken frenzy, and felt an unaccustomed sting in his eyes. So the man was a traitor. Not the lowest kind of traitor: a traitor for ideals he'd believed in. So he'd been a fool to believe in them; few people hadn't been fools in this way or that at some time . . . *Through the perilous fight*, thought Mendoza; perilous indeed for people like Thorwald, all ideals and no common sense. But Thorwald had made it home, in more ways than one . . .

He went up to the office; Sergeant Lake said, "That long-distance call—" and was interrupted by the phone. "Bert," he said, handing it over.

"Lieutenant? I've just seen Manton back to his job. He and Cardenas ended up in a bar on Broadway to have a quiet drink together. Scarne and I managed to get the next booth, but it isn't the quietest place in town and we couldn't hear much. They seemed to be arguing at one point, couldn't say about what—it was confused—but, reason I thought you ought to hear this as soon as possible, Manton said that Dvorzhak name a couple of times, and Cardenas seemed to be hushing him up."

"¿De veras—qué significa eso? I'll be damned," said Mendoza.

"Yeah. Then they split. Manton went straight back to International. I guess Scarne'll be calling in on Cardenas."

"Yes, thanks, we'll set up reliefs for you." Mendoza put the phone down. The Dvorzhaks. If Bert had heard right. Looking so very much on the edge of the case—what connection could they possibly—?

"This phone call," began Sergeant Lake.

"Tell me later," said Mendoza absently, and went out again.

Ruminating, he drove up to Willoughby Drive and rang the bell of the Dvorzhak house. One of the lucky refugees, you could say. Those jewels—plenty of money. Very foresighted of Mr. Jan Dvorzhak . . .

Anya Dvorzhak, going to see Gloria? Maybe. Why the hell?

He yawned and pressed the bell again.

The girl Anya opened the door to him. As she recognized him, her liquid eyes flickered just once, and then met his straight. "Yes?" she said. "Oh—you are the police officer who came before. What is it, please?"

"I'd like to ask you a few more questions, Miss Dvorzhak."

The older woman, her mother, pattered down the hall asking agitated questions in their own tongue. The girl replied soothingly. "You must forgive my mother, sir, she is so fearful—of course, however I can help you, I will be happy." The other woman was half-sobbing, gazing at Mendoza with terror-stricken eyes. The girl sighed. "Please, sir, will you come in here—into my father's study, we can be private here—and excuse me one moment while I explain to her, reassure her?" She smiled at him, taking her mother's arm. "She has had—very bad experiences."

"I understand." Mendoza went into the room indicated. It was not a large room, but a pleasant one. Paneled, two of the walls were lined with bookcases; there was a large old desk, somewhat littered, and several comfortable chairs. He could hear the women talking, out in the hall, in their rapid incomprehensible language . . . What, he wondered suddenly, is Anya doing at home when she should be at her college classes?

The one large window was open; it was a warm day. From outside he heard the irregular patter of ping-pong balls striking a table, a boy's triumphant shout: "That's game! I beat you!"

He strolled over to the window. Next door was the Farlow house. No, probably the property belonged technically to the boy, young Johnny Eininger. Odd to think, necessarily prying into private lives, what they knew about all these people, the people themselves unaware.

The window overlooked a very pleasant side patio belonging to the house next door. There was only a low clipped hedge between the properties. In the house next door, French windows gave onto a flagstoned rectangle at least forty feet long, with white-painted wrought-iron lawn furniture, a ping-pong table, a round table with a gay yellow umbrella over it. Toward the rear of the house, a widening driveway and a glimpse of a handrail told of a swimming-pool.

A big man and a boy had just finished a game. Farlow and Johnny; Farlow looked just about as you might expect from the reports on him. A big fellow in his late forties, starting to run to paunch a little but still good-looking. Wavy dark hair, regular features, mat of dark chest hair showing above his open-necked sports shirt.

The boy wore nothing but shorts, and his tanned, slim young body was smooth and muscled. "I *said* I could beat you! I've been practicing—let's play another!"

"O.K., kid, and this time I'll really take you—" Farlow was grinning happily.

Mendoza swung round as he heard Anya come in. "I am sorry," she said. "My mother is so fearful. She does not understand that here— Won't you sit down, sir?"

"I don't think this will take long," said Mendoza. "By the way, why aren't you at your classes, Miss Dvorzhak? I understand you're attending U.C.L.A."

She hadn't expected that; a muscle twitched in her cheek. "If it is of interest," she said, "I had a bad headache this morning, and stayed home."

"I see. Do you know Gloria Litvak? Did you go to see her on Saturday?"

"I am sorry, no. No, I do not know that name," she said. She didn't ask why he wanted to know; just stood waiting for the next question.

"That's surprising. She was mentioned in several newspapers as one of Valerie Ellis's friends, and her address given. I thought I recognized you at her apartment house."

"No. That is impossible, I'm afraid. I do not know her." Her voice was steady. He offered her a cigarette. "Thank you, I do not smoke. But please do not hesitate."

Mendoza lit the cigarette and smiled at her. "I wonder," he said, "whether you can give me any idea why a Mr. Paul Manton and a Mr. Ricardo Cardenas should have been discussing you and your family this morning?"

The little muscle jumped again in her cheek, but she met his eyes unwaveringly. "I am so sorry, sir, you must be mistaken. I do not know these gentlemen you mention. None of us has ever met them—or anyone of these names."

"Oh, is that so?" said Mendoza. "Did you know that they were both friends of Valerie's?"

She considered. "I do not think so, sir. I recall hearing her mention a man named Paul, but not what his surname is."

"I see." No—one like this, with such experience behind her, wouldn't shake easily; but he thought she was frightened.

What the hell about?

He didn't know. He didn't know anything more useful about this damned case than he'd known when the body got identified, that was the sum total.

His eyes held hers a moment longer. She was too calm, too co-operative, too incurious. "Thanks so much," he said, and started for the door. She saw him out politely.

He could hear, from next door, a new ping-pong game going. He wondered what the boy was doing out of school. He got into the Ferrari and started back downtown.

Odds and ends! And where the hell did they all fit in?

And he'd missed lunch; it was nearly two o'clock.

The third time round, Sergeant Lake managed to fill him in on the long-distance call. "Fellow named Poynter. He's president of the California bank, branch down in Blythe. He says one of their girls has been off sick, with flu, and not taking much notice of the papers in consequence, but now she's back, and when she saw the papers—and Valerie's picture—she says she's pretty sure Valerie's been in quite a few times, has a lockbox there—she's the one looks after the lockboxes, this girl. Only Valerie was calling herself Carol Burns."

"How very interesting," said Mendoza. "Blythe? Quite a way from home. Quite a little drive to get at her lockbox. Yes, but Valerie was a canny one, wasn't she?" He ruminated. "I think—I just think—I'll take a run down there and have a look around. Sometimes the personal touch—" He looked at his watch. "God knows I'm not accomplishing much here. Yes, I think so. I'll probably be back sometime tomorrow—tell Art. It's what, around two hundred and thirty miles or so? With any luck, make it by seven. See this girl— I wonder if the Ellises have got a better picture of her than we have? I'd better ask . . . Yes, see you tomorrow then."

"Well, O.K.," said Lake. "Good luck."

Mendoza went home for a clean shirt and his razor, and was greeted in the driveway by El Señor—an El Señor somewhat the worse for wear, having a shaven patch down one flank showing a couple of stitches and violent purple medication painted on. "¡Pobrecito! What happened to you, boy?" Mendoza picked him up. "Alison!"

El Señor started telling him all about it, at loud length. Alison had heard the car, and came flying to meet him.

"What happened to—"

"Oh, he's all right," said Alison breathlessly. "The doctor said so, it's just a little cut—it was that stray tom—but, Luis, it was like *fate* or something! Wait until you meet her—we've *got* one! A simply wonderful one! Wait until I tell you—"

"I'm feeling sort of superstitious about it," Alison had said uneasily. "As if we aren't intended to find anybody."

"Well, now, that's silly, Mis' Mendoza," said Bertha in a forthright tone. "Acourse you'll find somebody, sooner or later. Bound to. They can't all be thieves, or like that Miss Freeman. There's different agencies, like, to try, aren't there? You go to another one, 'n' just see."

"Well, I suppose I'd better," said Alison. She trailed off to get dressed, still wondering if it was fate. But after all, she'd only tried two—maybe the saying was so, third time's the charm.

She put on the new green plaid cotton shirtmaker, the green alligator pumps; checked the matching bag, and looked in the yellow pages. There was an Acme Employment Agency on Wilshire, she hadn't tried that one. She started to copy down the address, and sprang up dropping everything as all hell broke loose in the back yard—*Cats*—

It was, as she'd known it would be, that big yellow stray tom, a battle-scarred veteran. If it had to be any of them he jumped, thank God it was El Señor, not one of the females who'd try to fight back. El Señor might lord it over his harem indoors, but in the presence of another tom he was remarkably unaggressive. This time he'd fled under the lantana bush by the kitchen door and was wailing like a siren; the yellow tom was burrowing after him grimly.

Alison and Bertha erupted out the kitchen door, Bertha with a saucepan of water to throw; the stray tom squalled bitterly and vanished in a long yellow streak; and Alison lay down prone beside the lantana bush and started to coax El Señor out.

After ten minutes of reassurance he crawled out sulkily. He had a long bloody gash down one flank, and the tip of one ear was bleeding. There was blood on his blond muzzle and one blond paw. "Oh, dear!" said Alison. "*Poor* Señor! That cat! The poor thing, it's not his fault—people just turning them out to wander—but all the same, I'll call the pound again. Poor boy, I know it hurts—have to take you to the doctor, heaven knows what infection—*Come* on, poor boy—" She heaved him up in her arms. "Get the carrier, will you, Bertha? In the garage—"

El Señor snarled at being thrust into the cat carrier, which he hated. Alison felt ready to snarl at that stray tom. Not the tom's fault, no, but all the same— And the pound saying blandly, Well, you'll have to have the animal confined before we can send a man. Coax a wily old veteran like that yellow tom into a stout carton or something? And meanwhile he went around attacking defenseless pets. Mrs. Pettigrew up the hill was sure it had been that tom who'd slashed her silver Persian. On the other hand, the tom had made a big mistake (Alison thought in satisfaction) taking on the Hildebrands' Peke. That was where the tom had lost a slice out of one ear. He should have known better—a Peke . . .

"All right, be quiet," she said, sliding the Facel-Vega round the corner onto Los Feliz. "We're nearly there! You're not hurt that much."

"*Nyeouh!*" said El Señor. He knew perfectly well he was going to see Dr. Stocking, whom he hated. Alison reflected that it was another example of how unfair life was: that Dr. Stocking, like most other veterinary surgeons, who really liked cats, should be so bitterly hated by his patients.

She parked, and hauled the heavy cat carrier into the waiting room. There were several people ahead of her: a woman with an overfed dachshund, a man with a black-and-white mongrel, another man with a collie, and a woman just waiting. Alison announced herself to the receptionist, explained the circumstances, and sat down beside the lone woman, lowering the carrier to the floor between them.

"Ah, the poor boy," said the woman to El Señor, who wailed. "I do hope he's not badly hurt."

"I don't think so, by the way he's complaining," said Alison.

"Isn't he the pretty boy—*deas!*" She was gray-haired, with a round kind face, a pink-and-white complexion: a woman about fifty, in a clean starched cotton dress and sensible shoes.

."He's half Siamese and half Abyssinian," said Alison. You always got talking to people in a vet's waiting room.

"Now isn't that unusual!" She smiled at Alison. She had guilelessly childlike blue eyes and a soft Scots burr in her voice. "You do look worried— I don't think you need, *achara,* he's complaining so, the boy. When they're strong enough for that—"

"Oh, it's just that it's rather a nuisance," said Alison, and told her about the stray tom. "It's not that I'm not sorry for the poor thing, but you can see it's a nuisance. This is the third time he's jumped El Señor. And I was just going out—" Half the day wasted, she thought, so no new nursemaid tonight, and poor Luis— She added politely, "I hope yours isn't too—?"

"Ah, I'm only here to pick up my sister Janet's Jamie. Being as she doesn't drive." The woman had such a calm pleasant voice. The rough Scots burr reminded Alison nostalgically of her father. *Achara,* the woman said, friend. He had had a smattering of the Gaelic too, a Highland man, and said that sometimes. And *deas,* the pretty one. "We boarded the dear boy here while we went off on a little holiday, you see. But now I must be getting back to work."

The other three looked at them with the conscious superiority of dog-people to cat-people. The collie shook himself, rattling his chain collar.

El Señor wailed. "You be quiet," said Alison, "you'll be all right."

"Ah, now, let him get it out of his system," said the Scotswoman. "If it's any comfort to him. It's the same with babies—I always say, it's exercise for them to cry, you must just thole it. You hold them and comfort them, they settle down soon enough."

"You don't know my two," said Alison grimly. By the time she took El Señor home, it'd be afternoon, and the agency couldn't produce a nurse-maid right away, you couldn't expect—

"Well, they're all different, that's so. It's interesting to see how different —they're themselves right from the start, true enough. Two, you have?" She smiled; she was interested. "How old are they?"

"Twins," said Alison above El Señor's complaints. "Five months. And they start howling at 2:30 A.M. *every* morning, and they're nearly driving us mad. My husband— And I'm at my wits' end trying to find a nurse for them. Someone to walk the floor instead of us, you know—"

"Mr. Gulbrandsen," said the receptionist, holding the little hinged door open. The man with the mongrel got up and went through. El Señor yelled. The collie shook himself again.

"Well, now, you have?" said the Scotswoman in her soft voice. "Isn't that a strange coincidence? For that's what I am, myself—at least what I've been at since I was left alone and came over to be with Janet, and she a widow herself." She smiled at Alison. "I don't know whether you think I'd suit you, my dear, but we could see. If you'd like. Not wanting to put myself forward . . . And here's our Jamie." She got up to take the cat car-rier from the receptionist. Jamie was a fat black neuter with impressive jowls. "The poor Jamie, thinking we'd abandoned him! Home soon, my boy, *deas*—home to Janet." She opened her bag, paid the receptionist. Turning back to Alison, "If you'd care to try me, then."

Alison looked at her. Fate, she thought. The woman's steady blue eyes held all the calmness and serenity of a remote Highland loch; her slow voice with its Highland roughness was soothing.

"Not wanting to push myself onto you. I'm Mrs. MacTaggart, Máiri MacTaggart."

Alison heard herself say, "My father was born in Dunnett Bay. You remind me—excuse me, I mean the way you speak—"

"Ah, a Caithness man was he," said Mrs. MacTaggart. "And you'll have the red hair from some bold Viking back aways, then, if your mother wasna Glasga' Irish."

"A McCann," said Alison, smiling at her.

"Ah, now! And your twins with the red hair? No? What a pity!" Mrs.

MacTaggart picked up the carrier with Jamie. "Would you like me to look after them, Mrs.—"

"Mendoza."

"Mrs. Mendoza," said the receptionist, "you may come in now."

"A gallant Spanish man you're wed to, so. I've never had twins to see to."

"Please do come and look after mine," said Alison. Fate, undoubtedly.

SIXTEEN

"I'm sorry," said Palliser for the sixth time that evening, interrupting himself. "You're not interested in all this. I can't seem to get my mind off this thing . . . Damn it, there's something I can't put a finger on, something—"

He should have been feeling happy about Jackson, and that his ideas about Gertrude Dasher seemed to be checking out. Instead, the last few weeks of round-the-clock work were catching up with him, and he just felt tired and irritable. The Dasher thing was as clueless and up in the air as the Valerie Ellis business. Damn it, who could have killed the woman and why?

Roberta Silverman gave him her slow, calm smile. "Just shows what a good detective you are. I ought to be apologizing to you, holding you to a date. I know how hard you've been at it. Where you ought to be, John David Palliser, is home in bed."

Palliser yawned. "And that's where I'm heading as soon as we've had that cup of coffee you promised me."

"I'll bet," said Roberta, going into the kitchen. "Sit up half the night meditating on your new case, if I know you."

"Damn it, who could have killed the woman? No place to look—nobody knew anything about her. Damn all secretive old ladies."

"I thought you'd figured out that she'd been blackmailing somebody."

"Yes," said Palliser absently. It was the only answer to where the money came from; provisionally, it was all but proved now. No legacy, no capital investments, just the nice green cash; and he had talked to the postman on that route, who remembered the letters . . .

("We get to know things about people on a route, you know," he'd said. "You can't help noticing—it's not prying, we haven't got the time for that, but you can't help noticing. One reason I remember those letters for

Mrs. Dasher, they were the only personal mail she ever got. And always right at the first of the month. Depending what day the first was—if it was, like, a Sunday, the letter'd be postmarked next day. Like that. The envelopes were always typed . . . No, never any return address, but the postmark was always the central station—you know, the big main post office down by the Union Station.")

Well, all right, blackmail. The postman had gone on to say that he'd figured it was some relative, son or nephew or something, maybe sent her money in a letter every month. There wasn't anyone like that. If there had been, not only would Mrs. Powell have known, but whoever it was, living here (as witness the postmark) would have seen the news in the paper and come forward.

Oh, yes? Look at all the unlikely answers that were still possible. An illegitimate son or daughter, grown up, nobody who knew Dasher knowing about it. Voluntary contribution, but now mama is dead, no tie-up wanted, so keep still.

How wild could you get?

Roberta brought in the coffee on a tray. "You have exactly ten minutes to drink this and smoke another cigarette, and then you head for home. You look tired to death."

Palliser smiled at her. She had, paradoxically, a very restful effect on him, this tall dark girl with the still, unusual loveliness of a type not everybody would appreciate. And he hadn't asked her to marry him yet because he couldn't quite believe that Roberta would be interested in marrying a mere detective-sergeant (third grade) but maybe—"All right. Suits me. Even if we have caught up to Jackson"—he grimaced—"and what a type!—I've still got some work ahead of me, evidently. Damn it, Gertrude Dasher—I ask you—ordinary old woman living alone, pinching pennies . . . She liked money all right, but that's not—" Ever since this afternoon, through the abortive questioning of Jackson and through dinner with Roberta, something, some little idea, had been nagging at his mind, but he couldn't pin it down.

"Blackmail," she said. "A pretty good motive."

"Yes, but nothing to point to who she was— And then, you see, she'd been getting it without question, apparently, for six years. That's a long time for somebody being blackmailed to pay up so regular, before suddenly deciding to— *My God!*"

Roberta jumped. "What bit you?"

"My God," said Palliser blankly to himself. The little idea had suddenly got through to his conscious mind; but could there be anything in it? "Six years," he said. "Talk about wild ones—but I wonder—"

"Pull yourself together," said Roberta. "Five minutes to tell me about it before you start home."

Palliser took a deep breath. "Well, it sounds crazy—"

It was way out in left field, of course. But, depending on the times—he didn't know too many details about the Ellis case—there was a kind of logic in it.

"It's just a wild idea," he said to Hackett next morning. "There may not be anything in it at all. But all of a sudden it came to me—it's the same period of time."

"What is?" asked Hackett patiently. You always had to draw Palliser out, encourage him.

"That phone call, on the Ellis case. I heard something about it from Jimmy. I want to hear more details. But didn't whoever it was say something about Ellis getting killed 'because they killed that woman six years ago,' something like that?"

"That's right, why?"

"Well," said Palliser, "it was almost exactly six years ago that Mrs. Dasher retired, announced that she'd had a legacy, and started getting her five hundred per month all nice and regular."

"Oh," said Hackett. He considered, rubbing his jaw. He said he'd be damned.

"I mean, you could link it up—because she knew about the murder. The five hundred, that is. Whatever it was, whoever it was. And Valerie found out too. And put the bite on X, who didn't fancy the idea of paying out two sets of blackmail, so he handed her the spiked cocktail. And Mrs. Dasher, seeing the news in the paper, put two and two together and tried to get X to raise the ante. She did like the nice crisp cash, you know."

"It makes a story, in a way," said Hackett. He went out to the anteroom, Palliser following. "Jimmy—that anonymous call. What exactly did she say?"

Lake rummaged and found his scrawled memo. "What did she sound like?" asked Palliser, reading it. "Young, old? Any accent?"

"Lord," said Lake, "it was all so quick—only about thirty seconds, you know— Far's I remember, for what it's worth, I'd say not young. But then most anonymous calls and notes do come from the over-fifty group, don't they? No accent."

"Yes," said Hackett. "I do know that Luis thinks that call was made sole and simple to convince X she'd carry out her threat. It was bluff. So he says. If that's so, if there's anything to the call at all, she was telling a little piece of truth—there really was a woman murdered six years ago, and for some reason that had something to do with Valerie Ellis's murder a week ago . . . Of course he could be wrong. He sometimes is."

"What time did the call come through?" asked Palliser.

"I noted it down. Thirteen minutes to noon last Friday. I thought myself it could refer to the Overton case, only—"

"My God," said Palliser simply. "That convinces me. It convinces me good. The Overton case be damned. She died between eleven and one, so the surgeon said. By God, I can almost see it! She was asking for more hush-money, to keep quiet about Ellis—and X was arguing—and she made that call to let him see she meant business. So it was bluff—and he called it all right. She forgot that somebody who's killed once might not have any scruples about doing it again."

"There's not really an awful lot to back it up, John," said Hackett dubiously.

"I think there is," said Palliser stubbornly. "It'd be the hell of a coincidence, if she wasn't somehow connected—if she wasn't the one made that call—her getting murdered at just that time. The times are what sell me on it. I think he was so mad and scared that he killed her right after she'd made that phone call. And a few minutes later, maybe just as he was starting to leave, that Fuller Brush man came by and scared him all over again. And while he waited for him to go, he got the idea of setting it up to look like one of the rape-burglaries."

"You're going away out of sight of all the actual evidence," said Hackett. "I still say it's thin. You've got no time pinpointed for her death. Nothing at all says it was Dasher who made that call." He regarded Palliser disapprovingly. "Don't tell me you're growing into a detective who goes on hunches too! One is enough for any homicide bureau."

"But it could be—"

"Sure it could be, but that's a long way from proving it was. We'll bear it in mind, and when Luis gets back we'll see what he says about it. But the one thing we always come back to, on that phone call, is the thing that makes me doubt there's anything in it at all. The phone call, or your wild hunch."

"What's that?"

Hackett said, "You ought to see it for yourself. Six years ago Valerie Ellis was only seventeen, in her second year of high school. She hadn't gone on the bent yet, she was an innocent—or reasonably innocent—teen-ager living at home with well-off parents who gave her anything she wanted. Do you see a kid like that knowing anything about a murder—maybe a murder not even spotted as one by the police—and having any reason to keep still about it?"

Palliser looked even more stubborn. "Maybe not, but it's something to keep in mind." He took up his hat and turned for the door.

"Wild-goose chasing?" asked Hackett.

"I'm going out to find that Fuller Brush man," said Palliser.

After a little silence, Lake said, "Well, it does fit in a kind of way, Art. About the times, I mean."

"It's way out," said Hackett. "I only hope Luis doesn't pick it up as an inspiration because it's a hunch. He's so damn' superstitious about these things—if you want my private opinion, it's compensation. Because he claims not to have any religion. It's a kind of substitute . . . He ought to be back sometime today."

"I suppose so," said Lake. "He only went down to check that lockbox and so on."

They were both wrong. At half-past twelve a telegram arrived, addressed to Hackett. Hackett read it, said, "Now what the hell?" and showed it to Lake.

"Why the hell does he want to go over there for?" asked Lake.

And then they both did a double take and said simultaneously, "So *that's* what she meant!"

What with hearing all about the stray tom and Mrs. MacTaggart—who was to come at once, a perfect dear, and only Thursdays and Sunday mornings off—and making a detour to stop by the Ellises' and borrow a better picture of Valerie than they had of the corpse, and another detour to the bank to cash a check, it was a quarter to four when Mendoza started for Blythe. There was a certain amount of home-going traffic even at that hour, and at no time is the traffic anywhere in L.A. County light. It took him nearly two hours to make the sixty-odd miles to Riverside, even partly on freeways; but after that he was out of the big town and traffic thinned.

No choice: he had to climb through the San Bernardino mountains, and after he left Beaumont and Banning there wouldn't be much in the way of towns, excepting Palm Springs. He stopped in Banning for dinner, at a quarter to seven, and was on his way again at seven-thirty. He slid down the mountain road, in full dusk and then full dark, so early in the year, and then he was on the desert, and through Palm Springs, and even at night he could make time. But watch it, even on these lonely straight roads, because no man is infallible, and the Ferrari was insidious: before he realized, the big twelve-cylinder engine sliding up to eighty-five, ninety, ninety-five— *Look out!*

He stopped himself from swerving in a split second. Jack rabbit, bolting across the road. Thank God, hadn't hit it, but that was what caused accidents, swerving to avoid the animals; try to swerve at that speed, you'd be off the road in no time. These straight desert highways were always, sickeningly, littered with the little corpses—jack rabbits, prairie dogs, rattlers, the long-legged road runners, even occasionally a coyote. You couldn't help hitting them, traveling at the speeds such roads invited . . . He slowed to a meticulous seventy and kept it there, steady.

He was inside the borders of Joshua Tree National Monument, now. He crossed a short bridge over a nearly dry arroyo: the sign, picked out in reflected letters, said *Colorado River* . . . Come to think, the natives shouldn't be amused that visitors found California such a surprising place. It *was* surprising. The mighty Colorado, its waters trapped up there at Boulder Dam two hundred odd miles northeast, to provide half the water for Southern California—and here barely a trickle . . . He passed through a dark sleeping village, Desert Center. Only the occasional highway markers winked at him from the dark roadside now: the state markers, shield-shaped, with the bear in profile: *California 60-70.*

Call it two hundred and forty miles or so. He passed the sign saying *Blythe, pop.* 3,334 at a quarter to ten.

Obviously too late to contact the bank people tonight. At least, some compensations, he reflected: if no Alison, no twins either . . . He found a motel with a vacancy and went to bed.

But by a quarter to ten on Tuesday morning he had found the bank— one of two banks in town—and was waiting for its doors to open. At one minute past ten he was talking to Mr. Gerald Poynter.

Mr. Poynter was rather like a large egg—bald, round, and bland. When he learned who Mendoza was, the blandness fell from him. "Oh, my goodness, yes," he said. "You must see Greta—talk to Greta. A very nice, honest, truthful girl—did you say lieutenant? Yes— I could scarcely believe —a *murder* case—but when it was Greta, I— Absolutely reliable, you can believe me. German, you know, no imagination but ab-so-lute-ly reliable. Quite a sensation in our quiet little town—Communists—"

"I can imagine," said Mendoza. "If I could meet Greta?"

He was taken downstairs and introduced to Greta. The bank was a small separate building; in a town this small there wouldn't be much banking business. The vault was about an eighth the size of that in his L.A. bank, and there was only one attendant on duty: Miss Greta Krieger. Looking at her, Mendoza believed Mr. Poynter. She was a large blond young woman, with slightly protruding blue eyes, a firm square jaw, and a no-nonsense air. She was obviously destined to marry a successful farmer and raise a brood of blond, square-jawed children like herself—honest hard-working citizens completely devoid of any imagination whatever.

He produced his picture. Mrs. Ellis had given it to him tearfully. The Ellises still blaming themselves, which was ridiculous but human . . . She said it had been taken just before Fred and Amy were killed, so it was four years old; but it was still a better picture of Valerie than the one the papers had run of the touched-up corpse.

Greta Krieger looked at it and said, "That's her. She was wearing her hair different here, though. I thought it was—you know I said so, Mr. Poynter, when I saw the picture in the paper."

"You're absolutely sure?" asked Mendoza.

"Sure I'm sure. Absolutely. Only she said her name was Carol Burns. Isn't that illegal or something, Mr. Poynter? I mean, renting a deposit box—"

"I think we'd better get that cleared up first," said Mendoza. A little flustered at being involved in a case that had made such headlines, Mr. Poynter agreed. He summoned a junior vice-president as an additional witness, and they opened the box assigned to Miss Carol Burns.

They found in it twelve thousand nine hundred and eighty dollars in cash, and that was all. It was, reflected Mendoza, quite enough. He wondered whether the Ellises would come in for it: a nice windfall. If he couldn't fathom what the racket had been, who this crooked money might really belong to—

They got through the tiresome legal business, swearing out affidavits. No point in removing the money; he knew where it was, and left it there for the time being. He started questioning Greta, and after they'd been interrupted twice by people coming in to get at their boxes, Mr. Poynter summoned his own secretary to take temporary charge of the vault. Mendoza and Greta sat in two hard little chairs near the gate into the vault, with Mr. Poynter hovering excitedly nearby.

"Do you remember when she first came in? Was that when she rented the box?"

"Tell you by the record card," said Greta, and went back to the counter. After search, she came back with a six-by-eight card. "Here you are. Specimen signature and so on. I knew it was around then, couldn't have said the exact date. May seventh, 1962. About two years ago, little less. Yes, sure that was the first time she came in—that she rented the box, I mean. Why else'd she come in here? I remember, naturally, because, well, in a town this size most everybody knows everybody else. You know. And I'd never seen her before. And—" She hesitated, looking at him. Small towns apt to be insular: he read her mind. The big-city fellow, with his immaculate tailoring and narrow mustache and Latin name, something of an unknown quantity to Greta Krieger. "Well, you know, her clothes," she said. "She was a lot better dressed—I mean, what's the word, formal, kind of, than you usually see here—"

"Yes. Did she—if you remember—give any explanation of herself, Miss Krieger? She'd know that you knew she was a stranger, this small a town. Did she give any account of herself, why she—"

"Sure." Greta blinked her honest blue eyes at him. "She was kind of chatty. She said she was a saleswoman, wholesale like, for a big chain outfit that made cosmetics. And she was on the road a lot, going back and forth—she said she had the southwest territory. She said she'd come through here quite a lot, and figured it was a sort of handy base, you know, have a lockbox."

"I see. You believed her?"

Greta thought. "Well, gee, I didn't have a reason not to, mister. I don't guess I ever thought much about it. Except thinking it must be an interesting sort of job, traveling all around like that."

"How many times was she in, could you say?"

"Show you that by the records, too." She went up to the counter again . . . Valerie had visited her lockbox eighteen times in twenty-one months. Naturally, Greta wouldn't know whether she'd put something in or taken something out. Mendoza could have guessed. A very canny one, Valerie . . . He heard an echo of earnest James Ellis talking about how it was a good thing for young people, be on their own, learn the value of money. He thought, in a left-handed kind of way, Valerie had. He thought that every time she—or they, whoever they were—had taken a mark, on this caper, Valerie had socked some of it away. Had a ball with the rest, but some of it—maybe as much as half of it—tucked away under a false name. As security. So, even if she got caught up with, maybe got inside, she'd have something waiting.

("Often enough I told him—" James Ellis. Valerie more like her uncle than either of them suspected.)

"Were you here every time she came in?" he asked.

"I probably would be. Only times I'm off, for coffee breaks in the morning 'n' afternoon, and at lunch, Georgia comes down from upstairs. But I guess I must've waited on her every time she came, or Georgia might have remembered her too."

"Did she ever say anything else to you, that you remember? Personal things, anything?"

Greta stared at him, bovine. "Gee, I don't remember much of anything. I'd notice her when she came, of course. Just on account she was—you know—a stranger. Not a regular like Mr. Mancini or Mrs. Pell or Judge Newhall. You know. And her clothes, and all. Well, I guess I'd say she was friendly." He almost saw her slow, precise mind working, casting back. "She—one time I remember, wasn't so long back, maybe in October, November—she came in, and said like she usually did, Here I am, just passing through again, what a life. And I said it must be a hard job, all the traveling, and she said she didn't mind when it paid so good. I mean, it was all just ordinary things, like that."

"It's quite astonishing, when you *think*," said Mr. Poynter raptly. "All the time, this girl mixed up with *Communists*—that Thorwald—"

Mendoza didn't enlighten him. And he didn't suppose that Valerie had said or done anything to give the smallest secret away to unimaginative Greta Krieger. This was interesting to know, it was another something they hadn't known, but it didn't take him much further toward finding out what Valerie's racket had been, who—if anybody—had been in it with her, or why she'd been slipped the spiked cocktail by whom.

"You could've knocked me down with a feather," Greta was saying. "Honest, when I saw the picture in the paper— Why, I said to Ma, That's that Miss Burns that's got a box at the bank! I couldn't hardly believe it. A crook of some kind."

"And when Greta told me, and had convinced me she was absolutely positive, I thought it my duty—"

"Yes," said Mendoza. "Of course. We're very—"

"Oh, I guess maybe you'd want to hear about that," said Greta suddenly. "It just came back to me. About the first time she came in—the time she rented the box."

"Yes?"

"She told me this about her job and all," said Greta. "Like I said. She said it was a new territory for her, see, she'd been working back east. I just remembered this part. She was acting real friendly—I guess, looking back, and knowing now she was a real crook, like—I guess, she was trying to look natural, sort of convince me. You know?"

"Yes?"

"Well, she said that about her new sales territory, see? And she asked me what was the best road to take over to Vicksburg."

In the act of lighting a cigarette, Mendoza froze and stared at her. "Vicksburg—"

"Vicksburg over in Arizona," said Greta. "Tell the truth, I kinda wondered about it, because that's just a wide place in the road."

She had to be over at Vic's—Vicksburg, Arizona.

¡Qué demonio—! thought Mendoza. That Gloria knowing something indeed—knowing all about it—so, no wonder she'd nearly fainted when he heard that slip wrong.

She had to be over at Vic's. She had to be over at Vicksburg.

Why? Why the hell?

SEVENTEEN

These great bare stretches of desolate country made Mendoza feel absurdly uneasy. At least there were mountains to be seen in the distance. He had never realized what part a man's familiar physical surroundings played in life until that time he'd been sent back to Chicago to escort a wanted man home. He had felt uneasy all the time he was there, with no mountains on any horizon: rather as if he might slip off the edge of that great flat plain. He had something of the same feeling now.

Blythe was only a few miles from the Arizona border: he was in Arizona within half an hour of leaving, after sending explanatory telegrams to Alison and Hackett. This was real desert—a howling wilderness. He'd driven on this secondary road up and down through what the map told him were the Chocolate Mountains, and found himself on the flat desert floor again. Miles and miles he had driven without passing so much as a ranch house, let alone a town. Once he thought he saw a man on a horse, a couple of miles off the road, but otherwise he'd seen only jack rabbits.

They had advised him at Blythe to take along some sandwiches and a gallon of water. Even in February, they said. Just in case. Even if it was only about seventy miles over there. He saw what they'd been talking about, now.

He passed two wooden buildings, so far away he couldn't identify what they were, and the lone rider, between the California border and Vicksburg.

If there had been more rural building, he might have passed Vicksburg without noticing it. It announced its population: *pop. 47*, the sign said. At first glance Mendoza couldn't see any of them. There was a street, and on it there was a drugstore, a general store, a bar, and a hay-and-feed store, and down at the end an enormous ice-dispensing machine. But Vicksburg could boast of the railroad running through: it had a station, at the end of the street. A ramshackle old clapboard station painted yellow, with a little platform.

Mendoza drove down there, thinking that there must at least be a stationmaster. What the hell had drawn Valerie Ellis to this godforsaken hole, he wondered.

There was one man sitting in the station, a man whose age it was impossible to guess, his face was so lined and seamed and tanned from the sun. He was crouched over the counter, his nose almost literally buried in a large book. He put it down as Mendoza came in, but not before Mendoza had read its title: *Metallurgical Science.*

"Well, and who might you be?" he asked.

Mendoza introduced himself, showed credentials. If he'd said he was the King of the Fairies, he thought, the other man wouldn't have shown any surprise. He merely remarked, "You don't say. Name of Ben Jenkins myself. Do for you?"

Mendoza produced Valerie's photograph. He remembered that her jaunts away from home had kept her out overnight, sometimes over two nights. Would there be a motel or hotel here? Doubtful. "I have information that this woman came here, probably a number of times." Or was that a valid deduction? No, of course not. It might have been only once. "Do you know anything about her, have you ever seen her?" In a place as small as this—

Ben Jenkins took the photograph and held it within three inches of his eyes. "Oh, *her!*" he said, enlightened. "Couldn't say her name, prob'ly Mike knows. You could ask him, acourse. Or Ellie. Damn funny thing," he added conversationally, "last couple of years, I got to get so close to things to see plain."

"Maybe you need glasses," suggested Mendoza only a trifle sarcastically. "Mike who?"

"Well, I don't know as I fancy the idea," said Jenkins. "Have to go clear into Phoenix to get any, I guess."

"Mike who?"

"Mike Cassidy, acourse. Though it could be, there might be a doctor in Peoria or Glendale."

"Where would I find him?" asked Mendoza.

"Find who?"

"Mike Cassidy!"

"Oh, you want Mike. Well, why the hell did you come to the station, y' damn fool? If he isn't out with Bessy, he'll be at home or to Hank's bar. White frame house next to Sam Hart's place on First Street."

First Street, thought Mendoza, my God. First and last street. "What's the address?"

"Hey? Oh, you can't miss it, Ellie's got new pink curtains up."

Mendoza gave up and went back to the Ferrari. There was actually another street, turning off at right angles from the ice machine. There was actually a sign: First Street. There were seven houses on this block of it, and another block ahead boasted six or seven more. He found the pink curtains at the front windows of a white-painted frame house about the middle of the block, parked, and climbed the rickety steps.

A woman came to answer his knock—there was no bell: a thin, gray-haired woman about fifty, with the same seamed, tanned face as Jenkins, but more attractive: she'd once been pretty. Her angular body was neatly clad in twill pants and shirt. She looked as taken aback to see him as if he *had* been the King of the Fairies. "Oh!" she said, a hand to her heart. And added, "Mike's out with Bessy."

She didn't seem unduly upset at the idea. Maybe Mike was her brother, not her husband? Mendoza said, "Mr. Jenkins at the station sent me. He thought Mr. Cassidy might know—" And he introduced himself again, produced Valerie's photograph.

"Well, just fancy!" said the woman, looking at it. "A policeman, are you? From Los Angeles? My. Well, I suppose you'd better step in out of the sun." Mendoza had been noticing the sun; even in February—

"Do you recognize her?"

"Why, yes. I ought to say, I'm Mrs. Cassidy. Fancy coming all this way just to ask that. You'll have a drop of Mike's whiskey? He'd be the first to offer it. He's only gone up into the Buckskins for a couple of weeks. You sit down."

Mendoza sat down on a Victorian-looking love seat upholstered in something that looked like burlap and was extremely uncomfortable, and said, "No, thanks very much. You recognize the woman? How? Where did you meet her?"

"It wouldn't take a minute," said Mrs. Cassidy. "You're sure? Well, maybe a nice piece of blueberry pie then? They're canned blueberries, acourse."

"No, thank you. What I want to ask you—"

"Well, just as you like," said Mrs. Cassidy. "But it can't be said I ever welcomed a body under my roof and never so much as asked if they had a mouth on them. It's just out of the oven, the pie." She sat down at last, on a chair matching the love seat.

Mendoza felt rather as if he were wading through all that desert sand, taking one step back to two forward. "You *know* the woman?" he asked loudly.

"Oh, yes, I know her. Has something happened to her, poor thing? Not lost, is she? But there, I don't suppose she could be in a place like Los Angeles." She might have been saying The Fairy Isles. "And you wouldn't come here looking for her. It's a pity you missed Mike. Bessy wasn't over-mad to go, but he coaxed her along finally." Her faded eyes were placid on him.

Mendoza heard himself ask, "Who is Bessy?"

The eyes widened. "Why, the burro, to be sure."

The burro, of course. Presumably to carry the sleeping-bag and Geiger counter. "What do you know about this woman?"

"Why, it's Alice," said Mrs. Cassidy. "Alice Roberts, her name is. Didn't you know? What's happened to her?"

"Never mind, I just want to know everything you know about her, please."

"Oh. Well, that's soon told." Mrs. Cassidy settled herself for a comfortable chat. "She's a city girl, you could see that right off. There's some of these city folk, they like to come out 'n' poke around for the kind of thing they call gemstones. Call themselves rock-hounds, they do, maybe you know. Rough quartz, and fool's gold, and agate—that kind of thing. Foolishness. You heard of that?"

"Yes. She said— She was one of those?"

"That's right. A real greenhorn she was, at first. Didn't even know enough to carry water with her, fancy."

"When did she first come here?" He resisted the impulse to raise his voice as if she was deaf.

"When? Oh, it'd be a couple of years ago, about then," she said vaguely. "You see, she ended up here because I've the extra bedroom. Real surprised she was, find out there wasn't a motel or something around. Because sometimes she'd want to stay over, when she had a couple days off her job. She was a part-time secretary, she said. So finally, that first time, when she asked around, Bill at the drugstore sends her up here, knowing I could put her up. And I didn't overcharge, either. Two and a half dollars with breakfast and dinner, fair enough, don't you think?"

"Very fair," said Mendoza. "She was a rock-hound. She went out looking for quartz and so on? Where?"

"Oh, out east o' town, toward the Harquahala range, mostly, I guess. She wouldn't be going far off the road, acourse, not with just the car, and Mike told her all how to do, made her get a compass and all. Goodness, city girl like that'd get lost easy, fifty feet from the road. And he told her, get stout boots and all, for the rattlers."

Mendoza tried to visualize that good-time girl Valerie in boots and pants hunting for quartz and agate, and failed. Of course, probably no one in town took a newspaper regularly; the Cassidys didn't know anything about the case. He started to ask another question, but Mrs. Cassidy was going on placidly. "She liked this part o' the desert, said she found a lot of things here. She'd come as often as she could get away from her job, after that first time. Sometimes she'd stay over, 'n' sometimes she'd just be out looking four-five hours, and come back and say she'd decided to get home, the sun played her out."

"How often did she come?"

"How often? Now that's hard to say," said Mrs. Cassidy. "There wasn't anything regular about it. After that first time, she knew she could land here any time and find accommodations. It made a bit o' change too, somebody new to talk to. Not that she'd be around much. Drive up in her big white car, and say here she was again, and change into her other gear—boots and so on—'n' be off. Depending what time it was she got here, acourse. She said it took her two or three hours, drive up from Phoenix."

"She told you she lived in Phoenix?"

"Why, yes, that's where she was from. Mike did laugh at her, he thought it was a cute trick, way she kept her car registered in California, with California plates and all—because, she said, a cop catches you doing something a little wrong, he makes allowances for a foreigner. What sort of surprised me, you turning up like this from Los Angeles asking about her. Why on earth?"

It would take her, thought Mendoza, around seven or eight hours from L.A. Less? Marion Keller said she liked to drive fast . . . Call it three hundred miles.

Deductions. This was how she'd piled up all the mileage on the Dodge. In the last twenty, twenty-one months—since May of 1962. Valerie, driving clear over to this godforsaken one-burro burg, to put on boots and venture among the rattlers hunting for the pretty rose quartz? ¡No hay tal! That he couldn't see. But why the hell *had* she come?

"Maybe," he said, "about eighteen times since she first came—in May two years ago?"

Mrs. Cassidy thought. "It'd be about that," she agreed. "Funny what gets into city people. Worthless stuff like that. Instead of something you can stake a claim on. But she's a nice bright girl and pleasant company."

"She'd go out," said Mendoza, "daytimes? Not at night?"

She bent a surprised gaze on him that held indulgence for city people. "Well, naturally. You couldn't find anything like that in the dark."

"In her car. Yes. Do you know if she went far?"

"I suppose different places. I couldn't rightly say, I didn't pay notice. She'd mostly start out toward the Harquahalas, way I say."

"Did she ever show you and Mr. Cassidy any of her—er—finds?"

"We wouldn't be interested in anything like that," said Mrs. Cassidy. "Bits o' rubbish. Oh, some of the agate's pretty enough, but worth nothing. Mike used to laugh at her—she knows what he thinks o' that sort of thing. They polish them up and make jewelry, fancy. Pink quartz 'n' fool's gold. Foolishness."

"When was the last time she was here?"

Mrs. Cassidy reflected. "Let's see, do I recollect this is Tuesday? It'd be two weeks back tomorrow. Yes, because it was the same day that fool Mex Joe García got drunk at Hank's and made such a row. I remember. She showed up here about four in the afternoon, Alice did—"

Caray, a fast driver, you could say: Mrs. Montague said she'd left about ten in the morning.

"—And said she'd have a little hunt round even if it was late. She changed, and went off, and I remember I was a bit worried because she didn't come back until after it was getting dark. She stayed over Wednesday night, and went out first thing Thursday morning—I made up a lunch for her—and she was gone all day. And Thursday night she said she'd be leaving first thing in the morning, and so she did."

"She started out east? Hunting her rocks, I mean?"

"That's right. Now, just why are you asking, anyways? A policeman—there's nothing *wrong*, is there? I just hired her my spare room—"

"Nothing wrong about that at all, no. Thanks very much." Mendoza made his escape. He drove up to the main street, conscious of her staring after him from the porch, and parked, and consulted a map.

There certainly wasn't much of anything around Vicksburg. There was another town about the same size called Salome some ten miles northeast; ten miles beyond that, Wenden. Both on the railroad: the Atchison, Topeka and Santa Fe railroad. The Harquahala Mountains, a thin trickle called the Bouse Wash. And empty desert.

What the hell had brought Valerie over here? The city-lights girl?

He started out on the road east—the only road out of town. In five minutes he might have been alone on the moon. Not quite: a few scattered head of white-faced Herefords on either side of the road.

Eighteen times (was that a valid deduction?) Valerie had driven over here, passing through Blythe. No. She'd been in Blythe eighteen times, sure. But here, maybe the same number of times but not necessarily on the same occasions.

Work it out. She wasn't the genuine rock-hound; that he'd take a bet on. Valerie who'd done a little hustling, worked a tired old con game with Eddy Warren? City-lights Valerie? She had come here with that excuse on some crooked business connected with the racket she was working. How could it be connected, for God's sake? A God-forgotten spot like this? (The mountains were faint on the horizon and he felt uneasy again.)

All right. But the money was collected at home in L.A. Witness the address book. Before or after she came over here? For whatever reason?

And why the hell was he driving down this road? Presumably the way she'd come (or was that a blind?) but nothing to give him any clue. Empty country, rock formations, sand, and cows: nothing told him anything. Mendoza told himself bitterly that he was a fool.

She had to be over at Vicksburg. Why the hell?

That girl Gloria knew about it. She knew why. How? In the racket? What racket, for God's sake, necessitated irregular but periodic visits to the empty desert outside Vicksburg, Arizona? Gloria, a call girl—if the family was respectable. Valerie—liking money however it came . . .

He slowed. This was a very secondary road he was on, but just here another branched off—hardly more than a track across the desert to the right: it looked like an old road seldom used. Ahead, he could see that in places sagebrush had grown into the old ruts; but the brush had been crushed down by the passage of something larger than a horse. On impulse he turned the Ferrari into it. A hundred yards up he stopped, got out of the car, and inspected the terrain more closely.

God knew he was no expert tracker, outside city limits: but anybody could see, here, that sage and other underbrush had started to grow across the old ruts, and been crushed down and killed by a car's passing.

A ranch back beyond those rolling hills? He stood with the sun beating fiercely down on him and thought, No. Because in that case, the track in constant use, the brush wouldn't have had a chance to grow into it in the first place.

He didn't really think this was any clue to where Valerie had gone or what she'd done here, but you automatically tried every direction indicated, even when the indication was slight.

He got back in the car and went on down the track, slowly, in deference to the Ferrari's springs.

Tall yuccas sprang up on each side. The track curved aimlessly and presently started to rise into the little rolling hills.

Gloria Litvak, thought Mendoza. The hour he got back to civilization, he'd have Gloria Litvak brought in and put her through the mill. Let her pass out on him a dozen times, he'd get out of her what she knew . . . There was Anya Dvorzhak too. She knew more than she was telling, damn it . . . And Waltham said (and the Feds should know) the family was absolutely clean, genuine refugees.

Manton and Cardenas—Cardenas the stuffed shirt—talking about the Dvorzhaks. For God's sake, why?

The track was definitely climbing now. The going was rougher, the track barely discernible in places. This was senseless. Turn around right now before he broke a spring.

That address book . . . Quite suddenly it occurred to Mendoza that there was an aspect he hadn't considered. It was a funny little point that probably meant nothing at all, but there it was, and this was the first time it had occurred to him.

Vardas. Wilanowski. Dvorzhak. Names in the address book—fourteen names—Tronowsky, Klinger, Gsovskaya, Koltai, Imarosa.

Foreign names. What a lot of people would think of as foreign names. What about it?

He hadn't turned around. The track led him up and over a little rise, and there was more flat empty desert below. Not quite empty. A building: a small building, about two hundred yards ahead. A little wooden shack of some sort, with what looked like the ruins of a corral at one side. He started down toward it.

Well, what the hell did that say? Nothing. Names Czechoslovakian, Polish, Hungarian, Russian, Japanese. So what?

But those were the names associated with the collections, the meeting-places marked with the dollar signs.

Root of all evil, he thought.

A plane roared over noisily.

He drew up by the shack and shut off the engine. The plane had died away in the distance; the silence was appalling. There was only the flat land stretching away, the remote line of hills, the smell of sage in the hot sun, and silence.

Mendoza got out of the car. The shack was derelict, all right. Somebody, a long while ago, had lived here briefly: kept a horse, or horses, in the little corral: and had moved on (after establishing the track) elsewhere, abandoning the little thrown-together shack.

He walked toward it through rock-hard sand that yet drifted and got into his shoes; he felt gritty with sand. There were outcroppings of rock through the sand. The door sagged open on loosened hinges.

But it would be, he thought vaguely, a shelter of sorts from the merciless sun, while you waited— Waited for what?

Sometimes she'd stay over, and sometimes she'd just be out looking four-five hours—

He shoved the door wider and went in. Dirt floor. One window, without glass. Four walls and a roof: the whole place sagging, out of true.

But there in one corner a fairly new sleeping-bag, neatly rolled up. A squashy big plastic cushion propped against the wall.

He heard the plane again, in the distance.

Maybe, he thought, the first times she came, she'd taken care to carry everything away with her. But then she'd got careless—nobody ever came here—less of a bother, leave things here.

He walked across the packed dirt floor and looked at the corner of the one room. The sleeping-bag. (Not for Valerie, that.) The cushion. Plentiful scattered crumbs—sandwiches. Water she'd bring with her each time, fresh.

There was something else, lying on the sleeping-bag. A copy of *Vogue,* and it was the February issue, and they were just eleven days into February.

Two weeks ago tomorrow, the last time, Mrs. Cassidy said. Five days before Valerie died.

She must, thought Mendoza, have spent some damned boring hours here in this hut. Waiting. Waiting—

He went back to the sagging door and looked across the desert. The eminently flat desert.

And suddenly remembered just which Civil Service department Ricardo Cardenas' sister Maria worked in—The Department of Immigration. In the Americanization office. Dealing with recent immigrants.

"Oh, by God!" he said softly, suddenly. "By God, of course! ¡Con qué esas tenemos! Why didn't I see it before? So now we know—do we? By God, yes—it adds up, it's got to be that!"

The beautifully flat desert, where a light plane could sit down so anonymously, let out a single passenger—

Russian, Polish, Czechoslovakian names. Names from countries which hadn't a regular immigration quota for the United States. And people who

—they'd tightened the rules the hell of a lot, who they let in these days—might not conform to regulations, so if they were determined to get in—

Thorwald. Oh, yes, of course. The stateless citizen.

Paul Manton and his little Cessna. The very good pilot. And Ricardo Cardenas, the civil servant, whose sister— Didn't it add up! And Valerie the go-between—

A dozen pieces of the jigsaw puzzle fitted themselves together magically, all in one moment.

Hell, and very probably not a Western Union office between here and Blythe— Mendoza wrenched the Ferrari around and headed back for the road, too fast. But he was smiling happily to himself.

At the same moment Hackett was staring at a telegram. "I just thought you'd like to see it," said Waltham. "We're sending a couple of men down, of course. I don't suppose it's got anything to do with the murder, but—"

"No," said Hackett. "I don't see how it could be. But thanks."

The telegram was from the *Jefe de Policía* of Mexico City. In excellent English it said succinctly that one corresponding to the description of Osgar Thorwald had been placed in that city, resident in a modest hotel for some two months, up to two weeks and three days ago, namely January 26th, when he had flown up to the city of Chihuahua. It had been ascertained that there he had hired a car and driver to take him to, of all unlikely places, a small village called Puerto Peñasca on the east coast of the Gulf of California, in the province of Sonora. If the FBI desired, further inquiries would be pursued.

"What the hell?" asked Hackett.

"Exactly," said Waltham. "We're sending a couple of men down. Just like to ferret out all the details, you know."

EIGHTEEN

Palliser had identified the Fuller Brush man yesterday, but hadn't caught up with him in person until Wednesday morning. He had just come back to the office after a thought-provoking interview with him when Mendoza arrived. It was ten-thirty.

"I've had a couple of ideas I'd like to talk over—" began Palliser, as Mendoza came in almost on his heels.

"Later, later! ¡Ya está—Paso!" said Mendoza briskly. He swept into the office in a hurry and glanced into the sergeants' room. "All of you lazing around here," he said disapprovingly to Hackett, Dwyer, Scarne, and Landers.

"Well, welcome home from the wilds," said Hackett. "Did you find the murderer lurking behind a Joshua tree?"

"No, but I found a few very interesting things," said Mendoza. He was looking rather raffish—for Mendoza: he had on the same suit he'd worn Monday and the same tie; but his shirt was reasonably clean and he had shaved.

He hadn't, on second thought, bothered about telegrams: the personal touch required here too. It had been about five o'clock yesterday afternoon when he stood in that cabin doorway and had his inspiration about where the crooked money had come from. He'd driven straight back to Vicksburg and through it, and started home. Back through the desert to Blythe, and across the lonely empty country past Desert Center and the Joshua Tree Monument, the little trickle of the Colorado River. He'd stopped in Palm Springs for a late dinner at nine o'clock; but by the time he got to Beaumont the two days of long-distance driving had caught up with him (on top of the sleep he'd been losing lately) and he had to stop. He'd checked into the motel at midnight and left it at seven-thirty this morning to make the remaining seventy miles to L.A. as fast as possible. He hadn't been home at all.

"All right, boys, let's do a little work for a change," he said now. "*Pronto,* I want you to go out and bring in Gloria Litvak. I also want— how I want—Mr. Paul Manton and Ricardo Cardenas. And the Dvorzhaks—never mind the mother, the girl and her father will do. Wherever they are, whatever they're doing, haul them in. *Inmediatamente, por favor.*"

"What's the excitement?" asked Hackett.

Mendoza sat down at his desk and reached for the outside phone. "We now know," he said, "what the racket was. Quite an offbeat caper, but— I want Mr. Waltham, please."

"Oh? He may not be there, they had a wire from Mexico City—" Hackett explained that.

"Oh, really? Another little piece of the jigsaw," said Mendoza pleasedly. "Waltham? Come to Papa, friend, with some blank warrants. I'm about to talk to a couple of people you'll want to charge—it's out of my jurisdiction, a Federal offense. We've found out what the caper is—let's be honest, I've found out . . . They were running their own special branch of the Immigration Department—with their own regulations. Cash down."

An hour later, he faced those five across his desk. The Dvorzhaks were resolutely wooden-faced. Gloria and Cardenas were frankly nervous. Manton sat easily with one leg crossed over the other, smoking.

"So maybe I was a little slow getting onto it," said Mendoza, "and there was also, of course, Greta Krieger's flu. If she'd seen the picture in the paper sooner— But we've figured it out now. I've just got back from Vicksburg, by the way." Gloria uttered a little whimper. "I wonder how many you'd brought in, in twenty-one months? Like to tell me, Manton?"

"How many what?" asked Manton in a bored voice. Cardenas went a curious gray color.

"Aliens," said Mendoza. "People who for this reason and that weren't eligible for legal admittance to this country. When you come to think about it, there must be a good many like that— I know they've tightened the rules about it. I'd be interested to hear the exact details of how you worked it, and I know Mr. Waltham here—of the FBI—would be even more interested." He looked at Cardenas, hoping the man wasn't going to have a fit; he was clutching at his collar and whispering, "No—no—no—" in a frantic undertone.

Manton said, "D'you have any real proof of that, Lieutenant?" He sounded merely interested: a very tough young man indeed.

"I can deduce a number of details, of course," said Mendoza. "After seeing the terrain. You'll be telling us how you got into the business, and how you made arrangements to meet the—mmh—clients. Mr. Cardenas' sister, working in the Immigration Department, would know what immigrants had relatives and friends anxious to get here. Could introduce prospective customers. But when that was done, Valerie would hie herself over to Vicksburg, as the rock-hound Alice Roberts from Phoenix, and establish herself in that dreary little shack. She must have been damn bored, but I expect she consoled herself with visions of all that nice cash to come. I can see that there'd be a little uncertainty as to times. You couldn't keep as regular schedules as the commercial airlines. You might have engine trouble, the weather might be unfavorable—head winds—and so on. But eventually, you'd sit down alongside that hut—such a useful landmark—with your grateful client, and Valerie would take over. Because naturally you couldn't land openly back at International with passengers like that."

Gloria had gone green-white and had her eyes shut. The Dvorzhaks were impassive; Anya's eyes were grave on him. Cardenas now seemed to be praying.

"You make up fancy stories," said Manton, putting out his cigarette.

"And sometimes," Mendoza went on, "such as in the latest job you pulled, a couple of weeks ago, you'd sit down so late in the afternoon that it wouldn't look natural for Valerie to leave the Cassidy house that night. Hence the sleeping-bag in the shack. I expect a few of your clients had slept in more uncomfortable places. She'd pick them up next morning and ferry them over to their destinations. To the loving friends and relatives waiting—conveniently introduced by Mr. Cardenas, who would have learned names from his sister."

Cardenas said faintly, "No—oh, my God—"

"I might add," said Mendoza, "that there are a couple of Federal men now down in Puerto Peñasca poking around."

Manton sat up and after a moment laughed. It was a genuine amused laugh; he looked at Mendoza, at Waltham, and his reckless brows seemed to tilt devilishly. "Well, that does it. *Finis. Terminar.* O.K., you got us. I'll tell you all about it—"

"*Please*—" wailed Gloria. "Please, Mr. Manton—"

"Don't be stupid," said Manton. "As soon as they get to that *zafio* Pedro Estéban he'll come apart in their hands. Or somebody—the whole place knows about it. It'll all have to come out now and they may as well get a straight version. We've had the hell of a good run, and"—he grinned at Mendoza—"I've got nothing on my conscience, *amigo*. If you know what I mean. Except Thorwald, of course," he added thoughtfully. "But how the hell were we to know who he was? And by what I've seen in a couple of press stories, I don't figure Thorwald had any nefarious plans. Just homesick."

"Paul—" moaned Cardenas. Gloria just leaned back in her chair and shut her eyes.

"How did the business get started?" asked Mendoza interestedly.

"Well—" Manton glanced at Gloria. "Sorry, honey, but they won't be fobbed off with a fib, and tell you the truth I can't think of a plausible one on the spur of the moment." He lit a new cigarette. "It wasn't Gloria's idea, no, but it was her aunt. Older sister of her father's, got out of Poland into France and wanted to come here, but for some damn' fool technical reason she wasn't eligible."

"It wasn't fair," Gloria whispered miserably. "Honestly it wasn't fair— Daddy swore out an affidavit saying he'd be responsible and all, but it didn't make any difference, they said—"

"And she was moaning about it to Val, and Val thought of me." He laughed. "Said, suppose the woman got to Mexico somewhere, I could just fly down and pick her up, couldn't I? And probably the Litvaks would pay a lot—"

"Well, I don't suppose it was just as simple as that," said Mendoza. "Mr. Cardenas, would you like a doctor?"

"No—no," moaned Cardenas. "My job—I'll be *ruined*—and Maria—fired —go to jail—"

"Hell, you both knew what you were risking," said Manton contemptuously. "You ought to have enough socked away to make up for it . . . No, of course it wasn't that simple. I had to work it all out well in advance, sure—everything arranged for."

"I had an idea you masterminded it," said Mendoza.

"And I'd do it again tomorrow," said Manton. "I don't know if you know Mexico, Lieutenant . . . No? The little places—like Puerto Peñasca —miles from any kind of town. I happened to know that one because I'd been down that way fishing a lot of times. About two hundred people, in the village and scattered back in the hills—mostly full-blooded Indian— people, kids, and pigs all in one-room shacks—the little weedy gardens with corn planted and not much else—nobody in the place's ever seen electric light or more than one or two cars—don't quite believe in 'em. Priest the only official authority within a couple of hundred miles—nearest city of any size, Chihuahua, three hundred-odd miles across wild country . . . You get the picture?" He drew strongly on his cigarette. "Well, I happened to know the place. A very handy spot to operate from, because it's only about a hundred miles below the Arizona border. I went down and—fixed things up. With Pete Estéban. He's a good-natured—"

"*Zafio*," said Mendoza with a smile as Manton hesitated.

"Lout," translated Manton, grinning. "Fishes a little for a living, lets his wife do all the work on the land, plays a mean guitar, and thinks all this talk about a village school is *muy absurdo*. Nine kids."

"*¡Qué hombre!*"

"So I said to Pete, listen, *hermano*— Well, it doesn't matter what I said, upshot is he agreed to look after the clients there—overnight usually—for a little cash in hand. Nobody'd take much notice, except of the hired car coming in. The whole place'd know about it, as I said, but nobody in Puerto Peñasca knows much about *norteamericano* laws—or cares. Priest's a fat old half-Indian going around in a dream, not often out of the church. Easy enough to keep him from knowing. When I landed, I was just flying around on a little scenic tour and had engine trouble. You know? And then I went down to Mexico and fixed things with a friend of mine there."

"Mexico City?" asked Waltham.

"That's what I said. He agreed to take charge of 'em there and get 'em up to Chihuahua—nearest taking-off spot for the Gulf country—and tell 'em where to hire the car and so on."

"Name, Mr. Manton?"

"Uh-uh," said Manton, smiling. "You know about Ricardo and his sister being in it, and I don't suppose you'll come down too heavy on Gloria. But I don't spill on pals, *amigo*. Leave him be."

"Well," said Mendoza mildly, lighting a cigarette, "I don't flatter myself that I'm better than the Communists at persuading you to talk. *Sigue.*"

"After I set it up, we got going. It went smooth as cream, even the first time . . . For God's sake, Ricardo, can't you get it through your head they were bound to find out anyway? You came in with your eyes open, for the long green—"

"Which you didn't altogether," said Mendoza.

Manton looked at him thoughtfully. "Perspicacious," he said. "No, Lieutenant. You're perfectly right there. Val was only interested in the cash too . . . Even that first time, it went like silk. Val was the go-between, as you deduced. Nobody except Gloria ever knew about me—Val let that out to her. Never mind. I told her what to tell the Litvaks. Get the client to Mexico. They have the hell of a lot less strict laws about who gets in, see. Well, the Litvaks got the money together somehow—"

"Daddy m-mortgaged the house," murmured Gloria pallidly.

"And got her there. My boy saw her up to where I could pick her up, no questions asked. I'd made a reconnaissance tour over in Arizona, looking for a nice lonely rendezvous, and found that shack. It was a handy spot." He grinned reminiscently. "How damn bored Val got! She complained like hell—about the heat, about the boots and the rattlers and everything else—but she went. For the long green. You figured out that bit just fine, Lieutenant."

"Oh, God," said Cardenas. "My *reputation*—Maria—"

"It went so smooth, we got to thinking, maybe there's other people with friends and relatives like that—and Val had heard Gloria talk about Ricardo here, who was a cust—a friend of hers—"

"That's right!" said Cardenas bitterly. "Blacken my name every way possible! Really—"

"Oh, for God's sake," said Manton, "be your age, man! You can see—"

"Oh, yes, in an ideal position to give you names of possible clients," said Mendoza. "His sister would know of recent and not-so-recent immigrants who had the friends and relatives wanting to come here, barred for this reason or that. They'd be asking her advice—"

"That's the idea. Val sounded him out on it, and I may say," said Manton, looking amused, "that he jumped at it." Cardenas moaned some more. "You'll gather that I've known Val a good deal longer than I admitted, but I did meet her through Maureen, the way I told you. Just to get all the facts clear. I assure you, strictly business. She was built that way."

"So I gather. She was the go-between who made the actual contacts and collected the money. Mr. Cardenas, hearing that the Glessners or the Vardases had a cousin or sister or old mother panting to enter our portals and unable to, would pass the name on to Valerie. And she set up the bargain. Set rate?"

"What the traffic would bear at first. Since we're letting our hair down, we did a couple of cut-rate ones because I was sorry for the clients. Val and Ricardo set a minimum price—five G's. I argued them into doing a couple cheaper, by not taking a cut myself. We split even three ways usually, and I paid my boy in Mexico out of my cut, and Pete—that was the agreement."

"How the hell did you come by Thorwald?" asked Waltham suddenly.

Manton laughed. "Pure accident," he said. "How could we know? I deduce he had ceased to be all palsy-walsy with his Red comrades, or he'd have been slipped across the border by the brotherhood. As it was, he ran across my agent in Mexico—said he'd been hunting for a deal like that for weeks, did my boy know where he could get fixed up? Well, naturally it looked like extra gravy. We set it up—that was the latest job. Two weeks ago today, Val and I both took off. I got down to Puerto Peñasca about dusk on Wednesday—call it four hundred miles from L.A. He was already there. He didn't say much about himself, put on an East European accent —obviously, looking back, to forestall any awkward questions about a hundred per cent American who had to sneak back home. I figured to take off next morning, but the damn ignition was acting up and I had to do some work on it. We didn't get airborne until three o'clock, and it was getting on for six when I landed by the shack. Too late for Val to start back with him that night, so he stayed in the shack and she picked him up on Friday morning, drove him up to L.A.—he said that was O.K. with him, anywhere."

"And he bought her that bottle of Madeira as a little thank-you present?"

"That's right. Insisted on coming in with her and drinking her health. Filthy stuff, she said. God, what a sweat we got into when that broke— Thorwald! My God, if I'd known who it was—! But of course that was our only connection with him. You can see—"

"Yes. And I'd make a guess that your meetings in Valerie's apartment were to discuss the fees, new jobs?"

"Hagglers," said Manton darkly. "Ricardo would know the financial circumstances, more or less, from his sister. Bloodsuckers. People having to raise the money by borrowing—taking the second mortgage—any way. Sure. We'd just lately been noticing how hawk-eyed the landlady was."

"There was one Wilanowski—"

Manton threw his head back and laughed. "By God, I admired that old boy! Canny old bastard. We'd been—or Val had been—all innocently collecting on delivery, so to speak. When she went to collect from that one, he just said calmly, Nothing doing. The—er—client was in the country, and we couldn't speak up without denouncing ourselves, so we could whistle for the money. God, Val was mad! Tossed a bottle of Four Roses at me because I laughed. Mercenary little bitch. After that she made a rule—cash in advance."

"Yes. Well, now, let's have some names," said Mendoza. "I'm sure Mr. Waltham's itching to hear some names. We start with Miss Litvak's aunt. And—?"

Manton sat back and lit a new cigarette from the stub of the old one.

"*Terminar*, Lieutenant," he said. "No names. Not from me. You said I wasn't in this just for the long green—too right, as our Aussie friends say. Sure, we've got to have rules, but rules have a way of not allowing for human nature. I'll tell you this much. Six of those poor devils I ferried in were ineligible to come in the legit way because they'd served prison terms. Now that sounds reasonable enough, doesn't it?—keeping out the crooks. Only, what had they served terms for? Four of 'em for stealing food when they were starving, and the other two for inciting to riot against the Reds. Hardly pros, Lieutenant. But then I never was much of a man to go by the rules."

The girl Anya Dvorzhak broke her long silence. "You are a good man," she said quietly.

Manton looked more upset by that than anything that had been said before; he flushed, angrily embarrassed. "Well, hell," he said. "Those poor devils—"

"Did it ever occur to you," asked Waltham, looking very angry himself, "that you were maybe ferrying in secret agents? People actively dangerous to—"

Manton faced him, still flushed, and his heavy brows twisted to a frown. "No, it did not," he said coolly. "I've seen the comrades close to, sir. They've got their own routes and their own channels. Obviously. Any time they want to slip a man over the border, they don't leave it to chance he'll find a couple of amateurs running a ferry service."

Which was absolutely true, of course.

Manton turned on Cardenas savagely. "And you'll damn well keep quiet on any names too, you coward. Or you'll regret it, by God. I'm not going to give those poor bastards away now. Reasons!" he said to Mendoza. "Piddling little technical reasons. He's a stateless citizen, so he isn't eligible under any quota. She was once a member of the Nazi party. Who the hell in Germany didn't support the Nazis, if they wanted to go on living at home, running a business, keeping a job. Reasons! It was like—" He swung toward the Dvorzhaks, and shut up, and stabbed out his cigarette.

"Yes. I think Valerie was just setting up a job for you?" Mendoza looked at them.

They had listened to all this in silence, unexpressive. Now Jan Dvorzhak shrugged and spread his hands. "Since you know so much—" he said. His eyes were sad. "It was a last resort. We do not want to break the law. This country has been very kind to us. And I had foresight, I managed to bring away the jewels, so we are not poor. But—"

"I will tell him," said the girl gravely. "It is my cousin, Marya. She is in

Austria, she has got there safe, and she wishes to come to us. But there is a history of—of the tubercular, you understand, and they say she is not allowed to come in. It is—" She swallowed nervously, and the pilot uttered a rude word.

"Excuse me, but it's— What the *hell?* So they send her money to go to a sanitarium in Switzerland—*and* get charged for converting the damn check into francs or whatever! Instead of—and not everybody's got the money to spare—"

"It is not of the contagious type," the girl went on. "And we only wish to bring her here, to have her in a hospital perhaps on the desert where they say she will recover. It is not certain, in Switzerland. It—it does not seem fair—"

"Fair!" said Manton contemptuously. "It's damn nonsense." He looked at Mendoza and Waltham. "Everybody I ferried in was like that. Technical reasons, my God. And there were a lot more I wanted to bring in, but Val and Ricardo quashed it—the loving relatives couldn't raise enough cash. And I couldn't do it alone."

"Mr. Cardenas put you in touch with Valerie Ellis?" asked Mendoza of Anya.

"Yes, that is so. I must tell you, I see. It was a lie that I met her at that shop. And I did not much like her. She was—hard. But she said she would make the arrangements. We must send money for Marya to come to Mexico City, first. And then—"

"And then," said Mendoza gently, "Valerie was found dead, and you didn't know what to do. You went back to Mr. Cardenas, but I think he refused to help you—yes, he'd have been extremely nervous, especially when Thorwald entered the picture—"

Manton laughed. "Like hell!"

"—And so you went to see Gloria, who was mentioned in the papers as a close friend of Valerie's—"

"She told me of Mr. Manton, though she was frightened," said Anya. "I went to see him, and he said now it must be postponed for a while, because of the murder—he did not know anything about the murder, believe me, sir! None of us knew anything about that—but—" She stopped.

"And now postponed a while longer," said Manton. He smiled at Mendoza, and a teasing devil lurked in his eyes. "Damn it, when I think of that two hundred and fifty bucks I wasted on a phonograph and all those records, just to back up an artistic story—! How long d'you figure I'll get, Lieutenant?"

"I'm not up on Federal terms," said Mendoza. "I'd guess maybe a one-to-three."

Manton nodded. "Worth it," he said. "What the hell? Might be an interesting experience at that." He cast a glance at Cardenas, who had more or less collapsed, and grinned cheerfully at Anya. "Tell you what," he said. "You get Marya into Mexico—they've got some good sanitariums there, you know—and as soon as I get out we'll ferry her in past some other border. Texas or Louisiana, where they haven't got such smart-boy cops."

Two large tears started slowly down Anya's cheeks. "You are a very good man. I am so sorry you must go to prison. You—"

"Hey, now," said Manton. "Not to make any fuss. I walked into it, and I'd walk into it again. Only next time," he added to Mendoza, "maybe with different accomplices. If you get me."

"I do. Miss Dvorzhak, I don't think the FBI's so vindictive they'll be prosecuting you for anything—you're both free to go."

Waltham nodded shortly; they got up hesitantly. She went to the pilot, touched his shoulder shyly.

"I will think of you often, Mr. Manton. I thank you for your kindness. I—I will pray for you."

"Good God, girl, it's not as bad as that," said Manton. "Way the deal came out, that's all. Don't worry about me . . . You might write me a nice sympathetic letter or two while I'm inside. Just to bolster my prestige, you know—let the other fellows know I've got friends. Nobody else to do it."

"I will write you letters," she said. "Yes, Mr. Manton."

"Anya, come away," and her father urged her out gently.

"Nice girl," said Manton to nobody in particular. "But where do you go from here, Lieutenant? O.K., you've caught us—you know about the extra-curricular exercise. I assure you, neither Ricardo nor I murdered Val. That really caught us with our—well, came as a big surprise. Quite a little shock . . . Now listen to this. The last time I saw Val was about six o'clock that Thursday evening—two weeks ago tomorrow—when I landed Thorwald there. He paid off like a good boy, right there, and I took my cut then. He'd changed a wad into American currency in Mexico. I wasn't expecting to hear from her on the Dvorzhak deal until they'd got the girl to Mexico, so I wasn't surprised at not hearing from her, after she called to say she'd dumped Thorwald—of course we didn't know who he was then. Outside the racket, we didn't pal around any. When I saw that item on Wednesday night, body identified as Valerie Ellis, *hermano*, I got butterflies. But that's the whole story . . . I understand Ricardo's got a nice watertight alibi. Well, I really was over at Vegas, way I told you, that Sunday and Monday. If you want to know the main reason, I'm a man believes in clichés, from experience—you have a close call, best thing you can do is get right back in the air again or maybe you'll get windy. That damn tank springing a leak, just after I'd handed Thorwald over and started home— So, I'd taken Wednesday to Friday off, my bosses get used to that. I had my regular days off coming—Sunday and Monday. I really did fly over to Vegas, and get in a couple of hot games. I guess if you really looked, you could prove it—some of the house attendants might remember me."

"I wouldn't be surprised," said Mendoza. He found he liked Paul Manton, and in private sympathized with him.

"Who in hell killed her? And why the hell? It wasn't anything to do with all this. You do believe that?" For once Manton was earnest. "I just can't figure it. I didn't believe it, at first. That it could be Val, I mean. So far as I know, she wasn't mixed up with any characters who'd— Hell, she was greedy, she was like a kid—immature, grabbing at life, but—any reason to *murder* her I can't see—"

"It's still a little problem," said Mendoza meditatively. "So it is."

NINETEEN

"Mrs. Dasher?" he said to Palliser. "That's a new thought all right." Palliser had poured it all out to him as soon as they were alone. The hush-money sent in typewritten envelopes from the central station: the curious reticence of Gertrude Dasher: the Fuller Brush man who'd had no response to his ring at her door, at about noon that day.

"She *could* have been out, but the Flesches didn't see her go past and Mrs. Flesch had been in the living-room all morning where she would have seen her. And the times check—the time of that anonymous call, and then it was just six years ago that—"

"It's too far out," said Hackett. "We don't have one thing that says Dasher made that call."

"No," agreed Mendoza, "we haven't . . . So we start out on Valerie all over again, from scratch. Let's not miss any bets, however wild they may look. Damn it, now this little ride on the merry-go-round is over, we've got even fewer places to look than we had before! Cross out Manton, Cardenas, and her girl friends—no reason to want Valerie dead. Any of the people she knew, no apparent reason. Yes, we've been led up the garden path in more ways than one, but none of that had anything to do with the murder . . . Mrs. Mandelbaum, for instance. She never knew her, Cardenas just wanted a back-up on a plausible tale of how he'd met Valerie. Probably Mrs. Mandelbaum once bought a job from them. Quite possibly the young Hausners ditto. Yes, well, leave all that to the Feds. Maybe Cardenas' records will give them some leads, where to look. I'm not wishing them luck on it—I'm with Manton, leave the poor devils alone. But we can cross all that out. I had a hunch from the start that the motive for the murder didn't tie up to the racket."

"That's for sure now," said Hackett. "I don't see anything that ties up at all."

"Well, there's one indicated place to look." Mendoza passed a hand across his face; he was tired. "But I can't see any possible reason there, either. It just doesn't make sense. And as for your time periods," he added to Palliser, "Mrs. Dasher starting to get her hush-money six years ago when the anonymous caller says 'they' murdered a woman— Well, my God, a lot of things happened six years ago, John. They don't all necessarily link up. It was six years ago they found out about Osgar Thorwald's treason. Quite a few people got themselves murdered that year. I forget who won the Kentucky Derby, but I do remember that a minor miracle happened and a pro football player took a blonde away from me. There was a summit meeting . . . There's nothing to say this is anything but a wild idea."

"I *know*," said Palliser, goaded. "But the times convince me of it. Damn it, if she hadn't been so secretive! I don't even know who she was working for when she supposedly got the legacy—"

"You should be able to unearth that," said Mendoza, "from the banks. An employer would have paid her by check. Even if she didn't have a bank account somewhere then, those checks made out to her would duly wend their way homeward and get microfilmed."

"I know, I've got inquiries out to every bank in the county on it. But it'll take time. Either she never had a bank account before she opened this one—I haven't found one yet—or she closed it out and opened another at this bank with the first payment of blackmail money. That was on March third, 1958. She probably wasn't earning anything like five hundred a month before, she may never have bothered with an account. Husband didn't leave her anything but the house and enough insurance to bury him. And when we do turn up whoever she was working for then, well, whatever she was getting the blackmail money for might not have had one damn thing to do with them. Why should it? It might have been something she saw or heard somewhere else. But all the same, I'm looking—I've got a hunch—"

"Yes," said Mendoza. The more he looked at the Ellis case as it now stood, stripped bare of suspects or clues, the more irritated he felt. And this Dasher thing was just such another one. If she'd even kept one of the envelopes, so they had a sample from the typewriter! He said irrelevantly, "Valerie was a lot shrewder than her uncle thought. She was living in the cheap apartment so as not to attract the attention of the revenuers. Ditto the deposit box in a false name. All tax-free . . . What a mess *that's* going to be to untangle. Rather the Feds than me . . . Of course there is just one other small thing, John, that in a nebulous way could be a little link."

"What?"

"That postmark," said Mendoza through a yawn. "This is the twelfth of February. Valerie was murdered a week ago Sunday, the third. And somebody, being foiled by Mrs. Montague from staging a fake suicide in Valerie's apartment, instead stashed the body in that schoolyard, with the help of that mechanical monster. Whoever did that had to know the monster was there to be used. That men were working there along Garey Street. Well, they'd been there all that week, and whoever went down to the central post office, on Friday the first, to mail Mrs. Dasher's hush-money, might have noticed that. It's roughly the same neighborhood. Of course Garey isn't a main drag—it's two blocks up from the nearest main drag, Alameda—the street the post office is on. But they're short blocks. He could have noticed those big yellow machines up there at the corner. It's just a thought."

Hackett made a derisive sound. "Talk about reaching!"

"On a thing like this you've got to reach, in all directions," said Mendoza. "My God, I'm tired . . . Every little smell of a lead we thought we had just melting away. That visitor she was expecting on Tuesday, when Gloria and Mrs. Ellis came to call—of course it was Manton, telling her they'd start the newest job next day . . . At the moment, I don't see anything at all to do on Valerie. Nowhere to go and look. Except, of course— But what the hell could *they* have to do with it?"

"I kind of like that idea," said Palliser, still thinking of Mrs. Dasher. "Whoever mailed that letter could have done just that. And if he knew that school was there— Well, in a way that rather cancels out my idea about whoever was employing her at the time being involved."

"Why?" asked Hackett.

"Neighborhoods," said Palliser. "Money. She was working for people, then, who could afford to hire baby nurses. That wouldn't be anybody who'd know Garey Street—not the best part of town, down there."

"Very nice deducing," said Mendoza somnolently. He reflected irrelevantly that nursemaids had been a recurring theme through both of these recent cases, the time they'd been working them . . . A tune started running aimlessly through his mind, Little Buttercup's song from *Pinafore* . . . They'd gone to see that British company on tour: a very good company . . . *A long concealéd crime I would confess* . . . "Because they murdered that woman six years ago—" Yes? Anything to do with it? Not a crank or a nut?

"Some bank will come through eventually," Palliser was saying. "But it isn't likely that whoever was employing her then—if they weren't involved in the blackmail—would know much more about her when even her closest friend—"

A-many years ago, When I was young and charming, As some of you may know, I practiced baby-farming . . .

"I still say—" said Hackett.

Two tender babes I nussed, One was of low condition—

"All right, I'll bet you," said Palliser excitedly. "I tell you, I've got a hunch—I'll lay you ten to one on it—" It must be the hell of a strong hunch; Palliser wasn't a gambling man as a rule.

"In dollars," said Hackett. "I'll take you. Of all the wild ideas—"

Oh, bitter is my cup! However could I do it? I mixed those children up—

Mendoza shook his head at himself and got up. "I'm getting old, boys," he said. "Ever since those twin monsters came home from the hospital, I've been aging rapidly. I won't be fit to do any thinking until I've had a nap. I'm going home for a while."

He heard the woman's voice as he came down the hall, having left the Ferrari in the drive. The Highland burr that was oddly soft and harsh at once, curiously attractive.

"But that's Caithness folk for you—or any of us Highland folk maybe—never like to be beholden to any. A Weir, you say you were? That'd be a sept to any of three clans—Buchanan, or MacFarlane, or MacNaughton. My grandda himself was a MacNaughton . . . Ah, no, *mo croidhe*, we mustn't be pulling the pretty cat's tail."

"So maybe we're related." Alison's voice sounded as if she were smiling.

"Very likely then. All the Scots and Irish are seventh cousins or around there, the countries being small."

Mendoza stopped on the threshold. The twins were having their exercise in the middle of the living-room floor, and Alison and Mrs. MacTaggart were sitting on the sectional with cups of coffee.

"Luis! You're back—" She scrambled up and came to him. "*Amado* . . . she's a dear, do like her." That in a whisper. "And the new chair's come, and— Did you have a nice trip over to the desert? You look—" She swung him around to be introduced.

"And you'll be the lieutenant I've been hearing about." Mrs. MacTaggart gave him a nice smile, holding out her hand. "Now don't worrit the man with the new chair, *agradh*— Tired to death he looks, with catching murderers and all, and I never knew an honest man yet that was just so interested in the furniture. You look to me, sir, like a man needs to sit and relax maybe over a drop or two of good whiskey with not that much water to it."

"I see you're an addition to the household," said Mendoza, "a woman with so many of the right ideas! Barring the water. You heard what the woman said, *querida*—humor me. And not, Mrs. MacTaggart, catching murderers. Unfortunately. I'm stuck but very tight on this one, damn it." He sank down on the sectional and looked at the twins. "You really don't mind looking after these little devils?"

She twinkled at him. "You came to it late or you'd be boasting the roof down on them. Isn't young Johnny like you, now, barring his mother's eyes! I'll get you your drink, sir, that Bertha's busy over the stew." El Señor went out after her, hopefully.

"Isn't she a dear?"

"*Definido*—very nice woman . . . Either I'm losing my touch or this case is insoluble. All even higher up in the air than it was," and he brought her up to date on it. "Tell me where to go, what to look for!"

"Yes, I see," said Alison. "I'm sorry for Manton—I rather agree with him."

"So do I, but that's the Feds' headache. Damn it!" He got up and began to pace, automatically avoiding the squirming twins and the cats. "I'm thinking now about Eddy Warren. Funny little man, but he is a pro. If he's peddling reefers he may be tied up to somebody who's peddling H. And he was storing his stuff in her apartment. If she found out a little too much— No, not Eddy, but one of his tougher pals. The only thing is, would anybody like that do it that way? Sleeping-pills—*¡pues no!*"

Mrs. MacTaggart came back with his two ounces of rye in a jigger glass. "That cat, for all what you call him, maybe some Irish ancestors he had, liking the rye too. Here you are, sir. For all of that, you're always reading about the Spaniards being wine drinkers."

Mendoza laughed. "If we looked back, without much doubt we'd find other blood in me—those crafty old Aztecs. As far as that goes, I'm told it's a Basque name, not Spanish, and nobody knows where they came from. Thanks." He swallowed the rye. "I needed that."

"Well, now," she said interestedly, "is that so? My father was a great student of history, as it happens. Maybe that's so, but the historians make some guesses as to where those Basque folk went, you know, sir. What else does research tell them but that those Danaan folk that went to Ireland to rule the place, all that time back, they came over the sea from the Iberian shore? Basque or Spanish they were, no doubt."

"You don't say," said Mendoza. "So there, my love, not so strange a combination at all. Some of my ancestors were probably your mother's too." He made Mrs. MacTaggart a bow and she laughed.

"*An Fhir!* And now it is time these two were in their beds and you two having a bit privacy and comfort." She picked up Master John and went off.

"You can see," said Mendoza, "just how damned up in the air it is. Aside from the people connected with that caper, who did she know? People like Maureen Moskovitch, Eddy Warren. And also, everybody she knew might not have got into that address book. No way of telling. The snag I keep running into is the method—those sleeping-pills . . . Damn it, could it have been an accident, somehow? And somebody panicking when she passed out and—"

Mrs. MacTaggart came back and picked up Miss Teresa.

"No, by God!" said Mendoza. "It was a deliberate kill—I swear it was—a personal kill. It had to be. Bainbridge said at least ten capsules. Probably in a drink of some kind . . . It's natural enough nobody would have heard about it, I can see that—if she'd unexpectedly come across something that was—mmh—usable for blackmail, she wouldn't have confided in her erstwhile accomplices on the other thing. Not Valerie. She'd want all the profit for herself . . . Of course there's one obvious place to look, but I just don't see how they could tie up—"

"Where? *I* don't see."

"You disappoint me. That last notation in her address book. The Farlows. We said, before we knew what her racket was, maybe she'd seen the Farlows as new marks, and scribbled down those triumphant exclamation points for that reason. But now we know what the racket was, and it's unlikely that the Farlows have any anxious relatives abroad. Why was she so interested in the Farlows?"

"Oh, yes, I see," said Alison. "But, Luis—"

"I know, I don't see anything there either. The background looks very straightforward. Of course there's the money—all that Eininger money—and Valerie—"

"Excuse me," said Mrs. MacTaggart interestedly. She had come back for the blankets and toys, and straightened now with an armful of them. "I couldna help hearing the name. Would that be the Mr. Thomas Eininger that lived down in Bel-Air?"

"It would," said Mendoza, turning to look at her. "Why?"

"I was only interested because I looked after that baby when they were only just home from the hospital. A matter of a month I was with them, young Mrs. Eininger and the little boy. It was the first place I had after I came here, I was still that homesick, I remember. Not that I'm not that yet, whiles, for my own Kildonan and Ben Grian Mór on the horizon . . . But naturally I remember. And later on, I was reading about the terrible accident, with the boat he had, and both of them drowned dead. Nice folk they were—and the poor little baby."

"Why poor?" asked Alison. "I thought you said—"

"Well, of course in a way 'twas lucky it was a boy. A boy doesna think so much of such things. A fine healthy baby all other ways. The birthmark, it was."

"A birthmark," said Mendoza softly. "A—noticeable one?"

"Aye, you would say so. Lucky indeed, a boy, and so I said to Mrs. Eininger—a nice young thing she was, the husband older but a fine upstanding man for all that. A deal of foolish talk over what causes such things, marking and so on— I said, you just thank God the boy's strong and healthy. What they call a port-wine mark it was, spread all over his right shoulder and little back—and some marks they can do these grafts on, and take away, but not that kind—"

"¡Porvida!" said Mendoza in a near-whisper. "¡Qué casualidad—con qué esas tenemos! Talk about coincidence—if that stray tom hadn't jumped El Señor—if you hadn't— For the love of God. I will be damned. I will be—"

"Luis, what on earth—"

But Mendoza was catching up on his jigsaw puzzle. "Mrs. Dasher," he said raptly. "Oh, yes, of course—of course. She must have been— Perfectly natural. And that woman—inexperienced with babies, maybe? Yes. He'd have been, what, two, three? Nearer three . . . Six years ago. Six years ago. And the will—all that nice money . . . But where did they—how could they—" He stood staring into space blankly, and then he said in a triumphant shout, "Marion Keller! But what the hell was the name she said?"

They were both staring at him as if he'd gone mad. He laughed. All his tiredness dropped away from him; there was work to do. He swung Mrs. MacTaggart off her feet and kissed her on both cheeks. "Up the MacTaggarts!" he said. "You've just solved both mysterious cases for us!" He ran for the phone.

"Well, indeed!" said Mrs. MacTaggart. "Isn't it the bold man then!"

"I beg your pardon?" said Marion Keller, sounding bewildered.

"The name you said—that woman Valerie had a crush on—"

"Oh. Yes. It was Pitman—Nan Pitman . . . Yes, on the same street. I don't remember the exact address, I'm sorry . . . Who? Oh, the— Yes, of course I remember them on account of the yachting accident . . . Yes, it was the house on the corner of Bellaggio Road and Copa de Oro. Why? I don't— What? . . . Why, yes, I seem to remember that Mrs. Ellis knew them fairly well."

"Thank you very much," said Mendoza fervently, hung up and immediately dialed again.

"Broken?" said Palliser. "What d'you mean, b— Who's this Pitman?"

"Try the *Times* morgue. Snap into it! All they've got on it. It was evidently put down to accident. I don't know the exact date, but it'll be early in 1958. Probably not long before Mrs. Dasher opened that bank account. Get a search warrant for the Farlow house, *pronto*. I'll be down to get it and go up there with a couple of the boys. I don't expect we'll find any incriminating evidence left lying around, but you never know—there was Valerie's handbag, and all that stuff from Mrs. Dasher's house— And I want to talk to that cook or maid or whatever she is—I'll bet if she does live in, she's off on Sundays . . . My God, offbeat you can say, but we've got there now— And, John!"

"Yes?"

"Before you do anything else, you collect that ten bucks from Art!" He hung up on Palliser's puzzled voice, did some more dialing.

"Waltham? Mendoza. I know you've quit looking into backgrounds, but while you were still looking, did you get any more on Jack Farlow?"

"Farlow?" said Waltham blankly. "Oh, that one. Well, let's see . . . That's kind of old stuff, with all this new line to work we've— Hang on a minute . . ." More than a minute, and a vast rustling of papers. Waltham came back on the line finally. "Hello? There's odds and ends here, that's all. Not much. He played pro football a while. He's a native Californian. He's—"

"Where was he born, do you know? Parents?"

"L.A.," said Waltham. "May twelfth, 1916. Father was a carpenter—they lived down on Fourth Street then, if that means anything."

"Oh, very pretty," crooned Mendoza. Fourth Street was only a few blocks from Garey Street. "And?"

"Well, odds and ends . . . You sound a little excited."

"With reason," said Mendoza. "What kind of jobs did he hold before he married Grace Eininger, the millionaire's sister?"

"A good many, as far as we looked. Lifeguard, swimming teacher—he worked for the city a while—"

"He worked for the city a while," repeated Mendoza dreamily. "How nice. For the department of whatever they call it—street repairs, water-main repairs?"

"It just says here, the city," said Waltham. "Why?"

"He belongs," said Mendoza, "to an organization called Americans All. Do you know anything about it?"

Waltham made a disgusted noise. "That. Sure, we keep an eye on it. Just a casual eye, you know. Bunch of fanatic crackpots. They're agin a lot of things, but mostly it's on the religious basis. Mainly they're anti-Catholic. They don't like Jews either, or in fact anybody who isn't a hundred per cent white Protestant—they've put out some nasty brochures about Orientals and Negroes, as well as a lot more stuff about the proverbial Jewish conspiracy—but mainly they agitate about the Catholic Menace. Why? Have you—"

"That makes me very happy," said Mendoza. "I see. At least I begin to see. A lot of things. Thanks very much." He put the phone down.

"Luis, what on earth— Do you know *who?*"

"'*A long concealéd crime I would confess,*'" hummed Mendoza pleasedly. "And who would ever expect to find common-sense truth in Gilbert and Sullivan? Farce, in a way. My subconscious working overtime."

"Luis, if you don't tell me this minute—"

"'*Some day, no doubt, you'll rue it,*'" hummed Mendoza, "'*although no creature knew it, so many years ago!*' Always so satisfying to see things tidily cleared up . . ."

TWENTY

Mendoza got back to the office just ahead of Palliser, who came in still looking puzzled. "Well, I think I've got what you wanted, but what possible connection— Here, I copied it down. No follow-up story. I chased Bert over to the coroners' office for the autopsy reports, I thought if you were interested—"

"Good boy." Mendoza took the folded sheet from him.

From the *Times* of Friday morning, February 28, 1958.

"Mrs. Nancy Pitman, 29, and her two-and-a-half-year-old son Bobby both burned to death last night in an accidental fire which largely destroyed the guesthouse in which they were staying. The house was in the rear yard of a home on Cedarbrook Drive in Franklin Canyon, the property of Mr. and Mrs. Glen Hartfield, who are at present touring Europe. Mrs. Pitman, a friend of Mrs. Hartfield's, had been occupying the guesthouse since her recent divorce.

"Owing to the secluded position of the property, the fire was not seen and reported until it had nearly consumed the building. Sheriff's officers believe that Mrs. Pitman had been drinking heavily and started the fire accidentally, by dropping a cigarette or burning match.

"Her ex-husband, George Pitman, accountant, stated that he had called on her earlier in the evening and that she was then drinking. He had warned her to be careful.

"The bodies, all but destroyed by fire, were taken to the Hunter and Rose Funeral Home."

Mendoza sighed deeply and looked up. "I knew it," he said. "I knew it had to be that. And I don't suppose there'll ever be anything to say that that was murder—unless they come apart. The link—the missing link—was Bellaggio Road in Bel-Air."

"I don't get this," complained Hackett, taking the sheet from him.

"See if that search warrant's come through yet. I've got to call that lawyer, get details on that, and then let's get up to the house. I'll tell you about it on the way."

Grace and Jack Farlow came home at two-thirty, as Mendoza, Hackett, Palliser, and Landers were busy doing a thorough job on the house on Willoughby Drive. The maid, who had been dithering around asking agitated questions, flew to meet them.

"Oh, sir, oh, ma'am, I didn't know what to do—a warrant, they said, but I—"

"What the hell's all this?" asked Farlow. "What are you men doing here?"

Mendoza straightened from the contents of the top desk drawer in the living-room. "Welcome home," he said. "I'm glad to see you. I hoped you'd come in before the boy. So much better not to thrash all this out before him—though he'll have to know eventually."

"What do you want here?" Grace Farlow's voice went shrill with shock and alarm. "You get out of—" She stared at Palliser as he passed across the hall. "What right—"

"Search warrant, Mrs. Farlow. You thought you were so safe, didn't you? Everything taken care of—nobody suspecting anything." Mendoza smiled at her. "But murderers often get tripped up by the unexpected coincidence. The unforeseen witness."

"I don't know what you're talking about," she said furiously. He thought, looking at the vicious panic in her eyes, that she had been the brain and Farlow the brawn. The man's mind moved slower; he was panicky too, taken by surprise, but he just stood staring at them, waiting to take his cue from her. The maid began to cry nervously—a thin middle-aged woman.

"Let's not waste time," said Mendoza. "Come in and sit down. I can tell you the story almost without asking any questions."

"You've got the hell of a nerve," said Grace Farlow coldly, "walking in here like this." She came into the room. "Just what have you dreamed up, anyway?" Her long nose arched at him regally. Farlow followed her in.

"I think you're the one with the hell of a nerve," said Mendoza. "Sit down. It was quite a shock, wasn't it, when you found the boy was dead? One small thing I don't know is how, but maybe you'll tell me. You weren't very experienced at looking after small children—even when you'd been doing it for about nine months, since your brother and his wife had died. Were you? Died, leaving you and Mr. Harley Crawford, his attorney, co-trustees."

She went dead white, but said automatically, "I don't know what you—"

"How the hell did they find—" began Farlow in a rough bewildered tone.

"*Shut up!*" said the woman.

"Of course you only had to take care of Johnny Eininger on Mrs. Dasher's days off," said Mendoza. He could hear, they could all hear, the other men moving about the house. Landers came in and showed Mendoza a small plastic medicine bottle.

"Bathroom cabinet," he said laconically.

"Very nice. Without much doubt the same stuff found in Valerie. I see it's a prescription. Take it along."

"What the *hell?*" said Farlow. "What— I don't see—" He subsided, looking sullen, as she turned on him.

"It was disaster," said Mendoza, "for you. If the boy died while he was a minor, all that nice money went to various charities and you, as Thomas Eininger's sister, only got a lump sum of a hundred thousand. A nice piece of money, but nothing to live on the way you'd been living—the capital estate runs close to five million. As the boy's guardian, you—and Mr. Farlow—had been living very high indeed—Eininger's new house in Bel-Air, a car apiece, servants—the works. You were set for the rest of your lives, and with the boy looking on you as parents, naturally he'd go on seeing you had everything when he came into the money."

"You're just crazy! Where'd you get this lunatic idea, anyw—"

"I got it," said Mendoza gently, "from watching a ping-pong game, Mrs. Farlow. Last Monday afternoon. Incidentally, why was the boy out of school that day? Well?"

It was Farlow who said mechanically, "He had an appointment with the dent— Why the *hell?* I don't—"

"More coincidence," said Mendoza. "I got the idea, Mrs. Farlow, when I heard that the real Johnny Eininger had a rather noticeable birthmark. And the boy you're bringing up as Johnny Eininger hasn't."

"Crazy," she said contemptuously. "Don't you suppose, with all the money, we'd have had a thing like that rem—"

He laughed. "That particular kind of birthmark can't be removed, Mrs. Farlow . . . What happened? Did you let him drown in the bathtub while you answered the phone? Or maybe he got hold of some insect poison? Something like that. Anyway, it was disaster for you—the end of your high living." He looked at the man. "Mr. Farlow never earned much

of a living, did he? You'd fallen into a soft place and now you were about
to get tossed out of it.

"But only—when you came to think—for lack of a small boy between
two and three. You think fast, and after finding he was definitely dead
you thought about it before doing anything. It was Thursday, February
twenty-seventh, 1958. Mrs. Dasher's day off. The maid's day off. You were
alone in the house. You tried to think how you could conceal the death,
get a substitute Johnny. It'd be a long gamble, but I think you're the kind
prepared to take long gambles. And if any brawn was required, you had
your husband handy."

The man was frightened—very frightened. He couldn't hide it. Alone,
by now he'd be pouring out all sorts of self-incriminating statements, a
tangle of silly lies; but her stronger will held him silent. But he couldn't
hide the panic in his eyes.

"Well, you could conceal the body easily enough. A little boy not quite
three years old isn't very big. The other problem was the tough one. You
can't, these days, acquire a three-year-old child without leaving a lot of records behind. You can't steal one, to start a hue and cry—a three-year-old
can talk, knows his own name. I don't know what wild ideas may have
come to your mind before you thought of Nan Pitman. Who'd also lived
on Bellaggio Road up to a while ago. Whom you knew—casually or quite
well, Mrs. Farlow? I wonder. Nan Pitman and her little boy, not quite as
old as Johnny but approximately that age. Nan Pitman was a gift from
the gods, wasn't she? Living in that very secluded spot. Known lately to be
hitting the bottle a little."

"Jesus," said Farlow. "Jesus, they know—" He looked around wildly.

"You set it up and your husband did the rough work. If she wasn't already passed out, gave her a little tap on the head. Passed the boy—Bobby
Pitman—to you and put the body of Johnny Eininger in the house. Set
the fire, carefully overturning an ash tray for the firemen to find. It was an
easy job, wasn't it? A perfect setup for you. Sure enough, it was put down
as accident, and I don't suppose there was enough left of the bodies to
conduct autopsies on. And as for Bobby—well, a child that age might be
difficult for a while, suddenly set down among strangers, called by a new
name—but he'd be too young to know what had really happened, and he'd
get used to being Johnny instead of Bobby. They say there's a block, don't
they, at about the age of four, inhibiting the memory. There was, of
course, the birthmark. But it was in a place normally covered by clothes,
and not many people knew about it. It wasn't a thing Mrs. Eininger had
boasted about. The nurse who'd come in when she was just back from the

hospital knew—you didn't think of that, it was three years back and didn't matter. Mr. Crawford was merely your brother's attorney, not a personal friend, and didn't know about it. Of course, there was the baby's nurse, Mrs. Gertrude Dasher—"

"Oh, my *God,*" said Farlow. "Grace—" He turned to her. She was staring remotely at the wall past Mendoza's shoulder, blank and white. She didn't move or speak.

"But you made a good plan about that too. Crawford tells me that you told him you'd decided to sell the Bel-Air house and move because the doctor said Johnny's sinus trouble would be better away from the sea breezes. The Einingers had lived in that house on Bellaggio Road for about four years—a few of the neighbors knew them. Maybe a few of the wives knew about that birthmark. Move away, among strangers, and be safe.

"And Gertrude Dasher, who knew about the birthmark—make an excuse to discharge her. Only that was easier said than done, wasn't it? She suspected something fishy, and she found out about the substitution. And she wasn't a fool—when she heard about the Pitman fire she added two and two quite easily. But she was willing to keep quiet for hush-money. You couldn't pay her a lump sum, but out of your very generous allowance from the estate you agreed to pay her five hundred a month."

Hackett came in with Palliser and showed Mendoza a wide old-fashioned gold bracelet. "John thinks that Mrs. Powell can identify it as Mrs. Dasher's."

"That's mine," said Grace Farlow. "You can't—"

Hackett looked at her. "Well, it was in Valerie Ellis's handbag," he said.

"You can't prove—"

"You overlooked a note that'd got pushed down in the lining," said Hackett gently. "It starts out, Dear Val."

"Coincidence," said Mendoza, "played such a large part here. What a windfall. Isn't this nice. Awkward things to get rid of, that stuff from Mrs. Dasher's house. There's central heating, no convenient furnace. And they were so certain they'd never be remotely connected—and since they knew that Valerie had connected them by scribbling down the name and address, they'd be too scared we were keeping an eye out to try to dispose of it. Sit tight and take the gamble. Yes." He looked back at the Farlows.

"It worked out just fine for you—with the exception of Mrs. Dasher—for six years. You thought you were quite safe, it was all so long ago, nobody would ever suspect now. But there's a saying about the mills of the gods. There were still people around who knew about that birthmark. And Valerie Ellis happened to be one of them. Her mother had been friendly with Mrs. Eininger, had seen the birthmark and spoken of it—very likely Valerie had seen it too. It was just your bad luck that Valerie's latest unlawful occasions brought her to the house next door—that she saw you arriving home, and recognized you. And saw the pseudo Johnny with you—*without a shirt*. Isn't that so, Mrs. Farlow?"

It was the man who half whimpered, "Just been to his swimming lesson —oh, my God—Grace—"

"Valerie was no fool either. I don't suppose she'd thought about Johnny Eininger since she'd moved from Bel-Air, but when she recognized you she remembered that about him. She didn't know about the murder, but she did know this wasn't the real Johnny Eininger, and I think she tackled you about it right then. And you said, thinking fast, you'd have to discuss it with your husband, and maybe made a date to meet the next day, Sunday. Didn't you? And the more you thought about it, the less you liked the idea of paying out more blackmail. I could guess how you set it up. You didn't want her seen coming to the house, so I think you met her somewhere else and drove her back here in your own car, straight down the drive to the kitchen door maybe . . . We needn't go into the details, they're obvious. No, Valerie didn't know you'd already done one murder, or she mightn't have accepted the offer of a drink so unsuspiciously."

Palliser reappeared, looking pleased. This time he had a plastic bag; he held it open for Mendoza to look. The real English silver set—teapot, sugar, and cream jug. "In an old trunk in the garage," he said. "Mrs. Powell can probably identify it for sure."

"Very nice," said Mendoza, and went on to the Farlows. "Only you forgot Mrs. Dasher. You forgot that Mrs. Dasher, who'd been—I think we'll find—taking care of Johnny Eininger since before the Einingers' fatal accident, knew who Mrs. Eininger's neighborhood friends were. Knew that one of them was Mrs. Ellis who had a daughter named Valerie . . . In a way, they both brought it on themselves—Valerie and Gertrude Dasher. If they hadn't been quite so fond of money— When Mrs. Dasher read in her paper that Valerie Ellis had been murdered, she wondered about it. She couldn't be sure, but I think she wondered. And I think she got you, Mr. Farlow, to come to see her on some pretext, and asked you a few questions. And—excuse me—not being very quick on the uptake, you gave it away somehow. That was on Friday morning about eleven-thirty, wasn't it? Yes. And she pressed you for more hush-money, and when you argued she called your bluff by phoning us and started to tell the tale. She really should have known better. Because anyone who's already done two murders isn't going to worry much about a third one. You lost your temper, grabbed the phone away and hung it up, and hit her . . .

"And then, as you stood there with her body at your feet, the doorbell rang. Scared, weren't you? Grace not there to tell you what to do. But as you waited for whoever it was to go away, you got the idea—set it up to look like one of that series of rape-burglaries. You'd been prudent enough to leave your car down the street, come to the house on foot. With luck, you could slip off unnoticed— It wasn't a bad effort, Mr. Farlow. Only we're fairly bright these days . . . I'd take a private bet that Grace had told you off well and truly for being so clumsy about carrying out the bright notion for disposing of Valerie." He looked at the woman. "You should have gone with him," he said mockingly. "Mrs. Montague's sudden appearance wouldn't have rattled *you* into dropping the keys and running. You'd have thought of something. And you were quite bright in building that little plan—if Valerie had been found dead in bed, with an empty pill bottle beside her, we'd have written it off as suicide or accident. You show quite a talent for crime, Mrs. Farlow."

She didn't move or speak for a long moment, and then she began cursing him in a low voice, obscene and vicious.

"You lost the gamble in the end," said Mendoza, "as so often happens, because you had a stupid accomplice. We've got some nice solid evidence and we'll get more." He looked at Farlow. "I can even piece a little of that together. When the original plan was foiled, and you were left with the body still on your hands, for some reason—just general hatred of Catholics, Farlow?—you decided to stash Valerie in that schoolyard. You'd noticed the machines there, on your way down to the central post office on the Friday before. And I think you'd once operated a machine like that and were familiar with—"

And Jack Farlow broke his silence to utter one fairly coherent remark. He sounded utterly bewildered and sincere.

He said, "Grace said I was a damn fool. But I thought sure it'd work. Why, hell, everybody knows how *they* do! All those priests and nuns carrying on, and they bury the babies all secret in the convent grounds—anybody knows anything about *them* knows— I thought they'd hush it up! Natural thing. Wouldn't want the church connected, so they'd get rid o' the body like they do and—"

The woman had started to hush him, and saw it was no use. She looked at Mendoza, and there was savage resignation, fear, and a kind of cynical humor in her eyes and her voice. "Aren't you right," she said flatly. "A real smart boy, the partner I picked. I asked him did he believe in fairies too. He just doesn't know from nothing. But it was too late then."

And in the little silence, the front door opened and the boy's clear voice called, "I'm home! Anybody here? Aunt Grace?"

"Mrs. MacTaggart was terribly shocked," said Alison, massaging cream from her face with Kleenex.

"And well she might be," said Mendoza.

"She thought about the little boy first, and I must say I do too. What'll happen to him?"

"Yes," said Mendoza, "a tragedy there. Hospital records proved it, of course—he's the Pitman boy. Looks like a nice boy. His real father will get custody—a perfect stranger to him. But he's only nine, and maybe in time—"

Alison's tongue protruded pinkly as she rolled a few pin curls, sitting at the dressing-table. "Did you find out what happened to the real Johnny?"

"One of those unpreventable accidents. Farlow came apart, as I said. The real Johnny was trying to reach a plate of candy on the kitchen table, climbed up there, and fell off. Ordinarily, just a few bruises. But he evidently fell against the table leg at just the right angle to— Bainbridge said it was probably a skull fracture. He was dead when Grace picked him up."

"Poor little boy."

"The lawyer's having seven fits," said Mendoza. "Quite a legal mess to clear up."

"Yes. It's been a funny sort of case, hasn't it? Almost everything getting found out because of coincidences. It makes you think," said Alison, tying a gay blue scarf round the pin curls to match her blue waltz gown. "Like fate—or Nemesis, for the Farlows. All coming back to Mrs. MacTaggart in the end. Because you didn't have any idea where else to look, did you?"

"Certainly I did," said Mendoza. He was sitting up in bed smoking; El Señor sat on his lap and batted at the smoke as it rose, and Bast was established on the foot of the bed washing herself, while Nefertiti and Sheba wrestled with a catnip mouse on the floor. "I'd have looked at the Farlows—"

"But you mightn't have gone so far as to get a search warrant. There wasn't anything really suspicious about them. I still say it's like fate," said Alison. "Just think. If I hadn't caught that obnoxious Miss Freeman kicking Bast, and tossed her out—if my second choice hadn't happened to be baby-sitting Betty—I wouldn't have still been looking for a nurse. And if that stray tom hadn't jumped El Señor—remind me to call the pound again tomorrow—I wouldn't have been at Dr. Stocking's at the same time as—"

"If you want to go all the way back to first causes," said Mendoza, "you could take it back to the Garden of Eden and the Tree of Knowledge. If we hadn't—mmh—collaborated to produce that pair of iron-lunged infants, we wouldn't have been in the market for Mrs. MacTaggart in the first place."

"Dear Mrs. MacTaggart," said Alison, recapping the jar of vanishing cream.

"And speaking of collaboration," said Mendoza, "are you coming to bed at all?"

"I'm coming, I'm coming," said Alison hastily, and came.

"Yes, I told you all along," said Mendoza, reaching for the lamp switch, "that all our problems would be solved by a nice knowledgeable nurse-maid . . ."

MARK OF MURDER

. . . their works are works of iniquity, and the act of violence is in their hands. Their feet run to evil, and they make haste to shed innocent blood: their thoughts are thoughts of iniquity; wasting and destruction are in their paths. The way of peace they know not . . .

—Isaiah 59:6–8

ONE

"Such a blessing," said Alison, "to be able to walk right off, with never a minute's worry. Máiri's such a dear, and so reliable. Isn't it a beautiful day!" She sat up in her deck chair and conscientiously inhaled several deep breaths of the sparkling sea air.

Mendoza grunted. "All the same, you're worrying because there wasn't a card or letter at Norfolk."

"I'm not really," said Alison. "She probably wasn't sure of catching us, and will write direct to the hotel in Bermuda."

Mendoza grunted again.

"For goodness' sake, look at the pretty ocean or— You're supposed to be enjoying yourself, on vacation."

"I know, I know," said Mendoza. He sat up and looked at the calm blue Atlantic, bright in the sun of early July, said perfunctorily, "*Qué bello*," and leaned back again. "I wish the damn boat would go faster. Maybe I can get a *Times* in Bermuda."

"And the first vacation you've had in years," Alison went on. "From what I can make out, whenever you have taken a few days, you've found some excuse to go back and hang around the office, and never got a proper vacation at all. It's ridiculous—"

Mendoza turned lazily and looked at her, from her wind-blown gleaming red head to her frivolous green linen sandals, which matched her sleeveless linen dress, which in turn displayed her very satisfactory figure. "Things come up," he said. "You finally managed to drag me away, *querida*."

"Well, you might *enjoy* it a little more, that's all," said Alison.

"I am, I am." Mendoza sat up and looked at a man walking briskly past down the deck. "Well, fancy that," he said.

"What?"

"That fellow looked like Benny Metzer. We had the word he'd gone to working the liners since we chased him out of town the last time. I think I'll just—"

"You'll stay right where you are," said Alison firmly, "and enjoy the nice sea breeze. I swear you're more married to your job than you are to me!" She looked at him with her head cocked. "What's wrong, Luis? You did enjoy New York, and the first night and all. But ever since we've been on this ship you've been—fidgety. It can't be seasickness, you'd have succumbed by now."

"Damn it," said Mendoza, "it's just—three weeks. Out of touch. I wonder whether Art got anywhere on that body in the hotel. It looked damned anonymous. Damn it, I've just got the feeling I shouldn't be here, there's something going on that—"

"¡Qué disparate!" said Alison, and laughed. "And I know why, too. It's not that you're psychic, it's just that you're firmly convinced the L.A.P.D. can't operate efficiently without you there in the homicide office at headquarters. Egotist!"

Unwillingly he grinned. "And maybe you're right. But—" He stood up; he still felt undressed in the casual gray slacks and open-necked sports shirt; he felt uncomfortable without tie or jacket. "I'm going to take a walk," he said. "The way they feed you on these ships . . ." He didn't much care for the consciously superior service of the stewards and waiters either, as too, too British as this cruise liner. And he definitely didn't like—"Oh, my God," he said, looking up the deck, "I'm off indeed, here they come again. Those Kitcheners."

Alison giggled. "You've no idea how funny it is, watching you evade Evadne."

Mendoza said shortly that Kitchener ought to beat her, and fled up the deck; Alison was left to withstand the Kitcheners' onslaught. Evadne Kitchener had attached herself and her paunchy little husband to the Mendozas the first day out; professing to recognize Mendoza as a certain well-known actor incognito, she—as Alison put it—arched at him simperingly while her husband told Alison how vivacious dear Evadne was.

"Your charming husband not with you?" she called gaily now. "How too disappointing! I do trust he isn't straying toward that rather vulgar little blonde at your table. I must say, I thought—"

"He's brooding," said Alison gravely, "on all the murderers he might be arresting, instead of wasting time like this."

Evadne gave a little scream of mirth. "You *will* keep up your little joke!

Calling himself a policeman indeed, when we both know who the dear man *really*—but we won't give you away, my dear. *So* thrilling—"

Mendoza paced moodily down the deck, ignoring the bright sun on the beautifully calm sea. He wondered what Art was getting on that corpse. If anything. And there'd been that deliberate wrecking of the S.P. Daylight too. Homicide got the train wrecks. The engineer being quick-witted, it hadn't been a bad one, nobody killed; but that switch had been thrown deliberately, and they'd have to find out who had done it. There'd been a couple of prints, but not in Records.

Well, damn it, Alison was probably quite right. Other men went off on vacation and the force struggled along without them. But ever since he'd been on this damn cruise liner he'd had the irrational feeling, the nervous feeling, that he hadn't any business to be heading leisurely for Bermuda and the luxury hotel. That he was needed in the office, that something big was happening and they needed him. Damn fool, he said to himself now, standing at the rail and staring back in the general direction of New York. Just, probably, because he'd never been away from the job this long before, in all the twenty-two years he'd been on the L.A. force.

He'd enjoyed a week or so of the vacation, and so had Alison—when she wasn't worrying about the twins, though she wouldn't admit it. Which was silly too, because that treasure Mrs. MacTaggart was completely reliable. But suddenly now he felt—well, admit it, he thought ruefully, he felt homesick. For his own office, where he ought to be, in respectable city clothes, going over the latest cases with Hackett and his other sergeants, deploying men, making decisions.

There hadn't been much to get hold of, he thought, on that bloodily slashed corpse in the Third Street hotel room. The doctor had said, a distinctive knife, but . . . He wondered how it had turned out. The damn New York papers didn't print news from anywhere west of the Hudson, unless it concerned a national catastrophe.

They'd be in Bermuda tomorrow. Maybe Art had found time to write him a few lines. Maybe he could get an L.A. *Times* somewhere. Didn't most resorts stock papers from all over? Of course it was British territory. . . .

And, my God, there were the Kitcheners and Alison bearing down on him. Undoubtedly—he could see the words forming on Evadne's mauve-painted lips—to carry him off for pre-lunch cocktails. Foreseeing the present impossibility of detaching Alison without downright rudeness, Mendoza left her to her fate and, pretending he hadn't seen them, dived down the nearest companionway. He found himself at the door of one of the plush saloons and dodged in.

Almost at once he began to feel a little happier. Various groups, mostly of men, were sitting over cards here; in one corner he saw the man who looked like Benny Metzer just sitting down with four other men. He sauntered in that direction. That flat back to the man's head, and the left shoulder carried higher, and the lobeless ears . . .

It was Benny, all right. Dressed to kill in expensive sports clothes. Mendoza stood a little way off and watched with professional admiration as Benny, chatting genially with his companions, deftly got the innocent deck off the table and substituted his own—probably a deck of concave strippers. As another man cut the cards, Mendoza walked up and slapped Benny on the back.

"Well, fancy running into you, old pal, old pal!" he said heartily. "Introduce me round, friend, and invite me to sit in, won't you? I'm just in the mood for a few hands of draw!"

Benny showed his teeth like a cornered rat, recognizing him with starting eyes, an arm of the law that ought to have been thirty-five hundred miles away. "I—why, sure, *old pal,*" he said between his teeth. "I—gennelmen, like you to meet—"

A prosperous-looking middle-aged man in too gay sports clothes said that any friend of Mr. Johnson's was welcome. Mendoza said that was fine, leaned over Benny's shoulder and as he added, "Haven't run across this old pal in many a year," rescued the honest deck from Benny's specially tailored coattail pocket. Benny felt it go and wriggled in helpless rage. Mendoza drew up another chair, sat down at the table, and casually swept the doctored deck into his left hand. "New deal, gentlemen—first cut?" He laid the honest deck out, neatly stacked, before his neighbor, and smiled at Benny. The others looked as if they could afford to lose a little, and he'd enjoy taking some of Benny's ill-gotten gains.

It was better than walking the deck, feeling homesick for the homicide office and his real job. All the same, better tell the captain—and the Bermuda police—about Benny. Mendoza sighed. Duty. He never could get worked up about the Bennys, himself. Largely harmless; and any fool who sat down to play cards with a stranger was asking for it.

He looked at a fair-to-middling hand and wondered what was going on right now back home, at the office.

Hackett came into the office, set a cardboard carton on Sergeant Lake's desk, and said, "Get that up to the lab pronto, will you? God, I wish Luis hadn't gone gallivanting off. He might have one of his famous hunches on this one."

Lake looked at him and said, "Don't tell me—"

"That's right," said Hackett. "Looks like the same boy. That's four in ten days. The press boys've got him named now, in the afternoon editions. The Slasher. City terrified, et cetera. It looks like the same knife, on this new one. See what Bainbridge says, but it looks the same to me."

"I'll be damned," said Lake. "Another woman?"

Hackett shook his head, looking a little sick. "Fourteen-year-old Mexican boy. Everybody says, a good boy. On his way home from a Boy Scout meeting at the Y.M.C.A."

"Oh, my God," said Lake, "what a thing. And another one just came in."

"Oh, damn," said Hackett. By what they had on this Slasher—damn fool name to hang on him—that was going to be a tough one, a lot of plodding routine, using a lot of men. "What?"

Lake shuffled papers on his desk. "Call just came in, from the squad car. I was going to pass it to Palliser, he's the only one in, but— Man found dead in his office. A doctor, I think. Shot. They've just found him. Address over on Wilshire."

Hackett wrote it down. "You sent a doctor and so on?"

"Just finished that when you came in. Bainbridge, and Marx and Horder to do the printing, and Scarne."

"O.K." Hackett looked into the communal sergeants' office, which was occupied solely by Palliser at the moment. Palliser's desk was littered with papers and he was reading one, his long dark face looking gloomy. "Take a little break," invited Hackett. "Come look at another corpse with me. I may have to turn it over to you, so you'd better be in from the start."

Palliser didn't object. "We'll never get anywhere on that train wrecking," he predicted as they walked toward the elevators. "Even when we've got prints off the switch."

"Doesn't look promising? Where've you been looking, in general?"

"Everywhere there is to look," said Palliser morosely. "We've collected about a hundred and fifty prints from possible suspects, but none's matched up and all the possibles are just that—men fired by the S.P. or some other local railroad. Nothing really says—"

But it would be nice, thought Hackett, to drop on that X. That could have been one hell of a train wreck. . . .

Whoever had thrown that switch, just as the Daylight was past the Sun Valley intersection, had pretty evidently intended the train—traveling at a moderate clip there as its next stop wasn't until Glendale—to enter a short siding and plow into the rear of a chemical factory nearby. Owing to the quick eye of the engineer, who had spotted the switch standing wrong before they reached it and thrown on the brakes at once, the train had managed to stop before the end of the siding—four cars jackknifed, the engine derailed, minor injuries. Not a major wreck, as had been intended.

Somebody who had once worked for a railroad and knew how to operate a switch . . . And the hell of it was, of course, he'd been right there on the scene, had to be, because the switch had been used twenty minutes before for a freight dropping off a few cars there. The signalman hadn't seen a thing; and in the confusion afterward . . . They'd been plodding through the local railroads' records on past employees, concentrating on the Southern Pacific, but nothing said he was among those. He might just be somebody who liked to see train wrecks.

"You might know," said Hackett, "we'd get handed another one. July, after all. The rate always goes up in summer." Which, oddly enough, was true of other crimes as well as homicide.

The new one was at an address on Wilshire, close in downtown, just the other side of the Harbor Freeway. When they got there, in Hackett's car, they saw a rather elegant small building, new-looking, of stucco and synthetic decorative stone. The stucco was painted gray and the trim white. There was a sign swinging from a fancy wrought-iron post at the sidewalk: *Dr. Francis Nestor, Doctor of Chiropractic*, it announced.

A squad car sat in front of the building, and Hackett recognized Dr. Bainbridge's old Chevy.

The white door was open; they went in. The waiting room was well furnished in very modern style: gray carpet, low turquoise sectional, black plastic chairs, one of those modern paintings that to Hackett looked like the product of a kindergarten.

A woman sat on the sectional; she looked dazed and a little frightened. "But it just doesn't seem possible," she was saying, shaking her head. "Frank, dead. All of a sudden, like this."

The big uniformed man standing beside her came over to Hackett, who introduced himself and Palliser. "Glad to have you here, sir, I'm Bronson —I ought to be getting back on tour. That's the wife, by the way. See, what happened is, far as I can make it out, this guy—the chiropractor—had an evening appointment last night. He should've been in by at least midnight, only he wasn't. Naturally, I suppose, Mrs. Nestor sat up worrying, but maybe he used to step out on her once in a while, and she thought— well, anyway, it wasn't until about an hour ago she decided to do something about it and came down to his office. Found the front door locked, went round to the side, and saw that door'd been forced open—lock broken. She was afraid to go in alone, so she called in and I got chased over. And there he is, shot—and no gun, so I—"

"Well," said Hackett. "That about it? Wait a minute and show me that door, will you?" He went over to the woman. "Mrs. Nestor?"

She looked up at him. "Yes."

"We're from headquarters. I'll want to ask you a few questions, but not right now. Will you stay here or would you rather go home?"

"Oh," she said. "Of course. No, that's all right, I'll wait. It just doesn't seem possible, that's all. So sudden." She was a woman in her early thirties, he judged, and ordinary-looking: not very attractive, what another woman might call mousy. Her hair was dun-colored, fluffed out around her thin sallow face in a too youthful style; she didn't have on much make-up, and she wore a plain, neat blue cotton dress, no stockings, a pair of saddle shoes with white ankle socks. Interestingly, she didn't seem to have been crying.

The patrolman led him out the single door at the rear of the room, to a short cross hall with several doors. "Down here, sir." The second outside entrance was on the right side of the building. The door had been forced: crudely forced, with something like a tire iron or, of course, a jemmy. This building sat between two much larger ones; on this side its nearest neighbor, across a small parking lot, was a three-story office building. Without much doubt, nobody there at night. Hackett sighed, said, "O.K., I guess you might as well get back on tour."

He went down to the other end of the hall, past two open-doored examination rooms, to the scene of activity. This was a private office; there was a glass-topped walnut desk, a plastic-upholstered swivel chair behind it, a glass-fronted bookcase, a couple of other chairs. The floor was marble-patterned vinyl. This building, and the rooms they had seen, looked like class: Dr. Nestor had evidently been doing very well indeed with his practice.

"What does it look like?" he asked. In that confined space, several men were having difficulty avoiding each other or disturbing possible evidence as they went about their jobs. Dr. Bainbridge was squatting over the body. Scarne was taking flash shots. Marx was printing the top of the desk, and Horder was printing the flat slab door.

Bainbridge glanced up testily. "I've just got here. You can see he's been shot. Probably a small caliber, and until I've looked inside and so on I'll say roughly between—oh, call it twelve and sixteen hours."

Hackett looked at his watch. "Putting it between eight and midnight last night." He bent and looked at the corpse.

Frank Nestor had been, probably, around thirty-five. Hackett's first thought was that, even dead, he looked an unlikely husband for the plain sallow woman out there in the waiting room. You could see that Nestor had been a very good-looking man, the type you could call a ladies' man. Not very big, middle size, but he had lean, handsome, regular features, with a hairline dark mustache and curly dark hair. And he was dressed to the nines, in beige flannel slacks, an expensive brown sports jacket, white shirt, and a beige silk tie with brown horse heads on it; that was neatly confined by a gold tie clasp set with a piece of carved jade. He was lying on his back directly in front of the desk, almost parallel to its length. One arm, the left, was flung out and twisted so that the back of the hand was uppermost; there was a heavy gold ring set with a black star sapphire on the little finger. The other arm was across the chest, and that hand was clenched.

He'd been shot once in the forehead, very neatly. As Bainbridge said, probably a small caliber; there was very little mess.

Marx looked up and said, "It looks kind of ordinary, Sergeant. A break-in, and whoever it was didn't expect to find him here. There's a steel cash-box—the wife says he kept cash in it anyway—there."

"I see," said Hackett. The steel box, a smallish one about eight inches long, had evidently been kept in the left-hand top drawer of the desk; that drawer stood open, and the box was lying on its side a couple of feet away from the body. Its lid was open; a key was still in the lock, suspended from a ring that held others.

"His car's parked out there in the lot," Marx offered further.

That, of course, was just what it looked like: a simple break-in. The burglar running into Nestor, using his gun. Riffling the place, using Nestor's keys, and running. Only, equally of course, you had to look at all the possibilities. It could also have been set up to look like that.

Nestor the good-looking sporty type. Ladies' man? His clothes and this office spelled Success, spelled Prosperity. That unglamorous female in the waiting room didn't look like the kind of woman Nestor would have married. Conceivably, when they came to look, they'd find that he had indeed stepped out on her. Maybe she'd been jealous enough to . . . Or maybe somebody's husband had been jealous enough to . . . You never knew.

"Well," he said. "John, suppose you have a look through the desk and so on, and I'll ask Mrs. Nestor a few questions."

TWO

"Are you feeling well enough to answer a couple of questions, Mrs. Nestor?" Hackett sat down facing her, got out his notebook.

"Oh yes," she said obediently. "Of course it's been quite a shock, coming so suddenly. I can't realize it yet." Her eyes were a greeny brown, oddly flat and dull. But she hadn't, he thought, done any crying. Of course that didn't say anything: some people didn't cry easily.

"Your husband seems to have been doing very well here."

She looked around the waiting room. "Oh yes, he was, I think. People liked him, I suppose. He put up such a good appearance, and made people like him. He'd always said he knew he'd be a success at it, he'd wanted to be a doctor—a real medical doctor, I mean—but of course this was a shorter course and not so expensive. Not but what it cost quite a bit at that, it's a four-year course now."

"How long had he been in practice?"

"Oh, only a little over three years."

Hackett, asking these questions he didn't really care about, to get her talking, was surprised. This office must have cost something to rent. "How long had he been here, in this office?"

"Oh, he started out here. He had—it was lucky—a legacy about then, and he said it was better to invest it in the office, because a good front always impressed people."

"I see. Well, he had an appointment last evening?"

She nodded. She spoke flatly, emotionlessly. "He'd do that for people who couldn't get in during the day. I think it was for eight o'clock."

"Did he tell you what time to expect him home?"

"No."

"It seems you didn't get really worried until this morning," said Hackett. "Enough to—investigate. I'm sorry to ask you, Mrs. Nestor, but was that because he had—stayed away overnight—before?"

She looked at him thoughtfully, as if really seeing him for the first time; her expression didn't change at all. She dabbed at her pale lips with a wadded-up handkerchief and after a moment said deliberately, "I expect I'd better tell you why. It's not very pleasant, but I can see you'd have to know. I only hope it doesn't all have to come out in the papers. That wouldn't be very nice." She spoke like a woman of some education; but he thought that, whatever emotions she'd once had, they'd been driven out of her, or wasted away, somehow, for some time. "Yes, I'm sorry to have to say it, but he had stayed away like that before, without telling me."

"I see. Do you know of any other woman in his life?" Hackett felt like apologizing for the cliché, but how else would you put it?

"I wouldn't know any names," she said. "I didn't know many of Frank's friends. Not any more. I expect I'd better say how it was, or you'll think that's awfully queer. You see, my father had quite a lot of money, and that was why Frank married me. I didn't realize that until Father died and we found he'd lost all the money some way—I never understood exactly how. Frank was—very angry about that. I expect he'd have left me then, but he'd got used to me. And I kept a nice place for him, a comfortable home, and good meals and so on. And of course as long as he had a wife no other woman could catch up to him, if you see what I mean. It was convenient for him. And then, of course, there was Mr. Marlowe."

"Who is Mr. Marlowe?"

She dabbed at her lips again. "He was a friend of my father's. When— before Frank was doing so well, he'd drop around sometimes and give me little presents—to see we had enough to eat, at least." No trace of bitterness in her tone. "And he lent Frank the money for the chiropractic course. Of course Frank paid him back."

"I see. Your husband didn't keep any regular routine, about coming home?"

"Oh, you mustn't think we ever quarreled," she said. "It was just sort of understood. It wasn't like that—he was home to dinner most nights, or he'd call if he wasn't going to be. A few nights a week he'd be out somewhere, and sometimes—as I say—he wouldn't come home at all, but then he'd usually go straight to his office, from—wherever he'd been. He kept a razor and clean shirts there, I think."

"I see. Well now, why did you begin to get alarmed, Mrs. Nestor?" You ran into all sorts of things on this job, but you never got beyond surprise at the behavior of human people, the ways they lived and the compromises they made with life. That good-looking corpse in there . . . This woman had been alive once. Or had she? Probably—she'd never have been very pretty—she'd been wildly in love with him, and it had broken her when she found how he felt.

"Oh well, when I found he hadn't come to the office I did wonder. He was always prompt about that, because he really did like money, you see. And when Miss Corliss called and said he wasn't there—"

"Miss Corliss."

"She's his office nurse. She phoned me to ask why he wasn't there. She hadn't a key to the office, you see, and of course the front door was locked. Well, of course, as you can understand, I didn't care to have her know I didn't know where Frank was. I do hope all this won't have to come out in the papers." Her flat, emotionless voice was beginning to raise the hairs on Hackett's neck. "So I told her he wasn't feeling well and wouldn't be in, she might as well go home. But it did seem peculiar, because it wasn't like him. So I came straight here—"

"Why, Mrs. Nestor? Apparently he wasn't here, you knew that."

"I knew that, of course. The thought that just crossed my mind was that he had possibly decided to leave me, or—just gone away somewhere on a little trip, and he might have left a note here. I didn't know, but it was possible. But when I saw his car in the parking lot at the side, of course it looked even odder, and then I saw that the side door had been forced. I didn't like to go in alone. I thought—well, I don't quite know what I thought, but I walked up to the drugstore on the corner and called the police."

Hackett looked at her reflectively. That, he thought, was quite a story. From quite a female. Her dull eyes were unreadable. Had she still loved him enough to feel jealousy? Had she got to hating him enough to kill him? A very peculiar ménage that had been, to say the least. And did that ring quite true, about why she'd come to the office? Not a very natural thing to do, or was it?

He thought he'd ask her to let the lab give her a cordite test, though that wasn't always conclusive.

"Were you at home all last evening?" he asked. "Alone?"

"Oh yes." She gave the address readily: Kenmore Avenue. "Frank left after dinner, about seven-thirty. I watched TV a little while, and did some mending, and then I realized he probably wouldn't be in until late, so I went to bed. That was about ten-thirty. It wasn't until this morning that I realized he hadn't come home at all."

Home, thought Hackett. My God. "Do you have separate rooms?"

"Oh no, but, you see, I went to sleep."

He looked at her again. It was early to come to any conclusions; he wasn't sure exactly how he felt about her story. He said, "May I have your full name, please?"

"Andrea Lilian Nestor. My maiden name was Wayne."

He thanked her. "I think that's all I'll ask of you right now, Mrs. Nestor. We'll be in touch with you. I suppose you'd like to go home. Have you a car, or—"

"Oh no," she said. "I don't drive."

"I'll have a car come and pick you up."

"That's very kind of you," she said, sounding surprised. "I don't mind the bus. Could you tell me—I expect you'll want to do an autopsy, but should I make any arrangements?"

"For the—" That stopped him, the flatly practical question. He said, "Not until we officially release the body."

"Oh. I see. Well, thank you. I think," said Andrea Nestor meditatively, "I'll have him cremated."

Hackett went back to the private office down the hall. He felt shaken. He asked Marx if the phone had been printed; it had, and he called in for a car to take Mrs. Nestor home. He thought now, before he swallowed the obvious break-in and impersonal assault, he'd take a long hard look at Andrea Nestor and at Frank Nestor's social life.

And there was that Slasher, roaming around loose. Four in ten days. God. He wished Luis was home.

He said to Palliser, "Picked up anything?"

"Not much. His files look a little interesting."

"Oh? How?"

"Well, this all looks very much in the money, doesn't it?" Palliser gestured round the room. "But, according to his files, he didn't really have many regular patients. Maybe I'm no judge, but I'd say a setup like this should indicate quite a large practice—maybe, what, at least eighty, a hundred, more regular patients. Files on just thirty-six, and only about twenty of those seem, by the appointment book, to have been coming at all regularly. He charged six bucks an office visit."

"You don't say," said Hackett.

"All right to take it away?" The ambulance had arrived; a couple of interns were looking in the door. Bainbridge had already left.

Hackett glanced down at the body and said absently, "Yes," and then, "Wait a minute." He squatted down beside it. The right hand, closed, lay across the chest; he lifted it, turned it over. There was something clutched between finger and thumb; with some difficulty he pried loose the dead man's grip. "Now this I don't believe," he said. "The clue straight out of Edgar Wallace."

Palliser bent to look, and said he'd be damned.

It was a button. A very ordinary-looking button, very dark gray or black, with four little holes, and a tiny strand of thread still caught in one. A button about half an inch in diameter.

Palliser straightened up. "Are we supposed to read it that he made a grab at the killer and got this instead of the gun? Talk about too good to be true—"

"Well, it could happen," said Hackett. "Just because it looks obvious— You know as well as I do, it's usually just what it looks like."

"Sure," said Palliser. "So it is. You want to take his files along?"

"I'll see them later, here." Hackett looked at his watch, said to the interns, "O.K., he's all yours," and looked round the office. Nothing much more to do here right now.

Irrelevantly he thought of Roberto Reyes. Such a good boy. The fine marks at school. The priest talking about God's will.

In Hackett's book, the ones like the Slasher hadn't one damn thing to do with God's will.

Right now, he thought, his money would go—tentatively—on Andrea Nestor, as the X who had taken Frank Nestor off. Or maybe a jealous husband. Some work to do on it. But the hell of a lot more to do on the Slasher—as yet so very damned anonymous.

There was also the train wreck.

He said to Palliser, "Come on, let's go have lunch. I'll be concentrating on this thing for a while, and we'll let Bert or somebody take over the routine on that Daylight thing. Agree with you, probably come up with nothing definite in the end. But this Slasher—damn it, who made up that one, I wonder?—we'll be working but damn hard. You haven't seen all the statements—"

"No, I've really just seen the *Times*. You want me to take over the routine on that?"

"I don't know yet," said Hackett. "Look, let's drop by the office and get those statements, go up to Federico's, O.K.? You'd better be briefed, just in case." Yes, this Nestor business looked like being tricky, but on the other hand the press was howling about the Slasher—and that was indeed quite a thing. Four in ten days. . . . The berserk killer, the lunatic killer, who killed for little or no reason? Looked like that. And as yet practically nothing on him.

He wished Luis were here. He might just have one of his hunches about the Slasher. Which was wishful thinking, because you didn't get anywhere on one like that with irrational hunches. If you got anywhere it was by the patient plodding routine.

That woman. *I think I'll have him cremated.*

Let Palliser take over the routine on the Slasher? That was getting the hell of a lot of publicity, the sooner they cleared it up the better. If they didn't yet have *City Terrified of Random Slasher*, they soon would have, way the press boys were carrying on. . . .

He drank sugarless coffee glumly and watched Palliser reading the statements.

The first one had been the Skid Row bum, found in a cheap room in a shabby hotel on Third Street. They didn't even know his last name; a bartender down on the Row had identified him as "a guy named Mike," familiar down there, a wino. He'd been savagely knifed, and the body slashed and mutilated after he was dead. The desk clerk couldn't give anything but a very vague description of the man who had rented the room. "They come 'n' go, you know," he said nervously. The scrawled signature in the register was almost illegible; it might be Fred Rankin or Frank Tomkin or in fact anything you could make of it. The clerk did say he hadn't any luggage. Naturally, the clerk was pressed, as were the people on that floor. Nobody was at all helpful; the man just hadn't been noticed, and he'd taken the room only twelve hours before. Naturally, too, he hadn't been back.

That was the situation when they found Florence Dahl. Or rather when the woman in the next room found her and made enough noise to bring the nearest traffic cop on the run. They knew most of what there was to know about Florence—she had a string of arrests and fines for soliciting and resorting—but that wasn't any help in finding who'd killed her. Florence had gone downhill in twenty years at the game and was taking any customers she could get. She'd been living in a sleazy rooming house on Grand Avenue, and a couple of women, the same types as Florence, who had rooms on the same floor, had told them a little. From what they'd heard. Some man Florence had brought home that night, shouting and swearing something awful there in her room. Couldn't remember anything specific he'd shouted, except that one woman insisted he'd kept saying, "Every ham's gaining on me," which hardly made sense however you interpreted it. That had been about nine o'clock; only those two women and the landlady home, besides Florence. It hadn't gone on very long, or probably in due course the landlady—tolerant though she was—would at least have gone up and banged on the door. He'd stopped shouting, and maybe ten minutes later they'd heard the door of Florence's room slam, and heard him go downstairs and out.

None of them had laid eyes on him, of course.

And that was when he started to look more important, because Dr. Bainbridge and the lab had linked those two murders. On account of the knife, and the M.O. Florence too had been stabbed, slashed, and mutilated. "It looks like a very unusual knife," said Bainbridge. "From what we can figure out, measuring the wounds and so on, about half the edge is serrated—like a bread knife, you know. It's not a standard size—I don't think it's a commercially made knife, though that's just a guess. The blade's about eleven inches long, give or take half an inch, and unusually wide—about two and a half inches."

"Quite a snickersnee," said Palliser now, reading statements over coffee.

Hackett agreed glumly. In deference to his diet he'd ordered only a large salad and coffee, and was still hungry. He tried not to imagine what Angel had had for lunch.

They were still taking statements on Florence when the body of Theodore Simms was found in an alley on Flower Street, close in to downtown. All his identification left on him, but his mother said he'd have had a little over five dollars in his wallet, and that was missing. Simms had just lost his job as wholesale salesman for a small local firm—no fault of his, the company had been laying off, having hit a slump—and was looking for another. He was Number Three all right, treated just like the first two—stabbed, slashed, and mutilated savagely.

Several people vaguely identified him as having been in a small bar on Flower Street about nine o'clock that night. The bartender was more definite; he said Simms had had two beers, and that the man sitting next to him had started talking to him. Said Simms hadn't done much of the talking, and he hadn't heard anything of what the other man said himself, but they'd left together. What had the second man looked like? "Hell, sort of ordinary, I guess. I was busy, I just noticed out o' the tail of my eye, you know? About medium height, I guess, not very fat or very thin—hell, I wouldn't want to guess how old. Only thing I do remember, he had two straight whiskies and he paid me with a silver dollar and two dimes."

End of the line on Simms. That alley would be pretty dark at night.

By then Hackett had reached the conclusion that this was a bad one, the kind that killed on impulse for no reason, or a lunatic reason. Fourteen-year-old Roberto Reyes just confirmed that.

Roberto's mother had called in last night, when he failed to come home after the Boy Scout meeting at the Y.M.C.A. "Always he is so good, to come straight home, and it is only the few blocks he has to walk. ¡Dios me libre! God forbid it, but I think of the accident—he knows to be careful, but children—"

But they hadn't found Roberto until the middle of this morning. A couple of kids, taking a short cut through another alley facing on Second Street, had found Roberto. Number Four.

Eventually, with the priest soothing Mama's hysterics and the other kids standing around crying, Hackett had got a few pertinent facts out of Manuel Reyes. The boy was always prompt about coming home; he wasn't supposed to be out late. The meeting would have been over about eight o'clock, and the Y.M.C.A. was only four blocks away from the Reyes home on Witmer Street. Yes, Roberto would have walked down Second Street on his way home. But he would not have talked to a stranger, gone anywhere with a stranger. . . . Well, perhaps, if some person had asked him for directions, something like that—he was a very polite boy, he would always want to be helpful. "¡Ah, qué atrocidad! ¿Para qué? That this should happen to us—such a good boy always, such fine marks at school—"

"Se comprende," Hackett had said gently. "Lo siento en la alma. We'll find whoever did it, Mr. Reyes, and he'll be punished."

Which would mean a lot to Roberto, wouldn't it? he thought. And it was something to work, with practically no evidence on the killer. And no tie-up to any of the victims.

"A kid," said Palliser now. "No reason for it—you figure he just runs amok all of a sudden? And how the hell—"

"It's the only way you can figure it," said Hackett. "Come on, let's get back. And the hell of it is, no make on him at all. That damn bar so dark, nobody could say even what color he was. Though I suppose that desk clerk would have noticed whether he— Yes, the ones like Florence are used to funny customers, so nobody investigated right away. And Simms— Well, you can see there's practically no evidence on it, but we've got to work it. Because one like that—maybe those aren't the first people he's used that knife on, and they sure as hell won't be the last, unless we catch up to him."

"So, you have any ideas where to start looking?" asked Palliser.

"Some," said Hackett tersely. "For one thing, these four kills all happened inside a fairly small area—all downtown. Roughly inside about a twelve-block square. All right. We know that our Slasher—damn it, might as well call him that—once took a hotel room, and in that area. At least it's practically certain that the man who rented that room is the one who left the body in it. The fellow called Mike would probably go anywhere with anybody who promised him a drink, ¿cómo no? Anybody could get taken to Florence's room. The indication seems to be, on Simms, that this fellow got talking to him at the bar, for some reason followed him out. And we can't guess on the Reyes boy, but I want to talk to some of the other kids at that meeting, find out if any of them took the same direction. Or I did want to. Now, with this Nestor thing in our laps, I think I'll let you do that. See the kids. And we're also going to set every man we've got free looking at every hotel inside that area, for a signature to match up to the one in that hotel register. We've got photographs of it. Have some more prints made up if you need them, and send out some men."

"Hell of a job," said Palliser. "But, of course, the first thing to try, I see that. You're going to work the Nestor thing?"

"I think I'll go back and poke around his office some," said Hackett thoughtfully. "And it might be the obvious thing, just what it looks like, but on the other hand there are a couple of funny little things about it. And that woman— Yes, you get on with that, I'll probably be back about three anyway to see if they got any interesting prints. . . . Everything always comes at once. I wish to God Luis was here. . . ."

THREE

When Hackett turned into the parking lot beside Nestor's office he saw a second car there beside Nestor's. Nestor's white Buick convertible was parked in the slot nearest the side door, and the other car had been parked in the next slot, so the Buick's length partly hid it. There was movement there at its rear; a woman straightened and began to walk around the car, saw him turning in, and paused.

Hackett pulled his Ford in on the other side of the Buick and got out. He ought to have left a man here, he thought, angry at himself. He went up to the woman, who had waited for him. "Detective Sergeant Hackett," he said curtly. "Are you one of Dr. Nestor's patients?" He wondered suddenly about that; if Nestor was doing so well, he'd scarcely have had a morning free of appointments, but nobody had shown up.

"Oh no, I'm his nurse. Margaret Corliss." She was a woman about forty, and not trying to look younger. A little too plump, and careless make-up; she had short, straight dark hair and dark eyes behind plastic-rimmed glasses. She was in a white uniform and sensible flat-heeled white shoes. "Mrs. Nestor called and told me the awful news, about Doctor. I couldn't believe it at first. It just doesn't seem possible. But then I thought I'd better come down and call all the patients who had appointments. I expected the police would be here, and it would be awkward, having patients coming in. It's dreadful—have you any idea who the burglar was yet?" She sounded sincere, anxious.

"Have you been in the building?" he asked.

"Oh no, I just got here."

"Well, come in with me now, please, I'd like to ask you a few questions." Just as well she was here. He took her down to the private office. She was quick, coming in, to notice the small stain on the floor, and recoiled slightly.

"Oh, is that where— It's too awful! To think of Doctor—"

Palliser had left the top drawer of the one big file case open. Hackett drew it out and set it on the desk. "Sit down, Miss Corliss." He sat down himself in the desk chair and riffled through the cards in the file. They were stiff cards, lined, about eight by six; and most of them were blank. Only here and there, under different alphabet headings, was a card filled out. "Can you tell me who the doctor's appointment was with last night?"

"Why, I didn't know he had one," she said blankly. "Just a minute, I'll look in the appointment book." She found it on the desk and turned to the latest filled-in page. "There's nothing listed. He certainly didn't mention one to me, and usually when he did make an evening appointment, of course he'd ask me to be here too. It's better policy, you see—especially if it's a woman."

"Wasn't that rather inconvenient? I should think—"

"Oh, it wasn't very often," she said. "Goodness, I just can't believe such an awful thing's happened. Mrs. Nestor said it must have been somebody breaking in to burglarize the place. It seems to me people are getting more lawless every day. The things you read—"

Well, it was possible, thought Hackett, that Nestor had used his office as a meeting place for his girl friend. Or girl friends.

"Would you say that Dr. Nestor had a good practice?"

"Oh yes, very good. He was a clever doctor, people liked him."

"I see. Would you come and look at these files, please? It doesn't look like a very large practice to me. Not big enough to start paying his office rent." He watched her; he saw her eyes move behind the glasses. She looked through the file drawer obediently.

"But, my goodness," she said, "he's taken a lot of the file cards out. I wonder why? There should be ever so many more here—of course he had a lot more patients than just these!" She sounded concerned. And that "ever so many" gave her away: she'd been a long time away from England, but there remained the faintest trace of Cockney.

"Oh, is that so? Why do you suppose he'd do that, Miss Corliss?"

"Why, I've reely no idea, it does seem funny." That "reely" gave her away further. "Do you suppose the burglar could have done it? I mean, like vandals at the schools, you know—just out of mischief."

Hackett regarded her guileless expression. There was something about Margaret Corliss that smelled just faintly wrong to him, as this whole Nestor business did. And because, damn it, he'd had that Reyes kid and the Slasher on his mind this morning, he hadn't been giving full attention to this thing; he'd had no business to walk away and leave the office unguarded, with that side door open. They hadn't really looked around much here, just desultorily as yet. He hadn't, for instance, looked at the other file drawers. . . . Ought to have his head examined, doing a fool trick like that.

Had the woman been in the building? At the back of her car . . . He asked suddenly, "What were you putting away in your car trunk as I drove up, Miss Corliss?"

The brown eyes never flickered, only widened on him. "In my *trunk?* Why, nothing, Sergeant. What would I be—I'd just driven up and parked, reely I had."

"Then what were you doing behind the car? I thought you seemed to be shutting the trunk lid."

"Well, reely, all the fuss about nothing," she said fretfully. "I should think you'd be better getting after the burglar, that's the important thing after all. I suppose you can see I drive an old car. The trunk lid's got a way of coming loose and flying up, and of course usually in the most awkward places, when I'm in the left-turn lane or something. It did that just as I came in, so of course I went round to shut it." She sounded a little annoyed now. "Reely, I don't know what you think I— All I came down for was to call the patients and put them off."

"So you said," said Hackett. "It's now"—he looked at his watch—"getting on for two o'clock. It seems funny there weren't any patients scheduled earlier today, if he had such a large practice."

"But it's Wednesday," said Miss Corliss instantly. "Doctor always took Wednesdays off. It's the patients for the rest of the week I want to—"

"I see." Something just a trifle wrong, but he couldn't put a finger on it. Not worth a damn. "Could you do your telephoning somewhere else? I'll be looking around in here. I saw a desk in a little cubicle off the waiting room—"

"Yes, of course, that's my desk. Certainly, Sergeant, and I surely do wish you good luck in finding out what awful fiend did it. Just a dreadful thing, poor Doctor only thirty-six and doing so well. I expect it's all right to take the appointment book?" She picked it up casually.

Well, Palliser had seen it. He got up after she'd gone out, and gently eased the door open; she'd closed it after her. The little cubicle adjoining the waiting room had only waist-high partitions on the sides that faced the waiting room and the hall. He heard a chair pulled out, shoved in, and after a short pause the little click as she lifted the phone. . . . "Mrs. Vandenburg? This is Dr. Nestor's nurse, Miss Corliss. I'm so sorry, but I'm afraid—"

On the level? Had she been putting something in the trunk? Been in here already and taken away—well, what? Something wrong about this setup. Those files—that was just damned silly, suggesting that a burglar . . . Why would Nestor have lifted a whole wad of file cards out? It made no sense. Mrs. Nestor wouldn't have had a chance, the patrolman had been with her. And whatever the Corliss woman might have taken out of here, if anything, it hadn't been the file cards (if any), because Palliser had already commented on that to Hackett. What the hell, he thought blankly.

He opened the other three drawers of the steel filing case. They were all bare.

What could she have wanted to lift, here? Echo answers what, thought Hackett irritably. Had she been putting something in the trunk? Go and look. Sure, without a warrant, and get hauled across the coals for it. Ten to one the trunk was locked anyway. . . . Funnily enough, his sister's Dodge had a trunk lid like that. If she forgot to lock it, it was always flying up.

He walked down the hall, out the side door, and around Miss Corliss' eight-year-old Plymouth. The trunk was locked.

As he came back she was saying into the phone, "Mr. Weatherby? This is Dr. Nestor's nurse, Miss Corliss. I'm so sorry—" She had the phone on her lap, the appointment book on the desk before her.

Hackett sat down at Nestor's desk again. Nestor had been doing right well indeed, for a chiropractor in practice only three years. Of course, he gathered that some people swore by them, wouldn't go to an M.D. on a bet. But he seemed to remember that they were legally limited in certain ways; couldn't write prescriptions except for vitamins or give shots.

He opened the desk drawers. There wasn't much in any of them. A couple of prescription-form pads with Nestor's name and office address printed on them, a couple of ballpoint pens, in the top drawer. The next one down was filled with sample packages, mostly of different vitamins. In the bottom drawer he found a half-empty fifth of scotch, an expensive brand. The other drawers were empty. It looked as if Nestor hadn't used his desk much.

He got up and walked round the little office. The bookcase held mostly medical textbooks. But thrust carelessly on top of the books on the middle shelf was a large scrapbook with simulated leather covers. He took it out and opened it, and had a little surprise.

Evidently, and maybe it figures, Nestor had been a snob. Interested in high society. The book was half filled with clippings from newspaper society pages, and quite a few pictures. *Mr. and Mrs. E. Montague Fairfield have announced the engagement. . . . The Richard Priors and their twin daughters Jean and Janet were entertained at a formal dinner by our charming visitors from Paris, M. and Mme. . . . The well-known hostess and clubwoman, Mrs. Lyman Haines, in her Bel Air home, displays Loper's new informal at-home gown, while her daughter Sheila . . .*

A little funny, thought Hackett. There were several clippings not yet taped in; the uppermost one was quite a lengthy article, and the name Marlowe caught his eye. He scanned it briefly.

Mr. and Mrs. William Maxwell Marlowe have announced the engagement of their youngest daughter, Susan, to Baxter W. Stevens III. Miss Marlowe . . .

High society, all right. Hackett put the book down and did some more looking. Wandered down to the examination rooms. This kind of equipment, he thought, was probably damned expensive, and both examination rooms were fitted out the same. Both had tiled sinks. The steel examination tables, with handles to tilt them in various directions, and those gadgets for taking blood pressure, the latest type, attached to the wall. Steel lockers against the wall. Metal tables bearing glass jars of cotton swabs, tongue depressors, a lot of bottles filled with tablets and capsules. He opened the locker in the first room; it was empty. The other one had a padlock on it; he had Nestor's keys, found one that fitted the padlock. Inside the locker was a wrinkled white smock hanging neatly on a hook, and on the little shelf, folded together, a pair of rubber gloves.

Quite expectable, he thought sadly. What the hell was wrong here? Just something a little funny, that he couldn't put a finger on.

Palliser had found an address book in the desk. See what showed up there, but . . .

And back in the office, with Miss Corliss still telephoning in the background, he thought abruptly that those two examination rooms hadn't been quite the same.

He went back to the rear one, next to the office. Near the door stood an electric cabinet, squarish, about three feet high. That hadn't been duplicated in the other room. It was white porcelain, baked enamel, and across its front was a neat metal plaque. *Sterilizer.*

"I guess that musta been the guy killed Roberto all right," said Miguel Garcia. He was still half scared, self-important, self-conscious, genuinely awed at his own good luck. "I guess it was lucky I ran."

"Maybe it was," said Palliser, beginning to feel a little hopeful. It was after five; he wondererd if Bert or Landers had come up with anything at one of the hotels. He'd taken part of the hotel list himself, had drawn blank, and then started to hunt up all the boys who'd been at that Scout meeting. Miguel was the ninth one he'd talked to; none of the others had known anything. He'd found Miguel in this big schoolyard, pointed out by a couple of other kids, and was talking to him here on a rickety wooden bench in the still hot sun. Of course, he remembered absently, actually it was only a little after four, sun time.

"Tell me exactly what happened, Miguel." He lit a cigarette. "Everything you remember."

"Yes, sir. Excuse me, but nobody's supposed to smoke on the school ground." Palliser started to say that it didn't matter, it was after school hours and he was grown up, and met Miguel's solemn dark eyes, and stepped on his cigarette. A kid like Miguel, several counts on him already, who unlike some kids down here seemed to have some respect for the rules, and parents who encouraged him to join the Scouts—well, no harm to set an example. He smiled at Miguel, who was small for his fourteen years and a nice-looking boy, if slightly grimy at this end of a day. "Let's hear all about it."

"Yes, sir. Gee, it's awful—Roberto getting killed like that. When we heard about it, Danny Lopez was telling about it at lunchtime, gee, I thought right off it musta been that guy—and I better tell somebody about it, I was goin' to ask my dad when he gets home tonight—"

"Well, you tell me now."

"Yes, sir. See, like I was just tellin' you, I'm the only one went the same way as him, goin' home last night." A couple of the boys had been called for by a parent, an older brother or sister, but most of them hadn't been. Down here, kids were expected to be self-reliant pretty young. And it wouldn't have been quite dark yet, what with daylight saving—full dark about eight-twenty, in July. Dusk, deepening dusk, as the boys walked along Second Street. "So we went together, I mean, I kind of caught up to Roberto, he left first. At the corner of Corto, about there. See, I had a lot further to go, we live on Angelina."

Palliser produced a city map and made him point out the place. Miguel was unhesitant. "See, I'd go the other way, up Douglas Street, about a block further along. It was the middle of that block, just before I'd go the other way 'n' Roberto'd be turning up Beverly, see. There was this guy standin' there by the curb—just standin' there's all." He warmed to his tale now, and his dirty hands flew out in gestures. "I dunno why he scared me, it was just something about him—way he stood, kind of still, or something. Just as we come by, he stepped out nearer an' started to say some-thin'—he said something like, 'Hey, kids'—only then I looked at him, and when I saw his face I was all of a sudden awful scared, and I just went on, kind of fast. But Roberto stopped. An' I—an' I went on faster, up toward the corner, and then I looked back and Roberto was still talkin' to the guy—I thought I'd call him, tell him come on, but then I didn't. And, well, the light turned green an' I—just ran. But gee, it musta been *him*. The one *did* it. That Slasher, like they call him. Why do you suppose he wanted to kill Roberto, anyways?"

"We don't know," said Palliser. "Now, what did the man look like, Miguel?"

"Gee," said the boy regretfully, "I didn't have much of a look at him, mister. It was funny, what scared me about him, I mean he didn't try to hit me or have a gun or nothing. Kind of the way he *stood*. I dunno. It was almost dark, you know, and not anywheres near a street light. He—he was kind of tall and thin, I guess—I don't remember nothing about his clothes—except, well, they seemed kind of loose on him, like they didn't fit good. And he had this kind of red face, kind of nasty-lookin'—"

Palliser took him over it again, but nothing else emerged. Miguel couldn't say what kind of face, thin or round, long nose or short, anything definite. The man had had a hat on, he hadn't seen his hair. "It was just a *minute*, see—and it was nearly dark—"

It was the most definite information in yet, and what did it amount to? A tall thin man with a red face. And considering Miguel's size, a medium-sized man might look tall to him. And come to think, in the dusk how had the boy seen the red face?

He thanked Miguel and went back to his car. Get a formal statement from the boy tomorrow. Report in, see if they wanted him to stay overtime —if not, might go to see Roberta, if she wasn't busy correcting her fourth-graders' papers. He yawned. He wondered if Hackett had got anything on that chiropractor.

This Slasher. Hell of a thing. . . . "Manners maketh man," he thought. If that Reyes kid hadn't been so well brought up, to stop and an-swer the stranger on the street, he might have been as alive as Miguel Garcia, who had providentially got scared and run.

But this was a little something, from Miguel. Piece by piece you built it up.

He drove back down Vignes to First Street, up to Los Angeles Street, and parked in the big lot behind the solid looming rectangle of the Police

Facilities Building. He realized he was hungry. He took the elevator up to the homicide office and asked Lake if Hackett was in.

"No, he just called in. Said for you to call him at home."

"O.K." Palliser passed on Miguel's story. "Not much, but more than we had before. You might circulate that very vague description around." That was easily said; it would entail a lot of work. Every patrolman had to be briefed, and because you couldn't confine it to just the one area—the Slasher might turn up anywhere next time, God forbid—every precinct station, the sheriffs' boys, and suburban forces. Just in case. They were running an extra car tonight, around that downtown area.

Higgins was on night tour this month; he lounged up to hear about it, and said he'd start the phoning. "Hackett turn up anything definite on that new case?" asked Palliser.

"I don't think so," said Lake. "But he said he doesn't like the way it smells. Could be he's pinch-hitting for our Luis, havin' hunches."

Palliser yawned. "In Bermuda about now, I understand," he said. "I wish I was in Bermuda. Listening to some nice calypso over, say, a Cuba Libre. . . ."

FOUR

"You will," said Angel, standing on tiptoe to kiss him at the door, "have to learn to curb your language, Art."

"What? What have I been saying wrong?"

She laughed. "I scolded Mark for pulling the cat's tail a while ago and he distinctly said, 'Damn.' "

Hackett grinned. "Starting young. You all right? You left those trash cans for me to bring in, I trust."

"I did. Of course I'm all right. Once you get past the morning-sickness bit—I never felt better."

"Well," said Hackett doubtfully. It seemed quite an undertaking to him.

"Silly," said Angel, and her mountain-pool eyes that shaded from green to brown were smiling at him. Mark Christopher, who would celebrate his second birthday two months from now, fastened like a leech on Hackett's left leg and demanded imperatively, "Kitty-kitty!"

"How the hell did we get into all this?" asked Hackett plaintively. "We said two, but if this isn't a girl—I know you—and I'm not a millionaire like Luis, just remember."

"I don't mind if it's not a girl," said Angel. They wouldn't know about that for five months. "We can always try again."

"That's just what I said. Nothing doing. These days, they all expect college—"

"The more we have," said Angel logically, "the better chance that one of them will make a lot of money and support us in our old age. And there's a sort of exotic new French casserole for dinner. Yes, I remembered about calories—though I think the doctor's silly about that, you're a big man, you need lots of good food. You're not really too fat."

"Not yet," said Hackett gloomily. Ten pounds off, the doctor had said firmly.

"And you don't have to go out again, do you?"

"Well, there's a new one come up, on top of this damned Slasher thing. I'd better call in, anyway, and if anything new has turned up—"

Angel made a face at him. "Why did I ever marry a cop?"

"You want to be reminded?" He reached for her again but she laughed and backed off.

"Fifteen minutes—I'll just get it out of the oven."

"*Daddy* get kitty-kitty!" said Mark Christopher.

Hackett looked around and pointed out kitty-kitty: the big smoke-silver Persian curled in his basket by the hearth. "Kitty won't play!" said Mark tearfully.

"Well, old boy, I can't do anything about that," said Hackett, who had learned this and that about cats in the time since Mendoza had wished Silver Boy on them. He sat down in the big armchair.

That Nestor. The outside thing, or the personal, private kill? Something a little funny there, anyway. Those files . . .

Something nagging at him—some little thing.

Chiropractors. *A four-year-course now.*

The evening paper, the *Herald*, was unopened there on the ottoman. He didn't pick it up.

The Slasher. Quite the hell of a thing. The sooner they picked that one up . . .

Some little thing he'd noticed, there. And for some reason he didn't much like that Corliss woman. There was also the wife.

And . . .

"A *sterilizer*," he said aloud suddenly. "A *sterilizer*."

"Well, I try to keep the place reasonably clean," said Angel amusedly from the dining-room door. "Need we go quite that far?"

Alone out there in the night, a man walked a dark street. His mind was a confused jumble of thoughts, and all the thoughts were full of hate.

As long as he could remember, he had hated, and envied, and resented. He had learned to hate early, and learned why afterward.

He had hated the unknown mother who had left a baby to the orphanage. He had hated the unknown father who had begotten the baby. He had hated all the other children who laughed at him and called him names, and hated the women at the orphanage who called him stupid and punished him for breaking silly rules.

Other people had things, incomprehensibly and unfairly. Things he had never had and didn't know how to get—things he realized only dimly were good to have. Other people concerned about them, and homes, and settled existences. He didn't know why. He didn't know why about anything, except that he hated.

He walked the dark street, an entity full of vague undirected hatred against the entire world, and his hand closed over the knife in its sheath, hard.

They had called him names, the other children. Laughed at him. People didn't like to look at him, you could see it in their eyes. As if he was a monster or something. Ever since the fire that time in the school, and the pain—the awful pain . . .

Nobody, he thought. Nobody. Everybody but him. Everybody against him. Bosses, calling him dumb. Girls . . . Everybody hating him. He could hate right back, harder.

But there was always the blood. He liked seeing the blood. Things felt better then. He got back at them then. For a little while.

He came to an open door, hesitated, went in. It was a bar, dark and noisy and crowded. He shouldered up to the bar and found a stool, ordered whiskey straight.

He felt the weight of the knife in the sheath on his belt. The man on the stool next to him, raising an arm to light a cigarette, jostled him; instant red fury flowed through him like an electric current, but the bartender had put the shot glass in front of him and he picked it up with a shaking hand.

"Sixty-fi' cents," said the bartender.

He felt in his other pocket, threw a silver dollar onto the bar. He drank the whiskey, and as it jolted his insides he felt a little better.

"You like to buy me a drink, honey?" A hand on his arm, insinuating. He turned and looked at her. Another one like that last one—a kind he knew, knew all about, the only kind of woman he'd ever had, ever could have. She was a little high, her voice was slurred, she had a scrawny aging body and her lipstick was all smeared. "You buy a lil drink for Rosie, an' Rosie'll be nice to you, honey. I seen you before, ain't I? Around—"

He laughed and leaned into the light from the blaring TV above the bar, and she gave a little gasp and drew back.

"You seen me before?"

"No—maybe not." She'd have stepped back farther, but he put his arm around her and closed his hand cruelly round the thin sagging breast. "I buy you all the drinks you want," he said savagely, "an' pay you besides. Is it a deal?"

"Sure—it's a deal," she said dully. "Can I have a drink now, honey?"

"Sure thing," he said. He hated her, hugging the hate to himself. The way she'd gasped and looked away.

Everybody in the world, except him. His hand went secret and sure to the knife.

There was always the blood. . . .

Mendoza's turn at the newspaper and magazine counter finally arrived and the fatherly attendant turned his British beam in his direction. "Do for you, sir?"

"I see you stock some American papers—I don't suppose you've got a Los Angeles paper? A *Times*?"

The beam faltered. "Well, now, I'm afraid not, sir. I don't recall that I've ever been asked—"

"Well, could you get me one, please?"

"I really couldn't say, sir. I can try. Beg pardon, what was the name again?"

"The Los Angeles *Times*," said Mendoza hopefully. He looked around the vaulted immense lobby of the luxury hotel, the new sports jacket feeling uneasy on his shoulders, and felt homesick. Nearly two weeks out of touch now, and they were staying here another week before flying home.

"Beg pardon, would you mind—that's L-O—? . . . Yes, sir. Er—would that be California, I presume?"

"It's quite a well-known town," said Mendoza irritably.

"Yes, sir. I'll see what I can do, sir. 'Kyou, sir." The beam turned elsewhere.

Mendoza turned away and a diffident voice said, "Another Californian? I just flew in myself—if this is any use to you, you're welcome." A big hearty-looking man in city clothes, smiling, holding out a folded newspaper. "Kind of foolish to extend the feud this far from home." The paper was a San Francisco *Chronicle*, with yesterday's date on it.

"Thanks very much indeed," said Mendoza. The big man waved away gratitude.

Carrying his treasure under one arm, Mendoza wandered down the lobby toward the alcove where he'd left Alison. Alison was enjoying the vacation anyway, he thought gloomily. And probably, just as she said, it was only egotism.

Alison was chatting with Mrs. Garven; inevitably, they were showing each other snapshots. Of Mrs. Garven's two rather plain daughters back in Montreal, and—of course—of the twins. When the Kitcheners abandoned them in favor of a round of night clubs, Mrs. Garven had attached herself. Garven was a prosperous businessman, with an ulcer to prove it, and all he talked about was common stock, its vagaries and inner economics, which Mendoza knew as much about as he knew or cared about the migration of lemming.

It was a fine hotel, and the weather was nice, and the service excellent, if they did keep pressing exotic rum drinks on you. But he still felt self-conscious without a tie, and he still felt uneasy about being so far from home. Suppose something big had come up. Or Art should have come down with Asian flu or something. *Quizas,* and so what? Other good experienced men in the office.

He sat down opposite Alison and Edith Garven and lit a cigarette. "Just eleven months," Alison was saying rather wistfully. "But Teresa's walking already and Johnny probably is by now too. It does seem ages we've been away, but we have such a wonderful nurse—"

Mendoza opened the well-handled *Chronicle* and started to hunt through it for any news from L.A. The alleged feud was largely a joke, but for all that the San Francisco papers were a little chary of printing news about Los Angeles, and prone to treat it sarcastically where possible. The headlines were about forthcoming elections, a senatorial speech, an argument in the House. A socialite wedding. A dog show. He turned pages hopefully.

". . . must go up and dress, Ted and I are going to that amusing calypso place tonight. Have you been there yet?"

"Yes, last night. Well, I didn't exactly—"

"Of course the songs do tend to be *rather* . . . But I feel one should be *broad-minded,* my dear, especially in a foreign country. I—"

"¡Ca!" said Mendoza softly. The bottom corner of this page had been torn, but he saw the dateline, *Los Angeles,* and carefully held the torn pieces together to read the brief story tucked away on the third page.

Los Angeles, July 14.—A fourth victim of the latest mass killer roaming the City of Angels was found today, a teen-age boy. The Slasher, as he is locally known, has murdered and mutilated two men, a woman, and the boy within a period of less than two weeks. His first victim was left in a hotel room almost certainly rented by the murderer, but police as yet have apparently no clue to his identity.

"*¡Por Dios!*" said Mendoza to himself distractedly. "My God—that body in the hotel—I *knew* there was something about it . . ." He could vividly imagine all the desperate hunting, the try-anything routine, on a thing like that. And no details at all, of course, damn it—not from 'Frisco. He got up and paced down the lobby, muttering to himself. The Slasher. My God. My God, four people—a mass killer, one of those berserk killers. He wished to God there'd been just a few details. Damn.

He thought, I could call Art, long distance. And what good would that do, to know the details?

"*¿Qué ocurre, querido?*" Alison put her arm through his. "I do wish you'd cheer up and enjoy yourself more. You look—"

He told her, thrust the folded paper at her. "I know what sort of job one like that is, damn it. I should never have let you drag me this far from home. God knows what a mess that is, and don't I know it, the press needling us for not dropping on him inside twenty-four hours—probably damn all in the way of evidence—"

"Now look," said Alison reasonably, "there's Art, and John Palliser, and a lot of other perfectly capable men still there to cope with it, Luis. It's hardly as if you were—were shirking your duty or something like that. And it's silly to worry about it when there's nothing you can do. Look, it's nearly six o'clock. Let's go up and get dressed, and we said we'd try that Spanish place the taxi driver recommended. *¿Cómo no?* Come on, be sensible and forget it."

"Oh hell," said Mendoza miserably. He trailed upstairs after her, to the luxurious big room that he disliked further because it had twin beds, and shaved and got into the uncomfortable evening clothes she'd insisted on; but he didn't forget the Slasher. He could just imagine what the boys were going through. And a few other cases on hand too, probably.

He hadn't any *business* to be here. He ought to be home, joining the hunt.

He could call Art. He could—"*¡Mil rayos!*" he said to the very bad rye that the Spanish place had produced with prodding. He'd had a feeling all along . . .

There was a boy with a guitar who sang, but Mendoza hardly heard him. He was back home, with a harassed Hackett and all the rest of them, visualizing the routine they'd be setting up, the tiresome questioning, the eager follow-up of any small lead. On one like that. The Slasher. Hell. Thirty-five hundred miles . . .

"Well, you understand, I don't want to get anybody in trouble," said Mr. James Clay. "You couldn't help liking Frank, he was that sort of guy, but that doesn't say I exactly approved of all he did. Not that I'm a prude, but—"

Mr. Clay was being fairly helpful in building backgrounds, and Hackett drew him out hopefully. Frank Nestor had once worked as a salesclerk in Clay's sporting-goods shop on Hollywood Boulevard, and they had, Clay said, kept up. Clay only a few years older than Nestor, a friendly, pug-faced little man.

"He was doing real well the last few years, since he got to be a chiropractor. But from what he said here and there, I don't figure he was being just so ethical at it, if that's the word. . . . Oh well, he said once you'd be surprised how you could rook the old folks, selling 'em regular courses of special vitamins and so on, at ten and twenty bucks the bottle. Like that."

That figured right in with what Hackett was beginning to build on Nestor.

"Mind you, I guess most chiropractors are honest, like most M.D.s. I go to one regularly," said Clay, "chiropractor, I mean, for my sacroiliac, and he's good, too. I asked him about it once, after I'd heard Frank say that, and he said it's so, there are a few of 'em just in it for the money—well, like some M.D.s, I suppose—and they rake it in by overcharging for vitamin pills, supposed to be something new and different. I could figure Frank doing that, and just thinking it was smart. And yet you couldn't help liking the guy. He had what they call charm—you know?"

"That kind isn't usually shy with the opposite sex," suggested Hackett.

"Sure as hell he wasn't," agreed Clay. "That I can tell you. I started out feeling sorry for that wife of his, but in spite of everything I couldn't keep it up. And *my* wife said the same. So, anybody knew them knew he'd married her for the money—her old man was a millionaire, everybody thought then. Turned out he'd lost most of it before he died. Frank was working for me when he married her, you know—six, seven years back. She should've known what kind Frank was, when she'd been married a month. He was making a good salary here, but he always had expensive tastes—and he was always ready for a little session of poker. He didn't go out of his way to be mean to her, just the opposite—he wanted everybody to like him so bad he was nice to everybody, her included. But she just asked for it. Acting like a doormat, you know. Never complaining when he lost the grocery money at cards, or like that. Never standing up for herself, or trying to fix herself up a little. I never could take to the woman somehow. . . ."

It seemed that Nestor, Clay, and several others used to get together for poker a couple of times a month, and Nestor had talked, casually, about his girl friends, about his lucrative practice. "I don't mean he'd come right out with names and details—Frank wouldn't do that. On the women, I mean. But he'd say things like, he had a date with a hot number tomorrow night, or something like that. So I knew he was stepping out on his wife a lot."

"Did he ever mention a name to you at all?"

That was where Clay said again he wouldn't want to get anybody in trouble. "He did, once. About two weeks ago, last time I saw him, matter of fact. He had the tail end of a nice shiner—about three days old, you know—and I asked him about it. He laughed and said, oh, Ruthie's husband had caught up to him."

"Ruthie." There was a Ruth Elger, and an address, in Nestor's address book. "I see."

"I guess at that," said Clay, "even if he wasn't just so level, at that job, he'd have been good at it. He'd always wanted to be a surgeon, he used to say, and he was good with his hands, any hand work. I understand now it's not like it used to be, this chiropractic thing, a six-week course anybody could take—it's like a regular college course, and they have to take all the pre-med classes. He may have turned quite a few unethical bucks, but he was really interested in it and no fool, you know. I don't know how much it's worth to you, Sergeant, because I couldn't say whether it was so, but he told me once his family had had a lot of money, he'd always had everything, and been going to go to medical school and so on, but after his father died his mother got hooked by some con man and lost it all. He said he'd made up his mind to get his however he could—he was kind of bitter about it."

"And that might figure too," said Hackett. "Could be. Now, you knew him pretty well, Mr. Clay. This could be what it looks like, the break-in after drugs or cash, and the impulsive assault. But not so many burglars carry guns. It could also be a private kill. And generally speaking, in a case of murder, the deceased has done something—or been something—to trigger it off. Could you make any guesses as to who might have wanted Nestor dead? Off the record—just between us."

"Hell," said Clay, "that's a thing to ask me, Sergeant." He looked down at his scarred old desk there in the back room of his store, the untidy pile of invoices, business letters. "I don't know about any—you know—specific person. Far as I know, everybody liked Frank just fine. But I'll say this much. If it was like that, the private reason like you say, I'd make a guess that it was most likely over some woman. Some girl's husband or boy friend. He liked the girls—and they liked him."

"Yes. What about his wife? Do you think she—felt anything about him any more? Enough to—"

"His *wife?* Hell, I don't know," said Clay doubtfully. "That's—well, I don't know, I never could read that woman." That makes two of us, thought Hackett. He wanted to see Andrea Nestor again. "You think a *woman* might have—Lord, what a hell of a thing, old Frank getting murdered. . . ."

"Well, we'll see what turns up," said Hackett. He thanked Clay and went out to his car. One of the new Traffic Maids, on her three-wheeled cycle, was righteously making out an overparking ticket for him. Without compunction Hackett pulled rank on her and got the ticket torn up. No millionaire indeed, with another one coming along he needed every dollar he earned.

What, he wondered again, had Nestor wanted with a sterilizer? Chiropractors weren't allowed to give shots or do anything they'd need surgical tools for, were they? Instruments that would have to be sterilized. There was just the glimmer of an idea in his mind about that, but resignedly he thought there'd be no way to prove it—now. That Corliss woman. He could kick himself for such stupid carelessness, leaving the place wide open. . . . He wanted to see her again too. And he wanted another try at that desk clerk in the Third Street hotel, the man who'd been on the desk when the Slasher signed for a room. The man was hardly the world's greatest brain but he must have noticed more about the Slasher than he claimed to remember.

Hackett ruminated behind the wheel, uncertain where to go from here. There were a lot more places to look, on the Nestor thing, than there were on the Slasher. But that one was the one most urgent to catch up to. God, yes.

The prints in Nestor's office had been mostly his and Margaret Corliss'. It would be largely wasted effort, probably, to track down all his patients and get their prints to compare to the unknown ones in the office; probably X had worn gloves or wiped off anything he'd touched.

If it had been the casual thief, why hadn't he taken Nestor's starsapphire ring and jade tie clasp, along with the cash? Of course, it could have been juveniles after drugs; in the dark they wouldn't notice from the sign that Nestor had been a chiropractor and wouldn't have any drugs on the premises. But . . .

Margaret Corliss had said at first that she'd come to call and put off the patients because—how had she put it?—it would be awkward having them come in while the police were there. And then later on she'd said that there never were any patients on Wednesdays. Hackett got out his note-book, turned to the page where he'd written down the facts of that odd lit-tle encounter with Miss Corliss, and added that one.

That button. By the thread hanging from it, maybe already loose; so when Nestor saw the gun, made a grab for it, he got the button instead? Button from, probably, a man's jacket. Just an ordinary dark gray button.

He couldn't sit here the rest of the afternoon. Where now?

They had the bullet out of Nestor's skull, and not too much damaged: a .22. When, as, and if they ever found a possible gun, Ballistics could prob-ably say whether it was the right one.

Well, all right. Go and see Ruth Elger, whose husband had presumably given Nestor a black eye. Go and see everybody listed in his address book. See Mrs. Nestor again. . . .

While the berserk killer roamed around loose. Hell.

Hackett started the engine. It was Friday afternoon, getting on to five o'clock. He'd promised Angel he'd be home for dinner, but he thought he'd go out again afterward. See that desk clerk: he was on the night shift, wouldn't be on until nine o'clock. See Mrs. Nestor. See—

FIVE

Hackett went back to headquarters to report in, see if anything had turned up that looked interesting. Something had, and how much was it worth?

"I happened to be in," said Palliser, "so I talked to her. A Mrs. Constance Brundage. About fifty, too fat, nice motherly soul but not much in the way of brains. She made a statement. Your guess is as good as mine whether it's worth anything. She said she was waiting for a bus at the corner of Western and San Marino, last night about eight o'clock, when a man came up to her. She was alone on the corner. She said he looked 'sinister' because he had a hat pulled down over his eyes and his jacket collar turned up, which looked funny on a warm night. Said he had a sinister voice too, like a gangster, she said."

"Yes," said Hackett. "Naturally. *¿Qué más?* And how much of that is imagination?"

Palliser shrugged. "What with all this press hysteria— Anyway, she said he came and stood 'too close' to her, and she got nervous, and then he said he needed bus fare and she looked like a nice kind lady, would she give him a dollar? And she said no, and backed away, and he followed her—and goodness *knows*," said Palliser in obvious quotation of Mrs. Brundage, "*what* would have happened, except that the bus came just then and she got into it in a hurry, and the sinister stranger didn't. But on thinking it *over*, she was sure it must have been this terrible Slasher, and it was just the Lord's mercy she hadn't been his fifth victim. And—"

"*¡Basta!*" said Hackett. "Description?"

"Very vague—it was dark. Just one little thing made me think twice, and get a statement. She can't say anything about his features, and says vaguely he was about medium-sized. But she did say that his clothes didn't seem to fit, looked too big for him. And Miguel Garcia—who's a much better witness—said the same thing about the man Roberto stopped to talk to."

"So he did," said Hackett slowly. "Food for thought. I'll be damned. On the other hand, John, a lot of bums around town are wearing hand-me-down clothes that don't fit."

"True. I just mentioned it," said Palliser.

"And asking for money. Of course we don't know the hell of a lot about him. It could be. Corner of Western and San Marino—if so, out of the territory where he's been operating. Nice."

"You get anything new on Nestor?"

"This and that—maybe," said Hackett. "I don't know. I've got a funny little idea, but how the hell to prove anything? I want to see the wife again, and the people in his address book. And Ruth Elger's husband. I also want to have a heart-to-heart session with that desk clerk. He must have noticed something more than we've dragged out of him."

"I don't know," said Palliser. "It's not the kind of hotel where they give guests the eagle eye to see if they're respectable. And it was about ten o'clock at night."

"All the more reason for him to notice, damn it. Business'd be slow," said Hackett. "I want to talk to him again, anyway."

"Wish you luck," said Palliser, shrugging again. It had been a hot day, and he was tired. But he had a date with Roberta Silverman and was anxious to get away, to a cool shower and a shave and a clean shirt, and Roberta's dark eyes smiling at him across a table and a long cold drink.

He didn't know then that this was an important conversation, that tomorrow he'd be racking his brains to remember just exactly what Hackett had said to him. The night shift was coming on. He told the night desk man where he'd be and went down to the lot for his car.

That night, at ten minutes past ten, the man full of hate took his pleasure in blood again. He had been with the old lush Rosie, but it hadn't lessened the taut violence in him. He had taken the half-empty bottle with him when he left, and on the street he stopped to drink from it. The raw spirit didn't seem to get to him, though he'd had four or five drinks before, with Rosie.

He walked on down the dark street, the vague hatred churning inside him. At the corner he turned; he had taken a room at a place on this street, just today. But he didn't feel like going there, to sleep.

There was a full moon, a great silver circle of serenity riding high above the city, casting clear silver light on the streets. He walked under it, hating.

At a corner two blocks up, a young and pretty Negro girl waited for her husband to pick her up. She had been visiting her sister and her sister's new baby, just home from the hospital; and her husband, Joe Lincoln, would pick her up here on his way home from work as a clerk at a local supermart. She was smiling, thinking about her new niece, for she was expecting her own first child in two months.

It was a nice warm night, and there was a bench here; Joe would be along in a few minutes. Besides the moon, there was a street light at the corner, it wasn't dark.

The man full of hate came up behind the bench and stopped to drink from the bottle again. She heard his steps and turned her head, and saw him clearly. Small shock registered in her eyes, and she turned quickly away.

Another one, looking at him as if— And a nigger girl too. Everybody always—

His hand closed on the knife in his pocket and he lurched toward the bench.

Most of the night shift were out on that one from ten-twenty on. The husband found her there—not five minutes after she'd died, said the surgeon, in all probability, blood still flowing. She'd really been cut up, it was quite a mess, and they called every car in the vicinity to stop any and all pedestrians within six blocks. But again they drew blank—the Slasher seemed to have vanished into air.

When they'd been that close, it was irritating to say the least. They'd go on hunting, but the longer he stayed loose the colder the trail.

Higgins came back off that at twelve forty-five, talking bitterly to himself about it. Really a mess. By all rights they should have picked him up as easy as— He couldn't have been more than a couple of blocks away when the husband found her. Of all the Goddamned bad luck.

Sergeant Farrell, on the night desk, welcomed him in and said he'd go off for a coffee break, then, somebody to mind the desk. Higgins sat down at the desk dispiritedly and lit a cigarette.

He was still sitting there three minutes later when the call came in.

He said, surprised, "Why, yes, Mrs. Hackett. . . . What?" As he listened to the distrait, carefully controlled voice, his hard-bitten face went grim. "I see. All right, we'll get on it. No, he hasn't been in tonight so far as I know. . . . Yes, I see. We'll find out. I'll be in touch." As a realist, he didn't tell her not to worry.

He put the phone down. He thought something had happened all right. Not like Art Hackett, not to call her if he was held up this late somewhere.

Ten minutes to one.

Accident.

The first thing to think about. He called down to Traffic. "Just check it out, will you? Put an Urgent on it. . . . He'd have had identification on him, but just in case—better take it down—yes. Arthur John Hackett, thirty-six, six three and a half, two hundred and thirty, medium-brown hair, eyes blue. He'd be driving a dark blue four-door Ford sedan, 1957 model. . . ."

His voice was expressionless, relaying that also to the Georgia Street Emergency Hospital and the General. All they needed, he thought, Hackett out of action. If Hackett— Well, don't expect the worst. He looked up the license-plate number and relayed that to Traffic. In that first ten minutes, Traffic hadn't any record to tell him about. Farrell came back and went a little white, hearing about this.

"Does anybody know where he was going tonight?"

Which was a question that would be asked again.

"It's a heavenly beach," said Alison, groping in the closet for her beach sandals. "And morning's the best time really. Aren't you going to get up today at all?"

Mendoza was sitting up in bed smoking moodily. "What the British call coffee is no inducement. And I thought one point about taking a vacation is that you can sleep late. It's only seven-thirty." As a matter of fact he hadn't slept much. He'd lain awake worrying, coming a dozen times to the conclusion that he really couldn't ask Alison to cut the vacation short. And, damn it, they'd planned to stop off in Illinois and see the Lockharts on the way home. . . . "Furthermore," he added, "what's the point in my going to the beach with you? I can't swim. Am I supposed to enjoy myself watching every other male present ogling you? And if I wasn't the nice indulgent husband I am, I'd absolutely forbid you to wear that outrageous bathing suit."

"It's not a *bikini*, I wouldn't dare—it's a perfectly decent bathing suit," said Alison. "Well, at least get up and get dressed while I'm gone. Don't just sit there brooding." She came up to the bed. "Luis, *amado*, it's senseless. I know you feel you ought to be there, hunting down the murderer. You're not the only competent officer on the force."

"I know, I know!" said Mendoza. "Don't fuss, *amante*. Run along for your swim."

"We can have a nice leisurely breakfast afterward," said Alison, picking up her beach robe. And that was when the knock fell on the door; she pulled the robe around her and opened the door to a smartly uniformed boy who smiled at her.

"Mendoza? Cablegram f'r you—"

"Oh," said Alison.

But Mendoza was out of bed, finding small change on the dresser top, ignoring the polite, " 'Kyou, sir." He had the yellow envelope ripped open before the door was shut.

"*Luis*," said Alison, watching him. "What—"

He had gone white as death, and his mouth tightened to a grim line. He thrust the sheet at her, sat on the bed, and picked up the phone. "Travel service. . . . When's the next plane out? I don't care where, Washington or New York, wherever I can get the quickest flight to Los Angeles. . . . Well, look it up, for God's sake, and make it snappy!"

"Oh, my God," said Alison. She read it twice before she took it in. *Hackett attacked on critical list outlook bad hell of mess here can you fly soonest.* It was signed by the captain of detectives. "Angel," said Alison. "She'll be—" She stopped, looking at his face as he spoke impatiently into the phone. She opened the closet door, got out suitcases, began hastily to pack. Thirty-five hundred miles, she thought distractedly. Whyever did I say Bermuda? Not Art, she thought. Not *Art*—and Angel—

"Can you get seats on it? All right. Two. Make sure of that right now, will you? Give me the desk again. Mendoza, room 284. We're checking out in an hour, I want the bill made up, please. Yes. No. There'll be two tickets on the eight-forty plane to Washington, in my name, delivered at the desk. See they get into the right slot. I'll be down in twenty minutes." He flung off pajamas, started to dress.

"Luis—it'll be all right," she said, knowing how foolish that sounded. "Not Art—it couldn't be—"

"*¿Y cómo no?*" said Mendoza hardly. "It's not the safest job there is. You get on with that—we've got an hour or so to wait. God—ought to have some breakfast, I suppose. There's a plane to New York at noon, but this one being earlier, we might get better connections, get there sooner. We'll see."

"I'll never say you aren't psychic again," said Alison. She found she was

folding clothes blindly, through a haze of tears. Not Art, Art mustn't—
And Angel hadn't anybody, they had to get back.

It was the longest hour Mendoza had ever got through in his life. He
ate an anonymous breakfast; they were at the airport by eight-fifteen, with
twenty-five minutes to wait, but after several eternities the plane was
there, and taking on passengers.

They hadn't talked much; there wasn't much to say. He sent a cable,
and then they just waited. For the plane to take off, and then for the
plane to land in Washington. There wasn't any use making idle specula-
tions.

They landed in Washington a little before noon, and had all the nuisance of Customs to go through. There wasn't a flight direct west scheduled until nearly four, so they got the twelve-fifty flight to New York and
landed there at one fifty-five. And then they waited some more, for the
next flight scheduled to L.A., due to take off at three-ten.

"You ought to have something to eat, you didn't have any lunch," said
Alison. "Coffee, anyway . . ."

He felt empty but not hungry; he got down a sandwich without tasting
it, and a couple of cups of coffee. "At least with jet flights we can get back
in a hurry. Ten years ago—"

No use in speculating. They'd know when they got there.

The three-ten flight from New York to Los Angeles was scheduled to
land at International Airport at eight o'clock, but traveling east to west
they gained three hours, and it was just five-thirty by L.A. time when they
landed. "Can you cope with the luggage?" asked Mendoza.

"Of course, darling. Go and call right away."

He felt as tired as he'd ever felt in his life, and at the same time taut as
a coiled spring. It was nearly six o'clock before they got to the taxi rank
outside. Mendoza said to the cab driver, "Take all this stuff to 311 Rayo
Grande Avenue in Hollywood." He passed over a bill and took the next
cab in line from under the nose of an elderly dowager, thrust Alison in,
and said, "White Memorial Hospital," to the driver. "Take the freeway
for God's sake."

Alison held his hand tightly. "It's got to be all right," she said. "I don't
mean to sound like a fool, Luis, but—whatever happened—they know so
much more these days, and there's plasma, and—"

"Yes, *querida*. Wait and see."

It was six thirty-five when they got to the hospital. A brisk thin nurse directed them to the third floor, and a brisk fat nurse there directed them to a small waiting room at the end of a long corridor.

Angel was sitting there, dry-eyed, looking down at her clasped hands. She had dressed in haste, carelessly, and hadn't any make-up on; she looked as if she'd been sitting there, numbly, a long time. Hackett's older sister sat opposite her, and she'd been crying. Alison went to Angel at once. Mendoza went to find somebody who knew something, and ran into Scarne in the hall.

"Lieutenant—God, am I glad to see you! You must have made time back. They hadn't called in so long, I got chased up to see— They said they'd call if there was any change, but—"

"Let's find a doctor, for God's sake. What happened and when?" snapped Mendoza.

"It's a miracle he's still alive. He went down a cliff off Canyon Drive, in his car—the car's one sweet mess, you should—"

"¡Vaya por Dios! How—"

"He was sent over, Lieutenant. He didn't get found until 2 A.M. this morning, but then they got searchlights up there, the works, and you could see by the tracks. The car was aimed to go over—and he'd been tied up before—"

"¡Dios! You've got casts of the tire marks, you've—" Mendoza caught the arm of a white-smocked intern passing. "Doctor—"

"That one," said the intern when they'd identified themselves. "If he hadn't the constitution of an ox he wouldn't be still with us. I'm sorry, we aren't committing ourselves yet, he's still in a deep coma. There was an extensive skull fracture and internal injuries—broken pelvis, both legs, a couple of ribs, and one a bit nearer a lung than we liked. . . . Dr. Mac-Farlane operated to relieve the pressure, but as I say he's still unconscious. We don't know when or whether he'll be conscious. All I can say is— Well, you can see him, but—"

"Who've you got stationed here?" Mendoza asked Scarne. He knew there'd be somebody, to get whatever Hackett said when and if he regained consciousness.

"Fellow named Evans."

Mendoza knew Evans, a uniformed man bucking for rank. He nodded at him, installed in a chair beside the door not too far from the high bed. He stood over the bed and looked at Hackett. Hackett lay on his back, breathing slow and irregular. His face was drained of color; he looked gray. His head was bandaged, and one arm. A watchful nurse had a hand on his pulse, and they had an I.V. going.

"All I can tell you is we're doing everything we can," said the intern. "He's got a very sound constitution to help him fight. But we can't say one way or the other, not yet."

"Yes, Doctor. Will you please see that somebody calls in if there's any change? I know you've been briefed, but just remind the desk. You've got the headquarters number—ask them to call this number too, please." He scribbled their home number on the back of an envelope, handed it over. He looked at Hackett again and led Scarne out, to the little waiting room.

Angel was crying now. "I'm sorry, I don't mean— I c-couldn't, somehow, until you c-came in and I—"

"Yes, all right, darling." Alison looked at Mendoza and, seeing his expression, asked no questions.

"Angel said— I took the baby to your place, Mrs. Mendoza—your nurse—" Hackett's sister Elise Dunne looked at them helplessly.

"That's fine, Mrs. Dunne. Now, Angel—"

Mendoza came up and squatted down before Angel. "You're doing no good sitting here, either of you. They're doing all they can, and they'll call when there's any change. I've asked them to call our number too, and"—he looked at Hackett's sister—"you can give them yours. Come on now." He urged Angel up. "Scarne, drive them to our place, will you? O.K. Alison, you look after her. God knows when you'll see me, but I'll be in touch."

"Yes, darling. Come on, Angel, it's only sensible—"

"And get back downtown as fast as you can," said Mendoza to Scarne. He kissed Alison, held her hard for a second, and went out and downstairs. He called a cab and waited for it impatiently. He had work to do.

SIX

He walked into the homicide office at seven-forty, and he didn't feel any particular joy at getting back home; he was intent on the job. Most of them were there—Palliser, Dwyer, Higgins, Landers, Glasser, Farrell: on one like this they weren't punching any time clocks. And they didn't waste any time asking about the vacation, making welcoming noises at him. They all looked relieved to see him; Palliser said tiredly, "Thank God. You made time, didn't you?"

"I want a breakdown on it," said Mendoza without sitting down. "In detail. From one of you who knows the detail."

"Me," said Palliser. "We knew he was missing, from about twelve-forty. Mrs. Hackett called in. He'd left home about seven-thirty, and we're not sure where he was going. He said to me he wanted to see that desk clerk again, at that Third Street hotel. That was on the Slasher—" He gave Mendoza a terse briefing on that, enough to put him in the picture. "He meant to see Mrs. Nestor again, that's another business, and you'd better hear about that too—"

"I want the facts on Art, John."

"It's relevant," said Palliser, and told him about Frank Nestor. "Higgins called me back in and we had everybody alerted, everywhere around any area he might've been, but he didn't turn up until about two o'clock. An Edward Charlton, on his way home up Canyon Drive, spotted the wheel marks going off the road, in his headlights, and looked. The Ford had rolled about two hundred feet down—it's not a sheer cliff, just a steep hill, with underbrush and so on—turned over at least once—it was lying on its side."

"*Dios,*" said Mendoza softly. "Why wasn't he killed?"

"Coming to that. When we got the ident from Traffic, we converged up there in strength. Because Traffic said it wasn't an accident. Anybody could see that by the tire marks. The Ford was backed around to face the drop square—there's a two-yard soft shoulder either side, loose dirt that takes marks just dandy. And gunned over. Not a sign of any attempt to brake. Traffic's taking the car apart looking for anything, they're the experts on that. And we figure, with what the lab came up with, that the reason he wasn't killed is that he was already unconscious, lying across the front seat, face down."

"I did wonder why there weren't any facial cuts," said Mendoza. He sat down at his desk and lit a cigarette. The desk needed dusting, and somebody had overfilled his ashtray. He didn't do anything about it.

"So did the interns in the ambulance," said Palliser. "And for a civilian, we might not have committed lèse-majesté, but as it was we hauled Dr. Erwin himself out of bed and shot him over to the hospital. He saw him before they did the surgery, and went over his clothes." They were all avoiding Hackett's name; maybe the impersonal pronoun would help to keep this on the objective level, if anything could. As cops, they had all seen other cops killed on the job, and that was always bad; but this was something worse. Something really bad. The deliberate thing.

Dwyer got up in silence and took the lid off the shoe box sitting on the desk. "Erwin said," said Palliser, "he'd been tied up. Wrists and ankles. For one or the other, his own belt had been used." Dwyer lifted out the belt and passed it over. It was a worn brown steerhide belt with a plain buckle, and it was twisted out of its normal flatness still, where it had been used as a rope would be used.

The fifth hole in it was the most worn and frayed, but evidently more recently the fourth hole had been in use. Hackett and his diet . . . Mendoza's eyes stung suddenly. He put the belt down. He said, "Yes."

"He'd got the worst knock on the head at the back of the skull, a little to the side, not the front. The interns said he was half on the floor, head on the passenger's side of the car. Glass all over from the windshield but he hadn't a cut on him."

"Yes. I see. You've printed the car. Anything?"

"What do you think?" asked Higgins savagely. "His, that's all, and his wife's. Steering wheel and gear selector clean. Naturally."

"Naturally. All right. Why?"

Dwyer looked at Palliser. "It's your fairy story," he said. "Tell the detective man."

"And it's no fairy story," said Palliser equably. He sat smoking quietly; he looked relaxed, but his mouth was grim. "What else could it be, for God's sake? Nobody's got any private reason for murdering Art Hackett.

I'll tell you what it has to be—something he spotted on one of those cases. He was out looking, and he found out something, something definite, a giveaway. And somebody knew he had, right then. So he got knocked on the head then and there, and tied up, and the faked accident was set up later."

Mendoza was watching him. "I'll take that, John. What was he working on? Where was he?"

"We don't *know*, damn it," exploded Dwyer. "We couldn't press Mrs. Hackett too much, and she didn't seem to know anything definite anyway—"

"All he said to me—that was before he went home," said Palliser, "was that he was going to see the desk clerk, and maybe Mrs. Nestor, and maybe a couple of the people in Nestor's address book. He didn't like the way the Nestor case smelled—he thought it was a private kill, not the outside thing. We've got his notebook, with a couple of interesting ideas on that jotted down. But there's also the desk clerk, and that was on the Slasher, and *I* don't like the way the desk clerk smells."

"He denies Art came to see him?"

Palliser smiled bitterly. "You're ahead of me. Sure he does. I don't like him."

"This is where I part company," said Dwyer, "from our brain-trust boy, Lieutenant. I just don't see the Slasher, who we can build pretty easy as a hair-trigger lout with a low I.Q., setting up that faked accident."

"You'll have to convince me on that too," said Mendoza, stabbing out his cigarette and immediately lighting another. "Nobody, a hotel desk clerk or anybody else, is collaborating with the Slasher. That's the berserk, unplanned thing."

"So it is," agreed Palliser. "Let George tell you how the Slasher vanished last night. After Number Five. The pretty Negro girl, seven months pregnant. Only she wasn't so pretty by that time. At the corner of Third and Hartley, which is about two blocks from that hotel. The interns said she hadn't been dead fifteen minutes when they saw her, and the squad car couldn't have missed him by more than ten. Where did he go?"

"¡Demonios!" Mendoza sat up. "You scoured the neighborhood, George?"

"Sure we did," said Higgins bitterly. "Five squad cars and fourteen men on foot. For six blocks all around. What else? Christ, the blood couldn't have been dry on his knife!"

"Tell me a story about that," said Mendoza to Palliser.

"Of a sort," said Palliser. "Maybe he's just smart enough—hearing the sirens so soon—to threaten the desk clerk into hiding him? Clerk'd be scared afterward to admit it—or there could be some other tie-up between them. Hackett thought the clerk must have noticed more about the man than he admitted. Why was he chary of talking? Look. If Hackett was at the hotel, it'd have been after nine o'clock—the clerk didn't come on until then. The call on Number Five—Loretta Lincoln—came in at ten-sixteen. Say that Hackett had just left the hotel, was heading home. He'd go straight up Third, making for the freeway exchange and the Pasadena Freeway. He could have been at that corner about then, even, my God, spotted the Slasher at work. And followed him when he ran. So you say the Slasher isn't one to set up the faked accident. Maybe not. Maybe Hackett tangled with him, got that knock on the head, there in the hotel, and somebody else got stuck with an assaulted cop and set up the accident. All I say is, it being the same general area—"

"Same general area the Slasher's been roaming right along," said Mendoza. "Nothing says Art was there. He just might have been."

"That's what I say," said Higgins. "God, I don't know how we missed him—he couldn't have been five minutes ahead of us! But on this thing, if Palliser's right, and I don't see what else it could be, it looks the hell of a lot likelier to me that Hackett maybe went to see Mrs. Nestor and caught her talking over Nestor's murder with a boy friend or something. Or went to see Nestor's office nurse—we know he didn't like her either and from what's in his notebook neither do I—and spotted something definite. All I say is, I think it's likelier it was something to do with the Nestor case, not the Slasher."

Mendoza put out his cigarette, looking around the group. His gaze came to rest on Higgins. "Of all of us big tough homicide cops," he said mildly, "you're the biggest, at least, George. Six-three, about a hundred and ninety? Yes. Could you handle Art, boy? Half an inch taller, forty pounds heavier? Barring a fluke, a very lucky first blow that put him out, not very many men—even big men—could put Art down and out very easy. And I really don't see any female doing that. Presumably somebody had to lift him into the car too."

"Which we also thought of," said Palliser sardonically. "So she—whoever—had a boy friend. Or it was two people together."

"Yes. Damn it, if we only knew definitely where he'd meant to go, who he'd—" Mendoza lit another cigarette with a quick angry snap of his lighter. "All right, I'll go along with your story, John. It was something on a case he was working. Nobody had any reason to want him dead as Art

Hackett—only as a cop on a case. *Conforme.* So, *¿pues qué?* On the Slasher's sudden vanishing after Number Five, I might just buy—with a lot of reservations—your little idea of his scaring the desk clerk—or somebody—into hiding him. But I don't buy the idea of one like the Slasher setting up that faked accident. Of course, I will say that whoever set it up didn't take many pains with it. Didn't realize how obviously faked it looked. Which doesn't look like a brain. . . . You hadn't really settled who was handling which case. I see that. Art had been concentrating on the Slasher, most urgent, *naturalmente,* and then this Nestor thing came up and he got interested in that, sent you out on routine on the— Yes. All right. He might have gone to see anybody involved in either case. I'll talk to his wife, see whether— But I do *not* see one like this berserk lunatic—"

The office door opened and Marx came in. He had a couple of still damp five-by-seven prints in one hand. He asked, "How's Hackett?"

"No change. They'll call if— What've you got?"

Marx came up to the desk and laid the prints on the blotter. They were enlargements, a trifle fuzzy that big, of two fingerprints. "I've got a lot of imagination," said Marx. "I think Palliser's got something about that desk clerk. And on principle I don't like cops getting clobbered. Nice to see you back, Lieutenant—you made time home, I guess. These jets. So I did some overtime for you. I thought I recognized that print when I saw it blown up, so I checked."

"Well? What is it?"

"This one"—Marx lifted the first print—"is one of the prints we got off that S.P. switch. Whoever tried to wreck the Daylight. And this one, which is the exact same print of, probably, somebody's forefinger, I got off Loretta Lincoln's nice shiny plastic bag last night. After—like we know— our Slasher had rifled it. It's not hers or her husband's or her sister's."

"What?" exclaimed Palliser blankly. "For God's sake—you don't mean—"

Mendoza sat back and said, "*¿Y qué respondes tú a esto?* So the Slasher was the X who tried to wreck the Daylight. A hundred to one and no takers against. And that job called for a little planning ahead, didn't it? *Pues sí.* He had to know what time to be there, what trains were coming through before, to throw that switch at the right time. So our Slasher isn't quite the brainless lout he looks, is he? Yes, and maybe somebody who likes to see train wrecks might take it into his head it'd be fun to send a car over a cliff. Maybe, instead of using his knife on a cop who dropped on him, he did set up the faked accident. On a sudden whim." He looked round the group. "Who wants to bet?"

The outside phone rang and all of them stiffened to frightened attention.

It was Rhodes of Traffic, calling from somewhere unspecified to say sadly that they'd done what they could with the wrecked Ford and nothing useful had turned up. Just the lack of prints on anything a driver would touch, which of course said that somebody other than Hackett had last driven it.

"Yes," said Mendoza. He thought somebody had better notify Hackett's insurance agent to put in a claim on the car. He thanked Rhodes. He put down the phone and said, "I don't suppose you've just been sitting around mourning all day, boys. What have you got?"

They hadn't got much. The desk clerk's denial. Neither Mrs. Nestor nor Margaret Corliss had been located to question, nor Ruth Elger and her husband. They had seen about half the people listed in Nestor's address book, all of whom denied that Hackett had called on them last night.

"I went up there and asked around—that canyon road," said Palliser. "I don't know how much it's worth, but the people who live in the place nearest where he went over—a Mr. and Mrs. Roy Baker—say they heard a car evidently being turned around in the road, about ten forty-five. It's rather an exclusive district up there, big places—quiet road. But the houses are set back, and you'd think if they'd heard that, they'd have heard the car go over—though, of course, it didn't hit anything to make a loud crash, just plowed through all that underbrush on the way down. They say the car sounded old and noisy."

"Yes." Detective sergeants with families couldn't afford nice new cars. "Doesn't say much, no." Mendoza looked at his watch. "You've all had a day and so have I, but there's a little of it left. I want Art's notebook." Palliser handed it over. "I'll go see the desk clerk and check back on Mrs. Nestor. John, would you feel like checking back on the Corliss woman? O.K. The rest of you can keep trying to locate the other names in his address book." He got up.

The Ferrari was home in the garage. He went downstairs and commandeered a patrol car, drove over to Third Street. The hotel was called the Liverpool Arms, ostentatiously. It was a fourth-class place, old and shabby: probably had more semipermanents than transients. The block was solidly filled with parked cars; he left the squad car in front of a hydrant. It was just nine o'clock: the clerk would be here.

Inside, the lobby was narrow: bare wooden floor, a steep flight of stairs, uncarpeted, at the back; one ancient-looking self-service elevator. The desk was no more than a long narrow counter, with a sagging old armchair behind it, a makeshift shelf of mail slots hung on the wall. A door there led into some inner room. The register, closed and dusty, was on the counter; the clerk was in the chair, leaning back with closed eyes, half asleep.

Mendoza rapped on the counter and the clerk jerked upright. "Oh—all right, right with you," he said in a grumbling tone. He wasn't a very prepossessing specimen. About sixty, bald, with sagging jowls and a gross big paunch above his belt. His gray-white shirt and stained, wrinkled trousers had seen better days. He hadn't shaved that day or, probably, the day before, and he showed about five snaggly yellow teeth in his upper jaw, none below. He blinked at Mendoza. "You wanna room?"

"I want to ask you a few questions," said Mendoza sharply, and showed his badge. "A Sergeant Hackett's been here to question you before?"

"Yeah, but he wasn't here last night. I *told* 'em that. I ain't lyin' about it, why'd I lie about it?" The clerk's eyes shifted.

"I could imagine reasons," said Mendoza. "Look at me! What's your name?"

"Telfer. Adam J. Telfer. I got no reason—"

"Listen to me, Telfer. I'm in no mood to go the long way round on this! Look at me, not the floor. You know the man I mean?"

"I know him. Great big sandy feller. He's been here, but not last night. I ain't lyin'—" But his eyes kept shifting.

Mendoza reached out, took him by one shoulder, and shook him savagely. "Look at me! I can take you in, you know, and grill you better at headquarters! The truth, now!"

"You leave me be— Why'd I lie about it? He wasn't here."

"All right. You saw the other man—the one who rented the room where the body was found. Keep looking at me!" He tightened his grip.

"Yeah. I said so. But not good, see? It was only a minute."

"Tell me what he looked like."

"I *told* 'em—them other cops—I don't *know*. I didn't see him good at all. Honest I never. It was only a minute—he stood sidewise to the counter and he had a hat pulled over his eyes—I didn't—"

"He paid you two-fifty for one night and he signed the register. He was standing right here for at least three minutes, probably five, right under the overhead light. Tell me more, friend. What age was he? Dark or light? What was he wearing?"

"I didn't—" Telfer swallowed; he looked panicky. "I—they was a couple of bulbs out o' the light, it wasn't as light as it is now—"

"I don't want excuses, I want answers," said Mendoza very gently. He wanted suddenly, violently, to use his fists on this stupid creature obstructing him. He let go of the man's shoulder. "Begin at the beginning. It was about ten o'clock. He came in. What did he say?"

"Said he wanted a room, I guess. I *told* 'em all that before."

"You guess? Don't you remember?"

"Sure I remember. I remember that. But, like I say, the light wasn't so good then as it is now, and I—"

"Did you know him? Had you seen him before? Pal of yours maybe?"

"Jesus, no! Me, knowin' one like that? I said—"

"You saw him, God damn you, and you're going to tell me more or I'll take you in right now! Brace me, Telfer. We can help your memory down at headquarters—"

"I *told* 'em," said Telfer. He was nearly in tears. "He was—sort of medium, 's all. And he kept turned sideways, and he had this hat . . . And the light—"

"Anybody back you up about the dead bulbs?"

Telfer looked away, cringing. "I dunno if anybody else noticed, why should anybody—"

"Who put in new ones?"

"Damn it, I did. I don't hafta take— I *told* 'em all I—"

Mendoza looked at him, feeling very tired. He said abruptly, "You'll be seeing more of us," and turned on his heel.

SEVEN

The apartment building on Kenmore Avenue where the Nestors had lived was an old one but reasonably well maintained. According to the mail slots, they had the left-hand front ground-floor apartment. The small lobby was a little dusty; the whole place was very quiet.

He pushed the door button and heard the shrill buzz from beyond the door. After an interval he pushed it again. He wondered if she'd gone away somewhere.

But presently the door opened, a cautious few inches on its chain. "Who is it? What do you want at this time of night?"

He brought out his badge. "Just a few questions, Mrs. Nestor. May I come in?"

"Well, I must say it's a peculiar hour to come bothering at me. But I suppose if you must, you must." She unhooked the chain, stood back ungraciously to let him in. "I haven't seen you before. There were two other officers—"

"Yes. Lieutenant Mendoza. You remember Sergeant Hackett, who questioned you on Wednesday? You saw him again?"

"Why, yes. I expect we can sit down." She sat on the edge of the couch. She had undressed and was wrapped in an aged and ugly striped flannel bathrobe, hugging it round her primly. She had put her hair up in curlers, covering it with a pink scarf, and her sallow face was bare of either make-up or vanishing cream. She had on a pair of old run-down black mules with little pompons on the toes.

The room said this and that. Old furniture, most of it belonging to the apartment, very little ornament—the two pictures probably had come with the apartment too. But everything very neat and clean. The one floor lamp she had switched on in the living room cast light into the visible corner of the kitchenette, and it caught reflections from newly waxed linoleum there. She was, without much doubt, one of those persnickety house-keepers. He didn't wonder that charming, easygoing Frank Nestor had sought diversion elsewhere. He had a suspicion that when she'd made up her mind that he'd married her for her expectations and nothing more she'd subtly—and maybe unconsciously—taken revenge by turning herself into the obvious martyr.

He sat down facing her. "Where have you been all day, Mrs. Nestor? We've been trying to get in touch with you."

"Oh, have you? Well, I had to go up to Forest Lawn to make the ar-rangements about the funeral. They had the inquest yesterday, and then that other officer told me they'd released the body, so I could make the ar-rangements. And then I went to buy a black dress because I didn't have one, and it will look better at the funeral." Her voice was quite flat, ex-pressionless, and her shallow eyes were empty. "But I was meaning to get in touch with you too, because they told me at the bank that you'd been asking questions and they'd showed you all about Frank's account there. I shouldn't think that would be allowed. And I don't understand why I can't have that money—I'm his widow and he hadn't any other relations at all, at least I never heard of any. Do you know, he had nearly five thou-sand dollars in his account. I never suspected he'd saved up that much."

And it was another interesting thing, thought Mendoza. Considering that Nestor hadn't stinted himself in any direction—his star sapphire ring, the Buick convertible, the four-hundred-a-month office—he must have been raking it in from somewhere, all right. Just the marked-up vitamins?

"Did Sergeant Hackett come to see you last night, Mrs. Nestor?"

"Why, yes, he did. Just for a short time. Mr. Marlowe was here. Why?"

"Mr. Marlowe?"

"Mr. William Marlowe, he's a very fine man, he was an old friend of my father's."

"What time was Sergeant Hackett here?" He was watching her. She answered him readily, without hesitation, but without interest either.

"Why, let's see, it was early. About eight o'clock, I think. He asked me a lot of questions all over again, things he'd asked before. I must say it seemed very inefficient to me. And about Miss Corliss too. I don't know much about her, I never interfered in Frank's business. Come to think, it'd've been a little before eight, because I happened to notice the clock when Mr. Marlowe left and that was ten past."

"Mr. Marlowe was here when the sergeant came?"

"That's right. It was nice of him, he came to see if I might need a loan to pay for the funeral, you see. He's a very wealthy man." And all the

while her expressionless eyes stayed fixed on him as if she was memorizing
him.

"He left before Sergeant Hackett?"

"Oh yes. Mr. Marlowe said he knew I was tired and didn't want company, and he left, and Sergeant—whatever the name was—he took the hint
finally and left too, about half an hour later."

"And that was the last you saw of either of them?"

"Well, yes," she said. She dabbed at her mouth with a wadded-up
handkerchief. "Why do you want to know all that? I'm sure, you all ask
the oddest questions—I should think you'd be out looking for whatever
burglar it was shot Frank, instead of bothering me."

"We're wondering whether it was a burglar, Mrs. Nestor," he said casually. "Whether it wasn't someone your husband knew. Or someone you
knew."

"I?" she said blankly. "Why on earth should you think that? I don't
know any burglars, for heaven's sake. Of all the ridiculous ideas. And to
come asking questions at this hour of night, when I'd already gone to
bed—"

Essentially an ignorant woman? Concerned with the practical matters
only? The self-made martyr so wrapped up in herself she was oblivious to
anything outside? Or something a lot deeper?

The tiredness was catching up to him now. The long, long day, most of
it spent in enforced inactivity in the planes, with the frantic worry gnaw-
ing at his mind, Art . . . He got up, and he had to haul himself up by the
arm of the chair.

"All right, thanks very much, Mrs. Nestor," he said. "We'll be in touch
with you." He pulled the door open.

"I'm sure I don't know why," she said. "That's the queerest thing I've
heard yet, thinking I might know the burglar. I don't know why you have
to come bothering me."

"Don't you?" said Mendoza, swinging around on her suddenly. "Was
there a burglar at all? We don't think so, you know. Have you ever owned
a gun, Mrs. Nestor?"

She stepped back, but there wasn't any shock or fear in the shallow
eyes. "Well, for heaven's sake," she said flatly. "I should think anybody
could see how Frank came to get murdered. Of course I've never owned a
gun. I must say I don't see the point of all this. That sergeant getting me
down there for some kind of test, now I think it over, it's nothing more or
less than an insult. I'm a good Christian woman and—"

The cordite test. Negative, but it wasn't always reliable by any means.

"We'll be in touch with you," said Mendoza wearily, and went out. It was ten o'clock. He got into the car and drove back downtown to drop it at the garage. He called a cab and had himself driven home, to the house on Rayo Grande Avenue.

There were lights in the living room. It seemed years since he had last walked up this flagstoned path, opened the wide oak door to the square entry hall.

"You shouldn't have stayed up, *amada*," he said as he kissed Alison. Bast and her daughter Nefertiti ran to meet him, talking loudly, and he bent to pick them up, stroking the sleek heads. He sat down heavily in the nearest chair.

"You'll not sleep without you have a bit of whiskey in you," said Máiri MacTaggart. "Wait up indeed. Would we be going off to bed and you not in, as long a day as we've all had even so? I'll fetch it." Her kind, wise blue eyes smiled a little; she trotted out.

"Luis—"

"Well, they're not saying one way or the other," said Mendoza. "The longer he hangs on, of course, the better his chances—I suppose. He could stay in a coma for days." He roused himself to tell her the details, briefly, and what they thought about it.

"Oh, God," said Alison tiredly. She had, probably, had a bath and was wearing her newest housecoat; she had probably also had a meal, if he knew Mrs. MacTaggart. "We got Angel to bed—she'd been sitting there since three this morning, you know—and Máiri coaxed some hot broth and toast into her, and I got her to take three aspirins, I hadn't anything stronger. But if it's going to be that long before we *know*—" She wandered around the room distractedly, sat down on the couch to stroke Sheba, who was diligently applying herself to the last bath of the day. Bast and Nefertiti purred on Mendoza's lap; dimly he realized that it was nice to be home again, with the cats, and presumably the twins safely asleep in their own beds.

Mrs. MacTaggart came trotting back, looking like a plump little lamb in her woolly white dressing gown, gray hair standing out in little curls; she handed him an overgenerous supply of rye in a juice glass. "Get that down you, man," she said in her soft Scots burr. "You're doing nobody any good getting yourself fagged to death so you can't think proper. It's a caution, imagine you two traveling more than three thousand miles since this morning. You'll get that down and you'll both be going to bed. And," she added to Alison severely, "you will not be up at the crack of dawn worrying about that poor young thing in there, her man at death's door and her carrying. She'll sleep in, all the pills you gave her, and I'll see to her when she wakes."

Alison smiled at her wanly and said, "You're a tower of strength, Máiri. I don't know what we'd do without you. She even remembered Silver Boy, Luis—"

"Somebody's needed to keep a little common sense. Why wouldn't I? When Mrs. Dunne fetched the wee boy here and told me of it, of course I would think of Mrs. Hackett's cat. And that Bertha was here by then, so I just ran over in Miss Alison's car—knowing you wouldn't mind it, *mo croidhe*—and took him to Dr. Stocking's where he'll be safe until we can sort matters out. And you'd best take the man and put him into his bed, *achara*, or he'll fall to sleep where he sits."

It had been a long, long day. But he wouldn't sleep, not with Art . . .

He shook his head muzzily. The rye had hit his empty stomach like a small bomb. He thought vaguely, *Passing the love of women* . . . He hauled himself up to his feet.

"What would we do without you, Máiri? I haven't even said hello to you. . . . The twins O.K.? That's good. . . . *Déjelo para mañana*. . . . It's got to be all right, hasn't it? Alison—"

"Come on, darling, bed. You look like death. Máiri—"

"You'll not be fussing. I'll see to everything. The wee boy's snug asleep in his cot by my own bed. You see to your man. They're troublesome creatures to love," said Mrs. MacTaggart, "and often enough bringing sorrow on us, but nought to do about that but the best we can."

In the big master bedroom Mendoza flung off his clothes carelessly. The whiskey—damn the whiskey—had turned his mind numb; he couldn't think.

El Señor, the miniature lion, had officially retired on the foot of the bed hours ago, and gave them a very cold green glare for disturbing him at this hour. "Señor Malevolencia!" said Mendoza sleepily. "Alison—"

"Here, let me help you."

"Don't be silly. Quite all right. Alison, you talk to Angel, tomorrow. Find out what he said before he left—anything he told her about those cases. Explain—"

"Yes, Luis. All right."

He wouldn't sleep, because there was Art . . . *Passing the love of women* . . . But he slept, his last conscious thought that it was good to be home, to feel Alison's warmth close, and to feel the warm heavy weight of four cats at the foot of the bed.

He was in his office at eight o'clock Sunday morning, shaved and tidy in gray Italian silk with the newest discreet dark tie, mustache newly trimmed, back to civilization and the job.

The hospital said, No change.

He had read Hackett's notes, and he had read Traffic's official report on the Ford. He was now listening to Palliser, who had found Margaret Corliss in her apartment last night.

". . . said she'd been out shopping and visiting friends, and hunting a new job. Maybe natural. But there's something offbeat there, I can't put a finger on it but—"

"You haven't interpreted Art's notes. Maybe we can, with a little cerebration," said Mendoza. "I want to see that office. She said he hadn't been to see her?"

"That's right. She was home alone all that evening, nobody came to see her."

"Really. Poor girl. And she ought to be home alone at this hour too. Jimmy." He got up and went to the door. "Call that Corliss woman, tell her to be home at one-thirty, I'll drop by to see her then. . . . Here's one thing," he added to Palliser. "His wife told Art that about the time Nestor graduated from his chiropractic course he had a legacy. Which he used to fit out his very classy new office. She said to me last night he hadn't any relatives. Suppose you check that out—where'd the legacy come from? Fond godfather maybe? I'd just like to know. I'd also like to know something about Andrea Nestor's background. And the background of that Telfer at the hotel."

"Well, all right," said Palliser. He sounded a little surprised. "My own thought was, if we can find out something definite about who Hackett *did* see Friday night—"

Mendoza stabbed out a cigarette, his tenth this morning, and laughed sharply. "*Eso cae de su peso*. Sure. But how do we pin it down for sure? Margaret Corliss says he didn't call on her—so if she's lying, how do we know? Ask the neighbors if they heard her doorbell ring? If they saw a 1957 Ford parked on the block?"

"Well, hell, I know, but—"

"We've committed ourselves," said Mendoza, "to the premise that he got something very definite on somebody—real evidence. Enough for an arrest right then, maybe. On the Slasher, or on the Nestor thing. And that X knew it and took steps right then to stop him passing it on. All right. Nobody involved is going to hand us the information for the asking. Anybody who says right away, 'Why, yes, he was here'—like Mrs. Nestor—ten to one hadn't a thing to do with it. But we don't know how many places he'd been, because we don't know for certain what time he went over the cliff—or how long he'd been tied up before. ¿Cómo no? The only definite thing we're going to get is by following both of these up hard and heavy— get the Slasher, find out all about Nestor's taking off—and then we can put the finger on who sent Art over that cliff and why. And don't tell me it's the long way round. We'll be looking everywhere, but that's how it looks to me right now."

"Sense," said Dwyer laconically; he had just come in. "What chores do I get?"

"You work through the rest of Nestor's address book. Split it with Glasser—Nestor knew the hell of a lot of people. John, you look for the legacy. I'll be seeing Corliss and the Elgers. Who's on day shift? Let Galeano check into Telfer. And why in hell didn't somebody spot the one clue on the Slasher you were handed free gratis? Jimmy can check that out—"

"What? What clue?" asked Palliser blankly.

¡Porvida!" said Mendoza. "I caught that one as soon as I read the statements! I'm surprised Art didn't pick it up. Estúpidos—the silver dollar! That bar where, evidently, the Slasher got talking to Number Three— Theodore Simms. He had two straight whiskeys and paid with a silver dollar and two dimes. How recently have any of you seen a silver dollar?"

"My God," said Palliser. "I never thought— Of course you don't much any more. Only—"

"Only!" said Mendoza. "Exactly. All this Goddamned inflation. We'd all be a damned sight smarter to feel like that, hard money or nothing. But the fact remains, where do you see silver dollars these days? Can any of you smart detectives tell me?" Glasser and Scarne had come in now, were listening silently.

"God's sake," said Dwyer. "Vegas. For the high-priced one-arm bandits."

"All right," said Mendoza. "Where else? I'll tell you. Up north. Through the gold country—anywhere from Sacramento down through the San Joaquin—inland. All those conservative rural types who like the feel of the hard money. So let's find out if any more bars down around Second and Third have taken in any silver dollars lately, and if anybody remembers anything about the fellow handed them over, if so. And let's also send out some inquiries in the direction of Vegas and up north."

"On what?" asked Glasser. "I don't see—"

"¡Ignorante!" said Mendoza irritably. "Art saw that. It's in the cards our

Slasher hasn't gone off the rails so sudden. That our Number One in that hotel wasn't his Number One. Let's ask, anyway. Whether Vegas, or any place up north, has had some mysterious knifings—lately, or last year, or any time. Just for fun."

"Oh," said Palliser. "Yes, I see that. But—"

"¡*Largo de aquí!* Let's get busy and work this thing! Jimmy, get busy on all that—"

"Will do," said Sergeant Lake.

"And the rest of you, out! John, where's Nestor's appointment book?"

"Far as I know, still in his office, why?"

"I want you to look at it. Meet me at Federico's at twelve-thirty for lunch." Mendoza got up, reached for his hat, and was out of the office ahead of them.

EIGHT

He stopped to have a few words with the captain—Wiley, who had got that desk when Holmes retired last year. Wiley was always a little on the defensive with Mendoza; he thought it should have been Mendoza's promotion; Wiley had been a fixture in the Forgery office for years. As a matter of fact Mendoza had been as pleased to stay where he was; as captain he'd have had an even more sedentary job, and he always hated to delegate authority.

"I hated like hell to call you back," said Wiley, "but I knew you'd want to come anyway when you heard about Hackett—the hell of a thing—and, damn it, I'm a delegate to this Peace Officers' convention in Denver, flying out tonight." He turned the whole mess over to Mendoza with undisguised relief.

Mendoza went to look at Frank Nestor's office.

Hackett, the trained and experienced man, was also by nature a careful man. He remembered lessons and precedents. Unlike some others, he had it always at the back of his mind that through accident or some other cause another man might be taking over a case he was working; and sometimes you got asked tricky questions in court, too. Hackett took carefully detailed notes, not just cryptic jottings as self-reminders.

Sitting at Frank Nestor's desk, Mendoza opened Hackett's notebook again and reread two filled pages. He found the appointment book on the desk and looked through it thoughtfully. Quite an artistic job, he thought. He put it in his pocket and made a tour of the office.

The whole place had been searched, and the boys were usually thorough; but that was before Art had been sent over the cliff—maybe in connection with this thing. If they were doing it over now, they might take the place apart a bit more. Just in case, Mendoza looked. He upended the soiled-clothes hamper in the lavatory and was rewarded with a white smock that had a smear of old dried blood down its front.

He rather liked that, so he looked further. Stuck to the bottom of the metal wastebasket in the rear examination room he found a tiny scrap of paper with the two letters MO printed on it. It wasn't much, but he put that carefully away too.

He looked at the scrapbook full of high-society doings, and the start of a very tentative theory formed in his mind about that. He went down to the nurse's desk and looked that over very thoroughly, but evidently she'd been allowed to clear it of personal belongings. There were all five of the city telephone books there. A tedious little job for somebody, probably Sergeant Lake, but they'd have to be gone through; some people jotted down things in phone books, or underlined numbers. He took them out to the Ferrari.

He went back and looked at all the rooms again. He opened the top of the sterilizer; it was empty. He wished (as Hackett had before him) that Hackett hadn't overlooked the precaution of leaving a guard here that day, or had come back a little sooner. Couldn't be helped now. He took down the white smock hanging in the locker; it was unstained. But, after thought, he took the rubber gloves along with him. Give the lab boys a little more work.

He found, in the nurse's desk, a ledger. Whoever had kept the accounts had kept very sketchy ones. Maybe on purpose. He took that along too.

He had looked up the address and phone number before he left the office; now he dialed and asked whether Mr. Marlowe were home.

Yes, he was, who was calling, please?

Mendoza thought that sounded like a servant. Did anyone have butlers these days? A man's voice, anyway. He identified himself, said he'd be obliged if Mr. Marlowe could give him a few minutes, if he came by.

The address was on Kenniston Avenue, the other side of Rimpau. A very classy district indeed: wide quiet streets of big, very expensive houses. A good many houses sprawling over two or three city lots, with outsize pools behind them and walls everywhere for privacy. The Marlowe house, when he found it, was one of those. It looked vaguely as if it had been modeled on a French château, it had a three-car garage, and what looked like an honest-to-God butler opened the door.

He was a small man, pale-faced, in a neat dark suit; and Mendoza was a little surprise to him. He repeated his name doubtfully, taking a second glance at Harrington's tailoring, the Sulka tie, and the conservative black homburg he'd taken from Mendoza's hand. Mendoza suspected he'd check the brand name in that behind his back.

"If you'll come down to the library, sir," he said, wooden-faced. Mendoza followed him down a very wide carpeted hall, past a pair of double doors and several ordinary ones, all closed, to a door at the end on the right. The man opened this and stood back. "The—ah—lieutenant," he murmured. Very likely, before he saw the tie he'd have said, "The policeman."

Mendoza went into a large square room filled with heavy furniture that belonged in a British men's club and was another little surprise to the man who rose to welcome him. "Ah, yes—" said William Marlowe, and stopped as if he'd blown up in his lines. He eyed Harrington's tailoring and the tie too; he couldn't keep the brief flicker of surprise out of his eyes. Mendoza let his expression go very bland. He knew Marlowe's type at a glance, and he knew what Marlowe had expected to meet in a Lieutenant Mendoza.

"Well, and what can I do for you, Lieutenant? Do sit down, won't you?" Marlowe was not a big man—about Mendoza's own height, five-ten —but broader and stockier. He was about sixty, and well preserved: he'd kept his hair and not taken on much weight. He had a roundish face, regular features, the inevitable important-executive horn rims. His voice was an unfortunately high-pitched tenor, with the hint of a British accent. More probably New York and/or Harvard, thought Mendoza.

And Marlowe, prepared to condescend to a police officer, had expected one out of a 1930 detective story, had expected possibly the accent and low-class grammar, the deference to a rich man.

Harrington's Italian silk had shaken him.

Mendoza sat down, smiling at him. Marlowe was wearing a dark blue suit of excellent and conservative cut, and a plain navy tie. Mendoza glanced at his shoes and said affably, "Do you visit England very often, Mr. Marlowe?"

"I—why— Usually once a year or so," said Marlowe, taken aback. "How—"

Mendoza smiled. "The very British tailoring. Savile Row? Personally I like Harrington quite well, if you keep an eye on him." Marlowe would probably know how Harrington charged. "Just a few questions, Mr. Marlowe. You know Mrs. Nestor. You went to see her on Friday evening, I understand."

"Oh, it's about that," said Marlowe. "Yes, I did. I've always felt rather sorry for Andrea—I knew her father, poor man. She's always—" He hunched his shoulders. "She's one of those people, nothing ever turns out right for her. Perhaps it's partly her own fault—I shouldn't say so, but she's a rather stupid woman. That husband of hers, poor fellow, had all the drive and the brain."

"I believe you lent him the money for the chiropractic course?"

"Yes, so I did. I saw he was—in earnest about it, you see, and I had every confidence that he'd repay me. Which he did. That's a tragedy there. Such a wanton thing. I most certainly hope you'll find out who was responsible." Marlowe bent to proffer a silver bowl of loose cigarettes.

"Thanks so much, I'll have one of my own," said Mendoza. "When you were at Mrs. Nestor's apartment on Friday evening you met one of my men there—Sergeant Hackett."

"Yes, that's right," said Marlowe, leaning back. "Seemed a very pleasant fellow. He wanted to ask Andrea about a few things. That's a tragedy indeed, poor Frank getting killed that way. Just when he was doing so well. Probably one of these juveniles, or—"

"I understand that you left before the sergeant? Mrs. Nestor said—"

"Why, yes. Why?"

"I'd like to hear all the details," said Mendoza.

"Well, I'm afraid I don't quite see the point . . ." Marlowe looked puzzled.

"Sergeant Hackett had a most unfortunate accident later on that night," said Mendoza. "We're trying, just for the record, to trace his movements, see where he'd been and why he might have driven up to—the site of the accident, you see. Did he say anything at that time about where—" And that was very unlikely, but you never knew.

"Oh," said Marlowe. "Oh, I see. That's too bad, he seemed a very nice fellow. I hope he's not badly injured?"

"The hospital isn't very hopeful," said Mendoza. They had kept any hint out of the papers that it hadn't been an accident. Another accident wasn't very interesting news, and there'd been only a brief article about it on page eight of the *Times*. It was salutary that X should go on thinking that his faked accident had been accepted at face value.

"Oh, I'm sorry to hear that," said Marlowe politely. "Well, let me think back. I'm afraid I can't help you much. I only stayed, after he came, because I thought Andrea might—er—feel the need of a little moral support. He asked her a few questions about Frank, his usual routine and so on, and—" He stopped, and then went on, "And I saw he was, ah, perfectly polite and so on—"

"Not likely to bully the poor girl, in other words," suggested Mendoza, smiling.

"Oh well, we ordinary citizens so seldom come in contact with the police! You'll have to forgivé me, that *was* in my mind, the reason I stayed." Marlowe laughed deprecatingly. "Yes, when I saw that, I left."

"I see. And he didn't say anything to give you an idea where he was going next?" Of course he wouldn't have; that was clutching at straws. Marlowe said he hadn't. "Yes. Mr. Marlowe, you know Mrs. Nestor quite well, I understand. Did she and her husband quarrel much? Do you think she might have a—man friend outside her marriage?"

Marlowe stared at him. "What on earth gives you that idea? Absolutely not, I'd say. Oh, they didn't care for the same things, perhaps, but I think, between us, she was more or less resigned to his—call it extracurricular activities. And even if she hadn't been, I don't see what on earth you're getting at there. . . . After all, that could have nothing to do with—" Marlowe stopped, his mouth open foolishly. "Unless you're thinking it *wasn't* a burglary, that . . . ? Why, good God, it never crossed my mind—but *Andrea!* No, really, Lieutenant, if you're thinking along that line, it's quite ridiculous! I've known her since she was a child, and—" He stopped again, looking thoughtful, and then shrugged.

"Well, we try to be thorough," said Mendoza. "Do you mind telling me where you went from there?"

"Well, I came home," said Marlowe stiffly. "Here. I was here for the rest of the evening. Paul could tell you that. The rest of the family was out, but—"

"Thanks very much," said Mendoza, getting up leisurely. Marlowe hadn't quite recovered from his little surprise; covertly he was still studying Mendoza, from his sleek widow's peak, trim mustache, Sulka tie, and gold links to the custom-made shoes. And feeling puzzled. Let him, thought Mendoza. And he wondered what had suddenly entered Marlowe's mind just then, when he'd stopped and looked thoughtful, about Andrea Nestor.

He'd crossed her off—on Art—because she'd admitted he'd been there. But the assault on Art could trace back to the other case. So maybe Andrea had got fed up with her charming, crooked husband and got rid of him the permanent way.

Crooked. Pro crooked, he thought. And that was going to be one hell of a tricky thing to prove, all legal.

The Elgers lived at a nice upper-class address too, on Normandie in Hollywood. At eleven o'clock on Sunday morning he hoped to find them home.

Cliff Elger was listed twice in the Hollywood phone book: at the Normandie address and as Cliff Elger and Associates on Hollywood Boulevard. Mendoza deduced that that meant he was an agent of some kind.

The nearest parking slot that would take the Ferrari was half a block away from the apartment. Walking back, Mendoza was thinking that he'd been out of touch with the hospital for several hours. For a second something seemed to constrict his breathing.

Nothing he could do, nothing, but what he was doing. Trying to do.

How many years had it been? Art had just made rank—detective—and he'd been new in the homicide office, as sergeant, after eight years down in Vice. Eleven years. A little better than eleven years. You got to know a man damn well, working with him for eleven years.

Not the safest job in the world, no. But the risk of a random bullet from some hood's gun, the unavoidable crash in a high-speed pursuit, you expected. The deliberate, private assault—that was something different.

He had a moment of unprecedented black pessimism. This Nestor thing could easily be just what it looked like: the casual break-in. And that Slasher so damned anonymous. Trying to wreck the Daylight. Somebody who liked to watch train wrecks. So maybe somebody who'd set up another kind of wreck. And where to look for him? A thin man with a red face, said a boy. . . .

He thought it might be a useful idea to get the newspapers to run a photostat of that signature in the hotel register. Somebody might recognize it.

The apartment was a new one, very square and modern. There was a sign in front: Now Renting, 1 and 2 bedrooms, from $250. The hell of a lot of money to pay out every four weeks, he thought. He went into a square carpeted lobby and looked at the mailboxes. The Elgers were in apartment 1A.

It was the second door down, and there wasn't a bell, only a brass knocker, shield-shaped. He used it. He had to use it three times before the door was opened to him.

If this was Ruth Elger, maybe Nestor had figured she was worth a black eye. She was about five-five, with a luscious figure and big dark eyes, a tilted nose; probably mouse-brown hair originally, but she wasn't letting nature dictate, and it was an expensive attempt at imitating Alison's burnished bright copper. Dressed and made up, she'd be something to look at. Right now, she was wrapped in a rather dirty silk housecoat, and she looked pale and sick, with dark circles under her eyes.

"Well?" she said.

Mendoza introduced himself, said he had a few questions to ask.

"Oh, God, it's a cop," she said, turning into the room. "What did we *do* last night, Cliff? I don't remember going out anywhere."

"Didn't," said the man lying on the couch. He groaned. "Don't talk so loud, honey, I'm a tender plant 's morning." He was simply clad in a pair of red and white polka-dotted shorts, and he had an icebag balanced on his forehead. He opened one eye and squinted up at Mendoza, and groaned again. "False alarm. Maybe he's a cop, but I know why he's come. He wants to break into TV. It takes more than looks, brother."

"I really do want to ask you some questions," said Mendoza mildly.

"Oh, God, I feel *awful*," said Ruth Elger. "Why did we, Cliff?"

"Celebrate," said the man on the couch. Very slowly he rolled over, hauled himself to a sitting position, planted both feet on the floor. He pressed the icebag into place with one hand and managed to get both eyes open. He looked at Mendoza. "Looks, all right, you got. Latin lover-boy, mustache and all. Can you act? Can you sing? Besides, you're out of date. Ten years ago the Latin type was fine—maybe five years from now. Right now, what's wanted is clean-cut crew-cut red-blooded American boys, snub noses and all. God. They make me sick."

Mendoza produced his badge. "Hangover, Mr. Elger?"

"God," said Elger.

The woman came back from the kitchen with a cup of black coffee. She sat down and raised it to her mouth with both shaking hands.

"Celebration," said Elger. "I landed the Stoner contract for Jeffie. Bless little Jeffie's heart. Little two-hundred-grand-a-year Jeffie. Seemed reasonable at the time, celebrate. We didn't go out any place, I couldn't have hit anything or got a ticket, or did I?"

"About Frank Nestor," said Mendoza.

"Oh, my God," said Ruth Elger. "*That* awful thing." She put a hand to her head. "Poor Frank, getting shot by a burglar. Oh well, he was a bit of a bastard, but you couldn't help liking him."

"*You* couldn't," said Elger a little sulkily.

The room was—expectable, thought Mendoza. A lot of expensive modern furniture, everything wildly untidy, clothes flung over the backs of chairs, an empty gin bottle sitting on the color TV. "You gave him a black eye a couple of weeks ago," he said to Elger.

"That I did," said Elger. He put the icebag down on the couch beside him, stood up, and stretched. And Mendoza watched him, fascinated. Art Hackett was the hell of a big one, and it would take quite a lot of man to handle him. Maybe this was the man. Elger, naked except for the shorts, was quite something to see. He must be almost six-five, and he had a torso like the ads in the back pages of *True Detective:* You too can build muscular power. He might tip the scales at two-fifty, and all of it bone and muscle. Thick mat of hair on his chest, hairy legs. He had a square-jawed, nondescript face, shrewd blue eyes that right now were bloodshot and not quite focusing. "That I did," he said, and yawned widely.

"Oh, Cliff," she said, pouting. "I was mad at you about that idiotic Warren female. I didn't really think you'd— But when you got plastered at the Andersons' party you were pawing her like mad, and I— You know I wouldn't't've—"

"Damn right," said Elger. "That Goddamned little would-be charmer, twisting his damn mustache at you—" He broke off, looked at Mendoza again. "Of course," he said seriously, "your type's always useful for villains. Funny thing, seventy-four per cent of all heavies always have mustaches. I made a graph on it once. It's damn funny, because a lot of females go for them. I'll bet you do right well with the females, cop or no cop."

"So I used to," said Mendoza. "Some straight answers, please, Mr. Elger. You thought—or knew—your wife was, shall we say, dating Dr. Nestor on the side. You had a fight with him—"

"I only met him twice," said Ruth Elger defensively, plaintively. "I wouldn't have— But Cliff—"

"Suspected it," said Elger laconically. "Knew it was just to spite me. Didn't think it'd do any harm to teach him a lesson. Fight? Good God, man, him and me? I found 'em in Mike De Angelo's bar together, and sure I gave him a black eye. Pleasure. That's all. I hit him once and Ruthie and I left. What the hell? Ruthie said she was sorry, and I said I was sorry about the Warren girl—not that I'm admitting anything!—and that was that. What the hell are the cops sniffing around for?" He eyed Mendoza interestedly and patted his crop of dark curly hair. "I'm feeling better, Ruthie."

"Oh, God, I wish I was," she said.

"Did a Sergeant Hackett of my office come to see you on Friday night?"

Elger turned away and sat down again. Mendoza couldn't see his eyes, read his expression. "Never heard of him. Was he supposed to? What about?"

"Where were you on Friday evening?"

"Where were we?" ruminated Elger. "Friday. What happened to Thursday? Oh, I remember, I had lunch with that guy from New York— *that* won't come to anything—and we had dinner at Sardi's. Friday. Friday, I spent mostly with Jeffie, coaxing him to sign that Stoner contract.

God, that man. Why do I stay in this business? Thinks he can ask half a million guarantee because he's made one picture and sends the teens. Maybe he can, eventually. I was beat. And we were meeting the studio lawyers yesterday—was yesterday Saturday? I've got a dim recollection— Yeah, so I came straight home. Didn't I, Ruthie?"

"Friday," she said vaguely. "Yes, that's right. You said you needed a quiet night for once, on account of the lawyers next day. We had dinner here and didn't go anywhere."

"You were both here alone all that evening. And Sergeant Hackett didn't come to see you?"

"Nope, never heard the name. Why?" Elger cocked his head at Mendoza. "Now I look at you a second time—Knight Productions is doing a rehash of the Joaquín Murrieta thing, and you're just the type. You ever done any acting?"

"Only," said Mendoza, "in the line of duty, Mr. Elger. You were both home alone all Friday evening and no one came to see you."

"I said so," said Elger. He stood up again, towering over Mendoza, suddenly motionless, hands on hips. The only man Mendoza had run across in quite a while who would be capable of putting Art Hackett down and out. "What's it all about?" he asked.

"Oh, God, I feel *awful*," said the woman.

NINE

When he got to Federico's out on North Broadway he called the hospital. He was passed around a little, until an annoyed nurse told him that the patient's condition was unchanged, and while they realized that people were concerned, it would be helpful if they'd refrain from calling in more than once an hour. There had been four calls in the last twenty minutes, she said crossly.

Mendoza deduced with no difficulty men going off duty for lunch and taking the chance to call in. He didn't apologize, but thanked her. He went on into the restaurant, found Palliser at a table alone, and joined him. "Hospital says no change," said Palliser. "They still won't say yes or no."

"I know. Who'd you get, the nurse?"

"No," said Palliser. He looked very tired and grave; he spoke deliberately, looking at his cigarette. "I got a chatty young intern who's very interested in the case. He said that at this stage there's no way to be certain that even if he lives he won't have some permanent brain damage."

Mendoza didn't say anything to that. There wasn't anything to say. The tall Jamaican waiter came up and he said, "Bring me a drink, Adam. A double rye."

"Scotch and water," said Palliser.

Adam didn't remonstrate with Mendoza for drinking in the middle of the day; he said softly, "Yes, sir. We were all mighty sorry to hear about Sergeant Hackett's accident, Lieutenant. They know yet whether he'll get better?"

"Not yet," said Mendoza.

Adam shook his head. "I'll do some earnest praying for him, Lieutenant. I'll fetch your drinks."

Mendoza took Nestor's appointment book out of his breast pocket and laid it on the table. "Last Wednesday morning," he said, "the call came in on Nestor, and you and Art went over to look at it. While Art talked to the wife you looked around the office, as the Prints boys finished with things. You looked at this appointment book. Carefully?"

"Well, I looked at the last filled-in page to see if his Tuesday evening appointment was listed, to give us a lead. It wasn't. Then I just riffled through it."

"Look at it again, please." Adam brought their drinks; Mendoza swallowed rye and lit a cigarette.

After a minute Palliser said, "Somebody's added a good deal to this, I think. As I remember it, it hadn't much written in it—big gaps on the few pages that had anything on them."

"*Soy del mismo parecer,*" said Mendoza, and swallowed more rye. "And right under Art's nose too. He had the glimmering of an idea about it, and once I'd thought over what he'd written down in his notebook, I had more than a glimmering. . . . Small steak as usual, Adam. You'd better have a substantial lunch, John, we've got an afternoon's work ahead of us."

"Same for me, medium. What are we going to do?"

"Try to break down the Corliss woman. After I went through that office I thought any finesse would be wasted. I called Jimmy—Scarne and Bert will meet us at her place with a search warrant. I'm not gambling that we'll find anything, but you never know."

"And what did you see in your crystal ball about her?" asked Palliser.

"Where the money was coming from," said Mendoza. "And she's a very levelheaded, cool, shrewd female, is the Corliss woman, and something to tackle. The way she took that gamble—my God. And nearly brought it off too, because Art hadn't seen through it all the way. . . . That, I'll lay you any money, was a very high-class abortion mill, and I'll bet Nestor was getting some fancy prices."

"For God's sake," said Palliser. "How do you make that out? Any evidence?"

"A little, maybe. Short way round if we can induce Corliss to talk, but on that I'm not taking any bets. . . . Details later. What did you find out on the legacy?"

"Nothing, because there's nothing to find out. Nestor never had a legacy in California. But I've been back into his bank records, and it makes a funny kind of picture. About the time he told his wife he had that legacy he paid in five thousand bucks in cash—"

"It fell out of the sky on him, maybe?"

"He said, all gratuitous, he'd had some lucky windfalls at Santa Anita.

Now listen to this. For roughly the last two and a half years Nestor's been paying some nice round sums into his account every month. Paying some out too, but we know where that went—the Buick, the office, et cetera. It's run all the way between one and two thousand a month; lowest it ever fell was eight hundred. And about ninety per cent of it in cash."

"Yes, naturally," said Mendoza. "He'd ask for cash. He'd spread it out over each month, not to pay in a suspiciously large sum all at once. There'll have been a few checks for small amounts—he had some genuine innocent patients, the ones still on file."

"That's right," said Palliser. "And a couple of times when he did deposit a large amount told the teller—all very garrulous—he'd picked a lucky horse or had a lucky poker session. It does look as if you might have something. But what about this appointment book? When I looked at it before it didn't have a tenth of all those names in it—"

"Can you swear to that?"

"Yes, I can."

"Good," said Mendoza. "Right under Art's nose, by God. The nerve of the woman—I tell you, I don't think we'll shake her. I think we'll have to go the long way round to prove it."

"If Nestor was in that trade it'd be pretty certain she was in it with him, I see that."

"Almost without question. Because the money was coming in hand over fist—he must have been doing a roaring trade—and it's not the kind of business you put box ads in the *Times* about. Some woman helped him build up that trade. You notice it took a little while—about six months—and then the profits started rolling in. I could tell you a little story about it."

"You always tell interesting stories," said Palliser.

Mendoza looked at his steak meditatively. "Well, Clay said Nestor was out to get his, however it came. Also said that he'd probably have been very competent at his profession. I can see him, when he started in practice, envisioning possibilities in a mill, a first-class one, absolutely safe and reliable. Everything guaranteed. Aiming to draw the high-class females who could afford to pay a stiff price for the super service. I don't know where he picked up Corliss—she's not in our records but I think she may be in somebody's, because on all the evidence she's tough and experienced. I'll tell you what I think. I think that, round about three years ago, word began to get round here and there in the suitable places, about what number a girl should call if she was in the market for the super service. Around all the places where there'd be innocent daughters of wealthy fathers, any kind of money in combination with the kind of girls and women apt to find themselves in the market—married or not. In other words, he was trying to corner the market in that field, and I'd say he made a pretty good stab at it, judging by his income."

"That's quite a story," said Palliser. "Have we got anything to back it up?"

"The bank account. Overpriced vitamins wouldn't quite account for that kind of income. And at that, I expect all was grist to his mill, apologies for the pun, and he'd do some cut-rate ones to keep in practice. We've got a smock with a bloodstain on it, a pair of rubber gloves, a small scrap of a label which was once, probably, on an ampoule of morphine. And—"

"But listen," said Palliser, "if that was so we'd have found all sorts of evidence there! There'd be his instruments, and drugs, and hypos—"

Mendoza sighed. "We all make mistakes. Art was ready to kick himself when he began to suspect, from his notes. You started the usual routine on it, the photographs and printing and so on, but didn't begin an official search—and then Art sent you on the other case. And didn't bother to put a man on guard there while he went and had lunch." He finished his coffee and picked up the bill. "Come on, let's go try to scare Corliss."

"I'll be damned!" said Palliser. "You mean she— With him there? For God's sake. But—do you think she's the one shot Nestor?"

"I do not," said Mendoza. "In a left-handed sort of way, you've got to admire the woman. She must have had the hell of a shock when Mrs. Nestor called and told her. And what a gamble to take— I tell you frankly, in her place I'd have packed a bag and bought a plane ticket to Japan. And the fact that she didn't—well, I don't think we'll get much change out of her."

Margaret Corliss faced the four men unblinkingly, stolidly. "A search warrant?" she said. "Well, reely, I never was so insulted—as if I had anything to hide! What the world is coming to, with the police thinking they can accuse honest women—" And she looked like a very ordinary honest woman, plain and indignant, in the middle of her ordinary, rather shabby apartment living room.

"I haven't accused you of anything yet," said Mendoza. "But we're going to take some short cuts, Corliss, because I'm not feeling very tactful or talkative. Go over there and sit down. All right, boys"—he nodded to Dwyer and Scarne—"take the place apart."

"Reely, I—"

"Sit down, I said! I know all about it," said Mendoza, standing over her where she flounced into a sagging armchair. "And if you don't come apart and admit it, we'll go the long way round to collect the nice legal evidence to prove it. So one way or another you're due for a little holiday at the taxpayers' expense. I'd guess a one-to-three, if you've never been inside before. Now, Frank Nestor was operating an abortion mill and you were in on it. He—"

"I don't have to listen to your insults—dirty Mex—"

"Sit still and pay attention!" he said coldly. "You'd done some leg work on it, passing the discreet publicity. Between you, you'd built up a nice business, profitable as all hell because you were charging what the traffic would bear." Both he and Palliser were watching her for any betraying gesture or expression; she just sat, a plump plain fortyish woman, and stared back with cold eyes. But Palliser thought the eyes were watchful.

"I'm not asking you, I'm telling you," said Mendoza hardly. "This I know. I know the hell of a lot. Everything had been running smooth as silk—you'd been doing a land-office business. *Dios*, at the prices you probably got, two or three a month would make a damn nice living for both of you. And as word got round by satisfied customers—everything guaranteed safe, a real doctor—business picked up, didn't it?"

"Talk all you please," she said stolidly. "I don't have to listen."

"You'll listen. You had one hell of a shock when you heard that Nestor had been shot—"

"Oh, I thought you were going to say I shot him. Reely, blackening Doctor's name like this—wherever you got a nasty idea like that—"

"Weren't you at all surprised when his wife told you first that he wasn't feeling well, was at home, and then called to say he was lying murdered in his office? Did you know anything about Nestor's private life, or was it purely a business arrangement?" He looked her up and down, contemptuously. "Obviously he wouldn't be interested in you that way—probably nobody—"

She reddened indignantly: the one slur a woman might rise to. "Of course there wasn't anything between Doctor and me! I've got my own gentleman friend, he—"

"Oh, have you?" said Mendoza. "That's interesting. Was he here with you last Friday evening? What's his name?"

"I don't have to tell you anything! Coming here and— You've got me all confused—what's Friday got—"

"Never mind. When you heard Nestor had been murdered you knew you'd be in one sweet mess unless you could clear the evidence out of that office. You were taking the hell of a chance, but you moved fast and you had luck. You found the office open, and you found the evidence where it had been left, so you knew probably we hadn't searched the place thoroughly yet. You bundled it into your car trunk—and don't think I can't tell you what it consisted of!" He gave her a wolfish smile. "There'd have been a few surgical tools, probably in the sterilizer—and whatever supply was on hand of the morphine he used for anesthetic—and we'll find where he was acquiring that too, probably from some local pusher—and I really do think Doctor had kept a record of all his under-the-counter patients, and while he never let you lay hands on it, you knew where it was and you took that too. Once we had made any kind of search, the whole thing would have been obvious—and how obvious that you'd known all about it! As it was, there were a few more details you had to take care of, but just as you started back to the office your luck ran out. A big tough sergeant of cops drove up." Mendoza stopped; her silent tight-lipped watchfulness was raising wrath in him, Palliser thought. He'd heard that Mendoza was one of those, a drink or so turned him belligerent; and he'd had that double rye, and hadn't eaten much of his steak.

"My God, you had one hell of a nerve, didn't you?" said Mendoza. "You went on taking the chance—to save yourself. If that came out, you'd be tied into it tight. So, right under the sergeant's nose, you went on hiding the evidence—and planting false evidence. Talk about nerve—*eso ya es llover sobre mojado*, adding insult to injury! You knew the minute we saw those files, listing that slim number of legitimate patients, we were going to start wondering like hell where all Nestor's money came from. That worried you, didn't it, that you couldn't do anything about the files? The sergeant was in there, you couldn't walk off with them or start adding fictitious file cards, to make them look good. No. But you did what you could. By God, you did. You made the excuse of calling the patients, and you got hold of the appointment book. You sat there at your desk, the innocent efficient nurse, with that and the phone book, leaning over the phone so nobody could see you were holding down the tabs, talking to dead air—and while you canceled non-existent appointments you actually entered a lot of non-existent appointments in the book. Because on the surface it had to look as if Nestor had a large practice, to account for the income." He laughed sharply. "Unfortunately, somebody had already looked at the appointment book and is ready to swear it's been extensively added to since."

"You can't prove that," she said. "You can't make me out—"

"You don't think so?" said Mendoza. He laughed again. "We'll prove it, Corliss! Check out every one of those names in the book—and nine out of ten'll show up as non-existent. What was a chiropractor doing with a blood-stained smock? Some patient had a nosebleed? *¡A otro perro con ese hueso!* We'll prove it, and you'll be spending the next few years in Tehachapi."

Scarne came in from the bedroom. "Nothing," he said. "Nothing even unusual."

"I didn't expect it," said Mendoza without taking his eyes off the woman. "Corliss is a little too smart to keep incriminating evidence around, isn't she? Or thinks she is. What did you do with Doctor's records, Corliss? And all the rest of it? You might have got rid of the tools, but I think you'd hang onto the records. I think maybe you had the same bright little idea Doctor had about that, didn't you? Did you stash them away in a safe-deposit box maybe? If and when we charge you, I can get an order to open one of those, you know. . . . Well, don't just stand there!" he added to Scarne. "Go down and look at her car." He picked up the bulging handbag lying on the table near the door. "Keys probably in here."

"You leave my things alone! You—"

"Search warrant, Corliss," said Mendoza. "All nice and legal!" He took a step and stood over her close. "No, you couldn't do anything about those damning files—files showing just the few legitimate patients he had. You told the big sergeant one very damn silly story about that, but it was really all you could say, wasn't it?—that a lot of file cards were missing, had been taken out. You could point to the appointment book, all righteous, and say that showed how many patients he had—but it wasn't quite the same thing, was it?"

"You've certainly got a nasty imagination," she said shrilly. "Not one word of that—you can't prove—"

"Sooner or later somebody might have begun to wonder," said Mendoza tautly. He bent a little closer to her. "Look at me! You know something, Corliss? Somebody had begun to wonder about it. That big tough sergeant, Corliss. He didn't like you, he was wondering hard about you. He wanted to see you again, rake you over the coals a little. Did he, Corliss?"

"I don't know what you—" Suddenly her eyes showed a little fright, at his nakedly savage tone.

"Did he? Last Friday night— And did you, maybe, give yourself away somehow? So that you knew if the sergeant passed that on you'd be in one hell of a mess anyway? And was, maybe, your gentleman friend here to lend you a hand at—"

"I don't know what you're talking about," she said rapidly, nervously. "What if Larry was here Friday night? That cop never— I don't know what you *mean—*" But her dark expressionless eyes shifted at last, once, and her tight mouth worked convulsively.

"*¡Perra negra!*" said Mendoza violently—and Palliser moved. He saw Mendoza's eyes, and he took one step, between them, to seize Mendoza's upraised arm.

For an instant they stood breast to breast, and Palliser was the taller man but he wondered if he could hold him. He said quietly, "You haven't been haled up to I.A. the last couple of years, sir, you don't want to break your record."

Mendoza drew a long breath. "No. No. All right, boy."

Palliser felt the violence of effort as he regained control. He let go of him and stepped back.

"—sue you for slander!" she was saying breathlessly. "That's right, try to hit a defenseless woman! Of all things, I never heard of— All lies! You'll never prove—"

"You're wasting breath and effort, Corliss," said Mendoza. "We'll prove it on you. Larry who?"

"I don't have to tell you that," she said haughtily. "To drag him in. I never *heard—*"

"Are you a registered nurse? Where'd you train?"

"I don't have to tell you—"

Scarne came back, letting himself in with her key, and said, "The car's clean, Lieutenant."

"Yes," said Mendoza. "Just don't try to run, Corliss. We're watching you, and we'll get enough for a warrant sooner or later."

She was still sitting there, stolid and defiant, when they went out.

Dwyer dropped behind with Palliser. "Brother," he said *sotto voce*, "you took a chance there. I've seen him like that a few times. He might just as easy have knocked you into the middle of next week. For all he's not outsize, when he's in the mood he can be a tough one to take."

"Better me than a female citizen there's no evidence on," said Palliser tersely.

In the street Mendoza stopped beside the long black elegance of the Ferrari. He took off his hat and put a hand to his head as if it ached, and summoned a smile for the three of them. He said, "So we go the long way round. With the lab boys working overtime. A tail on her twenty-four hours a day, from now on. She knows we'll get there in the end. Somebody'll have to go through that appointment book, check out all the names. Get that set up, one of you, will you? Bert—you chase back to the office and start that. And when you and Scarne have finished checking your bit of Nestor's address book, I could bear to know the hell of a lot more about one Cliff Elger. Go talk to people about him. I'll see you back at the office at six."

"O.K.," said Dwyer casually. He and Scarne walked on toward Dwyer's car down the block.

"I'm *sorry*, Lieutenant," said Palliser. "It was just—I mean, I know how you felt, that damn woman, but I couldn't let you—"

Mendoza tossed his hat in the open window of the Ferrari. He didn't say anything; he reached for a cigarette, lit it.

"I mean, my God, you know—the headlines," said Palliser. "That juvenile thing last year—all blown up out of nothing, but the chief is so damn scrupulous about that kind of thing, and Internal Affairs—"

"I know," said Mendoza. "Thanks very much, John. Make a fool of myself—that never accomplishes anything. We'll drop on Corliss, with any luck. That doesn't say— Let's talk this over a little." He got into the car.

Palliser got in after him. "Yes, sir."

"Build it for me," said Mendoza. "The way you see it, on Art. How did it happen?"

"Well, I don't see that we can—"

"From what we know. Construe," said Mendoza.

Palliser considered. "One thing did occur to me. What was the last thing he wrote in his notebook?"

"You think, don't you?" Mendoza brought out Hackett's notebook. "But it's not much help. . . ."

TEN

It wasn't much help because Hackett didn't keep consecutive notes; he had used separate sections of the notebook for separate inquiries and people. There wasn't any way to know what he'd last written down. In the section on Andrea Nestor, the last thing he'd written was, "Any overheard quarrels with husband? Ask neighbors?" There wasn't anything about the Elgers at all.

"But of course," said Palliser, "wherever he was attacked, whoever did it, if we're right he probably wouldn't have had a chance to write any notes about that interview."

Mendoza agreed. It was always better not to produce a notebook at the actual interview with a witness, if you could avoid it, but to write your notes afterward; that would be what Hackett would have done.

"The only other thing that struck me," said Palliser, "is that it would have been a lot easier to set up that fake accident if there were two people involved. Because that canyon road's pretty long and winding. The site was about a mile up from where the road starts, above the end of Bronson. It's steep, too. When X had sent the car over, he'd be on foot, unless somebody had driven another car along to pick him up. And look, how would he know that the crash wouldn't be heard right away, bring people swarming around? How's he going to explain himself, there on foot? I think there must—"

"You said the houses, and not many of them, are set back. And that there wasn't really any crash, the Ford didn't hit anything big. A mile's not really very far. Of course it'd be more than a mile, maybe a lot more, because we don't know where X lives, where it happened. It'd have been easier for two people, but it wasn't at all impossible for a single X. I think we can make a few deductions anyway." Mendoza produced a folded paper from his breast pocket. "This is what Erwin had to say—and the surgeon at the hospital. The most serious injury is the head wound—massive skull fracture. They don't think he was hit with a weapon of any kind, and they don't think the injury occurred during the fall over the cliff. They say it's too big an area, and on account of certain technicalities and measurements they come up with the opinion that he was knocked against some hard, broad, flat surface with great force. That's Erwin—'with great force.' Thus adding his own weight to the force of the blow. Erwin suggests a cement wall, the side of a building, or a flat stone hearth. There's a slight bruise under the jaw too, which backs that up. They think that happened a little while before he incurred the other injuries—which was obviously when the car was sent over. Anything occur to you from that?"

"Not much. Except that it's likelier, isn't it, that it happened inside somewhere, not on the street? I don't suppose X had thought it all out beforehand—he probably struck that blow on impulse, and probably just after Hackett had let him see he'd given himself away somehow."

"I'll go along on that. We can deduce something else, John. Why did X have to take Art's own belt off to tie him up? Obviously, because he hadn't any rope or stout cord handy—or maybe only enough for either the wrists or ankles. What does that say? Possibly an apartment, instead of a house. A house can usually produce something of the sort—clothesline, et cetera—but people living in apartments, unless they habitually wrap a lot of parcels for mailing— Yes."

"Well, practically all of them do live in apartments," said Palliser. "The people we've come across so far."

"There'll be some of Nestor's friends living in houses, I suppose. All right. Say it was Corliss and her boy friend Larry—who I'd like to know more about too. We will. He was there. Suppose she somehow gave herself away to Art, or he spotted some evidence there while he was talking to her, and started to question her hard or even charge her—and the boy friend got mad and hit him, caught him off balance maybe and knocked him against that imitation marble hearth or even just the wall. I'll say this. I think we'll find that Larry is an amiable weak lout—Corliss' kind do pick up that type. Possibly he's had a few brushes with the law himself. So he'd be all too ready to help get rid of a cop."

"Um," said Palliser.

"And, if he is that type, it's a type that often comes apart fairly easily," said Mendoza. "I don't know but what I like the Elgers better, except that they look fairly normal—for *their* type—and there's nothing on them at all." He told Palliser about the Elgers.

Palliser said, "You know—what Dr. Erwin said—that he was probably knocked against something. That sounds to me as if he was taken completely by surprise. Because, after all, it's second nature, isn't it?—you're questioning a suspect, a pretty hot suspect, even if you've just found that out—you're watching for any tricks. Aren't you? We've just had a reminder about that, last month—those two fellows stopped for speeding, who shot up the squad-car man. He never thought to check them for arms."

"Yes?"

"Well, what it might say," said Palliser, "is that it was somebody he'd never expect to attack him at all. Physically. Such as a woman or—or an eighty-year-old man, something like that. So he was off his guard entirely, and that was how he was caught off balance. And you know—"

"I rather like that," said Mendoza, "because in the ordinary way he would be taking care. Not being a fool, and having some experience. What you were going on to say was that obviously, if he'd had any reason to be suspicious of Cliff Elger, he'd have been taking double pains to be careful, a gorilla like that—bigger than Art himself."

"That's just what I was going to say."

"And you'd be right. And come to think," said Mendoza, "am I right about that belt? People living in apartments wouldn't have any clothesline lying around, but a good many people do keep cord for wrapping packages. For—for tying up things to put away, like Christmas decorations and winter clothes. I don't know. Maybe it was just the first thing X thought of. But maybe not too. Because—it wasn't a very cunningly faked accident, was it?"

Palliser shrugged. "The squad car first on the scene spotted it right away. By the tracks. No skid, no try at braking—the car was backed around deliberately to face the drop."

"Yes. Not a brain, whoever set it up. So he might not have realized that we'd spot how the belt had been used either. On the other hand, it must have made him a little more trouble. When he got up there he had to take the time to put it back on Art—rather an awkward little job, rolling a big heavy man around getting his belt through all the little loops. I think we're safe in saying that he used the belt in the first place because he couldn't lay hands on anything else in a hurry. And why tie him up at all? Yes, why? Here was a badly injured man, unconscious—he wouldn't be getting up and walking away anywhere."

"Well, so X didn't have any medical knowledge, to know that."

"Yes, but also that says maybe he stashed Art away somewhere awhile, before he set up the accident. . . . Oh hell," said Mendoza, and started the engine. "There's not much in all that. I don't know. Let's go back to the office and see if anything's come in."

"By the way, you said to the Corliss woman you thought she'd had the same bright idea Nestor had had. What was that?"

"Maybe something to check—if we had any way of knowing where to look." Mendoza smiled. "That scrapbook full of the doings of high society. When I looked at it, one thing struck me. Every single clipping, whatever it was about, included a photograph. And every single photograph included at least one young woman. . . . I said I think Nestor was aiming at the moneyed women. He'd get others too, of course. Kinsey has alerted us to the fairly high incidence of abortion in unexpected places. And of course a lot of those customers would give false names. I think Nestor was keeping his scrapbook on the off-chance of recognizing former patients. I don't think he was above a little genteel blackmail."

"Oh," said Palliser, enlightened. "I get you. He recognizes Jane Smith, who came to him last year for a job, as being really a socialite debutante, and puts the bite on her—but how could he? Without giving himself away?"

"He couldn't, really, beyond threatening to tip off her parents, or boy friend, or husband for that matter, anonymously—but a lot of women in that position might not clearly realize that. I wonder if he'd found a victim yet, from all his diligent research? And, if he had, whether she'd paid up. Well, see what routine's turning up for us."

Routine had turned up a couple of interesting things. Sergeant Lake said, only half kidding, "I might have known things would start to move, Lieutenant, soon as you got home and had a hunch."

Landers, making the round of the bars in that downtown area asking whether silver dollars had been part of their take lately, had turned up two leads. A bartender at a hole-in-the-wall joint on Broadway remembered a fellow coming in several times who'd paid with silver dollars. He had made a statement, and if there wasn't much in it, there was something. He couldn't give any kind of description. "¡Naturalmente!" said Mendoza irritably. "They will keep bars so damn dark." All he remembered about the fellow was that he was very poorly dressed, in what looked like somebody else's clothes, and usually kept a hat pulled down low on his forehead. Maybe, oh, four, five times he'd been in. Always at night, and once or twice quite late, staying until the bar closed at 1 A.M. He was, said the bartender vaguely, medium-sized and kind of thin. And he always ordered bourbon, straight.

The other bartender worked at a place on Main. It wasn't quite down into Skid Row, but on the fringes; and he was a tough customer, who didn't much care for cops and was reluctant to open up with any information. Landers had persuaded him, finally, to come out with what he knew. And that wasn't much either, but again, something. There was this old bat, he said, kind of a regular—probably a setup, also a lush. He wasn't admitting that she was working out of his bar, naturally, because he didn't want to lose his license; but that, said Landers, was what it sounded like. Anyway, her name was Rosie—that was all the bartender knew. And the last couple of times she'd been in, she'd paid him with a silver dollar. He gave a vague description of her; no, he'd never heard her last name, and of course he didn't know where she lived—he could do the hell of a lot better than that for himself.

"Well—something, but what?" said Mendoza. "Put out a call on Rosie. Trace it down, and probably find the customer she got the silver dollars from just blew in from Vegas and has nothing to do with our Slasher. However—"

Nothing had turned up on that search of hotel registers in the downtown area. Mendoza called the city editors of the *Times*, the *Herald*, the Hollywood *Citizen*, and the Glendale *News-Press*, and requested them to run cuts of that signature they had from the Liverpool Arms register: promised to send over prints. He sent a man down to get the prints and deliver them by hand.

The first body had been found the day before he and Alison had left for New York; he hadn't heard many details on it. Now he settled down to reread all the reports on the five victims. . . . He said to Lake, "That stuff we picked up in the hotel room—is it still around? Lab send it back?"

"I seem to remember it did—probably be in Art's desk." Lake looked, and brought him a shoe box containing a few odds and ends. "No prints, nothing suggestive."

Mendoza looked at it sadly. No guarantee either—the Liverpool Arms being what it was—that any of these things was connected with the Slasher, who had occupied that room such a short time. Found in the room with the body, but ten to one the rooms there weren't so thoroughly cleaned between tenants.

A half-empty packet of matches. A single penny, dark with age. An empty crumpled-up cigarette package, king-size Chesterfields. A dime-store handkerchief, soiled. A crumpled-up paper cup that had held bourbon at some time.

He picked up the matches idly and opened the cover. He looked at the dozen matches left in it and said to himself, "¿Y qué es esto? Somebody's slipping, either the lab or us. Jimmy!"

"What now?"

"This Mike. The first victim. I suppose you couldn't tell me whether he was left-handed?"

"Nor I don't know what color eyes his grandmother had either. Why the hell?"

"We can probably find out," said Mendoza. "He seems to have been known down on the Row. And I'd like to ask Bainbridge his opinion on this one too. . . . Why? Have all of you so-called detectives gone blind? Look at this packet of matches. The ordinary right-handed person, tearing off a match, holds the book in his left hand and naturally reaches for the first match at the extreme right. ¿Cómo no? He gradually works his way through the book from right to left. All right. Whoever started to use this book of matches did it just the opposite—all the matches that have been torn out were at the extreme left. If Mike wasn't left-handed, there's a fair probability that these were the Slasher's matches and that he is left-handed."

"Oh," said Sergeant Lake. "That might narrow it down, sure. From about seven million to only two and a half."

"Well, it's another something," said Mendoza.

Dwyer came in at five-fifteen, Scarne and Glasser after him; Landers had just finished taking the second bartender's statement. All the people in Nestor's address book looked ordinary—other chiropractors who'd been in his graduating class, men around his own age, salesmen, clerks—some family men, some not. Of the women, a few looked like typical tramps, a few others were married; one of those women, a Mrs. Anita Sheldon, had been scared, said Glasser, and begged him not to drag her name in—nobody knew she'd known Nestor, her husband would kill her if he knew. "Husband's a truck driver," Glasser added. "National moving firm. Those guys are usually pretty hefty."

There wasn't much there. They'd look harder at the Sheldons.

Dwyer said he'd seen Elger's two associates in their office, and they'd given him names of a couple of others who knew him, another agent and a producer. The consensus was that Elger had the hell of a hot temper, was known to fly off the handle over any little thing. "The kind who gets mad quick and then cools down fast and it's all over, you know. But everybody seems to like him."

"Yes. And that kind sometimes cools down fast to find an unintended body around," said Mendoza. "Especially when they're as big as Cliff

Elger. Well, boys—any of you feel like doing a little more leg work to-night?"

None of them minded.

When he got home Alison met him at the door. "What's wrong, *querida?*" he asked, seeing her eyes. He held her close. The hospital was still saying, No change.

"Oh, Luis," she said shakily. "Nothing now. But—I didn't tell Angel, I asked the nurse not to. We were at the hospital this afternoon, and the nurse told me. They—they thought he was going, this morning. Then his pulse picked up, for no reason, and he—"

Mendoza put his head down on her shoulder for a minute. "Well, he's still here anyway," he said. "Maybe Adam was doing some extra earnest praying about then. I want to talk to Angel. Can she—"

"Yes, of course."

He went into the living room, where Bast greeted him loudly and El Señor contemplated him evilly through green slits, from the top of the phonograph. The record-cabinet doors were open and El Señor had dragged out four albums. Mendoza said absently, "Señor Molestia!" and put them away.

Mrs. MacTaggart came trotting in with a shot glass and a saucer. "I heard the car," she said. "You'll be needing a drink before dinner, and that unnatural cat giving you no peace unless he has his share." She set the saucer down for El Señor, who had an unaccountable taste for rye and lapped eagerly. "And the longer the man hangs on there, the better chance there is, as I needn't be reminding you. Mercy on us, what's—"

Pandemonium broke out in the hall. Mark Christopher staggered in clasping a wildly struggling Sheba around the middle. "Kitty-kitty!" he was announcing triumphantly. Miss Teresa Ann, still very uncertain on her small feet, staggered after him wailing loudly, and bringing up the procession came Master John Luis on all fours, also wailing.

"Now what is all this indeed? Like banshees the lot of you— Mark, put the kitty down now—" Mrs. MacTaggart hurried to Sheba's rescue.

El Señor finished the rye, thoughtfully licked his whiskers, and looking slightly cross-eyed jumped down to cuff Sheba, who was indignantly smoothing down her coat. She shrieked and spat at him.

"The happy home," said Mendoza resignedly to his drink. "Talk about the patter of little feet . . ."

When Angel came in with Alison he eyed her and said, "I think you could stand a small drink before dinner too."

"I'm all right," said Angel.

"Cocktails all made, waiting," said Alison with a show of briskness. "I thought we both could. I'll get them."

Mendoza sipped rye, looking at Angel. He and Art's nice domestic little wife had never appreciated each other to any extent; he couldn't say he knew her very well. He was rather surprised she wasn't weeping and fainting all over the place. She looked pale, but she'd put on make-up and combed her hair. Just another pretty dark-haired woman: but for the first time he noticed the firmness of her jaw and her steady eyes.

Alison came back with two glasses, and he waited until Angel had taken a sip. "Now, I expect Alison told you I want to hear every detail you remember, about what he said to you that night."

"Yes, of course," said Angel. "The worst of it is, I wasn't paying too much attention—of course I couldn't know it was important then. And what with coping with Mark pounding the table legs with one of his pull-toys—but I've tried to think back as well as I can. I know definitely he said he was going to see that hotel clerk." She sipped her cocktail; her voice was steady. "He was worried about this mass killer, on account of all the fuss the newspapers have been making, what they were saying about the force. He said something about Nestor's wife too, and a woman named Corliss. And he mentioned somebody named Elger. That's all I remember, I'm sorry."

"That's fine," said Mendoza. "He said definitely he was going to see the clerk at the hotel?"

"Yes, that I remember. He—" She stopped, and finished her drink rather quickly. "He left about twenty past seven. He kissed me at the door and said, 'Think I'll try those Elgers first, or the Nestor woman—and, damn it, I'll be late because that clerk's not on until nine. Probably be home about ten-thirty.' That's—"

"O.K.," said Mendoza. "That's something. But he must have gone to see Mrs. Nestor first, and we know he was all right when he left there. Gives us a sort of *terminus a quo*, anyway." He stared into his nearly empty glass.

Suddenly she got up, came over to stand in front of him. "You'll find out, won't you?" she said.

Mendoza looked up at her. "We'll find out. Whatever happens."

"Yes. I never—never liked you very much," said Angel. "It seems a little funny, but I guess now I can see I was a little jealous of you. Not just of you. All of them. The office. You because you're the important one there. And he—thinks—so much—of you."

"Yes," said Mendoza. He stood up. "Yes, Angel. I know that."

"He thinks—you're so good," she said. Her eyes were very bright. "I never thought— But the way all of you have— They've all called me, you know, to say— There was even a letter from the chief. I never really understood how it is—with all of you. I—I used to resent the job, sometimes."

"As most cops' wives do," said Mendoza. "Which just makes it all the tougher for the cops."

"Yes. I wouldn't feel that way any more," she said. "It's like—I see that —soldiers in line of d-duty. All together."

"And there is no discharge in that war," said Mendoza with a crooked smile.

"So you will find out who. You'll just go on until you do. Whatever happens. And I guess—maybe—he was right about you too. I didn't think you ever felt things much, that you were the kind of man who— But you do. I see."

"Now I'll tell you," he said gently, "I never thought much of you either, but you're a good girl, Angel. I wouldn't have thought you'd stand up to this so well. Whatever happens, we'll get him, I promise you."

After a moment Alison said with a little catch in her voice, "Well, if the mutual admiration society'll break up, I think dinner's about ready. . . . I suppose it's silly to ask you if you're going out again."

"*Tú debeas saberlo,*" said Mendoza. "I'm going out on what the British call a pub crawl."

"Bars?" said Alison. "Good heavens. You can't go into bars without drinking, and you know what three drinks do to you. You'll end up getting picked up for disturbing the peace, or assault and battery."

"*¡Dios me libre!*" said Mendoza. "I just hope to God we can turn up something useful."

ELEVEN

They were out in force down there tonight, most of the night shift and some of the day men, wandering in and out of the bars in the Slasher's territory. Palliser was stationed in the bar where the bartender said the lush Rosie dropped in; he'd stay until ten-thirty when Higgins would take over. The bartender didn't like it, but agreed to point her out if she came in. Piggott was sitting in the bar on Flower Street where the bartender remembered the fellow who had paid him with a silver dollar and walked out with Theodore Simms. The rest of the men had only a very vague description to work from, but they'd be checking on anybody who matched it, getting names and addresses. That was the kind of dogged routine that often got you there in the end, especially on one like this.

Mendoza went first to the bar on Main, the bar Rosie frequented. Palliser was sitting in the rear booth, and getting surly looks from the bartender for occupying a whole booth instead of a stool. He didn't come over to take Mendoza's order right away.

"Nothing yet," said Palliser.

"Couldn't expect it," said Mendoza. "Too early. If she's working tonight at all, she's still fixing herself up in her room. . . . No wonder nobody could offer any descriptions. I can hardly see you, let alone anybody across the room. These damn places—" He looked up as the bartender slouched over and said, "Nothing for me, thanks." The bartender almost snarled at him. Palliser was taking an occasional small sip of a highball.

Mendoza drifted over to the bar on Flower Street, to have a word with Piggott. Piggott was the day tail on Margaret Corliss, and he greeted Mendoza with something like excitement. "I was just wondering was it worthwhile calling in, Lieutenant. See, I—"

"Something? . . . Straight rye," said Mendoza to the bartender, sliding into the opposite side of the booth.

"Not on this, no. It's that Corliss dame. You know I got a pretty good memory for faces. Well, when I first laid eyes on her today I thought right off I'd seen her before. Only I couldn't place where. I been thinking about it on and off all day, you know how a thing like that bothers you. Like some name you can't remember, but it's right on the tip of your tongue. It kept bothering me something awful, because I got to thinking it might be important. Well, I said to myself, lay it at the Lord's door and ask for help on it." Piggott looked at him earnestly over his glass of plain water; Piggott was a pillar of the Free Methodist Church and wouldn't have dreamed of touching the jigger of whiskey at his elbow. "And just five minutes ago, as I was sitting here not really thinking about it, the Lord came through and I remembered. I saw that woman down at headquarters once, Lieutenant. I couldn't tell you when, but I can tell you where—it was in the corridor right outside the Vice office. I'd been down there, some reason, and I saw Lieutenant Andrews with her—he had her by one arm, they were just going into his office."

"¡No me diga!" said Mendoza. "That's very interesting. That all you remember? Well, we know it wasn't a charge because her prints aren't on file, but if she was brought in for questioning even once, maybe Percy will remember something about it. Probably be somewhere in his records anyway. I'll ask him in the morning. That's very interesting indeed. . . ."

From there he wandered over, looking around several other joints on the way, to the bar on Broadway where the barkeep remembered the fellow with the silver dollars. He found Higgins sitting on the end stool there, over a nearly empty glass, watching the crowd. "He said he'd give me a signal if the guy came in, but he's not very sure he'd know him again."

The bartender came up, but only to take Mendoza's order and suggest a refill. Higgins shoved over his glass and Mendoza said, "You'd better nurse them along slower, George, it's still early."

Higgins laughed. "My God, place like this gets about sixty-five high-balls out of a fifth, and only eighty proof to start with. . . . You sure see the types in these joints. Makes you wonder about people, how they get this far down."

Presently Glasser and Scarne came in, and took a good look at all the customers. There was a man alone, round the horseshoe curve of the bar, who matched what there was of their vague description: medium height, thin, in rather loose-fitting old clothes. Glasser went up to him, they exchanged a few words, and the man, looking very frightened, went out with Glasser. Five minutes later he came back in, looking shaken, and ordered a new drink. Glasser would have his name and address.

Routine. It usually got you there in the end. Sooner or later. . . .

About ten forty-five Mendoza stepped into the lobby of the Liverpool Arms. The armchair behind the counter was empty; the inner door stood open.

Suddenly he felt that small cold bite up the spine that told him he was onto something, a new card was about to be handed him; and though he hadn't the remotest idea what it might be, he obeyed instinct blindly and stood still, making no move toward the counter.

The old shabby building was very silent at this time of night. From what he could see through the half-open door, the small room behind the counter was a storeroom of some kind; he had a glimpse of dusty shelves.

He heard the glassy clink of bottle on glass, and something was set down with a thud. A minute later Telfer the clerk came out and shut the door behind him. He moved with exaggerated care, and he was wiping the back of his hand across his mouth.

Mendoza walked up to the counter. Telfer noticed him then and stood swaying only a little, smiling his yellow-snagged smile. " 'D evening, sir," he said. His eyes were glassy and there was the saccharine-sweet smell of port wine about him. "Do for you?" He didn't seem to recognize Mendoza at all.

"Never mind," said Mendoza, and turned and went out. For God's sake! he thought. Every little lead they had turning out to be useless. Telfer a wino, and the odds were that was why he couldn't tell them anything about the man who'd taken that room. Probably so high he didn't remember a single damn thing about him. Of all the Goddamned bad luck . . .

But, damn it, was he going senile, not to have tried that? Like Art walking off and leaving that office wide open—sometimes you caught yourself forgetting the most elementary things.

Where was the Slasher sleeping? He hadn't signed into any other hotel in this area. He could be staying in a different flophouse every night, the fifty-cents-a-night, men-only places on the Row. Nobody asked for signatures in those places. But he could also have taken a room in some cheap rooming house. What was he living on, too? Did he have a job—or an unlimited supply of those silver dollars? Well, cover the rooming houses, anyway; ask about recent arrivals.

And the ordinary citizen might think that one like the Slasher would be easy to spot, that he'd behave so queerly or look so different that anybody could spot him at a glance. Unfortunately not so. As Higgins said, you ran into some funny ones down here, and a lot of them looked odd.

At eleven-thirty he wandered back to the bar on Main and found Higgins where Palliser had been sitting. Higgins had probably, of necessity, drunk four or five highballs this evening, and he looked and acted as sober as the proverbial judge. Mendoza, who had ordered five drinks and contrived to empty three of them inconspicuously on the floor, ordered a sixth and said, "You can drink it for me."

"I don't like rye," said Higgins.

"But I've already had two," said Mendoza. "You know what it does to me. We're on a job, damn it."

Higgins looked at him benevolently and said he'd look after him if he started picking a fight with the bouncer. The bartender came back with the rye and jerked an ungracious shoulder.

"You want Rosie, she just come in. There by the juke box."

Higgins got up. "I'll bring her," he said.

Thirty seconds later he ushered her into his side of the booth and slid in after her. "You said you'd buy me a drink, honey," said Rosie.

"Sure." She wasn't very high yet; she could probably take a good deal more. "You like rye? You can have this." He reached and set Mendoza's glass in front of her. "Cigarette?"

"Thanks lots," she said. She put the rye down in one swallow and leaned to Higgins' lighter. "You just buy drinks for Rosie 'n' Rosie'll be nice to you. *Both* of you," she added, discovering Mendoza across the table. She beamed at them muzzily. "You're cute," she said to Mendoza.

"We'd just like to talk to you awhile, Rosie," said Higgins. He looked at Mendoza and they exchanged a silent opinion. They'd both seen about all there was to see, down here and elsewhere, of the bottom of things; but nobody ever quite got used to it.

She might have been pretty once, a shallow-eyed little blonde with the pert figure, out for the fun times and the romance. There were a thousand reasons for it, for the Rosies; this was a long time later.

She giggled up at Higgins a little foolishly. "Order me another drink, honey." Mendoza signaled the bartender, who shrugged and began to build a highball.

She might be no more than in her forties, but she looked sixty. That was a long time of too much careless make-up and too little washing. She was too thin, shoulder bones standing out sharply, her wrists and ankles like a child's. She hadn't much on under the old, mended, cheap black rayon evening dress, and the thin breasts pushed relentlessly out by the padded bra, the too thin body, were hardly provocative: only a little pathetic. Her hair, bleached too often and washed too seldom, was dry and uncurled, hanging untidily to her shoulders. She smelled of old sweat and cheap cologne and whiskey, and the coy painted smile was somehow a little obscene, as if a death's head had winked at them.

"We just want to talk to you," said Mendoza. The bartender came up and slapped a highball in front of her.

"Sure. That's what they all say," said Rosie, and giggled again. She drank thirstily.

"About silver dollars," said Higgins. "You've been spending a few lately. Don't often see silver dollars any more."

Rosie didn't say anything. She looked at him, setting her glass down, and small fright was in her eyes.

"Where'd you get them?" asked Higgins casually.

"H-how d'you know I had any silver dollars?" Suddenly she read them; Rosie would have had this and that to do with cops in the course of her misspent life; and she gasped and shoved violently against Higgins. "You're fuzz—you leave me be, I haven't done nothing—let me go!" She made no impression whatever on Higgins' solid bulk; but her voice rose, and the bartender came over in a hurry.

"I said no disturbance in here, bloodhounds! Listen—"

"We don't want you, Rosie," said Higgins. "Quiet down, you stupid little— We just want you to answer some questions, damn it. We've got nothing on you, see? Take it easy—here, drink your drink."

She shrank into the corner of the booth. "I haven't done nothing," she said sullenly.

"You've spent a few silver dollars, Rosie," said Mendoza. "That's all we want to know about. Where'd you get them?"

"Why's it matter to you, anyways?" She reached for her glass.

"It matters. Where?"

"From a friend o' mine," she said.

They could translate that. A customer. "What's his name, where'd you meet him?" asked Mendoza.

"I don't have to—it's no damn business of yours—"

"We'll go on sitting here," said Mendoza, "until you tell us, Rosie." Sharp savage irritation rose in him: obstructed every small step of the way! And Art— Don't think about Art. "All we want to know is what he looks like."

"None o' your business. I didn't mean nobody gave 'em to me, I—I got this friend o' mine to change 'em for bills, see—" She was still busy defending herself on the obvious vice count.

"I don't care how you came by them," said Mendoza. "Who did you get them from? Do you know his name?"

"What the hell are you insin-sinuating about me?" she flared up. "I know lotsa people, no reason I shouldn't—I'm a *model*, see, I got a good job all lined up, you guys can't—"

"Sure, honey," said Higgins, "we can see you're a real high-class girl. We just want to know which friend gave you the silver dollars." He sounded patient.

Mendoza wasn't. He leaned across the stained, scarred old table. "Listen to me, you stupid female! I don't give a single damn who you go to bed with, how often or for what price. There's the hell of a good chance that the man you got those silver dollars from is this killer, the Slasher. You can tell us what he looks like, and that's all I want from you, if you can get that much through your—"

It didn't penetrate at once, and then when it did she half screamed, "The— Oh, *my Christ!* No—I never saw him, I don't know who— Let me outta here for God's sake! Jesus, you don't—"

"I told you what I mean," said Mendoza coldly. "We think that man's the Slasher. Now will you tell us all about him or shall we take a little ride to headquarters?"

She made one sudden, convulsive effort to squeeze past Higgins again; she looked almost witless with fright. Then she said faintly, "O.K., O.K., you take me in and I tell you. Please take me in, mister—on account of if he knew I told—"

"Whichever way you want," said Mendoza. He dropped a couple of bills on the table and slid out of the booth. Higgins took her by the arm and followed.

They went single file down the narrow aisle to the door, the woman between and Higgins' hand on her arm. They came out to clean fresh night air, and Mendoza said, "Where's your car?"

"Up the block to your right— *God damn!*" said Higgins. Rosie was out of his grip like an eel, leaving a torn edge of her tawdry dress behind; she fled up the block wildly, dodged around the corner there, and was gone. They ran after her, swearing, and turned into the darker side street. They heard the clatter of her high heels, sharp on the sidewalk ahead, and then lost them.

"Go call up a car," panted Mendoza. "God damn the little—"

She was gone. He stood there waiting for the car, to start the futile block-by-block hunt. She'd be diving into whatever cheap rented room she called home, bundling her few possessions together to run on—maybe out of L.A.—thinking of her own skin, Rosie. The Rosies did that. And, being Rosie, she'd know how to go to ground, anonymous, in some other Skid Row.

Damn her, damn her. She might have given them a very damn definite description—if that was the Slasher—and he knew they'd never pick her up.

But he set up the routine hunt. You had to try.

That night he didn't sleep much. He lay and stared into the darkness and, senselessly, his mind went back over every detail of every case he and Art had worked together.

A lot of cases. You got to know a man pretty well in that length of time. *No way to be certain . . . permanent brain damage . . .*

He was still lying there at five-thirty when light outlined the window, and El Señor got up, yawned and stretched, trampled over Bast and went to sit on the window seat and make chattering noises at the early sparrows in the tree outside. Bast sent a disgusted glare after him, wrapped her tail round her nose, and went to sleep again.

Alison was heavily asleep still, lying motionless. He got up, shaved, and dressed. Went out to the living room. Hospitals were always awake. At six-fifteen he called.

No change. They had said it could be days. And no way to be certain. . . .

When he heard faint sounds from the kitchen he wandered out there, and the brisk little Scotswoman smiled at him. "Coffee in five minutes. And it's a senseless sort of thing to be saying to you, but it's never any bit of good worrying over a thing that's out of your hands entirely."

"I know, Máiri," he said. "I know that."

"It's a great pity you've no religion to depend on. I don't know," said Mrs. MacTaggart, "but what I haven't stayed in this heathen household with the hope of reconverting you, my gallant man. And I'm making a novena for the sergeant, so you'll have to find your own breakfast if you want any. . . . I've taken the wee boy in to his mother, and our two are fast asleep still and likely'll stay so until I'm home."

"Yes," said Mendoza. . . . He drank the coffee too hot. He watched her hurry off to the garage for Alison's car. Damned ridiculous, he thought. Superstitious . . . On her knees at the nearest one, the Church of Our Lady of Good Counsel, obeying the ancient meaningless ritual.

What happened or didn't happen, to Art or Luis Mendoza or anybody else, it was just according to how the hands got dealt round.

They hadn't picked up Rosie.

The reproduced signature had made the front page of the *Times*, blown up twice life size. It was certainly an odd signature, almost totally illegible. Fred, Frank, something like that, and whether the second name started with a T or an L was hard to say, or what the rest of it might be. Anyway, there it was. See if anybody recognized it. It'd be in the afternoon and evening papers too.

Routine was churning out background information, the kind of thing you collected automatically; none of it was at all suggestive.

William Marlowe was fifty-nine, and a Harvard graduate. He'd inherited an estimated ten or twelve million from his father; there'd been money in the family for some time. Oil money and other interests. They came originally from Connecticut, where the family had been since pre-Revolutionary days. He was married—his wife was a D.A.R. member—and had one son and two daughters.

Andrea Nestor's father had been a self-made man. Self-made by gambling on the stock market. He'd died broke six and a half years ago. She had attended local private schools. No close friends had shown up; the neighbors hadn't known much about the Nestors. She seemed to be a neutral sort of woman—nothing to get hold of, good or bad.

Frank Nestor had come here from New Jersey about ten years back. No background showed at all before that; he never mentioned any relations, wrote no letters back home.

The only interesting thing turned up overnight was Larry Webster. Corliss had met him at a bar and grill on Grand Avenue for dinner, and they'd gone back to her apartment. The tail had got his name and address from the registration in his car, and called in.

Webster had a record. Mendoza rather liked the record. Lawrence Richard Webster, forty-four, Caucasian, six feet one, one ninety-five, complexion medium, eyes blue, no distinguishing marks. He'd served six months for aggravated assault in 1947, been picked up three times on a D.-and-D., and done a one-to-three for burglary.

Very nice, thought Mendoza. Just the boy friend for Corliss. And she said he'd been at her apartment on Friday night. . . . He thought he'd like to have a little talk with Larry Webster. He put out a call on him.

He phoned down to Vice. Lieutenant Andrews had been out on a stakeout last night and wasn't expected in until about eleven. "O.K., tell him I want to see him—I'll be there."

That damned—that *Goddamned* stupid lush Rosie. Who could have given them a description.

A description . . . You just had to try everywhere.

Mendoza stood up abruptly. Palliser was a good man, but . . . He said to Lake, "If they pick up Webster, hold him for me. I probably won't be long."

"I know it was almost dark," he said to Miguel Garcia. It was nine-thirty. Miguel was attending summer school; he'd talked to the public-school principal, who had called Miguel out of class for him. They sat here in an empty classroom, Mendoza uncomfortably perched on the edge of a too small desk, and Miguel looked at him with round solemn eyes. "Maybe it's easier for you to tell it better in the Spanish, Miguel? I—"

"It doesn't matter, sir." They were speaking English. "My dad says we got to know English real good, to get on, see. So we do good at school and all. Well, I mean. Get a good kind of job, see. My dad works for the city, for the parks department, keeping it all nice and the grass watered, see."

"Well, I suppose you could say I work for the city too," said Mendoza. Miguel gave him an uncertain grin. "Yes, sir. You carry a gun?"

"Well, no," said Mendoza. "I'm afraid not. Now look, Miguel. You saw this man—the one who probably killed Roberto. He's killed other people too, and we'd like to catch him."

"I sure hope you do, sir. That was just an awful thing, Roberto. My dad said I should help the cops—oh, gee, excuse me, he said you shouldn't say cops, you don't like it—the policemen all I can, and I told that other one—"

"Well, we're cops, like it or not," said Mendoza, smiling.

"I told him all I knew, sir. All I remembered."

"Try again, Miguel. Think back, hard. He said something to you, and for some reason you felt scared of him, and walked on past—"

"Yes, sir. I don't know why I got scared. He just stood so kind of *still*— and then stepped out and said something like, 'Hey, kids.' Like that. I—"

"You told the other officer he was thin and had on clothes that looked too big for him, and had a red face."

"Yes, sir."

"How did you see that, Miguel? It was nearly dark, and the man had a hat on. You said there wasn't a street light near. And what exactly did you mean, his face was red? Like a drunk?" Miguel, living down here, would know about that: the broken red veins of a lush.

"No, it was—gee," said the boy, "I don't know how to say about it, sir. It wasn't very light, almost dark, sure, but there was *some* light, from the drugstore on the corner—and he— Well, I guess it was that sort of scared me. It was silly. I could see—it was red all over his face, and—sort of puckered, like. Like Pokey."

"Pokey?" said Mendoza softly.

"Yes, sir. My dad says you shouldn't make like you don't like looking at him, it isn't polite," said Miguel. "It's not his fault he got burned so awful bad like that, one time, on his face. He looks real awful, sir, one side of his face all drawed up like, and all red. But this was even worse, see, it was all over the middle of his face, and I guess it was that sort of scared me, it was silly."

"Who's Pokey?"

"Oh, he sells papers at Figueroa and Third, sir. I guess my dad's right, but—well, anyway, this guy was worse, see. I told the other policeman. Red all over his face, and—"

"Thanks very much, Miguel," said Mendoza fervently.

TWELVE

"A real break," he said. "Something more than definite—it might lead us to him in the next twelve hours. Evidently a bad scarring, from an old burn—red scar-tissue and the skin puckered, you know what I mean. God, if we'd had this before—"

"My fault," groaned Palliser. "Damn it, if I'd had the sense to press the kid more—"

"You couldn't know. It was just one of those last-resort hopes that paid off. And of course it's not a hundred per cent sure, but damn near, that that fellow Roberto stopped to talk to was the Slasher. We'll get this on the wires right now—tell everybody. Yes, and no wonder it wasn't spotted in those bars, you can't see your hand in front of your face—"

"But why the hell didn't that desk clerk spot it?" said Dwyer.

"Telfer didn't spot it," said Mendoza exasperatedly, "because that night he was probably so full of cheap port when the Slasher came in, he wouldn't have noticed if the man had been painted bright green with red polka dots. I dropped in on him last night. I'd have a guess that, with cops all around, maybe last night's the first time he's dared risk drinking on the job again. It's not a very high-class place but all the same, if the owner or manager found out, Telfer would get fired safe enough. He's the kind who can carry it off—he looked just a little high, you know, and probably if I'd asked for a room he'd have assigned me one and found the right key, automatically. The way they say sleepwalkers never fall over anything. But he'd seen me before and didn't recognize me. I don't think he'd remember now that I came in last night."

"Tight enough to pull a blank, in other words. That's something all right," said Palliser. "I'll be damned. And of course that's why he was so cagey about giving a description. But at least he didn't mislead us by making up some description, and now we've got this—"

"You think he hasn't misled us?" said Dwyer. "So maybe last night wasn't the first time he'd taken the chance since. Maybe he was carrying a load on Friday night and doesn't know whether Art came in or not."

"*¡Qué demonio!*" said Mendoza. "I haven't got that far. My God, that could be so. And we'll have to tackle him on it to make sure. . . . Hell. Jimmy, get this news about the Slasher's scar relayed out—with every cop in town looking for something as noticeable as that, we ought to lay hands on him inside twenty-four hours anyway."

"I've only got one head and two hands," complained Sergeant Lake. "Sure, that's urgent, I'll get it out, but could somebody give me a hand on this damn appointment book? I've been phoning for two days and haven't made a dent in it."

Which was understandable. Building up the fictitious large practice for Nestor, the Corliss woman had scribbled down nearly a hundred names throughout the book. Under the circumstances, most of them had been very common names, and throughout the county area the same names made up long lists in all five phone books. And every name had to be checked out, that its owner had never been a patient of Dr. Nestor's, if they were going to prove that on her. It was, in fact, one hell of a job. Mendoza suggested that Dwyer lend a hand, and Dwyer groaned.

But as he started downstairs Mendoza felt a great relief at this new break: something as glaringly obvious as that disfigurement ought to mean that they'd pick up the Slasher within hours. Not too many people, even in a city as big as this, would possess such a disfigurement; and he seemed to be keeping inside the one area. Check every rooming house, every flophouse—run extra cars . . . With any luck, and God knew they were due for some luck, they should get him now. And before he used his knife again. . . .

He found Lieutenant Andrews just arriving and followed him in. "When did you get back?" asked Andrews. "I thought—oh, sure, they'd let you know about Hackett. How is he? . . . Hell of a thing. Do I come into it?" He yawned and sat down.

"Late night?"

"I sometimes wish I was down in Traffic or somewhere," said Andrews. "Or Records—that must be a nice peaceful place. I never used to believe it, but I'm beginning to—that sins don't get committed until after midnight. I didn't get home until five."

"Too bad. Well, what I want to know is, Percy, do you remember a woman named Margaret Corliss? I don't know whether she was calling herself that then, but an unspecified while ago you evidently had her in for questioning." He described her in detail.

Andrews leaned back and shut his eyes. "It rings a bell," he said. "It definitely rings a bell. Wait a minute, now. Traces of a Cockney accent, you said? What the hell was it on? Oh, my God, yes, sure, it was that Sally-Ann thing. Pierce"—he raised his voice to the sergeant outside—"look up the records on that beauty salon thing—two, three years back—you know, the Finn sisters."

"Have to dig for it," said Pierce. "O.K."

"Twin sisters," said Andrews, "named Finn. Ran this Sally-Ann Beauty Shoppe. Which was a blind for an abortion mill. The Corliss woman was an employee—the only employee. It comes back to me—"

"Very nice, very nice," said Mendoza. "You couldn't prove she was in on the deal?"

"We tried, but no. She is, if I remember rightly, a very canny customer. Kept her head, registered shocked indignation all the way, and there wasn't a thing to tie her in. Just the strong probability, you know."

"That's my girl," said Mendoza. "I think, with luck, we'll get her this time."

"They will go and do it once too often," said Andrews. "She tried it on her own and got involved in a homicide, I take it."

"Not exactly that way," said Mendoza. He was outlining his ideas about that when the sergeant came in with a manila folder. "Dates," said Mendoza. "Let's look at some dates."

Vice had got interested in the Sally-Ann Beauty Shoppe in May of 1961, three years and two months ago. The sisters had been arrested in mid-June, and investigation had continued for a week or so.

"Yes," said Mendoza. "How nice. Frank Nestor graduated from his chiropractic course that very June. He also had a legacy about that time—a little earlier—only it wasn't a legacy. Five thousand bucks. I do wonder, now, if that doesn't represent his first job in this line."

Andrews made an incredulous sound. "Five G's? For a lock-picking job? I've run into a lot in that trade, but I never heard of prices like that."

"No, it does seem a bit steep. Well, anyway, for whatever reason, he's thinking it might be very profitable to set himself up in that trade. He's inexperienced, and he sees right away that the main difficulty is publicity. The right kind of publicity. And—I suppose the Sally-Ann business got press coverage—one morning he opens his paper, and lo, here's mention of a woman who's recently been involved in such a business, and reading between the lines he could make out that it's only for lack of evidence you're not holding her. Very likely her address was given—it usually is. I'll have to check with the papers. But, yes, I can see him waiting for the all-clear, until he saw she'd been released without charges, and then going to see her and propositioning her. Another little piece of the puzzle, explaining how they could have got together. Well, this fills in a little, thanks very much."

"Good luck on it," said Andrews through another yawn.

He got back to his office just in time to take Alison's call. When he heard her voice he found he was gripping the phone too hard, and felt a sudden constriction in his chest. "Luis—Luis darling—they just called, the hospital I mean—"

"Yes, *amada.*"

"They think he's just a little better! Oh, the nurse was awfully cautious and—you know—roundabout, and said it didn't mean he'll be all right, he could easily have a relapse—you know how they are—but his blood pressure's up a little and his pulse is better. I didn't know if they'd call you, and I— But it's got to mean—"

"Yes," he said. "Good news. We don't know whether it means— Thanks, *querida.* . . ."

He'd just put the phone down when Palliser came in, smiling. "The hospital just called, he's better, his pulse—"

"I know. But they're still not waving any flags. And there's the other question."

"Yes, there's that. But it's something."

"Something," said Mendoza. "And the more I think about that, the more—confusing—it looks. How the hell did it happen, let alone why? I don't know—" He passed a hand over his forehead. "Like to take a little ride with me before lunch?"

The first difficulty about it was, he thought, how had Art been put down and out? If it had been Elger, no question there; so, on one like Elger, if he'd had reason to suspect him, Hackett would have been watchful—but Elger was enough bigger to have taken him.

But anybody else they knew of in either case would scarcely be a match for Hackett. Larry Webster was big, and he might be tough, but the women . . . Of course there was that truck-driver husband of one of Nestor's girl friends; he ought to go and see her, get what details on that he could.

And he hadn't asked the Elgers where they'd been on Tuesday night.

Cliff Elger, who had the hell of a temper. And also a reputation and a good business, which he'd want to protect.

"Just ahead," said Palliser beside him. "Stop here."

Mendoza pulled up the Ferrari and they got out. "We can probably see some traces," said Palliser. He led Mendoza up thirty feet and pointed silently.

This road wound up into the hills above Hollywood, through one of many little canyons. The lots were cut out of the hillside, and many of the houses looked down on the road from twenty or thirty feet up; a good many of them were set back, behind trees, fifty or sixty feet. Here and there the hill at one side or the other fell away, and dropped rather abruptly down to a tiny box canyon. There had been a cycle of dry winters, and the underbrush looked scrubby and brown—tall wild grass, a little sage, wild flowering shrubs. Few trees; these foothills didn't grow many trees except those deliberately planted.

At the roadside here, above a steep drop of several hundred feet, there were still traces in the loose earth where they'd taken casts of the tire marks. Some of the marks still showed. Palliser led him across the road and showed him others—the wheel marks of a car pointed straight across the road toward that drop. There had been a two-bar post and rail fence, and about ten feet of it was carried away. It had never been intended as a barrier, being only a couple of feet high; white-painted, it was meant for a guideline at night. No street lights up here, and not every house had a light by its drive.

Where the Ford had gone over, a great swath was cut in the underbrush, ending about two hundred feet down where a young pepper tree had been violently uprooted.

"If that hadn't stopped him," said Palliser, "he'd have gone on down another hundred feet. God. And the ignition on—it could have gone up like—"

"Yes. Maybe that was intended," said Mendoza. "X wouldn't have noticed that tree in the dark." He looked around. The nearest house was just a glimpsed roofline about fifty yards away. "We've been very glib about this," he said slowly.

"I don't get you."

"Well, in the first place, this is something very damned unusual," said Mendoza. "Not a cop getting attacked, but getting attacked in this way. Why did it happen?"

"He found out something on—"

"Yes, I know we said that. But, so he did, and X somehow managed to put him down and out. Why did X go to some trouble to fake this accident?"

"Because, obviously—"

"How much easier it would have been simply to—well, for instance, bash him again until X was sure he was dead, and leave him in the handiest dark street. Or—well, the point is, to start with, this is probably a long way from wherever the first attack happened—"

"Which is probably why," Palliser pointed out.

"Yes, that could be. What's in my mind," said Mendoza, "is a funny little discrepancy. Look, John. After the initial attack, wherever and whyever and however it was made, X could have disassociated himself in several much easier ways. He didn't need to make it look like an accident in order to disassociate himself. As I say, he could have bashed Art's head in, left him in an alley, to make it look like a mugger. But he went to all this trouble instead. What does that say?"

"He's overcautious?" guessed Palliser, following slowly. "I don't see what—"

"We said, to disassociate himself, he set up this faked accident. If he was working alone, he went to quite a little trouble on it. Another thing, was there any reason he picked this particular road? Was he familiar with it, for some reason? It'd be lonely and dark, but I don't think it's the kind of road to appeal to neckers, somehow. . . . Quite a little trouble. He'd have to drive up here, from wherever it happened. Stage the accident. Then he'd have to walk down, in the dark, to where he could pick up a bus—because he wouldn't have risked a cab, he might be remembered if we ever did ask—though at that he might have, considering. And you know, John, if it was after ten-thirty or so, there wouldn't be any busses running. Except a very occasional one to L.A.—I'll look it up—only about two between midnight and 6 A.M., I think."

"Well . . ." said Palliser. He didn't get what was bothering Mendoza. Mendoza with quite a reputation as the smart boy, but for the first time Palliser got what Hackett meant when he said that Mendoza had a tortuous mind, looked for complexities and imagined subtleties where they didn't exist.

Mendoza got out a cigarette and lit it, carefully stepping on the match to bury it in loose earth. "I will grant you," he said, "that anybody wanting to set up a fake accident around here would be likely to think right off of a car going over a cliff. Brakes failing, or a moment's inattention, on a lot of roads around here . . . My own first thought would be, somewhere up in Griffith Park. But it's the summer season, the Greek Theater's open, and there'd be crowds up there, maybe to notice something. Or maybe, as I say, he knew this road for some reason."

"Yes," said Palliser patiently.

"Anyway, he was taking pains at it. Some effort and time spent. ¿Conforme?"

"Yes, sure."

"And then," said Mendoza, "when he came to the actual faking of the accident, our clever, cautious X did it in the damnedest silliest way possible. As if he thought we'd take one casual look, and say, 'Too bad, the poor fellow must have missed that bend in the road,' and never take a second look. As if he hadn't any idea that the Ford would leave tire marks for us to see, that we can take casts of—that we'd obviously look for skid marks and not find any. He'd used Art's own belt to tie him up, and he took a little trouble putting it back on him. It wouldn't have taken another thirty seconds to get Art's prints on the wheel and gear selector, but instead, he just wiped them both clean, and of course that told the story right there. He had heard of fingerprinting. But apart from that—"

"I don't see what you're getting at," said Palliser.

"Apart from that," said Mendoza, "either he didn't know that police forces are quite bright these days, with scientific labs and all the rest of it. Or he didn't care."

"I don't—"

"We built up a nice theory here," said Mendoza, and he was looking tired, a little sad, a little grim. "We said, wishful thinking maybe, it must have been that Art had found out something definite on one of these cases, and whoever he'd dropped on managed to jump him, put him out of action. And set up this fake accident so he couldn't pass on the information. . . . You've been a cop long enough to know that the obvious thing is generally what happened. Just look at the surface facts here and tell me whether we weren't reaching a little far out, toward the detective-story plot."

"Well, it's damned offbeat, sure, but—"

"He meant to see Telfer," said Mendoza. "We don't know whether he did. But that's not a very savory district around there. And didn't we say, not many men could put Art down and out just so easy. I'll tell you what's in my mind. Just a little easier than I can see that offbeat, implausible plot, I can see him—maybe on the way back to his car—getting jumped by three or four or five louts. Juvenile louts, maybe riding high on liquor or H. And the louts, rolling him, finding out he's a cop, and saying, 'Hey, let's have some fun with the cop.' And talking it over, forgetting about his

wallet—I know he wasn't robbed—looking for his car, finding it. Tying
him up in case he came to, while they argued about how to have fun with
the big cop— Maybe riding around in both cars awhile, talking it over.
And finally— And by that time so high they didn't take any special care
about it. They'd have been disappointed the gas didn't explode. Can you
see that?"

Palliser said, "Damnation. That's a story. Looking at it like that—just as
a separate thing, I mean— Hell, I've got to say it'd be just a little more
likely— I mean, well, expectable, if that's the word for it. But there's nothing to say—"

"We're like lawyers," said Mendoza. "We have to go by precedent. The
obvious is usually just what happened. . . . I'll just say, let's keep open
minds. It could be the way we thought—but it could be something altogether different too." He dropped his cigarette and stepped on it carefully.
"Let's get back and see if they've picked up Webster."

At about the same time, Sergeant Nesbitt of the Wilcox Street detective
bureau was feeling pleased with himself. There'd been quite a spate of
break-ins lately, with practically nothing to go looking on, and it was gratifying to have enough to make a charge on one of them. Three young
punks just starting to accumulate records; a good many cops would be seeing a good deal of them from now on. He just thought about that in passing; he wasn't a particularly imaginative man, and crooks were just crooks
to him. It was his job to deal with them. He dealt with them very
efficiently.

These particular crooks had had a couple of weapons on them—two
guns and a switch-blade knife.

He finished writing up his notes on it and said casually on his way out
to lunch, "Oh, Bill. You better send those cannisters down to headquarters
Ballistics. They're so damn fussy about checking everything. Just in case."

"O.K., will do," said Bill, and subsequently sent them, by way of an annoyed plainclothesman who had hoped to finish the *Times* crossword puzzle before anything came up.

The man full of hate was feeling something new and pleasant now.

He was important. He was the Goddamnedest most important guy in
L.A.

He was in all the newspapers, by God.

It was exciting, it was the most exciting thing that had ever happened
to him.

He couldn't make out why. Maybe it was different in a big town? Because there'd been others—he thought back, vaguely, to the others. He remembered a girl, a pretty girl, who had fought him and said, "Please." There had been that guy, Dago some kind, he'd been pretty high and hadn't fought him. And a while before that, another woman. He didn't remember where that had been, but in the country somewhere.

Not much fuss made about them. But of course he hadn't stayed around. Maybe there had been at that.

He got out his knife and looked at it. He was proud of the knife. He had made it himself, back at Marlett's old farm workshop. Out of a piece of old iron he'd made it, in his spare time, and Jesus, he'd sweated blood over setting them teeth in it, like a saw. It was a good knife.

It had made him somebody important.

He was in all the papers. When he'd heard some guys talking about it, in that bar last night, he'd gone out and bought a paper, and managed to spell out what it said. Some of the long words were hard, but he could read most of it. Right on the front page, it had been. Him!

The Slasher, they called him. He liked that. He liked the new, exciting feeling of being important.

It was a thing he hadn't expected, hadn't reckoned on at all. He liked looking at the blood, but it was a personal, temporary thing. In a vague way he'd known that if they caught him they'd kill him—the law—just like he'd killed. He didn't mind. No. His life hadn't been so good a thing to him that he minded. Ever since the fire in the school, back there when he was just a kid . . .

But now—now he was so important to millions of people!—he would mind. He thought back to the best one, the kid. Oh, Jesus God, he had liked that one, the feel of doing it. The kid, the damned little Mex kid, calling him sir. It had been all there ahead of him, the whole bit—his whole life, sex and fun and liquor and money—why the hell should he have it, when I never had nothing? I took it away from him, he thought. Like God or something.

Important. Hell, the whole state was talking about him, thinking about him. Just because . . .

He wouldn't have minded, a couple of days ago. Now, he thought furiously, delightedly, he'd like to do a lot more before that happened. Really show them—pay them all back, the whole world, for what they'd done to him.

So he minded, now. He was thinking about that now.

They'd be looking. Every man's hand against . . .

But it had always been that way.

He thought, and he made a plan. So they wouldn't find him.

He'd stayed in a lot worse places.

He hadn't much to pick up, in the room. He still had the money he'd saved on that job up north, a lot of money, nearly four hundred bucks. He put the bottle of bourbon into his pocket; and the cigarettes, the paper bag full of doughnuts, the extra shirt and sweater went into the little canvas bag.

He went out of his room, down the hall, and out the back door. Four houses up, along the little alley there, was Los Angeles Street. He walked up it to Temple, and on his way he passed the massive rectangular bulk of the Police Facilities Building, but he didn't know what it was.

As he walked up Temple a plainclothes detective was talking to the landlady in the house he had just left. "He *had* such a scarred face? What name did he give you?"

THIRTEEN

Just after four o'clock a very angry man burst in on Sergeant Lake and demanded, "This is the murder office, where they hunt the murderers? I will sue you all! Every man in the police I will sue! *Infame!* You call me a murderer, and it's a lie! You slander my good name!" He waved a copy of the *Times* in one hand and shook his other fist under Lake's nose. He was a little fat man about fifty, with a few strands of black hair plastered across a round bald head, a round olive-skinned face, and a pair of luxurious braggadocio mustaches. "Scoundrels!" he said richly. "I denounce you!"

Every man in the office heard him and came to find out what was happening. Mendoza said, "What's this all about?" and the little man swung to face him.

"Who is the chief man here? It is an outrage! My name you publish in the paper, and say it is that of this madman who kills children! I will sue you all—"

"Now just quiet down and come into my office, and let's hear all about this, Mr. . . . ?"

"Oh, you pretend you don't know my name! I am Tosci as you very well know— Francesco Tosci—isn't it plain to see in my own writing here? And I'm a respectable man, never in my life have I killed anyone—it is infamous!" He glared at Mendoza. "In all the newspapers, plain to be read, *my* name!"

Mendoza exchanged a glance with Palliser. "Let's see what you're talking about," said Mendoza.

Mr. Tosci was more than willing. He flung down the *Times* and with a shaking finger pointed out the reproduced illegible signature from the Liverpool Arms register. "My signature, it is—this I admit—but I do not kill people! It is—"

Mendoza and Palliser got him soothed down between them, with elaborate apologies, and Mr. Tosci sat down, sizzling only gently. Mr. Tosci was, it appeared, a barber, with his own shop over on Flower Street, and he had never so much as had a moving-violation ticket. He had not seen the newspapers today until a customer left a *Times* behind and, in tidying up, Mr. Tosci had picked it up and to his horror recognized the reproduced signature on the front page. He had rushed straight out, leaving the shop in his assistant's charge, to come here and accuse them of slander. He—

"Libel," murmured Palliser.

"Me!" said Mr. Tosci. "*My* name all over the papers, and saying I am this fiend who—"

Mendoza apologized again. "But you were at that hotel that night, Mr. Tosci? You signed the register when?"

The little barber calmed down enough to explain. They would understand as fellow men that these things happened, it was a great pity but one was only human. He had had a little argument with his wife, and there had been a few hot words, and in the end Mr. Tosci had stormed out of the house and decided to spend the night at a hotel. "Women," said Mr. Tosci with a sigh. "Always the one word more. I thought by the next day she would be cooled down." He had gone to the Liverpool Arms more or less at random, and been given a room, spent an innocent night in it, and gone to his shop at nine the next morning, after having breakfast at a Manning's coffee shop on the way.

"And why you are thinking—"

"Yes," said Mendoza. "I want Telfer, and I want him now. Somebody go and get him! Now, Mr. Tosci, if you'll just wait a little and let me explain—"

"Who is this Telfer? It is an outrage—"

But they got him to wait, with explanation. Scarne went out in a hurry to pick up Telfer, who was located in his shabby room at the hotel, reading a sports sheet and drinking port. Scarne hustled him into his clothes and brought him in.

"That's the man," said Tosci instantly as Telfer was ushered into Mendoza's office. "He will say, he was the man I paid for the room, and he gave me the key."

"Well, Telfer!" said Mendoza. "Did this man come into the hotel the same night the Slasher did?"

Telfer looked acutely uneasy. "I—guess he did. Sure."

"You don't remember, do you?" Mendoza's tone was cold. "You don't remember because you were drunk. You were so drunk you pulled a complete blank. You carry it fine, you look just a bit high, but it was the hell of a lot more than that, wasn't it?"

The man licked his lips. "No, it wasn't—I was all right—I wouldn't do a thing like that, I promised Mr. Morley—"

"Oh, so you'd been found drunk on duty before?"

"No, I—only once," said Telfer sullenly.

"You're going to stay here until you admit it," said Mendoza. "You were drunk. When Mr. Tosci here came in— What time?" he broke off to ask Tosci.

"It would have been about ten o'clock, sir."

"—you were still competent enough to get him to sign the register, give him a key. But when the Slasher came in, some time later, you were blind drunk. My God, you don't even know whether he came alone, do you? You said so, but he might have brought that first victim with him. Yes. You handed him a key at random, and he never signed the register at all. Did he? Look at me! Did you remember that you'd handed out two keys that night, to two different men, or was it a complete blank? Well?"

"No— I—you got it all wrong. There wasn't—it was just him, I remember all right—"

"Stop trying to cover up and let's hear the truth for a change! Do you remember *anything* about that night? Do you remember what room number you gave Mr. Tosci?"

"No, it's too far back, I—"

"It was number 118," said Tosci.

"Yes," said Mendoza, suppressing rage. The room where the body had been found was 214. As that had been the last signature in the register they'd taken it for granted it belonged to the Slasher. On Telfer's word.

"Damn you," he said rigidly, "do you know how much you've delayed us on this? Those other four victims are your direct responsibility! If you'd been in your right mind you could have given us a full description that next day, and ten to one we'd have got him within hours. How does it feel, Telfer, to be responsible for four murders? Two women, one of them pregnant, and a man and a little boy? They'd probably all be alive now, Telfer, if you hadn't been drunk that night! Do you realize that?"

"You can't lay it on me!" gulped Telfer. "I—that's not so—"

"You *were* drunk, weren't you? If you go on denying it, you know, I'm going to begin to think that you knew the other man—the Slasher—and had some reason to let him have a room without registering. Did you?"

"Jesus, no, I— All right, if I got to tell you, I guess I was high. Only for

God's sake don't go telling Morley, or he'd throw me out! I didn't mean to, and it was the first time since— I'd had an awful bad headache all that day, see, and I thought maybe a couple glasses o' wine'd settle it, that's—"

"Medicinal purposes," said Mendoza sardonically. "You'd had a good deal more than that by the time Mr. Tosci came in, hadn't you? Do you remember him at all?"

Telfer looked at Tosci and said, "Kind of. Listen, you won't go telling old Morley, will—"

"I wouldn't doubt he'll be finding out for himself. Do you remember anything about the man who came in later on? Anything at all? Such as a scar on his face?"

Telfer suddenly came apart. "I mighta never *seen* him, I pulled a real blank—see, first I knew about that at all, when they found the body, and it was 214, and 214'd been empty last I knew—and there was this name on the register I didn't remember so I figured I musta waited on him sorta automatic— I never—"

"Didn't you know that two rooms had been rented overnight? The maids—"

"I don't go talking with them," said Telfer sullenly. "How would I know? I'm only on the desk at night. If there wasn't no other name on the book—"

"You don't remember anything at all about the second man?"

"Mister, I pulled a blank, I said. I don't know if he was white or black. Listen, if old Morley—you won't go and give it out, will—"

"All right, that's all," said Mendoza. "You can go. But you might give some thought to what I told you, Telfer—if you hadn't been drunk that night those four people would probably still be alive today, and the Slasher would be in the County Jail instead of roaming around loose."

"I didn't have nothing to do—it was this real bad headache, see," whined Telfer.

"¡Basta!" said Mendoza. "Get out of my sight—somebody else can take a statement from you."

Telfer shuffled out quickly, and Tosci, wholly soothed and friendly now, shook his head gravely and said that he had always believed it, foolishness caused more evil than wickedness.

"A profound remark," said Mendoza wearily. "We're very sorry you've been upset, but you can see how the mistake was made."

"Naturally, naturally! If I had not been so outraged, sir, I would have realized that our fine smart policemen would not make such a mistake without reason—and I must apologize for anything I said when I—"

"Yes, yes, quite all right, Mr. Tosci."

When they'd got rid of the little man Palliser said disgustedly, "It shows you how even what looks like solid evidence can be misleading. That damned old lush—my God, if he'd given us a description then!"

"Way the hand got dealt," said Mendoza.

Sergeant Lake looked in and said they'd finally picked up Larry Webster and he was here.

Mendoza said, "O.K., shoot him in." He felt very disinclined to talk to Larry Webster, and his head was aching slightly.

Palliser asked, "Anything wrong? You look—"

"Nothing. Nothing new," said Mendoza.

He had dropped in at the hospital after lunch, and for the first time got hold of the senior doctor on the case— MacFarlane, who had done the operation. MacFarlane, unlike some doctors, didn't mind explaining to laymen. He was a tall cadaverous old man with shrewd blue eyes. "You understand," he had said, "that there's no certainty about such a case. He is holding his own, but I'm making no predictions as to whether he'll ever regain consciousness. If and when he does, it then remains to be seen whether there's any permanent brain damage."

"What effect might that take, Doctor?"

"Quite impossible to say. It would depend on what area of the brain was most severely damaged. We might find that his memory was entirely gone, for instance, or his speech. We're beginning to find out more about the brain, you know, and we do know that—in layman's terms—each section controls different functions. I have known of cases where the learned skills, such as reading and writing, were lost. I'll not minimize the situation, sir. At worst, if there's permanent damage, he could be a hopeless mental invalid, if he lives. At best, he could come out of this coma safe and sound with his mind intact. I was hoping to see his wife—"

"I don't think she should be told that," said Mendoza.

"I've always found that a policy of frankness is best. If the worst should occur, it would not be as great a shock. I—"

"Well, I don't agree with you," said Mendoza bluntly. He remembered how his grandmother used to say, "Don't run to meet trouble." "If she's got to be told sometime, I'll do it. I'll ask you not to tell her, Doctor. For one thing, she's expecting a child."

"Oh, I hadn't realized that. Well, perhaps in that case . . . And of course we'll hope that she need never know. It's quite possible that he'll recover entirely, though it was a massive fracture." MacFarlane shook his head.

"When will we know?"

"When and if he regains consciousness. Frankly, I'd be feeling much more hopeful if he wasn't keeping in such deep coma. It's been, what, around sixty hours now, and he's showing no signs of restlessness, which would be encouraging as a symptom of returning consciousness. When and if he should seem to be regaining consciousness we'll inform you at once, as I want someone who knows him, preferably not his wife, to be there when he does. That would be the immediate test, you see. Whether or not he would instantly recognize an old friend, understand what was said to him by such a friend."

"I see. Could you give me any idea how long it might be?"

"Sir," said MacFarlane sadly, "there are cases in a number of hospitals where a person has lived in a coma for months. He might regain consciousness tomorrow and recover quite normally, or he might lie like this for weeks—or he might die tonight. I don't know."

"That's frank anyway," said Mendoza evenly. "Thanks very much. . . ."

He looked at Larry Webster with dislike. The ordinary part-time, small-time pro, and looking it. A grown-up lout, with a graying crew cut, powerful shoulders; he had a rather stupid, weak face, with a loose mouth and small eyes. He was dressed neatly in working clothes, tan cord slacks and a shirt to match. You wouldn't have turned to look at him on the street, but Mendoza knew the type.

"Sit down, Webster," he said flatly.

Webster sat. "This is my day off, see, I din't know you fellows wanted to see me about anything, naturally, how could I? I been going straight ever since I got out last time, I got a good job at a garage, sir, the boss'll tell you. If I'd known you'd wanted to see me— I'm clean, you ask me anything you want—"

That type. Mendoza looked at him reflectively and then without speaking to him went out and told Sergeant Lake to put in a rush on a search warrant for Webster's living quarters. "Where does he live, by the way?"

"Cheap apartment hotel out on Olive. They picked him up at a bowling alley."

Mendoza went back to his office. "You know Margaret Corliss, Webster."

"Sure, sure, I know Madge. Madge is a nice girl; we been, you know, going around some together."

"How long have you known her?"

"Oh, gee, quite a while, I guess."

"Make a guess."

"Well—four, five years maybe."

"So you knew her when she was working at the Sally-Ann Beauty Shoppe?"

"I guess that was the name of a place she worked once, yeah."

"Where the proprietors were running a little mill."

"The cops said so," said Webster. "I don't know anything about that, nor Madge didn't either. Madge never suspected such a thing, she told the cops all she knew and they saw she didn't know anything about—"

"Insufficient evidence," said Mendoza, and laughed. "Sure. Did you know about the mill Dr. Nestor was operating? The doctor she was working for until he got himself murdered last Tuesday night?"

"Well, I knew she was working for this doctor, but he wasn't up to anything like that, Madge wouldn't—"

"She was working as a beauty operator at that shop? She's a qualified operator?"

"Sure, I guess so. That's right."

"Then how come she took a job as an office nurse? Quite a switch."

"Oh well, she said she thought she'd like a change, kind of. I guess it was like that. And this doctor, he didn't need a regular trained nurse, it was just somebody to—you know, answer the phone and put down about appointments and—"

"She certainly did that," said Mendoza without a smile. "Where were you last Friday night?"

"Friday night—well, I'd have to think—"

"Then think," said Mendoza. . . . Because, he thought, while the Corliss woman wouldn't have had any reason to murder Nestor, still there was something in that part of the puzzle. Art Hackett was no fool. He had started to suspect what was behind the Nestor setup, and maybe by Friday night he'd seen through it. And seen that possibly, if Nestor had kept any records of his illicit patients, that list would bear looking into. It could be that some frightened, ashamed young innocent had confessed to her parents, who had threatened Nestor with exposure—something like that. Hell, they didn't even know that the gun hadn't been Nestor's. Or there could have been an argument about money with a new patient's boy friend. Anyway, that list would be interesting: and if Hackett had seen through the Corliss woman's actions that Wednesday morning, he could have guessed that she'd have it. If, of course, there was one. And gone to see her . . .

"Think hard," he said. "Miss Corliss says you were at her apartment."

"Sure, that's right," said Webster. "I remember now. We had dinner together—"

"Where?"

"Uh—some grill out on Olympic. And we went back to her place and— and played cards—"

"¡Dámelo!" said Mendoza. "All very innocent. And how late did you stay, playing cards?"

"I don't know. Maybe midnight."

"Did anyone come calling on Miss Corliss that night while you were there?"

What looked like genuine surprise showed in Webster's eyes. "Why, no, sir."

"A sergeant of detectives? Sergeant Hackett?"

"No, sir. I never heard that name. Excuse me, why you asking all this, sir? Madge wouldn't be up to anything wrong, honest, sir. She was awful sorry about Dr. Nestor getting shot like that, it was some burglar broke in, wasn't it, and—"

"I'll bet she was sorry. Suddenly losing a profitable job. Do you know what cut he gave her?"

Webster shifted uneasily. "I dunno what you mean. Listen, we're both straight, Madge never—"

"That's fine," said Mendoza. "Then you won't object to my having your apartment searched, as we searched Miss Corliss'."

After a moment Webster said, "Why, I got no objection. I'm clean."

"Let's just see if the warrant's come through. . . . Did Miss Corliss ever give you anything to keep for her?"

"No, sir."

"If she did, better tell me now," said Mendoza.

"No, she never. I don't know what you're getting at. I told you all I know, can I go now?"

"No," said Mendoza. "You'll stay right here until a couple of men have looked through your place." He looked at his watch; they'd be night-shift men. He took Webster out to the anteroom. The search warrant was on its way up; Sergeant Lake was just leaving. Mendoza told Sergeant Farrell, just coming on, about the warrant, to send out a couple of men.

He went back to his office and called Alison to tell her he'd be late. Possibly not home at all until God knew when.

"All right, darling, we won't expect you. . . . Yes, she's fine, we've been so relieved ever since they called this morning." Alison laughed. "And, Luis, Máiri's taking all the credit for it—her solemn novena beginning to work, you know!"

"One good Christian soul to intercede for the heathen," he said. "Yes. Expect me when you see me, *hermosa*." Time enough to tell them, if . . . He put the phone down.

It was a definite headache now. He hadn't wanted much lunch, and come to think he hadn't had any breakfast. Ought to go out and get something.

Sixty hours, said Dr. MacFarlane. My God, thought Mendoza in vague surprise, is this still only Monday? These long, long days, since he'd ripped open that yellow envelope in the Bermuda hotel room . . .

It was seven-fifty, and he'd taken two aspirin Sergeant Farrell had found for him, which hadn't done much for the headache, when Glasser and Higgins came back from Larry Webster's apartment. Higgins said, "Sorry, we'd have been here before but we thought they ought to be checked for prints, just in case. Webster's are all over most of 'em—they checked Records." He laid a manila envelope on the desk; he was looking pleased.

Mendoza upended it and a dozen little glass ampoules rolled out. The kind containing one set dose each, for convenience in filling a hypodermic syringe. They were all neatly labeled. Morphine.

"*¡Qué bello!*" said Mendoza. "Where?"

Higgins smiled. "In the middle of a couple of pounds of sugar in a cannister in the kitchen. A lot of people don't realize we're halfway bright."

Mendoza said, "Fetch him in."

Webster came in smiling ingratiatingly. "Now you found out I'm clean, I never—"

Mendoza crooked a finger at him. "Come here, friend. Where'd you get these pretty little things? Are you breaking in on the big time, with dope?"

Webster looked at the ampoules and said despondently, "Oh hell. Hell and damnation. I never figured you'd find 'em where I hid 'em. But they're not mine. Honest, sir, I never— Madge asked me to hold 'em for her. I'm not taking no narco rap, not even for Madge. I'm leveling with you, they're hers, see—"

Mendoza said resignedly to Higgins, "Go bring her in, George. Fast. Tell Farrell to get the warrants, Webster and Corliss—narco possession. And he might send out for a sandwich and coffee."

"With pleasure," said Higgins, and went out.

"You can't hold me— I didn't have anything to do—it was Madge! I—"

"Sit down, Larry," said Mendoza tiredly. "You're going nowhere for a while."

FOURTEEN

Margaret Corliss didn't come apart as easily as Webster had, of course. She went on stolidly denying it, calling Webster a liar, saying they couldn't prove anything. Mendoza kept at her for some time before the sense of what he was saying seemed to reach her.

"We will prove it, you know. We're already on the way to proving that most of those names in the appointment book are fakes, and who else could have put them there and why? On that bloodstained smock, we're going to find that no legitimate patient ever bled in his office, and we know it's not his type of blood, but it is his smock. Why did he want a sterilizer? Why did he want morphine? And so on and so on. You'd be surprised what evidence the lab can find when they go looking, and they'll be taking those examination rooms apart. Now we've charged you with something, I can get an order to open that safe-deposit box you've got at the Bank of America, and I'll bet I'll find some interesting things in it."

That was what got to her. She shrugged and sat back, accepting it coolly: a gambler who'd lost this throw. "I guess you will," she said calmly. "You win. I did all I could—it was reely very awkward, Doctor getting shot like that, you can see it was. But if you open that box, well, you'll get the evidence all right. Just how the luck goes. Can I have a cigarette?"

He gave her one. "Now, let's have some straight answers."

"I don't know why I should tell you anything."

"Look," he said. "You'll get a one-to-three and serve the minimum term, on a first offense. You're still ahead in a way—I expect you've saved some of your cut. But whoever killed Nestor, again in a way, put you in this spot, didn't he? All I want to know—"

She was quite informative, eventually. Once she saw she couldn't get out of it, she told him what he wanted to know; and he thought she was telling the truth.

Frank Nestor had approached her much as Mendoza had imagined, seeing her name in the paper in connection with the beauty shop. He'd said frankly he intended to set up a mill and needed a woman contact. She'd sized him up and thrown in with him, and it had turned out a very profitable venture. In one way, thought Mendoza, those two had been much alike: all business, taking the main chance.

"Doctor was very clever," she said. "He had a lot of ever so clever ideas. You know those ads in the personal columns that say, Any girl in trouble call this number? Well, of course they're put in by real charities or social workers, like that, and they don't exactly mean the kind of help Doctor meant." She smiled. "But he had a lot of cards printed with that on, and my phone number. I left them all sorts of places, places he picked out—at the college libraries at U.S.C. and U.C.L.A., and so on, and in ladies' rooms in all the expensive night clubs and big hotels—"

"Quite the little publicity agent," said Mendoza, "wasn't he?"

"Oh, I said he was clever. And once you get a business like that started, you know, the women tell each other—it gets around. Not that I ever had any experience of it before," she added hastily. She wasn't, at this late date, going to connect herself again to the Sally-Ann business. "And he was good, too. Never the hint of any trouble, he was always so careful, everything all sterile, and he always put them right out with the morphine. . . . I don't know where he got that. No, that's level, I reely don't. I know he'd have liked to use a regular anesthetic, like sodium pentothal or something like that, but there was no way for him to get hold of it, you see. He was very careful, about the morphine—he always tested their hearts first and took their blood pressure. He'd have made a good surgeon. Right from the first, it all went as smooth as could be. . . . You'd be surprised, how many of the girls who called me, who'd meant to go on and have the baby and put it out for adoption, because they didn't know where to go, you see—they jumped at it, when they found how Doctor wanted to help them."

"How did he charge?"

"Well, that was the only trouble there ever was," admitted Margaret Corliss. "Not all of them could raise the kind of money he was asking. You see, the—well, call them patients—he wanted to get, he said from the first, were the ones with money. Who could pay anything up to five hundred or more. You know, the college girls with big allowances, or society girls and women. Like that. And we did get some of those, too. Sometimes he'd be sorry for a girl and do it for less. The way we worked it was, I'd meet the girl outside somewhere, like in a park, and size her up, what she was good for, and make the deal. Then, when she'd raised the money, we'd make an appointment at my apartment. Doctor'd meet us there and drive us to the office—it was always at night, and he'd go round all different ways so she wouldn't be quite sure where she was, see—and do the job, and then I'd keep the girl overnight. But he was so careful, there was never any trouble. They never knew a thing about it, under the dope, and it was just like in a regular hospital, everything sterile and all. They never knew his name, of course. . . . The lowest I ever remember was two hundred, he was sorry for that girl. He always asked five at least and if we could see it was a woman with real money he'd get seven-fifty. A couple of times we got a thousand. Because it was all guaranteed absolutely safe, you see. Those two were older women, and we figured they were married —maybe society women of some kind, you know."

"Did he keep a list of them?"

A little reluctantly she said, "It's in the safety box. Of course most of them gave wrong names, I suppose."

"Just about as he started practice—both legitimate and otherwise," said Mendoza, "he claimed to have had a legacy. Do you know anything about that five thousand bucks?"

She shook her head. "Not reely. He spent a lot of money fixing up the office, and I did ask him how he could afford it, because he paid cash. He just laughed—he was always laughing, Doctor, such a handsome man . . ." She brushed away genuine tears. "And he said something about casting your bread on the waters."

"Oh, really. Well, and so who was the appointment with on Tuesday night?"

"There wasn't one. No, reely there wasn't. I'd know, I was always there, just like I told you. There wasn't any job set up for that night. I don't know what he'd be doing at the office."

"All right. You knew he was stepping out on his wife—did he use the office to meet women?"

"I wouldn't know," she said primly. "It was just business between Doctor and me— I'd heard him say things about women he went out with, but not to reely know anything about them, or where he took them or like that. He might have, but I wouldn't know."

He accepted that. Quite a story, he thought; Nestor had been an enterprising fellow. Saw where there was money to be had and went for it the shortest way. And when you looked at it from one angle, it could be he'd saved a lot of suffering and maybe a few lives, those women coming to him, instead of some drunken old quack or dirty midwife.

"Was there any recent trouble over a patient? Over the payment, or anything else?"

No, there hadn't been, she said. There had been a couple of girls lately who'd had difficulty raising the money, and one of them—this had been about a month ago—had somehow managed to get it, and came back, but Nestor had refused to do the job because it was too late, he said—over three months. "You see how good he was, he said it wouldn't be safe for her. She was awf'ly mad, and argued with him a long time, but he stuck to it."

Nestor a very canny one, too. Legally speaking, the abortion of a foetus more than three months old was manslaughter. Which Nestor had undoubtedly known.

"Well, what do *you* think happened?" he asked suddenly. And he'd once thought, maybe it was this woman and Webster had assaulted Art, if . . . But he was a long way from being sure about that now. He thought she was leveling, and at a second look he didn't feel she'd be capable of that. "You hadn't any quarrel with him—"

"The idea! Of course not, we got along fine, Doctor was reely a very nice man."

"Did he keep a gun in the office? He didn't. Well, who *do* you think shot him?"

She looked a little surprised. "Why, it was the burglar, wasn't it? Did you think it might be some—some private reason? Oh, that reely couldn't be. Nobody had any reason to want him dead. Everybody liked him. He had ever so many friends, he was always going to parties. . . . Well, sometimes it'd be with his wife, sometimes not, I guess, from what he said. Nobody seemed to like her much, she's a funny kind of woman, the little I've seen of her. But he was popular. . . ."

She was helpful, but not to the extent he'd hoped. Still, it cleared this part of the puzzle out of the way; and he thought she'd spoken the truth when she denied that Nestor had had an appointment—a professional appointment—that Tuesday night.

Meeting a woman in the office, maybe, and her husband suspecting, following her?

Glasser took Margaret Corliss up to the County Jail and saw her booked in, with Webster. Mendoza sent a routine note up to the Narcotics office about them, though the narco charge wasn't anything really, a formality.

It was ten-forty; he ought to go home. He sat on of inertia, reading reports. . . . There'd been men out, covering this crowded downtown area, asking questions wherever rooms were rented, at hotels, at random. They had reported evidence from several places of men with burn-scarred faces, and they had turned up three such men, all on Skid Row. Considering the importance of that, all were being held overnight for the Garcia boy to look at in the morning. One little lead looked more promising, even though it had come to nothing. A man with such a scarred face had taken a room at a house on Boardman Street, giving the name of John Tenney. The landlady had thought he was in, but when they looked, he wasn't, and all his few possessions were gone. It was possible he'd overheard the plainclothesman asking questions and slipped out the back door. But of course that didn't say he'd been the Slasher—and it didn't say where he'd gone.

Ought to go home, thought Mendoza. He wasn't accomplishing anything here. . . . He heard the phone ring on Farrell's desk, and Farrell's voice. And then, "Lieutenant? Call in from a squad car—another Slasher job, but the woman got away—"

"¡Dios! Where?"

"San Pedro, between Emily and Myrtle. It just happened ten minutes ago."

"I'm on my way. Send another car."

When he did get home, at two-thirty Tuesday morning, he was feeling the way Higgins had felt on Friday night. How the hell had they missed him? The men in the first squad car couldn't have been five minutes behind him, and they'd had four other cars there within ten minutes, and men on foot to search that whole area.

Etta Mae Rollen had sobbed, "It was like he come up out of the ground —all of a sudden he was just *there*, and g-grabbed for me, and I saw his knife—"

Etta Mae had been very damn lucky indeed. She had managed to tear herself away from him, and she had run. A block up she had seen a squad car coming toward her, and run to it screaming. The men had called in for assistance at once and gone back with her to where he'd been, but if he'd appeared out of thin air he'd disappeared that way too.

They weren't doubting it had been the Slasher, because Etta Mae had got a good look at him, and she offered a description before they asked any questions. She'd been coming home from her job as waitress at a coffee shop on Broadway. Just past the corner of San Pedro and Emily streets, where there was a good bright street light, there was a TV store where the lights were left on all night. She'd had a good look at the man with the knife. "He wasn't awful tall but he was mighty strong, only he just had hold of a piece of my coat mostly, and it tore all down the seam—you can see—when I got away from him. Oh, he had a terrible sort of face— I'll never forget it to my dying day!—it was all thin and sneery and he had this great big red scar, all puckered, right across the middle of his face, and his eyes kind of glittered—"

Her coat hadn't been torn, but partly cut with a knife where he'd missed his first stroke. Probably the lab would tell them it had been a partly serrated blade.

They'd covered all the alleys and back yards, they'd routed out the few night watchmen left in warehouses, to search the premises; they'd really covered that area. And nothing had shown. Where the hell had he gone? At least he hadn't killed again. But if they didn't get him soon . . .

Mendoza had been tired, earlier this evening. Now he wasn't conscious of tiredness—he'd worked past that point—and he ought to sleep but he knew he wouldn't. He ought to have something to eat, too, but he wasn't conscious of hunger. His mind kept going over and over all this—what they had, on both cases, and on Art. Was the assault on Art linked with either, or had that been the extraneous thing? He didn't know; he couldn't make up his mind.

Canyon Drive, in Hollywood. The Hollywood hills. Very exclusive, expensive houses up there. Had X been familiar with it, or picked it at random?

He slid the Ferrari into the garage; he went out, pressed the electric-eye button to close the door. Very quietly he let himself into the dark house. But as he went down the hall he saw light there under the nursery door and softly opened it to look in.

"Well, you are late and no lie," said Mrs. MacTaggart.

"What's wrong, Máiri?"

"Nought at all much. I've been up a bit with young Johnny, but they run a wee temperature for nothing at all, times. He's gone off peaceful as you please now, you can see. Just a bit fretful like." El Señor, self-appointed guardian of the twins, had joined her sleepily and was sitting on the foot of Master John's crib, playing watch cat.

"Sure?" Mendoza looked down at the flushed sleeping twins. It was very odd, suddenly, the idea that they were his; he could hardly disown it, young Master John with that uncannily identical widow's peak, if he had Alison's hazel-green eyes. He didn't know much about the twins, thought Mendoza suddenly. The little monsters who'd kept them awake at night until they found that treasure, Mrs. MacTaggart. Of course at this age, he supposed, they hadn't developed very distinct personalities maybe. He wasn't around them enough to say, really.

Miss Teresa moved restlessly and one pink thumb found its automatic way to her mouth. Mendoza yawned. He thought vaguely, start any sort of job, you ought to see it's done properly. He ought to know more about them. Try to be around more.

But things came up. . . .

"You are tired to death, man," said Mrs. MacTaggart softly. "Can I not get you something? A nice cup of hot broth now? Or a hot whiskey and lemon maybe?"

"No, thanks, Máiri, I'm fine."

She surveyed him calmly, drawing him out to the hall. "If a lie could have choked you, that would have done it. We are only waiting on God's will. Go to your bed, man."

He went on down the hall. El Señor had opened the bedroom door to join Mrs. MacTaggart when she'd first gotten up to check on the twins. Mendoza shut it and began to undress. Alison was asleep, but stirred and muttered his name drowsily as he got into bed.

He would not sleep, of course. Another full day tomorrow. Go and see that Anita Sheldon? No, first get the court order to look at the Corliss woman's safe-deposit box. That list. Yes, and what would that tell him? Nothing really. No real lead there; she'd said there hadn't been trouble over a patient. Hell.

Cast your bread upon the waters . . . How did it go on? Something about, *it shall be returned to you in many days.* That didn't sound quite right. Scriptures. Prayer. Only there was nothing to pray to. . . . Just the way the hand got dealt round.

He decided quite suddenly that if Art died he'd resign from the force. Even apart from this thing—working overtime at the job, the fascinating job, when it wasn't necessary. Not fair to Alison; not fair to the twins, as time went on.

He lay thinking about that, staring into the darkness. And El Señor, shut out from his mother and sisters, rattled the doorknob impatiently until he tripped the latch, slid in, and landed with a thud on the bed on top of Nefertiti, who spat at him sleepily.

Who might get his desk? Mendoza wondered. If? Higgins was the next senior sergeant after Art, but they'd probably bring in somebody from outside—the senior sergeant from Vice or Narcotics. Little shake-up all round. If.

What would he do with himself all day? Learn to live a new kind of life. Play a little. More time with Alison and the twins.

More than half his lifetime, jettisoned. And God, he'd seen friends killed on duty before, but . . .

He had known he wouldn't sleep, but he slept, heavily; and woke feeling stupid and slow. It was six o'clock. That much sleep anyway. Six o'clock Tuesday morning, and—

He got up, shaved and dressed, went out to the living room and called the hospital. The patient's condition was unchanged.

He thought, Friday night. Call it eighty hours. MacFarlane: *be feeling much more hopeful if* . . .

He went out to the kitchen. Mrs. MacTaggart was already there, making coffee. Of course, of course. Her damned novena: out to the church first thing for nine days.

"You will stop for breakfast somewhere," she said severely.

"Yes, all right." Suddenly he realized he was ravenous. He did stop, at a Manning's coffee shop on Vermont, and had three eggs, a double order of bacon, and four cups of coffee. When he got to the office he was feeling more like the old Mendoza, the boy with a little reputation on this force.

By the time the lab man came in he'd got quite a bit done. He'd started the machinery going to get that court order on Margaret Corliss' safe-deposit box. He'd looked over the night reports—they'd had four men looking all around that area of the Slasher's latest job, but they'd turned up nothing. He had got the other warrant on Corliss, charging her with complicity in Nestor's abortion trade. He'd talked that over with the D.A.'s office, and the charge on Webster. The D.A.'s office didn't think they'd press an accessory charge on Webster: too vague.

He had called Mrs. Anita Sheldon to ask if she'd be at home this morning; he wanted to talk to her. She had sounded very frightened. "You can't come here! Oh, please—if Bob ever got to know, he'd— And it's his day off, I can't—"

"Would you prefer to come to my office? Say eleven o'clock?"

"Oh dear. Oh, I guess so—if I've got to—there won't be any *reporters*, will there? *I* don't know anything to tell you about Frank, really, I didn't know him very well—"

He had called the Elger apartment and got no answer. Called Elger's office and been told Elger was out somewhere with a client.

When the lab man came in Mendoza was studying the official shots of Nestor's body. They weren't telling him much. He had a little box full of the contents of Nestor's pockets on his desk; he looked at it and picked up the button. That ordinary little button that had been clutched in Nestor's dead fingers. The clue out of the detective story.

"Morning," said the lab man, whose name was Duke. "Say, I've got a little something, I—"

"Hold it a minute," said Mendoza. "Jimmy! I must be going senile. Jimmy, I want search warrants for the quarters of every male in the Nestor case. Let's see, Webster, Elger, this Bob Sheldon, every legitimate male patient he had, every man listed in his address book, every male he knew. To look at their clothes. Just in case. It's possible X didn't realize he'd lost a button. You never know where you'll hit pay dirt. Damn it, it's a very long chance, but—" He looked at Duke. "What have you got?"

Duke laid a pair of shoes on the desk. "We're always damn busy," he said, "but we've been concentrating on Hackett the last couple of days. As you can imagine." Duke was snub-nosed, freckle-faced, and right now looking pleased with himself. "We've been going over his clothes, for any little thing that might show up. Now it's your job to say what this might mean, but for what it's worth, it looks kind of interesting to me. Not to say suggestive. These are his shoes, I just got to them this morning."

"Yes?" said Mendoza.

They were a pair of black moccasin-type shoes, middling expensive, well worn but polished. Mendoza thought absently, Size 11B.

Duke lifted them and held them toward him heel first. "Look at that. They're not new shoes, but they've been taken care of. Kept polished. But here, on both heels—that is, the back of both shoes above the heels—is this deep scrape. The surface of the leather's entirely gone, violently scraped off—more on the left than on the right one."

"Yes, I see."

"Well, that wasn't done when he went over the cliff in his car, you know. It wasn't done on anything in the car. I've had these under the microscope, and I took scrapings to look at closer. You know what was in those scraped spots? Asphalt. Asphalt and," Duke added dreamily, "crankcase oil, and bird droppings, and decayed leaves. Traces, you know."

Mendoza sat up. "What the hell? Does that say—"

"Me, I'm only a chemist," said Duke. "You're the detective. But we aren't exactly disinterested in this one, and I saw what Dr. Erwin said about that skull fracture. The back of the skull, more to the left side. I think this does tell us a little something."

"*Asphalt—*"

"The way I read it," said Duke, "and stop me if I don't make sense, is that he got that first blow outdoors, on the street. Literally on the street—a blacktop street. He got knocked backwards, maybe tripped over something or it was just a very hefty blow—and his feet went out from under him, scraping the street, and he went down hard on something—as Erwin said—broad and hard and flat."

"But not the street itself," said Mendoza slowly, "because there wasn't a trace of anything like that in the wound or on the scalp. Of course he had on a hat, but you didn't find anything like that on it. Nothing extraneous."

"That's right," said Duke. "I just thought I'd pass it on."

"And isn't it interesting," said Mendoza. "Thanks very much. . . ." He thought about that story he'd built up, on Art. The louts jumping him. The outside thing? Or, if you were bound to link it with another case, had he shown some suspicion, and been followed outside?

The nice neat detective-story plot—Art stumbling across the X in the Nestor case, or the Slasher—he had bought it, but now he wasn't so sure.

Art attacked in the street. A blacktop street. Like how many thousand streets in L.A. County?

What the hell?

And that was when the man from Ballistics came in. A paunchy, elderly fellow named Hansen, who said, "I think we've cleared one up for you, Lieutenant. That chiropractor that got himself shot. We've got the gun."

"¡Parece mentira! Don't keep me in suspense—where the hell did you—"

"Well, the Wilcox Street boys sent it down, and I fired a few test slugs, and they looked sort of familiar—I did the tests on that slug out of the chiropractor. It's a Harrington and Richardson Sportsman 999—nice little gun. Nine-shot revolver, retails for about fifty bucks." He laid it on Mendoza's desk.

"And where did the Hollywood boys get it?"

"Attempted break-in at a drugstore, Saturday night," said Hansen. "Three juveniles. They got this off one of them."

"¡Un millón demonios!" said Mendoza exasperatedly. "¡Ya se ve! So it was the outside thing on Nestor—just what it looked like. The outside thing—too."

FIFTEEN

Mendoza called Wilcox Street and set up an immediate date with Sergeant Nesbitt at the County Jail. Damn it, this turned the whole case upside down. The facts that Nestor had been an abortionist, had been cheating on his wife, didn't matter a damn; he hadn't been murdered for a personal reason; it had been just what it looked like, the break-in, the burglars finding him there, using the gun in panicky impulse. So the Nestor thing hadn't anything to do with the assault on Art; he hadn't stumbled onto the personal killer there because there wasn't one. And there wasn't any way he could have stumbled onto these actual killers, either.

So, a hundred to one, the assault on Art had been the outside thing too. Because, to hell with the train wreck, Mendoza didn't see one like the Slasher setting up that faked accident—elementarily faked as it had been. If Art had stumbled onto the Slasher that night, the Slasher would probably have just yanked out his homemade knife and . . .

And, buying the detective-story plot, they'd wasted three days on that. Where to look now? Nowhere. They hadn't a clue as to where or when the first assault on Art had happened.

He said to Sergeant Lake, "If I'm not back when Mrs. Sheldon comes in, ask her to wait, will you?" He went downstairs to the lot and headed the Ferrari for North Broadway.

Wait a minute. Were there any leads? Even small ones. It could have been the way he'd outlined it to Palliser, a little gang of juvenile louts drifting the streets, jumping Art on impulse. In that case, a very small chance indeed that they could ever be identified, charged. But—the *terminus a quo*. He was all right when he left Mrs. Nestor's apartment on Kenmore. He'd meant perhaps to see the Elgers, see the Corliss woman, see the desk clerk, but they didn't know where he'd actually headed from Mrs. Nestor's. But Mendoza thought that Margaret Corliss was leveling with him now, and she'd denied again that Art had been to see her that night. All right. Mendoza was thinking again about Cliff Elger. None of these people had had anything to do with taking Nestor off, and it looked pretty farfetched that any of the rest of them could have had anything to do with the assault on Art; but Cliff Elger? That big boy, bigger than Art, who had the hair-trigger temper? Could he have got so mad at something Art said—about his wife, probably—that he struck that first violent blow, and found himself stuck with a badly injured cop? And with the reputation to preserve . . .

Art attacked in the street. His heels scraping a blacktop street as he fell —but he hadn't fallen onto the blacktop, or there'd have been the same traces of asphalt and so on in the wound.

"I'm a fool," said Mendoza to himself suddenly, braking for a light. It was, when you thought about it, obvious. Whoever had struck that blow. Art standing at the curb or in the street—he could see it—car keys in his hand, ready to walk round the car to the driver's door. Either he'd been already facing someone, talking, or someone had spoken to him and he'd turned. And the blow struck—the violent blow—and he had fallen backward, feet sliding out from under him, and gone down hard on the broad, flat expanse of the car trunk. There wouldn't have been traces on the car, after the accident; he'd been wearing a hat.

That said a little more, but it wasn't any lead to who. Cliff Elger, roaring mad at something Art had said, following him down to the street, getting madder when he couldn't rouse Art's temper in return . . . Maybe. Normandie was a blacktop street.

So was the street Madge Corliss' apartment was on. So were a lot of streets—including Third and the side streets around there. Wait a minute again. If that little build-up about how it happened was so, didn't it say probably that the car had been parked along the curb, not diagonally? And that wasn't much help either, because on most streets in L.A. and Hollywood the street parking wasn't diagonal. You got that in a lot of towns around—Glendale, Pasadena, Beverly Hills—but not much here.

"Hell," said Mendoza, and parked, pocketed the keys, and walked up to the jail.

Sergeant Nesbitt was waiting for him at the top of the steps. "Lieutenant Mendoza? Nesbitt." He was a square, solid man about forty, with a square stolid face. "I understand you're going to claim my young punks on a murder rap. Well, glad to oblige. They're all under eighteen, though, you won't be getting the gas chamber for them."

"What's the story?" They went inside.

"Well, we've been having quite a little wave of break-ins up in my stamping ground. Drugstores, independent markets, dress shops, and so on. The cheaper stores where the buildings are old and the locks not so good, you know. It's been mostly petty stuff, we figured it was juveniles— not much cash, and stuff they wouldn't get much for— I think myself some of it was stolen to give away to their girl friends, make them look big. You know. Cigarettes, liquor, clothes from the dress shops, and so on. Well, Saturday night a squad car touring out on Fountain spotted what looked like a flashlight in the rear of this drugstore on a corner, took a closer look, found the back door forced, and picked these three up in the stock room. They had an old Model A Ford sitting by the back door, half full of stuff they'd already piled in it." Nesbitt rummaged and produced his notebook. "One Michael Wills, Joe Lopez, George Kellerman. They're all from down around your part of town, and they've all been in a little trouble before. Wills was picked up and warned once for carrying a switchblade, and the other two have one count each of Grand Theft Auto —little joy riding, you know. Probation. Wills and Kellerman are seventeen, Lopez sixteen."

"Well, they've got into big trouble this time," said Mendoza. "Who had the .22?"

"Wills. I'd say he's the ringleader."

"O.K., let's go in and look at them."

Nesbitt told the desk man whom they wanted to see; in a few minutes they were let into one of the interrogation rooms, and the boys were brought in by a uniformed jailer.

Mendoza looked at them coldly, resignedly. They were about what he'd expected to see, from the black leather jackets and wide belts and dirty jeans to the expressions on their faces. And there was a lot of talk about it, from a lot of different people, and a lot of different solutions offered to cure the problem. It was a problem all right. They said, clean up the slums. A fine idea, but it wasn't going to cure the problem, because quite a lot of very respectable citizens—Luis Rodolfo Vicente Mendoza among others—had grown up in the slums. They said lack of discipline, which was a little more realistic, but it was theoretically a free country and you couldn't tell people how to bring up their kids. They said prejudice, they said inadequate public schools. What nobody among all the do-gooders would ever admit was that some people just came equipped that way, and that more people were just naturally the kind who'd play along with any strong character to be one of a gang; and you weren't going to change character overnight.

Wills was tall and thin, with an angular pale face, sullen pale eyes, and lank dark hair; he looked older than seventeen. Kellerman was a fat lump, big and awkward and blond. Lopez was a little runt of a kid, skinny and dark, with terrified eyes. They just stood and looked back at him.

"Well, let's get the show on the road," said Mendoza sharply. "Which of you shot Nestor last Tuesday night?"

They looked surprised; and then Lopez looked almost idiotic with panic. "We n-never shot nobody, mister. *¡Se lo digo, no! Honestamente,* we never—we never do a thing like that—"

"You got rocks in your head?" said Wills coldly. "What makes you think we shot a guy?"

"I don't think, I know," said Mendoza. "There's no point going the long way round here. You've been pulling a series of break-ins. Probably in other places than Hollywood. Last Tuesday night you broke into the office of Dr. Frank Nestor, on Wilshire Boulevard. Only you found the office wasn't empty—Dr. Nestor was there." Why had he been there, by the way? Not very important? "Wills, you had the .22. When Dr. Nestor showed up, did you panic and shoot on impulse, or did you kill him deliberately? You *did* have the .22—it's your gun?"

"For Christ's sake!" said Wills incredulously. "That's crazy, man! We was never near no doctor's office, Tuesday night or any other! We never heard o' that doctor. Why the hell'd we want to break in a doctor's?"

"I can think of reasons," said Mendoza.

"Oh—dope. We don't go for that crap," said Kellerman. "Not me, boy! I seen what it done to my brother. You're nuts—we'd never do a real bad thing like that. Gee, what was a couple cartons cigarettes and—"

"I said, let's not go the long way round," said Mendoza. "I've got other things to worry about than you three louts." He took a step toward them and Lopez cringed back. "Now listen—"

"You c'n beat me all you want!" cried Lopez in a high frightened voice. "Just go on 'n' try—you never make me— *¡Santa María y Josefo—* I never—"

"Oh, for God's sake, Joe," said Wills contemptuously, "they don't dare lay a hand on us!" He gave Mendoza an insolent leer. "They got to stay little gents—ain't that so, bloodhound?"

Mendoza pasted a careful, bland smile on his mouth. Never let them see they were getting to you. It was sometimes difficult. Sure—that juvenile thing last year. All the careful rules and regulations to protect the citizenry—and the L.A.P.D. with a lot of private rules on that too, especially about the minors, and what it came to was that the punks could call you every name in the book, tell the most obvious lies, accuse you of anything from wife beating to sodomy, and you had to take it without even a word or two in reply. Sometimes a man lost his temper a little and roughed up one of them—which was the only way to reach a lot of them—and then you got the press screaming about police brutality and the tenderhearted public excitedly demanding investigation. Mendoza smiled at these three young punks, pityingly. The only other way to reach them was to talk to them like the immature children they were. "Look, Mikey boy," he said very gently, "I've got no time to waste playing games with little boys. I'll give you just five minutes to tell me a straight story, but whether you do or not, I'm getting warrants on all of you for murder. As of now. That .22 is the gun that killed Frank Nestor, that we know, and it was in your possession on Saturday night. Which of you had it on Tuesday night?"

Evidently he reached them with that. Lopez started to say a fervent Hail Mary, with his eyes shut; Kellerman just looked worried. Wills suddenly dropped his sneer and said, "Listen, is that on the level? Somebody got killed with that gun? Jesus—"

"I told you there was somethin' a little funny about it, Mike," said Kellerman.

"That's level," said Mendoza. "What fancy story are you going to tell me now?"

"Jesus," said Wills. "I'm not taking no murder rap! I never had that gun until Thursday night, bloodhound, and that's level in spades. I never laid eyes on it till Thursday."

"¡No me tome el pelo! Don't kid me," said Mendoza skeptically. "So where'd you get it?"

Wills licked his lips. "We found it," he said.

"Oh, for God's sake," said Mendoza, "can't you think up a better one than that?"

"No, honest—honest, mister, we did!" said Lopez eagerly. "It was down on Main, we was all together—we saw this guy drop something, just ahead of us, see, and Mike picked it up—I saw him—honestamente—"

"That's right," said Kellerman stolidly. "I saw him too. It looked like a swell gun, not so old either—but I told Mike, see, when I see the serial number's filed off, I said, get shut of it, maybe it's hot."

"You've got all the answers," said Mendoza. "Do you really think I'm going to buy that one?"

"It's the truth!" snarled Wills. "It's all I can tell you. Jesus, I wish now I'd tossed it in the first alley we passed, but I didn't. It was mostly loaded, too—eight slugs in it. That's God's own truth, this guy dropped it and I picked it up. Right in the street, see—on the sidewalk."

His tone was passionate. Mendoza looked at him. "So now suppose you produce a nice tight alibi for all three of you for last Tuesday night."

"*Hell!*" said Wills violently. "You Goddamn cops—"

"I ain't taking no murder rap either, Mike," said Kellerman. His broad forehead wrinkled painfully with thought. "It ain't sense. So maybe we get hit a little tougher if we tell them, it's still not *murder*. Gee, none of us'd do a bad thing like a murder!" He looked at Mendoza earnestly. "We couldn't've, because we was down in Boyle Heights last Tuesday night, we cracked a TV store and got a lot of stuff. You can check it, I guess—lessee, we was with them girls up to about nine, and then we did the store, and we sold a lot of the stuff at a pawnshop on Whittier Boulevard, that'd be about ten-thirty, wasn't it, Mike? And—"

"Oh hell!" said Wills sullenly. "Well, all right. That's where we was, just like George says."

"That's right, mister, *honestamente—*"

Mendoza looked at Nesbitt and raised his eyebrows. Nesbitt shrugged.

"We'd sold stuff there before—the old guy's name is Behrens. Honest, he'd tell you we was in, about ten-thirty, and—"

"All right, what's the address?" Mendoza wrote it down. "I'll probably be seeing you again." He turned on his heel. Walking down the corridor, he asked Nesbitt, "What do you think?"

"*Finding* a gun," said Nesbitt. "I ask you."

"Down on Main," said Mendoza absently. He thought suddenly, suppose you had a gun you wanted to get rid of? A hot gun. Maybe one you had a license for, so the serial number could be traced. You could sell it, but the transaction would be traceable too. You could pawn it, but all pawnbrokers were supposed to keep records of serial numbers. You could just dump it somewhere, in an empty lot, but there was always the chance of someone seeing you, or finding it and reporting it. Really, a very excellent way of getting rid of it would be to file away the serial number and then drop it somewhere, casually, in a district like Skid Row, where the chances were that whoever picked it up would keep it for his own nefarious purposes or pawn it for drinking money.

He wished now he'd asked those punks if they remembered anything about the hypothetical man who'd dropped the .22. But it had almost certainly been after dark, and they wouldn't remember any details. Hell. And no way to . . .

"We'd better check," he said to Nesbitt. "The pawnbroker, and his stock. Just in case."

"Sure," said Nesbitt sadly. "We have to check everything."

Boyle Heights—Whittier Boulevard. That would be the Hollenbeck station, and Mendoza thought he'd get them to check it out for him. He thanked Nesbitt for cooperation and drove back to headquarters, thinking about the gun.

The Sheldon woman hadn't shown, though it was after eleven. He called the Hollenbeck station, and the sergeant he talked to groaned but said he knew they were keeping busy with this Slasher down at headquarters, and they'd check out the pawnbroker for them. "How's that sergeant of yours doing in the hospital?"

"Not so good," said Mendoza. But a sudden queer warmth spread through him, for the real concern in the man's voice. That sergeant over at the Hollenbeck station had probably never laid eyes on Art Hackett. This was a big police force, though perennially undermanned for the population it served, and it took pride in itself for being, for all that, the top force anywhere. He realized suddenly that every man on this force who had read that brief newspaper story—*Veteran Homicide Officer in Near Fatal Accident*—was pulling for Hackett. Just because he was another cop. Cops had to stick together.

He put the phone down. Palliser came in, looking annoyed, and said that Miguel Garcia hadn't recognized any of the three men with burn-scarred faces they'd held overnight. "I got the Rollen girl to look at them too, she said definitely no. So wc lct thcm go."

"Yes. It won't be as easy as that," said Mendoza. "Have those search warrants come through yet?"

"A few. Your idea was that button? Well, if that *is* a real clue," said Palliser, "and Nestor really did snatch it off his killer, I should think X would have felt it go. And—" He stopped.

"Yes," said Mendoza. "Belatedly, I saw that too. If he realized that Nestor had snatched it, maybe in reaching for the hand that held the gun, how easy simply to take it back when Nestor was dead. So he doesn't know it's gone from his jacket or whatever. Or didn't then. So maybe he's hung the jacket away in his closet for us to find. . . . I thought for a little while we'd cleaned up Nestor, but I'm having second thoughts." He told Palliser about the young punks, about the gun.

Palliser said thoughtfully, "Well, I'm bound to say, if I had a hot gun to get rid of, that might be a damn safe way to do it. Down there, nobody'd be likely to hand it to the nearest patrolman and say, 'Look what I found.' Of course you're checking with the pawnbroker."

"*Naturalmente*—or rather, Hollenbeck is. You and Bert and whoever else is available had better go out on these warrants. Of course, there's every chance that since the murder X has noticed the missing button and, taking no chances that he dropped it somewhere incriminating, has got rid of the jacket or suit—or replaced the button. Anyway, have a good look for that—a button that doesn't quite match the rest. . . . I want to see Elger again—and this damn Sheldon woman—"

The outside phone rang, and Sergeant Lake looked in and said, "It's your wife."

All Mendoza's muscles seemed to tighten. If the hospital . . . He said, "O.K.," and picked up the phone, seeing his fears mirrored in Palliser's dark eyes. . . . "*Querida?*"

"Luis," she said. "Luis—we're at the hospital. Angel's just got the doctor to tell her—how it really is."

"Oh," said Mendoza. Some of the tension went out of him, and Palliser, seeing it, drew a breath and went out. "I'm sorry about that."

"He kept looking so serious, and— When we'd thought— And he tried —but Angel kept at him, and he finally told us—how it might be. Luis, it can't happen, can it?"

"I don't know, *belleza*. It's a thing, we wait and see."

"I know—but—"

"How is she taking it?"

"All right," said Alison. "It's no good fainting and having hysterics, but— She's—all right, so far. But I can't bear—"

"Yes," he said. "There's more to Art's Angel than I'd thought. She's a good girl. But I'm sorry she knows. I'd hoped—"

"*Protecting* us!" said Alison with a little angry half sob.

"Just not running to meet trouble, *amante*."

"No. I know. But—"

Neither of them said anything for a moment; there was nothing more to say. The line hummed between them, a small comforting contact.

"Alison," he said. "Alison."

"Yes."

"How would you feel about it—if I resigned from the force?"

There was another little silence. "You mean . . . ? I—I don't know, darling," said Alison. "Would you—want to? I mean—"

"I don't know," he said.

"What would—you do with yourself?"

"Something, I suppose. Find something. *Esa es cuestión aparte.* I don't know."

"If you really wanted to—" she said. He heard her draw a little breath. "Will you be home at all? I know how you're working at it—"

"I don't know that either, my darling. I'll call. You take care of Art's girl—and yourself."

"Yes," she said forlornly. "Yes, Luis."

He put the phone down. He looked around the office. He really didn't know. Twenty-two years. Riding a squad car. In plain clothes, down in Vice—spotting the pro gamblers mostly, because maybe he was half a pro gambler himself. And eleven years in this office, sergeant and then lieutenant.

He'd sat at a desk up here for eleven years, working the cases as they turned up. Always plenty of cases to work.

He wondered how it would feel, to be plain Mister instead of Lieutenant. To have nowhere special to be at a specified time every morning. To have no work to do at all. Just time to play.

The job wasn't necessary. All that nice money, in gilt-edged securities, in real estate. No. But . . .

Sergeant Lake looked in and said, "That Sheldon woman's here, Lieutenant."

Lieutenant. He had a place in life, as *lieutenant.* But maybe not fair to Alison, to the twins—and if Art . . .

But meanwhile, thankfully, he had the job to do. He said, "O.K., Jimmy, shoot her in." He snapped his lighter, lit a cigarette.

SIXTEEN

Anita Sheldon was a vapid-looking little blonde with china-blue eyes, and she was very frightened. She hadn't known Frank Nestor very well, she didn't know anything about him really, it'd just been like meeting him for cocktails somewhere, nothing *bad*, but Bill had got so mad about that Youngman guy that time, there hadn't been anything *in* it, but Bill—if he got to know about this—He didn't *understand*, him away off on some job maybe four or five days, and a girl liked a little fun . . .

Within five minutes Mendoza put her down as a shallow little tramp; and when he heard that she'd been married to Bill for five years he provisionally crossed off Bill, who must have found her out in that time if he wasn't mentally deficient. Bill hadn't got mad enough to shoot any of her other pickups; it wasn't likely he'd shot Nestor. When he learned that Bill had been on his way up to Santa Barbara with a truckload last Tuesday night he crossed him off definitely.

Well, she had met Nestor in his office on two occasions. "But not to *stay* there, of course, we'd go on to some nice restaurant, somewhere like that."

When Mendoza thanked her, told her she could go, she shot off like a scalded cat. Evidently, he thought, Nestor had picked up whatever came handy: and from all he knew of him, that ran true. Ladies' man, not too particular. The ones like Anita Sheldon flattered and caught by his charm —but Ruth Elger had been something else again. Going out with him because she'd had a fight with her husband. Using Nestor. And maybe the first time she'd strayed, and Elger . . . But would Elger have *shot* him? Hair-trigger Elger more likely to have beaten him up, maybe?

Mendoza took out the button and looked at it. Well, see what turned up there. He felt harried; he was getting nothing on all this at all, and time was catching up to him—he had the worried feeling that there was something, some relevant fact, right under his nose, if he wasn't too stupid to see it.

He forced himself to sit still, take a couple of deep breaths. He was trying to go at it too fast, do everything at once. Sit and think calmly over the evidence, take it easy.

Nestor's high-society scrapbook was lying on his desk along with a few other things; he picked it up. It occurred to him that possibly, if his guess as to its purpose was the right one, and if Nestor had even once recognized a patient, he might have indicated it in some way. Either in the scrapbook or on that list in Madge Corliss' safety box. Idly he started leafing through the book.

The first item taped to the page was short: *Miss Susan Marlowe, daughter of Mr. and Mrs. William Marlowe, spent a delightful Easter weekend cruising aboard the yacht of the J. Haskin Treadwells.* No pictures on that. Of course Nestor would have been interested because of his slight connection with Marlowe. He went on looking; the year-in, year-out social affairs, the races, operas, first nights, teas and dinners and lectures. A lot of pictures, but Nestor hadn't scribbled anything in the margins. "¡Nada!" said Mendoza, and shut the book.

And the outside phone rang on Sergeant Lake's desk. . . . "It's another one, Lieutenant. Another Slasher job. Just found."

"Hell!" said Mendoza. There was nobody else in the office. "Where?"

"San Pedro and Fifth. Squad car just got there."

"All right. Rout out Bainbridge."

There was quite a crowd around when he got there; a second car had arrived and two uniformed men were rather helplessly trying to move the crowd on. The press had also arrived; he saw the flash bulbs going off, and Wolfe of the *Citizen* gave him a tight-lipped humorless grin as he pushed into the crowd.

"They do say the population's rising too fast, Lieutenant. This is one way to cure it, I guess. But we always thought you boys were a little smarter."

"Like to change jobs?" said Mendoza curtly. "Let me through, please. . . . What have you got on it so far, boys?"

They hadn't got much. The body—looking much the same as all the other bodies the Slasher had left behind him—hadn't any identification on it. It was the body of a middle-aged man, and the only items on him were half of a Greyhound Bus ticket from San Diego to Los Angeles, three single dollar bills and some change, in an otherwise empty wallet, and a flat pint bottle of scotch, nearly empty. His clothes were old and shabby, and he looked unkempt.

The body had been left where, probably, it had become a body, in the middle of a narrow alley between two buildings. It had been found by a couple of truck drivers backing in there to make deliveries.

Nothing much to be done on the spot. Quite impossible to say whether an item or so among the many dirty, miscellaneous items in the alley had been dropped by the Slasher.

"All right," said Mendoza. "You know the routine." Lake would be chasing up somebody to come and take pictures. "When the surgeon's seen him and we've got some pictures, let the ambulance boys take him. Drivers' names? . . . O.K. We'll try to identify him through the bus ticket—I'll take that stuff now."

But as he pushed out through the crowd again a hand touched his arm timidly. "Please, you are one of the *Polizei*, sir? I—I—maybe I know something about this terrible man, sir. I—"

He looked down at her. The careful English was thick with German accent. She was a little plump blonde, a real blonde, about thirty-five; she looked like the illustration on bars of very good Dutch chocolate, pink cheeks and all. She was wearing a mightily starched white apron over a very neat blue house dress. "Please," she said anxiously, "I am Gertrud Flickschuster, sir."

The interested crowd surged nearer, and Mendoza said, "For God's sake, can't you get these ghouls to move on? Mrs.—Flickschuster?—come over here, please. What is it you think you know?"

"I hear the poor man is found, it is another from—by this terrible murderer, so I come. To find a—the word I don't know—*Geheimpolizist*—to tell. I think I have seen this man. In our delicatessen he comes"—she pointed up the street—"last night."

"You'd better come back to headquarters and make a statement," said Mendoza.

She hesitated. "You will—I may come out again? There is Rudi alone in the shop—"

"Yes, of course." He smiled at her; by the accent, she hadn't been in the theoretically free country long. He put her, starched apron and all, into the Ferrari, drove back to headquarters, and took her up to his office. "Take some notes on this, Jimmy. Now, Mrs. Flickschuster?"

It seemed that the Flickschusters, who had come here four years ago, kept a delicatessen. They stayed open until nine most evenings, and one or the other of them or both were always behind the counter. And just before they closed last night a man had come in and bought a half pound of sausage, a pound carton of potato salad, and a quart of milk. Gertrud had waited on him and remembered him well—"Because he is so ugly, sir, a terrible face. It has the hollow cheeks like a death's head, and this terrible mark on his face—*vernarben—die narbe* on his face, from the burn, it looks—all red, across the nose. But it is not until Rudi has been reading the newspaper that I have known—it is saying about this man—"

"Yes." And that might be a more interesting and significant little story than it looked at first glance. Mendoza got her signature to a statement, phoned for a car to drive her back to the delicatessen. . . . The Slasher, buying precooked food at night. The man was staying somewhere, damn it, but with the press relaying his now known description to the public, he hadn't rented another room as yet—that they knew. Nobody was likely to rent him one when they'd had a look at him.

Etta Mae Rollen attacked at San Pedro and Emily. The latest unknown corpse near San Pedro and Fifth. Mendoza frowned at a city map: about four blocks apart. The Slasher holed up somewhere, in hiding? Sense enough to read the papers, know he had to hide? But where, for God's sake, in that rabbit warren of crowded downtown streets? Business of most kinds was thriving—there wouldn't be many empty buildings. And, true enough, the population increasing at such a rate that there wouldn't be many empty houses, either. In that section people lived cheek by jowl, there wasn't much privacy. What hole could a loner like the Slasher have found?

Hell. He wondered what, if anything, the Hollenbeck station was getting from that pawnbroker. It would be a help to clear those juveniles out of the way, know definitely they had an alibi for Nestor—if they had. Which would say that their story about the gun was probably gospel truth. He decided it was too soon to call Hollenbeck and ask.

Sergeant Lake came in and said that Nestor woman was here, asking to see him. "You haven't had a chance for lunch at all, shall I tell her to wait or come back?"

"No, that's O.K.—shove her in." He was curious to know what she wanted.

As Madge Corliss put it, a funny kind of woman indeed. He didn't think any disillusionment with Nestor was responsible for her flat emotionlessness. He remembered what Marlowe had said of her and silently agreed: rather a stupid woman.

She came in and sat down in the chair beside his desk. Her mouse-brown hair in its old-fashioned shoulder-length bob hung lank about her face. She had on a printed cotton house dress, bright pink, and a shabby green cardigan over it; white ankle socks with the kind of cuban-heeled black oxfords made for old ladies with fallen arches. She hadn't any make-up on except lipstick, and most of that had worn off.

Nestor's essential character aside, reflected Mendoza, it really wasn't hard to see why he had . . .

"Yes, Mrs. Nestor?"

"Well, I'd just like to know," she said in her flat nasal voice, "when I can get into his office. You people have put a seal on the door. The rent'll be due in ten days and of course I don't want to pay another month's rent. And there are some valuable things there I could sell for quite a lot of money. To another doctor."

"Well, I'm afraid I can't tell you anything on that," said Mendoza. "We don't know, it may be we'll want to have another look around there. But I see your position, and we'll try to arrange to free it before the end of the month."

She did not thank him. "It's been a nuisance, I must say," she said. "The bank not giving up that money and so on." The news of Madge Corliss' arrest had made minor headlines this morning, the revelation of Nestor's undercover trade; evidently Mrs. Nestor didn't read newspapers and had no kind friend to tell her about it, for she didn't mention it at all. But with one like that, who could say? She might, if he asked her, say, *Oh, that. I'd suspected it all along.*

"As long as you're here, Mrs. Nestor, I'd just like to go over it with you again—about Friday night, when Sergeant Hackett came to see you. . . ." He took her all through it again, and she gave him the same answers, disinterested.

He let her go, dispiritedly. His head had begun to ache again. He couldn't see where to go from here—if nothing turned up on that button. But he didn't know yet that those juveniles were in the clear, of course. And if they weren't, where else to look on Art?

It was one forty-eight. It seemed to him that lately, the last few days, time had slowed down somehow so that there were twice as many hours in a day. He wondered what the boys were getting on their searching jobs.

Sergeant Lake came and looked at him disapprovingly and told him to go get some lunch.

"Yes," said Mendoza, and dialed the offices of Cliff Elger and Associates. He was told that Mr. Elger was out to lunch with a client. Where? Well, probably Frascati's on the Strip or the one on Wilshire.

Mendoza tried Frascati's on the Strip first, as the nearer place, and

spotted his man at once. Elger's great bulk, clad in loud tweed, was
perched on a bar stool. He was doing most of the talking, gesturing
widely, laughing. The man sitting next to him was much smaller, present-
ing a thin, narrow-shouldered back and a bald spot.

Mendoza climbed up on the stool at Elger's other side. Elger was halfway through a martini: probably not his first. The other man, a depressed-
looking middle-aged man, was staring silently at a glass of beer.

"—just got to take it in your stride," Elger was saying heartily. "You
know? Script writers always change a book around some. What should
you care, you've got the money. You worry too much, friend."

The depressed-looking man said in a surprising Oxford accent, "But she
wasn't a chorus girl, she was the vicar's daughter. It all seems quite point-
less to me, and *rather* silly."

"Now you just stop worrying, old boy," said Elger.

The bartender came up and Mendoza said, "Straight rye. Mr. Elger!"
Elger swung around, looking surprised. "Oh—it's you," he said.

Mendoza smiled offensively at him. "Business as usual? I thought you'd
be keeping a closer eye on your Ruthie. Or have you hired a private eye?"

Instantly Elger's expression darkened. "What the hell d'you mean by
that? That bastard Nestor—*and* I wasn't surprised when I saw the *Times*
this morning! Ruthie told you how it was, she hardly knew the guy, it was
just to spite me she—"

"Naïve, Mr. Elger!" said Mendoza cynically. "They can sound quite
convincing, that sex."

"Damn you—"

Mendoza picked up the shot glass and swallowed half the rye. "Don't
sound so upset," he drawled. "Happens in the best of families—"

Elger swung on him and he ducked, alert for it, and caught the man's
wrist in both hands. It had been an awkward swing, from a seated position; but if Elger had been on his feet . . .

He said incisively, "Hold it, Elger! Take it easy. Now what did I really
say? Nothing much. You lose your temper that easy very often? Because,
if you do, I'm surprised you haven't got stuck with a corpse—or a near
corpse—long ago!"

"What the hell," said Elger sullenly. He shook his arm free of Mendoza's grip. The other man was watching interestedly. "You talking about
Ruth—damn cop—"

"To see what little thing might set you off. Look at me!" said Mendoza
sharply. "Did you lose your temper last Friday night, Elger? Did you? Because of some little remark Sergeant Hackett made to you? Did—"

"I told you I never heard of that guy!"

"Did you follow him down to the street and attack him there, Elger? And then find you'd nearly killed him? And there he was, right in front of your apartment—and if he came to, he'd talk—or he might just die, so we'd get you for manslaughter if nothing worse—and there's your business and reputation gone. Was it like that?"

"I don't know what the hell you're talking about," said Elger roughly. He threw the rest of his martini down his throat so fast he nearly choked on it.

"So you thought of the clever little plan— If you did that, Elger, by God, I'll get you for it," said Mendoza. In that moment he was nearly persuaded that Elger was his man: Elger so quick to hit out in blind fury, over very little; and the suppressed savagery in his tone, the expression in his eyes, made Elger draw back a little.

The bartender was looking worried. They didn't like disturbances in a high-class place like this. Mendoza finished his rye. "Make no mistake," he said, "if it was you, we'll get you. I'll be seeing you again, Elger." He slapped down a bill and stood up. . . .

And where had that got him? He knew that a very small thing might trigger Elger's temper.

The lab, he thought. They really did work miracles these days, those boys. Would there be any difference in the composition of blacktop—could they tell its age, or degree of wear—something to pin down the locality? A forlorn hope. He could ask.

He ate a flavorless sandwich at a drugstore and went back to the office. Sergeant Lake was leaning back reading a teletype.

"Here's our boy," he said, handing it over. "Not that it helps us much on catching him."

Mendoza read the teletype standing. It was from the sheriff of El Dorado County up north of Sacramento. The inquiries on any known knifings with the same M.O. as the Slasher's had been out for nearly three days; this was the first response.

What Sheriff Jay Hampton had to tell them was that there'd been two murders in a little place called Georgetown, about three months back. Quite a surprise to Georgetown, which had a population of about eight hundred—Mendoza found on consulting an atlas—and probably hadn't had a murder since the frontier was officially closed in 1890. You could read between the lines of Sheriff Hampton's terse statement. The first victim had been Betty Riley, a local girl well known and liked. Engaged to the son of the town's bank president; her father was one of two doctors in town. A pretty girl, popular and virtuous. She had been to see a girl friend, Martha Glenn, a block away from her own home, on the night of April thirtieth. Had left there about nine o'clock to walk home, and next turned up dead on her own front lawn, at ten-forty. Found by her father as he came home. She had been stabbed and slashed to death, and mutilated afterward. The sheriff had called in the state boys, the B.C.I. from Sacramento, and their crime lab had said that the knife used had a partly serrated edge. Absolutely no clue had turned up; it looked like the random killing of a lunatic. She had not been raped, and evidently hadn't had time to scream.

"¿Y pues qué?" said Mendoza irritably.

The second victim, found next day in a field outside of town, had been one Giorgiono Cabezza, an itinerant agricultural laborer who'd just been fired from his job on a local ranch. Here they turned up something more definite. Cabezza had been seen in several bars the night before; he'd been talking about leaving town, finding another job farther south. Toward the end of the evening, around midnight, he'd been seen with another man, a transient just passing through—nobody in town knew him—possibly a hobo. Nobody in Georgetown had ever seen him before, and nobody had heard his name. But the surgeon said Cabezza had been killed about 2 A.M., and the transient was the man last seen in his company. They had a good description of him: a man about forty, very thin, hollow-cheeked, middle height, and he had a very noticeable scar from an old burn across the center of his face. No evidence actually pointed to him as the murderer, but he had not been seen anywhere around since, and Georgetown had had no more knifings.

"What the hell does that tell us?" demanded Mendoza. "For God's sake!" He'd been hoping that if the Slasher had killed before, especially in a small town, something more definite might have been got on him. This was just nothing but confirmation of what they knew. And he should have known it wouldn't be anything more; if any other force had got anything definite on the man there'd have been flyers sent out.

And the papers yelling their heads off about inefficient police. Mostly. Spare a moment to be grateful to the *Times*, which had run a thoughtful editorial pointing out all the difficulties of the hunt for the random killer.

He put the teletype down and dialed the Hollenbeck station. "Well, I was just about to call you, Lieutenant," said the sergeant he'd talked to before.

"Anything?"

"It seems your Ballistics man gave you a false alarm. Our boys just got back from checking. I looked up the record on that break-in—TV store on Soto Street—and it didn't close until eight-thirty so the break-in was after that. This Behrens, the pawnbroker, naturally didn't know from nothing about those three juveniles, never laid eyes on them, never bought anything off them—but he hadn't expected any check, of course, and there were four transistor radios and a portable TV in his back room, and the owner of the TV store could identify them by the serial numbers. From his place, all right. Well, you said your chiropractor was getting himself shot between eight and midnight. Kind of tight times, when you think— and not very likely the kids would pull two in one night, so close together. They probably broke in that store between nine and nine-thirty, or a bit later. The pawnbroker's not talking, but they say they were in his place about ten-thirty. Well, they'd probably—"

"¡Basta ya!" said Mendoza. "I know. Go out on a little spree with the cash from the pawnbroker, with or without girls. Not go looking for another likely place to break in. So the fancy story about finding the gun is probably—definitely—true. Thanks very much."

"Sometimes you get a tough one," said the sergeant sympathetically.

Mendoza stared intently at the desk lighter. So it was back to the private thing. Was it? Not those juveniles, but maybe an older pro? Entirely too coincidental that those juveniles should end up with the gun. No, it had been the private kill, on Nestor.

Well, what about Elger for it? A gun used, and then that canny, cautious plan to get rid of the gun . . . Not in character?

Andrea Nestor, now . . .

Some other jealous husband?

Look thoroughly at everybody in Nestor's address book. That Clay had sounded quite level, but there might be . . .

Palliser came in. He said, "I don't know what anybody else may have turned up, but I've drawn blank on your button."

"More good news," said Mendoza. "Sit down and tell me who you've eliminated."

SEVENTEEN

The man who wanted to kill was seething with hate and anger, where he lay hidden in the place he had found for himself. He had thought of killing, more killing, to pay them all back, but his slow mind had told him that they would come hunting him, they would hunt him out—a place like that room. He needed a secret, safe place to be when they came hunting. So he had come here.

But for the rest of it, it had all gone wrong. He had only caught one of them to use the knife on, make the blood come. A man more than half drunk, who came lurching up the street toward him in the dark, and was easily pulled into that alley.

And people looked at him queerly, even more than usual, almost as if they knew what was in his mind. That woman at the place he'd bought food, last night . . .

He'd gone into a bar and heard some men talking. They were talking about him—him, the big important one, the Slasher, and what they said did not fill him with panic but with rage. How they knew what he looked like now, there'd been an artist's drawing in the paper, they said, and how they were telling everyone not to go walking alone at night, to be careful.

There hadn't been people out, near as many as usual—he'd noticed that. He'd drifted, a dark shadow, in the shelter of buildings around many streets, and when they came past him it was in groups, two or three together and walking fast.

On account of *him*. Dim pride rose in his mind; but it was no good, it spoiled everything, if it stopped him killing any more of them. He wanted in sudden furious rage to kill and kill—pay them back. They mustn't hunt him down, to stop him.

He had almost reached out for the nearest of those two women who had come along, hurrying, not talking—he could take her, let the other one scream and run, he could be gone before . . . But he was some way off from his safe, secret place, and he didn't.

Instead, he had taken out his knife and looked at it: not really looked, there in the dark, but felt it. He liked to use it to make the blood come, and it came quiet and easy. But you had to be near, to kill with the knife. . . .

He'd had a gun of his own, once. Back the first place he'd worked after the orphanage, old man Haskell's farm outside of Younker, back in Georgia. You went out shooting birds, come fall, everybody did, and he got to be a pretty good shot on an old gun Haskell let him use, and he saved up and bought himself a new gun. It was a .22 rifle, and he'd been pretty good with it. That was a long time back. He didn't remember how long, he'd been a lot of places since, and he didn't remember what had happened to that rifle.

You could kill from a ways off with a gun. With guns. It wouldn't be as good, there wouldn't be as much blood, but you could kill more of them and still keep safe. . . . He'd laughed and laughed excitedly, thinking about it, how it would be, do it like that. Slip out at night, and he could be maybe half a block away, and get them maybe two, three at a time, and then while they were running around like a flock of scared chickens, hunting him, all the time he'd be back in his secret place—waiting for the dark and to go out again. It would be like that.

And he knew where he could get the guns. There was a place not far away, guns in the window.

Vague memory stirred in his mind, about guns. . . . He'd been a lot of places, but mostly country places, because he couldn't do many city jobs. Country places, where people hunted things. Rabbits and birds. Going out rabbit hunting, a man would say, passing along the fence by where you were. That's a nice stand of corn—and you with a day's work ahead. . . . Going out people hunting, he thought to himself, and shook with laughter again.

So he'd started up through his secret place, to go there and get the guns. This was a big, dark, strange place, with him the only one in it. He came out from where he'd made a kind of bed from an old broken-down sofa left there, and he was in a vast empty underground room cement-floored and walled. There were shapes against the walls, a big square furnace, pipes disconnected and rusty, a row of ancient refuse barrels, and empty shelves all along one wall. At the far end of the big room were stairs.

He'd drifted up them silently, though he knew there was none to hear anywhere around. At the top he was on a little square landing and there was a door, but it was half off its hinges, hung drunkenly open so he could see beyond. He stepped past the door, onto bare dusty flooring, to an irregularly shaped wide corridor. There was another door to the right there: it had something painted on it but a couple of letters were partly worn away and he didn't know what it meant—it said L D ES. Down at the middle of the corridor it widened out and there was something like a bar standing there.

He didn't go that way. He turned to the left and went through an open arch into another vast dark place: but he knew the way. He felt along carefully by the wall, until his feet told him he was nearing the door. The door was very heavy and had an iron bar across it inside; he pushed against that hard, and reluctantly the door creaked open and he came out into the night.

There was no moon, but he knew where he was. He was standing at the side, almost at the very end, of a big brick building, and ahead of him was a steep cement ramp leading to the street. He went up it.

It was late; he'd lain a long while thinking about all this, before deciding. There wasn't anybody around at all, streets dark and empty, and he walked quickly. After he'd got the stuff, he thought, he'd like to do one tonight, but it was too late—nobody around, nobody at all. . . .

And he'd had a little job, to get it all back to the safe place. Because he was going to kill, and kill, and kill . . . They'd never find him, and he'd need lots to kill so many. . . . But he had it all there at last, and he was satisfied. Only, too late to go out and hunt any of them tonight. Have to wait for the dark again. . . .

All day he had lain here, waiting for the dark. Now he was hungry, and what he'd got at that store last night was gone. He sat up, thinking about that slowly. For the dozenth time he picked up the newspaper and carried it to a place under the ventilation grill in the ceiling where light came in.

He'd spelled out the words under the picture. *Artist's sketch of the Slasher from his description. Have you seen this man?*

It didn't look an awful lot like him, he thought. Except there was the mark—the terrible red mark—right across the face. . . . They'd laughed at him, they'd called him— And there had been a pretty girl named Ellen, who had screamed and run. In sudden red fury, he crumpled up the paper and flung it away into a corner.

It wasn't dark yet. It wouldn't be dark for a while. But he was hungry. But they mustn't hunt him down. He was going to—

After hesitation, he started up through the dark, for his door to the outside. He had his hat pulled low over his eyes, and he thought he could pretend to have a cold, keep his handkerchief up.

There was a hamburger joint a block up where you could take it away with you, didn't have to eat there. He walked up to it fast. There were some other people there, eating or waiting for their hamburgers. He asked for two; when they were shoved across the counter at him he put down a silver dollar.

"Buck an' ten cents, mister."

He found the extra dime. He walked back quickly, carrying the food. Down in his safe place he ate slowly, enjoying the greasy hot flavor of beef and onions and pickle. . . .

Now he was lying here hungry for something else. For the dark. For the dark to come down, so he would know it was time. The right time to go out and start his night's hunting.

He held a gun on his lap, and now and then he touched it almost lovingly. The knife was good, but the gun would be good too. Better, now. Better for him.

I'm a people hunter, he thought, and laughed.

Most important guy in the whole Goddamned town. In all the papers. Everybody talking about him. The Slasher. Be the hell of a lot more important before he was done. . . .

Laughing at him. Not wanting to look at him. Stupid, they said. The girls, the pretty girls looking at him and—

He was on his feet, pacing excitedly, cradling the gun.

A pretty girl named Ellen, screaming when he tried to kiss her . . .

Suddenly he yelled in a high savage voice, *"What d'you think of me now, you bastards? All you Goddamned bastards—show you—show all of you—"*

Nobody heard him at all, and after a while he stopped.

Jesus God, wouldn't it ever get dark tonight?

Dwyer and Scarne came in while Palliser was still talking. Nothing had shown up, of course. Palliser had been a little excited to find a button missing from Cliff Elger's topcoat. "But it was a bigger button, and a different color, and who'd be wearing a topcoat in July?" And as for asking whether anybody had given away any clothes for salvage lately, you couldn't expect anything on that. If X had belatedly realized he'd left that button behind, and couldn't replace it on the jacket or cardigan, and gave it away to be rid of it, he wouldn't say so. The canny way he'd got rid of the gun . . .

Mendoza agreed inattentively. He had a county guide open in front of him and was studying the big detailed map of the downtown area.

"I only dropped in to report no progress too," said Dwyer. "I'm on my way down to Santa Monica to have a look at the wardrobe of a fellow named Ross. Don't know how well he knew Nestor—he's just there in the address book. And you'll likely be getting a formal complaint from a Wall Street type by the name of Marlowe. He wasn't home when I got there—seems he has a butler who also acts as his valet, all veddy-veddy, but it was his day off; the maid was scared of me and my warrant, and let me in. The master arrived just as I was looking over his second-best evening jacket, and he didn't like me at all. He said so. *Police*, he said, and it was a dirty word coming from him, pawing over his clothes—very highhanded, and the idea of trying to connect *him* to a sordid crime— Quite a little pile there, I'd say."

"Money *and* family," said Mendoza, sounding faintly amused. "But you're not going anywhere else. All that can be put off—our Slasher is the hell of a lot more important. That one we've got to get, and in a hurry."

"You have any bright ideas how to do it, beyond what we're doing? Somebody'll recognize him and say so—he's got to eat, he'll be showing somewhere—"

"Eventually!" said Mendoza. "It's not good enough. Yes, I've got a bright idea. Jimmy! Call down to Traffic and ask Fletcher to come up here. Now look." He pointed at the map. "He's stuck to the downtown area up to now, and never above Third. This is his part of town. Incidentally, remembering what we got from up north, the part of any town where that sort does land—the drifters, the almost bums. On and around Skid Row. All right. We had one quite promising lead, you remember, from that leg work on men with scarred faces. A man like that had rented a room over on Boardman, said his name was John Tenney. Had, we subsequently found, paid the landlady partly in silver dollars. Only he skipped before we laid hands on him. He could have skipped because he heard our man questioning the landlady—we don't know."

"Are you heading any particular direction?" asked Dwyer.

"*Paciencia*. After that we got the attempt on the Rollen girl and the murder of this late unknown. Both along San Pedro, four blocks apart. I'll tell you where I'm heading. I think he's just smart enough to have realized that, with his description in circulation, he's got to have cover, some safe hole to lie up in. I think he's found one, and it'll be somewhere not too far from where he attacked those two. I can't offer a guess where it might be, an empty building—if there are any—or what. But he's got to be some-

where around there, and he won't be coming out of his hole until after
dark. We're going to get a lot of men, the more the merrier, and conduct a
building-to-building search in a twelve-block square between Main and
San Pedro, between Temple and Third."

"For God's sake!" said Scarne. "Do you realize how much territory that
covers?"

"Some of it," said Mendoza, "is taken up by the Civic Center. We're
sitting on one perimeter of it right here. I know. A lot of residential
streets, a lot of business—and part of Skid Row. Nevertheless, we're going
to do that. We're going to pry into every nook and cranny—"

"Now?" said Dwyer.

"There's four and a half hours of daylight left. Set it up, get it started.
After dark, they can search in pairs. And—" Mendoza stopped, and said,
"Yes. The dogs. I want the dogs. Damn it, where's Fletcher?"

The L.A.P.D. had been slow to start using dogs. Maybe some prejudice
of the chief's; the chief liked dogs and maybe was reluctant to see them
used that way. But with increasing evidence of their great usefulness, the
force had finally acquired a few. Officially they were under the Traffic
office; Mendoza wasn't quite sure how many there were yet, fully trained
and ready for action. But on this kind of action, as on many others, a
trained dog would be worth two men—seeing and hearing and smelling
where a man wouldn't.

"My good Christ," said Dwyer mildly. "Look at it." He flung the map
down. "Dozens of little side streets and courts—rooming houses, apartments—along the main drags, warehouses, all those joints on the Row with
flophouses *and* a few cat houses, probably, upstairs—my God, with a hundred men it'd take three days to be sure you'd covered—"

"So we take three days, or three weeks!" said Mendoza. "Did you like
the afternoon headlines, Bert? We're going to work this the only way we
can. Damn." He massaged his temples, elbows on the desk. "I've fumbled
around at this . . . I thought Art's business tied up to the Nestor thing,
I've been concentrating on that—but—I don't know . . ."

"Who's called the hospital last?" asked Palliser.

"Jimmy. Just before I came in," said Mendoza. "They say he's getting a
little restless, which they seem to think is a good sign. But of course—"

"Yeah," said Dwyer. They all knew about that. A clean dying one
thing: the permanent brain damage another. "You don't think now it was
tied up to either case?" He looked at Mendoza thoughtfully.

"*¿Qué sé yo?*" said Mendoza. "I don't know. There's nothing really that
says yes or no. I'll say this much, I doubt very much whether that is

linked with our Slasher. In spite of his being the one who derailed the
Daylight. It doesn't fit—it isn't the right shape. But it could have been the
outside thing. And if it was"—he sat up straighter, automatically brushing
ash off the desk, aligning the desk box and blotter—"if it was, by God, or
if it wasn't, we'll get the X on that and get him but good. But—"

"Amen to that," said Palliser.

"But in the meantime we've got the Slasher on our hands. I say, let's go
all out to get that one, and then we'll have the slate clear—and the damn
press off our necks—to hunt down the other one. Plural or singular? Hell,
I don't know," said Mendoza. "I don't even know whether the motive on
Nestor came out of his abortion trade or something else—his girl friends,
his marriage. ¡Basta! Forget about that for a minute—" He looked up as
the door opened.

"What's the urgent summons to my lowly office?" asked Fletcher of
Traffic. He was a big, heavy, amiable man, about due for retirement.

"How soon can you get me about fifty men?" asked Mendoza. "More if
you can. And all the dogs available? For a house-to-house search of about
one square mile of downtown?"

Fletcher just looked at him. "Are you serious? Right now? What the
hell on? Not—"

"That's just what," said Mendoza. "We've got to get this boy, Jack, and
the sooner the better. I've got a hunch he's holed up somewhere inside
that area, and I want a thorough hunt. Leave the rest of the citizenry to
its own devices awhile, and haul in some men off tour. I can't make rules
for your department, but everybody in this office is working round the
clock as from now. Maybe you saw the afternoon headlines too."

Fletcher laughed shortly. "I did. The citizenry! It's been told often
enough, by a lot of people who should know, it's got one damn good
police force, but let a thing like this come along, you'd think we're a
bunch of morons, way they talk."

"Some people," said Mendoza, "just naturally think we've got to be morons, to be cops in the first place. Sometimes I almost agree with them."
And he thought, If Art died . . .

Fletcher rubbed his jaw. "Use your phone," he said, and it wasn't a
request. He used it, ruthlessly, for ten minutes. When he put it down for
the last time he said, "God help the innocent citizenry tonight. And bless
the Hollywood boys—they can pull men off a lot of nice genteel places
where nothing ever happens, without much danger. . . . Crews of twenty
cars to report in within fifteen minutes, that's thirty-six men. Another
twenty called in from stationary traffic duty, and God help the drivers at

downtown intersections. Lessee, it's four-forty. Call it five o'clock for briefing. Where?"

"Your sergeants' office. I want every man issued with extra ammo," said Mendoza. "I know our Slasher isn't on the Most Wanted list—not on any list, his prints unknown—but he's the hell of a dangerous boy. We don't want any more casualties, do we?"

"I'll see to it," said Fletcher briefly. "O.K., twenty minutes." He went out.

"We're going to be fairly busy for quite a while," said Mendoza. "Maybe you'd all better snatch a sandwich or something while you can." Dwyer and Scarne drifted out after Fletcher. The outside phone rang and Mendoza picked it up. . . . "Yes, *querida*," he said. Palliser watched him for a moment, saw he wasn't getting any bad news, and went out unobtrusively.

"They said he's been restless. They seem to think—it might be a sign that he'll be conscious soon. I—oh, damn," said Alison. "I *know* they're doing all they can, and—and they know so much more now, but they're so horribly impersonal about it. That afternoon nurse—they've got specials on, you know—talking about the patient this and the patient that when it's *Art*."

"I know," said Mendoza. "Just how they are, *amante*. All in the day's work to them."

Alison said forlornly, "She's a Seventh-Day Adventist. She gave us some Improving Literature to read, about vegetarian diets. Well, she seems kind enough, but—"

"Yes, darling. What about Angel? I said she ought to see her own doctor."

"Yes, he gave her some tranquilizers but she won't take them. Luis. Did you *mean* what you said—about r-resigning? I don't know what you'd *do*. I don't know—"

"*No se preocupe*," said Mendoza. He thought, Have to borrow a gun somewhere. He couldn't go home for his own .38 in the handkerchief drawer, the shoulder holster, or Alison would know . . .

"—Luis?"

"No," he said. "I won't be home. We've got a little project on down here. It's expect me when you see me, I'm afraid."

"Yes," said Alison. A little silence, and then she said, "It's just, it feels as if everything's in slow motion, somehow. That it's days since I've seen you, and—everything taking so long to happen—Luis—"

"Yes," he said. "It does feel rather like that."

"Máiri says to tell you to get a proper dinner somewhere." Alison uttered a little laugh.

"I will if I have time."

"And El Señor broke that jardiniere you don't like. The green one the Mawsons gave us for a wedding present. He knocked it over quite deliberately—"

"¡Señor Comedido!" said Mendoza. "How tactful of him. . . . I don't know when I'll see you, amante. Take care. . . ." He put the phone down and said to Sergeant Lake, "Get me a gun somewhere, will you? And a cup of coffee if you can."

"See what I can do," said Lake, and got up. In the doorway he collided with Lieutenant Goldberg of Burglary, just coming in.

EIGHTEEN

"Well, and what can we do for you, Saul?" asked Mendoza.

Goldberg asked first about Hackett and shook his head at the latest report. "It's more the other way around, I'm afraid. I just thought it'd be neighborly to mention it, in case anything does happen."

"Make it short, we've got quite a night's project mapped out."

"Well," said Goldberg, "there was a break-in last night at a gunsmith's shop over on Spring. Quite a lot of stuff gone, and—"

"Your problem," said Mendoza.

"It could turn into yours. I don't like it," said Goldberg. "All they took was guns—and the hell of a lot of ammo for them. There was other valuable stuff there—he had a color TV in the back room he was keeping for his wife's birthday, and he does a side line in transistor radios, there were about twenty of those. And he'd left a few bucks in the register. Well, the first thing a burglar looks for is cash, usually. But all somebody, or several somebodies, was interested in, was guns. We've been all round the suspected fences and pawnbrokers today, and not a smell has turned up. Which makes it look as if whoever the somebodies were, they just wanted guns—as guns."

"Oh," said Mendoza. "I begin not to like it too. My God, on top of—"

"Listen to the list," said Goldberg, unfolding a sheet of paper. "They or whoever took an old Springfield .22 rifle, a Ruger Standard Single-Six .22, an S. and W. .357 Magnum, a .38 Colt Trooper, an Ivor-Johnson Supershot .22, a Whitney Lightning .22 automatic, and three of the gunsmith's own target revolvers—he's a pro shot—a Colt Python .357 Magnum, a Colt Officers' Match Model .38 revolver, and an S. and W. Target .45. And about twenty rounds of ammo for all nine guns."

"¡Santa María!" said Mendoza. "Is he starting a little private war?"

"That may be too close for comfort," said Goldberg soberly. "Tell you what just crossed my mind—a gang of juveniles. Planning a rumble with something new added."

"*¡Por Dios!* And you could be right," said Mendoza. "God, on top of all the rest of this— We can only hope, if that's so, the rumble isn't planned for tonight. Thanks for the warning, anyway."

"I could be just woolgathering," said Goldberg, sneezing and groping for the inevitable Kleenex. "Just thought you ought to know. All but one of them handguns, you know, and all that ammo—"

"Yes indeed."

Sergeant Lake came back and handed Mendoza a .38 Police Special, a shoulder holster, and a box of ammunition.

"Hey, what's up?" said Goldberg. "You never pack a gun unless it's something damn serious."

"I think," said Mendoza, taking off his jacket, "we're on damn serious business tonight, Saul."

Nobody else thought so for quite a while. Dwyer said to Scarne, "Work our tails off on an all-night job, just because he gets a wild hunch! There's nothing to say the Slasher's holed up in that area. Why just that area?"

"First cast," said Scarne gloomily, "I guess."

"My God, sure, we sweat it out all night and don't find him because he's a block outside the line our Luis drew on the map!"

But Mendoza was the one who gave the orders.

They set it up, with the fifty-six men from Traffic and those available in the homicide office—Dwyer, Scarne, Palliser, Piggott, Landers—and Higgins and Galeano would be in later.

There were some residential streets in the area they were covering, but more of it was business. The residential streets were shabby and poor, and a lot of those old houses had derelict shacks built at the rear of the lots; a few still had henhouses standing from years back before the town was a city. But along the main drags—San Pedro, Main, Los Angeles, Third and Second, First and Temple—were many kinds of small business and some large: a solid block of warehouses, some, they discovered, empty. Store owners were called, keys to the empty buildings were sent for, the men were briefed. They assigned one crew of men, in pairs, to two-square-block sections, and started them out. It was, of course, very unlikely that their boy was holed up in a private residence; but if there was an empty house somewhere even that was possible.

They got the men all down there by five-thirty, with seven cars roaming at random, and the operation started.

Dwyer, paired off with Landers, was still grumbling. They were let out of a squad car with the other two men, both uniformed, who were on this particular block with them; Dwyer looked at the building on the corner, a four-story warehouse, blank-faced. "Hell of a waste of time," he said. "Just because Mendoza the brain gets a hunch—"

"Hey, I've heard of him," said one of the uniformed men interestedly. "Is this one of his deals?"

"One of his wild deals. We're supposed to look for an open window or something this boy could have got in by—but I've got the keys. You go round to the side and look, and then come back."

In many streets other men were dropped, began their search. They made polite requests of householders and shopkeepers; in almost all cases they met no resistance. Over on Stevens Street, Officers Carlson and Ramirez ran into a belligerent householder who tried to start a fight, so they hailed a patrol car, put him in it to cool, went through the house, and found several hundred gallons of homemade beer in the garage. But there weren't many cases like that.

The dogs and their handlers arrived. By that time the word had got out that a mass raid of cops was in the neighborhood, and people came out to stare, form little crowds. The dogs fascinated them, of course.

And then it was getting on for eight-thirty, and the dark had come down full, not insidiously and reasonably as it does elsewhere; the sky changed from pink-streaked silver blue to full dark within fifteen minutes, and after that the dark was studded with the men's flashlights, little eyes of light moving along the sidewalks, and, here and there where a house or building was empty, moving past windows inside.

Mendoza was over on Temple Street with Palliser then. "For God's sake," he said to the driver of a squad car at the curb, "can't we get these people off the streets?" Little knots of people stood about, at front doors, under street lights. "They've been warned—they ought to know—"

"You think he might try another one, with all this force out and about?"

"We don't know," said Mendoza. "With one like that, who can say?"

"Well, we can tell 'em to go home," said the driver, "but it's supposed to be a free country." He gunned the car up to the nearest little group, got out, and began to talk to them.

That kind of job was always a tiresome one; at the same time, tonight, the men were all a little keyed up at the thought that they might, just might, find themselves unexpectedly facing the Slasher. . . .

It was ten twenty-three when Patrolmen McLelland and Leslie, both of the Wilcox Street station, came out of an ancient brick office building on Los Angeles Street and paused to light cigarettes. The office building was on a corner, and a little wind had got up; they went round the side of the building to get their lights, and Leslie said, "Half these old places ought to be knocked down. Did you see the state of those lavatories?"

McLelland opened his mouth to answer, and there was a sharp crack; Leslie staggered, dropping his cigarette and shoving McLelland against the brick wall. "Jesus!" he said. "That was a—" A second shot barked and the slug hit the building an inch from McLelland's right ear.

Both men dropped flat in the next second. "You hit?"

"Just nicked me, I think." Leslie explored, said, "Went through the shoulder padding. What the hell— Where's he shooting from? Can you—"

"Over there—kitty-corner across the intersection, I think. Try to cover me." McLelland, gun out, crawled up toward the corner and around it. The side street was all dark, across there, and the street lamp at the corner was out. This block of Los Angeles Street was deserted at night, and not well lighted.

About four buildings up, just passing under one of the feeble street lights, were two men walking in his direction. McLelland debated about calling to warn them to stop. Then a gun spoke again—a heavy gun, by the sound—and one of the two men spun round and fell flat. The other one stopped in his tracks and then stooped over the first man, so the second bullet flew over his head and made a sharp *spat* on the building front.

McLelland turned and sent a snap shot toward where he thought the gunman was. This thing had started so suddenly that he'd hardly had time to feel surprise. He just found himself thinking blankly, What the hell? Now, lying there, he heard footsteps across the intersection—soft, but audible; steps walking, then running—away.

Leslie heard that too. He came up panting. "For God's sake—" he said. "You hit? What—"

The other man came up to them. "You're cops?" he said, seeing McLelland in uniform. "Thank God. Mac's dead. Did you see that? He's *dead*. We were just walkin' along, talking about politics, and he'd just been saying about all this lousy foreign aid, and then— He's *dead*. And his eye's all—his eye—" He leaned over, retching, and Leslie took his arm. McLelland, gun still in hand, ran down to where the man lay; he'd been neatly drilled through the left eye, probably a fluke shot.

He looked up the street and saw a black and white squad car coming. It screeched to a halt beside him. "Were those *shots?*" asked the driver.

"Sounded like a .38," said McLelland. "This poor devil's a D.O.A. A sniper— I think he was just shooting at anything that showed, way it—"

From about a block away a gun began to talk—a fusillade of shots, in rapid succession. "For God's *sake*," said the squad-car driver, "has war been declared?" He picked up the hand radio. "Car 104 at L.A. and Woods. Sniper just shot a man here. Shot at two of our boys."

"He went up Woods," said McLelland.

"He went up Woods toward Main."

The radio crackled excitedly at him. They heard more shots, a little farther off. "*Awk!*" said the radio as if in comment. "Join car 194 at junction of Main and Woods. Repeat—"

"What about us?" asked McLelland. But the radio didn't say anything about that, so they stayed there and got the names of the two men, quick and dead, and after the ambulance came they went on with the search. That had been their orders.

Mendoza and Palliser were in an empty factory on Third Street when they heard about the sniper. A uniformed man came down the corridor looking, said, "Lieutenant? They sent me over to find you. There's a sniper loose. Last they heard of him, he was on Woods Street somewhere —killed a civilian and shot at two of our men. Then he took some shots at a squad car along Main—"

"¡*Porvida!*" said Mendoza, and then he said suddenly, "That's our boy. Come on. You've got a car? Let's get going."

"But how could— A sniper?" said Palliser incredulously. "You mean like that Corning thing last year? Just some nut loose with a gun? I don't—"

Mendoza was hustling him along. "¡*Vamos, vamos!* It's our boy—I see how his mind works, *pues sí*. I said, just enough sense. He wants to kill, he likes to kill with the knife, but we've told people what he looks like now—and you can kill people from a distance with a gun. With guns. My *God*, yes—Goldberg's boy too, and that young arsenal—"

They got over to the corner of Woods and Main at about eleven o'clock. Men were looking at the squad car, whose right front door was riddled with bullet holes. A uniformed man was propped against it with his jacket off and a makeshift bloody bandage round one arm. "For God's sake, isn't anyone following him up? Any idea which way he went?" demanded Mendoza.

A shattering explosion of shots in the distance answered him. He commandeered the nearest squad car, piled three men in the back and Palliser beside him, and gunned it in the direction of the shots. They roared up Main, with its lights and crowds thinning here, to Winton Street; down there to the right were three squad cars, slewed around in the street, and a little crowd, and four uniformed men. Mendoza swung the car down there.

"For the love of God, haven't you people any *sense?*" one of the men was demanding impatiently. "Scatter—get away—" A second man in uniform was leaning against the side of a car, clasping his shoulder; blood seeped between his fingers.

The gun barked, and the other man's plea was heeded. Several women screamed, the crowd scattering back into the shadows of hedges and houses. This was a residential street. The sniper was apparently behind a hedge across the street.

There was a woman lying in the street beside the cars. "She's only winged," said one of the patrolmen. "I put a tourniquet on, and the ambulance is on its way. Now let's have a look at you, Bill—"

They were all crouched down, now, behind a squad car, and they all had their guns out.

"What the hell *is* all this, anyway?" asked the wounded man, sounding indignant. "All of a sudden—"

"It's our boy," said Mendoza calmly, peering round the bumper long enough to fire a shot at that hedge. "I know. We've flushed him."

"The— That's crazy," said the other patrolman. "Excuse me, sir, but he's always used a knife, I don't see—"

"I think he's beyond caring how he kills," said Mendoza, firing another shot. Two more bullets hit the other side of the squad car, and then there was silence. The woman lying in the street moaned. "Don't tell me we've got him? Cover me, please." He moved around the car, bent low, made a dash for the shelter of the hedge across the street. His flashlight flicked on briefly; he straightened. "Gone—fan out after him—all directions! John, come with me—call up some more cars, will you?"

Palliser ran to keep up with him as he started down toward San Pedro. "I don't see how you make this out—all of a sudden—"

"He wouldn't have expected all this," said Mendoza. "He didn't know we were out hunting too. His first night's target practice with the arsenal—yes—but maybe getting his fire returned has shaken him a little. Damn, I'm out of condition. Wait a minute. Listen."

There were distant sirens; Palliser couldn't hear anything else. Then from the corner of San Pedro down there a squad car came bucketing around the corner fast, and its headlights caught a man running diagonally across the street. Just one flash, and he was gone; he'd been nearly at the opposite curb; but they both saw the guns, one dangling from each hand. The squad car braked loudly, and Mendoza fired across its hood. "Searchlight, for God's sake!" he snapped.

The light came on, swung to point where they'd seen him. Two men scrambled out of the car. A bullet came out of the dark and hit the top of the light, and they heard a man running.

"One of you follow me—the other call in a Code Nine," said Mendoza, and plunged across the street. Another shot plucked at Palliser's sleeve as he ran beside him.

"He's heading back—to his hole," panted Mendoza. "Bet you—" But these damn dark streets, and they were only guessing he was ahead of them. . . .

Then they saw him, for just another half second. There was a street light at the corner, and they saw him—a darting thin figure in clothes that flapped loose about him—turn left there, running awkwardly in great strides. They came round the corner after him, and skidded to a halt.

"Where the hell did he go?" gasped the uniformed man. This silent empty street was fairly well lighted; along here all the buildings were dark, but they could see the full block ahead, and no living thing moved on it.

"Dan!" said Mendoza. "Into one of these buildings. The nearest one, for choice. I want men—a lot of men—we're going through every building on this block—"

A squad car screeched to a stop beside them, with one man in it. "O.K.," said Mendoza tautly. "You call up reinforcements—tell them where we are. You two go round to the side of this place—and be damn careful, no flashlights! John, let's see what we've got here." He moved to the front of the corner building. "I think this has got to be it, we weren't thirty feet behind him—he didn't go far past the corner. What in God's name is this place?"

It was an old building; and they saw now, in the yellow light from the old-fashioned street lamps, that this whole block of buildings was waiting for demolition. In the last few years a good many of these shabby old streets had come in for renovation; the city was building itself new city and county buildings, and big companies were buying up this valuable downtown land to knock down the derelict old buildings, put up shiny new skyscrapers.

A start had been made on demolishing the buildings near this corner. A great pile of knocked-apart lumber and twisted metal lay in a heap alongside the corner building, which had two wings enclosing a square open entrance. For a second that looked vaguely familiar to Palliser, but he couldn't place it. A department store of some kind? But no sign of display windows. The whole place looked ready to fall down, and up there past the wings it was dark as the mouth of hell. But Mendoza was walking up toward where the door would be, quite cool, gun in hand.

"He'll be lying quiet," he muttered, "hoping we won't realize this is where he's got to be."

There had been a door, probably; it was missing now, they found by feeling along a rough stucco wall. They went in shoulder to shoulder—into whatever it was, and Palliser thought, an extra-wide doorway.

Bare wooden floor. Mendoza wasn't trying to be quiet. He took a few steps straight ahead and, holding his flashlight at arm's length away from his body, switched it on briefly.

"Christ!" said Palliser involuntarily.

It sprang at them out of the darkness, terrifying, incredible—a dark-skinned giant in a great feather headdress and long glittering cloak, double life size.

He heard Mendoza take a breath, and then laugh. "Wall mural," he said. "Polynesian god of some sort?" His voice echoed oddly. "Where are we, anyway, John?"

Palliser held his own flashlight out and pointed it to their right. A long wide corridor, thick with dust. There was a door, closed, at the far end: they could just make out, painted on it, the mute legend GENT ME .

Nothing stirred: no gun spoke out of the darkness.

Mendoza turned his flashlight ahead, lower. There was a wooden counter there, like a bar; fittings of some kind had been removed from it. The light flashed around nervously, here and there, and a pair of giant hula dancers seemed to undulate at them from another wall.

"I think—" said Mendoza, and at that moment the light showed them a face. A face not fifteen feet away—a face of nightmare. The man was pressed against the wall there, rigid, looking toward them. Not a big man: a thin man in ragged clothes too big for him, nondescript clothes. His face was a mask of blind hate and rage and terror: and splashed across it was the mark—the red scar mark of death, that in the end had triggered death.

For an instant they all stood there motionless; then the Slasher made one quick, convulsive movement and vanished out of the circle of light. Mendoza plunged after him, the flashlight sweeping a wide arc.

Black as the Earl of Hell's weskit, thought Palliser ridiculously, hurrying after him. His grandmother used to say that. Black as . . .

But the flashlight showed a rectangular blackness—and another—and then they were through the nearest one, and he understood where they were.

This was a derelict movie theater. That had been the candy and pop-corn stand out there. All the fittings taken out—carpets and curtains—probably the plumbing—and, here, the seats.

It was a vast, black, empty great place, with the floor sloping sharply away under his feet. The two flashlights found the man again, running diagonally across the uneven floor, stumbling, turning up toward the arch-way that had once led to the last left aisle. Mendoza fired at him and evidently missed.

Then the quarry was out of the light, and the roar of Mendoza's gun was echoed by another—a bullet slammed past Palliser's shoulder, close. He fired blindly.

They were running, up the slanting floor now, and Mendoza fired again. Dimly Palliser was aware of sirens somewhere in the distance, and loud excited voices nearer. . . .

He rammed into a wall, and swore. He had missed the archway—he groped for it and came out into unexpected light.

They had parked two squad cars directly in front, and headed their searchlights up here. It wasn't very bright, but you could see in here now. Palliser saw.

The man who liked to kill was standing against the wall there twenty feet away, his terrible face contorted. He still had both his guns. Mendoza was facing him, ten feet down from Palliser.

Men were coming, pouring into the lobby excitedly.

The man fired, and missed, and raised the other gun.

Then a shot spat at him from another direction, and he fell back against the wall and slid down it slowly, and sprawled full length.

"Thanks very much, Bert," said Mendoza. "That was my last slug. I never claimed to be a marksman."

Dwyer walked up to the body and looked down at it, gun still in hand. "You can say I told you so if you want," he said. "You and your hunches!"

NINETEEN

There was quite a bit of clearing up to do; Mendoza didn't get home until two-thirty again. There were all the reporters swarming around. And they found the Slasher's secret place and the rest of his arsenal; they found out who he had probably been, from an old union card in his wallet. The Railroad Brotherhood. So for a start they looked for that name, John Tenney, on the list of former S.P. employees, and there it was—he'd been hired, briefly, as a trackwalker, some years back.

"In a kind of way, you might feel sorry for him, if he hadn't . . ." said Palliser, leaving that unfinished.

And Mendoza said, "That damned lush Telfer! Look at all this mess! Seven people killed—I don't suppose anyone's missing the wino or Florence, or the other Skid Row type we found this morning, but there's the boy, and Loretta Lincoln, and Simms—and several more hurt, including a couple of cops. My God, and if Telfer hadn't been drunk that night we'd probably have picked the Slasher up inside twenty-four hours, with a full description."

"It isn't going to trouble Telfer's conscience," said Palliser dryly.

"No, probably not. . . ."

And when he did get home he couldn't sleep. Had the assault on Art been tied up to Nestor? How and why? Had to get at that thing again in the morning. . . . Cliff Elger? He still didn't know where the Elgers had been on Tuesday night when Nestor was shot. . . .

But, he thought suddenly, coming to complete wakefulness from an instant's half-sleep, it had to come back to that appointment in Nestor's office that night. Didn't it? He had told his wife he had an evening appointment. It might have been a date with a girl, but—*vide* Anita Sheldon—they wouldn't stay there. Naturally. So if it had been that, then he must have been killed very close to the eight o'clock margin Bainbridge gave them, or he wouldn't still have been in the office. But if it hadn't been a girl friend . . .

That scrapbook. He'd been thinking, Nestor not above a little blackmail. Had it been something like that? Have a good look at that list of patients, when the court order came through. . . . By what Bert and the others said, the other women in Nestor's address book had been casual pickups, not exactly the kind to inspire the grand passion—to the point of murderous jealousy. But of course you never did know. People . . .

Art. If that wasn't linked to Nestor, was the outside thing, where the hell to start looking? Dead end. Hell.

Andrea Nestor?

No. No. A man. They knew that much, because it had been a man who got rid of that gun. Maybe two people? Andrea Nestor scarcely a woman to do murder for, either. . . .

He drifted off uneasily at last, but woke for good at six. El Señor was chattering at the birds outside the window. Mendoza shaved and dressed, went out to the living room and called the hospital. Established routine now, he thought. Part of these long, long days. . . . The nurse's impersonal voice said, "Oh yes, sir—just a moment, Dr. MacFarlane wants to speak to you personally, if you'll wait a moment."

"All right," said Mendoza. He waited, wondering academically how far his pulse rate had shot up.

"Lieutenant? Yes. He's been increasingly restless," said the doctor. "I think the chances are good that he'll regain consciousness sometime today. I'd like either you or someone else who knows him well to—er—stand by for a call, as it were. You understand."

"Yes, Doctor."

"You'll be called as soon as we know. . . . Well, we're still not making any guesses, of course. Wait and see. You'll have someone standing by?"

"Yes." Much as he would like to be the man, he couldn't; he had things to do today. "Thanks very much, Doctor."

"We'll just keep hoping," said MacFarlane sadly.

Even Mrs. MacTaggart wasn't up, this morning. He got out the Ferrari and stopped for breakfast at the Manning's on Vermont, but he couldn't get much of it down; he had three cups of coffee and began to feel slightly more alive.

He got to the office before the night shift was off; told them the latest news. When Dwyer came in he said, "You're taking a little holiday, Bert. Stick around in case the hospital calls." He explained.

"O.K.," said Dwyer, looking grim.

Mendoza looked at the clock irritably; he couldn't decently arrive at the Elgers' apartment before nine o'clock. He sat at his desk thinking about that appointment of Nestor's on Tuesday night.

An appointment with Ruth Elger? And Elger—

So X discovered belatedly that he'd lost a button and, just in case he'd lost it in Nestor's office, gave away the jacket if he couldn't replace the button. How were you going to prove it?

A button. Suddenly, now, Mendoza was wondering whether that might have been what Art had spotted. If there was a tie-up. Whether X hadn't noticed the missing button until Art noticed, and questioned him about it. Whether . . .

Such a very ordinary little button. He got it out and looked at it. And another thought crossed his mind about it too, as a faint possibility of a lead—probably very faint. In these days of mass production. However . . .

All the morning papers had screaming headlines about the capture of the Slasher.

Nine o'clock found him using the knocker on the Elgers' apartment door.

Ruth Elger let him in; she wasn't dressed yet, but looked better this time—no hangover, and make-up. "Well, for heaven's sake, what do *you* want?" she asked rather crossly.

"Answers to a few questions, Mrs. Elger, if you don't mind." The room wasn't much neater than when he'd seen it first, and it hadn't been dusted in some time. She told him ungraciously to sit down, perched herself on the arm of a chair.

"Well?"

"Do you remember what you and your husband were doing on Tuesday night a week ago? A week ago yesterday?"

"Heavens, *I* don't know. I suppose we were here, if we weren't— Oh no, the Werthers' party was on Wednesday, wasn't it?"

"It's not so very long ago," said Mendoza.

"Why on earth you want to know— Oh. That—that was the night Frank was shot, wasn't it? For heaven's *sake*. You can't be thinking *we* had—"

"Just try to remember, please."

"Oh well! It was—yes, we went out to dinner—to the Tail o' the Cock, I think. *Tuesday.* Oh, I do remember, yes, as a matter of fact we were arguing all through dinner about that silly charge-account thing, and all the way home for that matter, and it wasn't long after we got home that Cliff got really mad and sort of slammed out—"

"Arguing over a bill you'd run up?" said Mendoza. "And he left the apartment. When?"

"Heavens, I wasn't watching the clock, about half past nine, I suppose. . . . No, I don't know where he went. What does it matter? I expect to a bar somewhere, he was a little high when he came home."

"At what time?"

She shrugged petulantly. "About midnight, I guess. I was in bed."

"Mrs. Elger, has your husband ever owned a gun?"

"A— Well, of *course* not," she said. "What on *earth*— You simply can't be thinking— *Frank?* Good heavens, it was just—just an episode. Not important."

"What's important or not," said Mendoza, "depends on who's looking at it. Thanks very much. . . ."

He sat in the car thinking about that. Cliff Elger in a temper, and he might be quick to hit out at a man, but probably not the type to knock a woman around; so, rushing out, in his temper. To a bar? Or had he, on the way, started brooding over Ruth and Nestor again? And . . .

Wait a minute. How could he have known Nestor would be in his office at that hour? Had he known Nestor's home address? Well, it was in the phone book. He'd have tried there first, wouldn't he? But he hadn't.

Mendoza was still liking the idea of Cliff Elger for Nestor, because—admit it—he'd like to think the Nestor thing was behind the assault on Art, and Elger was the only man they'd run across so far who could certainly have handled Art without too much trouble.

All right, he thought. Suddenly he saw another, more plausible picture. Elger rushing out to a bar. Downing three or four highballs. Maybe it affected him the way it affected Mendoza; but whether or no, say he was brooding. And worked up a rage at Nestor. Maybe she'd been lying about the gun, or maybe he kept one at his office and she didn't know that, maybe Nestor had had the gun unknown to Madge Corliss. That sounded more plausible; a man Nestor's size might well reach for a gun, if he had one, when a gorilla like Elger came in mad. Yes, say that whatever Nestor's appointment had been, it was over, and Nestor was maybe just about to leave when Elger burst in—

Why Nestor's office? How had he known—

Say he was drunk, but—

Hell.

He drove back to the office. The hospital hadn't called. They had, however, got an ident on that unknown victim of the Slasher, through the Greyhound Bus office and the San Diego police. His name was George

Snaid, and he'd been picked up for vagrancy in San Diego and given the usual twenty-four hours to leave town. Nothing more was known about him. Another of the victims who wouldn't be missed.

The court order to open Madge Corliss' safe-deposit box hadn't come through yet. "Damn judges," said Mendoza. He wanted to see that list.

He sent Lake out for coffee. He sat at his desk chain smoking nervously. Dwyer, with nothing special to do, was playing solitaire desultorily, laying out the cards on top of a filing case, wandering over to stare at the phones on the desk every five minutes. He wasn't much of a cardplayer, and his inept, awkward shuffling of the deck got on Mendoza's nerves.

"I did think of something," he said presently. "A little thing. You know how that dame in the room next to Florence Dahl said the Slasher kept shouting something like 'Every ham's gaining on me'? It came to me what it was. Every man's hand against me. Out of the Bible, isn't it?"

"I couldn't say," said Mendoza. "Very likely. Yes, that's probably what it was. I wonder if we could trace him back at all. Where he started, how he got that way. That landlady on Boardman Street said he had a Southern accent." But he wasn't thinking about the Slasher; that was over and done, and there was other work to do. "Bert?"

"Well?"

"You talked to those old pals of Nestor's who used to play poker with him. Any of them mention anything about that?"

"About what?"

"What kind of poker player he was."

"Oh." Dwyer considered, looking at the deck in his hand. "One fellow —another chiropractor—said he was a wild gambler. Take any long chance, he said. So he lost oftener than he won."

"Yes. That kind of poker player," said Mendoza. "But that wasn't why he lost oftener than he won. That was because he didn't play enough poker. The man who's playing any game regularly, day to day, always has an edge over the occasional player. . . . Do you *have* to try to tear the deck in half every time you shuffle? Look." He took the cards from Dwyer and shuffled them. "Gentle and easy, see?"

"I'm not a pro gambler," said Dwyer.

"No." Having the cards, Mendoza kept them; absently he shuffled, squared the deck neatly, cut it, and turned up the ace of diamonds. "*Tuerto*," he said. "A lucky card." He shuffled the deck again, squared it and cut, to show the ace of diamonds again.

"Don't ever ask me to play cards with you," said Dwyer.

"It's just a trick." Mendoza shuffled again, using a different method, and began to deal him a poker hand, calling the cards as he tossed them face down. "King of spades. Deuce of clubs. Ace of hearts. Four of hearts—"

"Wrong. Three of clubs."

"Hell, I'm out of practice at crooked deals. . . ." The cards moved restlessly between his hands. "Did I tell you about meeting Benny Metzer on that cruise liner? I took twenty bucks off him—he could have killed me." Mendoza laughed sharply.

"One of your pro gambler acquaintances? Do tell." Dwyer was watching the telephone again.

"That's right, you came up here from Forgery, didn't you?"

"And a damn dull job that was," said Dwyer absently.

"Sometimes it can be." Mendoza dealt himself a straight poker hand and quite by chance drew a full house. "So it can happen," he muttered.

Think about this thing, damn it. Nestor. If that nice story he'd built up about Cliff Elger was so, then—when Nestor was still in his office—his appointment, whatever it was, must have taken up some time. Not the usual job, because Corliss hadn't known about it. The spot of genteel blackmail? And, naturally, the blackmailee arguing, and the sparring back and forth about the price?

Only, really, why bring in Elger, in that case? Blackmail was quite a reasonable motive for murder.

Only what did the blackmail have to be? Threat of revealing an abortion. These days, with the relaxed morals . . . And besides, Nestor couldn't have carried out such a threat without revealing himself and his part in it, which anybody with common sense would . . .

All right. All *right*. Some featherbrained woman, not seeing that, shooting him in panic? A man had got rid of the .22. So, the woman confessing to some protective male—father, husband, boy friend—who had thereupon set up the bogus burglary and got rid of the gun.

And that would say for pretty sure that the assault on Art had been the outside thing.

Wouldn't it? Well, for ninety-eight per cent sure. Art hadn't known about those illicit patients—couldn't have known who they were, of course. Hard to see how he might have inadvertently stumbled across . . .

Mendoza shuffled and cut, and turned up the knave of clubs. He stared at it for a moment, slapped the deck together, centered it on his desk, and stood up. "Do you know what the knave of clubs means in cartomancy?"

"I don't even know what cartomancy means," said Dwyer.

"Fortunetelling with cards. The knave of clubs," said Mendoza, "stands for a bearer of unexpected news. I'm going out to find him. I probably won't be long."

"Let's just hope it's good news," said Dwyer after him.

This was a will-o'-the-wisp, of course. Just an idea. But sometimes you grabbed at any small hope there might be, looking for a lead.

He went straight out Wilshire, and there wasn't much traffic this early. It wasn't ten o'clock yet. Just on ten. The street signs changed to elegant black on white, and he was in Beverly Hills. He turned left on Beverly Drive and went down four blocks to a line of expensive-looking shop fronts. Miraculously he found a parking slot, and found he had a nickel in change. He yanked the handle on the parking meter; nothing happened; he shook it hard, and it condescended to bury the red *Violation* sign in its insides. He walked back to the most expensive-looking shop front of all. It presented a genteel pale fawn façade with tinted glass double doors. There was no legend on the doors at all; the only designation it offered to reveal its commercial purposes was a single discreet name in lowercase gilt letters above the door: *harrington.*

Mendoza went in. There was pale fawn carpeting, nothing so vulgar as a counter; this room, an anteroom to the high mysteries beyond, was only about fifteen feet square. An exquisite young man in pale fawn dacron drifted up, identified him, and murmured, "I'll fetch Mr. Harrington, sir. Do sit down."

Mendoza didn't sit down. He wandered over to one of the full-length triple mirrors and decided absently that the Italian silk was too dark a gray. He adjusted his tie.

"You again," said Harrington abruptly behind him. "Good God, I just made you two new suits and those evening clothes. You're a vain bastard, Mendoza."

Mendoza turned around. "You malign me. No, I don't want anything new. I want some information."

Harrington was a solid, round little man of some heft, with a bald round head and pudgy little hands. He also had a pair of very sharp black eyes. He cocked the bald head at Mendoza. "Oh?"

"Which you probably can't give me," said Mendoza. He handed over the button, the little ordinary button. "Can you tell me anything about that? It occurred to me it's in your line. You're quite a specialist on anything to do with male attire, aren't you?"

Harrington looked at the button, turning it over in his fingers.

"I know it's a very ordinary sort of thing," said Mendoza apologetically.

"My God, and you a detective!" said Harrington. "Of course, maybe only a specialist would spot it. I can tell you this and that about it, of course. To start with, it's obviously a button from the sleeve of a jacket. Too small to be an ordinary jacket button. It's—"

"The *sleeve* of a— But—"

"No, I know. Those conservative bastards," said Harrington with a chuckle. "Grandpa had buttons on his sleeves, so naturally you go on putting buttons on sleeves. No scope—no progress. I haven't put any buttons on sleeves since, lessee, about 1939, but they still do. Most of 'em. I get some of their stuff in for repair occasionally."

Mendoza was staring at him. "Harrington," he said, "did you ever wonder how that fellow in the Bible felt when his ass started to talk to him? Not that I mean to imply— Whose stuff?"

Harrington tapped the button thoughtfully. "There you are," he said, "something else. Bone. Old-fashioned. Practically everybody uses plastic these days. Well, I could give a random *guess*. Either Rowlandson, or Herrick and King, or possibly Shattuck. Savile Row, of course."

"Of course," repeated Mendoza gently. . . . And quite suddenly, in one single lucid moment, everything fell into place and he saw it unreel before him like a moving picture. Of course.

"Say something to you?" asked Harrington interestedly.

But Mendoza was raptly placing the pieces of the jigsaw puzzle where they belonged. "A delightful Easter weekend," he said absorbedly. "Oh yes . . . . *have announced the engagement* . . . Five *thousand* bucks, but he'd be willing to pay high for— Oh yes, I see. Smart up to a point. And then—and *then*—" His eyes turned cold, and he whispered to himself, "The bastard—just a cop—to cover it up. And naturally, cops being morons or they wouldn't be cops, and he—"

"Did I say something?" asked Harrington, sounding more interested.

Mendoza focused on him with a little difficulty. "Harrington," he said earnestly, "you are indeed the knave of clubs. A bearer of news. I forgive you that tweed monstrosity you palmed off on me two years back. I forgive you— Well, never mind. My heartfelt thanks. Give me that thing." He almost ran out.

"Knave of *clubs?*" said Harrington after him, blankly.

Mendoza gunned the Ferrari up Beverly as fast as the law allowed. By God, he'd have a siren installed in this thing before he was a week older. . . . He got onto Wilshire and headed back downtown, and all the way the jigsaw pieces went on fitting themselves together, so nice and neat. . . .

Oh yes. Andrea Nestor. The belt, of course. And the button. Kenmore Avenue—but a dark stretch along there . . . And—

It was ten-fifty when he came fast into the office and looked round. Palliser was just coming out of the sergeants' office with a teletype sheet in his hand.

"We've got in a little more on Tenney. The S.P. told us he listed his birthplace as Younker, Georgia, and we—"

"¡No importa!" said Mendoza. "I only dropped in to pick up somebody —to keep an eye on me while we drop on the X who shot Nestor and sent Art over that cliff. Might as well be you, John. ¡Pues vámonos ya! Let's be on our way!"

Palliser stared at him and dropped the teletype. "You know—"

"I know all about it," said Mendoza grimly. "Let's go and take him. And if I will be resigning from this force, I'd like to leave a fairly clean record, so if I start to lose my temper, boy, you restrain me. . . . That Goddamned self-important stupid bastard! That—"

"Evidence?" said Palliser.

"Oh, there'll be evidence," said Mendoza. "By God, there will! Has the hospital called?"

"Not yet."

"Come on—let's go and take him," said Mendoza.

TWENTY

The impassive manservant blinked up at Mendoza. "I'm afraid Mr. Marlowe has just finished breakfast, sir, I don't know whether he'll see you—"

"Oh, he'll see me!" said Mendoza. He walked in past the man. "Where is he?"

His tone made the man blink again; a rather sly smile crept over his mouth. "In the library, sir."

Mendoza led Palliser down to that door and opened it. Marlowe, in a handsome tailored silk dressing gown, was sitting at the desk opening his mail. He glanced up, and his expression darkened. "What do you—"

"I've come for you, Marlowe," said Mendoza. "I've run across a lot of stupid killers before now, but you're one of the silliest. I want you on the charge of murdering Francis Nestor and assault with intent to murder on Arthur Hackett. Will you wait for the warrant here or downtown?"

Marlowe went an ugly red. "You must be a lunatic, sir. I don't know what you're— That's quite absurd! Why should *I* have wanted—*Paul!* My servant can tell you that I was here all that evening, and I'm sure you must— Ah, Paul. Just—"

"I'll do the asking," said Mendoza. "Was Mr. Marlowe here, from about eight forty-five on, a week ago Tuesday night?"

The man said, wooden-faced, "He certainly came in around then, sir. He came to this room and said he didn't want to be disturbed. I didn't see Mr. Marlowe again that evening, sir."

"Interesting," said Mendoza.

"But of *course* you knew I was here, man! Why on earth—"

"I can tell you the whole story now," said Mendoza. "And I don't give a damn about Nestor, but for what you did to Hackett, we're going to get you but good. It's never very smart to try to kill a cop, Marlowe. First let me ask you if you own a gun?"

Marlowe said coldly, "You needn't think you'll get away with such highhanded— Yes, I own several guns, but—"

The manservant coughed. "There is a small amateur target-shooting range in the basement, sir, beside the recreation room. The young gentlemen—"

Marlowe said furiously, "You may go, Paul!"

Mendoza sat down on the arm of a chair. "And that just about puts the lid on your stupidity, doesn't it? You did get rid of the gun, and the way you did that wasn't such a bad idea either, but you never really expected to be connected to the case in any way. You stupid bastard, don't you realize we can dig all those slugs out of the sandbags or whatever your target backs up to down there, and find quite a few to match up to that gun that killed Nestor?"

Marlowe took a step back, and his mouth tightened. "I had no reason—"

"You had a couple of very good reasons. You want to know what I know? I'll tell you," said Mendoza. "A little over three years ago you found that your youngest daughter Susan had got herself, as they say, in trouble. You think the hell of a lot of your fine old family name, don't you? Yes, so maybe you didn't think the young man was good enough for her—inconceivable that he wouldn't have jumped at marrying this kind of money! Well, you didn't have any contacts with an abortionist, and anyway you wanted to be sure of a good safe job. And you thought of Frank Nestor, the bright young man you'd staked to the chiropractic course. It's quite a serious training these days, and he'd know enough to do the job and do it nice and clean. And you didn't think he'd jib much at it. He didn't, did he? Maybe it wasn't that Easter weekend she was supposed to be yachting, but maybe it was too. Anyway, he obliged you—and Susan— for, I think, the cancellation of his debt and the nice round sum of five grand. . . . How am I doing, Marlowe?"

Marlowe sat down again in the desk chair. "That's—no, I—"

"We'll cut this short," said Mendoza abruptly. "That was that. I don't suppose you knew you'd put ideas in Nestor's head and he'd set up a profitable little abortion mill. But he did like the long green, didn't he, and when your daughter recently got engaged he saw how he might get some more out of you. For his silence." Mendoza smiled. "Has she, maybe, caused you a little trouble, Marlowe? The wild type? So you were only too pleased at the prospect of getting her respectably married? And in this one case Nestor could have told what he knew. Could have told the young man—or his parents—how he knew she'd once been in the market for an abortion, because you had asked him to do it, which of course he'd righteously refused to do. Not a thing a young man—or his parents—would like to hear about his fiancée, was it? Especially a young man named Baxter W. Stevens III. And you saw right then that if you paid him once—this time—every time Nestor ran a little short, or was in the mood, he was going to threaten that again. And, yes, you're very proud of your name and your social position, aren't you? You'd feel a lot happier if the one outsider who knew about that was—out of the way.

"So you agreed to pay, and you set up an appointment at his office, a week ago last night. But you didn't bring money—you brought a gun. You shot him, I think, almost as soon as you got into the office. And just before you fired, when he saw the gun, he tried to grab your arm. But you didn't know he'd got a loose button off your sleeve, did you? No. You didn't know *that* until—

"You set up the fake burglary by breaking open the door, stealing the petty cash. And you came home satisfied that the dumb cops wouldn't look beyond the end of their noses. Oh, just in *case* there was any little investigation, you got rid of the gun—or did you do that hoping some shady character down there would pick it up and after his next arrest get charged with Nestor on the strength of the gun? Very possibly. You're only smart up to a point, Marlowe.

"Then on Friday night—"

"I won't listen to this—this rigmarole," said Marlowe rigidly. "Insulting me like this in my own—"

"You'll listen! On Friday night you played friend of the family, paid the little call on Andrea Nestor. It was just bad luck—and not all his, Marlowe!—that you were wearing the same suit, and that Sergeant Hackett came calling just after you. . . . Yes, you were a little surprised yesterday when a man came to paw through your wardrobe, weren't you? And considerably upset. It was just chance again that it was your servant's day off and you could tell the dumb cop, no, you hadn't given away any clothes recently. I think I'd like to hear what your Paul has to say about that."

"*No*—" said Marlowe in a high frightened voice.

Mendoza jerked open the door, which wasn't quite shut. As he'd expected, the manservant was just moving away from it. Mendoza spoke his name, crooked a finger at him. "In."

"Yes, sir?" The man looked from him to Marlowe, bland and inquiring.

"You look after Mr. Marlowe's clothes?"

"Yes, sir, you could say so."

"Has he told you to give away any of his clothes recently, or have you noticed any missing?"

"Paul—"

"Why, yes, sir," said the man in a colorless tone. "The gray summer-weight tweed, sir. He told me it was getting too shabby, to give it to the salvage people. But as a matter of fact, sir"—he coughed gently—"as it had quite a lot of wear in it still, I gave it to my brother-in-law, who is much the same—er—build as Mr. Marlowe."

Marlowe said thickly, "You're fired! Get out of this house—damn you for a—"

The manservant looked at him thoughtfully, blinking, and faded silently from the room.

"More nice available evidence," said Mendoza, smiling. "Shall we go on with the story? On Friday night, at Mrs. Nestor's apartment, Sergeant Hackett spotted that button missing from your sleeve. And you noticed him staring at your sleeve, and for the first time realized you'd lost a button. And the fact that the sergeant looked interested in that more or less told you where you'd probably lost it, didn't it? Now, he didn't know it was anything but a coincidence, it didn't tell him right away that you were the X who had shot Nestor. But he wanted to ask you questions about it, and look at the other buttons on that jacket to see whether they matched. He'd have come to see you about that later—he let you go then. But you hung around there, waiting, after you'd ostensibly left, to go back and ask Mrs. Nestor whether the sergeant had asked any questions about you. Didn't you? And you didn't keep enough out of sight, and he spotted you when he came out, so he started questioning you then. Maybe more suspiciously than he would have before, because why were you hanging around? And you panicked, didn't you? You knew that that button would be very easy to trace to you, because of your British tailoring. All we had to do was look. And this big tough sergeant knew you had a button missing—but he was the only one of us who *did* know. And in panic and desperation, you were idiot enough to attack him."

"I—" said Marlowe. He was shaking and white. "Please, I don't understand—how you—"

"Ordinarily, of course, you'd have stood no remote chance of putting him down, far less out. But I can see just how that happened, too. He didn't know what he had, he didn't know its importance, and he wouldn't be expecting any physical trouble from one like you, he was off guard. Shall I tell you how it went? He was standing in the street, behind his car —maybe thinking he'd almost finished with you for the time being—and you were on the curb where you'd both been standing talking. Which brought you about level with him. You hit out as hard as you could for his jaw, and you hit hard enough to catch him off balance—maybe he slipped on some oil left there—and his feet went out from under him and he crashed down on the trunk of his own car.

"And when you found he was unconscious, a really desperate notion occurred to you. You'd done one murder. If the sergeant should, say, be killed in an accident, nobody would ever know about that missing button. You could get rid of the suit, cover up.

"Well, you acted at once. Kenmore's very dark and quiet along there, there wasn't a street light near, only the little light from the apartment entrance. Nobody had heard or seen. But a dog-walker or somebody might come along at any minute, and you hurried. He was a big, heavy man, and dead weight, but they do say"—Mendoza smiled—"needs must when the Devil drives. And you look to be in pretty good condition. You pulled him around and dragged him into the car somehow. The one thing you saw at all clearly right then, I think, is that you'd have to underline the fact that he'd driven off in his own car. So you found his keys, and you drove the Ford up a block or so, to another dark, lonely spot, and parked it. He was still out—but you didn't know how badly he was hurt, you had to—immobilize him. You hadn't any rope to do it with, so you used his belt and yours. And I think you also gagged him, just in case."

Marlowe was watching him, gray-faced, as if hypnotized. "No, you can't do this to me," he muttered distractedly. "My name—my family—disgraced— I have influence with—"

"Nobody influences the cops in this town," said Mendoza coldly. "Which you'd know if you knew more about us. But you don't know much about us, do you? . . . You tried in a clumsy sort of way to give yourself an alibi, but you never really thought anybody'd look at you, did you? You left him there, and you drove home, to set up your crude little alibi here. We've just seen how easily it went to pieces. When you were sure the servant was at the back of the house you slipped out, having left your car parked in the street, and you drove up to the vicinity of Bronson and Franklin and parked it. I wouldn't put it beyond you to have left it in a public lot with an attendant! And then you took a cab back to the vicinity of Kenmore where you'd left the Ford. We'll find the cab driver without much trouble. And into the Ford again and up to that steep canyon road—"

"No, please, I—" Marlowe gasped. "The disgrace—my wife would—" He turned suddenly, blindly, pulled open a drawer; Mendoza was on his feet in a flash, but Marlowe turned holding a small revolver in shaking hands.

"I hope you won't be silly enough to use that," said Mendoza. "But you seem to be silly enough for anything. Didn't you think we had *any* sense, Marlowe? To look at the tire marks, test the car for prints? You had heard of fingerprints—you wiped yours off everything a driver would touch. But that in itself looked very funny, you know. . . . Why Canyon Drive? Maybe you know somebody who lives in that very classy section, and knew the road? Anyway, you"—he stopped, controlling his voice to steadiness—"set up your accident, and a very Goddamned stupid way you did it too, and you walked down the mile or so to where you'd left your car. You knew the rest of the family would be out late—yes, there are probably quite a few prenuptial parties going on for Susan, aren't there? . . . For God's sake, do you really think we're all such fools, Marlowe? I think you really did put us down as a bunch of morons. The way you went to work at it. Well, as you see, we've got a lot of nice evidence on you now, and I'm taking you—"

"No," said Marlowe. His eyes were wild, but his hand had steadied on the gun. "No—I can't face that—the disgrace, my wife, Susan—this can't be happening—there was no *way* for you to find out—"

"Give me that," said Mendoza softly, advancing on him. "Let me—"

"*No!*" shouted Marlowe in sudden savage desperation. He sprang up and plunged for the door, slammed it behind him before Mendoza could reach it. And before Mendoza could turn the knob there was the sharp crack of a shot in the hallway outside. . . .

They looked at the sprawled body in silence for a moment. He had put the muzzle of the gun in his mouth, and there was a little mess. "God damn him to hell!" said Mendoza viciously. "So he does get away after all! I was looking forward to seeing him pulled down in the mud—"

"Vindictive," said Palliser wryly. "Not so good for the family. . . . How much of that was bluff, by the way?"

"Not much of it," said Mendoza, "really. Once I knew by the button it was Marlowe, there was only one logical motive. Only one way it could have happened. Damn him. Of course, if he hadn't caught Art off guard, he'd never have stood a chance of—but—"

The colorless manservant came quietly up the hall and looked down at the body. He said to Mendoza gravely, "I thought that was a shot. The rest of the family is all out, sir. I trust you'll be attending to the—er—formalities?"

"Quite right," said Mendoza. "Are you accustomed to your employers committing suicide?"

"Dear me, no, sir," said the man. "What a tragedy. I presume, sir, you'll be wanting that suit back from my brother-in-law?"

"You presume quite right," said Mendoza, and went back to the library to call the office and an ambulance. . . . The bastard, slipping away from him at the last minute . . .

He left Palliser, Scarne, and Landers to go through the house, pick up any more desultory relevant facts. So, on this one, there'd be no publicity after all, just the relevant evidence quietly attested to and the file put away marked *closed*. A nice discreet verdict of the usual suicide while temporarily insane, and that was that.

God damn him. To protect his precious name and position . . .

Still filled with cold wrath, he came into the office. "Understand you've broken the Nestor thing. Who and how?" asked Sergeant Lake.

"Marlowe—damn him." He was in no mood for long explanations. He went into his office. Dwyer was still there, fiddling nervously with the cards. It was five minutes past one. Of this new long, long day.

"I keep expecting it to ring," said Dwyer. "Damn it, they *said*—"

And at that moment the outside phone rang. And Sergeant Lake called in to them, "Hospital, Lieutenant."

Mendoza picked up the phone. His hand tightened on it, and his mouth drew to a grim line. "Yes, Doctor. . . . Yes. I'll be there in ten minutes—"

"Let me go," said Dwyer.

"No." Mendoza almost ran out, toward the elevators, and went all the way down to the garage; he commandeered a patrol car and had the siren going before he was off the ramp onto Temple Street. By God, he'd have one installed in the Ferrari tomorrow.

He made it in just over ten minutes. The doctor was waiting for him; they started for the elevators. "You understand, Lieutenant, if he doesn't recognize you, or seems mentally hazy in any way, it doesn't tell us definitely that he won't make a complete recovery. After all, he has been in a deep coma for something like five and a half days. And we know something about mental therapy, too, to help. But this will be a useful—ah—test."

"Yes," said Mendoza. The elevator landed; they walked down the corridor. The hospital atmosphere was thick all about them. No noise, only a faint hint of ether, of medicines, in the air; but the aura of professional busyness, of impersonal efficiency.

There were two nurses in the room, at the far side of the bed. The rails were up on each side. One of the nurses said, "I'm sorry, Doctor, we had to discontinue the I.V. He was so restless—"

"Quite all right," said MacFarlane absently.

Hackett's big bulk was moving uneasily on the bed; he had thrown off the sheet. His color was bad, an ashen gray, and all the bandages looked alarming. He was muttering incoherently. "His pulse is up to nearly ninety," said the other nurse.

"Yes," said MacFarlane. "I think it should be very soon now. I'm sorry, Lieutenant, we just have to wait—"

"Yes," said Mendoza.

"Mmh . . . mmh . . ." Hackett was mumbling; he sounded to be making a desperate effort.

"How is his wife standing up?"

"All right," said Mendoza, watching Hackett.

They watched in silence as Hackett tossed and muttered. Five minutes. Ten minutes. The nurse said, "His pulse is *very* fast, sir, I don't like—"

MacFarlane bent over the bed and used a stethoscope. "Constitution of an ox," he murmured. "His heart's sound enough. Don't worry."

Hackett quieted down and lay still for a little while, and then quite suddenly he opened his eyes. He stared vaguely up at the ceiling for a moment, and the doctor touched Mendoza's arm and mouthed, "Wait a minute."

"His pulse is down to normal, sir," said the nurse. Hackett turned his head weakly in her direction.

Mendoza stepped closer to the bed. He had his mouth open to speak Hackett's name when Hackett said, "Nurse. You're a—"

"That's right," said the nurse, smiling at him.

"Marlowe," said Hackett with great effort. "Tell—"

"Art," said Mendoza. "Art?"

Very slowly Hackett turned his head on the pillow. His blue eyes looked slightly unfocused still, and his voice came weakly in little gasps. "Luis," he said. "They—hauled you back—off vacation. Sorry. Have—a nice—time?"

Mendoza managed a grin. "I never want another one like it, boy," he said. And then the doctor was leading him out, and he sat down rather suddenly on the bench along the corridor.

"Very satisfactory indeed, of course," the doctor was saying. "He'll probably make a quite normal recovery now. Say three months. Very gratifying indeed—such a deep coma, and that massive fracture—but that looks very conclusive, of course."

Mendoza thought, Ought to find the nearest phone: let the girls know, call the office. Everything O.K. He heard himself laugh, and belatedly realized why: Art could forget his diet for a while, anyway.

"—as I said, Lieutenant."

"Yes," said Mendoza. *Lieutenant.* It sounded a lot better than *Mister:* the hell of a lot better. He started to get up, to go and find that phone, and suddenly all the lack of sleep, the worry and strain, the long, long days had caught up with him, and he had to lean on the bench. "Doctor," he said, "maybe you'd give me a shot of benzedrine or something? I might just manage to make it home. . . ."

"I am *not* going to wake him up," said Alison's voice. "I should think you'd *realize*—"

Mendoza opened his eyes. He knew where he was at once. On the long sectional in the living room of the house on Rayo Grande Avenue. He'd just made it that far before it all caught up to him and he went dead out as if he'd been knocked on the head.

It was almost dark. A little past eight o'clock, he thought vaguely. Around there. Somebody had taken off his jacket and tie and shoes, and unbuttoned his collar. And there was a cat coiled up on his chest, and he thought another one near his feet.

"You *know* what he's been through," said Alison's voice. Alison trying to keep her voice low. Sounding annoyed.

Mendoza lifted his head an inch and squinted down at his chest. He identified El Señor by the blond mask and slitted green eyes. Automatically he lifted a hand and rubbed behind El Señor's ears.

"I absolutely *refuse*—" said Alison.

Mendoza yawned and sat up, bringing El Señor with him in one arm. Annoyed to have his position changed without his official consent, El Señor hissed at him and escaped to the far end of the sectional, where he sat down on top of Bast and began to smooth his ruffled coat.

Nearly dark, but light enough still to see Alison with her back to him, shoulders looking very stiff, at the telephone table across the room. And Angel in the entrancehall doorway watching her.

Somewhere in the distance one of the twins was wailing. "He can't possibly—"

Mendoza yawned again. He felt, he decided, all right. He got up and crossed the room, put one arm around Alison, and took the phone away from her. The twin stopped wailing abruptly.

"*Oh!*" said Alison. "Luis—"

"Mendoza here."

"Well, I'm sorry to wake you up," said Higgins, "but we've got a sort of funny one down here. Just turned up."

"*Luis!*" said Alison. "You are *not—*"

"Mmh?" said Mendoza. He felt, on the whole, pretty good, he thought.

"Woman strangled with her own belt, it's obviously murder, but there was the damnedest odd note left beside the body—"

"*¡Qué interesante!*" said Mendoza. "All right, I'll come down and look at it." He put the phone down.

"Luis, no!" exploded Alison. "You ought to sleep the clock round—"

"But you've got," exclaimed Angel from the door, "to have something to *eat* before you—"

"*With,*" said Mrs. MacTaggart firmly, coming up the hall, "a wee drop of whiskey to hearten you beforehand."

Mendoza kissed Alison and started toward the bedroom for tie, jacket, and shoes. "Get me a cup of coffee, that's all. I'm O.K."

And Alison and Angel sent one unanimous bitter comment after him. "*Cops!*" they said.

THE DEATH-BRINGERS

Then shall two be in the field; the one shall be taken, and the other left. Two women shall be grinding at the mill; the one shall be taken, and the other left.

Matthew 24:40–41

ONE

Alison Mendoza smiled out the front window of the house on Rayo Grande Avenue, as Máiri MacTaggart, that jewel of a housekeeper-nurse, hurried up the front walk, trowel still in hand. Mr. Warbeck, with a backward glance at her, continued on down the street. He was a funny little man, with his shock of untidy hair and overearnest manner.

"I believe," she said to Máiri, "you've acquired an admirer."

"Ah, get on," said Mrs. MacTaggart. "And me in shouting distance of sixty? What I——"

"No, really, but he does always stop to talk to you if you're out in the yard."

"Two, three times, is it? He admires the twins, is the truth. Daft over children the poor man is."

"You don't convince me—you didn't have them out there right now."

"Tosh," said Mrs. MacTaggart roundly. "The man's lonely, is all—retired and not knowing what to do with himself. He talks to most people roundabout. What I—"

"Mmh," said Alison. Mr. Warbeck had become a tolerably familiar sight in this area for only a few months. This was a newly subdivided section, but Laurel Canyon was an old residential site and down the hill were older, shabbier homes; Mr. Warbeck, it was understood, rented a room in one of them. He seemed to walk a good deal, and all the kids and dogs for blocks around knew him. A nice little man, thought Alison vaguely; and if he was getting up the courage to lay siege to their Máiri, who was a widow, she didn't sound very receptive, which was a good thing.

"What I came in to tell you, if you'll stop joking a minute, he had his transistor radio on, and it was the news. There's been another one."

"Not another——"

"Another bank robbery is what I'm saying. Right downtown, the Security-First Bank on Spring Street. At noontime again, like all the rest, a couple of hours ago, and the villain got clean away."

"Oh, dear," said Alison inadequately.

"Clean away again, can you imagine it? But thanks to God he didn't shoot anybody this time."

"It doesn't seem possible . . . And I suppose that means," said Alison, "that we won't be seeing Luis until midnight again."

Lieutenant Luis Mendoza had never, as he expressed it, brought himself to resign from the honest job, despite the unexpected fortune his grandfather had left him; he was still, dapper as ever, holding down his desk at the Homicide Bureau at Central Headquarters downtown.

"Very likely," agreed Mrs. MacTaggart with a sigh. "All things considered. It does seem a great pity they can't be spaced out more sensible."

"Homicides, you mean?" said Alison gravely. "It does seem that way. But all this—it doesn't seem *possible* he can go on getting away with it. Maybe they'll get a useful lead this time——"

"The Invisible Man, the newspapers are calling him," said Mrs. MacTaggart. She looked serious. "And if they don't, then, maybe I'd best make a novena for it. The poor lieutenant, not in until one last night— ruining his health he'll be!"

It was the fourth bank robbery in twenty-seven days. All the jobs had apparently been pulled by the same man. He was a loner, and it just didn't seem possible that he could so utterly vanish moments after each job.

As if they didn't have enough on their hands already. As if September wasn't about the damnedest month of the year anyway, with the temperatures hitting a hundred degrees and over and the homicide rate naturally rising too. As if . . .

It was, in fact, turning out to be one hell of a month for the cops at Headquarters Homicide. Hackett, the senior sergeant, was still in the hospital, due to go home in a couple of weeks and spend another month convalescing before he came back on the job. Landers was on vacation, and so was Farrell. And Piggott, impossibly, was home in bed with the 'flu.

"The 'flu," said Palliser bitterly. "How the hell could he catch 'flu in September, for God's sake?"

But that was the way the ball bounced, so they were undermanned to start with. And there'd been that shooting over on San Pedro—that was three weeks old and looked like coming to a dead end; the corpse had been a near-Skid-Row drifter and anybody might have had some reason to cool him, good or bad—and the suicide that just possibly wasn't—though after a lot of probing into it Palliser was almost convinced that it was—and the teen-age gang rumble with two kids dead and several in the hospital, and yet another child-beating with the baby dead. And just this morning somebody, probably in some kind of car, had held up a Shell station on Figueroa and left a corpse behind him—the corpse of a nineteen-year-old kid who'd have been back at his classes at L.A.C.C. three days from now, if somebody hadn't wanted a little ready cash.

John Palliser didn't like to talk to bereaved parents. He was a young man for a sergeant, and a sympathetic young man who liked people. He didn't mind talking to the bad boys, and he could get as tough with them as need be, but he never knew what to say to people like Mr. and Mrs. Walsh.

"Why did it have to be Jimmy?" asked Mrs. Walsh. "Why my Jimmy?" And Palliser didn't know, so he couldn't tell her.

"He was a good boy," said Walsh numbly. "A good boy. Earning his own way through college. He wanted to be a lawyer. He'd've been a good lawyer. Never in any trouble, even if we don't live in too fancy a neighborhood." Walsh was a clerk in a Bekins' warehouse.

Palliser asked the questions that had to be asked. Jimmy had worked at the station two summers. The owner, Mr. Hammer, had liked him, treated him well, trusted him. "Why did it have to happen to Jimmy?" Walsh asked blankly. "Why did it happen at all? He said Mr. Hammer always told him—Jimmy and this other guy works there, the mechanic—anybody ever tries to hold up the station, play along, don't get brave, hand over the money. So Jimmy wouldn't have—— Why?"

There wasn't any immediate answer; possibly there never would be. The shooting had been done, as near as they could figure, about nine this morning, and you'd think that in those teeming city streets, in broad daylight, somebody would have seen something; but by noon it was apparent that nobody had, among immediately available possible witnesses. The shooting had been done not in the glass-enclosed station office but in the garage, set back farther from the sidewalk. The lab team was still going over every square inch of everything in there. The shooting had been discovered about ten o'clock when the mechanic, Mike Partridge, came on duty and found young Walsh's body. The owner, summoned down then, thought the heist man had got away with somewhere around forty dollars.

Palliser left Higgins and Dwyer still asking questions in the neighborhood and called the morgue from a drugstore phone. They hadn't, of course, got to an autopsy yet, but they had dug the bullet out. It was too much damaged for Ballistics to identify, thought the doctor, but he'd send it over anyway.

"Oh, great," said Palliser gloomily. He left his drugstore sandwich half eaten and went back to the Homicide office. As he came in, Sergeant Lake slammed down the phone and got up in a hurry.

"Lieutenant—another one! The same bastard—Security-First at First and Spring—just now, the guard called in——"

"¡Bastante! ¿Qué es esto? For God's sake, it's less than a week since he hit that Bank of America——" Mendoza seized his hat and caught Palliser's arm. "All right, call the Feds and the lab, but we'll get damn all this time, too, I'll just bet. For God's sake. Come on, John."

"Well, I just——"

"Nobody else here, damn it," said Mendoza.

"It's hot as hell outside," said Palliser plaintively. "Where do you suppose he gets the energy? And how in hell does he do it—disappear like that?"

"By all we've got so far," said Mendoza, "he's found out how to dematerialize, is all I can figure." They got into the elevator.

Homicide, with quite enough on its plate, thank you, had not been concerned with the first bank job. That had been the Broadway-Washington branch of the Bank of America, and nobody had got hurt. The loner had just walked away and vanished with twelve hundred and fifty-three dollars of the bank's money, so that headache had belonged to Lieutenant Saul Goldberg of Robbery.

But exactly a week later, on August nineteenth, the loner had walked into the Security-First National Bank at Main and Commercial, showed a gun to the chief teller, collected a little under three thousand bucks in the inevitable paper bag, and started to walk out. The bank guard, belatedly catching on, had run after him and collared him at a side door, whereupon the loner had calmly fired three bullets into him and pulled his vanishing act again.

The guard died just as the ambulance got there, so that laid it right in Homicide's lap, and the headache had been getting worse ever since. Of course the Feds were on it, too, but there was an old saying that you can't make bricks without straw, and while they had a rudimentary kind of description, it didn't give them any leads.

"It all happened so fast——" said the chief teller helplessly. And it was the same story five days ago, at the Bank of America at Ninth and Main. This time one of the male tellers had spotted what was going on and had quietly slipped out into the main part of the bank and waited for him—followed and tackled him before he got to the door. If the teller had hoped to be called a hero in the headlines he'd been sadly mistaken; what he was called in the headlines was dead.

They got all sorts of descriptions from various witnesses, which was par for the course; the general public, Mendoza thought, when asked to remember details, usually wound up proving the truth of that bit from Holy Writ: *They have eyes and see not.* But one thing the witnesses all agreed on was that the man was bald. Very bald.

But bald, curly-haired, white, black, or green, how the hell did he get away so quickly and completely? Somebody should have noticed him—which direction he went, at least—and unless he'd had the devil's own luck every time he'd never have found a parking space on the street near those banks, and even if he went off on foot, among the usual crowds somebody should have seen him . . . Although, of course, anonymity could hide in a crowd easily.

And very probably, thought Mendoza grimly, they wouldn't get anything more suggestive on him from the new set of witnesses.

They didn't. They got just about what they'd got before. As far as it went, it was helpful, because it added up to the same boy—again allowing for the variations of the witnesses. They discounted the hysterical female at the bank last week, who claimed he was a big black man over six feet tall with a scar on his face, and the man who insisted the loner wore a beard. The descriptions they had from those who'd had the best looks at him roughly said the same thing. And there was nothing very useful there.

"Was he bald?" Mendoza asked the chief teller. Palliser was talking to the guard and the bank manager, and a handful of Feds had turned up and were questioning the other tellers, the few members of the general public who'd been here.

"Oh, yes, sir." The chief teller was a pretty youngish woman, brown-haired and brown-eyed; she had on a bottle-green linen sheath and a chunky five-strand necklace of green beads. She kept clutching at the beads nervously. "But it all happened so *fast*—"

"Just tell me what you remember for sure, how he looked."

"Well—well, he wasn't a *young* man, I don't think. I think his eyes were light . . . I couldn't say about his coloring, I mean, he was a white man, but I wouldn't like to say, I guess he was sort of medium—and he was bald as could be, I remember his bald head sort of shining . . . And he had on a dark-gray suit and a white shirt and a tie—a—a black tie, I think. Dark anyway. It was all so *fast*—I got the shakes when I saw that gun. Mister, I really got the shakes. With those two fellows shot dead, I mean! It looked as big as a c-cannon——"

They knew about the gun, at least, and it would look something like a cannon to anybody not familiar with guns. The doctors had recovered bullets from both the guard and the teller, and Ballistics had examined their lands and grooves and looked in their records and come up with a make on the gun. It was a Smith and Wesson 1955 target revolver; it had a six-and-a-half-inch barrel, and it fired .45 ACP caliber slugs. It was a big gun. It was a heavy gun. In the hands it was now in it was a damn dangerous gun.

"What did he say?"

"He didn't s-say very much." Another similarity. What the hell good did it do them to find out it was the same boy? "He showed me the gun and just said something like—oh, 'You know what I want,' like that—and honestly, I was so scared and surprised—I mean, even reading in the papers about this guy, even knowing somebody like that's around, you just don't *expect*—I just started grabbing up money. I don't know to a penny what I had, but I usually have more on hand than the other—— Honestly, I just wanted it *over*——"

"He had a paper sack?"

"Yes, he did. It was, oh, a sort of medium-sized one, not really big. Now wait a minute," she said. "Wait a minute. That was kind of funny. See, I was stuffing bills into this bag, and all the time I was thinking—as well as I *could* think, you know—I mustn't let anybody see what's going on, Jean at the next cage, or Bill Harding over at Money Orders—they're nearest me, see—or somebody might try to get smart like that fellow last week and wind up dead. So I was trying to be real quiet and easy about it, see. And I got the bag full, and there was still a little pile of bills left in my drawer, but he says, 'That's fine, Miss Thomas'—you see, there's my name plate right inside the window, he saw that—and before I could try to get any more bills in, he took back the bag and shoved it under his jacket and put the gun away, too, and off he went. I don't know, he didn't seem to walk fast, but he was just—gone."

"He saw the bag was full and took what was already in it. I see. Not a greedy fellow. You can't remember any of his features near enough to describe? Nose? Ears? Jaw?"

She shook her head. "I didn't really look at him but just at first, you know. After that I was concentrating on the money. Naturally. He had a sort of roundish face, I think."

"Which way did he go?" Mendoza looked around the bank. It was a large bank; this main-floor office was perhaps a hundred by a hundred and fifty feet, with marble counters around most of three sides. There were two doors giving onto Spring Street and one onto First. There was also a door out of the bank into the lobby of the building; it was, of course, an ordinary office building above the main floor.

That was the door she pointed at. And the lobby had a street door of its own, too, onto Spring.

"Mmh," said Mendoza thoughtfully. "You didn't happen to notice his hands?" No, she hadn't. They had a witness from the first job, a sharp-eyed private dick who'd been standing at the next window, had seen what was going on and had the sense to stay still. He said the loner had worn strips of flesh-colored adhesive tape on his finger tips. He could be right, though nobody else had noticed that. In this weather gloves would be conspicuous. . . . But, nothing. No lead. Here was the same dark-gray suit, the same dark tie they'd heard about from the other witnesses before. And she went on to give him more of the same. As far as she could tell, he wasn't either very big or very small—average. She couldn't guess his age; she wasn't very good at that. His voice—well, he hadn't said much—it was sort of average. Just an ordinary voice. No accent or anything. He wasn't very fat or very thin—average—"Of course we only see customers about from the waist up. I couldn't tell——"

¡Mil rayos! thought Mendoza irritably. And this was the one who'd seen him nearest to, this time. This time nobody had realized what was happening—had happened—until after the loner had got clear away and the chief teller had gone into hysterics.

"And besides," she said tearfully, "it's not Miss Thomas, it's Mrs. Thomas!"

People.

Mendoza thanked her and went over to the Feds. They hadn't got much of anything either.

"The Invisible Man," said one of them disgustedly. "Argh, maybe he is."

"Well, there's this and that," said Mendoza, lighting a cigarette. "All in the downtown area. Why? Probably the most crowded section of town. And he hits at the lunch hour—between twelve and one, a peak period when he'd be least likely to be noticed. But why pick banks in this area in the first place?"

"He hasn't got a car," said the Fed wearily, "and you know how the bus situation is. He can't figure out where to catch a bus for anywhere else."

"Very funny," said Mendoza. "What it suggests to me is, he'll keep hitting banks in this area."

"So?" said the Fed. He was a big fellow with rough-hewn features; he reminded Mendoza a little of Hackett. "Do you see a lead there?"

"Stake out all the banks in the area bounded by, say, Washington and Sunset, Union and San Pedro?" Mendoza sighed. "Trained observers to describe him better, at least?"

"*Compadre*," said the Fed gently, "how many men you got? How many men you think *we* got? An army? Banks—there are thousands of them. Thousands."

"Nineteen, twenty in the downtown area," said Mendoza.

"Argh," said the Fed. "So four times he hits downtown. So next time he hits Federal Savings in Glendale or the California Bank in Culver City. Who can tell? *Compadre*, we got other things we're working on, you know, and just so many men."

"*Amigo*," said Mendoza, "so have we. So have we."

They would have to get a formal statement from Mrs. Thomas. They would be comparing what she said with what the other witnesses had said. They would—a waste of time so far—include Mrs. Thomas in the group being shown thousands of mug shots at Records, hoping for a possible ident.

At least this time the loner hadn't killed anybody. No telling when he might again.

A loner, for God's sake.

Hitting banks. Such very public places, with people all around. And then disappearing. How?

Mendoza and Palliser went back to Headquarters. "This gas-station thing," said Palliser. "The hell of a thing. By all that shows, a nice young kid—ambitious and hard-working. I wonder if the lab came up with anything. Damn shame. Probably one of these damned hopheads, hunting easy money to support his habit."

Mendoza yawned and punched the elevator button again. He said, "Detective novels."

"What? What about them?"

"Mostly about the private homicides. ¿Cómo no? Nice intimate killings. Largely very implausible. They do occur—but how many of that kind to the kind we mostly see—the impersonal, random, wanton kills?" He sounded dispirited.

They got out of the elevator and walked down to the door marked *Homicide Bureau*. Sergeant Lake looked up.

"You've got a new one, boys. Higgins came in just after I got the call. I sent him out on it."

"What now?" asked Mendoza resignedly.

"Over on Allen Street. Teen-age girl shot. Colored. Looks like something a little funny, what the squad-car man said. I don't know."

"All I need," said Mendoza. He picked up his hat again.

The city had tripled its population in the last ten years; the chief was clamoring for more money to hire more cops. The city was policing a territory ten times the size of New York City with a quarter as many cops, and the city had the top police force in the world; but it could only stretch so far and do so much. And of all the public services the city fathers granted money to, the cops were always last on the list.

Naturally.

TWO

When Mendoza and Palliser got to the house on Allen Street, the ambulance had just arrived; they wouldn't move the body until the lab team had seen it. Higgins, looking very hot and uncomfortable in the stuffy little living room, was talking to Mrs. Coffey.

It was an old frame house on a block of old frame houses. This was one of the oldest sections of L.A., and while you couldn't exactly call it a slum, you couldn't exactly say it wasn't, either. Whether or not a given block fell into the category of slum depended a lot on what kind of people lived there. Negro section or white section or Oriental, that held true.

Most of the houses on this block were kept up fairly neatly. A couple had been recently painted, but the strips of dry grass in front yards were faintly brown, in September, and a few other houses looked run-down, a pane of glass cracked in a front window, a curtain showing tears. L.A. had quite a population of Negro elite society, professional people who lived in some of the best residential areas of the county; but just as not all the white population belonged to elite society, neither did the people like the Coffeys.

"I don't know what happened, sir," Mrs. Coffey was saying now, agitatedly. She still had on a faded blue apron over her house dress, and she kept bunching it up between her hands, unaware of what she was doing. "I didn't hear anything like a shot. You're saying Carol was shot, and I guess you know, sir, but I didn't hear no shot. I was right out in the back yard. I don't understand—and you're saying she's dead, but it don't seem possible——"

She was a big woman and still handsome, with regular features, a medium brownish color—some white blood, thought Mendoza. There was a young boy in the doorway across the little room; the open door gave on a much smaller bedroom—glimpse of a narrow cot-bed neatly made, a cheap painted chest of drawers.

Higgins glanced at Mendoza wearily. "Mrs. Coffey, this is Lieutenant Mendoza, Sergeant Palliser. What——"

"How do you do," she said mechanically. "I've been out back. I never heard a thing. I just come in and found her laying there——"

"This was about twenty-five minutes ago," said Higgins to Mendoza. He went over to the two interns crouched over the body, and Mendoza followed him. "How long do you figure, boys?"

"Can't have been dead long when she was found. Call it half an hour ago, thirty-five minutes. Looks as if she got it right through the heart."

Mendoza looked down at the body. It was the body of a young Negro girl, eighteen, nineteen. She wasn't pretty now—her mouth gaped, her blind eyes stared—but very likely she had been pretty; she had a slim, rounded figure. She lay on her back almost up against the rear wall of the living room, between the open door to another bedroom and the right end of the shabby chintz-covered sofa on that wall. She was wearing white shorts and a red halter-necked bra—a very nice figure indeed—and there was blood all over the halter and her warm brown skin and down on the shorts and on the worn beige rug.

"How could Carol be *shot?*" asked Mrs. Coffey. "I don't understand—who'd want to shoot *Carol?* Everybody likes Carol——"

"Were you here, son?" Higgins asked the boy.

The boy was sixteen or seventeen. He was darker than Mrs. Coffey or the dead girl and not as good-looking. He had on jeans and a clean white T shirt. He said, "I was in my room. In there." He nodded behind him to the little bedroom. "The door was shut. But I heard this noise. I didn't know it was a shot—it didn't sound loud like that, like you think a shot would be. Just a kind of pop, like. Naw, I didn't get up to look out the window or nothing. Little kids always fooling around with cap pistols. That's what—what it sounded like."

"Here's the lab boys," said Palliser, looking out the window.

"But everybody liked Carol——"

"You're the girl's brother?" asked Higgins.

"He's my son Verne," said the woman. "Yes, of course Carol's brother." There was a little crowd collecting from all over the neighborhood now outside. The squad-car men were out there. "You're telling me she's *dead.*" She sounded nakedly incredulous; she was trying to see the dead girl beyond the interns' bent shoulders.

"I'm sorry, ma'am," said Higgins gently.

"In her own home—quiet neighborhood like this—— She was doing the dusting for me," said Mrs. Coffey. "We're having June and Frank for dinner, that's my married daughter and her husband. And I said to Carol if she'd straighten up a bit in here and dust things, while I went out back to cut some roses fresh——"

The lab team was in now. Mendoza said, "If we could go to another room, Mrs. Coffey? Maybe the kitchen? This is getting a little crowded in here, and you won't want to watch all this."

"Yes," she said dully. She turned and led them into the second bedroom off the living room, from there across a short dark hallway into a narrow kitchen. It was an old house, but the kitchen had plastic tile on the drainboards and looked very clean and neat. It was about the size of the living room and in one corner was an old-fashioned round oak table with four chairs around it. There was a plastic lace doily on the table, and sitting on it a cheap glass bud vase with a single perfect yellow rose in it. "Is this all right?" She glanced at the vase; her hands still bunched up the apron, nervously, unconsciously. She said, "I just picked that a while ago. It's Carol's favorite one—she always cuts one of them to pin on her dress, going to a dance or something, you know. It's called Peace, that bush is." There was a little pile of fresh-cut roses lying on the drainboard on a sheet of newspaper.

"Mrs. Coffey——"

"I better call Sam," she said suddenly. "My husband. Oh, my God, he'll be—— He's real proud of Carol. Real proud. Her going to college and all. This was going to be her second year. She went partly at night so's she could hold a job and earn the money, you see. She works at the Newberry's over on Central. Please, can I call my husband? I mean, ask somebody to—— I wouldn't know how to tell him. I just wouldn't know." Grief was taking the place of shock in her eyes now. "But she's only *nineteen*," she said.

Just like the kid the heist man had shot this morning.

"Of course, Mrs. Coffey," said Mendoza. "We'll want to talk to him too. It's just possible he might know of someone who had some reason to—— Where does he work?"

"He works at the General Hospital. He's what they call an orderly there. You know, he helps take the meals around and cleans up and like that. He'll be——" Mendoza nodded to Palliser, who slipped out to find a pay phone. Suddenly Mrs. Coffey drew a deep, deep breath and exhaled slowly. She turned to Mendoza almost as if by groping instinct; perhaps even in this confused moment she selected him as also one of a minority which had known prejudice, and she said, "Excuse me, sir, I want to ask you—I got to ask you—you take it easy with Sam, sir. With my husband. Questions and all. There's nothing like what you think, there's nobody had any reason at all, shoot our Carol. We all knew everything happened to her. She's a good girl, there's nothing like that, sir. Sam, he'll be just wild. Just wild. But I got to ask—— My husband, he's from Alabama, sir. I was born here, but he's from Alabama. A place called Kinston, he's from— little town. And—and you see, sir, he don't know that—that policemen are different, different places. He don't believe it. Why, you got colored police- men here, but he still——" She stopped with a little gasp. "I mean, I don't want for you to think, if he acts scared of you or—or anything——"

"We won't upset him, Mrs. Coffey. We don't like to bother you at a time like this, but we do want to find out who did this, you know."

"Yes, sir," she said in a low voice. She had stopped bunching up her apron. She sat down in one of the chairs at the table. "I know."

"Did your daughter have a boy friend?"

"Not a real regular one. She's gone out with Dick Watkins, and Eddy Loman, and a couple times with the Kingsley boy—Glen Kingsley down the block. I guess she went with Dick mostly, but it wasn't like going steady. She d-didn't go out an awful lot. Carol's a serious girl. She's going —she wanted to be a teacher. That's what she was studying. She got pretty good grades, do you know? She got an A in English last year. Sam was pretty set up about that, him only having a couple years' schooling him- self. Real proud of Carol——" For a moment her features crumpled and they waited for her to break down, but she controlled herself. "Not that Sam isn't a steady worker—he's always held a job, what job he could get. But college and all—it was something." She looked up at Mendoza a little blindly. "You go to college, sir?"

"No."

"Oh. A Mrs. Lyons my mother used to know, her boy went to college and then he joined the police here. I thought——"

"Yes," said Mendoza. Higgins looked a little grim. Neither of them had known Joe Lyons personally, but they remembered how he'd been killed, by a hopped-up j.d. he'd stopped for speeding. His name was on the Honor Roll at the Headquarters building.

There was a little silence; they gave her time. Presently she said, "There's talk, you know—a lot of talk. And down in the South, no ques- tion, it's bad—like where Sam comes from, he's all the time talking about it. But when our Carol was going to college, fixing to be a teacher, and no trouble about her getting in, why, half the ones in her class was colored—

and colored getting in the police and all . . . I don't know, looks as if here anybody got any ambition and brains can get to be anything. . . . She got good grades, did I tell you that? She got an A in English——"

They sent the body down to the morgue. Palliser and Higgins started asking questions up and down the block. Depressingly, they heard from the neighbors just about what the girl's mother had said. A good girl, quiet and respectable and ambitious, helped her mother in the house. A nice family, always went to church regular, and both the elder Coffeys were death on liquor, real temperance—good Methodists they were, as the Reverend Williams would say too.

It got to be five o'clock, and the temperature was still something like ninety-seven, and Palliser gave up and went back to Headquarters to see if the lab had come up with anything on the gas-station holdup. Mendoza had been scheduled to join a meeting with the Feds to discuss the bank jobs.

Of course, Palliser reminded himself as he rode slowly up in the elevator, it was really only four o'clock by sun time. But since the population had shot up, what with the increased amount of water in use, and all the square mileage of new cement, the damn climate had changed—the nights didn't cool off the way they used to.

He had a date with Roberta tonight. He only hoped he'd get to keep it.

Mendoza was still with the Feds presumably. There wasn't any lab report waiting. He called the lab and was asked did he think they were miracle men. "Yes, I think you are miracle men," said Palliser. "Let's have what you've got."

"Tomorrow," said the lab man.

Palliser sighed and decided to call it a day. The night men were starting to straggle in. But before he left the office the phone rang and it was Dr. Bainbridge at the morgue asking for him. Palliser looked at his watch: five-forty. "Yes?"

"I think I've got something for you," said Bainbridge. "On this Walsh boy. Damn shame—well-set-up young feller. So damn young. Sign of age, I suppose, when the kids begin to look so very damned young."

"Yes. What is it?"

"I can't show you over the phone, damn it. I was just leaving. You stay put ten minutes and I'll come up."

"All right," said Palliser.

Dr. Bainbridge bustled his tubby little self into the Homicide office fifteen minutes later. He sat down in Mendoza's desk chair and said,

"Maybe this'll say something to you. I don't know what the hell it is, but then I'm not a trained detective." He fished an envelope out of his pocket and handed it over. Palliser upended it cautiously over the desk blotter, and a little something fell out. He turned it over curiously with one finger.

It was a small piece of metal. Very small. Between a quarter and an eighth of an inch long. But "long" was the wrong term, because it was curved slightly. It was straight for a little bit, and the inner surface rounded gently in a curve while the outer edge showed a definite point and then turned upward. Steel, steel alloy, darkened aluminum? Palliser fingered it. "Where'd you get this?"

"Out of the wounds," said Bainbridge, leaning back comfortably. "The boy was shot, but he was also beaten up. First. Banged over the head, to be non-technical. With something, not just fists. He was struck four or five times by our old friend the blunt instrument, and I think—from the angle of the shot—he was then shot as he lay prone and probably unconscious on the floor of the garage."

"Nice," said Palliser with a grimace. And why? Jimmy's father said that both Jimmy and the mechanic had been told not to show fight to a holdup man. So? Had the heist boy, just possibly, been somebody Jimmy knew and could identify? It was a thought.

"That," said Bainbridge, nodding at the little strip of metal, "was in the deepest head wound. I would assume it was broken off the blunt instrument. By the force of the blow."

"Yes," said Palliser, "but what the hell is it?"

"That," said Bainbridge, "I really couldn't tell you, Sergeant. You're supposed to be the detective."

"¿Cara?"

"You're going to say you won't be home," said Alison.

"Well, I wasn't," said Mendoza. "With a little provocation I might quote Omar Khayyam."

"That'd be a change. What part?"

" 'Myself when young did eagerly frequent Doctor and Saint, and heard great Argument about it and about, but evermore Came out by the same Door as in I went.' These bank jobs. I've been sitting around talking it over with the Feds. Very unproductively." Mendoza was at an unprotected public phone at a drugstore on Hill Street. A narrow aisle separated him from the lunch counter with its long mirror behind it; he could see the reflection of the slim dark man in the sharp-tailored gray Italian silk, the man with the narrow mustache and deep widow's peak; automatically he lifted a hand to straighten the discreet dark tie. The blonde waitress behind the counter smiled widely at him.

"When we heard about the new one we thought we wouldn't see you until after midnight again. Did you get any leads at all?"

"*Nada.*"

"But it seems impossible he should just *disappear*—— You should have got him the first or second time, by all——"

"*Presonar vino y vender vinagre.* I am," said Mendoza, "being ogled. By an emphatically blonde waitress. I can't see her legs, but she has a very fetching figure."

" 'Lover Boy Mendoza they used to call me.' *Mi hombre amoroso,* come home."

"I don't know," said Mendoza. "I got damn bored with the Feds, and she's a very pretty blonde. The way she's eying me——"

"I'll bet," said Alison. "Teresa walked six steps today without falling down. I think she's getting the hang of it at last."

"Babies," said Mendoza, "are also boring."

"Then why," asked Alison, "did you want those negatives to have wallet-sized prints made?"

"A pure reflex," said Mendoza with dignity. "In our present culture, any man who has been so foolish as to—mmh—give hostages to fortune automatically carries photographs in his billfold."

"So he does," said Alison. "It's nothing to do with the fact that Terry looks like you and Johnny like me."

"Nothing at all," said Mendoza.

"Are you coming home at a decent hour?"

"Well, this blonde—— What have you got for dinner?"

"Chicken and avocado salad? Vichyssoise? Máiri's making scones, and there's unsalted butter and that imported jam."

"I'll pass up the blonde," said Mendoza. "After all, I can pick up a blonde any time."

"*¡Amador!*" said Alison, and her voice turned serious. "You're tired. It's a bad one—a tough one?"

"They're all being tough ones," said Mendoza. "One of these times."

"Máiri's going to make a novena for you."

"*¡Maravilloso!* These superstitious females."

"And she has an admirer. That funny little Mr. Warbeck."

"He's not going to take her away from us?" asked Mendoza anxiously.

"I doubt it. She's not interested."

"Good."

"Come home," said Alison firmly.

"Half an hour."

THREE

"At least," said the Fed, "we know our boy won't be working today." It was Saturday morning. The Fed's name was Dale, and he was a tall thin young man with a long nose and a humorous mouth. He sat down beside Mendoza's desk and brought out a long yellow teletype. "What do you think of this? The Washington boys just passed it along. This Alfred Siegal, five-ten, one-sixty, hair—oh, well, this is out-of-date anyway. Siegal has a pedigree—assault, armed robbery—and back in 1932 he pulled several singlehanded bank heists. As far as anybody knows he's never been mixed up with the big boys, no contact with the Syndicate at all. He's served time. The last anybody heard of him—on our side of the fence anyway—was back in 1949 when his latest probation ended. He was then forty-two. But add fifteen years, he might be bald by now, and God knows we haven't got very much else definite to go on."

"No. Anybody have any idea where Siegal might be?"

Dale shrugged. "Who knows?"

"Well, that's very helpful. Look." Mendoza sat up abruptly. "You missed our conference yesterday. What do you think's happening with the money?"

"Because none of it's been passed, or none we can trace? Hell——" Dale rubbed his jaw. The banks, of course, had records of the serial numbers of all the bills above singles. The loner had got away with more big bills than singles, but none of them had been passed so far anywhere in the country. And that was helpful in a negative kind of way.

Dale said, "He could be sitting on it until he figures we'll stop looking. Maybe he doesn't know we never do."

Mendoza shook his head. "What kind of people hold up banks? Much the same sort of people who steal, period. Not really very smart people—as Saul Goldberg could also say. Ninety-nine times out of a hundred they start right in enjoying themselves with the proceeds, throwing it around. And of all thieves, your bank robber is apt to be even more so—being more aggressive and more of a gambler by nature. I don't think he's sitting on it. I think he's selling it to a hot-money man."

"But, my God," said Dale, "the piddling amount he's got away with——"

"Call it that to the banks! I know, I know. He's taken exactly seven thousand, one hundred and eighty-two dollars in four hauls. Not a fortune, but a nice piece of change. He——"

"A hot-money agent wouldn't give him a third of that. Too much trouble for too little profit—channeling the actual bills out of the country, in a long series of elaborate deals, where eventually they turn up, completely untraceable, in Switzerland or North Africa. What the hot-money men largely deal in are the really big hauls, ransom money, that kind of thing."

"I know," said Mendoza again. "But let's try to read him from the very little we do know. I make him a very cautious fellow."

"*Cautious?*" said Dale. "Holding up banks all by himself?"

Mendoza grinned. "No, but look at the precautions he takes. He knows a lone man can't hope for a really big haul this way—getting into the vaults, for instance. But he does pick the chief tellers, who usually have more cash on hand than the other tellers. And by what they say he's very cool, plays it slow and easy. I think he might very well be a type to play it even safer by taking the loss and getting rid of the incriminating evidence. Anyway, we've got feelers out to all the stool pigeons. See what they come up with. We don't know, but of course there'll be at least one hot-money man here."

"Um, I don't know," said Dale. "You want to do anything about this Siegal?"

"What the hell could we do? No place to start looking for him, you said."

Sergeant Lake came in and handed Mendoza an envelope. He opened it; it was the formal autopsy report on Jimmy Walsh. Ballistics said the bullet was considerably damaged, no make on the gun. There was nothing else new from the autopsy. "Hell," said Mendoza, and reminded himself to be sure Palliser saw it. "Do you ever have spells like this when everything goes wrong?"

"We're human too," said Dale dryly.

"And who the hell wanted to shoot that nice little colored girl? It doesn't make sense."

Dwyer came in and nodded at Dale. "Think we might have something," he said.

"Don't tell me, a break at last!"

"Well, I won't say for sure." Dwyer had broadened out in the last couple of years and started to lose his sandy hair, which worried him; he'd developed the habit of fumbling with it, perhaps unconsciously checking to see how much was left, and one hand strayed to the top of his head now as he hoisted one hip to a corner of Mendoza's desk. "We've got eleven witnesses going through all those mug shots. Two of 'em picked out this same one about an hour ago. Well, two out of eleven—the others weren't sure. But the two who picked it were two of the chief tellers—Mrs. Thomas and the man, Clark. Which looks——"

"It does indeed. Who is he?"

Dwyer produced an envelope. "I pulled his pedigree for you. He's not a very nice boy. Daniel Fisher, first arrest at sixteen, back in 1930, car theft. Two, three, four more counts on that—probation—six months on the Honor Farm—probation—hell, you can tell the story for yourself. First arrest as an adult, break-in at a liquor store. Maybe he had a good lawyer—he got a suspended sentence, more probation. These judges. Then he got picked up for burglary—this was in 1936—and did a one-to-three. He's out about a year, probation just over, when he starts pulling heist jobs. He got picked up on that in 1941 and did a three-to-ten—additional count, resisting arrest. Matter of fact, he half killed a patrolman. He got out in 1947, and the year after that he was charged with knocking down an old lady and stealing her bag—in MacArthur Park, at night. She couldn't identify and he got off. Then in 1950 he got picked up for armed assault. It was a hung jury and the thing dragged on on the calendar and was finally dropped. He got picked up on the same charge six months later, did another three-to-ten, and got out in 1960. About a year later—he was still on probation—he was found with a gun on him—a .45 incidentally—and spent another six months in the clink. Since then apparently he's either gone straight—and I never did believe in miracles," said Dwyer, "or he's been too careful to get caught."

"Mmh, yes," said Mendoza. "Yes. He's always worked alone, he's not averse to using violence, and he's a thief. And once carried a .45. Men who carry guns at all usually have some preference. Is there an address there for him?"

"Old one—1961—but, sure. Over in the Atwater section."

"So let's go see if he's home," said Mendoza, and stood up. "Or at least ask questions about him if he's not there."

"According to all this," said Dwyer, "I'd say the chances are good. He's never moved around much. Same address in 1930 as when they picked him up in 1941, and he moved to this place in 1955. Went back there when he got out of jail last, I guess."

"I kind of think I buy Mr. Fisher," said Dale. "Does he match up otherwise to what we've got?"

"Well, we haven't got much, have we? He's five-ten, one hundred and eighty, medium coloring, blue eyes, no scars or deformities, and in 1961 he was going bald."

"I buy him," said Dale with decision, getting up. "Come on."

Mendoza took up his hat and started for the door. Dwyer stepped in front of him and said, "Uh-uh."

"What?"

"Art not being here, I figure I got to substitute for him. I'm the next senior sergeant, after all. Go get your gun."

"Oh, for God's sake," said Mendoza.

"Go get it or you can't play. This is not a little snotnose kid hopping cars we're going to see. And we need you around here, Lieutenant—you and your crystal ball. Not to mention that I kind of like that nice redheaded wife of yours."

"I suppose you've both got guns, and he's only one man."

"Maybe Art's right—you just don't like to spoil the set of your jacket," said Dwyer. "Go get the gun."

"Bullying me in my own office——"

"Sure, sure, so we get there and find this guy hopped up or something—he seems to've tried a lot of different kicks—and you get shot up, and everybody blames me."

"Now, Bert——"

"That butters no parsnips," said Dwyer firmly. "The gun."

"Oh, for *God's* sake," said Mendoza. He flung his hat down on the desk, took off his suit jacket, opened a drawer, took out the shoulder holster and strapped it on, checked the .38 Police Positive, and shoved it into the holster. He put on his jacket. "Satisfied?"

"Okay," said Dwyer mildly. "Let's go."

"Bullying me!" said Mendoza bitterly. "*Se lo digo,* it's no joke! Between you and Art——"

"We need that crystal ball of yours."

"And I have a hunch right now that this is all going to be very tame indeed," said Mendoza.

But his hunches weren't always right. Not by any means.

Palliser was not thinking about the bank robber. He was thinking about Jimmy Walsh. He wanted very much to find out who had killed Jimmy, the nice bright kid who'd wanted to be a lawyer. The little colored girl, Carol Coffey, that was something to think about, too, but he'd wait for the autopsy report, see if Ballistics could make anything of the slug; then he'd want to talk to some of her friends—she might have confided something suggestive to a girl friend. Everything seemed to be happening at once, the last couple of days, and nobody could be in two places at the same time. Higgins was out talking to Carol's boy friends, he thought.

And right now he had what looked like a very hot lead in the Walsh case.

"Let me get this straight," he said to the man sitting across the desk from him here in the communal sergeants' office. "You live on this street, Fig Court?" It sounded a rather improbable name, but the county had a lot of those.

"Yeah, that's right. Right off Figueroa. It ain't even a whole block long, you know. Just our apartment, and two others same side o' the street, and a couple houses across the way." The man across the desk bore the elegant name of Rosario Jesus del Valle; he was a short, scrawny little man obviously dressed in his Sunday-best suit for this call on the cops, a cheap navy-blue suit, and a very clean white shirt, and a gaudy tie. He had a lot of curly black hair and earnest brown eyes; he was almost a handsome little man. He said, "I work for the railroad. The S.P. In the yards."

"Yes. And your apartment's in the rear of the building, so your side windows look down on that Shell station."

"That's it. See, I didn't hear about that poor young kid getting killed till I get home last night. That's a terrible thing, ain't it? Why, he filled up my car lotsa times just this summer. I just got a car last year, saved up for it, you know, and Margarita, she likes drive out around in the country, get outta the city, down to the beach, like that. She says it's not healthy for kids, all this city air. Crazy. I grew up in the city, it never hurt me none. But I love her, what do I do? I buy gas, drive to the country." He shook his head. "Gotta drive fifty miles any direction, get outta the city nowadays. And what's when you get there? Fields with cows in them. Fields with tomatoes in them—string beans, lettuce."

"Listen," said Palliser, "you said——"

"Oh, yeah, yeah, sorry, I was getting to it, sorry. So Margarita tells me about the kid, says isn't it terrible, and I right away think about what I seen yesterday morning, and I think, Jesus, he could've been the one did it. Because the paper said it was about nine A.M."

"That's what we figured," said Palliser.

"O.K. So I figure to myself, I better come in and tell you about it, see.

Just in case it was the one. Jesus, a guy going around killing kids like that —nice kid he was, always polite. And besides, I happen to know that this Hammer who runs the station tells 'em all, don't get smart if a holdup happens, stand still for it. So why shoot the kid? I mean, maybe he's a nut."

"Maybe. What did you see?"

"So," said del Valle, "I say I better come in. That Margarita. She's *extranjera*, you get me, born down south of the border, and right off she gets the jitters, me mixed up with the cops. I got to take a while, calm her down, explain you're right guys and all, and then I got to see the foreman and explain this is a legit excuse. You get me. So that's how come I don't get here until now." It was ten minutes to eleven.

"Sure," said Palliser impatiently. "So what did you see?"

"The baby was sick," said del Valle maddeningly. "Nothing serious, a little colic, but I guess we're both kind of foolish about her, see—she's a real doll, you know? Only six months, but a real charmer. She's got these eyelashes—— Well, anyways, it was my day off. I get a weekday and Sunday, see, and we usually sleep late the weekday on account of having to get up early Sunday for Mass. Father Rodriguez only has seven and nine o'clock Masses, but we was up early yesterday account of Elena. The baby."

"Yes, yes," said Palliser. "And so?"

"Well, Margarita says we got to take her to the doctor. Be sure it ain't something serious. So I'm in the bedroom getting dressed, and I forgot to wind my watch the night before, and it's run down. So I yell to Margarita what time is it?—so's I could set my watch, see—and she yells back it's twelve after nine, so——"

Palliser sat forward in his desk chair.

"—I go over to the window so's I got good light to set the watch and I set it and I wind it and I put it on, and then—you know how you do things just sort of casual like—I look down outta the window." He paused. "No, I didn't hear no shot, but——"

"Yes?" said Palliser.

"Well, I see this guy come outta the garage there. He looked like he was in a hurry. I didn't see anybody but him—not the kid, not the mechanic Hammer has. Just this guy. He comes outta the garage, and he walks real fast across the blacktop past the station and gets into a car, and off it goes."

"Wait a minute. You said, 'off it goes.' Was he driving it?"

"No, no, there was a couple other guys in the car. He got in beside the driver, and there was another guy in the back seat."

"All right. Can you describe him?"

"I saw him, didn't I? Sure. I couldn't say at all what size he was, 'cause I was looking down at him, see? But he wasn't fat or thin, just average, and he had on dark pants and a green sports jacket. A light-green shirt, no tie. No hat, and he had kind of sandy hair."

"Good. What about the car? Did you get a good look at it?"

"Sure," said del Valle. "Look, I said I just got a car last year—in December. Cars I been lookin' at and studying on a long while. I can tell you most any make and model, one look at it. On account I was trying decide what'd suit me best, see. Good mileage and all. What I ended up getting was that six-cylinder Plymouth. Good car. What d'you drive?"

"A Rambler," said Palliser. "What was the car?"

Del Valle nodded. "I thought about that one too—nice car," he said. "But I like the Plymouth O.K. Well, this car, it was one I'd looked at, so I knew it, see. It was an English Ford—the Anglia De Luxe—and it was light green. This year's. Yeah, solid color. And it had those things, you know, to carry skis like, on the roof."

Palliser felt a little excited. "I don't suppose you noticed the plate number, but that's very helpful, Mr. del Valle. There were three men in the car?"

"Yeah, I'm positive of that. Counting this fellow in the green jacket. And I did notice the plate number. Not all of it, naturally, because who does? But these new ones now, with three letters, sometimes they sort of spell words, and you do notice. If you get me. And this one, it started out HAH, like somebody laughing, which was sort of funny."

"Thanks very much," said Palliser fervently. "It was very good of you to come in—we appreciate it."

The Atwater section address turned out to be a very old and shabby four-family apartment. Fisher's apartment was Four, at the rear on the second floor.

They climbed uncarpeted stairs.

"I want to go and see Art this afternoon," said Mendoza. "He claims he's going stir-crazy, shut up with all those nurses calling him 'We.'"

They walked down a dingy dark narrow hallway where dust rose from an old, thin carpet. Dale said, "Art?" There was a door with a single tarnished numeral: 4. He knocked on it.

"My senior sergeant. He's still in the hospital. He got assaulted a couple of months ago. Won't be back to work until November, damn it."

"These thugs."

"Not exactly a thug."

Dale knocked again, loudly. The door opened suddenly.

"Yeah, what you want?"

This was undoubtedly Daniel Fisher himself. He had lost the rest of his hair. He was wearing a pair of polka-dot shorts and nothing else, and what hair he lacked on his head he had on his chest. He looked a little flabby but sufficiently formidable.

"Mr. Fisher?" said Dale. "F.B.I." He proffered his I.D. "We've got a few questions to ask you——"

"What the *hell?*" said Fisher hoarsely. He stepped back, to the middle of the room. His eyes moved nervously, wildly. He shouted suddenly, "Goddamn all you bastards, hounding a man—hounding——"

And quite suddenly there was a gun in his hand, and quite suddenly bullets started flying.

Dale ducked behind a nearby armchair, reaching for his own gun. Dwyer dodged over toward the left wall, and before Mendoza got his gun out Dwyer had jumped Fisher from the side and had him down. Dale piled onto the clawing tangle; they hauled Fisher up to his feet and took the gun away from him. Fortunately Dwyer had a pair of cuffs in his pocket.

"Whoosh, that was close," said Dwyer, inspecting the powder burns on the shoulder of his jacket. Fisher stood staring at them sullenly. "Well, they do say only the good die young."

FOUR

"All right, Fisher, let's have some answers," said Mendoza.

"I didn't do nothing. Why can't you guys let me alone? I ain't been in any trouble since I got out last."

"You're in trouble now, brother," said Dwyer dryly. "You didn't act just so smart, shooting at cops like that."

"What other cops have been hounding you?" asked Dale.

They'd brought him down to Headquarters and stood around him now in one of the interrogation rooms. Dressed, Fisher didn't look so formidable: just a shabby, paunchy, unshaven man on the wrong side of fifty.

"I didn't do nothing," he said sullenly.

"You pulled a gun on us." The gun had been sent down to Ballistics, but it wasn't the gun used in the bank jobs; it was a Ruger Black Hawk .44 Magnum. But a man who had one gun might have two, though if so it hadn't been in his apartment. They didn't bother to ask him about a gun permit—a waste of time. In California you didn't need a permit to keep a gun on the premises, only if you were going to carry it in a car or on your person; and anyway, what pro hood ever had a permit?

"Yeah, well, I was nervous—you comin' in like that. I'm sorry," said Fisher. "You gonna give me the gun back?"

"Are you kidding?" asked Dwyer. "To a guy with a pedigree?"

"Where were you yesterday between twelve noon and one o'clock?" asked Dale.

"Betw——" Instant panic flared in Fisher's eyes. "Why? I dunno. I didn't do nothing. Honest."

"Where were you?" asked Mendoza patiently. "Think."

"I—— Listen, there's something all cockeyed here. I dunno why you guys—— Listen, we come through that door out there, it says Homicide! That's murder, ain't it? I never *killed* nobody! I didn't do nothing——"

"Matter of fact," said Dwyer thoughtfully to Mendoza, "you'd have to figure from about ten-thirty to eleven. He's got to get down there, and he hasn't got a car, and you know how the buses are."

"Mmh," said Mendoza. "So prove it to us, Fisher. Where were you between, say, ten-thirty and one o'clock yesterday?"

"Why? Was there a murder done then? I— Oh. Oh, them bank jobs. Jeez, I never done nothing like that! You got me all wrong! Honest, I never——"

"Two witnesses identified you," said Mendoza.

The panic flared again, but also there was bafflement, anger, in Fisher's eyes. "Two— That ain't possible! They're plain cockeyed! I never done no such thing! I don't get— Listen, you got my gun. They got a way to test, like on slugs, don't they? Match up—so you'll find out it wasn't my gun killed them guys. That's nuts! I never——"

"So where were you between ten-thirty and one o'clock?"

Fisher was silent, thinking. Judging from his expression, it was a painful process. Finally he said, "I was at my apartment. I didn't get up till late."

"Mmh-hm," said Dwyer. "Anybody with you?"

"No. No, I was alone."

"That's a pity," said Mendoza. "Make any phone calls? Any way to prove that's where you were?"

"Well, I'm telling you that's where I was."

"Brother, this one's a comedian," said Dwyer.

"What time did you leave the apartment—or did you?"

"Yeah. Yeah, I went out later on—got some cigarettes and——"

"See anybody around when you left? What time?"

"Oh, I guess about—about two o'clock. No, I didn't see nobody."

"Too bad," said Dale. "When'd you get home?"

"Well, I did see the landlady then. Around five o'clock, I guess."

"And she saw you."

"Well, sure."

"So you can't really prove where you were between ten-thirty and one, can you?"

"I just finished telling you I was home! That's all. You damn guys—a fellow makes a couple little mistakes and you're all down on him, don't——"

"Little mistakes," said Mendoza, "such as hitting an old lady over the head and robbing her."

"I never done that. Jeez, the way you guys——"

"I'm getting rather tired of you, Mr. Fisher," said Mendoza. "I suppose we could go on asking all over again—and hearing the same answers—but we're damn busy right now, so I think we'll just book you into jail. Bert——"

"Hey, hey, what for? I didn't do nothing——"

"A real comedian," said Dwyer, "this one. He pulls a gun and shoots at three cops, and he wonders why he's going to jail. Armed assault to start with, and then we'll have these witnesses take a look at you in the flesh and see what they say."

"Nobody can say I pulled them jobs—I never——"

"Oh, take him away, Bert," said Mendoza.

Dwyer obliged.

Mendoza went back to his office and sat down at his desk. Dale sat down opposite him and lit a cigarette. "And at that I don't know," said Mendoza. "Wait and see. But a lout like that—they never expect to be caught up with until they are, you know—would he have bothered to cache the operative gun somewhere else? And eyewitnesses—we've both known a lot of cases where they . . ." He let that trail off. Not so very long ago the state of California had executed an innocent man, and Mendoza would not soon forget what that had led to. . . .

"Yeah, I know," said Dale.

"I want to hear what Wolf says about him." Wolf was the sharp-eyed private dick who'd witnessed the first job. "He's trained to remember faces, notice details. I'd sooner take his word than that hysterical female's."

"Yeah. Well, I suppose we'll herd all of 'em down to take a look at him after lunch. Which I guess we've earned."

"I'll let you and Bert do that—visiting hours at the hospital are two to three. Come on, I'll buy you lunch."

Palliser had sent an urgent teletype up to the D.M.V. in Sacramento, asking about Anglia De Luxes with plates starting out HAH. The D.M.V., of course, didn't keep any record of what colors cars happened to be, nor was it interested in the various accoutrements on cars such as ski carriers, luggage carriers, and the like. Those two points of description would be useful in identifying the particular car from the list they would give him.

He devoutly hoped they had some electronic machines up there to get out such a list, because otherwise he wouldn't get it for a month. Maybe six months. The state of California, whose population had been shooting up astronomically of recent years, had the highest rate of car ownership anywhere in the world, and it was highest in L.A. County. L.A. County had a population of around seven and a half million people, to which population was registered approximately three million automobiles. Even taking into consideration the very large selection of automobiles on the market, domestic and foreign, there were probably a number of Anglia De Luxes registered in the state and county. There wouldn't, of course, be too many which bore plate numbers starting out HAH. And there would be, he hoped, no more than two or three which were also light green and had ski carriers on the roof.

Mr. del Valle had done his good deed for the month.

Palliser went up to Federico's for lunch and ran into Mendoza and Dale. He told Mendoza about the Anglia De Luxe. "A nice hot lead," approved Mendoza. "But three men? So why shoot the kid?"

"Could be he knew one of them—the one that apparently did the job?"

"But then he'd have known the Walsh kid would be there. Why pick that station?"

"Oh, hell, I don't know," said Palliser gloomily. "And another thing, why pick such a funny time as nine in the morning? Anybody with any sense would know there wouldn't be much in the till so soon after opening time. There only happened to be the forty bucks there because a guy who owed Hammer for a windshield replacement had dropped in first thing to pay his bill. But I'd like to talk to those fellows."

"*Obvio*," said Mendoza.

"And would you have a guess as to what this is?" Palliser brought out the little curved piece of metal Dr. Bainbridge had given him.

Mendoza took it, looked at it, weighed it in his hand. "What *is* it? I've got the feeling I ought to know—it looks familiar in a way—but I'm damned if I——"

"Let's see it," said Dale. "Um. Would it be a part off a tool of some kind? Broken off? Where'd you get it—is it a clue to something?"

Palliser told them. "Piece broken off a wrench—a jack?" asked Dale thoughtfully. "I don't know."

Palliser took it back. "Maybe somebody at the lab will have an idea. And that's another thing, of course—why would the heist man beat the kid before shooting him? That looks as if it might have been something personal, doesn't it? I want to talk to his friends—see if there'd been any trouble over a girl, something like that. It could have been a private kill and the holdup staged to cover up."

"Anything's possible," said Mendoza. "We ought to get the autopsy report on the Coffey girl some time today. Let's hope the Ballistics boys can spot the gun."

"But even if they do—— Higgins saw two of the boy friends—didn't get much. I'm going to hunt up the one he missed this afternoon. God, this weather—— Tell Hackett I envy him. Nice air-conditioned hospital, nothing to do all day but sleep and eat and read . . . *Iced* coffee, please," said Palliser.

"That's Glen Kingsley back there, working on the green Dodge." The manager of Gus's Kar-Wash, Best in Town, looked at Palliser curiously. "He do something?"

"Not that I know of—I just want to talk to him."

"Well, don't take too long, you don't mind. We like to keep 'em moving. He's the one in the red berry."

Palliser walked down to the end of the lot, where a very black young man in white coveralls and a red beret was industriously polishing the hood of the Dodge. "Mr. Kingsley? I'm Sergeant Palliser—I'd like to ask you a few questions." He got out his badge.

Kingsley straightened up. Pain came into his eyes. "That'll be about Carol," he said. "Sure, sir. It's just an awful thing—just awful. You find out who did it yet?"

"Not yet. I understand she'd gone out with you sometimes?"

"Some," said Kingsley. He was very black, but his features were not those thought of as typically Negroid; he had a lean jaw, a high-bridged nose, very thick hair, a small fuzzy mustache. Palliser put him down as twenty-two or twenty-three.

"Were you serious about her?"

"Well, man, I was," said Kingsley. His mouth was still twisted with grief. "I might's well tell you right off—I know you got to ask around, ever'body knowed her—I wanted Carol to marry me. She was the nicest girl I knowed. Ever. Just—nice. Even if she was awful religious." He smiled a small smile.

"She turned you down?"

"Well, man, she did. She sure did."

"So I guess you'd feel a little resentful about that? Mad at her?"

Kingsley looked down at the wet rag he still held. He squeezed it absently and a small stream of dirty water dropped to the black asphalt of the lot. Nearby the automatic sprinklers on the car-wash line roared into life as another car entered the tunnel. "I wasn't mad at Carol," said Kingsley in a low voice. "Not like that, man. No. You couldn't get mad at

Carol. She tried to be nice about it, she did. We—you could say we didn't go for the same things, 'n' I saw that O.K. I guess she was right, but—heart 'n' head ain't exactly the same thing."

"What do you mean?"

"Well, like I ain't much for the education bit. They tried tell me in school, get a better job and all, but all the book stuff I just don't make. I get along—I get jobs O.K. I coulda kept her O.K., but she got this college thing in her head. Wanted to be a teacher. Well, sure, she was a lot smarter 'n me, I knowed that. I mean, I guess I knowed from the first, her and I just didn't match up, but—but—I loved that girl," said Kingsley. He blinked down at the wet cloth. "Carol—I loved her, man. I just wish I had whoever—done that—right here in my two hands. I could—— An' I wouldn't give a cuss what you done to *me*. Anybody kill *Carol*—— She was a nice girl." He looked at Palliser earnestly. "Man, I c'n go pick up a floozy off the street any time I want. You don't get the ones like Carol so very offen, man. Like—like I tell you a f'rinstance. I don't talk so good, like by the book, y' know. I talk good 'nough for me, so what? But alla time Carol'd be with me, I could see—I ain't *dumb* even if I don't have the book stuff in my head—I could see she was just itchin' tell me, Don't say ain't—an'—an' like that, but she never. See? She was too—too kind, Carol was."

"I see," said Palliser. "Where were you yesterday afternoon about three o'clock?"

"When she was—was—? Oh, man, don't waste your time on me! Mister, I cried like a baby when I heard about it. Me, do a thing like—— I loved that girl."

"But where were you?"

"I was prob'ly down at Lee's pool hall 'bout then. Yesterday was my day off. Mister, but I cried like—— I loved her, mister."

Yes, thought Palliser. But *love is strong as death; jealousy cruel as the grave.*

"Do you own a gun?" he asked.

"Me? A gun? Hell, no, mister. What would I want with a gun?" asked Kingsley.

Mendoza had just got back from the hospital when Lieutenant Goldberg drifted into the office, sat down, sneezed, and looked at him sadly, groping for Kleenex in his breast pocket.

"How are the allergies?" asked Mendoza.

"The allergies are doing just fine," said Goldberg. "Me, that's another question. What did I ever do to you, Luis? I try to co-operate with Homicide, act like a right guy. Why do you have to butt in and foul up one of my arrests?"

"¿Cómo se dice? Scout's honor, I don't know what you——"

Goldberg sneezed, blew his nose, dropped the Kleenex into Mendoza's wastebasket, and said, "This pawnbroker. Down on Union Avenue. Yesterday. He gets hit over the head by a pseudo customer and robbed of about two hundred bucks in cash, four transistor radios, some miscellaneous jewelry, and a mink stole."

"Yes? What have I got to do with it?"

"So we go over the place. Just in case it's some ignorant lout who hasn't heard about fingerprints. As if," said Goldberg, "there were any such. But we have to go through the motions. Just in *case*."

"Yes."

"I really thought better of you," said Goldberg. "Of course it's the same charge, and mine is even a little heavier, theft added. But it was sort of frustrating."

"¡Qué diablo!" said Mendoza. "I have a nasty foreboding—— What are you talking about, Saul?"

"Well, fortunately for us a lot of them are very damn dumb," said Goldberg. "Aren't they? There's a quotation—you ever hear it?—'The reason there are so many imbeciles among imprisoned criminals is that an imbecile is so foolish even a detective can detect him.' Somebody named Austin O'Malley."

"I never heard that one," said Mendoza, "no. Who was O'Malley?"

"Who knows?" Goldberg shrugged. "Anyway, the point is there were some prints. On the cash register. On—well, never mind the details. And so when I got the word from Records, I go out to pick up the guy, and what do I find? I find that our star sleuth, the great Mendoza himself, has had a running gun fight with him a couple of hours before and carted him off to the pokey."

"Oh, hell!" said Mendoza. "Hell *and* damnation. So that's why he didn't have an alibi. And *has* he got an alibi? And it wasn't me—I was an innocent bystander. Bert put the collar on him. Do you realize what you've done? The only lead we'd turned up——"

"I can claim him. A heavier charge, like I say. But what I'd like to know," said Goldberg, "is what the hell was Homicide's interest?"

"Two witnesses," said Mendoza, "identified him as our bank robber."

"Fisher?" said Goldberg. "This smalltime hood? Don't kid me, boy. That's wild."

"Well, there's his record—and he pulled a gun . . . You've really nailed him tight for this pawnbroker thing? Damn it. *Un momento*. When was that pulled?"

"About half-past twelve yesterday," said Goldberg, and sneezed. "Pawnbroker was just eating lunch in the back of his shop when the customer came in."

"*¡Diez millón demonios desde infierno!*" said Mendoza violently. "So we're right back where we started!"

"Pity, but these things happen," said Goldberg.

The autopsy report on Carol Coffey arrived at almost the same time as the ballistic report, and Palliser, who'd been about to leave the office, sat down to read both.

After digesting them, he began to realize dimly that he had a little problem on his hands.

The autopsy report said, to paraphrase the technical language, that Carol Coffey had died instantly from a single bullet in the heart. She would not have been capable of movement after the bullet struck; she had died and fallen instantly. That was the gist of it. Carol Coffey, the report added impersonally, if anyone was interested, had been constitutionally a very healthy teen-ager, and *virgo intacta*.

The ballistics report on the bullet which had killed her was also informative. The slug had been recovered virtually undamaged. It had been fired from a Colt Official Police .22 caliber revolver, a practice target gun.

The autopsy report said that it had not been a contact wound; there was no vestige of powder burns. So the shot had been fired from a distance of at least ten feet.

And Palliser had made a little sketch of the room at the time, of the body's position. And he looked at it again now and realized that they had a little mystery on their hands.

Nice. In all this heat.

FIVE

"John," said Mendoza, "has a little problem."

"He certainly has," said Alison. "Going to have to explain his ancestry to everybody he meets. Whoever heard of anybody named Mendoza having green eyes?"

"I didn't mean our Johnny. Palliser," said Mendoza somnolently. He was lying on the sectional with the Sunday *Times* scattered on the floor beside him and El Señor curled up on his chest. El Señor was half Siamese and half Abyssinian and had turned out, surprisingly, with Siamese markings in reverse like a negative, his blond mask, paws, and tail making him look somewhat like a miniature lion. "He's getting fatter," he added, prodding behind El Señor's ears. "Crack a rib for me some day when he lands on me."

"Palliser?"

Mendoza didn't deign to answer that one. "Of course it's not John's own personal problem. Belongs to all of us. He told me all about it—reason I was on the phone so long. Little teaser of a thing. What you might call a problem in—mmh—space relations." Mendoza reached into his shirt pocket, which was under El Señor's forequarters, and El Señor, disturbed, said, "Yah!" "I made a little sketch. I've been ruminating on it, but damned if I can see the answer."

"You will," said Alison absently. Master John Luis, industriously crawling about the room, discovered Sheba curled up under the coffee table and squealed with pleasure. El Señor sat up and glared around at everybody. When he was taking his morning nap, he wanted peace and quiet. Miss Teresa Ann, taking off after her brother, added her squeals to his. She got a firm grip on Sheba's tail and Sheba hissed and fled.

Ostentatiously El Señor curled up the other way round and draped his blond-tipped tail across Mendoza's face. Mendoza pushed it away and El

Señor muttered dark threats. "I thought I'd put it up to you," said Mendoza. "In a kind of way it's a domestic problem."

"I thought you said guided missiles or something." Alison put her book down. The twins had now discovered Bast on the credenza and were playing with her tail; Bast, as a settled older matron, put up with them more patiently than her offspring.

"What? Oh, well, what I probably meant was spatial relations," said Mendoza. Nefertiti drifted in, licking her chops, from the direction of the kitchen, and pounced on Sheba who had just resettled herself in the green armchair. They both fell off to the floor and rolled over, feinting at each other.

The twins were entranced. El Señor muttered.

"Well, look," said Mendoza, and Mrs. MacTaggart came bustling in.

"You're not wanting to keep those magazines, *achara*? The old ones of *Life* and the women's magazines and the fashions and so on?"

"No, I weeded them out the other day and put them in the garage."

"Then he can have them and welcome. It's Mr. Warbeck——"

"Again? He *is* courting you, Máiri. A respectable widower—I wonder if he's got any money?"

"You'll have your joke," said Mrs. MacTaggart indulgently. "It's for his children, he says. He's been telling me all about it—a kind little man he is. It seems he and his wife never had any, but he's all wrapped up, as they say, in this association—it's a volunteer organization of some kind, for needy children. He says it's surprising how many there are that aren't eligible for regular charity for some reason, yet the families can't afford things they'll be needing—special doctoring and so on, even with all the clinics. And orphans in homes, too. They make up special little treats for them, take a personal interest, you see. This association helps the ones like that. A kind man—he goes visiting them, takes them little presents and so on. Would you guess why he comes walking up the hill? There's a little orphan girl in a home downtown, she likes to press flowers—you know, the old-fashioned way—and he comes hunting wild flowers for her. There's poor orphans in the hospitals, too, he says, nobody to come and cheer them up a bit. He wants the old magazines to make scrapbooks for the children."

"Of course he can have them," said Alison. "What a nice little man."

"Indeed he is."

"Now don't go falling for him and deserting us!"

Mrs. MacTaggart gave her another indulgent smile, checked with one glance that the twins were behaving reasonably well, and went back to the kitchen.

"You know," said Alison, "that's real charity—real public service, isn't it? His own time and interest. I feel awfully guilty sometimes, *amado*. Just amusing myself—seeing friends—— That reminds me, we must have the Mawsons for dinner, we owe them. I really ought to——"

"So do a little work for a change," said Mendoza. He sat up, holding El Señor with one hand, but this was one disturbance too many for El Señor. To have his choice of Place for Nap suddenly move from under him just as he was finally settled down . . . He said bitterly, "Yow!" and kicked Mendoza hard on the chest as he left him in one spring. He stalked across the room, leaped up on the credenza, and cuffed his mother on the ear. Forgivingly, Bast started to wash him. The twins sat quiet as mice and watched.

"Sometimes they're almost as good as baby sitters," said Alison. "Except that El Señor will keep washing the twins."

"*¡Atención!*" said Mendoza.

"Your domestic problem," said Alison obediently. "Yes."

"Well, it's a funny little thing. This Coffey girl, shot on Friday afternoon. Leave out the fact that it looks odd because it's a nice upright Methodist family, there doesn't seem to be any reason for anybody to want her dead. It's the physical facts that pose a little mystery." Mendoza lit a cigarette. "Come here and look at this. It's a sketch of the house plan. Palliser——"

"What an inconvenient one," said Alison, sitting beside him. "You have to go through the front bedroom to get to the hall——"

"One of those old places, probably added onto. Probably minus a bathroom to start, and they took the front end of the hall to make one. Never mind. Now, we know what the girl was doing when she was shot—she was dusting in the living room. The dustcloth was under her body, she dropped it as she fell. We know from the autopsy report that she was killed instantly—the only moving she did after the bullet hit her was to fall. So we know where she was standing when she was shot. She was found—by her mother, five or ten minutes later—lying just here." He put an X at the spot. "The living room is ten by fifteen, the long way across the front of the house. There are three doors and three windows in it. One of each on the front, both giving onto the front porch. You go directly into the living room from the porch, and the front door is almost at the end of the front living room wall and almost opposite the door in the rear wall leading to a bedroom."

"Well, what's the point?"

"There are two windows at the side of the living room, and on the inside short wall—just up from the front door—is another door leading to the bedroom occupied by Carol's brother, Verne Coffey. Now, she fell where she died, that we know. And she was lying on her back right here, in this space against the rear living room wall between the door to the bedroom behind the living room and the end of the sofa against the rear wall. So we can even guess what she was doing—or had just been doing—before she was shot. She wasn't dusting the sofa—it's upholstered. The only thing she could have been dusting is a framed picture hanging on the wall in that space, because there's no end table at that end of the sofa. What we don't know is what direction she was facing."

"Oh. She was shot from in front?"

"From directly in front—the way she was facing—and the slug took a very slight upward path. We don't know from how far away, but more than ten feet or so—no powder burns. When she was dusting the picture, she'd have been facing the wall, wouldn't she?"

"I should think so," said Alison.

The twins had discovered the Sunday paper and were making noisy little tunnels out of it, amid chortles of glee.

"But then—well, you see the difficulty. I haven't explained the full beauty of it yet. For one thing, as with most of these old frame houses, the house is well off the ground—those steep wooden steps up to the porch, you know. I'd say the living room and of course the other rooms are a good ten feet from the ground. So in order to get a direct shot through any of the windows, you'd have to be standing on a ladder or something like that. Now, the boys went up and down asking questions, of course. Other than about the family. And——"

"If," said Alison, "the picture is under glass, she could have stepped back and to one side or the other to get the light on the glass, see if it needed washing."

"That doesn't make any difference, cara. My first thought was a sniper in a car. That would account at least partly for the height and the oblique upward path. But it was a hot afternoon and most of those old houses are like ovens—a number of people were out on their porches. It's a quiet side street, and we've got half a dozen witnesses that no car had passed for at least twenty minutes. The Coffey house is quite close to the houses on either side—those are narrow lots, you know—and the woman on the left side was out at that side of her house. In fact, she'd been talking to Mrs. Coffey across the hedge only a few minutes before. The people on the other side weren't home, but there were at least four people sitting on their porches across the street, who'd have seen anybody strange—or anybody at all, come to that—either in front of the Coffey house or at that side. Got that? So tell me what direction she was shot from?"

Alison studied the sketch. "That *is* a little funny," she said. "I don't see how it's possible at all. You've got all the directions covered by witnesses. If she was on her back—if she just fell backward when she was shot—that says she must have been standing sideways to that bedroom door, just *past* where the picture is, and——" She stopped.

"Yes," said Mendoza. "More or less facing the door to her brother's bedroom about six or seven feet away."

"But you said they're a nice upright family. What possible reason could the boy have?"

"*¿Quién sabe?* And even more to the point, how the hell could he have got rid of the gun? He says his door was closed, but it could have been open. He could have shot her from inside his room, which would make up the distance to ten feet. But what about the gun? If he immediately passed it to some accomplice outside his bedroom window, that'd have been seen from across the street. *Although*," said Mendoza suddenly, "there is a tallish hedge around the Coffey yard, and just maybe—— All right. She wasn't shot from the front door or the porch window, because those people across the street would have seen it. She wasn't shot from the two side windows of the living room because Mrs. Robinson was out there in her side yard, not twenty feet away—and quite possibly also Mrs. Coffey, who was cutting roses and came around there from her back yard. But on the other hand, Mrs. Coffey says she wasn't in her side yard more than two or three minutes—they didn't have a long gossip over the hedge, just 'Hello' and 'Isn't it hot?' So there wouldn't have been time—and it's the longest chance anyway—for somebody to have come into the back yard and shot her through the rear window of that bedroom which is exactly opposite the doorway to the living room, where she might have been standing looking into the bedroom."

"Then I don't see——"

"What it comes down to," said Mendoza, "unless all the neighbors are in a conspiracy, which seems unlikely, is that Carol could have been shot, inside the house, by her brother from his bedroom—or she could have been shot by her mother from that rear window. Only what the hell happened to the gun?"

"But that seems fantastic. You said they're perfectly nice, respectable people. What reason——"

"I'll say this. It seems just slightly less fantastic that it was the brother. If Mrs. Coffey shot her daughter, the stage has lost a second Sarah Bernhardt. But Verne——"

"Luis. They could have moved the body. Just not thinking, not realizing she was dead."

"They say not, and the ambulance boys said not."

"Oh."

"We'll take a long, hard look at Verne, anyway. You never do know. But how the hell could he have got rid of the gun? Search? Sure as hell we searched the place. We're not such innocents as to take stories at face value. The house was searched, and the yard was searched. No gun."

"Did you look under the house?" asked Alison.

Mendoza stared at her. "*Under* the house? There's no basement."

"Don't tell me I've found something you don't know. Of course, you haven't been a householder long. No, my darling, few California houses have basements, but they do have foundations. And there has to be a space between the foundation and the floor for pipes and things like that. And there'll either be a couple of trap doors in bedroom closets as access or a trap door outside, and in very old houses like that it's usually trap doors in bedroom closets."

"*¡Dios mío!*" Mendoza smote himself on the forehead. "Either I'm getting old or marriage is unsettling my mind. My God, I once found a corpse under a house too. And so we look, and there's no gun, that doesn't say there wasn't one on Friday. My God." He got up. He tripped over Master John who shot between his legs after Sheba; he clutched at the coffee table to save himself and shoved it hard against Miss Teresa's upended rump. Terry shrieked, Johnny grabbed Sheba's tail, Sheba spat, and Mendoza said, "I was out of my mind—voluntarily giving up the gay life of a bachelor!" He clutched his shin, which had come in violent contact with the table. "This place is a madhouse. I'm going down to the office."

He went down the hall to the bedroom after a tie and his jacket and disturbed El Señor who was napping on the bureau top. El Señor hissed at him.

"A madhouse," said Mendoza. "*¡Esta no tiene remedio!*"

He found the office empty except for Sergeant Lake who was having Sunday duty this month. Lake told him that Higgins was out getting some additional statements on that gang rumble; the kids charged would be coming up for indictment some time this week. Dwyer had got a vague sort of lead from a stool pigeon on that San Pedro Street shooting and gone out to see what was in it. He didn't know where Palliser was.

"That thing," said Mendoza. "Ley—Lee—Leigh, with an i-g-h, wasn't it? Walter William Leigh. No pedigree with us, anyway. Drifted down to Skid Row the last few years—panhandling for half a buck for a gallon of cheap *vino*. Anybody could have cooled him."

"Yeah, but you remember there was some evidence that he'd been in the money a few days before. Looked a little funny."

"I'll tell you, Jimmy, I don't care one hell of a lot who shot Walter William. God knows he wasn't much loss. I would very much like to know who killed Carol Coffey. Is anybody here at all?"

"Galeano was in a minute ago. I suppose Palliser'll be in some time."

There was, of course, no vital urgency now about looking under the Coffey house. Though you never knew—people did stupid things; if Verne had shot his sister and then dropped the gun down a convenient trap door, he might just have left it there. Some time today they would look.

The lab report was in on the Walsh thing. The lab boys hadn't found anything extraneous in the garage: no nice fresh beach sand, or grains of flour, or quarry dust—or footprints in oil, or of course any strange fingerprints. Well, there were a lot of fingerprints in both the rest rooms, which opened off the garage, which didn't belong to the owner, the mechanic, or Jimmy Walsh; but that was only natural.

Mendoza sighed. Tomorrow somebody would have to appear in court when that child-beater came up to be indicted. Either Dwyer or himself —they'd both been on that. People—they sure as hell came all sorts. Beating a six-month-old baby because the baby cried. Beating the baby to death. The baby's father, saying sullenly, "I gotta get my sleep, ain't I? Working man like me, I work hard, I get tired. I just sort of slapped her, 's all. Didn't go to hurt her none."

People.

Omar Khayyam, he thought.

> Impotent pieces of the Game He plays,
> Upon the Chequer-board of Nights and Days;
> Hither and thither moves, and checks, and slays,
> And one by one back in the Closet lays.

At random? Sometimes, in his job, he couldn't help thinking so. But any cop had enough to think about without thinking about philosophies.

Palliser came in and said hello absently. "Jimmy said you were here."

His long dark face with the heavy eyebrows and mobile mouth wore a look of abstraction. He said, "You going to the hospital today?"

"No, Alison's going with Angel—Angel'll leave Mark at our place. Look, I've just had a thought—or to be honest with you, it was Alison's idea—the——"

"I thought I'd go see Art," said Palliser. He felt in his pocket, brought out an envelope, looked at it, and said, "Oh, damn. I meant to take that little thing up to the lab, see what they can make of it. I got sidetracked. I wonder how much it means."

"What?"

"Well, I asked Walsh who were Jimmy's closest friends and if he'd been going with any girl and so on. Those poor damned people. An only son. Why the *hell* things like this have to happen——" Palliser was silent, fumbled in his pocket again, and found a pack of cigarettes. "So I went to see a couple of the boys, and I heard the same story from both of them. You know I said yesterday it could have been a private kill. And del Valle —when I checked back with him just now—said he thought the guy he'd seen leaving the garage was somewhere around thirty. He's a pretty good witness. Good on details."

"Yes? What was the story?"

"Both the boys—Eddy Beckwith and Howard Thompson—said that Jimmy had been pretty interested in a girl named Diane Rush. They were all in high school together, Jimmy'd known her since then. They said he was serious about her. Said Diane was kind of the flighty type and dated a lot of boys, and just lately she's been going out with an older guy, a fellow about thirty she met on her job—she's a waitress at The Nest, which is a fairly fancy place. They said Jimmy had 'sort of' thought of Diane as being engaged to him and had raised quite a fuss about this. They also said that probably Jimmy's parents wouldn't know about that because they didn't approve of Diane and Jimmy wouldn't have told them."

"Mmh," said Mendoza. "Diane the flighty type. Evidently the older guy—*Dios*, it does depend where you sit how you use these terms, thirty, my God—was doing all right with Diane, and Jimmy on the short end of the stick. So why should the other fellow shoot Jimmy?"

"God knows," said Palliser. "I just wonder if it means anything, that's all. All they could tell me was the fellow's first name is Humphrey."

"Come on," said Mendoza. "Let's go look under a house."

SIX

Dwyer came in just as they were leaving, so they took him with them. "I don't know, but it doesn't look as if there's much in it," he said in the elevator. "I got the word from Tommy—you know that one." Mendoza nodded: a part-time Skid Row bum who on occasion turned pigeon. "He said this Walter Leigh had been acting a little funny about two, three weeks before he got it. Dropping hints that he was going to be in the money—and he'd been going to see certain people, like a bartender at some joint down there who, rumor says, can fix you up with anything from an abortion to a collection of feelthy pictures. I saw the bartender. I wouldn't doubt the rumor, by his looks, but there's nothing on him, and of course he never laid eyes on Leigh, according to him."

"Small loss," said Mendoza. "At the moment I'm more interested in Carol Coffey."

When they got to the Coffey house the boy Verne opened the door to them. He was not as easy and forthcoming with them as his mother; maybe he'd swallowed some of his father's uneasiness about cops. He said his mom and dad were at the funeral parlor—"you know, making arrangements."

"Yes," said Mendoza. "Now, we haven't got a search warrant, Verne, but we'd like to look around here a little. Do you think your parents would mind, or is that O.K.?"

Verne shrugged. "Who's to stop you? You're the cops."

"Well, we don't like to play rough unless we have to. John, suppose you and Bert have a look. I'd like to ask Verne a few more questions." He sat down on the sofa. He saw that all the chalk marks had been scrubbed out, where the body had lain, but there were other stains that would be harder to clean. "Sit down, Verne."

"I'm all right here. I was—was goin' over to see Benny pretty soon, anyways. We got a sort of date." The boy was nervous. Just because he didn't like cops?

"Has there been any trouble in the family lately, Verne?"

"I don't know what you mean. We never have n—any trouble. You mean like fights?"

"Just anything. Maybe Carol staying out too late and your dad being mad? Or you staying out too late? Or some new boy friend of Carol's your parents didn't like?"

Verne shook his head. He was a big boy for his age; he'd be as big a man as his father when he filled out. "There was never n—anything like that," he said. "You got any idea who did it yet? It was so sudden—and there wasn't n—any reason, anybody kill Carol."

"We don't know yet," said Mendoza, watching him. "Did you love your sister, Verne?"

"She was my sister," said the boy. He looked a little embarrassed; maybe in this upright Methodist home the emotions were considered a little embarrassing to discuss. "Sure, Carol was O.K. Sometimes—sometimes she was a little bossy, but I guess—sisters——"

"You ever have any quarrels with her?"

"Why? That d-docsn't matter now . . . I don't know nothing about this, why you're asking——"

"Did you?"

Verne swallowed and rubbed his hands along his jeans. "I—I guess so, sometimes. When we were littler. Nothing serious. Why? Listen, I really don't know nothing at all about it. It's just an awful thing to happen, and sure, I'm awful sorry and all, but how would I know anything? And I've got a date—sort of—to meet Benny. Can I go?"

Mendoza looked at him meditatively. Sam Coffey was undoubtedly scared of cops—any cops. Mrs. Coffey, who had lived here all her life, knew there were cops and cops; but maybe the boy had naturally taken his dad's word before hers. Maybe that was the only reason for his nervousness. He said, "Don't you think you ought to stay while we're here? You don't think your parents would mind your—mmh—leaving us in possession?"

"What's to mind? Mom seems to think you're all heroes—and what could they do, anyways? You're trying to find who did it—I guess."

"We're trying, Verne."

"Yeah. I was s'prised see you," said the boy suddenly.

"Why?"

"Oh—well—I dunno. I guess you just naturally figure, you guys aren't going to lay yourselves out over—somebody like Carol."

"Why not?"

"Oh—you know—because."

"Because why?"

"You know."

"Anybody who gets murdered in this county," said Mendoza, "we want to know who did it. That's damn foolish thinking, Verne. Did your sister have any trouble getting into college? Has anybody ever tried to keep you out of school? Pushed you around? Stopped your father from getting a job? Don't take any bets we won't be in there pitching until we find out all about this."

"Can I go?"

"You can go." The boy went without another word, slamming the front door after him. Mendoza looked after him thoughtfully. This was a very opposite response to the one they'd had from Mrs. Coffey. Just the husband's fault? Palliser said nervous, very nervous of cops—on Friday, too much upset and shocked to show it much, but it was there. And so the boy was surprised to see them back. Hadn't thought they'd bother much about Carol's murder. That was interesting.

He went into the boy's bedroom. Evidently Alison's little suggestion had paid off: neither Palliser nor Dwyer was there, but there were ghostly noises from under the house. The room was about eight by nine, very neat and clean; it held the cot-bed, the cheap chest of drawers, a small plastic-topped desk, and a straight chair. There was a small rag rug on the floor and a narrow door in the front corner of the room. It was open. Mendoza looked inside.

A small walk-in closet. It was sparsely filled with clothes. At the far end a shoe rack had been moved and a square trap door lifted up. Mendoza knelt down alongside it. "You finding anything?" he called down. He remembered the time he'd found the corpse under the pink stucco apartment house. A case with a lot more class than this, he thought.

"Give us time!" Dwyer's voice sounded muffled. "Lot of space down here." Mendoza caught the reflections from their flashlights.

He got up and went across to the front bedroom. Probably Mr. and Mrs. Coffey's room. It was also very neat and clean, and it also had a walk-in closet. And the closet also had a trap door in the floor.

He went from there into the hall, looked into a small bathroom with chipped plastic tile in bright pink, went into the spotless kitchen. The third bedroom—it was an odd house plan—opened off the kitchen, between that and Verne's bedroom, but had only the one door into the kitchen. Carol's room. Starched white curtains, a white bedspread on the twin-sized bed, a dressing table with a white organdy skirt. A rag rug on the floor. A walk-in closet, minus any trap door.

He came back to the living room just as Palliser stepped out of Verne's room. He looked hot, dirty, and disgusted. "What a hell of a place to chase us on a day like this! I'll bet it's ten degrees hotter down there. And no gun. Bert's still looking, but it's not there. For one thing, if the kid did drop it through that trap door, it'd have been somewhere right underneath —it wouldn't grow wings and move twenty feet back under the kitchen or——"

"*De veras.* Well, that doesn't tell us it wasn't there once. Bert might as well come up."

"*Cobwebs!*" said Palliser. He was still brushing at his suit. "Maybe I had a traumatic shock at three years old or something, but I've always had a horror of cobwebs. And the dust and dirt down there——"

"It's an old house," said Mendoza. He went into Verne's closet and shouted down to Dwyer to come up. The doorbell rang.

He heard Palliser's voice at the door and came out to find a pretty girl holding a large round Mexican-clay casserole on a tray before her and looking somewhat confused. The girl was nearly half-white and very pretty indeed, and she was looking confused, he thought, not solely because Palliser had opened the door instead of one of the Coffeys, but because she had on only shorts and a bra.

"Oh!" she said. "I just—where's Mrs. Coffey? I'm—— I met you on Friday. You were——"

"That's right, Miss Webb. Sergeant Palliser. We're just having another look around. Mr. and Mrs. Coffey are at the funeral parlor."

"Oh," she said. "Isn't anybody here? I mean——"

"Verne went off to see a friend of his," said Mendoza. "Someone called Benny. Would you know who that is?"

"I guess—most likely, Benny Lincoln. Over on the next block."

"Lieutenant Mendoza," said Palliser. "Miss Nancy Webb. She knew Carol very well."

"H-how do you do. Have you found who did it yet? I just can't get *over* it," said Nancy Webb. "It just seems impossible. Carol murdered! Please, do you mind if I come in and leave this? It's Beef Stroganov, and it's hot. I'd like to——"

"Certainly," said Mendoza. She seemed to know the house; she went straight back to the kitchen, looked in the right drawer for a hot pad, and set the casserole on it on the drainboard. The yellow rose had disappeared from the table. "You knew Carol well, Miss Webb?"

"I knew her all her *life!* Why, we started out Sunday School together when we were four." Tears stood in her eyes. "I never knew anybody nicer than Carol. Kinder. She was a really good person."

"You might describe yourself as her best friend?"

"Yes, I think I was."

"Well, I'd like to ask you . . ." Mendoza hesitated. He smiled at her. "Just take it that we have to ask all sorts of questions, Miss Webb. With our nasty suspicious minds. It doesn't really imply anything. But I think you know this household well—and you would know most of what Carol was thinking and feeling, what was happening to her."

"I guess so. Yes, we were back and forth a lot, doubledated sometimes. You see, our families have lived on this block a lot longer than some others, since Carol and I were just babies. Of course, since she was going to college we didn't see each other quite so much—I went to secretarial school, I'm a stenographer at Knott, Wiley and Conger—they're lawyers. Over on Washington Boulevard. What d'you want to *ask?*" She looked at him curiously.

"Was there any sort of family trouble here lately?" he asked, purposefully vague. "Any really serious argument, or——"

"Oh," said Nancy Webb in a dropped voice. "Oh. You mean about Verne?"

"That's right," said Mendoza coolly.

"Well—I don't know that I'd best tell you about that. I mean, it's a private family thing—Carol only told me because it upset her—and besides, well, excuse me, but what business is it of yours? It's not as if it had anything to do with——" Her eyes widened incredulously on him, and he wondered why on earth this girl wasn't trying out for T.V. parts as Lola Rodriguez or Maria Alfonso and decided she was too honest and nice a girl. "But you're not *thinking*—— Why, that's impossible! Just——" She made a helpless gesture. "If you knew the Coffeys! It's——"

"But I don't, Miss Webb. We have to look everywhere, and naturally we look in a lot of wrong directions. We have to look at everything. To be sure when we find out the truth. You see? So I'd like to hear about Verne."

She looked at him carefully, in silence, for a while. Then she said unexpectedly, "I used to be crazy about *Dragnet.* It surely made out you're a real crack police force."

"Well, we are," said Mendoza. "Highest requirements for rookies of any force in the world."

"Honestly? A cousin of mine got turned down at Headquarters. Because he didn't have twenty-twenty vision. He joined the Santa Monica force instead." She was silent again and then said, "Look, it was silly. It wasn't anything much. I mean, we go to church, too, and—and so on, but Mother and Daddy aren't as strict as the Coffeys are about some things. Not as if they *drink*, but a glass of wine on Christmas and birthdays—like that, you know. But Mr. and Mrs. Coffey are really death on it. And—what it was, you see—about two weeks ago Verne didn't come home at the usual time for dinner, so Carol went looking for him. And—well, look, Lieutenant, kids like that, it sounds exciting to them. Goodness, you know as well as I do, in *some* neighborhoods down here, by the time kids are twelve or fourteen they've done *everything*—the real slums. But kids like Verne, that've been pretty well brought up——"

"So what was he up to?"

"Well, he and Benny Lincoln and Marvin Cross had got a half gallon of cheap wine from an old fellow over on Main, and they were sitting behind a billboard on that vacant lot down the block. I don't know if they were really—you know—high, maybe so. Probably the first time Verne, anyway, had ever tasted it. But Carol—brought up the way she was—she was just horrified. I mean, I don't want you to think I approve of people getting drunk, because I don't. Naturally. But I'm not a *fanatic* about it. It was the kind of trick kids that age do."

"So what happened?"

"Well, I don't really know. Carol just told me that and that she 'gave him an earful,' that's how she said it, and made him come home. I expect she told the Coffeys, or anyway, if Verne was tight, they'd have seen it."

"Yes. Was he punished in any way?"

"I don't know. Really. And really, Lieutenant, to think that *that* could have anything to do—— Please, don't think that. They're really awfully nice people, after all," she said earnestly.

"Well, we like to think we're smart enough to tell good from bad," said Mendoza. "Thanks very much, Miss Webb."

"Because it must have been a—a nut of some kind. Who *did* it. Just wandering around. Because nobody could have any *reason* to kill Carol——"

"We'll find out," said Mendoza.

They waited for the Coffeys to come home. They asked questions and met unexpected resistance from both of them. Unexpected because Mrs.

Coffey had been very co-operative before, and because Sam Coffey was very leery of the boys in blue and before had been inclined to fawn a little on them, sycophantic.

"I don't think that's any of your business, Lieutenant," said Mrs. Coffey. She looked very tired and she'd been crying. "It's nothing to do with what happened to Carol, and it's a—a private family matter, how we raise our children. How we believe in raising children."

"I realize that may be how it looks to you, Mrs. Coffey," said Mendoza gently. "But we have to look at everything that had happened to her lately, how she'd been feeling and thinking. And——"

"That didn't happen to Carol, it happened to Verne," said Coffey. "It happened to him good!"

He was a big man, a broad man, deep brown; his son looked more like him than like the mother. He had a deep bass voice and a Deep South accent.

"Did you punish him, Mr. Coffey?" asked Mendoza.

"That makes no never mind to you, Officer," said Coffey. "He's my boy —I raise him way I think right. Wine is a mocker and strong drink is raging. I just try raise my children in the right way."

"Yes, sir," said Dwyer. "Did you punish him?"

Coffey looked very confused for a moment; Mendoza thought that *sir* had stopped him dead in his tracks. "That don't matter now," he said. "Boy do somethin' wrong, he got to expect punishment. Why you askin' about that? It ain't nothing to do with Carol. My little Carol laying there dead." Tears sprang to his eyes, coursed down his cheeks; he did not lift a hand to brush them away. "My little girl, never did nobody no harm all her life, just sweet and kind—an' some basser come along an' shoot her— It don't make no sense! Nothin' don't make no sense!" A deep wrenching sob shook his big frame.

"Sam," said the woman quietly. "Sam, it's just God's will."

"An' God's will don't make no sense either! Oh, the Lord forgive me, I don't mean be a blasphemer—I know that, Amy—but—but——" He stood silent, with bowed head.

Mendoza turned to her. "Verne was punished, Mrs. Coffey?"

She didn't answer and then said woodenly, "It's a private family thing, sir. I'm sorry, but I don't see what——"

Coffey raised his head. "The boy got what he deserved," he said dully. "Have to raise children right. They stray off the way you show 'em, you got to chastise them. My wife, she said I was too hard, but you got to be strict with children, they start going wrong. I whupped the boy good, I did."

"Sam——"

"I see," said Mendoza.

"You see, you see!" shouted Coffey. "What you see, white man? I told 'em—I tell my children—we got to set an example! Let the white man see we ain't needfully lazy drunken niggers—don't I know how you all think——"

"Sam!" said the woman.

And the savagery died from the big man's eyes, and fear came there, and he said in a mumbling voice, "Oh, now, I'm sorry, sir. Nevah meant offend you, sir. I guess the shock kinda unhinged my mind——"

Mendoza opened his mouth and shut it. There was nothing he could say to this man: this man, with provocation enough, who had built an Enemy in his mind and perhaps would never wholly believe that some of the Enemy were men of good will, regardless of color. This man who, resenting authority, automatically assumed that authority was venal and would seek vengeance for words—mere words.

Sticks and stones, he thought. Words could be dangerous things. In the wrong mouths.

He said evenly, "Thanks very much, Mr. Coffey. That's all right now." They went out.

"What do you think?" he asked Dwyer. They got into the big black Ferrari. The Ferrari had attracted all the little boys in the neighborhood, who were lined up, staring.

"I think it's possible," said Dwyer. "Not that I exactly approve of seventeen-year-olds getting drunk on cheap wine, or anything else—but it's an age where they're naturally experimenting with the grown-up things. And me, I'm all for morality and going to church and so on, but a set of parents who weren't quite so strict about it would have understood better, handled it more sensibly. When will they learn that that kind of thing usually just turns the kids in the opposite direction?"

"You find your boy with a half gallon of cheap *vino* and just lecture him?" asked Palliser.

"Steve's only ten," said Dwyer. "Hell, no, I'd take him down to the emergency hospital and show him some of the results. But I can see that kid Verne feeling resentful of his sister. Who told on him. After all, Papa's still the boss—until the kid gets a little older, anyway—so I can see the resentment centering on stool-pigeon Carol. Who found him and hauled him home tight." He ruminated. "The gun could have been dropped down there and then hidden somewhere else after we left on Friday."

"Or given back to whoever he borrowed it from," said Palliser.

"All right, let's find it," said Mendoza mildly.

"See all his friends." Dwyer sighed. "Ask around. God, in this heat. Why do all the tough ones come in hot weather?"

"Law of nature," said Palliser.

"Let's just hope our bank robber doesn't pull another one this week," said Mendoza.

"And I hope to God," said Palliser, "the D.M.V. gets that list out by tomorrow or Tuesday—— A nineteen-year-old kid——"

"Two nineteen-year-old kids," said Mendoza, and they were silent.

SEVEN

The Fisher thing, negative as it looked, was helpful in a way. They had not attempted before to use an artist and/or the Identikit, in trying for a possible sketch of the loner, because all the witnesses they had were too vague on details. Now, when two of them had, if hesitantly, picked out Fisher's picture, they knew at least that the loner must look a little like him.

Wolf, their private-eye witness, hadn't been in on the parade of witnesses who were taken to look at Fisher—that had been before Goldberg had pitched his little bombshell. Seeing Fisher in person, Mrs. Thomas had said no, Clark had said not sure, and nobody else had had much to say at all, but then nobody had had a really good look at the loner.

Wolf had been off on a job; Mendoza got hold of him first thing Monday morning and haled him up to his office. Mendoza had a little idea about all this. Maybe not one that would pay off, but sometimes you never knew what would pay off.

He had Fisher's mug shots, full-face and profile, on his desk; he passed them over to Wolf. "How much does he look like our X?"

Wolf smiled. He was a lean, rangy fellow, very dark, with a good deep voice. "This is the guy the two tellers picked out? Bad luck, Lieutenant. Well . . ." He discarded the full-face shot and looked at the profile. "It's not him, of course. Not the same profile. I only saw him in profile, you know, and the boy you want has a nice straight nose and not so much jaw as this bird here. But it is something like him."

"Yes. Well, I'd like to try to get out a sketch," said Mendoza. "If possible. We know now he looks something like Fisher, and with you adding what details you can, we might get a fairly good one. Frankly, I'd rather rely on what you remember than the rest of them—trained observer." Wolf was an operative with a big firm which had a good reputation, and he was an experienced man. "I realize it's a gamble. Pity you didn't see him full face. But we might get *something*."

"I don't know—do my best for you, but—— For reproduction in the papers, you mean?"

"No, we probably couldn't come close enough for that. How many thousand men of that general type are walking around? No, my idea was to pass the sketches to every bank guard—in the general downtown area to start with. A good many of them are retired cops, and most of them are pretty good men, in an unobtrusive sort of way. If one of them spots somebody resembling the sketch, he can walk, not run, to the nearest phone, we send over the nearest squad car, and—well, it'd give us a hell of a lot better chance, even if we wound up accosting a few innocent citizens first."

"I see that. Well, do my best."

"Such as it is?" Mendoza smiled. "I'm putting a lot of faith in your experience, Mr. Wolf. Your trained eye. You gave us a couple of things nobody else noticed at all, and I just hope the trained eye wasn't taking a few minutes off and all the other witnesses aren't right after all."

Wolf looked interested. "Where did I stray off the rails?"

"Everybody else says a suit. On every job. We've got a whole range of colors to choose from, black to light brown, but you know eyewitness accounts as well as I do. All the tellers and one guard say a gray suit. But you said he had on a gray corduroy jacket and gray slacks."

"That's right," said Wolf. "I'll swear to that. The jacket was the first thing I noticed about him. Because it *was* corduroy—on a day as hot as that. What else did I notice nobody else did?"

"You said he put the paper bag full of bills into his *outside* pocket. Where the tellers said anything at all about that, they said the inside pocket."

"Sure of that, too," said Wolf comfortably. "I was only about three feet away, you know, at the next window to his right. Nobody else but me knew what was happening. He was alone at the chief teller's window and he held the gun close to him, in front. The girl at my window was typing up my money order, with her back turned. I spotted the gun, and so I looked him over carefully. With just this in mind. And when the teller handed over the bag, he took it with his right hand and all in a hurry shoved it way down in the outside jacket pocket. Another reason I know it was a sports jacket—the ordinary suit jacket wouldn't take a parcel that large, but you know the big patch pockets they put on sports jackets."

"I'll take your word," said Mendoza. "But I hope you're as good as I think you are." Wolf laughed. "So, we'll get an artist up here, and he might like to try using an Identikit, too—and you feed him whatever you have."

"O.K. by me," said Wolf. "I only hope we can come up with something reasonably good."

Mendoza saw him settled down with the police artist, in one of the interrogation rooms; they'd probably have a long, long session. And come up with anything bearing the remotest resemblance to their boy? God only knew.

Palliser and Higgins had both left reports on his desk. They had both gone calling again on Carol Coffey's boy friends. Dick Watkins had said he and Carol had got along fine, had discussed marriage, "but not seriously," because they were both interested in getting an education first. He was a second-year law student at L.A.C.C. Eddy Loman had said he'd only dated her a few times; she was a nice girl but damn strait-laced, and he hadn't felt this way or that way about her—just another girl. And why anybody'd want to shoot her, he couldn't imagine.

But Glen Kingsley, who had told Palliser he was probably at Lee's pool hall about the time Carol was shot, couldn't be placed there. Maybe he was, maybe not, said the proprietor; he'd had quite a crowd in that afternoon and he just couldn't say.

But how in hell could Kingsley—even if he'd wanted to—have shot Carol? With neighbors covering the front and both sides of the house, and Mrs. Coffey out in back? Mendoza sighed. He'd never believed there were such things as Locked Room Mysteries in real life, and he didn't feel like getting credulous at his age. He thought he'd buy Verne for it. Verne, resentful of what he might regard as Carol's holier-than-thou attitude, acquiring a gun somewhere and shooting her. And where was the somewhere?

And on the other hand, the boy wasn't stupid by any means, so why do it in such a damn-fool way? With his mother not thirty feet away, neighbors all around to say nobody had approached the house?

Where could he have got a gun? Palliser now was out with Dwyer questioning all Verne's friends. He might have said something; one of them might have helped him get a gun. How? Crooked pawnbrokers—they tried to keep a check on them, but in a city this size . . . And then again, it looked as if money was tight in that household. Where would Verne have got the cash to buy a gun?

And also, if Verne really thought that the cops wouldn't bother much about a little colored girl shot, he just might have done it that way.

The D.M.V. (and he could almost hear the names those clerks in Sacramento were calling Palliser) had made a start on that list of Anglia De Luxes with plates starting out HAH. At Palliser's suggestion they were starting out with Los Angeles County. The list wasn't very long yet, but it was growing. And what the hell of a list to check once they had it. Short cut, set Jimmy to phoning all the owners—we're taking a poll of preferred colors for automobiles?

Had this Walsh thing been a private kill? Mendoza thought he'd go out and see some of the people in it, find out what it smelled like.

He put the reports tidily away, brushed ash and tobacco off the desk, emptied the ash tray, lined up the desk box with the blotter. There was a small folded envelope on the blotter; he frowned at it and picked it up.

Palliser's little metal clue out of the Walsh boy's head wound. He'd left it here, all absent-minded; it ought to be up at the lab. Well, it was damned hot weather and they were being run off their legs; a little absent-mindedness could be forgiven.

Mendoza put it in his pocket and went out to see Mr. and Mrs. Walsh.

When he dropped back to the office at twelve-thirty he found Wolf just emerging from seclusion with the artist. They both looked tired and irritated. "Well, we got sketches," said the artist. "Your guess is as good as mine how accurate they are."

"Let's see." Mendoza studied them interestedly.

The first sketch showed the head and shoulders of a man who looked to be in the middle fifties. He had a roundish face with a suggestion of jowls, and a good straight nose, not too prominent, and a straight mouth a little small for the rest of the face. The man was smiling slightly. There were four sketches; the first showed the man wearing a soft felt hat pulled down over his eyes. The second showed him hatless, and he looked like another man, with a dome of a bald head above a high forehead. The third showed him in profile—"That's a good likeness, I'm sure of that," said Wolf—with the hat on, and the fourth showed him in profile hatless. He had small ears, the lobe joined to the cheek.

The artist said gloomily, "Of course we can't guess at the shape of his head. You see some funny ones, and it makes a hell of a lot of difference."

"The profile is good," insisted Wolf. "It's O.K."

"If you say so," said the artist, shrugging. "So what do we do with them, Lieutenant?"

"I want copies run off—make it a couple of hundred to start with. Oh, hell, I suppose the Feds'll be offended if they don't get some—make that two hundred and fifty. Then we pass them out to all the bank guards in the downtown area and also the vice-presidents and stock advisers—you know, the fellows who are sitting around waiting to arrange loans and so on—they generally have a good open view of the whole bank. And we wait for somebody to spot X. On his next call."

"O.K.," said the artist. "I'll set it up. Probably get them out for you"—he looked at his watch—"by four-thirty, five."

"Good. You two have had quite a morning," said Mendoza, surveying them. "Suppose," he said to the artist, "you set this up and meet us in the lot in ten minutes. I'll buy you lunch, and I might even run to a drink beforehand."

"You've got a deal," said Wolf and the artist simultaneously.

Back in July, Art Hackett had got himself assaulted. He'd been sent off a cliff in his car, and everybody had been surprised he hadn't been killed. He had a broken pelvis, a lot of things broken, and a severe skull fracture, and for a while there it had looked as if Art Hackett wasn't going to make it.

But he was a big man and a tough man, and he had a good deal to live for, including a wife named Angel and a son named Mark and another baby due in December. And he had made it. Just a question of time now, said the doctors; and at this stage of the game Hackett was getting very damned sick and tired of that phrase.

He was sitting up in the hospital bed when Mendoza came in that afternoon, looking even bigger than he was in white nylon pajamas, a big broad sandy man dispiritedly leafing through the new *Reader's Digest*. "How do I feel?" he echoed bitterly. "I feel fine, Luis. I want to go home. They won't let me out. I tell you, I'm going nuts. I'm tired of reading, and there's nothing on T.V. I can get around on crutches, and at least at home I'd have a different view out the window. *And* Angel's cooking. Damn it, I know I'm spoiled, but the *meals* here—if you can call them that! I walked down the hall this morning and weighed myself—I'm down to a hundred and ninety."

"Well, congratulations," said Mendoza. "You can forget about dieting for a while."

"Damn right," said Hackett with a sigh. "When I get home . . . And they say I can't go back on the job until November fifteenth. Hell, as soon as I can get rid of these crutches I'll be O.K. And get some decent food in me." He moved restlessly. "I understand you're being kept busy. These bank jobs—hell of a thing."

"And other things. You're jittering to get back to the rat race, Arturo?"

"Oh, I know," said Hackett. "When you're on the job, it gets you down sometimes. John's upset as hell about this Walsh kid, and I know how he feels. But it is the job, and if you're a cop——"

"So all right, do some armchair detecting," said Mendoza. He sat down beside the bed, gave Hackett a cigarette, and told him about Carol Coffey, produced a sketch of the house and yard. Hackett frowned at it.

"Now that is the hell of a funny little thing, isn't it? I'm with you. I can't see any answer but the boy, but if you can't tie him up with the gun, you'll never get him. And you said he's a well-brought-up boy, respectable family—would he know where and how to get a gun?"

"Mmh," said Mendoza. "Neighborhoods—overlap, down there. He's probably going to school with a few j.d.'s, even if they aren't pals of his."

"Yes, but even so—— Is that enough motive? Don't answer that," said Hackett wryly. "I know the stock answer—what motive is enough, it depends who has it. You'd better be lucky in tying Verne up to the gun."

"And if so," said Mendoza, "what a hell of a shock to the parents . . . The job. Why the hell are we doing this dirty thankless job, boy? Dealing with the dregs of things? The muck at the bottom of the human pool? I sometimes wonder."

Hackett smiled. "You remember what Lockhart said? That good cops are like good sheep dogs, they just come equipped with the urge."

Mendoza laughed. "He's right about a lot of things . . . They've got a new grandson." He smiled, thinking of Lockhart; if it hadn't been for Lockhart, a while back, Alison wouldn't be waiting for him in the house on Rayo Grande Avenue, or a lively pair of twins.

"Good," said Hackett absently.

Mendoza reached into his pocket for his cigarettes and brought out instead the envelope with Palliser's mysterious little metal bit. On impulse he dumped it out into his palm and looked at it. What the hell was it? Something almost on the tip of his tongue . . .

"Art?"

"Hum?" Hackett was still studying the sketch of the Coffey house. "What is this?"

Hackett looked up and Mendoza laid the little thing in his hand. Hackett looked at it casually and said, "Bit off the trigger guard of a gun. Revolver most likely."

"*¡Válgame Dios! ¡Naturalmente—ya lo creo! ¡Vaya con el mozo! ¿Sabe* *una cosa?*—you know what? You're a very, very smart cop, my Arturo, and all the rest of us have been blind! *Adiós*—I've got work to do!" He snatched up his hat and fled.

Hackett stared after him.

It was no trouble for the Ballistics man to identify the gun. "If you'd brought this thing to us in the first place, anybody up here could have told you—"

"We acknowledge our sins," said Mendoza.

Palliser was still muttering, "But I should have *seen* it—am I going blind? Of *course* it's part of a trigger guard—"

The Ballistics man was studying it interestedly. "Just have to look in our books," he said. "Shouldn't be too difficult—you don't often get a guard that isn't completely round. That little point on the outside edge—if you'll just give me a few minutes . . ." He went away.

Four minutes later he came back and said, "It's that J. C. Higgins Hi-Standard .22 nine-shot revolver. Comes in either a four-inch or six-inch barrel."

"Oh, *hell!*" said Palliser. "That's the brand Sears, Roebuck sells, isn't it? My God, anybody at all— Between Maine and California! For God's sake—"

"This just isn't our week," said Mendoza ruefully.

The Ballistics man smiled at them gently. "I'd advise you," he said, "to take this up to the lab. The Higgins people have just brought out a new model of this particular revolver, and it utilizes a different alloy than the old model. It's only been on the market about two months. If this is from one of the new models—"

"*¡Dios se lo pague!*" said Mendoza. "Come on, John!"

The city is alive; the city is exciting, and it is as addictive as the big H. You can get hooked by this city without loving it, without hating it. But the city itself is a bringer of death, and never twenty-four hours pass without death by violence in the city.

Sometimes it strikes with intention—a violent man points a gun, circles a neck with his two hands, raises the blunt instrument. More often it strikes at random; death is wanton. A child runs after the ball into the street—a shriek of brakes, driver not held, involuntary manslaughter. Brakes fail on a hill, the blaring warning horn, the scattering crowd— death choosing at seeming random, driver not held, involuntary . . . The sleeping pill swallowed, just one more cigarette before turning out the light, and the sirens screaming in the night and the flames towering to the sky, vying with neon. My dad's got a real gun, I know where he keeps it, naw, it's not loaded, but we can play like—— Bam, you're dead! You are. Did I turn off the wall heater? Sure, must have, good night, honey. And death comes quietly, so quietly, in the dark night.

The city is a place of death, because it is a place where many, many people come together, all kinds of people doing all kinds of things.

And there is the in-between death. At random, wanton death, but born out of violence.

The shopkeeper hit just a little too hard, so somebody can get at the cash register.

The throat squeezed just a little too long, so the mugger can grab the handbag.

The noisy child beaten. I didn't mean to *hurt* her.

The argument with the wife, the husband—— I guess I was a little tight, Officer, I didn't know what I was doing.

The city can be beautiful, and sordid, and rapacious, but it is death-ridden. Death visits the country, too, but more often the city, because there are more potential victims in the city.

Any city.

Cops are always potential victims. They all know this. But the incidence of cops running into violence, while it is higher than that of the average citizen, is not all that high; and they get used to living with it.

Bert Dwyer, this hot Tuesday, was not thinking about violence. He was thinking, as he walked along Grand Avenue from the lot where he'd left his car, that he'd be lucky if he got home in time for dinner—or at all, for dinner. Thursday was his wife's birthday, and after he'd made this call he was going to steal a little time off to buy her a present. She'd be thirty-six, but she didn't look it, and even after twelve years and two kids they were still in love, so it was going to be a present where she'd say, "Bert! You shouldn't have—we can't afford——"

He was nearing the corner of Seventh Street. The bank was on that corner—the Security-First Bank. All he had to do was hand over the sketches, explain, ask them to keep an eye out.

Much good this would do, he thought. Well, maybe.

The bank was a bank on the main floor and mezzanine, an office building the rest of the way.

Dwyer pushed open the first street door he came to. It let him into the lobby of the office building. There were stairs going up at the end of the lobby and two elevators in the left-hand wall. There were double doors to the right, leading into the bank.

He came in and saw the man. The man standing beyond the elevators, at the foot of the stairs. He saw what the man was doing.

His eyes widened in astonishment and understanding. Involuntarily his right hand went up under his jacket after his gun. He said, "Hold it right there, mister!" and he brought out the gun.

He had time to fire twice before the .45 slugs hit him.

He lived for one minute. To the bank guard who was first to reach him he gasped something that sounded like, "Two——" and then he died.

EIGHT

The squad-car men found his I.D. in his wallet and called in.

Lake got hold of Mendoza and Palliser at Federico's. Higgins walked into the office three minutes later, to hear the news; he got to the bank before anybody else from Homicide. Detective Bob Schenke was on night duty and it was Detective Nick Galeano's day off, but they both showed up after Lake called them.

Mendoza and Palliser got there just as the ambulance arrived. In the narrow lobby there was a little crowd, with Higgins and two uniformed men holding them back away from the body.

Dwyer lay a few steps inside the door, on his right side, feet toward the door. His gun had fallen from one outstretched hand. The interns came in and Higgins said in a taut voice, "Just a minute, boys. I make it four or five slugs in him, Luis. There are two shells gone out of his gun. They hit up there by the stairs, I think. A couple of chips out of the marble stair well there."

"Yes." Mendoza came up and looked down at Dwyer. "God damn this bastard," he said softly.

"Amen," said Higgins heavily. He stared at Dwyer's outflung hand almost touching the gun. "Oh, God, Bert." There were tears in his eyes. "We were at the academy together. Fifteen years back, do you know? God——"

Somewhere in the crowd a woman was exclaiming hysterically, "There were seven shots—I counted them. I stepped on the alarm as soon as he went out the door, and then there were seven shots—loud shots——"

"God," said Palliser. "Half the blood in his body——"

There was a lot of blood under Dwyer and around him, soaking his clothes. Forty-five-caliber bullets make big holes in a human body.

"Fifteen years——" said Higgins numbly. "This son of a bitch bastard, we got to get——"

"Yes, George," said Mendoza. He had to step in the blood to bend close over Dwyer's body; gently he probed in pockets and found the big envelope of the artist's sketches Dwyer had been carrying and his parking-lot ticket. Both were bloodstained. He said remotely, "His wife will want the car."

The interns took over then.

"Excuse me, sir, I'm Tripp—Donald Tripp. I—I was here when he died. Who is he? You——" The bank guard, in uniform. A uniform bloodstained where he had knelt over Dwyer.

"He was a cop," said Mendoza in the same remote voice. "A very damned good cop, Mr. Tripp, and he leaves a big hole, Mr. Tripp."

"Oh, my God!" said Tripp. The woman was still talking about the seven shots. "Oh, God, that's terrible. I saw it all, inside, I mean, and I was running for the phone and Mrs. Von Papen started to scream, and then I heard the shots and I came——"

"Did you see anyone else here?"

"No, sir, no, there was just this man lying here, and all the blood—but I saw he was alive. I went to him—and he said just one word, he said *Two*. I don't know what it meant—and then he died, and I——"

"We'll want a statement later on, Mr. Tripp. There was a holdup here, yes. Did——"

"The same—the same one, sir, yes, the same man—but it was very odd, what made me notice him—and I thought, with the gun and all and the people he's shot, better let him get out quietly and then—— And *this* has to happen! Oh, my God——"

"Bert walked right in on his getaway," said Higgins savagely. "He must have spotted him somehow, and—— *Two*. What the hell——"

"There's time for speculation," said Mendoza. "Right now let's get that marble stair well dusted for prints—very unlikely, but it seems to be where X was standing when Bert spotted him. Spotted him for some reason. Let's for the love of God clear this crowd away—hang onto anybody who says they saw him." He picked up Dwyer's gun and put it in his pocket. He said, "After we've sorted out the story, George, you can trail me in Bert's car. His wife."

"I could——"

"You know it's my job," said Mendoza.

That was when Schenke got there, and a minute later Galeano. They helped herd the crowd back into the bank; they asked if anybody besides the teller and the bank guard had had any kind of look at the loner, and three women and a man said yes, so they asked them please to wait. Then they came back and stood around the interns, reasonlessly, because it didn't seem exactly right to leave Bert Dwyer there alone with strangers, while they got on with the job—even the job of trying to locate his killer. The interns handed Mendoza his wallet, which was covered with blood, and his watch. Then they got him onto the stretcher and covered him up and took him away, and all there was left was a lot of blood all over the marble floor.

They went up to where a couple of slugs had chipped pieces out of the marble stair well. A man was coming down the stairs and Higgins said, "Please don't touch the banisters, sir. Police." The man looked very surprised but came on down without touching the sides of the enclosed stair. When he saw all the blood on the floor, he turned green and bolted into the bank.

"Nothing to say Bert nicked him."

"No. I think it could be he fired before Bert did, and Bert was falling as he fired," said Mendoza.

"The Prints boys are on the way," said Schenke. "My God, I can't believe this—this Goddamned—— He must have just walked into it blind! If he'd been a minute later, probably this bastard would have made his getaway——"

"Or ten minutes earlier and Bert might have been out of the bank when our boy showed up. No profit in thinking if, Bob," said Mendoza.

"He said *Two*," said Galeano. "What did he mean? If I know Bert he was trying to tell us something——"

"He *told* us, all right," said Higgins angrily. "He told us how the vanishing act is done! It's a pair, not a loner. One man walks in and gets the money, comes out, and immediately hands it over to a second man who walks out with it, while the first guy probably goes upstairs in the same building and hangs around until all the excitement's over. Doesn't it say that to you, Luis? Bert saw two men here, and I'd take a bet he saw the loot being handed over, and that's what——"

"That's what it might sound like," agreed Mendoza. "But let's not jump to any conclusions."

"Well, that's sure to God how I make it! So we're going to have a look in Records for any pair that's ever pulled a heist job, and we're going——"

"We're certainly going to do that," said Mendoza.

They did what had to be done. They asked the questions and wrote down the answers. They got names and addresses for all the witnesses.

The boys from Prints came and dusted the teller's cage where the heist man had stood, and all around the end of the lobby out there, and the door the man had used, and came up with a lot of confused prints, all too smudged for identification.

They heard only one new and rather odd thing, from the bank guard. "It was the reason I noticed him first, see? I don't suppose I would have noticed if I hadn't happened to be facing that direction, because he was very—very unobtrusive about it. I saw him come in, you see—he came in by the same door he went out, the door into the lobby of the building. He came in very—oh, quietly, and as soon as he got in he turned around and pulled down the shades on both the doors there. Just the way I do when we're closing at night, you know? Naturally I noticed that, and I thought it was very funny, and I started toward him, but by the time I got across to that side he was nearly at the chief teller's window—Mrs. Von Papen's window—and I think, Oh, boy! He's *that* guy, and I think about those people he's shot, and I think I'd just better watch until he gets away. If you take me. God," said Tripp, "if I'd known what was going to happen— I don't wear a gun, but my God, looking back, if I'd alerted a couple of husky guys—we could've jumped him from behind——"

"He pulled down the shades? Why the hell?" wondered Galeano.

"Look at the position of those doors," said Higgins harshly. "Right in the middle of that side wall, and all glass. Anybody watching him—as at least the teller would be—could see which way he turned when he went out. And we're pretty sure he turned toward the stairs, not the street door as he'd be expected to. He didn't want anybody wondering about that, about why. We know why—he turned the other way to meet his partner and hand over the loot. And——"

"And just then Bert walked in on it. Of all the lousy Goddamned luck," said Schenke.

That was certainly what it looked like. And by three o'clock there wasn't anything more to do at the bank. There had been reporters, but Mendoza hadn't given them anything yet. He didn't want Dwyer's wife getting it over the radio first.

"Oh, Christ, I don't *want* to see her," said Higgins. "I don't want to do this, Luis. Don't tell me, nobody does—you don't. It's just a hell of a thing. We all know it can happen to any of us any time, but when it comes like this—just the bad luck to walk in on that, not expecting it, not——" They walked up Grand Avenue, and the people passing in both directions passed uncaringly; they did not know that violent death had walked here three hours ago.

"He came to Homicide ten years ago. From Vice. He was a detective second-grade then. The boy had just been born," said Mendoza. "I remember. Have you ever met his wife?"

"No," said Higgins. "I don't want to meet her now. Her name's Mary. Christ, I don't. There's a girl too. Seven or eight, I think. What do you say to them? There's never anything to say."

"Never, that makes sense. But somebody has to say it."

Dwyer had lived up on Silver Lake Boulevard in Hollywood. It was an old single house on a mixed block of apartments and houses. There was a boy's bike in the driveway, and a black Scotty yipped at them from behind the driveway gate.

She knew, of course, when she saw Higgins get out of Dwyer's car in front. She didn't know how bad, but she knew. But somebody eventually had to say the quick, brutal words. *I'm sorry, he's dead.* Such very final words. And she didn't go to pieces right then—there were the children to think of; there was so much to think of.

. . . That she wasn't thinking of right now but would have to sometime. Such as the payments on the house, and on the car, and the grocery bills, and—— There would be a pension, of course, but not a very big one, because even on this force, which paid its cops good salaries, they weren't as high salaries as could be earned in easier, softer, pleasanter jobs.

What in hell's name, wondered Mendoza again, made a man want to be a cop? Ever?

And she did go halfway to pieces, and Mendoza managed to get the names out of her and called her mother up in Spokane and her sister in Portland; they would fly down at once, but that wouldn't get them here until tomorrow at least. He called the house on Rayo Grande Avenue and talked to Alison.

"You'll ask Máiri to come over at once, *amada?*"

"Yes—yes, of course, Luis. She'll look after them until—Luis, I——"

"Now. Don't make it tougher, *cara.* It wasn't me this time, that's all."

"No. But—Art was bad enough. I know Sergeant Dwyer isn't quite so—close to home, for you, but——"

"I worked with him for ten years," said Mendoza.

"Yes. Will you be home?"

"I don't know, *cara.* I'll call if not."

"Yes. Take care."

"Of what? I wish to God we knew."

"You'll get him. You'll get him now."

"We'll be looking hot and heavy. Send Máiri."

"Yes, love."

They waited until Mrs. MacTaggart came. Both the children were at a nearby playground, for which they could only thank God. But even Higgins felt they'd be all right with Mrs. MacTaggart. He got into the Ferrari with a little sigh. He said, "She's pretty. Even when she's all broken up like now. God, what a thing to happen . . ."

Palliser, Schenke, and Galeano had gone straight to Records and were pawing through all the different kinds of holdups for years back, looking for a pair who habitually worked together, looking for any pros who liked to work in pairs. They hadn't called in with anything yet, said Sergeant Lake. He was looking pale and grim. He asked questions; Mendoza told him what they'd pieced together.

"God, of all the rotten damned luck, just walking in that particular minute——" The phone rang; Lake picked it up. "Homicide, Headquarters . . . Oh, sure, just a minute." He looked at Mendoza. "Art."

Mendoza went into his office and picked up the phone. "Art."

"Luis, I just heard it on the radio. My God, how did it—— What happened?"

Mendoza told him, tiredly. "Christ!" said Hackett. "He had to walk in just *then*—— Oh, God. His wife?" Mendoza told him about that. "Well, that's—— What do I say? God. God, I wish they'd let me out of here. I couldn't do any of the leg work, but I could at least help out typing reports, looking—— Oh, hell. And I suppose they won't even let me go to the funeral——"

"Don't fuss about that, Art," said Mendoza. "Bert won't be there either —just the corpse. . . . Well, it looks like a pair. From what he got out to the guard. I don't know, we'll dig at that awhile anyway. See what shows. I expect Bainbridge has got the slugs out and sent them up to Ballistics by now. Small doubt it'll be the same gun. But that's a long way from collaring him. Or them."

"Angel called. She heard it too. She was—upset."

"Yes, wives will be. It makes the headlines when it happens, but it doesn't really happen all that often. Most of us die peacefully in our beds."

"We were at the academy together," said Hackett. "George Higgins and Bert and me. We always said, funny we should all three end up at the same place. God, I wish there was something I could do——"

"Lie still and get well, *hermano*. There'll still be work to do two months from now."

"But Bert——" Hackett was silent and then said, "I forgot to ask Angel to bring me some stationery. I've got to write a letter at least."

"Yes," said Mendoza. "Just concentrate on getting well. I'll try to drop in sometime tomorrow." He put the phone down. Letters, he thought. The chief would write a letter of condolence to Mary Dwyer, saying nice things about Bert. The mayor would write a letter. Quite possibly the governor would write a letter. Almost every man in the Homicide Bureau would find time to pay a little duty call, awkwardly, say what a right guy Bert had been. And they'd take up a collection from the whole force for Mary Dwyer. And the name would go on the Honor Roll downstairs. Albert Dwyer, another cop killed on duty.

By one of the violent men. One of the death-bringers.

So there was a big hole left in the personnel of Homicide. George Higgins would move up to first-grade sergeant, and Landers, next in line, to second-grade, and presently they'd get a replacement, a new and probably green detective third-grade out of Forgery or Robbery or somewhere. Mendoza wondered who it would be.

Sergeant Lake came in with a longish yellow teletype. "More on that D.M.V. list," he said.

"What?" said Mendoza blankly. "What—— Oh. That."

The D.M.V. list had completely slipped his mind. *Of all the lousy God-damned luck,* they had all said. But death was random—violent death. There was no sense in it, no sense at all. That intelligent, reasoning men could divine. Jimmy Walsh beaten and shot and dead on a dirty garage floor. Carol Coffey senselessly and impossibly dead, dusting the living room for her mother. Nineteen years old.

Bert Dwyer dead on the marble floor, his blood around him, thirty-seven, the wife and two kids—— Mendoza remembered suddenly that Bert had been a transfer to Homicide after Sergeant Conchetta had been killed by that hood.

He looked at the new addition to the D.M.V. list of Anglia De Luxes. It seemed, suddenly, vastly unimportant.

Palliser had got to Homicide by way of Auto Theft, which bureau didn't often run into violent death, and although he'd been on the force for eleven years, this was the first time he'd had the experience of having a colleague killed on the job. He had liked Dwyer and respected him as a good cop, and the sight of Dwyer there on the floor with the blood all around had shaken Palliser more than he would admit.

In a queerly sharp sort of way he suddenly understood the job better.

For the first time in those eleven years he saw that, whatever else you could say about police work, it was life stripped down to the raw essentials. There were no fuzzy edges to police work. Very simply, it was Good versus Bad, whatever fancy titles you might dream up: it was order against anarchy, reason against violence, sanity against mindless impulse; the drawn lines were stark; there were no fuzzy edges.

And there was (did he remember Mendoza saying that sometime?) no discharge in that war. You had to declare, one side or the other.

He worked with Schenke and Galeano and the Records men, hunting out names and past crimes, until past six o'clock. They turned up a few possibles. One from away back, 1946. And then there wasn't anything more immediate they could do. Except start looking for the men to match the names they'd turned up.

Schenke and Galeano went out to look up a pair of brothers who'd pulled a bank stick-up in 1952 and were just out of the pen, and Palliser dropped into a drugstore for a hasty meal of sorts and went back to Homicide to leave a report for Mendoza.

Sergeant Thoms said Mendoza had gone out for dinner, would probably be back, and there was a uniformed man asking to see Sergeant Palliser.

"Oh?"

"David Laskin. Squad-car man."

"Oh?" said Palliser blankly.

"I've got him waiting in the sergeants' room. Figured you'd be back."

"Oh," said Palliser. He went into the sergeants' room. The patrolman stood up, a big, good-looking young man, fingering his cap.

"Sergeant Palliser? You put a request in to Traffic, anybody on the beat that takes in Allen Street, as to whether we've ever had anything on this colored kid Verne Coffey . . ."

"Oh," said Palliser, adjusting his mind. "Yes, sure. Sit down. You got anything?"

"Sorry, sir, but nobody recognized the name. He's never even been picked up for a street scuffle or anything like that."

"Oh," said Palliser. It had just been a thought. And right now Verne Coffey seemed vastly unimportant.

NINE

Mendoza got home at half-past ten. He slid the Ferrari into the garage beside Alison's Facel-Vega and went in the back door. It hadn't cooled off much even after dark, and the temperature was nearly ninety. The house was still and mostly dark. He switched on the kitchen light and stood there for a moment, lax.

Alison came hurrying from the front of the house. A transparent green nylon peignoir swirled about her; the light was soft on her shining red hair. Coming toward him, she said, "You're tired to death, *amante* . . ."

He kissed her. "Twins asleep?" At thirteen months, blessedly, the twins had learned to sleep at night—sometimes.

"Thank God, yes. You've had a day. Luis—I'm so sorry. But it just makes the rest of us—well," and she sighed. "Angel was upset too."

"So Art said. I need a drink," said Mendoza. Unprecedentedly he stripped off his jacket and hung it carelessly over a chair, followed it with his tie. He opened a cupboard and got out the bottle of rye; inevitably El Señor heard the clink of glass on bottle neck and arrived in a hopeful rush for his share. Mendoza regarded him resignedly and poured half an ounce of rye into a saucer for him; El Señor settled down to it happily, purring. For once neither of the Mendozas commented on their alcoholic cat.

"But I *never* can understand," said Alison, "why everyone just—just submits to it so tamely. Bank robbers. Especially a man alone, like this. Why, there must have been quite a few men in the bank, every time he's come in—just stand around and let him get away with the money, instead of ganging up on him! And the people behind the counters—heavens, all they'd have to do would be to duck down—no bullet would get through those——"

Mendoza drank rye. "You can never be quite sure what a man with a gun is going to do, *novia*," he said dryly. "And you can never be quite sure where a bullet's going to go. He's shot two people before today, and everybody knows it. Nobody wants to get to be a hero the hard way."

"Well, I see that in a way, but—— I'd better go to see Mrs. Dwyer," said Alison unhappily. "And I thought afterward, how you said it happened, he just walked in on it all unexpected. Two minutes later, and he might still be alive. Why? It's senseless."

"A lot of things seem to be. No business of a cop's to philosophize," said Mendoza, "but it looks as if the time's marked out for each of us. This much and no more. For some reason or no reason."

" 'To everything there is a season, and a time to every purpose under the heavens'? I'd like to think there *is* a reason."

"But that goes on, 'A time to be born, and a time to die.' " Mendoza finished the rye. El Señor finished his and thumped down to the floor from the drainboard to find another cat to cuff. "I don't know the answer, *chica*. But he may have helped to break the case. It looks as if he was try-ing to tell us it's a pair, not a loner. . . . Come on, let's get to bed."

But in the middle of undressing he suddenly stopped with his shirt in one hand and said, "*Only*——"

"Only?" Alison was hanging up her robe.

"Only—what? It's a very little thing," said Mendoza, "I grant you. But Bert was a cop, and he talked like a cop. If it was that—that he saw two men, one passing over the haul and maybe also the gun—wouldn't he have said, or tried to say, 'a pair,' instead of 'two men'?"

"I don't see that at all," said Alison. "For one thing, he was dying—he must have known he was badly hurt at least. He'd say the natural thing, two men."

"*Es posible.* A lead, anyway . . . We'll get this bastard if it takes ten years."

He was tired, but he didn't sleep very well.

He'd known Bert Dwyer a long time.

Piggott came in on Wednesday morning. "I wasn't coming back until tomorrow," he said, "but I figure you need all the help you got. I'm all right." He looked a little pale and wan, but then he'd known Dwyer for some time too. "God, what a way to get it! Are there any new leads at all?"

Sergeant Lake was telling him about that when Tom Landers walked in. He'd been up visiting his sister in Oakland, heard it on the radio at eleven last night, and got the midnight plane down. "You've still got five days of vacation," said Lake.

"Vacation hell," said Landers, looking grim. His tall, lank figure looked taut, and the boyish face that was the bane of his existence, making him look ten years younger than he was, didn't look so boyish now, mouth a thin line and brows drawn. "It was Bert Dwyer got me to try for rank. I was on the point of quitting the force, but he talked to me—— I want the son of a bitch who killed him! Who's seen Mary? Is she all right? And have we got any leads on it at all?"

If that *two* meant what it sounded like, they had some leads. Palliser, Schenke, and Galeano had turned up fifteen possibles—men with records of heist jobs who worked in pairs, and a few pairs who usually worked together. There were other names of men like that in Records who could be eliminated on account of age or looks—though of course they didn't know what their present X's partner might look like.

If a pair was working it that way, and it would be a very damned clever way, the vanishing act was explained. Nobody on the street had seen the man who'd actually pulled the job come out, because he didn't leave the building; the man who left the building with the loot and very probably the gun was the second man. So even if the building was searched, or even if later on somebody from the bank spotted the first man, say, leaving the building, and raised a hue and cry, he'd be clean: no money, no gun— mistaken identification. If it was like that, this was a very cute pair indeed.

Item, first, this pair of brothers. Walter and James Senk. Long records of burglary, heist jobs. They had both started out as usual with grand theft auto and graduated to bigger things, both doing time before they pulled the bank job in 1952. They'd knocked over a bank in South Pasadena and been collared a block away by two squad-car men. They'd both drawn three-to-tens and got out in 1961.

Item, one Lester Cullinane, a pro from away back; he had a record of burglary, armed assault, forgery, grand theft auto. On nearly all his jobs he had worked with a pal: somebody to stand lookout, or help carry away the loot, or just for company.

Item, one Leandro Lucasta, another old pro with a monotonous record of heist jobs; he had hit liquor stores, supermarkets, bars, and might conceivably have decided to try banks. Nine out of ten jobs he had pulled had been in the company of his brother Joe or one Mario del Rojas. They had all served time.

Item—well, there were about fifteen men they wanted to haul in for questioning. For Wolf to look at in profile. Men with records like that, who by age and description could be their boy, or one of them. For one

thing, the man was not a young man but at least in his middle fifties, and
it wasn't very often that a man that age suddenly went on the bent; the
chances were that he had a record.

And this was urgent—it was very damned urgent now, with Bert Dwyer
lying in a mortuary—but at the same time they had these other cases on
hand, and they couldn't just forget about them. Somebody had to go on
giving some attention to the Walsh case and the Coffey case. There was
unfinished business there too.

Mendoza kept Palliser and Piggott for that and told them so. "I'm sorry,
I know you want to get after this boy, but we can't just ignore all other
business. And maybe a fresh mind on this Coffey thing—— Matt, will you
go and see this Verne's pals again? Get a little tough, see what you can
get."

"Sure. I see that, Lieutenant. But I'd like to look over somebody's notes
on the case. I'm not familiar——"

"You can have mine," said Palliser sourly. "And I wish you joy of it. I
can't see how anybody else could have killed her, but I don't think we'll
ever get enough evidence to prove it." He handed over his notebook.

Piggott was a plodder, but tenacious; he usually got there in the end.
"I'll get with it, then," he said, and went out.

"That D.M.V. list," said Palliser. "I see it's grown some more. It doesn't
seem to mean much to me. With Bert—— That kid, God, yes, we've got to
get whoever—but——"

Mendoza leaned his forehead on his palm a moment. "I know, John.
It'd be nice to believe, all firm and comfortable, in some very orthodox
creed. The benevolent old gentleman in the nightshirt, sitting up there ar-
ranging everything just the way it ought to be. Whether it seems that way
to us at the time or not."

"I don't think any cop ever could, all the way. The things we see every
day, every week."

" 'A time to weep, and a time to laugh,' " said Mendoza. "And that at
least is true. Everything passes. . . . I liked Conchetta. He was a damn
good man. When I caught up to that bastard who gunned him, I brought
him in half dead. And you know, John, I was thinking last night, I don't
remember Conchetta much any more. The way he looked, the way he
talked and laughed."

"That's not—that's all the more reason—— Oh, hell," said Palliser. "All
right. I know somebody's got to stay on these other things. What do you
think about Walsh?"

Mendoza sat up. "I don't think it was a private kill. I saw the parents. I saw a couple of his friends. He shows up as a nice ordinary bright kid. Sure, he was involved with this girl, but he was only nineteen, evidently he had some respect for his parents' opinion, and he'd probably have gotten over her. Nothing shows up of any kind of personal motive—nobody was jealous of him, anything like that."

"But he wouldn't have put up a fight to the heist man—he'd been told not to. So——"

"So," said Mendoza, "how many cases have we had where somebody played along with the heist man, handed over the money, and got it anyway? Because he might identify X afterward, or because X was hopped up —or just because X felt like it?"

"But the way he was beaten up—— Well, I know. I called the Higgins outfit yesterday morning, I told you that? Got hold of their sales manager. Seemed like a very nice guy, and he understands it's urgent. One thing might be a break for us. This new model of their nine-shot .22 hasn't been distributed all over the country yet—just to the western states. But——"

"No, you didn't tell me that. That could be a break," said Mendoza. They knew now, from the lab, that the piece of trigger guard had come off one of the new-model Hi-Standard revolvers.

"Well, with Bert—— And is it? By western states he meant everywhere west of Kansas," said Palliser gloomily. "How many is that? Colorado, Wyoming, Montana, New Mexico, Arizona, Nevada—er——"

"Idaho, Oregon, Washington——"

"Oh, Utah," said Palliser. "Yes, and us. For God's sake, how many stores sell guns in that territory? And I don't know how all the state laws read—it could be that some place like Montana, you can just walk in and buy a gun over the counter without even signing your name."

"I shouldn't think so," said Mendoza doubtfully. "I think they've all got laws of some kind, about showing I.D., even if they don't require a permit. But look, better check that first, because obviously it's no good asking for any information if that's so in any of those states."

"And if so, that'll be just the place our boy got the gun."

"Don't be so pessimistic."

"Pessimistic!" said Palliser. "So we check, how many of those guns have been sold in that area, even in just two months? So I go gallivanting all over on a tour of the West, chase them all down—oh, well, not that necessarily, we can get other forces to check—to find one with a broken trigger guard. Two hundred, three hundred, more? Oh, that was another thing. The sales manager did say—one ray of comfort—that nobody could have that repaired without buying a whole new unit, so eventually we'd know about that too. Maybe."

"Which is nice," said Mendoza. "What about this D.M.V. list? Maybe a short cut—if the gun belonged to the fellow del Valle saw. Easiest way, put Jimmy on the phone. Ostensibly a poll-taker or maybe a salesman for a car-painting outfit. The owners wouldn't be suspicious of that, tell us what color the Anglia was right away. You're going to have to narrow it down some way."

"All right," said Palliser dispiritedly.

Higgins and Galeano brought in the Senk brothers about eleven o'clock. Landers had just come back from an abortive hunt for Cullinane, so he stood in on the questioning too.

Walter Senk was fifty-seven, almost totally bald. He was five-eleven, a hundred and seventy, light-eyed, and he had a lot of tattoo marks all over him, but of course their bank robber had been pretty well covered up. James Senk, who could be the silent partner, was fifty-five, five-ten, a hundred and fifty-eight, light-eyed, and also bald, minus the tattoo marks. Both of them had been married and divorced and were at present sharing a room in an old rooming house on Flower Street, where they'd been picked up.

They didn't like being picked up and said so. "You got nothing on us," said Walter. "What's the beef now?"

"Maybe nothing," said Higgins. "Where were you both between noon and one o'clock yesterday?"

"What the hell?" said Walter. "Noon and—— Why? I don't hafta talk to you, bloodhounds. I don't hafta——"

"Talk," said Higgins gently. Higgins was almost as big and broad as Art Hackett, which was saying something, and he was smiling at the Senk brothers, but it wasn't a very nice smile. "You'll talk, brother, or I'll make you."

Walter Senk looked up at him, half surprised and half sarcastic. "You'll make—— A guy on *this* force? One o' you real gents? I'm laughing."

"So stop laughing," said Landers. "There was a cop killed yesterday, Walter. Maybe we're not playing real gents today."

"Listen," said James nervously. "Walt, maybe——"

"The *bank* jobs?" said Walter blankly. "Oh, Jesus, you ain't tryin' to tie us up to *that*? Oh, Jesus. There's a laugh. You can't—besides, that's a loner. You know that."

"Well, just maybe it isn't," said Galeano. "Let's hear where you both were between noon and one o'clock yesterday."

"Oh, Jesus," said Walter. "You're not gonna pin that one on us, bloodhounds. We learned our lesson, dint we, Jim?" He smirked at his brother.

"Yeah, I'll just bet," said Galeano. "Both holding nice regular jobs. Where?"

"Well, I—we come into a little money," said Walter. "Not much, just so we don't hafta work. If you——"

"A little money," said Higgins, "from jobs we haven't dropped on you for. Yet. Where were you?"

"Look, Walt, all we gotta do is tell them. They can check easy. Mac's a right guy, he'll say we was there."

"Where?" asked Galeano.

"Oh, for Christ's sake," said Walter disgustedly. "It's a crime to eat lunch? We was in Mac's bar and grill on Third. All the dee-tails you want, I had a corned beef on rye and a couple beers an' Jim had a Swiss cheese on rye and three beers."

"This Mac know you by name? Serve you personally?"

"Yeah, yeah, it's legit, he'll say. Jesus, tryin' pin somethin' like that on us——"

Higgins nodded at Galeano, who went out to check the alibi. "So we'll just wait and see what Mac says." Neither he nor Landers showed disappointment. That had come too easy and quick to be anything but the truth. But then, this kind of thing didn't break first time round.

Galeano came back forty minutes later. He said Mac had backed them up; and he'd checked downstairs: Mac—who was Robert Bruce MacDonald, incidentally—had no record, had a good reputation with Traffic.

They let the Senks go. The Senks went hurriedly.

Bob Schenke brought Leandro Lucasta in at one o'clock. He brought him in with some difficulty, because Leandro Lucasta was noisy drunk and fighting mad, and he'd given Schenke what would develop into a beautiful shiner. Schenke had picked him up at home, in the middle of a fight with his wife.

They wouldn't be able to question Leandro until he'd sobered up. They plied him with black coffee, finally gave up and stashed him in a cell at the new jail a couple of blocks away for safekeeping.

There were, so far on the list, seventy-eight Anglia De Luxes registered to owners residing in L.A. County which bore plate numbers starting out HAH. Rosario del Valle had said this year's model, but there wasn't all that difference between the 1963 and 1964 models, and Palliser had asked for coverage on both. Sergeant Lake was doggedly looking up phone numbers, dialing. "Mr. Baron? We are making a survey of——"

These days, what with all the polls and statistical surveys, the public wasn't surprised at anything and remained surprisingly polite and co-operative.

Sergeant Lake had made twenty-three calls and hadn't yet found a light-green Anglia De Luxe.

Higgins brought in Jan Czimchyk at four forty-five. Czimchyk had a long record—armed assault, robbery, burglary, Peeping Tom, rape, name it and he had it—and on most of the assault and robbery counts he had had a pal along. He was four months out of San Quentin. He was fifty-nine years old and he'd spent thirty-three of those years behind bars. He was five-nine, dark complexioned, blue eyes, a hundred and fifty pounds, and bald. Higgins had found him, via his parole officer, in a cheap room on Alpine Street.

"I never done nothing," he said sullenly.

Higgins asked him, "Where were you between noon and one o'clock yesterday?"

"I dunno why you got to pick on me. I done nothing. I do something, they put me back there—parole man says. I done nothing. I get job—dishwasher, drugstore on Broadway—I go straight O.K."

Until parole was up. They knew about that. "Where were you?" asked Galeano. "Between noon and one o'clock?"

"Please, I go straight O.K. You got me wrong. I done nothing bad. I dunno——"

"Then tell us where you were," said Higgins. These punks. These—— Unconsciously his right hand balled to a fist. God, these punks. In the fifteen years since he'd taken the oath he'd never laid hands on a suspect unless he'd been attacked, but it sometimes needed one hell of a lot of self-control. This one was just stupid, not like the arrogant can't-touch-me-I'm-under-eighteen juveniles, or some others, but right now, with Bert Dwyer at—— "Where were you? Just give us a straight answer, for God's sake."

"When? Where I was when, please?"

"Between noon and one o'clock yesterday, you stupid bastard!" shouted Higgins.

"Noon—this is twelve, O.K.? Yes. I done nothing bad—swear on my mother. One o'clock? I am at work—washing the dishes—drugstore on Broadway—they say, O.K."

"So we'll check it," said Higgins tiredly.

So they checked it. And four waitresses and two other dishwashers said that Czimchyk had been on the job between noon and one o'clock on Tuesday. Visible. Indisputably there.

Routine, it was called. It broke a lot of cases—in the end. But it took a lot of time, and it was damn boring.

Only the boys at Headquarters Homicide didn't find it so boring right now. The next man they brought in might be the man who had shot Bert Dwyer, and that man they wanted bad.

TEN

On Thursday morning the coroner held an inquest on Bert Dwyer. They would hold his funeral on Friday.

Carol Coffey's funeral had been on Wednesday.

Galeano brought in Lester Cullinane at ten o'clock Thursday morning. Mendoza was still at the inquest over at the Hall of Justice, and nobody else was there but Schenke, so they took turns questioning him.

And that turned out very unsatisfactorily, because Cullinane couldn't offer any alibi at all. With much prodding, he said he'd had the hell of a hang-over on Tuesday morning and hadn't got up or gone out until after two o'clock. He lived in a funny old rooming house near the Plaza; the men in the rooms nearest his couldn't say whether he'd been there or not. Nobody at the place could say. Nobody had heard Cullinane either staying in or going out.

That wasn't so good. It didn't say Cullinane was their boy; it just said he could have been. They hadn't one solitary thing otherwise to say he was. They couldn't hold him indefinitely without making a charge; they didn't have anything to charge him on, and if he went on saying, 'Don't know nothing about it,' they never would.

They let him go, but they'd keep him in mind. They would take a look at his pals, and requestion him, if somebody else more promising didn't turn up.

Mendoza came back to the office in time to see the last of Cullinane as he scuttled out and heard about that. "Pity," he said absently. "But I've got a few odd little thoughts in my mind, boys. That's a beautiful eye, Bob."

Schenke touched it tenderly and said, "All for nothing, too. When Lucasta sobered up, he gave me a straight story. He was at a wedding—his niece's wedding. About the time our boy hit that bank, Leandro was sitting in a pew at St. Michael and All Angels, solemn as could be." He looked at Mendoza. "What kind of little ideas, Lieutenant?" Sometimes Mendoza's little ideas turned out to be interesting.

"Well, I don't know," said Mendoza absently. He went on into his own office and they both followed. "Listening to that teller this morning, I kept thinking of what the other tellers said, and a couple of points struck me. First"—he sat down and lit a cigarette—"on all the jobs, he hasn't used the standard technique of handing over the little note saying, This is a stick-up. Of course, he's always gone to the chief tellers, who aren't as likely to have a line waiting in front of the cage, with somebody behind X to overhear him. But it's a point—he's just announced himself in a few brief words."

"Well?" said Galeano. "What's the point?"

"And then all of them said something to the effect that he spoke in a very polite and cultured voice. No, cultured isn't the word I want—grammatical. No profanity, no threats—and twice he used the tellers' names, seeing their name plates propped in the windows. That does strike me as just a little offbeat."

"I see what you mean," said Schenke, "but does it say anything in particular?"

"It might," said Mendoza meditatively, "say something very damn discouraging. It might say that he's a man of middle class and some education, who's just recently taken to a life of crime. It might say he's an amateur."

"Oh, my God," said Galeano. "If that's a hunch, I hope to Christ it's a dud one! I don't see it, anyway. What that says to me, he's got some education, sure, maybe before now he's pulled the kind of jobs your better-class crooks do—con games and——"

"Offhand, do you recall any con man who ever went on to armed violence?"

"Well——"

"Heist men don't usually bother to say please. That's the point. I just wonder why this one does, that's all."

"And then shoot people without turning a hair . . ." Schenke felt of his eye again. "Higgins and Landers are out looking for that Scott guy. Oh, and Scarne called . . ." Scarne, somewhat against his will, was back in Washington, taking a course at the F.B.I. academy. "He's wild. He can't get back until next week."

"We started this one handicapped all right," said Mendoza.

And then Higgins came in with Bill Scott, another one out of Records, so they all sat in on the questioning.

Palliser, cursing the heat, cursing deadly routine, cursing bad luck, was just entering the San Fernando Valley via the Golden State Freeway, bound, of all places on a hot day, for Chatsworth.

Sergeant Lake had turned up a green Anglia De Luxe, 1964 model. It was registered to a Richard S. Wembley who lived in Chatsworth. Chatsworth was way out at the end of the valley; the valley was always about ten degrees hotter than L.A. even at the Glendale end, and the farther west you went the hotter it got. Palliser estimated that it was about a hundred and ten degrees in Chatsworth.

He found Richard Wembley's address with the help of a county guide. It was an old house on about an acre of ground, and a sign in front read *Sunaire Kennels, Yorkshire Terriers.*

The green Anglia De Luxe was parked in the drive. It didn't have ski carriers on its roof. Palliser went up and rang the bell, mopping his forehead.

Mr. Wembley was at least sixty, tall and thin and white-haired. He was surprised and curious to find a police sergeant on his doorstep, but by using the just-routine bit, Palliser got answers out of him.

Last Friday morning Mr. Wembley had been en route up to Santa Barbara, with four of his Yorkshire terriers, to attend the Santa Barbara dog show over the weekend. He had driven up in the Anglia. He never drove the Anglia in downtown L.A.—he never had occasion to go there.

Routine.

Palliser thanked him, got back into his Rambler, and found that the few minutes of sitting in full sun had turned the steering wheel so hot he could hardly touch it.

He started back to L.A.

You just had to keep looking everywhere. Eventually, maybe, you'd hit the jackpot.

Bill Scott went on for quite a while saying sullenly they hadn't nothing on him and so what if he couldn't prove he was just home that Tuesday noon? Unfortunately he lived alone, in another cheap room, and there wasn't any way to prove it. He wasn't the world's biggest brain, and it was some time before it penetrated his mind why they were asking about that particular time. When it did, he started talking.

"Them *bank* jobs? Jeez, is it about that? Oh, my God, fellas, I'd never pull nothing like that, you oughta know me better! I'd never knock off nobody, I'm not as dumb as that! Jeez, they get you for life for that! Jeez, you got my record, fellas—I hardly ever even *hurt* nobody, did I? Did I, now? You oughta——"

"Well, there was that woman you hit over the head," said Mendoza. "Back in 1950, wasn't it?"

"Oh, my God, that was sorta an accident like. I never go to hurt nobody. Listen, jeez, you ain't gonna say *I* did them jobs? I'm clean, honest to God, I never—— Listen, for God's sake, *I* don't want no trouble with Benny, but he'll just hafta see—— Look, fellas, I was in a crap game. At Benny Guttieriez'—this pool hall down on Main. It was the hell of a hot game. I was really riding high, see—— Jeez, I ended up with half a century! Look, if Benny won't say, you ask some of the other guys was in the game—there was Jim Lopez, an' a guy named Moreno, an' Ray Foss, an'——"

He added addresses where he knew them, and Higgins and Landers went out to check. Probably he'd been there. And they'd pass on Benny's name to the Vice office, which was a necessity most men on the force considered ridiculous, but there it was; it was the law. It did seem pretty ridiculous that it should be legal to place bets inside the fence around a race track and illegal to start a friendly crap game or even a hand of poker anywhere else—except down in Gardena where you could legally play poker and nothing else. Probably nothing very drastic would happen to Benny.

But it would take some time to check out that alibi. Mendoza sighed and asked Sergeant Lake to send out for some sandwiches and coffee and added, "And then there's another thing. That bank guard."

"Yeah? . . . Ham all right? Egg salad? Chicken salad?"

"Chicken salad. You might have them send up ham for Scott . . . The bank guard," said Mendoza, wandering around the anteroom to his office, "is a former cop. Retired as sergeant from the state force in Pennsylvania. That's a pretty good outfit. He's a trained observer—like Mr. Wolf—and as he says, he spotted our boy when he came in, because of his pulling down those curtains and making straight for the chief teller's cage. So, having decided to play it safe—for which I can't blame him—and not interfere while our boy was at work, he kept his eyes on him, to notice everything he possibly could. And he tells us just what Wolf told us. He says a corduroy sports jacket with big patch pockets, and he says that the man not only shoved the bag of money into an outside pocket, he is also pretty sure he put the gun in the other outside pocket."

"Oh, he does?" said Sergeant Lake. "That strikes me as very funny,

Lieutenant. I've never seen a couple of thousand bucks cash close to, but even if most of it was in fairly big bills, seems to me that much in a paper bag would make a pocket bulge out some."

"It would indeed," said Mendoza dreamily. "He got twenty fifty-dollar bills, fifty-seven tens, nine one-hundred-dollar bills, and about twelve singles. It was a sizable parcel. I wonder why an outside pocket." And then he said suddenly, "But I'm a fool. Of course. If we're right about how this caper is pulled, that explains itself. He's going straight out to the lobby of the building to meet his partner and hand over the haul and the gun—he wants both of them handy, because they can't waste a second. Yes, of course, I see that——"

They had gone back and checked the plans of all the banks. It looked as if their reading was right, because in each case X had left by the door into the building lobby, and on one other occasion he had evidently pulled down the shades there, too, though nobody had noticed that until afterward. In that bank the teller would have had a clear view of him past those doors; in the others the tellers couldn't have seen which way he turned. So that, of course, made it look as if they'd figured out his M.O. in detail.

Scott's alibi checked out; he had been in that crap game. But Higgins and Landers didn't track down all the witnesses until nearly five o'clock that afternoon.

Then they let Scott go.

At three-thirty Piggott came in, looking pleased with himself. He had in tow a tall, thin, shambling colored kid about seventeen. He met Palliser just going into the Homicide office and said, "It just takes a little brains, you know."

Palliser glanced at the kid, who was looking scared to death. "Don't tell me you turned up some evidence?"

"I sure did. Want the lieutenant to hear it."

"My God," said Palliser, "maybe I ought to get religion." Piggott just grinned at him; Piggott was a staunch Free Methodist and got a little puritanical sometimes, but then (a lot of L.A.P.D. men thought ruefully) so did the chief, who happened to be a devout Catholic.

Mendoza was reading reports. He looked up as they came in and looked as surprised as Palliser. "Something? ¡No me diga—don't tell me!"

"Something," said Piggott. "Sit down, Lee." The colored kid didn't move or look up. "Go ahead, sit down. We just want to talk to you. Just hear over again what you told me before."

The boy's eyes moved sidewise, warily. He was poorly dressed, in shabby torn jeans and a dirty T shirt; he wasn't a bad-looking kid, but his expression was wooden and his eyes were panicky. He sidled nervously over to a chair and sat down as if he expected it to explode under him.

"This is Lee Roxhite," said Piggott. "He ties up the gun to your Verne Coffey. *A* gun, anyway."

"The hell!" said Palliser.

"How very gratifying," said Mendoza. "How? And how did you reach in and put the finger on him inside a few hours?"

"Well, I used my head," said Piggott. He looked complacent; he had reason to. "You said this Verne was from a good home, wouldn't know himself how to get hold of a gun. But there were bound to be some tough guys in the same school he goes to—school opened last Monday, you know—and could be he'd contact one of them. So I went to the school and saw the principal, and he picked out some names from their records, kids who've been in a little trouble and so on, that Verne might know. I've been talking to 'em ever since. No dice until I turned up Lee here. Now, look, Lee, we just want you to tell the truth. Understand? What you told me before?"

The boy said in a hoarse voice, "I—I say ennathing you want me to, suh. That right. Suah. You doan do nothin' if I say what you want? Do nothin' to me?"

"Nobody's going to do anything to you, Lee," said Piggott patiently. "Now, you know Verne Coffey? He's in your English class, isn't he?"

"Man, that teacher mean. She doan like me. I can't help, I don't dig that bit."

"Verne Coffey. You know him, don't you?"

Lee blinked nervously. "Yes, suh."

"Has he ever talked to you? Asked you something?" Piggott looked at Mendoza. "This is how I heard it first, see."

"Yes, suh."

"Did he ask you about a gun? How to get hold of a gun?"

Lee blinked again. His eyes shot to all three of them in turn. "Y-yes, suh."

"You've been in a little trouble, haven't you, Lee? For carrying a switchblade. Yes. And your dad's done a little time for burglary. You belong to that Knights gang down on Fowler Street? Yeah. So Verne might sure enough think you'd know where to lay hands on a gun."

"Man, I ain't—I ain't got no—I didn't——"

"Did Verne Coffey ask you where he could get a gun?"

"Yes, suh," said Lee docilely.

"Did you tell him or get one for him?"

Silence. "I—I——"

"Did you?"

"You gonna do somethin' to me?"

"Well, that depends. You just tell us what——"

"I tell you ennathing you want, you don't hafta beat nothin' out of me, suh, I tell you—just whatever you want me say——"

"Well, that's fine, Lee. Did you?"

"I'm right sorry, suh, did I do what?"

"Did Verne ask you where he might get a gun?"

"Yes, suh," said Lee meekly.

"And what did you tell him?"

Silence. "I—I—I dunno what you want me to say, suh."

"Did——"

"Just a minute, Matt," said Mendoza. He got up and came to stand in front of Lee Roxhite. "What else did Verne ask you, Lee? Did he ask you where he could get a switchblade too?"

"Y-yes, suh."

"I see. Did he tell you he was planning to kill his sister Carol?"

"Yes, suh."

"Mmh. Did he tell you," asked Mendoza, "he'd met some Martians off a flying saucer and was going back to Mars with them?"

"Yes, suh. I tell you whatever——" And then Lee blinked and half grinned. "Hey, man, what you mean, flying saucers?"

Mendoza grinned back at him. "So, whatever you think we want to hear, you tell." He looked at Piggott, whose mouth was open. "You should remember rules of evidence better than that, Matt. All leading questions!" He looked back to the boy. "You've got some funny ideas about us, Lee. We don't beat up people these days. Not colored people or white people —or even Martians. All we want to hear is the truth. Now let's start over, Lee. You were scared to death when the police officer started asking questions, and you thought if you just told him what he wanted to hear, he'd be satisfied and let you go. Then you got in a little too deep. Right? You haven't been telling the truth, have you?"

Lee swallowed. "No, suh."

"What is the truth? Do you know Verne Coffey?"

"No, suh. Nevah spoke a word to him."

"All right, Lee. Matt, suppose you drive him home. And, Lee! Another time, don't get funny ideas."

Without a word Piggott ushered the kid out.

"Maybe not too bright, but maybe just scared," said Mendoza. "Maybe another dad like Sam Coffey—of course, man with a record—all the boys in blue are bullies, kowtow to them."

"I will be damned," said Palliser. "But I thought it was too good to be true."

"Has that information on retail gun dealers come in from the Higgins people yet?"

"Can't expect it until at least tomorrow. Their home office is in Hamden, Connecticut."

"Nor I can't get that poor woman out of my mind," said Mrs. MacTaggart. "Mrs. Dwyer. Like a lost soul she is. A nice woman." She picked up Master John's plastic rattle from under the coffee table and Miss Teresa's cuddly soft stuffed poodle from the credenza. "The mother wants her to come back and live with her, but she was saying she'd take time to decide."

"I think that's wise," said Alison. "You shouldn't make decisions like that in a hurry."

"Indeed not," said Mrs. MacTaggart. She wrinkled her short nose. "The mother is all right, in a manner of speaking, but an awful autocratic body and spoils the children terrible." She went out with the toys.

"Luis——"

"¿Amada?" Mendoza was stretched out on the sectional with Bast the Abyssinian purring on his chest. He stroked her whiskers and the purr increased in volume.

"I'm superstitious," said Alison. "We're too lucky."

"Mmh?"

"We've got too much. Some awful thing's bound to happen to us. We've got too much. I mean—each other, and the twins, and Máiri to look after them, and Bertha coming in so faithful to take care of the house, and—— It can't last. Something awful——"

Mendoza laughed. "Todo lo cual no es verdad. Don't be silly, querida. Superstitious!"

"Well, I am. But maybe it does go by luck. Some people born lucky—under the right stars—and some unlucky. Under Saturn or whatever. I just feel—— That poor woman. I just suddenly felt——"

"Yes, cara," he said gently. Mrs. MacTaggart came in again, detached Master John from Sheba's twitching tail, and bore him off. Miss Teresa squealed excitedly as El Señor stalked in and pounced on his sister. Sheba rolled over and began kicking him furiously with both hind feet. Nefertiti sat placidly on the credenza, front paws well tucked under her, and watched the mock battle detachedly.

"I left some catnip out," said Alison in explanation, also watching. "Are you getting anywhere on it?"

"Routine," said Mendoza with a sigh. He squeezed Bast's ears gently. She redoubled her purring.

Mrs. MacTaggart came in and collected Miss Teresa from under the coffee table. "Nah!" said Miss Teresa rebelliously.

"Talking before we know it they'll be. Yes, love, time for beddies it is."

"But you've got some leads?" said Alison.

"For what they're worth."

Alison sighed. The rear door chimes sounded. "Now who on earth——"

"You forgot to pay the milkman," said Mendoza lazily.

"And he comes at eight o'clock at night? ¡Necio!" said Alison.

Mrs. MacTaggart came and stood in the doorway. "It's Mr. Warbeck," she announced perplexedly. "Of all things, at the back door like as if he wasn't good as anybody. I've mentioned your job to him, and he's saying he wants to ask your advice, that just maybe he's knowing something about this bank robber. Though I don't see——"

Mendoza sat up.

ELEVEN

"I'm very sorry to intrude like this, Mrs. Mendoza—Mr.—oh, no, Mrs. MacTaggart said it was——"

"Lieutenant. Now just how do you happen to know something about this bank robber, Mr. Warbeck?"

"Well, I don't know that I *do*, actually. But I feel very badly about this, sir, if I *have* any information for the police, of course I should have gone immediately and told them, but you see I didn't know anyone had been killed. I didn't even know about the robbery, and then I thought—— Oh, dear, I'd better explain . . ." Mr. Warbeck looked alarmed and upset. He was a medium-sized man about fifty, sallow-skinned, with a rather untidy head of thick dark hair and weak blue eyes behind gold-rimmed glasses.

"Why don't you take Mr. Warbeck to your den and talk comfortably?" said Alison. "Can't we offer you a drink, Mr. Warbeck?"

"Oh, no, thank you, no, I am a teetotaler." He trotted after Mendoza to the seldom-used den down the hall and sat down obediently when invited. "I must explain, Mr.—Lieutenant?—I seldom trouble to read the papers, and just lately I have been so worried about Marion Holderby's teeth, I really haven't—but I should tell you properly. You could tell me if it's anything at all the police should hear, and I'm afraid I wouldn't even know—er—*which* police to go to. I know there are different—ah—stations——"

"Central precinct. Headquarters. My office," said Mendoza. He smiled at Mr. Warbeck. "Suppose you tell me all about it, and we'll see."

"Oh, really? Oh, how very fortunate. What a coincidence! Well, it was like this, you see. I am a member—in fact, I am the treasurer—of this little philanthropic group. We call ourselves the Good Samaritans. It would surprise you, Lieutenant, even with the charitable civic groups, the city relief and all such services, how many poor children are not able to have needed medical care and so on, and the children are our chief interest. For one thing, we feel that many boys and girls from poor sections can be—er —set on the upward path, children who might otherwise be led into antisocial behavior, by the little things we do for them. Such as Marion Holderby's teeth——"

"Mr. Warbeck, if you'd just——" But Mr. Warbeck was well launched.

"They need straightening, you see, very badly. And while Mr. Holderby is gainfully employed—he drives a refuse truck—he is quite indifferent to the situation and refuses to supply the money. His wife is a downtrodden little woman and of course she has no money of her own. I am happy to say," said Mr. Warbeck happily, "that we have found the money—Mr. Holderby was concerned only for the money, you see, as long as someone else pays the bill he will not object—and she is to go to the clinic next week for her initial examination. It is the children like this, you see, we try to help——"

"That's very laudable," said Mendoza, "but——"

"Oh, dear, I do apologize. I'm afraid I get carried away. So many people *are* indifferent, or think the Health and Welfare Departments provide all the necessary services. But there are many who—— My wife and I never had any children of our own, but we were always active in charitable groups working for children, as both of us were so fond—— That was back in Auburn, of course. Auburn, New York. I was for a good many years the head floorwalker at Websters', an independent department store there. But then the owner died and it was taken over by a chain, and naturally they had their own personnel to bring in, one couldn't expect—— Most fortunately I have a small private income left me by my father, enough for my needs, and Emily being gone then—and I have so much bronchial trouble, the doctor advised a warmer climate, so I——"

"Mr. Warbeck——"

"I do beg your pardon, that's really irrelevant, of course. But you see, since I have been here I've been very interested in our little group. I had to explain this to explain to you how I came to see this man at all. You see, we maintain a very small office—one room, actually—on the eighth floor of that office building at Seventh and Grand Avenue, Lieutenant. A *very* small office—just a mailing address and a place for Miss Corsa, our very able secretary, to make up her mimeographs and so on. We send out appeals for donations quite often, but the response, I'm afraid, is not very good." Mr. Warbeck took off his glasses and began to polish them with his handkerchief. "I am generally there for a little while at least two or three days a week, and occasionally—if I am making up our accounts or drafting a new appeal—I am there all day. And as it happened, I was there most of last Tuesday afternoon. First I was calling clinics all over town, trying to discover what the lowest figure might be for Marion Holderby's braces, you see, and then I drafted an appeal for Miss Corsa to mimeograph and mail out, and then I was looking over our current account——"

Mendoza opened his mouth to ask a pertinent question but was over-ridden.

"And perhaps I have too narrow interests," said Mr. Warbeck apologetically. "But somehow, since retiring and coming out here, I don't seem to take much interest in the news any more. So much trouble, so much trouble! Occasionally I see Mrs. Tranter's paper—I rent a room from Mrs. Tranter, down on Oakdawn Avenue—but more often not. I—er—had heard about these bank robberies, but none of the details. Which is why I feel so badly about this, Lieutenant. If I *had* heard, if I *had* known, I would have realized sooner that what I had seen might be important——"

"What did you see?" asked Mendoza in a voice rather louder than usual.

Mr. Warbeck put his glasses back on. "Well, at first I wasn't sure that it is at all important, because it was *in* the building—on our floor, the eighth floor, you see. It didn't seem likely that this bank robber would stay *in* the building after holding up the bank. But the more carefully I thought about it, the more it seemed that it must have been almost immediately after that, and immediately after he'd shot that police officer—a terrible thing!—and I said to myself, Eugene, you had better take some advice on this at least, perhaps it *is* important. And then I remembered that Mrs. MacTaggart had mentioned that you are a police officer, and I came straightaway." He sighed. "I don't, of course, know a great deal about policemen or police work. My—my older brother was a little wild, there was trouble with the police over him, before he left home—my poor mother was so embarrassed—but of course that was back in Auburn, years ago. You see, at the *time*—on Tuesday, I mean—I never heard about any of the excitement. I didn't leave the building until after five o'clock, and by then it was all over. I didn't hear about it, in fact, until this afternoon, from Mrs. Roberts, who is also a member of our little group, when she called to tell me about little Jamie's adoption. A sweet child. I'm so happy we have found parents for him at last. And she did not mention the—er—time it had happened. But I had thought it a trifle queer at the time, and so when I came home tonight I looked at the newspapers—Mrs. Tranter always keeps them at least a week—and that was when I began to think it might be important." He looked at Mendoza anxiously.

"*What?*" asked Mendoza.

"The man I saw. You see—I went back in my mind, to be sure of all the details, and I am sure it cannot have been more than ten minutes after—after all the shooting down in the lobby. A terrible thing," said Mr. Warbeck. "I left Mrs. Tranter's house at a little after ten. I walked down the hill to Hollywood Boulevard and got the bus there, at the corner of Fairfax Avenue. I knew the schedule, of course, as I frequently take it, so I didn't have to wait long. And I must say, for so large a city, the public transportation is extremely poor. However! It generally takes the bus between thirty and forty minutes, at that time of day, to reach the corner of Spring Street and Seventh Avenue where I get off. And it seldom takes me more than ten minutes to walk the two blocks down to Grand and get up to our office. So I must have reached the office at very nearly eleven-twenty or a few minutes before. Yes. And I had been there for over an hour. In fact, I had only just glanced at my watch a minute or two before I got up, and it was then twenty-five minutes to one."

"Yes?" said Mendoza impatiently. Possibly it was Mr. Warbeck's fussy and maddening manner, but he had the growing feeling that something important was about to emerge. "Yes?"

"And you see, Miss Corsa had said she would be there at twelve forty-five, and I was rather anxious to speak to her about that Mrs. Riley, who—well, well, I mustn't be irrelevant! Anyway, I knew my watch had been running slow, and when I heard steps in the corridor—it's not carpeted, you see, and I hadn't bothered to latch the door, being there alone—I got up and went to the door to see if it was her. And I saw this man."

"Yes?" By piecing together what various witnesses said, and the surgeon, they had placed the bank heist as occurring between twelve twenty-five and twelve-thirty and the shooting about two minutes later. "How slow is your watch, do you know?"

"Oh, perhaps four or five minutes, I think. I saw this man——"

All right, they guessed that the actual heist man stayed in the building. If it was really twelve-forty when Warbeck's watch said twelve thirty-five, that gave him about eight minutes to reach the eighth floor. Reasonable?

"—And he looked so—queer—that I really did notice him, if you know what I mean," said Mr. Warbeck. "There's a skylight, too, the corridor is fairly well lighted. He was coming along from the direction of the elevators, but very slowly. Our office is on the left-hand side of the corridor as you come from the elevators—which are self-service elevators, of course—and so I was looking out the door to my own right. This man was all bent over, with one hand sort of holding himself under his jacket, as if—as if he were hurt, or in pain——"

Bert winged him, by God! ¡Claro es! thought Mendoza triumphantly. They had found the two empty shells from Dwyer's gun, but neither of the slugs—they had taken it for granted that both had ricocheted off the marble and gone out the rear door of the lobby, which was open, into the parking lot. They'd hunted around for them, but since at that time it didn't look as if X had been hampered in getting away, it hadn't seemed too important. Now . . . !

"In fact, when I first saw him, he was leaning on the wall. I thought perhaps he'd been taken sick suddenly, or even had a heart attack—and then he came on past me, but walking as if he *was* in pain, bent over, as I say, and one hand—— Well, you can see why, Lieutenant, when I did hear there had been shots fired and a man killed, I thought at once——"

"Yes. Did you see where he went?"

"Oh, I spoke to him. Yes." Mr. Warbeck adjusted his glasses. "As he came past, I asked if I could help him, if he was taken ill. He didn't answer, just sort of shook his head and—er—shuffled on past. Well, it was queer, and I watched him. He went into the public lavatory at the end of the corridor."

"Did you see any blood on him?"

"No, that I did not, Lieutenant—if I had I would most certainly have realized there was something wrong *then* and reported it."

"Can you describe him? His clothes and so on?"

"Oh, yes, sir, I can do that. Spending so many years as a floorwalker, one gets into the habit of noticing things, you know. I think he was taller than I am, even if he was bent over like that, I would guess he was five foot ten or a bit more. Quite thin, I would say. Of course I didn't see his face too clearly, and just for a moment, but it was—er—more full than thin. He had on a gray suit, a white shirt, and some kind of tie, I think. I couldn't see that because his hand was over it, inside his jacket like this." And Mr. Warbeck demonstrated. "Do you really think it could have been the bank robber, Lieutenant?"

"It sounds like one very damn hot lead, and I wish to God we'd had it before," said Mendoza. "Was——"

"Oh, *dear,*" said Mr. Warbeck. "I am so sorry. If I had only heard about it at the *time,* of course, I'd have told someone."

"Yes. Was his right or left hand inside his jacket? In other words, what part of him might have been injured?"

"Oh, dear, that's rather difficult to——" Mr. Warbeck shut his eyes, evidently trying to think back and visualize. "I *think* it was his right hand. As if he were holding his left shoulder, or a spot just below, you know. But I'm not absolutely sure."

"He had on a suit? Not a sports jacket and slacks of the same color?"

"Well, I *think* it was a suit," said Mr. Warbeck. "I do feel so horribly guilty that I didn't realize before it was—— But as I've explained——"

"Yes, yes," said Mendoza, getting up. Owing to Mr. Warbeck's ramblings, it was past nine o'clock. "I want a detailed formal statement on this *pronto*, Mr. Warbeck. Come on, I'll give you a ride down to Headquarters. And then I think we'll rout out the cleaners responsible for that office building——" He took Mr. Warbeck's arm.

"Dear me," said Mr. Warbeck, looking flustered. "You really think this is important?"

"Very damned important!" Mendoza hustled him to the living room where he'd left his jacket and shrugged into it.

Alison was attempting to read with El Señor and Sheba sharing her lap. She eyed Mendoza. "You look as though you'd just found the pot of gold at the end of the rainbow. Don't tell me——"

"Maybe we have," said Mendoza. "Expect me when you see me, *querida!*" He hustled Mr. Warbeck out to the garage.

Thoms was there, of course; Schenke was there, and Galeano was there of inertia—a bachelor, he hadn't much to go home to and had hung around, keeping Schenke company.

"By God," he said, hearing Mr. Warbeck, "I thought it was damn funny Bert would have missed the bastard entirely. He wasn't an extra-money marksman, but he wasn't that bad a shot either." They all, of course, had to keep up to a certain standard on the range.

And they all were feeling a little excited at this break. They got a formal signed statement from Eugene Howard Warbeck, who twittered excitedly and obviously felt very important himself, and sent him home in a squad car. And then they got hold of the manager of the office building, with some difficulty. He wasn't at home; he was enjoying a session of poker with some pals, but his wife reluctantly parted with the phone number.

The manager, one Frederick Reising, snarled at Mendoza. "Now who the hell are you and what do you want? The first time I've held any cards in weeks—three jackpots I've took, I'm really hot—and why anybody has to come bothering——"

"Congratulations, Mr. Reising," said Mendoza, grinning into the phone; a poker ace himself, he meant it. "Lieutenant Mendoza, Headquarters. I——"

"Oh," said Reising. "Oh-oh! Oh, my God. Listen——"

"Nothing to do with your poker game, Mr. Reising. Homicide, not Vice. No raid."

"Actually I'm at a poker palace in Gardena," said Reising casually.

Mendoza laughed. "At a Madison exchange? Quite a trick! Don't worry about the poker—I like a few hands myself occasionally. Look, what we want . . ." He explained.

"Oh, hell," said Reising. "Hell and damnation. Listen, Lieutenant, I'm hot—really hot. I don't want to miss this. Is it O.K. if I just call my wife, tell her to give you the keys? Is that all right? I'll answer all the questions you want tomorrow, though I don't see what *I* can give you, but—— The cleaning people will be there now. It's the Ace-High Service——"

Mendoza took pity on him—he'd had winning streaks himself—and said that would be O.K. "You're a right guy," said Reising fervently.

They collected the keys from a sleepy Mrs. Reising at midnight, out on Cumberland Street in Hollywood, and drove on down to the tall dark office building at Seventh and Grand.

As they came into the lobby, in the reflected glow from street lights and advertising neon, they all involuntarily looked at the place where Bert Dwyer had fallen. The blood had all been cleaned up now, of course, but they could see it.

"But he got the son of a bitch," said Schenke in grim satisfaction. "He winged him."

Mendoza was spotting a flash around, looking for light switches. As they had come up, they had seen that there were a few lights in the building, on upper floors. The cleaners. Reising had said only the upper floors, not the bank, which had its own cleaners. The Ace-High Service came every weekday evening to clean the rest of the building.

"And what a forlorn hope," said Mendoza now. "If anybody had noticed anything on Tuesday night, we'd have heard before."

"You think so?" said Galeano. "I don't suppose anybody on that kind of job is just so awfully damned brilliant. Look at a mess of bloodstained paper towels and figure some female had maybe been caught short by her period or something——"

"In a men's rest room?" asked Mendoza.

"Well——"

It was an eerie place at night, a big office building. It seemed to have echoes, secrecies not apparent during the busy daytimes when it was crowded with people. They rode up in an elevator; they found the cleaning women, who were surprised and disturbed to see them. The cleaning women didn't seem to be mentally deficient, just tired, hard-working women who didn't have the education or training to be anything but

cleaning women. Eventually they found the two who would be responsible for the eighth-floor public rest rooms. A Miss Rubio and a Mrs.
Marx.

"When you cleaned that men's rest room on Tuesday night," said Mendoza, "did you find anything—different? Unusual? Such as bloodstained
towels?"

Miss Rubio looked at Mrs. Marx. "Why, no, sir, we didn't, did we,
Rita? Just the usual mess. People are like pigs in public lavatories, honest,
the things we find! I wouldn't like to tell you, sir. You're *police*? Well, I
know there was that awful shooting here that day, but——"

"No bloodstains? Anywhere?" asked Galeano.

"Why, no, there wasn't. Naturally, if there had been, we'd have *said*
something—told somebody, like Mr. Reising. No, there wasn't. Why do
you think there was?"

"So he was cute," said Schenke. "They're very cute boys, this pair. He
took the bloodstained stuff away with him to dispose of outside. Elsewhere. But with a bullet in him—even if it wasn't so bad, and he got away
—he'd have needed a doctor. A crooked doctor. Or if he couldn't find one,
maybe he's a lot worse off by now. I *said* Bert couldn't have fired twice
without hitting *something*——"

In a house on Emma Street, an old frame house, the tall brown woman
said, "Pork chops. Your favorite. What's the matter, you sickenin' for
something?"

"No'm," said the brown boy. "I'm all right." And that had been six
hours ago.

"Well, you sure don't act all right. Moonin' around like you was only
half here. You miss your dad, I guess." Her voice had softened. "I know,
honey. The good Lord knows, so do I. So do I. But we got to believe it's
just God's will. You're not in any trouble at school?"

"How would I be? No, I'm O.K. Stop fussing."

"Well," she sighed, "you bein' kind of off your food, like. You feel all
right?"

"I'm all right!" he said angrily. He began to eat. The pork chops had
given him indigestion. He still didn't feel too good, even after all this time
later.

He didn't want to go home. He ought to, but she'd fuss some more.

He stood across the street from the Coffey house and stared at it. He
was thinking about what had happened there last Friday.

TWELVE

Half the men from Central division were at the funeral. The sheriff's county boys were co-operative at such times, coming in to patrol the area for a couple of hours so the men could get away. All the Homicide men were there, and Goldberg, and Pat Callaghan from Narcotics, and Fletcher of Traffic, and men from other offices.

Mendoza, sitting between Alison and Angel Hackett, wished he could believe all that the minister was saying. He hoped maybe Mary Dwyer did; he didn't know. And the minister, oddly, chose to read from Ecclesiastes.

" 'To every thing there is a season, and a time to every purpose under the heaven: a time to be born, and a time to die; a time to plant, and a time to pluck up that which is planted . . . a time to embrace, and a time to refrain from embracing . . . a time to love, and a time to hate; a time of war, and a time of peace. What profit hath he that worketh in that wherein he laboreth? I have seen the travail, which God hath given to the sons of men . . . That which hath been is now; and that which is to be hath already been; and God requireth that which is past . . . I said in mine heart, God shall judge the righteous and the wicked: for there is a time there for every purpose and for every work.' . . . Let us pray."

And presently they all drove up the hill to the grave, and listened to the minister again, and saw the coffin lowered. And then it was over, and it was time to remember life again. Mary Dwyer went quickly away in the limousine.

Alison and Angel had come together. "We're going to lunch somewhere and then to see Art. I don't suppose you know whether you'll be late?"

Mendoza shook his head. "I'll call, *cara*." He added to Angel, "You'd better look more cheerful than that for Art."

"Cheerful!" said Angel broodingly. "I know better than anyone how that woman feels. When they called about Art, that time——"

"Well, he was lucky—and lightning never strikes twice in the same place," said Mendoza. He kissed Alison and went on down the hill toward the Ferrari.

The Homicide boys all went back to the office and made up hasty plans, glanced over their lists, and started grimly to work again.

There were eight men on their list of possibles from Records whom they hadn't located yet. "I added a couple more this morning," said Galeano. They were still looking at Records; there were a lot of pedigrees to go through down there.

"So I see," said Mendoza. "That one rings a bell—Eric Blaine. An offbeat one, I seem to—— Is this a current address, I wonder. It's an old one." He stared at the name for a moment. "I'll go check on him. The rest of you——"

Palliser was sending out teletypes. Thousands and thousands of teletypes, he felt; it wasn't really that many, but there were quite a few. The information had come in, special delivery, from the Higgins head office where that new model Hi-Standard revolver was made. It listed every retail outlet which had been supplied with the new models. They might have a couple of small breaks, by what the rest of the information said. Sears, Roebuck wasn't, of course, the only retail firm which sold these guns; hardware stores, gunshops, a few other places sold them, too, but the largest supply of the new models had gone to Sears. Palliser knew that in California at least all handguns sold by Sears had to be ordered through the catalogue and all orders had to be accompanied by a voucher signed by an officer of the law, that the purchaser was and was not this, that, and the other. He doubted, therefore, that the gun had been purchased in California. Practically all of the guns sold by Sears, however, were purchased through their catalogue; and one small break here was that while the new model had first been distributed from the manufacturer two months ago, owing to the fact that a new Sears catalogue had not been printed until a month ago, to all intents and purposes the gun had only been on the market for four weeks, as far as the Sears outlet went.

But he sent teletypes everywhere—to all the retail Sears stores in the unfortunately large area concerned, to all Sears central warehouses, to a great many sheriffs and chiefs of police, asking urgent co-operation. Covering that area, that took him most of the afternoon, and even after all those other people sprang into action, there was going to be a deadly lot of routine to get through and it might get them nowhere in the end. In that area

how many of those guns might have been sold? He couldn't guess. A .22
handgun was popular with a lot of men. Try to have somebody, in all
those places, get a look at the actual guns which had been sold, to locate
one with a broken trigger guard? God. It looked hopeless; but given the
leads, you had to go through the motions.

About four o'clock, as he was taking a break over a cup of coffee, Piggott wandered in and sat down. "Ah, air conditioning," he said. He looked
hot and untidy. He said, "What kind of service was that for Bert? The
minister had robes on." He made it sound sinister.

"I don't know. Episcopalian, I think. Or Presbyterian."

"Oh," said Piggott darkly. "Robes."

"Well, why not?"

"Trappings of luxury," said Piggott. "I sometimes wonder what Luther
and the rest of them would think, come back and see how far away from
original Protestant principles——" He shook his head. "It *was* a Protestant
service, wasn't it?" He looked suddenly alarmed. Palliser reassured him
and said in any case he didn't think Piggott's immortal soul would have
been endangered if it hadn't been. Piggott looked sinister again but said,
"It's too hot to argue . . . I can't make head or tail of this Coffey thing.
But one thing did occur to me—when I was looking over all the statements
and so on. I hadn't seen the house, you know. And I thought, what about
the screens? I mean——"

"Oh, didn't I put that in? All the screens——"

"Yeah, yeah, I know now. Coffey had taken all the screens off to paint
the frames. Funny time to do it, hot weather and all the flies. I mean, just
like the lieutenant said at first, it could have been a sniper in a car. Only
if the bullet came through an open window, there'd still have been a hole
in the screen. Only there weren't any screens. So it could still have come
through a window."

Palliser shook his head. "I don't see it, Matt. They're all pretty high off
the ground, that old house. And while the slug took a slight upward
course, it was a very slight one. To get a straight shot through any of the
windows, you'd either have to be on the front porch or standing on a ladder. And we know nobody approached the house from in front, so——"

"Well," said Piggott, "I read a story once. A funny kind of story—it was
in a collection of stories I happened to pick up at the library. It was about
this Catholic priest who's a kind of detective, supposed to be, and there
was a lot of highfalutin talk and so on, but the point is, it was kind of the
same situation we've got here, man killed and a lot of witnesses all swore
nobody had gone near him. And you know who it turned out to be? The

mailman. Everybody'd seen him go up to the door, but he was just such a familiar figure nobody mentioned him."

Palliser, who did not read detective novels and had never heard of Father Brown, looked skeptical. "That seems very thin to me. *Somebody* would have mentioned him—he couldn't have counted on it. Are you supposing the mailman shot Carol Coffey and none of those neighbors saw it?"

"Well, somebody familiar in the neighborhood, you know—so familiar they'd all look right through him. A neighborhood kid? A—somebody like that Webb girl?"

"And what reason would a neighborhood kid or——"

"*I* don't know," said Piggott. "All *I* know is that the only other answer is Verne, and I don't think we'll ever tie him up to a gun. The right gun. We can bring him in and grill him a little and maybe in time he'd break down, but maybe he wouldn't too. My only suggestion is to get him to take a lie-detector test."

"Yes, I thought of that too. Tell us right off, yes or no, and when they can see we've proved they're lying, a lot of times they do break down and tell all."

"I'm going to ask the lieutenant."

"More to the point," said Palliser tiredly, "ask the Coffeys. We can't force anybody to take a lie-detector test if they don't want to, and of course it's not admissible evidence. Verne's a minor. Even if he agreed to take one, Sam Coffey could say no, and we'd be stymied. Of course," he added thoughtfully, "Sam Coffey might not know that."

Piggott looked as if he'd like to swear, if he had been a swearing man. "And you know as well as me we'd have to tell him. Tell people all their rights under the law. You know, I'm all for law and order, but I think sometimes we play too nice. All the—what d'you call 'em?—Queensberry Rules. I mean, sometimes, what with all the rules about evidence and prisoners' rights and all, it looks like *we* haven't got many rights working for us."

"How well I know what you mean," said Palliser. The outside phone rang and he picked it up. "Headquarters Homicide, Sergeant Palliser."

"Oh, hello, John," said Hackett. "Luis out?"

"Like everybody else. Piggott and I are sitting here deciding that all the citizens have got rights except cops hunting the bad boys. Rules of evidence and so on."

"You just discovering that?" said Hackett. "Add in those softhearted judges who rap us over the knuckles for charging the juveniles who are just being normal mischievous kids."

"Oh, yes," said Palliser. "How are you feeling?"

"I'm all right, but I tell you, some night I'm going to break out of here. Find out where my clothes are hidden and get *out*. Home. I've never been so sick of a place in my life. And when I did get one nurse who didn't have a face to stop a clock—in fact, a very cute little blonde—what the hell do they do but transfer her to Maternity! I——"

"Oh-oh," said Palliser. "I guess you are coming along all right, if you're taking notice of females again."

"Purely reflex action," said Hackett. "I'm a respectable married man. But I didn't call about that. I was lying here just now—Angel and Alison just left—and that Coffey thing came into my head, and all of a sudden I wondered about the screens. Weren't there any? On the windows, you know. Because that would be one way to tell whether she *was* shot inside the house——"

"Yes, it would have been," said Palliser, and told him about the screens.

"Oh," said Hackett. "Well, it was just a thought."

"Yes. You need cigarettes or anything?"

"I need," said Hackett, "some clothes and a military pass out of this damned place. Well, see you."

"See you." Palliser put down the phone.

Sergeant Lake came in and said he'd found another light-green Anglia De Luxe. He added apologetically, "In Pomona."

"For God's sake!" said Palliser. "Doesn't anybody down at the beach buy Anglias? Pomona! *Twenty* degrees hotter out there!"

Mendoza had spent a somewhat irritating afternoon tracing the Blaines back, address by address, sixteen years. The man he was hunting, Eric Blaine, interested him just faintly as a new possible because he had been a funny one, an unpredictable one, and just might have taken to bank robbing as a new kick. True, he didn't have a record of violence—but that might be his partner.

Eric Blaine and his older brother Charles had lived with their widowed mother. There was money—not millions, but a substantial amount of money. The boys hadn't had to work. Boys they remained until well into their thirties, enjoying themselves, but all strictly legal—oh, they'd both been picked up on D.-and-D. counts now and then, but that was all. Until Eric got the idea it might be fun to pull a holdup. Just for kicks, he said airily later on. It could be suspected that Mama held the purse strings a little too tight. At any rate, Eric had done a heist job on a liquor store in Hollywood and got himself a criminal record at the age of thirty-eight, which was unusual. He'd left his prints all over the place, and as he'd obligingly also left his thumbprint for the D.M.V. on his driver's license—— When he got out, ten years back, Mama had been dead and he and his brother had had a high time running through all the money. During that period they'd made a few headlines—wild parties complete with call girls, the attempted theft of a private plane ("'Always wanted to know how it felt to bail out,' says ex-con seriously"), and one rather unsavory episode involving the suicide of a twenty-year-old girl. Charles was sued by somebody for alienation of affections; for a while they both ran around with the coterie surrounding an ex-Syndicate hood who'd retired to Beverly Hills. Then, when the money was gone, they'd both dropped out of sight.

Mendoza didn't really think Eric—or Charles for that matter—was the particular X they wanted now; but you never knew. Eric certainly had the boldness this X needed to have, and maybe with encroaching years he had developed the caution.

They were now pretty certain that Bert had winged one of the pair. A waste of time to circulate flyers to all doctors; an honest doctor would already have reported treating a gunshot wound, and a crooked one never would. But because most doctors were honest, the chances were that the wounded man hadn't risked one at all. That he'd tried to take care of the wound himself, or some pal had. And if that were so, the chances were also good that the wound was a lot worse by now, infected—maybe the slug still in him (pray to God!). So they'd haul in every possible on their list and then take a long hard look at all the pals they'd ever run with, and then they'd take another look through Records for more possibles.

This one they'd never stop hunting for.

The Blaines had moved around a lot, Beverly Hills to Hollywood to Venice to Santa Monica to, finally, Bellflower. They had left forwarding addresses—apparently they'd stayed together—but because a number of different post-office branches were involved and phone calls were never satisfactory on a thing like that, Mendoza did a little traveling around in traffic, cursing the heat. The Ferrari wasn't air-conditioned because as a very cautious driver he felt it was dangerous to drive with all the windows up, not to hear the sirens maybe, or catch their direction. There were always a lot of sirens going in L.A. While he drove, he ruminated on that once-overheard remark of a stout matron touring Olvera Street on a hot day, to the effect that Mexicans didn't feel the heat.

It was a convenient theory.

God, it was hot.

He came to the end of his hunt, surprisingly, down on Bellflower Boulevard, at about four o'clock. Of all things he would have expected the
unpredictable Blaine brothers to be doing, running a tavern was the last
choice. And he wondered how in hell they had managed to get a liquor license. Well, Charles hadn't any record, of course, and it wasn't too un-
common a name—he could have claimed he was a different Charles
Blaine, and with Eric well in the background—— He could also, of course,
have bought the license under the counter before the new, stricter law was
in effect.

Anyway, there he was behind the bar of a very classy-looking tavern,
smartly advertised in neon as the Five O'clock Club. It had synthetic-stone
panels on its front, a stained-glass window in its front door, and inside it
was paneled in synthetic oak and liberally furnished in Ye Olde English,
with red-leather banquettes and captain's chairs and little round tables.
There was another barman and two very attractive cocktail waitresses—at
least attractive in this dim light.

There were only three customers in the place at this time of day.
Doubtless they got a brisk trade starting about an hour from now. A man
sat alone at the bar, slumped over a half-empty glass, and a man and a
woman bent heads together over a table, holding hands, full glasses forgotten.

Mendoza strolled over to the bar, hat in hand, and ordered straight rye.
He recognized Charles Blaine from his resemblance—his quite remarkable
resemblance—to Eric's mug shots. Both were biggish men, not so tall as
broad, with round faces and solid jaws; both were fair. Charles had lost
most of his hair; Mendoza wondered if Eric had too. That ran in families,
didn't it? He smoothed his own thick black hair absently, sipped the rye,
and wondered how to get at Charles. Was Eric in on this deal, or had
they at last parted company? No sign of Eric.

Come out all open and ask? He drank rye. He decided that no finesse
was necessary, and just then the man sitting on the bar stool five feet
away said, "Hey, Charlie, how 'bout 'nother shot? I'm good for it, you
know that."

"Sure thing, Joe." Blaine came up with the bottle.

"How's old Eric doin' these days? Still livin' it up with the dames? Boy,
he sure does make a hit with the dames, don't he?"

"He's got a touch of 'flu right now, in bed upstairs," said Blaine casually.

Upstairs, thought Mendoza. They lived here, over the tavern? A touch of 'flu, he thought, and suddenly his heart jumped a little and he thought, Or a slug somewhere in him, by God? A slug Bert Dwyer had snapped off as he fell dying?

Upstairs . . . He finished the rye and went out unhurriedly. There was a parking lot behind the place, and at one side was an outside staircase going up to a small landing and a door painted bright green. There were curtains at the two windows there.

He went quietly up the wooden staircase. The door was locked. He knocked on it gently and then sharply. After an interval he knocked again.

"Who is it?" Cautious voice just inside the door—a man's voice.

"Police!" said Mendoza peremptorily. "I want to see Eric Blaine."

There was a little silence—he could almost feel it to be a panicky silence —and then the voice said breathlessly, "He's—he's not here. He won't be home until—until about eight o'clock. You—'d better come back then."

"Let me in," said Mendoza.

"No. You've got no right—this is his apartment. I'm—just a friend. I can't—— What the hell *police* want with Eric?"

"I can get a search warrant," said Mendoza.

"So go get your search warrant!" The voice was angry and very frightened. "What the *hell*—police——"

"I'll be back in an hour," said Mendoza sharply, and clattered noisily down the stairs. He went back into the tavern. He stopped just inside the door and watched Charles Blaine behind the bar. He thought, *¡Adelante— no digo que es verdad,* but if so, God, let me be the one to get him! The one to get him, for Bert.

Within a minute the phone rang behind the bar. Charles Blaine answered it. Mendoza could not see his expression, but he didn't talk long. He hung up the phone, said something to the other bartender, clapped him on the shoulder, and went out to the kitchen through the door behind the bar.

Instantly Mendoza went out of the tavern. There was a narrow alley beside it, on the side where the staircase rose, which gave access to the parking lot behind. On the other side of the alley began another row of shop buildings all joined. The first one was a gift shop. Mendoza stood in front of the window and fixed his eyes on a pink china poodle wearing a silly expression and a straw hat garlanded with daisies. Hands in pockets, he contemplated the poodle and wondered who would consider paying out five ninety-eight (plus tax) for the creature, and out of the corner of his eye he kept a watch on the staircase. He could just see part of the green-painted door at the top.

Dios, had the luck turned? Was there a man up there with a bullet in him? A bullet out of Bert's gun? God, let me get him, he thought.

Next to the poodle was a white china Persian kitten, sitting in a yellow china basket. The basket had blue daisies wound around its handle, and the kitten wore an idiotic simper. Mendoza decided that it was a libel on all felines. Even the poodle was preferable.

Charles Blaine came around the rear corner of the alley and climbed the stairs. He had taken off his bar apron.

A man up there with a bullet in him, and police knocking at the door—for whatever reason—what would they do? If the Blaine brothers were sharing the apartment, Charles Blaine would have to know—

Next to the cat was a rather amusing owl. It was really a sewing kit. Its big eyes were the hollow handles of a pair of scissors, and its body was a pincushion. The owl stared at Mendoza and Mendoza stared back. He began to feel a little conspicuous; this wasn't the kind of shop a man would find so fascinating. Oh, well, he could be shopping for his wife's birthday. He could see his reflection in the glass, and straightened his tie, and reflected absently that at least *he* wasn't bald—nothing so aged a man as losing his hair; but he didn't, in fact, look his age at all. He felt superior. He smoothed his mustache.

The green-painted door opened and three men came out.

Three? thought Mendoza.

Two men, much alike, were supporting the third between them. Those two glanced out anxiously toward the street; Mendoza dodged back. Then they all had their backs turned, going down the stairs, and it was evidently an awkward job for the outside two. The stairs were narrow, and the third man, between them, seemed to be scarcely conscious, hanging limp. They got him down step by step, supporting him by the arms; his feet dragged; they were both panting.

Mendoza watched and timed it. The stairs went straight down; when they had got the man three steps from the bottom, he abandoned the gift-shop window, quietly walked down the alley, and stood at the foot of the stairs.

He smiled at Eric and Charles Blaine as they lifted the man down the last step. He had his badge in his hand, held out. "Mendoza, Headquarters," he said, smiling gently. "Do please introduce me to your friend, won't you?"

THIRTEEN

The man with the Blaine brothers was one Luther Foote, and he didn't have any kind of record, but he did have a gunshot wound in his lower right shoulder. He was forty-seven, five feet nine, a hundred and sixty, brown-haired, and blue-eyed; he was divorced from his wife; he was a plumber and had his own shop with three employees.

That information, and a welter of more information, came out at once, from the Blaines.

The surgeon told them that the gunshot wound was approximately as old as sometime last Tuesday. There wasn't any slug in the wound—it had gone straight through him; but that was helpful in a way, as showing it had probably been a high-caliber slug; a .22 or something like that probably would have stayed in him. The wound had had some amateur care but was infected; the man wouldn't die, but he wasn't in too good a condition. They could question him tomorrow.

They hardly had to question the Blaines at all. "What the hell d'you think we'd do?" burst out Eric, angry and scared. "This was Joe Sebastian! He's got contacts—everybody says—like with the Syndicate. Big-time gambler like him. Look, neither Luther nor me wanted any repercussions from Sebastian, for God's sake! D'you think Luther'd have looked twice at that dame if he'd known she belonged to Joe Sebastian? Like hell! But she and this redhead came in to the place—our place—alone, and they gave Luther and me the eye, and how should we know who the blonde was? My God." Eric mopped his brow. He hadn't lost his hair, and he looked a vigorous forty instead of the fifty-three he was. Somebody—that customer—had said he was quite a guy for the dames. Mendoza could believe it.

"My God," he said. "So there we were at this apartment, big fancy place right on Hollywood Boulevard, having some drinks, when this guy came in——"

"When was this, Mr. Blaine?"

"Last Tuesday night. And he's a big guy, and he just tells us calmly to get out. I was ready to go, believe me—I didn't like his looks—but Luther gets a little feisty after a few drinks, and he began to argue with him. That's when the guy says that no two-bit punk is going to play around with a girl of Joe Sebastian's, and he hauls out this cannon and takes a shot at Luther. I'd guess the place is soundproofed—nobody seemed to take any notice. I got Luther out O.K., but my God, Lieutenant, am I going to yell 'Cop' and lay a complaint against Sebastian? And get a couple of hoods come gunning for us for real? I'm not that big a fool! I——"

"That's the way it was," said Charles Blaine. "Eric brought Luther home with him, and we've been doing what we could for him. We knew a doctor would report it——" He passed a hand over his face.

"Sebastian?" said Mendoza, and smiled. "Don't believe all you hear. He's not a Syndicate man and he's got no Syndicate contacts. If he had he wouldn't be let inside L.A." This was the only big city in the world where the Syndicate had never got a toe hold. Of course, this last year or so the F.B.I. and other forces had cleaned the Syndicate out of a number of places. Mendoza knew Sebastian's name, vaguely, as that of a reputed big-time gambler who came visiting L.A. occasionally; supposedly he had undercover business interests here, silent partnerships. But he didn't know if he bought this story or not from the Blaines.

"My God, Lieutenant, if you——"

"We'll hear what he has to say. Where were you and Foote last Tuesday between noon and one o'clock?"

Eric Blaine was an intelligent man, if unpredictable. He leaped off the straight chair they'd given him and said wildly, "The *bank* robberies? Oh, my God, you don't think—— Luther and me? Oh, my God, how crazy can you get? The papers say it's a man alone—— That's *crazy* . . ."

"We've got evidence that our man winged him," said Mendoza. "Where were you?"

"Dear *God* . . ."

"Sit down, Eric," said his brother. "They were both with me in our apartment eating lunch. I've been thinking of expanding the tavern, and Luther was going to invest a little money in it."

"I see," said Mendoza. "You just chose the right tense, friend. I suppose you realize you'll lose your liquor license over this and won't be able to get another?"

Charles Blaine nodded tiredly. He looked at his brother and said, "You and your women."

"Well, how the hell was I to know——"

"You and your *women*."

So they went out and picked up Joe Sebastian, who wasn't nearly as big a man as he thought he was, and asked him about that story. Sebastian, a dapper big fellow with a booming voice, heard them out and denied the whole thing. The blonde they'd found with him denied everything too.

"Prove it," said Sebastian coolly.

They tried to. They got a search warrant and went over his apartment. They didn't find any bullet holes anywhere. They heard from the superintendent of the building that a window had been broken in Sebastian's living room last Thursday—an accident. Conceivably it could have been broken by a bullet on Tuesday; the superintendent said no bullet hole, but Sebastian wouldn't have left that there. After the first heat of the moment had passed, he'd start thinking about an attempted-homicide charge. Knock out some more glass with a chair, wait to report it until Thursday. They didn't find a gun on him or anywhere in the apartment.

"You've got nothing on me, gentlemen," said Sebastian. "Those two guys I never heard of in my life. Probably one of 'em shot the other and 's trying to cover up, drag my name into it." He winked. "A lotta people know my name who I don't know."

They didn't find a gun in the Blaines' apartment, in the tavern, or in Luther's apartment. And of course that was all very unsatisfactory indeed, because it left them right up in the air. Anything could be the truth. Maybe Eric and Luther were the pair of X's they wanted and that had been Bert Dwyer's slug that went clean through Luther. Maybe the story Eric told was true blue right down the line. No proof either way.

"Well, what does everybody think?" Mendoza sighed. The two Blaines had been taken over to the new jail—failure to report attempted homicide; they'd be out on bail presently.

"Oh, hell, pay your money and take your choice," said Galeano morosely. "But I guess I think not. Because for one thing, this Luther Foote, by what we hear, built up his own business, started as an apprentice and now owns the place, and that's not the type of guy—steady and hardworking—to suddenly go off the rails. It looks like he just has a weakness for skirts. As per little Eric."

"Well, there's nothing to *say*," said Schenke. And that was late Saturday afternoon. His eye was still faintly discolored; he felt it absently. "I guess I go along with Nick. There sure as hell isn't enough to charge them with the bank jobs."

"Mmh. One thing," said Mendoza. "If they are the boys we want, I think they'll start lying very low. Our boys have been going at it hot and heavy—five in a period of thirty-two days, and the last three not a week apart. I made it that they found out how easy it was and couldn't resist just one more. God, I wish we had the men to stake out every bank downtown they haven't hit. But if it is Luther and Eric, I don't think they'll pull another, after this little scare. Keep an eye on them, anyway."

"The Feds——" said Schenke doubtfully.

The Feds, sitting in on all the Blaine business, had been skeptical from the first. There had just been a kidnapping back East, and flyers sent out to all the western states where it was suspected the kidnappers might have headed, and the Feds had dropped L.A.'s bank robbers back into the lap of Homicide and gone back to their own work. Their, by implication, far more important work. Occasionally the Feds got to acting a little superior and upstage.

Mr. Warbeck had looked at Luther Foote and said, "Oh, dear, I can't really be sure——" And Wolf had looked and said briefly, "No." Well, it had looked too good to be true.

They sat around dispiritedly discussing it for a while. Of course, there were the sketches, in the hands of a lot of bank personnel—in the end that might pay off; and there were men they still hadn't found, whom they wanted to talk to. There was Lester Cullinane, minus an alibi; they were asking around about his pals; they would see them too. There was still a lot of routine to do on it.

After a while Schenke and Galeano went out to snatch some dinner and go looking for one Robert Rhys who had an interesting record and was currently on parole. Landers hadn't been heard from since noon; he was on the track of one Alfred Hardcastle who also had a record of interest. Nobody knew where Higgins was—doubtless after another one like that.

Mendoza sat on in his office, brooding over the Blaines and trying to calculate coincidences, until Sergeant Lake came in and said, "There's a guy out here asking to see you. Says his name's Tommy Canaletti. Ring a bell?"

Mendoza sat up with a jerk. "¿De veras? Now what—— O.K., shove him in, Jimmy." Abruptly his mind began to tick over on all cylinders again.

Tommy Canaletti was a sad little man who'd never got very far in life and realized it and minded it. Unlike most Skid Row bums, who lived day to day and had long ceased minding anything but the lack of fifty cents or a buck for another skinful of *vino*, Tommy realized that he was a failure—

a weak, ineffectual little man—and that made him all the sadder. He wasn't exactly a wino and he wasn't exactly a bum; sometimes he worked, making deliveries for markets, something like that; more often he just drifted around. And probably one reason why Tommy had turned pigeon was that it made him feel important, helping the cops. He didn't work at that all the time either, just sometimes.

Now what in hell was Tommy doing here? Like all pigeons, he never visited Headquarters—or any precinct house.

He drifted into Mendoza's office and looked around sadly. He was a little man, no more than five-three, very thin and dark, and he had the great mournful dark eyes of all Italian madonnas. "Hello, Lieutenant," he said in his soft voice. He hadn't shaved for a few days, and his Hawaiian sports shirt was dirty, if gay, and his jeans were torn. He had on dirty white tennis shoes. "I was sorry as hell to hear about Sergeant Dwyer," he said sadly. "He was a nice guy."

"Yes, he was," said Mendoza. "Thanks, Tommy. Was that what you came to say?"

"Well, not all of it," said Tommy. "On account, I could do with a sawbuck. Or even two. And I thought this was kind of interesting myself, so maybe you'd think so too. You wouldn't have a cigarette, would you?" Mendoza gave him one. "Thanks. You know the sergeant had been asking all around about this guy got shot over on San Pedro one night? Leigh, his name was."

"Oh." That little thing had more or less died a natural death. "So?"

"Well, like I told him last time I saw him—gee, that's awful, his gettin' shot like that, nice a guy as you'd ever want to meet, wasn't he?—like I told him, the word was this Leigh had gone to see this guy Broadbent—ain't that the hell of a name?—who's a bartender at the Acme Grill, but the word is he's got contacts, you want anything under the counter, you——"

"Yes, Dwyer told me about that."

"Sure. But it seemed kind of funny to me, he was just a cheap bum, what'd he be up to? You know. An' I been askin' around, just casual, you know, like I was just curious, an' I got this word from a guy—another cheap bum—this Leigh shared a bottle with one night. And I think he's nuts, because it don't make no sense, only this particular guy is so far gone on *vino*, Lieutenant, he just couldn't 've made it up, see? So I come to pass it on for what it's worth. Maybe a sawbuck?" he added wistfully.

"Well, what is it?"

"What the guy said was, this Leigh told him he was lookin' for a guy to buy money. Leigh said he was gonna be rich, he could just find a guy to buy the stuff. Like, you know, an agent—a hot-money man."

Mendoza sat up abruptly. "*¿Y qué es esto? ¡Porvida!* Now what the hell—— Is that level, Tommy?"

"I know—it smells. A cheap wino. A bum. But that's what this guy said. I thought it was just funny enough that maybe it'd be worth——"

Wordlessly Mendoza took out his billfold and handed Tommy Canaletti twenty-five bucks.

"Well, gee, thanks, Lieutenant! And I'd like to say again how awful sorry I am about Sergeant Dwyer——"

Walter William Leigh, shot over on San Pedro Street about midnight one night and left dead in an alley. Nobody important. A Skid Row bum.

Trying to locate an agent to buy hot money. The kind of pro crook right at the top of the tree, one of the elite of crookdom.

Why, for God's sake? The bank jobs. My God, the bank jobs.

A hot-money man might take such piddling little sums, if he had a deal going already or expected one, a big fat deal so he could just slip the hot bank bills in with the rest. (That kidnapping?)

Leigh, for God's sake. What the hell was the connection? A third man mixed in? Seven, eight, even ten thousand bucks—so far—wasn't such a hell of a take split three ways, and it'd be watered down considerably if they'd sold it to an agent. Call it between three and four thousand.

So they'd killed Leigh, the other two, to up their take? Or because he was a cheap bum who'd talk too much when he was high? Then why cut him in in the first place? This just didn't make sense, any part of it. But things Tommy Canaletti had come up with in the past had checked out. So . . .

Mendoza went out to the anteroom to talk this over with Sergeant Lake —he had to talk it over with somebody—just as the phone rang. Sergeant Lake picked it up and immediately it started to make loud angry noises at him. Presently Sergeant Lake started to laugh. He laughed helplessly; helplessly he handed the phone to Mendoza.

"—and none of these Goddamned sons of bitches at the new jail knows me, and I thought we had some Goddamned *rules* about prisoners' rights, and can *I* help it if I happen to look like a bum at the moment? All right, all *right*, I'm entitled to one call, you bastard. Now listen, I couldn't help it—the son of a bitch started the fight—was I supposed to just stand there and let him maul me?—and he's a big bastard too, I didn't—— Who is this? Jimmy, for the love of Christ, if that's you laughing——"

"Where are you, Tom?" asked Mendoza.

"Lieutenant, thank God, will you for Christ's sake come down here and identify me?" howled Landers. "I'm at the new facility on Alameda, where else? I'm after this Hardcastle character. I get chased around a lot of places he might be. I've been in more dives than—— Well, I catch up to him awhile ago in a joint down on Macy. He's with another guy, and when I go up to him to pick him up, bring him in, he gets all excited and yells Fuzz, and you see this joint isn't exactly the kind where all the customers like cops just so well, and so there's a little Donnybrook, and——"

"I see," said Mendoza. "Very natural."

"*Listen*," said Landers, "there's no law says how *long* I can talk, you stupid bastard! Look, Lieutenant, so he gives me a poke in the eye, and rips my jacket half off, and everybody's yelling and there's quite a crowd in there—it's not a very big place—and I knock him down and get out my gun, and about then a squad car comes up, and what *kind* of Goddamned stupid rookies are we getting these days, anyway?—because, my good Christ, I *tell* them who I am, and I—— But some Goddamned son of a bitch has picked my pocket, and my badge—— And for God's sake, they've got me booked for carrying a concealed weapon and D.-and-D., and I've had exactly two drinks all day and no dinner, and will you for God's sake——"

"Yes, Tom," said Mendoza gently. Sergeant Lake was still speechless, red-faced. "I'll come down, Tom. Right away."

Landers was spluttering. "So all right, it's the newest and biggest damn jail facility in the country—maybe in the world—*which* says something about L.A., for God's sake—and we staff it with a Goddamned bunch of stupid cretins who—— Yes, I mean *you*, you bastard! And take your hands off this Goddamned phone. I've got a right to——" There was a loud final click at the other end of the wire, and Mendoza handed the phone back to Lake and began to laugh.

"And he's still—technically—on his vacation," gasped Sergeant Lake. Sergeant Thoms came in and stared at them both.

"I'll go down and rescue him," said Mendoza. "Hello, Bill—Jimmy'll tell you all about it. If they don't believe me, I'll send you an S.O.S. and you can call the chief. You might call my wife and say I'll be late."

He identified an incoherent, raging Landers, who looked the complete tough minus a jacket, sleeve torn out of his shirt, and needing a shave, and calmed down a dozen suddenly agitated jailers, and sent Landers home. Hardcastle was safe in the new jail; they'd get to him tomorrow. He went back to Headquarters to see if anything new had turned up; also, he wanted to send out a pickup on that bartender. Sergeant Lake was gone; Sergeant Thoms was sitting at his desk reading a paperback. Higgins had come in, towing one Robert Bandhauser who was one of those on the list from Records, so Mendoza sat in on that questioning. It wasn't very productive. Bandhauser hadn't any alibi either.

At ten o'clock he went home, still dinnerless, and was fussed over and fed. Something, he thought, to be said for marital domesticities, even if it was productive of howling twins.

Palliser was now receiving teletypes. Thousands and thousands of teletypes. Not really that many, but—— *Full co-operation soonest,* Sheriff, Butte County. *Checking soonest,* Sheriff, Alameda County. *Immediate check,* Chief of Police, San Francisco—Sacramento—Fresno—Denver—Portland—Spokane—Helena, Montana—Phoenix—Boise—Las Vegas—Santa Fé—Salt Lake City . . . Sheriffs, hundreds of sheriffs all eager to help him out, hundreds of police chiefs . . .

Eagerly co-operative Sears' store managers. He was buried in teletypes. And nothing he could do much personally until all the results of the co-operation came in.

Find the one right gun, in that immense territory? Hopeless.

He went home. His mother's arthritis was better in this heat. It was at least good for something. He felt a little better after he'd had a shower. He called Roberta Silverman at eight o'clock.

"What are you doing?"

"Need you ask? Correcting papers, of course." Roberta taught fourth grade at a South Pasadena school.

"Oh."

"You don't sound your usual bright self. Well, I know, this thing—this sergeant. Did you know him well, John?"

"Yes, I knew him well," said Palliser. "There's nothing to say about that, is there?"

"Except that some of us—who are a little bit involved with any of you— even a *little* bit," she said with a smile in her voice, "sometimes wish you were driving buses or working on assembly lines instead."

"It doesn't really happen so often. Roberta——"

"I said a *little* bit."

But they both knew he'd ask her to marry him when he got his next automatic pay raise. And she liked his mother; they all got along fine.

"I'm supposed to be off Monday, but with all this— I don't know. I'll call you."

"Yes," she said. "It's all right, John."

Palliser presently went to bed and dreamed that he was drowning. He was drowning, but not in water; it was all yellow; it was a sea of teletypes, long strips of teletypes, more and more being poured on top by a diligent Sergeant Lake, and he was screaming, "Jimmy, don't do this to me——" and Sergeant Lake kept adding more teletypes.

He woke up, sweating—God, it was hot; nights didn't cool off any more —and took an aspirin. He overslept, and he was late into the office; he didn't get there until eight-twenty.

Sergeant Lake, comfortably solid and round-faced and (of course) basking in air conditioning, said, "Morning. I just turned up another one for you. Light-green Anglia. In Pacoima. Sorry."

Pacoima. The very damnedest hottest spot of the valley.

Palliser uttered a very rude word.

FOURTEEN

About nine o'clock on Sunday morning the bartender at that dive where Landers had got in trouble showed up and gravely handed in Landers' wallet, complete with badge and I.D., but minus any money. Landers said philosophically there'd only been about four bucks in it anyway.

The other bartender, they were still looking for. Schenke had gone looking for him, but it was his night off and he wasn't home. Schenke lingered until Mendoza came in that morning, to talk about that, and Galeano, Higgins, Landers, and the rest of them heard about that fantastic bit then.

"That Leigh?" said Galeano incredulously. "Tied up to the bank jobs? That's crazy! A cheap bum like that?"

"I know, I know," said Mendoza. "Even Tommy said it was crazy. But there it is. I don't know what it means, but I've thought since the second job that the bank money is being exchanged somehow, and that means a hot-money man, and here's a very funny sort of link to one. Maybe. We treated Walter William a bit casual, because it was such an anonymous kill, there weren't any leads at all, and he wasn't much loss. Right now I'm damn sorry Walter is dead and can't be questioned, and I think we ought to backtrack and find out a little more about him."

"We looked," said Schenke defensively. "There's never much you *can* find out about bums like that. They're—anonymous. That might not even have been his right name. Everything we got's in the files—I seem to remember he lived in a cheap rooming house over on First."

"Yes. I want to see all you got, refresh my memory. His prints weren't in our records, but they could be in somebody's. Let's ask the F.B.I."

"Anonymous!" said Higgins disgustedly. "What the hell could a bum like that have to do with——"

"I haven't the slightest idea, George. But any lead, we ought to——"

"Look, we don't have anything to say this pair *are* selling the loot to an agent."

"I still think so," said Mendoza stubbornly. "I know we haven't, but I think they are. And that being so——" Higgins exchanged a silent glance with Galeano. The boss got funny notions sometimes, and he could be stubborn. If he said follow this up, they hadn't any choice, even though it was reaching way out into space and the rest of them didn't see anything in it at all. On the other hand, sometimes the boss reached out into thin air and came up with something hot. "That being so," said Mendoza, "I'm making up stories about it. Walter William looked like an ordinary Skid Row drifter, but was he conceivably a former pro? In touch with pros? Once the member of a gang of hoods, fallen to Skid Row? On the other hand, what pro in his right mind, intending to knock over a bank, would trust somebody like Walter in the deal? And you know I said awhile ago, this could just conceivably be a pair of amateurs. All right. Did they know about Walter's possible record and, not having any idea themselves where to find a money agent, figure Walter might know? Or——"

"Oh, for God's sake," said Higgins. "Look. How many amateurs—people on the right side of the fence—know there are such things as hot-money men?"

Mendoza reached behind him for the new County Guide and turned the first page. He contemplated a scale map of the welter of surface streets and freeways that was downtown L.A.—mostly their beat except for a little corner to the left that came under the Newton Street precinct. The tangle of the railroad yards, the Civic Center, the monumental freeway exchange, and all the little narrow old streets everywhere—the oldest part of L.A. He said, "Good and bad in this territory, all mixed together. Rubbing shoulders. Some people just poor, and some pro crooks, and some on the fringes. You think anybody living down here couldn't not know a lot of things—pro talk, pro habits?"

"And what says they live——"

"Nothing," said Mendoza. "But it's in the cards, isn't it? The ones like Walter William rarely leave the area—how would anybody else know him?"

"Well——"

"I want the file on him," said Mendoza. That had been a minor sort of kill; he'd just been cleaning up the Brent business at the time, and he hadn't followed the Leigh thing very closely—Dwyer and Schenke had been on that. Schenke brought him the file; Higgins and Landers went off to question Hardcastle, and Galeano to hunt for Rhys some more.

The first thing the file told Mendoza shot his eyebrows up. Leigh had been shot by a .45. "*¡Qué interesante!*" he said to himself, and picked up the inside phone and asked for Ballistics. The man he talked to had nearly forgotten the case, but of course, like the lab boys, the boys up there were very tidy and organized and they never threw away clues, even after years, so they still had the slug taken out of Leigh, all neatly labeled and filed away. "Good," said Mendoza. "Will you do me a little favor and compare it with the slugs from our bank robber's .45?"

"The *bank* robber?" said the Ballistics man. "Aren't you reaching a little, Lieutenant? I understand this Leigh was a Skid Row——"

"You know my hunches," said Mendoza. "It came to me in a prophetic dream. Just have a look, will you?"

"Oh, I'll look if you say so. We're just here to serve you big brains. But I don't see—— Oh, I'll look."

Mendoza read through the file. Leigh had been found by a couple of squad-car men who thought he was a drunk. A lot of people around the area had known him: a drinker, but not as bad as a lot down there. Everybody said amiable, nice fellow, quiet little man, who'd want to shoot him? He'd had a room, a cheap room. He usually had a little money, nobody knew from where. Nobody knew anything about his having an argument with anyone lately, anything like that. It would have looked like the usual Skid Row killing for what was in the victim's pockets, except that he was shot: nobody who had a .45 to pawn would take the trouble to kill a drunk just on speculation. But there hadn't been any leads at all.

Mendoza collected his hat and went out to call on the rooming-house owner.

It was an old, big frame house, probably originally set back farther from the street, before progress had widened that. It badly needed a coat of paint; it had a wide front porch with some old chairs lined across it, and a dingy sign under the second-floor windows said *Rooms*. A very fat and very bald old man was the sole occupant of the porch; he sat and rocked rhythmically back and forth, fanning himself with an old-fashioned palm-leaf fan.

"Good morning," said Mendoza, climbing warped wooden steps. He'd left the Ferrari half a block away, but he had the feeling the man's eyes had observed his whole progress along the block. "I'm looking for Mr. Jason Frick."

"Set," said the fat man. He had on an ancient pair of black trousers held up with suspenders and an old-fashioned silk undershirt. His paunch was tremendous, and he was sweating freely. "I'm Frick. You're fuzz."

"Yes," said Mendoza, thinking again how things overlapped in this kind of neighborhood. Frick probably a perfectly honest man, but using the pro talk. "I want to ask you some more questions about Leigh." He sat down.

"Um. Told you boys about everything I knew before. Not that it wasn't kind of funny, why anybody'd want to cool *him*. I didn't know much about him. Don't figure nobody did. The kind I get renting my rooms, they're the ones alone—nobody to take much notice of 'em—not much money. Nothin' very interesting about 'em. They come 'n' go, and why should I notice, long as they pay me?"

"But you did say Leigh had lived here for some time."

"'Bout five years. Somebody sent him money ever' week. I'd see the envelope come in the mail. I dunno how much, but it was allus cash and he was allus right there to take it from the mailman."

"But you never saw a return address on the envelope—or noticed the postmark?"

"Maybe I just ain't curious, mister," said Frick, fanning harder. "Jesus God, it is *hot*. I figured somebody, like some of his family, you know, just didn't want him around, paid him to stay away. Well, he liked his booze, sure. But he wasn't a falling-down-drunk drinker. He got awful happy when he was tight—there wasn't any harm in him. He allus got home under his own steam. He allus paid me on the dot, an' that's all I could tell you. Except——" The fat man stopped fanning and scratched his nose. "I didn't think o' that when the other cop was here that time. Not that I s'pose it's got anything to do with his gettin' killed. But about two, three weeks before that he got a phone call here one afternoon. Only time anybody ever phoned him up, all the time he lived here."

"Oh," said Mendoza. "Did you answer the phone?"

"My house, ain't it? Sure."

"Was it a man or a woman calling?"

"A man. Sounded like, anyway. Just asked to talk to Mr. Leigh, so I went and got him."

"Did you hear anything Leigh said on the phone?"

Frick shook his head. "Was just on my way out here to set and have a cold beer. But he wasn't on the phone long. About five minutes later he come out, dressed to go out—he hadn't so many clothes, but he allus kept himself pretty neat, know what I mean?—and off he went somewheres. But anyway, he usually went out about then."

Mr. Frick was a very incurious man. Mendoza sat in the Ferrari, ruminating and baking gently in the really remarkable heat, and finally drove down to Second Street to the Hi-de-Ho Bar, which was one of Tommy Canaletti's favorites. He left the Ferrari in a lot and went into the bar. Tommy was there. Mendoza waited patiently until Tommy turned and saw him and lifted a quiet finger. Three minutes later Tommy joined him on the sidewalk.

"You maybe decided it wasn't worth the quarter century?"

"No, not at all," said Mendoza. "What I'd like now is the name of this bum who told you the funny story."

"You wanta get it from him straight? That's sad, Lieutenant," said Tommy. "I'm real sorry. For you, not him. I told you he was real far gone. They carted him off to the General last night and I unnastand he's dead. You could see. His name was Buddy Pargeter."

"Hell and damnation!" said Mendoza.

They picked up Alfred Broadbent, the bartender who reputedly had contacts, at four o'clock that afternoon. Broadbent was a real tough, even if he hadn't a record. He looked as if he'd been everywhere and done everything, and it looked as if he'd had experience with cops before, because all he did was sit stolid and unmoved at the battery of questions they threw at him and continue to repeat, "I don't know nothing about it."

He didn't know Leigh; Leigh had never come to ask him anything; he didn't know nothing about nothing.

They had to let him go, and they all agreed it would be no use at all to put a tail on him. He was a wise one and he was going to be keeping very clean while he thought the cops were interested. And they couldn't keep a tail on him forever.

But about five o'clock the man from Ballistics called, sounding incredulous. "How do you do it, Lieutenant? With the gypsy fortunetelling cards?"

"By God, it checked?" exclaimed Mendoza. "Don't tell me——"

"It's a match. The slug from Leigh is out of the same gun that shot the guard and the teller and Sergeant Dwyer. That S. and W. 1955 target revolver."

"¡Como!" said Mendoza softly. "¡Aquí está! Now just fancy that. Thanks so much." He put down the phone and looked at Higgins and Landers. "So I'm reaching," he said. "So we've got nothing to link Walter William with the bank jobs and I'm just peering into my crystal ball again and being obstinate about a hunch. They're not all duds, you know. So now we know that the same gun which got the guard and the teller and Bert also fired the slug into Leigh."

They stared at him. "I will be Goddamned," said Higgins. "I'll be——What the *hell* could be the link?"

"I don't know. I just can't imagine," said Mendoza. "But there it is. Let's keep working and find out, boys. If it's humanly possible."

Before that, when he'd got back from his abortive talk with Tommy, Mendoza had been cornered by Piggott, who argued that they ought to get Verne Coffey to take a lie-detector test. Mendoza had thought about that himself. "But there are a couple of factors to consider," he pointed out. "It's not absolutely infallible, you know. Usually, yes—but there are factors that can—mmh—nullify it. And if Verne is already very nervous of cops, and authority in general, he could tell nothing but the gospel truth and still his heart would go jumping around and his blood pressure shooting up, to give us the wrong picture."

"I see that, but those fellows are pretty smart about interpreting reactions. I still think we ought to."

"And I think I agree with you. They're not," said Mendoza, "going to like it. But it does seem indicated. I'd better go with you."

But at the Coffey house they got an unexpected reaction. They found all the Coffeys home and for the first time met the married daughter June and her husband Frank Best. Mendoza did the talking, as tactfully as possible, and whatever he had expected the Coffeys and Verne to say, it wasn't what he heard.

They were incredulous at first and then they got mad. Even Sam Coffey. Mrs. Coffey faced them like a brown avenging Valkyrie.

"You mean to say you got it in your heads my Verne murdered his own sister? *Verne?* I never heard anything so crazy in my life! I thought policemen are supposed to be halfway bright these days, but when you come saying *such* a thing——"

"My boy never done such a thing, crazy's right, all right—where d'you suppose he'd get a gun, anyways? How d'you suppose——"

Verne just stared, openmouthed. Obviously it came as a complete surprise to him. "You think *I*—what for 'd I want to hurt *Carol?*"

"Well, it seems to *me*," said June Best, her eyes flashing dangerously, "you can't be looking very hard for whoever *did* do it, when you can get such an idiotic, downright foolish idea—Verne! Why, he——"

"Now, Mrs. Coffey," said Mendoza, "we're not saying he did—we just want to be sure, you——"

"Sure!" she cried. "Well, I should most certainly say you're going to be sure, Lieutenant! Verne'll take your old lie-detector test any time you say— I never *heard* such nonsense, respectable people like—— And he'll tell you the truth like he's been taught, and your machine'll tell you he's told the truth! He'll go along with you right now and take your silly test. Verne——"

"Why, sure," said the boy, looking a little scared but more bewildered. "You think *I*—why, I never figured you'd—I never wanted to hurt Carol! Why'd I—— I take your test whenever you say——"

"You take him *now!*" stormed Mrs. Coffey. "We'll get this foolishness cleared up right away! Maybe you'd like *me* to take the test, see whether I killed my own daughter! Maybe you'd like *Sam* to take it! You——"

"Now, Mrs. Coffey——"

"You go 'long right now, give Verne the test——"

But a lie-detector test was a delicate sort of thing, and the victim had to prepare for it twenty-four hours in advance. They gave the Coffeys instructions—no stimulants, eight hours' rest, and so on. Verne would take the test Monday afternoon; they set it up with the lab.

Verne took the test. The lab men said he was a good subject. And they fiddled around with their graphs and figures, and they told Homicide something which put the Carol Coffey case into the realm of the impossible.

They said Verne Coffey was telling the absolute truth. He didn't know anything at all about how his sister came to be shot.

Carol Coffey had been shot, in her own home, while people were round about to watch all four sides of the house. Nobody had approached the house; no car had passed, and the only person inside the house with her at the time really didn't know anything about it.

On those facts Carol Coffey shouldn't be dead at all.

But she was.

And just where else were the Homicide boys to go looking?

And then everything died on them, in all the cases they were working. They didn't have much of anywhere else to look, and yesterday the high had reached a hundred and one at the Civic Center, and today it was going to reach a hundred and two, and the morning *Times* said no relief in sight.

And it was Tuesday, and a week ago Bert Dwyer had been alive, walking down a street thinking about the birthday present he was going to buy his wife, and now he was dead and cold and rotting in the ground, and they wanted the bastard who had fired that gun. They weren't finding him or any lead to him.

Palliser wanted to get him, too, but he'd been assigned to the Walsh case and he would also like to find out who had beaten and shot nineteen-year-old Jimmy Walsh. The best lead he had, of course, was the light-green Anglia.

At four-thirty on Tuesday afternoon he found it.

The D.M.V. had found one hundred and four 1963 and 1964 models of the Anglia De Luxe with plate numbers starting out HAH, registered in L.A. County. Sixteen of those were green. None was the right one. So then they found forty-seven Anglias registered in Orange County, and four of those were green, but none of those was the one either. So then they found thirty-one Anglias registered in Ventura County, and only two of those were light green, one registered to an owner in the town of Ventura and the other to an owner in Oxnard.

So on Tuesday afternoon Palliser drove up the coast highway, enjoying the brilliant sparkle of sunlight on the calm Pacific to his left, to check those out. He came to Oxnard first, of course, so he looked up the address and found it with a little difficulty. It wasn't a town address: it turned out to be an old ranch house on the outskirts of town, a handsome old house in the middle of a lot of landscaped land, with an impressive line of poplars behind it as a windbreak.

The Anglia De Luxe sat in the driveway. There was a three-car garage behind the house, and in it, in lone grandeur, sat a brand-new Mercedes-Benz sports car.

It was the right Anglia. It had ski carriers on its roof.

"*Police?*" said Mr. Richard Brock. "Well, what on earth——" He stared at Palliser's badge. "Well, anything I can do—— My God, it isn't Johnny, is it? My brother—not an accident?"

"No, sir, I just want to ask you a few questions. I'm from Los Angeles, not local."

"Oh," said Brock. He was a tall, good-looking man about thirty, dressed in very snappy sports clothes. Palliser wondered if this was the same green shirt Rosario del Valle had noticed. He was beginning to have the dispirited feeling that this hot lead—and God, the work the D.M.V. had done on it!—was going to peter out before his eyes. This man, this house, said Money. This man, holding up a gas station for forty bucks? Beating and shooting a kid?

"Well, what can I do for you? Sit down—did you say Sergeant? Can I offer you a drink?"

Palliser could have stood a drink. God, after the routine they'd done on this—— "No, thank you, sir. I'd like to ask you—a week ago last Friday, were you in L.A.? On Figueroa Street, at about nine in the morning? With two other men, in that Anglia De Luxe out there in the drive?"

"Why, yes, I was," said Brock. "Why on earth? We didn't get a ticket, or——"

"No, sir. You stopped at a Shell station, at a few minutes after nine. But not, evidently, to buy gas. Why?"

"Oh," said Brock. He looked still more bewildered. "I guess it was a Shell—I didn't notice. Yes?"

"Why did you stop there? What were you doing in L.A., and who was with you?"

"For God's sake," said Brock, "what is this? I don't—— Well, I suppose you've got a reason to ask, come all the way up here! Sure, it seems—— But anything you want to know. I was with Johnny and Bob, my brothers. We live here together, none of us married. Bob had been up north looking at a parcel of land we're thinking of buying. He has a thing about planes—he never flies—so he'd come down on the Owl and Johnny and I drove in to meet him, there was another business deal we had cooking with a man in L.A. So we met him at the Union Station when the train got in and we started uptown to check in at a hotel—we were staying over the weekend. What the *hell* this is all about——"

"The Shell station on Figueroa."

"For God's sake!" said Brock. "I needed a rest room. Sudden attack of diarrhea. I told Johnny, pull into the first one he came to. He did. I went in and used the rest room. Matter of fact, the damn thing kept up all day, it was damned annoying—don't know what started it. I was O.K. the next day. Now what's all this about, Sergeant?"

"Did you see any attendant there at all?"

"Don't recall that I did. I wasn't looking for one—I was in a hurry."

Palliser stared at the floor. He wondered why he'd ever thought of joining the force. Land deals. A Mercedes-Benz. Money. Man perfectly open and frank.

"Do you own a gun, Mr. Brock?"

"A—— Now what? Yes, I own a couple of guns. I own a rifle I use for deer hunting, and somewhere around here is a .32 automatic we keep in case of prowlers. What——"

Palliser sighed. The one nice hot lead they had, petering out to nothing.

All Rosario del Valle had given them was a lot of practice at the routine. The deadly routine.

All they had now, on the Walsh thing, was the gun. The gun—somewhere—with a broken trigger guard.

FIFTEEN

"But that sounds just impossible!" said Alison. "What possible connection could there be—— Don't you know anything more about this Leigh?"

"Let's hope we will. Nick found a fellow this morning who used to pal around with him a little. One time, says this fellow, something came up about Fort Worth, Texas, and Leigh mentioned that he'd been in jail there once. So we wired back to Fort Worth, but they'd never heard of him—under that name, anyway. And they don't keep records on vags, it could have been just that." It was nine o'clock on Wednesday night; the twins were asleep, blessedly. Three cats were spread out decoratively on the credenza, and El Señor was asleep on Mendoza's stomach. "We've sent his prints to Washington. If he ever accumulated a record anywhere, we'll hear about it sooner or later. But right now it all looks like a very peculiar setup indeed." His tone was absent.

Alison eyed him. "But you're brooding about something. Have you had an insp——"

"¿Por qué no? ¡Válgame Dios!" said Mendoza violently. "Yes, I am brooding over something. God." He lifted El Señor to the sectional beside him, sat up, and felt for cigarettes. El Señor complained bitterly about being moved and ostentatiously retreated to the farthest end of the sectional from Mendoza. "That morning," said Mendoza. "We had those sketches to get to the banks. I told Jimmy to make up lists, and what other way would he do it? He looked them up under their individual names, of course. Eleven branch banks, Security-First National. Eight branch banks, Bank of America. Four branch banks, Bank of California. And two Federal Savings, and a Coast Federal Savings. And what the hell else would I do? I cut up the list to roughly eight or nine apiece and handed them out at random. I thought at random. So it was Bert who got the one at

Seventh and Grand, the Security-First. Why didn't Higgins get it, or Galeano? Both bachelors."

Alison was silent and then said, "Destiny. Who knows? It's nobody's fault, Luis. It just happened."

"No, but what made me hand *that* list to Bert? I don't remember if he was nearest or what. I don't know, *querida*—it all seems so damned at random, that's all." Mendoza passed a hand over his eyes. "And either we're not being very bright these days or the luck's running dead against us, or both. Damn it, unless Washington can give us something on Leigh, where do we go from here?"

"Can't you do anything about tracing the gun—the one from the bank jobs, I mean?"

And just how? He—whoever—could have got it under the counter years ago, or two months ago, just anywhere. These damn scaremongers," said Mendoza, "talking about stricter laws on possession. Senseless. New York thought they were being smart with the Sullivan law, but anybody can still get a gun there any day, under the counter." He sounded savage; he felt savage. The whole machinery of routine had ground almost to a standstill on this. They were still looking at those men out of Records, the ones without alibis, and tracking down all their pals; but they'd nearly run out of them, and they hadn't found any more gunshot wounds or anything suspicious at all. Palliser's case looked very dead, too, and as for the Coffey thing—! And for one matter, this kind of fumbling delay, however hard they were working, didn't make them look so good to the public reading the headlines, NO CLUE YET FOUND. Mendoza swore and ground out his half-smoked cigarette.

"*Amante,*" said Alison, "you'll get him. You'll get them all."

"When? A year from Christmas?"

She came and sat beside him. "Suppose you stop bringing cases home with you and start remembering you're a husband."

"Mmh," said Mendoza. "Are you by any chance propositioning me—or complaining?"

"You figure it out."

"Well, it might take my mind off other things, true."

"What a compliment," said Alison. "I *am* flattered. Of course, you've been a husband for some time. Maybe it's starting to pall."

"Well, I wouldn't exactly say——"

"Well, what would you exactly say?"

"Well, what do you think?" said Mendoza, and reached for her.

On Tuesday they had set up a lie-detector test for the Blaine brothers. Foote was still in the hospital. The Blaines took the test on Wednesday, and on Thursday they got the results from the lab and all uttered some rude words about it.

Neither of the Blaines was lying. The artistic little tale about Joe Sebastian was gospel truth.

Among other things, it was annoying because lie-detector tests were not admissible evidence and they still couldn't charge Sebastian with attempted homicide.

The heat wave still held, and the weather forecast each morning still said no relief in sight. But at least Scarne was back, another man to help with the routine.

The routine had taken them just about as far as it could.

"So I'm thinking now," said Mendoza to Hackett that afternoon, "that I may just have rung a bell with the little idea that it's a pair of amateurs. Hell. If either of them was in Records we'd have turned him up by now, surely to God."

"I don't see that at all," said Hackett. "We know one of them at least is in the fifties. How many times does somebody that age suddenly go on the bent? On bank robberies yet, for God's sake! And no hesitation about using a gun. It could be a pair from somebody else's records. We've got no way of knowing until we get them." They hadn't, of course, any prints or much of anything else to ask Washington about. "And what in the name of God this Leigh is doing involved in *that*—it's wild! So all right, you said if it's amateurs maybe they knew he had a record—and we don't even know that—and got him to find the hot-money man. You said they might know about that possibility because of living down there, rubbing shoulders with pros. Then why for God's sake—when they've been so cute otherwise—let a bumbling old guy like Leigh in on it? Why not just go out looking for one themselves?"

"Which is a point," said Mendoza. "All this—it's like walking in quicksand. Slipping and sliding around. No landmarks. Nothing to get hold of. I hope to God Washington can——"

"You know how it goes," said Hackett. "We both know. Objective view, Luis. Remember all the times something's been tough going, not one single lead, but you go on worrying at it and all of a sudden it comes unstuck and there's X staring you in the face."

"Playing Pollyanna."

"No, but it does." Hackett readjusted his pillow. "In the long run we don't muff many of them, boy. And it's funny, too," he added thoughtfully, "lots of times when we do uncover X, he's so damned obvious you want to kick yourself for not seeing it before. There was that funny business about that Greek coin collection—hell, it was all such a tangle, not one thing to it made any sense, what with that ex-con and that idiotic French woman and the Greek and all. And then when we pulled the right string, why, it was all simple and obvious as—as broad daylight."

"So you advise us to sit it out patiently and wait for the right string to come along for pulling?"

"It'll come," said Hackett. He added seriously, "I don't think whatever arranges things will let Bert's killer get clean away, Luis."

Palliser was still getting teletypes. All those sheriffs and police chiefs so eager and willing to help out the L.A. boys with their holdup killing had gone out to check recently sold Hi-Standard .22 revolvers. They had among them (in that wide area) looked at a lot of guns, but none of them had so far seen one with a broken trigger guard.

Palliser was looking at guns too. In Los Angeles County, he was informed late Wednesday by the giant Sears central warehouse, six of those revolvers had been sold in the last four weeks. They had, of course, been sold through the catalogue, and each order had been duly accompanied by the voucher clipped from page 739 of the catalogue, filled out and signed. This voucher read:

"I certify to the best of my knowledge that —— who resides at —— and who desires to purchase a .22 caliber pistol or revolver from Sears, Roebuck and Co., is a citizen of the United States, over 21 years old and of sound mind; is not under indictment, nor a drug addict, nor a fugitive from justice, and has never been convicted of a crime of violence." Under this was an indicated line for "signature of officer of law" and for "official position or title" and "official address" and the date.

For which reason Palliser was more or less certain that none of the six people who had purchased one of those guns was the X who had beaten and shot Jimmy Walsh. But of course you had to do the routine on it.

All those vouchers were enclosed with the other information, names, and addresses. So on Thursday Palliser went out and about looking at guns himself. The new owners were wildly scattered all over the county; some of them weren't home, and he ran into one suspicious housewife who refused to let him see the gun. But by four o'clock he had managed to see four of them, and they were all quite intact.

Piggott had quite frankly given up on the Carol Coffey case; he said in his opinion the thing would never be solved and they might as well write it off. Maybe, he said, God had struck her dead from heaven; he couldn't figure out who else could have remained invisible. He had gone down to that Shell station on Figueroa to ask more questions all around. He said you never knew what might turn up.

Palliser, at four o'clock, was in Highland Park, having just seen his fourth gun. On the other two, he had his choice of La Crescenta or Arcadia, and he chose La Crescenta as the lesser evil. He got on the Pasadena freeway and drove back to Glendale, found La Crescenta Avenue, and started up the hill.

The house was on Altura Avenue, and it was a shabby sprawling old ranch-style in need of paint, with a wide front yard in need of watering. A man and a woman were standing at the front steps talking. Neither was young; the man was nudging fifty, the woman perhaps the same age. Palliser got out of the Rambler wearily—of course it was hotter up here, too—and went up the front walk.

"Mrs. Adler?" he asked.

They both stared at him. "Why, no," said the woman. "I'm Mrs. Page. Mrs. Jane Page."

"Oh," said Palliser. "But a Frederick Adler does live here?"

"Well, not now," said Mrs. Page. "Why?"

Palliser nearly said, "Oh, hell." He introduced himself, showed his badge. The man looked interested. "Sergeant, hah? Well, I'm Don Kimball, Detective second-grade, Glendale force." He held out his hand.

"Then you signed this voucher," said Palliser, and produced it.

Kimball peered at it and said sure. "What about it?"

"Well, we've got the hell of a job on our hands," said Palliser, "tracking down all these .22's sold the last couple of months. I needn't go into details, but I'd like to see this Adler's .22. He's moved, you say?"

"That's right," said the woman. "He decided to go home. He's only a boy really, Freddy. I mean, he's twenty-two, but he don't look it, and this was the first time he'd been away from home. He's a nice boy, but he was lonely, didn't make friends out here."

"Where," asked Palliser, "is his home?"

"Oh, Plainville, Kansas."

"Do you know his address there?" Of course she didn't. He looked at Kimball. "You hadn't any hesitation in signing that voucher for him?"

"Why, no, I didn't, Sergeant. See, I live right next door. I'd seen a good bit of Freddy when he roomed here. He was here nearly a year, wasn't he, Janie? I wouldn't say he's a big brain, he didn't finish high school—he was a box boy down at the Thriftimart on Glendale Avenue all the while he lived here—but he's a nice enough kid. I felt kind of sorry for him, the way he couldn't seem to make friends. Reason he wanted the gun, he said, he used to work late some nights, and a couple of times he'd been roughed up a little by some big kids hanging around the street corner where he got the bus. He said he figured if he just showed them the gun, they'd leave him alone. No, I thought he was O.K. to have it."

"When did he leave to go back to Kansas?"

They consulted. "It was a week ago last Monday," said Mrs. Page. "He seemed to get fed up with California—he said so—he didn't like the job too well, and then he was lonely. He left that morning, along about nine o'clock. I think he was going back on the bus."

"Well," said Palliser, "thanks very much, anyway. Nice to have met you," and he nodded at Kimball.

Routine, routine. Try gun number six this evening?

It was ten to six when he got back to Headquarters. He sent off a teletype to the chief of police of Plainville, Kansas, requesting co-operation. Would somebody please locate Frederick Adler and have a look at his Hi-Standard .22, see if it had a broken trigger guard? Thank you very much. He started out of the office, and Sergeant Lake beckoned to him. He was on the phone; he handed it over to Palliser.

"I got something!" said Piggott excitedly. "This you'll never believe, but I think we got a break at last! I found this woman—Mrs. Ruth Watts, Lebanon Street—and she saw a kid go into that station that morning just before nine. She even knows the kid's name—she——"

"How come she didn't say so before? There's been enough publicity about it."

"Yeah, but that's it. She was leaving on her vacation that morning—her boss let her take off Friday because these two girl friends she was going with don't work and they'd gone and got reservations over on Catalina for that night, without consulting her, see, so he let her go. She works at a restaurant over on Hill. So she was waiting for them to come and pick her up, about eight-thirty, when she remembers she's forgotten to get some of this special tea she likes to take with her——"

"Look, have you got a point to make?"

"I'm getting there," said Piggott. "So she figures she's got time to walk down to this little grocery on Figueroa that carries it, and she hurries off, and the grocery is a block down from that station and two blocks from where she lives, and she says as she came past the station she saw this boy just going into the garage. He's a neighborhood kid, she knows his name—

Alvin Cooper—and she never thought anything of it at the time, just thought maybe he knew the boy who worked there."

"Be damned," said Palliser. It could be a lead. After the letdown over the Anglia and Richard Brock. He'd worked it out that the Brocks must have stopped at the station after the holdup, if only just after. Jimmy Walsh had been beaten and shot at the rear of the garage, and his body had been partly concealed by a Ford sedan the mechanic was working on. The public rest rooms opened off the front of the garage, just inside the door. Brock could easily, in the dimness after bright sunlight, never have noticed the body.

"And she just got back to her place in time to meet the girl friends— what am I saying? They're all well into the forties—and she says you know how it is on vacation, she never looked at a paper, didn't hear about Jimmy getting shot until she got back yesterday, and she was figuring maybe she ought to tell us, except that a nice boy like Alvin wouldn't do anything like——" Piggott's silence was eloquent.

"She's definitely sure it was this boy?"

"Says so."

"Well, so where do we find him? He go to school?"

"Widney High on Twenty-first, but——"

"But he wouldn't be there now—damn, I'm too tired to think straight." Palliser yawned. "Got an address for him?"

"St. Paul Court, other side of the Harbor Freeway." Piggott added the address.

Palliser said, "I'll meet you there in twenty minutes." This could be a hot lead.

It was an unpretentious neighborhood of old houses. Next to it was another old house with an enormous sign in front, *Chinese Herb Doctor, Len Fen Yu, Best Remedies.*

The Cooper family was having dinner. There were, it seemed, a number of Coopers—parents, six kids, one set of grandparents, and an uncle. They were all seemingly very surprised and bewildered to be invaded by police officers. "*Alvin?*" exclaimed Mrs. Cooper. "Has Alvin *done* something? Why, he'd never——"

"We'd just like to talk to him," said Palliser. "Please." But all the Coopers were so concerned that they followed Alvin en masse from the dining room to the living room.

"I never done anything, sir," said Alvin. "Why'd you think I'd done something?"

Palliser looked at him. Certainly anybody who knew Alvin Cooper should recognize him even at a glance. Alvin was about five feet eight, perhaps eighteen, and too fat. He had a round moonface, a slight case of acne, and he was a good forty pounds overweight. Glandular, thought Palliser; somebody should have taken Alvin to a doctor long ago, but that wasn't any of his business.

He said, "We have somebody who says you were going into that Shell station garage—you know the one, where Jimmy Walsh was shot—between eight forty-five and nine o'clock that morning. How about it, Alvin?" He and Piggott stared at Alvin hard: the first moment of surprise sometimes revealed something.

"*Me?*" said Alvin. His voice shot up to a squeak. "Me, in that—you mean, that same *day?* Why, I never was there—I never went into that place in my life! I didn't know the Walsh kid. That's a lie—who said I was there?"

"Where were you at that time that day?"

"Gee, I don't remember what day——"

"Two weeks ago tomorrow." It seemed, thought Palliser, like two years. God, and Carol Coffey shot that same afternoon (who the hell *had* done that and how the hell had it been done?) and then the next Tuesday, Bert. God. Dead ends, nothing but dead ends. But here, maybe another lead.

"Oh," said Alvin. "Oh." He looked at his mother; there was sudden great relief in the expressions of all the Coopers. "Oh, then you just got the wrong guy, 's all. It must be, maybe, somebody looks like me? Because if that was the day, mister, I wasn't here. Father Whitley or anybody else'll say."

"That was the day you left," said his mother. "Friday. Sure. See, mister, the father—the church, it sponsors these weekend camp trips for city kids. Just up in the Angeles forest, you know—Friday to Sunday. Alvin went that weekend. The father picked up all the kids about maybe seven o'clock that morning, in his jeep. He'd say—it's St. Luke's over on——"

"Musta been somebody just looks like ole fatty Alvin," piped up one of the younger kids. Alvin flushed darkly.

Palliser nearly said, "Oh, hell," again. He looked at Piggott, who just shut his eyes. Even Piggott, reflected Palliser, probably wouldn't feel like trying to grill a respectable Catholic priest.

They said all the indicated things and bowed out. "Well, it *looked*——" said Piggott.

"Sure," said Palliser. "Hell. So it *was* somebody who looks like Alvin?

Possibly the Watts woman needs glasses and won't wear them? So, maybe somebody too fat?"

"*I* don't know," said Piggott gloomily. "I'm fresh out of ideas. Seems like every time we turn up a new lead on one of these things, it peters out right away."

"Yes," said Palliser. "Oh, yes, indeed." He sighed.

At eleven o'clock on Friday morning the inevitable happened. Mendoza had foreseen it, but there was an old saying about omelets and eggs.

An excited bank guard at the Security-First branch at Sixth and Spring called in incoherently to say he had the bank robber. He'd spotted him from the artist's sketch and collared him, and he was now all safely tied up in the president's office and they could come and collect him.

Mendoza, Higgins, Galeano, and Landers, and two squad cars, hared over to the bank, to confront an incoherent red-faced man under the grim surveillance of a dozen tellers, vice-presidents, and assorted executives.

"An *outrage*—I have never experienced such—— Just what you think you are doing—— And I assure you, I shall remove *all* my business affairs from this bank at once—— I have *never* considered," spluttered the portly man amateurishly bound to the desk chair with hastily commandeered neckties and belts, "I have *never* considered doing business with the Bank of America—America indeed, it was the Bank of Italy and that Democratic scoundrel Giannini—but I *assure* you, after this *outrageous*—— I am Henry Reinholt Snyder, Junior, and I demand——"

He was, of course, Henry Reinholt Snyder, Junior. As ample evidence in his billfold confirmed. Unfortunately he bore a superficial resemblance to the sketch.

Mendoza apologized profusely; the bank personnel apologized. Mr. Snyder was not appeased.

It all took up some time, and it was another dead end.

"But the sketches may pay off in the end," said Mendoza. "Sometime. You never know. Art said, wait for it. For—whatever arranges things—to show us the right string to pull."

He wished he could believe it would show up.

It was being a tough one.

But they'd never stop hunting and looking. Not when X had got one of their own.

SIXTEEN

There had been a suicide at a hotel on Grand yesterday. On Thursday some people named Brent had reported their eighteen-year-old daughter missing, and on Friday she'd turned up dead of an overdose of heroin at another hotel, so there was that to go into. The situation at Headquarters Homicide was very seldom static.

When Mendoza came in on Saturday morning, Galeano was waiting for him. "How do you like Lester Cullinane for the bank jobs?" he asked flatly. "I like him fine, since about seven o'clock last night."

"¿Por qué?"

"I didn't like him the first time we had him in. And that time he was fairly cool. But since this Warbeck character tells us for pretty sure Bert winged one of them, and we've been taking a look at all the pairs as well as the single possibles, I wanted to talk to Cullinane again. I did, on Wednesday. And that time he was very damn nervous. And I also find out just yesterday that a guy he went around with some, drinking and womanizing, hasn't been seen around at all for the last week or ten days. And so I figure he could be the one with the slug in him, because he lived at the same place as Cullinane, and it could be Cullinane's got him tucked away at a cheap hotel some place, trying to nurse him. At their own place somebody might have got curious."

"Now you don't tell me," said Mendoza. "That could be, all right."

"And it could also be," said Galeano grimly, "that some maid is going to get a little shock finding the pal's body—his name is Knuth, by the way, Pete Knuth—because now Cullinane has blown town. Apparently. Last night, I find when I went to see him, he paid off the landlady and, pffft."

"You *don't* say," said Mendoza. "That's very interesting, Nick." All the possible suspects had been told not to leave town, of course.

"He left some stuff from his room, the landlady says, asked her to keep it for him. I want to go through it and ask her some questions, but she raised a little fuss and said I'd have to get a warrant." Galeano's broad dark face broke into a humorless smile. "I asked for it overnight. Here it is. Want to come?"

Mendoza held open the door and they went out. "It's suggestive, you know," said Galeano. "Very suggestive. And just the way you said, too— you notice we haven't had a bank knocked over since Bert got it. X wouldn't have known who he was, even when Bert hauled out a gun—it would have been a little shock to find out they'd shot a cop. They'd know how we feel about that."

"If it was Cullinane and Knuth," said Mendoza, "they can't run fast enough or far enough to get away clear. But how the hell would that Leigh tie up to them? What's the address?"

It was a very old and very large sagging frame building, looking almost derelict, on a queer little old narrow street not far from the old Plaza. This was the very oldest part of L.A. down here, and this place might, on looks, almost have dated from the founding date of 1781, except that it wasn't Spanish architecture.

The woman who opened the door to them told them about the building. "Oh," she said, seeing Galeano, "you're back. You got that warrant?"

"I've got it, Mrs. Buckley."

"Well, come on in, then. It's just I like things to be legal—no offense meant." She was about fifty, a strapping, tall woman with a lot of grayish hair, which had once been blond, in a large careless bun on the nape of her neck. She was wearing a crumpled cotton dress and dirty rubber thong sandals on bare feet. "Who's this one?"

"Lieutenant Mendoza, Mrs. Buckley."

"Hum," she said. "Mexican and Eytalian. Force sure is broad-minded these days. No offense. You interested in my place?" Mendoza was looking around the surprisingly large room—or lobby?—they had come into. "It's a real interesting old place. I was lucky to get hold of it, picked it up for a song, fifteen years back. D'you know it's over a hunnerd years old? Believe it or not, this was one o' the first hotels built here—by Americans, I mean— after we got California from Mexico. It was for the old stagecoaches, you know. Built in eighteen fifty-eight. Ain't that something? There's thirty rooms here, besides this one." There wasn't much furniture in the room; a large old desk in one corner evidently served as a counter for registering guests. Oblong strips on two walls showed bare plaster where some built-in had been knocked out. "D'you know it's even got a basement?—kind of a scary place. I guess they used to keep the liquor there—it was a saloon, too, you know—this room and that one there. I had the bar knocked out—that's where it was."

"Very interesting," said Mendoza. "Now, about Mr. Cullinane and Mr. Knuth——"

She answered questions, incurious. In fact, here was another rooming-house keeper who seemed singularly lacking in curiosity. Cullinane had lived here about two years, she said, and Knuth only about a year; she guessed they'd made friends because their rooms were side by side. She didn't know what kind of jobs either of them had or if they had jobs. Knuth had gone—she thought and made it a week ago last Wednesday. (Mendoza glanced at Galeano.) "Did he give you any reason for leaving? You saw him, I suppose, when he——"

"Well, no, I didn't," she said. "It was Mr. Cullinane told me he'd gone. He had to go home, see a sick mother or something. Mr. Cullinane asked me what he—Mr. Knuth, I mean—owed me, and I told him, and he said Mr. Knuth'd asked him to pay me, and he did. You see, he left in a hurry."

"So he seems to have," said Mendoza. "When was the last time you saw Mr. Knuth?"

"Well, that did make it seem a little funny," said the woman. "Because that was when him and Mr. Cullinane was having a fight. Going at each other hammer and tongs when I knocked on the door. That was the Tuesday night. As a matter of fact, I'd come up to ask him for the rent—he was nearly a week behind."

"This was in Mr. Knuth's room?"

"Well, sure. You could hear 'em alla way down the hall. No, not really fighting, just cussing each other, you know. It was over some girl, I think —they kept talking about some Helen, Mr. Cullinane saying what he'd do to Mr. Knuth, he didn't keep away from her."

Mendoza raised his eyebrows at Galeano. This was off the track. "Did you see Mr. Knuth? Did he look all right?"

"All right? Whaddaya mean, all right? Sure he was all right, except he was mad and kind of red in the face. They'd been arguing, see? Mr. Cullinane looked awful mad, too, but they shut up when I come in, and I—— What you asking all this for, anyways? I asked about the rent and he said tomorrow for sure. He'd allus paid up before, so I said O.K. So then the next day about one o'clock Mr. Cullinane come down and I was just takin' in the mail, and it was then he said Mr. Knuth had left, and paid me. So I figured they musta made up their argument."

"Oh." Mendoza was a little puzzled. Another something that had looked interesting and might still look a little interesting. "Look, Mrs. Buckley. I'll be frank with you. We think Mr. Knuth might have had a gunshot wound on him somewhere. Did you see him, oh, favoring one arm, or—did he look pale, or anything like that?"

She stared at him, brushing back wisps of straggly hair. "A gunshot—— Why, for the lord's sake, why ever should you think such a thing? Quiet sort he was, come home high once in a while, but—— Well, of *course* he never had no such thing! You mean, when I saw him then, a week ago Tuesday?" She laughed, shrill and high. "It was a hot night, mister. He'd taken his shirt off, he come to the door in nothin' but his skin and a pair o' shorts. Not that he had such a big chest to show off—he looked kinda weedy, especially next to Mr. Cullinane. If he'd had a bullet hole in him I'd've seen, and he didn't. Only, like I say, as I went back down the hall I hear 'em goin' at it again, swearin' at each other something fierce, so I did think it was just a little funny about Mr. Cullinane, when he come next day and paid up Mr. Knuth's rent. But men," she added philosophically, "do all sorts o' funny things. I don't pay no mind. I run this place myself since Buckley died, got three-four strong Mex girls do the cleaning, and ever' one o' my roomers knows I don't stand no funny business, chippies brought in or like that. Otherwise I don't pay much attention to 'em. Not such a fancy place maybe, but there's gotta be cheap, nice, clean rooms for men like my roomers, don't have a lotta money."

"Yes," said Mendoza. Galeano had stopped smiling.

"He did go off in an awful hurry—Mr. Knuth," she said. "Somebody sick, I think Mr. Cullinane said. Left everything in his room, guess he just went off with what he had on. I went up there the next day, see if it needed cleaning bad, and there was Mr. Cullinane packin' up all Mr. Knuth's clothes. Mr. Cullinane said he'd asked him—Mr. Cullinane, I mean—to do that and send them on. Even left his transistor radio. No, I dunno where he went. Mr. Cullinane didn't say."

"Oh," said Galeano suddenly. He looked at Mendoza. "Are you thinking what I'm thinking?" He looked incredulous.

"Mrs. Buckley," said Mendoza, "you told Detective Galeano that when Mr. Cullinane left last night he left some of his things with you? What are they and where are they?"

Again she stared. "Why, I don't know—odds and ends. When he come, he had this old-fashioned steamer trunk, he asked could he put it in the basement, and it's been there ever since. He just said he was leaving a couple things. I s'pose whatever he didn't want to take with him he put down there. What's a little space down in the basement to me? I don't use it for nothing, don't keep nothing down there myself— No, I didn't see him go down there before he left, but—"

"And I don't suppose," said Mendoza, "this place is centrally heated? No furnace in the basement?"

"Well, no. I got a couple gas heaters put in——"

Galeano was looking faintly horrified.

"Mrs. Buckley," said Mendoza gently, "I wonder if we could see your basement?"

"Why, what *in* the world——"

"We do have a search warrant, you know."

"Well, for the lord's sake! You're about the queerest pair of cops I ever met! Sure you can see the basement." She led them through old, dark, musty-smelling passages (the place must be ridden with termites, thought Mendoza, and he only hoped it wouldn't fall down while they were in it) to an enormous dark kitchen which still had its original cavernous hearth on one wall. She pointed out a narrow closed door. "It's prob'ly locked, but the key's in it."

The lock, interestingly, had recently been oiled. They went down breakneck rotting steps to the great dark cave of the basement. Mrs. Buckley had rummaged and found a fading flashlight.

He was there, of course—Pete Knuth, not a very big man, who fitted quite neatly into the old steamer trunk. There wasn't, as far as they could tell, any bullet wound in him; it looked as if he'd been bludgeoned to death. But of course it was damned hot weather and he'd been dead about ten days.

"For God's *sake!*" said Galeano. They didn't say much; they got out of there in a hurry and called up reinforcements.

Mrs. Buckley was openly fascinated. A murder in her house—reporters flocking around—envisioning headlines and personal interviews, she beamed steadily.

"So now we know why Mr. Cullinane was nervous the second time you picked him up," said Mendoza.

"And also why he has run. I will be damned."

"So, some more routine." Mendoza sighed. "Senseless little argument over a girl—probably some cheap chippy at that—but it makes a little work for us. Get flyers out on Cullinane. Find out who Helen is. And so forth. Why the hell do you have to be such a smart detective, Nick? Probably nobody's going to miss this fellow any, he could have quietly rotted away here until Judgment Day. Whereas now we've just made more work for ourselves by finding him. Oh, I know, I know—just as well to get hold of Cullinane and stash him away before he loses his temper with somebody else."

Dr. Bainbridge arrived, looked at the corpse, and asked acidly why they couldn't just once find him a nice whole clean one, who'd died quietly in bed and been found ten minutes later. "In this *weather*," he said testily. "One like this."

They set up the routine on it. They got the Prints boys going over both rooms, the steamer trunk, and so on. They got up a flyer on Cullinane, to be copied and sent out in all directions, at once. They got a formal statement from Mrs. Buckley. They issued a formal statement to the press boys. They notified the Feds, who might have a new vacancy on their Ten Most Wanted list: Cullinane was a prime candidate.

"With everything else we've got to worry about," said Palliser disgustedly, coming in about two o'clock to hear about their trunk murder. "Any teletypes for me?" There weren't. "Hell," he said. "I'm getting nowhere fast on this Walsh thing." He stared glumly at Galeano. "So you're the smart boy around here, making deductions. Maybe we ought to turn you loose on the Carol Coffey thing. Nearly everybody else has had a whirl at it. Maybe——"

But, as it happened, they weren't destined to have the Carol Coffey thing on their hands much longer.

At a quarter to three that Friday afternoon, just two weeks nearly to the hour since pretty, respectable, ambitious Carol Coffey had been shot to death in her own living room, Sergeant Lake put his head in at the door of Mendoza's office and said, "Somebody to see you. I think maybe could be something important. On Coffey."

"Oh?" Mendoza put down the report he was reading. "O.K."

Two people came slowly into the office. He stood up. The woman was black—no question of that. She was a small woman, deep brown, about forty. She had been crying and still clutched a crumpled handkerchief in one hand. She was very neatly dressed in a crisply starched blue cotton dress, and a little blue straw hat with flowers on it, and Cuban-heeled black oxfords. Mendoza thought, her best clothes.

The boy had been crying too. She was holding him by the hand. He was a boy about twelve, and he was deep brown too. He was a nice-looking boy, and he was also very obviously dressed in his best clothes, a blue wool suit, very neat, with a white shirt and a tie.

They came in drearily and looked at Mendoza.

"Mrs. Catesby," said Sergeant Lake.

"Mrs. Catesby?" said Mendoza. "You wanted to see me? Won't you sit down?" He smiled at the boy.

"Yes, sir, thank you, sir." Her voice was still a little thick from weeping. "This is my boy Norman, sir. I didn't catch your name, I'm sorry."

"Lieutenant Mendoza."

"Yes, sir. I——" She looked at him imploringly. "I—it's about this terrible thing that happened to Miss Coffey, sir. I—we got to tell you. I've always been a law-abiding person. I was brought up that way, you've got to be honest. We had to come, I said that—as soon as I *knew*—what had happened. But I want to say, sir, it's part my fault—it's not all Norman's blame, sir. Because I ought to have thought, about how boys are about guns. They can't help it, I guess—something built into them." She stopped, her eyes filled, and she gave a deep dry sob. "I'm sorry, I'll try—tell it better."

"Please, Mom," muttered the boy, "I could——"

"I better tell it, Norman. I guess they'll want to—ask you questions and all, but——" She lifted sorrowful dark eyes to Mendoza. "You see, sir, I—I lost my husband last May. Joe worked for the city, he drove a truck and so on like that for the Parks Department, you know, keeping all the parks nice all over town. And he g-got killed last May, when his brakes went out on the freeway. So Norman and I, we was left alone, and it's been hard——" She swallowed convulsively; her hands clasped each other tightly on the cheap plastic bag in her lap. "I'm sorry, I don't mean go into that, it's our own trouble. Well, you see, sir, people were nice and there's a little pension but not much, and I've got to work. And Norman's twelve, old enough I can leave him days. I graduated from high school, but it's hard to get a job like clerking in a store, and I've got a domestic job for a lady in Pasadena, I take the bus. I don't want take up your time, sir, but I got to explain how—how it come about."

"Yes. That's all right, Mrs. Catesby. Take your time."

She took a deep breath. "We live on Ceres Street, sir. We were paying on the house before Joe—and I'm trying keep up, finally get to own it. It's a nice block there, lots of nice quiet neighbors, but I guess I don't have to tell you, sir, there's streets and people around there that aren't so good. I never worried about prowlers and such when Joe was—— But after, last July, we had a couple like that, and a man tried to break in one night. You know, it gets around, about a place where there isn't—isn't a man." Her hands clutched tighter. "There's some folk down there, and coming from further off, too—like these drug addicts—they'd do anything. And

I—and I—got a little nervous about that—I mean, I know your police are awful good, they come quick as could be when I called that time, and they were nice and polite—but I figured maybe best I'd have a—a—a gun in the house, ready." She stuck again.

"I never *meant*——" gulped the boy.

"Yes, Mrs. Catesby. That was very natural," said Mendoza. "You got a gun?"

"I don't—I didn't know anything about guns. I asked Mr. Clay. He lives next door. I told him—I asked—— And he said he thought it was a good idea, a woman alone and just Norman—— He went with me—to this Leiter's pawnshop—it's on Main Street. Mr. Clay has a grocery store down our way, and he always keeps a gun in case of holdups, you know? So he knows something about them. And I found out all about the regulations," said Mrs. Catesby anxiously. "They said I didn't need a permit for it unless I was going to be carrying it around, but I thought how sometimes the lady I work for has late parties, and I'm coming home after dark, and maybe sometimes I'd want to—— So I got a permit. I've got it right here. Right in this building, downstairs, they gave it to me—there wasn't any trouble about it." She bowed her head. "I should have *thought*—how boys are about guns. Just something in them."

"I never *meant*——" said the boy. He began to cry.

"I know you didn't, honey, but we got to tell the truth. No matter what they do to you for it. He never *meant*—but I should have known——"

The boy raised anguished wet eyes to Mendoza. "I—I never saw a gun close up before, and I thought how it'd be to really fire it off, how it'd sound and all—— Mom always said, don't meddle with it, it was always in the drawer of the table in the hall, but I kept wondering how it'd——"

"I knew something was wrong," said the woman pitifully. "With Norman. He was acting funny, picking at his food like—and I thought, maybe something at school. But when he stayed out so late, scare me half to death—he's always good about coming home on time—and I could see he was worrying at something, and I finally got it out of him and I knew we had to come tell you the truth whatever you do to him for it, and please, sir, he never *meant* anything bad, and oh, dear Lord, those poor people—that nice young girl—we never even *knew* the Coffeys, next street over, but——" Suddenly Mrs. Catesby began to cry.

The boy burst out, "I never meant to *aim* at nothing! I just kept wondering how it *felt*, fire off a gun, and it was in the table drawer and Mom was gone all day, and I was with her when she bought it and Mr. Clay and Mr. Leiter showed her all about loading it and all, and there was a box of extra cartridges—— And I thought—I thought I could just shoot it off once and see how it felt and put another cartridge back in so Mom'd never know, and I—and I—and I—*I never meant shoot anybody!* I didn't *aim* at nothing but a—but a—but a ole tin can I put on top of our back fence! And I didn't hit it—but—but—it said in the paper, the same kind o' gun—I heard Mr. Leiter say what ours was—and—and——"

"The Coffey place," said Mrs. Catesby with difficulty. "It—their property—it's right back of ours, on the next street. Please, sir, Norman never *meant*—— But we knew we had to——"

Mendoza said softly, "*¡Pares o nones!*" And who or what decided the throw of the dice? A one-in-a-million chance. Young Norman, curious to know how it felt to fire a gun. Firing a gun, at a tin can on a fence.

Sam Coffey taking off the screens to repaint the frames. Just then.

Carol Coffey, who got A's in English and wanted to be a teacher, dusting the living room. Standing in that doorway, facing it and the rear bedroom window—just the few moments when her mother was in the side yard . . .

The moment young Norman fired the gun. A nice well-brought-up boy, who never meant to hurt anybody.

The millionth chance. The wild bullet, wide of the innocent target, going across the narrow back yard there, into the open bedroom window, into Carol's heart.

At random. Death was so random.

You could ask, Why? That list of banks—why Bert Dwyer? And Carol. Ambitious Carol, a nice girl, with her A's in English. Who would probably have been a good teacher.

You could ask. You could wonder. And also about the bank guard and the teller.

Besides Bert.

Death was wanton. There was no sense at all to where or when or how death came.

"I—I brought the gun," said Mrs. Catesby falteringly. "I know there's tests you make and all." She reached into her purse and laid the gun on Mendoza's desk. It was of course, a Colt Official Police .22. "Please, sir, I know Norman's got to be—to be—punished. But when he never *meant*—when it was really a kind of *accident*—please, sir——"

Mendoza stared at the gun. There really seemed to be, he thought, no sensible order to life. To life or death. As a man with a very strong sense of order himself, it confused him. He felt angry about it. It was all wrong that someone like Bert Dwyer, someone like Carol Coffey, should die for such trivial reasons. In such trivial circumstances. Because they had been at a certain place at a certain time.

Death was so very damned at random.

It would be nice to be able to believe that—whatever arranged things—had some valid reasons.

SEVENTEEN

"Oh, my God," said Alison, looking sick. "The answer as simple as that. As—as appalling as that. Just random chance. That poor woman—and the Coffeys. What will happen to the boy, Luis?"

Mendoza shrugged. He was drinking black coffee and staring absently at Alison's own portrait of El Señor, sitting beside a witch crystal, which hung above the credenza. The house was very still; apparently the twins were asleep. "What can we do? The boy's only twelve, and there was no intention. It was an accident, pure and simple. And don't make with the psychological double talk and tell me there's no such thing. Accidents happen all the time—this was just one more. It's a little as if Carol Coffey had been knocked down by a bus as she crossed the street . . . Norman. Poor Norman. There'll be a hearing in juvenile court, thrash out the whole sad story, and very probably the judge will remand him in his mother's custody, put him on probation until he's eighteen, something like that. Which won't make the Coffeys feel any less bitter."

"No. What an awful thing. It makes you wonder—why was she standing there, just that second? And——" Alison broke off and uttered a little scream as Sheba landed on her shoulder from behind her chair. "Don't *do* that, you little monster!" Sheba unconcernedly walked down her to her lap and settled down to manicure her claws.

"Ifs," said Mendoza. "No profit, *chica. ¿Para qué?* And what is the answer to the answer? If Norman was a wild kid, had been in trouble before, was a potential troublemaker, would it make any more sense? If Mrs. Catesby didn't live in a district like that, where she had cause to want a gun handy—— If the normal twelve-year-old boy wasn't fascinated by a real-life gun—— What's the profit in saying if? It's just a senseless, meaningless accident that's brought tragedy to two families. It's no good asking why."

"I don't," said Alison, "*like* the idea of destiny. I don't like to feel that every last little thing that's ever happened to me or is going to happen is all—all blueprinted out already, and nothing I can do about it at all. It's not fair."

Mendoza laughed. "What is fair about life, anyway? No rules say anything's got to be fair. You like the idea any better that things happen because you were born under a certain star? What *I* don't like is the—the untidiness of it all." He sounded angry. "All I can say is, if there is something making all these arrangements, it's being done in a very damned disorderly way."

Alison laughed and sobered. "Nothing. Only you sounded as if you were complaining about a careless maid sweeping dust under the rug."

Mendoza got up and wandered around the room, hands in pockets. "And it is rather like that. Careless planning. When there must be hundreds of, for instance, senile old people nobody would miss—idiot children —psychopaths——"

"High-pressure door-to-door salesmen," said Alison.

"And unrealistic judges, and all those silly people who want to set up a Police Board of civilians to watch over us——"

"Art critics," said Alison dreamily.

"Instead of Bert. And Carol Coffey. Nobody can know the answer . . . That poor damned woman. Yes, of course we had to hold the boy. He's at Juvenile Hall, which is ridiculous because it's crowded as hell and he wouldn't run, but technicalities—— This fine new jail they build us, and do you know what it cost? Seventeen million bucks. And the nice new women's jail over in east L.A., at ten million. But do they consider a new Juvenile Hall? *Porvida*, no, have to think of the taxpayers' money! So the kids are sleeping on mattresses in the halls. I wonder why the Fire Department hasn't got after the council . . . Yes, I saw the Coffeys."

"I suppose I don't have to ask how they felt. I know how I'd feel."

"Why did this have to happen to us? Yes. But why does anything have to happen to anybody? Why to Bert? Why to Mary Dwyer? I don't like the only answer either."

"I ought to go to see her," said Alison somberly. There was a silence, and she added with an effort at lightness, "At least a few people are—getting something out of all this. You said that Mrs. Buckley was thrilled at the idea of a murder in her house. What another senseless thing, but louts like that—— And Mr. Warbeck stopped by today to ask if you'd found the man yet. He was quite proud of himself, giving important evidence to the police."

Mendoza smiled. "Important all right, but it doesn't seem to be taking us anywhere, damn it. And Art could be right, that they're in somebody else's records and not ours. Which is a cheerful thought."

"I still can't see how on earth that Leigh comes into it."

"You are not alone, my love," said Mendoza sardonically. "Of course, if we could count out all the vague talk about Leigh wanting to find a hot-money man and so on, we could explain him away very easily. The X who carries the gun doesn't seem hesitant about using it. So we could say either that Leigh was just somebody who got into an argument with him at a bar somewhere, or we could say that Leigh had——" He stopped with his mouth open. "Oh," he said. He started on and tripped over El Señor who had suddenly decided to abandon the green chair and make a beeline for Alison's lap. "Hell," said Mendoza, stumbling against the sectional and feeling his thigh. "That cat——"

"Inspiration has just visited you, *amador*? No, Señor, now Sheba got here first. There isn't room for both of you——"

"Well, I was going to say, maybe Leigh stumbled on the fact that X was the bank robber—or one of them—and was blackmailing him. And then it just suddenly occurred to me that we've blithely passed up one way of maybe getting some more information about Leigh. That money he had sent to him every week . . ." Mendoza went out to the hall, to the telephone table. He looked up the number and dialed.

"Hey?" said an indistinct voice.

"Mr. Frick?"

"Yep."

"This is Lieutenant Mendoza. I was asking you some questions the other day about Walter Leigh."

"Oh, yeah."

"Well, you said that every Monday he got some cash through the mail, but you'd never noticed a return address or the postmark. Have you noticed since?"

"How d'you mean, have I——"

"Well, let's see, he was killed on a Saturday night. If the cash was mailed locally, it'd have to be mailed on Saturday some time to be delivered on Monday, and if it was mailed from outside the county, it'd have to be mailed on Friday at least, and from anywhere farther away, probably on Thursday. So at least one more envelope had to reach your house that next Monday, before whoever sent it knew he was dead. What did——"

"Nope," said Frick. "Didn't ever another one come after he was killed . . . Sure I'm sure. I thought o' that myself, and I watched out for the mailman and looked all through the mail, that Monday after. Wasn't nothing there for Leigh."

"I see. Thanks very much," said Mendoza. He put the phone down slowly. That might say several things. Frick dishonest, holding onto the nice anonymous cash? He didn't think so; the man hadn't impressed him that way. If the cash sender was local, that said one very funny thing: it said that the cash sender knew Leigh was going to be killed on Saturday night, so he or she hadn't troubled to mail the usual cash on Saturday. Did it, could it say that the cash sender was his killer *and* one of the bank robbers? That sounded utterly ridiculous. Didn't it say that the cash sender had to be local or at the very least somewhere in southern California, because Leigh's death wouldn't have been reported in any other papers and the cash sender wouldn't have known he was dead? But that didn't matter, because the cash hadn't been mailed to reach Leigh on Monday. The cash sender knew he wouldn't be needing it by then.

Which in turn said, thought Mendoza (because the cash would have had to be mailed locally by Saturday afternoon, for Monday delivery), that whether the cash sender had been his killer or had just learned about it from the killer—Leigh's murder had been premeditated.

One more wild and impossible element—now whoever had, for a long time, been generously sending Leigh money suddenly turned out to be involved in his death. Why?

There didn't seem to be any answers to anything anywhere.

"Teletypes!" said Palliser with a groan. "I've started dreaming about them." He looked at the sheaf waiting on his desk and groaned again.

"I looked through this latest batch," said Mendoza. "All negative. You're getting a lot of nice co-operation from all these upright officers of the law. I hope you're thanking them properly."

"My mother always impressed on me never to forget please and thank you," said Palliser. "Right now I don't feel so damn much like adding the thank you to Chief Roland Cunningham of Plainville, Kansas."

"What's he done to you?"

"Handed me another deadly piece of routine to do. I told you about this Frederick Adler? The box boy at the Thriftimart? Who bought one of these Hi-Standard revolvers only about a month ago? And then decided to go back home to Kansas?"

"Yes. What about him?"

"Well, it means damn all, you know. I don't see whoever killed Jimmy Walsh, for no reason at all probably, after holding up that station, as being anybody who applies all legal to carry a gun. This Kimball on the Glendale force, who signed that voucher for Adler, told him he'd need a permit to carry the gun and helped him get one. Then all of a sudden, couple of weeks later, Adler decides he's fed up with California and heads home for Kansas. And I doubt very much that he's our boy, but he did have one of those new models, so I have to check it out. So I ask Chief Cunningham back in Plainville to find Adler and take a look at his gun." Palliser sighed. "And what do I get back? Yesterday morning? A nice tele-type from Chief Cunningham saying he's found Adler, who's back home with his parents at such-and-such an address, and asked him about the gun, and Adler hasn't got it any more."

"How frustrating," said Mendoza. "What did he do with it?"

"He tells the chief he figured since he was coming home he'd have no further use for a gun, and he sold it to a fellow he knew, the day he left. A fellow named Max King, who used to work at the same Thriftimart."

"So now you're chasing Max King, all in the sacred name of routine. Any luck yet?"

"No, and what's so damn frustrating about it, of course, is that when I do eventually find him, he'll haul out the gun all innocent and it'll have its trigger guard just as intact as it was when the factory shipped it out."

Higgins came in and said, "Morning. You got any suggestion for action?"

"There's a little more routine on our trunk murder," said Mendoza. "Somebody from the F.B.I. is coming over to copy down Cullinane's record and get extra mug shots of him."

Higgins sat down at his desk here in the sergeants' office and drummed on its top restlessly. "Haven't we *anywhere* else to——" And then suddenly he got up again and looked beyond Mendoza and Palliser, who turned around.

Mary Dwyer had come in and hesitated just inside the door. She gave them all a faint smile. "I just—I wanted to come and thank you all, for all your letters and so on. You've all been so good and helpful."

"Won't you sit down, Mrs. Dwyer?" Mendoza laid a hand on the nearest chair, but she shook her head.

"I won't stay. I just wanted to stop and say thank you." She was a very pretty woman indeed, and she must, Mendoza thought, have been some-what younger than Bert—in which he erred, but then he'd been married awhile and had maybe lost a little of his old sure touch with females. She wasn't very tall, and she had a very nice figure even in the sober brown linen sheath she wore. She had a creamy complexion and the true black

hair so seldom seen, and big gray eyes and a short straight little nose. "I'm
—going away," she said. "I'm getting the eleven-o'clock train for Portland,
so I thought I'd just come over here from the station a minute to say thank
you, Lieutenant."

"We haven't done much," said Mendoza. "How did you expect to find
us all here on Sunday, Mrs. Dwyer?"

She smiled faintly again. "Lieutenant, I was married to a cop for twelve
years. I knew you'd all be here."

"You know we'll get him, don't you?" asked Mendoza abruptly.

"Yes. I know that. You almost always do."

"Are you—moving away for good, Mrs. Dwyer?" asked Higgins.

Her eyes moved to him. "Oh, no. My mother wanted me to come and
live with her, but I don't like Portland much, and the children are settled
in school here, and we like the house. And then my mother doesn't like
dogs, and there's Brucie—— No, I'm just going up to stay with Mother a
week or so, while my sister stays with the children. Then I'll come back
and start looking for a job. I'll have to. The pension will help, of course,
but——"

"Yes," said Mendoza. "If you need any help there—a recommendation
or——"

"Yes, thank you, I'll remember. But I don't think I'll have too much
trouble there, Lieutenant. I worked for a while after—after Bert and I
were married. I'm a pretty good photographic retoucher, and there's nearly
always a job open in that line." She sighed, touched the little tan pillbox
hat she wore, with its nose veil, and said, "The children are pretty responsible and old enough to leave alone during the day. Laura's only eight, but
she's—mature. Well, just—just thanks for everything, all of you." She
turned.

"Now look," said Higgins. "Don't you—don't hesitate to call in now,
anything we can do. Me. Look, I know how it is for a woman alone, and
that's not a very new house, Mrs. Dwyer." His tone was earnest; he took a
step toward her. "Faucets needing washers, plumbing going wrong, electricity—— Look, I'm pretty handy at things like that. You need any help
with anything like that, don't you hesitate to call me, see? I mean, I know
—Bert did most of the work like that himself—and electricians and
plumbers, they come damn high these days. I'd be happy to——"

She looked a little surprised. "Well, that's awfully good of you, Sergeant."

"You remember, now."

"Yes, I will. Thank you again, and good-by."

Mendoza and Palliser swung to stare at Higgins. "Well, she's a nice girl," said Higgins. He sounded defiant. Higgins, supposedly the confirmed bachelor at thirty-seven, was not a handsome man. He had started out with craggy, irregular features, and a twice-broken nose—once in a melee in high-school football and once at the hands of an ex-heavyweight turned junkie—hadn't improved his appearance. No girls turned to look at him in the street, or if they did it was for his impressive shoulders and seventy-five inches. Now he flushed a dark red under the stares of his colleagues. He said, "So what *about* it? We ought to do what we can for her."

"*Pues sí,*" said Mendoza.

"Besides——" said Higgins. "Oh, well, hell." He passed one of his massive hands across his face. "What have we got to do today, anyway? Let's get started."

"God knows," said Palliser, "I've got enough to do." He eyed the mass of teletypes gloomily and went out without reading them.

And Mendoza, eying Higgins where he sat hunched over his desk reading a report, wondered a little amusedly if Higgins had been captured at last, too. He also wondered just what kind of a chance George Higgins would stand with a girl like Mary Dwyer. A girl who had been married to one cop for twelve years and knew a lot about cops. About their work. About their lives. About the statistics, and how any city is jam-packed with potential victims of violent death, but how any cop runs just a little better chance of getting involved with violence.

With the random death.

Higgins looked up and stared at the wall opposite him. "My God," he said, "anyway, she could take her pick. Couldn't she? And why the hell should she ever want to—get involved—with a cop again? Another cop?"

According to the teletype, young Adler hadn't known Max King's address. Palliser had gone, yesterday, to that Thriftimart where, said Adler, King had once worked as a box boy. The manager there gave him, after search, an address in Montrose. So Palliser had gone there, and it was a private house belonging to a widow who took in roomers, and found that Max King had moved away six months ago.

So Palliser had gone to the Montrose post office, which of course had been closed on Saturday afternoon, but he'd got in by knocking on the door and holding up his badge. He asked about change-of-address cards, and after a long search they had turned up an address for him in La Crescenta. So Palliser had, late yesterday, gone there, and it had been another private house belonging to an elderly couple who took a roomer, and they had told him that Max King had left about a month ago to go back to Montana where his brother lived and had a ranch. Actually, said Mrs. Keller helpfully, it was a half brother—no, she never recollected hearing Max say his name and couldn't say what town——

A couple of four-letter words formed soundlessly in Palliser's mind.

"Wait a minute, Mother," said Mr. Keller suddenly. "Now don't you recall me telling you, just the other day it was, he's back. Max is. Nice young feller. You recall, I ran into Frank Foster down in Montrose—he runs a restaurant there, Sergeant—though what in time the *police* want of Max I can't think, nice a young feller as you'd want to meet—and he was telling me Max came back. Didn't like the ranch work. I know he always said—Max, I mean—as how he'd like to get to learn T.V. repair work. He's good with his hands, a real smart boy."

"Well, thanks very much," said Palliser. The deadly dreary routine. It had to be done. Somebody had to do it.

And that had been at nine o'clock last night, and when he got to the restaurant Frank Foster ran, it had been closed, and so he'd looked up Foster's home number and called and got no answer. So then he had gone home.

So this morning he drove back up to Montrose and found the restaurant open, and found Frank Foster, and asked about Max King. Sure, Foster said, Max was back, he'd been in just the other day, and no, he didn't know where Max was living, but he had a job at a lumberyard down in Glendale and was going to school nights, to learn electronics. Going to Glendale College nights, Max had told him.

And the only lumberyard in Glendale was, of course, Lounsberry and Harris, so Palliser went there, and of course it was closed on Sunday, but there was an emergency number posted on the door, so he called that and eventually got the superintendent's name and routed him out.

"Really," said the superintendent. "Really, for such a trivial—— I was planning to take the children to the zoo——"

"Well, this could be important," said Palliser wearily. He didn't think. The damn routine.

So the superintendent looked for Max King's address, and so Palliser—in ninety-nine-degree heat—drove back up to Montrose, to Briggs Avenue, to the house where Max rented a room.

He found, at long last, Max King.

A pleasant-faced middle-aged woman let him in, not without surprise at the sight of his badge. Max King was watching a golf match on T.V. in the living room. He was a husky blond fellow about twenty-two, ruggedly good-looking.

"*Police?*" he said, looking astonished. "What the hell? *Me?* What've I done? Oh-oh. The car. Is that it? But I didn't think I had to re-register it until January, even if it has got Montana plates. I bought it from my brother, been over there awhile, but those open empty spaces I can't stand. Brother, give me the big city any time! Is it the car? I didn't——"

"No," said Palliser. "You used to work at the Thriftimart, and you knew a fellow named Frederick Adler, and——" He explained about the gun. "I'd just like to see the gun," he said. This deadly routine.

King stared at him. He said flatly, "Mister, you fell for a real snow job. That smells. I never bought a gun from Fred Adler. Nor from anybody. I don't have a gun. I never have and I never will. I had a kid brother shot all accidental by a gun that couldn't be loaded. I don't like guns, mister. Somebody told you a fairy tale."

EIGHTEEN

Palliser stared at him. Quite suddenly the routine stopped being so very routine. "Is that a fact?" he said. "You could be lying to me, Mr. King."

"Oh, for God's sake. Anybody who knows me knows *that* about me. Could tell you. It's Adler who—say, what is this anyway? Has that lout pulled something and tried to put it on me?"

"Mr. King," said Palliser, "I haven't got a search warrant, but would you allow me to look through your room, please?"

"Still think you're going to find it?" King was half angry and half puzzled. "Sergeant—did you say Palliser?—you can look anywhere you want to. All over the house—I don't think Mrs. Wechsler would mind, because none of us has anything to hide. Sam Wechsler agrees with me about guns. And I just moved in here ten days back, and Mrs. Wechsler was in and out of the room while I was unpacking, and she could say——" He turned and led the way to a good-sized room furnished as a den with a studio couch and desk.

Palliser looked, and there wasn't any gun.

"What *is* this, anyway?" asked King. He stood smoking, watching Palliser go through the chest of drawers. "That Adler—trying to push something onto *me*? I didn't know him hardly at all, just to know his name, you know. I don't figure anybody did."

Palliser looked up. "Why not? What was wrong with him?"

King shrugged. "Oh, hell, I suppose it's not his fault. Glands or something, but he's a funny one. Not anybody a real guy 'd want to pal around with. Slow, for one thing, no brain you know, and then he's so fat and sloppy. A slob. I was surprised he even got that job, and I think they were going to fire him at that. This was maybe a month back, when I quit and went to Montana. But why the hell he picks *me* to—— What did he do?"

"We don't know that he's done anything," said Palliser, "but this all looks interesting. You say he's fat?"

"A real fat boy." King nodded. "Why, don't you know him? I thought you'd picked him up, you said——"

"He's in Kansas." Unfortunately. "Go on. Fat?"

"Fat," said King. "Unhealthy-looking, know what I mean? You know how some peoples' glands go wrong, and they get fat. I knew a girl like that once, only she kept a real nice figure, taking these thyroid pills. I wondered why this Adler lout didn't see a doctor. Because he must be fifty pounds overweight—— Listen, and I wish I had him here right now, telling you a fake story like——"

"Mr. King," said Palliser, "you're not planning to leave town, are you?"

"I am not. You'll find me right here any time you want me. Or at my job. Or three nights a week in room three-fourteen at Glendale College. What the hell——"

"That's just fine," said Palliser. "Thanks very much. Now if you'll just give me your brother's name and address, that'll be it for now . . ." He got back into the Rambler and started downtown, thinking how suddenly the routine could sometimes turn up a big surprise.

He also thought about Mrs. Ruth Watts, who said she had seen a boy named Alvin Cooper going into the garage of that Shell station the morning Walsh had been shot, at about the right time. And the boy hadn't been Alvin Cooper, but Alvin Cooper was a big fat boy whose glands had gone wrong, and here was another big fat boy . . .

He came into the office and found Mendoza grumbling to Piggott about the slowness of the Feds back in Washington: they hadn't heard yet from the F.B.I. about anything they might have on Leigh. "Listen, Lieutenant," said Piggott soothingly, "they got requests coming in every hour from all over the place, and there's only twenty-four hours in a day. If they've got anything, we'll hear about it sooner or later."

"Well, it's aggravating. I try to make up stories about how he could be tied up to a pair of bank heisters, and there's just no plausible way—— You look a little excited about something, John. Something hot?"

"Could be," said Palliser, not stopping. He went straight on to the communications room and sent off a long teletype to Chief Cunningham in Plainville. Up to now, of course, all these co-operative law-enforcement officers had been working blind; now Palliser gave Cunningham a detailed account of the gas-station holdup and the connection with the gun. Frederick Adler claimed he had sold the gun to King; King denied it; King didn't have the gun and looked clean. (There was, of course, the chance—

the very small chance—that King had not actually been at his brother's ranch in Montana on the day Jimmy Walsh had been killed, that he was that particular X and had since ditched the gun somewhere. Palliser would check that out.) Now he would like Chief Cunningham to question young Adler again, and he'd also like to know something about young Adler. Had he ever been in trouble, and so on.

"And damn it," he said to Mendoza, after bringing him up to date, "I don't know what sort of cop this Cunningham is, whether he's competent or a hick-town fool. He——"

"Plainville doesn't look so small on a map. And some of those hick-town cops are as smart as they come," said Mendoza, thinking of John Lockhart. "It all looks suggestive, anyway. What about King?"

"He smells all right—he acts all right. But of course I'll check him too." Palliser looked at his watch; it was ten minutes to one. "Don't suppose I can expect anything back from Cunningham until tonight or tomorrow. I headed it urgent, but he might be off on a picnic or something, on Sunday, or if he isn't the Adlers might be. I think I'll get that other teletype off and then go get some lunch."

"All right, I'll wait and go with you. I wonder," said Mendoza, "if those Washington boys are pawing through their records by hand."

Palliser sent off a teletype to the sheriff of Lewis and Clark County in Montana, requesting co-operation. Mr. Max King claimed to have been at the ranch of his half brother, Mr. Alexander Ross, in that county, on such and such a date. Would the sheriff please verify?

Then he and Mendoza went up to Federico's and had lunch.

Nothing showed up from Washington on Leigh on Monday. But this break in the Walsh case continued to look good.

At eleven o'clock Palliser had a teletype from the sheriff of Lewis and Clark County, Montana. About a dozen people could swear that Max King had been just where he said he'd been on the relevant date. Palliser teletyped back brief thanks and thought about Frederick Adler. But what sense was there in Adler for it? Such a damn fool way to—— Well, he thought, were they ever very bright, the smalltime pros? But on the other hand, Don Kimball, a plain-clothes man on the Glendale force, had thought Adler looked sufficiently O.K. that he'd helped him get a gun, and the Glendale boys weren't bad as a rule. What added up?

When he got back from lunch he found a teletype waiting from Chief Cunningham—a long one. Cunningham didn't sound like a backwoods hick cop; he seemed to be on the ball. He sketched backgrounds: Frederick Adler was twenty-two, the only son of a local Civil Service clerk and his wife. Modest circumstances. He had dropped out of high school in his second year, had held a few lowly jobs but never for long. School authorities had recommended medical treatment for his obesity when he was fourteen, but the parents belonged to some obscure religious sect which didn't believe in all this newfangled doctoring (Palliser read between lines) and nothing had been done. The boy didn't have the education or evidently the brain to hold much of a job. He'd been picked up once, with a couple of other boys, for a little street scuffle, and once again on a D.-and-D., only last year. He'd left town after his father had paid his fine on that and just returned about a week ago.

And he was still insisting that he had sold the gun to King.

Palliser sent back a brief message to Cunningham: *King absolutely clean. Press Adler on gun.*

He hadn't really anything to do but wait for answers to come in. He sat at his desk and thought. He thought about Roberta Silverman and decided they could get along nicely, really, on what he was making now, and anyway, she might want to go on working a year or two so they could make a down payment on a house.

After a while Higgins came in, looking tired and hot, with a dumb unshaven lout who was a drinking pal of one of the possibles from Records, and it was always better technique for two or three men to sit in on a questioning, so Palliser and Landers, who had been arguing with Sergeant Lake about baseball teams, had the chance to do a little work.

Nothing came in from Cunningham by six o'clock, so Palliser went out for dinner. The hospital Art Hackett was in wasn't too far from the Civic Center, so afterward he dropped up there and brought Art up to date.

"*Nothing* else on the bank jobs at all?"

"We've run it into the ground," said Palliser morosely. "And you notice they're lying low—no more jobs. Bert scared them. I'm beginning to think the lieutenant's right—it's a pair of amateurs. For one thing, isn't it usually the amateurs who start spraying bullets all around? Your typical pro heist man plays it cool, he isn't asking for a homicide rap."

"Well, I don't know," said Hackett. He was lying here counting the hours; on Thursday he was going home, to be cosseted and fed by his Angel. "There's the other heist job, where it looks like a senseless kill. How's that?"

"Hot," said Palliser, and told him about that. "I want to get back and see if anything more's in from Cunningham."

"You'd better also start thinking about extradition proceedings," said Hackett. "That's clear as glass."

"Well, I don't see it's quite as certain as——"

"It's obvious," said Hackett impatiently. He shifted his bulk restlessly in the high bed. "You said King didn't know Adler well, or vice versa. But King quit his job and went to Montana while Adler was still here. It could very well be—maybe in overhearing talk between King and some others at the market—that Adler knew King was going to a ranch—his half brother's ranch—in the wide open spaces—and even that it was a different name. He could figure that King might be almost impossible to track down, to find if he *had* that gun or not. Adler might figure that even if we did eventually track down King, it would be so long after Walsh was shot, memories would be confused, we'd think King was just lying to us, had dumped the gun. One thing sure Adler didn't know was that King was going to get fed up with wide open spaces and come back so soon."

Palliser stared at him. "Maybe we ought to establish you permanently as an armchair consultant. How right you are. I hadn't got that far. Of course, you are sitting here in refrigerated air conditioning all day. Maybe once you're at home, sweltering like the rest of us, you won't be quite so bright."

Hackett laughed. "I tell you, for four different walls to look at and a few of Angel's meals, I wouldn't mind the anteroom of hell!"

"That's what you think now," said Palliser wisely.

At eight o'clock that night there arrived a teletype from Chief Cunningham. Adler had changed his story. He now said that he'd told the tale about King because he hadn't thought they'd ever find King, and what he'd really done with the gun—the reason he'd told the lie—was, he had sold it to a fellow he knew in L.A., and he was a nice enough fellow, but he'd been in trouble once and had a little record, so he wouldn't be allowed to have a gun, and Adler couldn't remember his last name but his first name was Joe.

Palliser could almost read the sardonic tone of Cunningham's voice as he'd dictated that. The story, of course, smelled very rank indeed.

He teletyped back: *Oh, yes? Do you use lie detector? If so try.* He sat and thought a little. Adler was looking very hot indeed.

Palliser had often enough heard Mendoza's maxims about detective work. He tried to use one of them now. The one that said, What detective work comes down to in the end is the story about the idiot boy and the lost horse. If you were a horse, where would you go?

All right, said Palliser to himself. I am Fred Adler, the fat boy nobody wants to make friends with. I have just committed the very serious crime of murdering somebody. My first serious crime, apparently, because Plainville didn't have anything much on me and there's no gap between then and when I showed up in California. I am not a very bright young man, and I am probably scared and confused. (Why, by the way, downtown L.A.? I have been living in La Crescenta and working in Glendale.) I know the gun can tie me in, because (for God's sake) I bought it openly, and the serial number is recorded on my permit and the bill of sale. Also the gun has a piece broken off the trigger guard. I want to get rid of the gun. Permanently. What would I do with it?

Some fifteen minutes later Schenke came in and said, "What the hell are you doing, Sergeant, daydreaming about your best girl? Or is it just indigestion?"

Palliser, who had jumped nervously and opened his eyes, said, "Hello, Bob. That was quite a large yard, and a lot of trees at the end of it, and it didn't look as if she took much care of it. Not a gardener." His tone was absent.

"Is that so?" said Schenke.

"Kimball's place, and most places along that block, are kept up," said Palliser to himself. "Grass kept watered, and bushes trimmed. But that place—it wasn't. Lawn needed cutting too. Looked as if she doesn't pay much attention to the yard."

"Naughty naughty," said Schenke. "Everybody ought to keep up their yards. What're you talking about?"

"Mrs. Jane Page," said Palliser, and he got up and went out to where Sergeant Thoms was monitoring the phone with his feet up, reading a paperback, and he said, "Bill, I want a search warrant. For tomorrow. I'll give you the name——"

Mrs. Page was upset and concerned and bewildered. "Freddy *Adler?*" she said. "You think Freddy *Adler* did something wrong? Why, he's a nice boy, he wouldn't do anything—— Why, he never even went with girls, he's not——"

Palliser reflected a little sadly that, if this was so, that was probably one reason. If this was so. Not that he went along with all the psychiatric jargon, but anybody with common sense could see that the physical handicap of any sort, maybe call it a social handicap, too, in this case, would set up frustrations which might somehow lead to violence.

And it was the hell of a big yard to hunt through, a grove of trees at the end of it, a disused garage, and another outbuilding—but they had brought along a metal detector. All very scientific these days.

It was an old house and a lot of things had got buried on the property over the years. They turned up broken rusty tools, a tire rim, a shoe with metal cleats, and assorted nails, nuts, bolts, screws, a dog collar with a metal plate and license tag, half of an old brass watering can, a broken toy pistol, a rusty alarm clock with the works missing, and a lot of stuff like that. Piggott and Galeano, who were manning the shovels, got very sarcastic with Palliser; it was another hot day, and one of the reasons they'd both studied to make rank was to get out of so much physical labor.

"I'd rather be back riding a squad car," said Piggott mournfully. He mopped his face.

"Hold it, here's another spot," said Palliser. "Here, I'll take a hand awhile." He took Piggott's shovel.

"Well, well, he's actually forgetting he's a sergeant," said Piggott.

"All very democratic," said Galeano.

"Lay off it," said Palliser, and drove his foot against the shovel. They had worked their way down from the rear of the house, past the garage, and were now—searching in horizontal strips across the property—just coming up to the disused outbuilding. Palliser dug and turned up a tarnished broken-apart picture frame made of aluminum.

"Hah!" said Galeano. "Big deal." Mrs. Page was standing on her back porch watching them.

"All *right*," said Palliser. "We've got to cover it." He took back the metal detector. He considered the terrain. They were standing a couple of feet from the little ramshackle building. He thought probably it had been built for a chicken coop, before the town grew and outlawed the keeping of livestock within city limits. He walked over to the fence at the left side of the yard and came back slowly, holding the detector out before him. He brushed against the front of the building as he passed, to the fence at the other side. Nothing.

"Getting hunches just like our Luis himself," said Piggott, "yet."

"Well——" said Palliser. He looked at the little building and then ducked his six feet two to enter it. Part of the roof was gone, so he could see.

The detector said strongly, Metal. Here.

"Hand me a shovel," said Palliser.

"I will say you're a stayer," said Galeano.

Palliser dug. He didn't have to dig far. The shovel clinked metallically with its third mouthful, and something fell from it to the hard-packed earth.

Palliser squatted and looked at it. He sighed. He said, "Hunch be damned."

It was a J.C. Higgins Hi-Standard .22 nine-shot revolver, and its trigger guard had a tiny piece broken off it.

A lot of times the slogging routine paid off.

He went back to Headquarters and gave the gun to Ballistics. There were a good many prints on it, it turned out. They didn't have Adler's, but they would. It would turn out that the prints were Adler's.

He sent off a teletype to Cunningham asking about extradition procedures.

As it happened, they didn't have to go through all that rigmarole. Cunningham had already given Adler the lie-detector test and proved he was lying six ways from Sunday, and after some persuasive talk Adler agreed to waive extradition.

Chief Cunningham flew out with him on Tuesday night and they listened to him on Wednesday morning, at an interrogation room at Headquarters.

Neither of his parents had accompanied him, which said a little something.

"I didn't think you'd ever find the gun," said Adler. "I guess maybe you're smarter than I figured." He blinked nervously.

"I guess maybe we are, Freddy," said Mendoza. Palliser, Piggott, Galeano, Landers stood around. Cunningham, a big good-looking man with a shock of gray hair, was in on it, too; he was looking around surreptitiously, taking in this immense, very modern Police Facilities building. Probably quite a contrast to his own headquarters.

"What were you doing in downtown L.A. that day, Freddy?" asked Palliser.

"I—I tell you how it was," said Adler. "I see you got me for it, I didn't think—but—but—you see, how it was, I'd just got fired. Off that lousy job." His eyes filled with tears. Frederick Adler certainly wasn't a very prepossessing character. He was about five-seven, and he weighed around two-fifty, and it was soft, unhealthy fat; under his blue cotton shirt you could see the flabby suggestion of feminine breasts, and his hips wobbled as he walked, and he had a sallow moonface with tiny eyes and a wet mouth. "I—never keep a job," he said resentfully. "The way I look. People don't like me. It's no wonder. I don't like *myself* so good. It's all my *dad's* fault! It's all *his* fault! I—I—that teacher at school said a doctor could do something, and I asked Dad, and he said—he said—about against God's will, I'm just meant be fat, and—— It's not *my* fault!"

"We'd like to hear about Jimmy Walsh," said Mendoza.

Adler blinked up at him. "Who's he?"

And it came to them then, he hadn't even known the name of the man he'd killed.

"The gas-station attendant," said Palliser. "That Shell station."

"Oh," said Adler. "I—I tell you how it was, I guess I ain't got no choice. I'd got fired, see. I didn't know what to do. I didn't tell Mrs. Page where I roomed. I just went off usual time like I was going to work, I——"

"Did you buy the gun because you were planning a holdup, Freddy?"

"No, no, I wasn't, I—not then. It was because these guys, they went and roughed me up, where I hadda wait for the bus, see, they made jokes and they said I was—was—was—you know, like no good with girls, and—— It's not *my* fault! No, I never—— But then I thought I'd go home. That day. My dad said about washing his hands of me, that time I went and got tight and the cops—— But at least I knew *some* people back there, and maybe—— I'd got fired and I didn't know where to go to get another job— some kind—and I didn't have any money. I'd spent all I saved up on the— the gun. And I didn't sleep very good that night, and so I got up early and I thought I'd go down to the railroad station and find out how much it'd cost to go back to Plainville. And I took the bus downtown, and that was about eight o'clock when I got there, and the man at the station said by chair car it was forty-nine fifty, and I didn't have that much. All I had was six dollars. So then I thought—I thought the Greyhound bus would be cheaper, but I didn't know where a ticket office was to ask, so I was just walking along then thinking and there was this gas station and a phone booth right on the sidewalk and I went in to look up the—the address. Of the Greyhound, see? And while I was in there I thought all of a sudden maybe I could hold up the station—there was just this one guy there that I could see—and maybe there'd be forty-nine bucks in the register. It was just a—just a sudden *idea* came to me, see?"

"Yes. So you did?"

"I—I—that guy, he wasn't in the little office, so I went into the garage part. I——"

"You had got into the habit of carrying the gun?" asked Palliser.

Adler licked his wet lips. "I had it, sure. I—it always made feel sort of *better*, feel it there. You know. I mean, people could laugh, but *I* knew I had the gun there on me. *They* didn't know—*they* didn't know—what I could do if I wanted. There was this kid there. In the garage. I showed him the gun. I thought it was easy. Listen, if I'd been like any other guy I'd never *be* into all this! If a doctor—— *I never meant* get into all this!" Tears started running down his fat cheeks. "I—I—the kid didn't put up a fight. We went to the office and he give me the money. Out of the register. Then I—then——"

"Why did you kill him, Freddy?" asked Mendoza hardly. "He gave you the money. You didn't have to kill him for it!" Nineteen-year-old Jimmy Walsh, who had wanted to be a lawyer.

"I—don't—know," said Adler dully. "Yes, I know. He laughed at me. He didn't put up a fight, but he laughed at me. He said—he said—I sure didn't need the dough because—I was starvin' to death—— And I made him go back to the garage and I—and I—— It's not *my* fault!" And that was a half-hysterical scream.

Mendoza straightened up slowly. He looked at Palliser. And they both wondered whether Jimmy Walsh might be alive today if Frederick Adler's father hadn't belonged to a funny religious sect which taught that all this newfangled doctoring was sinful.

Random chance. Just chance—a combination of circumstances.

NINETEEN

"Now you are not saying," said Mrs. MacTaggart, "that you're not going to catch that pair of robbers?"

"You must have *some*——" said Alison.

"Tell me," said Mendoza savagely. He sipped rye. "Tell me how and where! Especially if they're a pair of amateurs, no records. We've checked out nearly seventy possibles out of our own records and the Feds', and it's no dice. *Absolutamente nada.* So sure, sure, some of those—a lot of those—haven't got an alibi. There's no positive evidence to say yes or no."

"But, Luis——"

"It doesna seem *right*," said Mrs. MacTaggart, picking up Master John.

"Sure, sure," said Mendoza, "so if we've guessed right on the M.O., and if they pull another job, we might have a better chance. We think one man, the one who actually pulls the job, stays in the building. So the next time a bank gets knocked off, we shoot a lot of men over there *pronto* to go through that building, screen everybody there. But that's just *if* they pull another one. We haven't had one since Bert was killed, and it could be that finding out he was a cop scared them off. But good. Damn it, they could have left town—they could be in New York. They could have——" He uttered a startled grunt as Sheba landed on his shoulder from behind. The glass toppled from his hand; rye splashed over the coffee table. El Señor appeared as if by magic, leaped onto the table, and began to lap rye. "You little devil!" said Mendoza to Sheba.

"I can't imagine," said Alison, "where she picked up such an obnoxious trick. She's doing it more and more. She even did it to the meter reader today, scared the poor man out of his wits. If she'd give some *warning*, but—— It's really that tough, *amante?*"

Mendoza passed a hand over his eyes. "Nothing in yet from the F.B.I. on Leigh. Maybe they haven't got anything, but then why the hell don't they say so? And if they haven't, that's our last lead gone dead. Nobody here knew much about Leigh, we don't even know where he came from or if he was a native son. Nothing but dead ends, damn it. And there's this new one come up to work—that high-school girl dead of heroin. Not much there either, damn it."

"But if some of those men you've checked *could* be, if you got them in and really grilled them—searched wherever they live for the gun and so on——"

"*Cara,* haven't you been married to a cop long enough to know we've done all that? We haven't just been sitting around making wild guesses, you know. It's going dead on us. Dead as—as Caesar."

Mrs. MacTaggart came back to fetch Miss Teresa, who was lying on her back on the floor, dreamily sucking one big toe. "And there's a word about rending unto Caesar," she said severely. "And rendering unto God. Maybe if you was to be making a few sincere prayers about it, you'd be given help. And you needn't be sneering at that, you heathen man. I'll drop into St. Mary's first thing tomorrow and put up a prayer or two to St. Joseph, he being the one to find lost things, which to all intents and purposes is what you are all trying to do. I'll not believe that God would not let you find these villains, shooting a policeman and all."

Mendoza laughed as she went out, and she frowned at him over her shoulder. "Just what Piggott said. Lay it on the Lord's lap and have faith. Well, with both the Catholics and the Methodists working on it—— I don't know. The routine usually gets us there in the end—as per that Walsh thing I was telling you about—but on this, right now——" He shook his head. Sheba had walked down him onto his lap and was making bread on his knee steadily, doing no good to his trousers with her long claws. "It may sound funny, but I'm hoping to God they will try another one—with what we know, or think we know, it could give us a chance to pick up one of them at least, and knowing one, we'd probably lay hands on his pal without much trouble."

"But if one of them was wounded I should think you could——"

"So it looks now, over two weeks later, that it can't have been a very serious wound. If he'd died of it, the body would have turned up. The chances are now it was superficial. Oh, sure, when and if we pick him up there'd be evidence of that, but——"

Alison eyed him and said, "You really needed that drink you didn't finish. I'll get you another, and then dinner'll be ready." She picked up the glass and went out.

And Mendoza, who hadn't set foot in a church for twenty-five years, wondered fleetingly and tiredly if maybe Mrs. MacTaggart and Piggott might be just a little help, at that.

In a situation like this you needed help *wherever* it came from.

Whether God had anything to do with it or not, the very next day he got his wish.

The call came in from a squad car at seven minutes to one. Bank robbery at the Security-First at Pico and Alvarado. The guard had called in as soon as the man was out the door—the chief teller had run over to him as soon as the man left his window—and the squad-car man thought they couldn't be less than five minutes behind him, because the car had been just past the corner of Twelfth on Alvarado when they got the call, only a block away.

Before Sergeant Lake had finished telling him, Mendoza was on the inside phone. "Get me Traffic, *¡inmediatamente!* Jimmy, chase everybody here straight over there—I'll be right behind them . . . Mendoza, Homicide. I want at least twenty men in the nearest cars shot over to Pico and Alvarado, *pronto!*—it's the bank heisters. Send all you can get over there. I want that building searched—a cordon around it five minutes from now! Step on it! A man at all doors to the building, and everybody——"

When he had set that up, he snatched up his hat and fled. Higgins, Palliser, Galeano, and Piggott were three minutes ahead of him. When he got to the bank, traffic was snarled and drivers cursing, six squad cars double-parked in both narrow streets and one uniformed man at the intersection trying to keep traffic moving.

Mendoza ran to the nearest door, leaving the Ferrari double-parked; the door was the door to the lobby of the building, and a uniformed man was there, talking to a stocky elderly man in the first derby hat Mendoza had seen in years.

"I'm sorry, sir, you can't leave the building. There's been a little——" The uniformed man turned to Mendoza. "I'm afraid you can't come in, sir. There's—— Oh." He looked at the badge. "Excuse me, sir, could I ask you—uh?—"

"Lieutenant Mendoza."

"Yes, sir. We had orders to stop everybody going out, sir, but this—uh—gentleman——"

"What in the name of God *is* all this?" demanded the elderly man. "I happen to have an important lunch engagement, and I must say if the police think they can act so highhanded as to—— After all, it is lunch time and there are quite a few people working in this building who eat lunch.

Outside the building, Officer." He was only a little angry; he looked curious and annoyed.

Mendoza hesitated. That was indeed going to pose a little problem.
This was a ten-story building and God knew how many offices it had:
doctors, dentists, lawyers, tax consultants, all the usual tenants. Right now
there'd be people coming back from lunch, people wanting to go out to
lunch, and if they tried to hold them all at the doors, they'd have crowds
milling around to impede them—crowds through which one man might
more easily slip through.

He said, "Yes, I see that. All right—what's your name?"

"Slocum, sir. Patrolman."

"Anybody who wants to go out, Slocum, get the full name and address
and occupation—office number here where he or she belongs. O.K.?" He
wheeled to cover the other doors.

He heard the elderly man giving information imperturbably. "I am
Henry J. Barker. General practitioner, office six-oh-six. You want my home
address? It's——"

At the other four doors of the bank he found there had already accumulated several people wanting to leave or enter. He issued the same orders
and went into the bank.

It was in a kind of orderly confusion. Higgins and Galeano were talking to two men in front of one of the counters; whispering knots of tellers
stood about inside the counters; patrons, sensing something unusual going
on, stared. Palliser and Piggott were talking to a couple of men at another
counter, and evidently Jimmy had called the Feds, because Dale was just
coming in at a side door. Higgins turned, saw Mendoza, and beckoned
him urgently.

"Something, George?" One of the men with Higgins and Galeano was
the uniformed bank guard; the other was a tall, good-looking youngish
man, who was looking excited.

"Mr. Lamarr, the chief teller," said Higgins. "Lieutenant Mendoza."

"How do you do, sir. I can only tell you," said Lamarr, "that I am sure.
I've got a very good eye for details, always have had. And as soon as he
showed me the gun, I said to myself, you're going to inventory every last
little thing you can about this fellow, for the c—the police. I don't lose my
head very easy, Lieutenant."

"Mr. Lamarr gives us something new," said Higgins. "Something
funny."

"Let's hear it."

Lamarr was appraising Mendoza's beautifully cut gray silk suit. "That

set you back something," he observed. "I'm interested in clothes myself,
Lieutenant. We're expected to dress pretty well, you know. One reason I
spotted this. That bird wasn't wearing a suit, he had on a corduroy jacket
and slacks, almost matching. Gray. But the jacket was a reversible one."

"A rev——"

"Sure. They're kind of the latest sports craze—two jackets in one. Solid
color one side, plaid or stripe on the other. All finished, seams and pockets
and so on, both sides. I'm sure of that because I was looking at one myself
just the other day, and you see, in order to get an ordinary-sized inside
breast pocket—a fairly deep one, you know—on both sides, the breast
pocket you can see on the outside is about twice as deep as usual. You can
see the stitching. And I can tell you something else, sir. When I handed
over the money in the paper bag, I'm pretty sure he put the bag in his
right-hand outside pocket——"

Which Wolf, their smartest witness, had also said.

"And when he did that, he"—Lamarr gestured—"pulled the jacket down
and a bit to the side—see what I mean?—and I just caught a fast glimpse
of the inside pattern of it."

"Jacket unbuttoned? Yes." Dale had drifted up and was listening intently. Mendoza slid a hand into his jacket pocket, looking down, and saw
that as pressure pulled the jacket down on that side, the same side of the
unbuttoned front turned back very slightly. "So what was it?"

"It was a dark-green plaid," said Lamarr, without hesitation. "Something like the Black Watch but not exactly. More like—oh, the Douglas
tartan, or the Forbes . . . Yes, sir, I know tartans. My mother was
Scottish."

Mendoza reflected resignedly, so now they'd have to get Máiri MacTaggart to help, tell them all about the Douglas and Forbes tartans.

"I didn't notice a thing, not a *thing*," said the guard excitedly. "I was
standing over there next to New Accounts, and Mr. Lamarr came running
across and told me—the man was just going out the door then, I only saw
his back—and *then* I noticed that the curtains on that door were pulled
down, and I couldn't imagine——"

"¡*Abran paso!*" said Mendoza. "By God, we're right behind him,
George, keep your fingers crossed! We've spotted the M.O.—he doesn't
leave the building—he pulled down those curtains again so nobody could
see which way he turned. *Por Dios*, he's got to be here yet—handed the
loot and the gun over, and X number two sailed out, but the first one is
here somewhere, I swear it, and by God——"

The whole building was jumping now. More squad cars had arrived.

Palliser and Piggott, and presently Higgins, were organizing the search. They weren't going to leave so much as a private office lavatory unlooked at. It was quite a job, but they had about thirty uniformed patrolmen and it was being done systematically, floor by floor.

People coming in from lunch, mostly girl secretaries and stenographers and receptionists, stared curiously and lingered to ask questions. "You work here, miss? I'll just ask you to go straight to your office, then, please. This is just a routine——"

It took them over four hours, until long after the bank had officially locked its doors for the day. After a while Traffic got a little irate at all those patrolmen off regular duty, but the Feds filled in with a few more men. They covered it. Very thoroughly they covered it. By five-thirty one or more cops had poked his nose into every office, lavatory, public rest room, coat closet, and broom closet in the entire building.

Approximately sixty people, in that period of time, had left the building by one exit or another. People coming away from dental appointments, doctors' appointments, lawyers' appointments, salesmen from calling on prospective clients, people like that. Every solitary last one of them left a name, address, and occupation with one of the uniformed men manning the exits.

And they didn't turn up one damned thing.

Mendoza swore. He went on swearing.

"We *couldn't* have missed him!" said Palliser violently. "We're pretty damn sure he stays in the building awhile—that's the object of the whole exercise, let his unseen side-kick get away—we said, my God, probably he stays until all the excitement's over and the cops have all gone! And this time we couldn't have been five minutes——"

"Longer," said Mendoza. "The first squad car got there within minutes, but we didn't really get the exits guarded for at least ten to fifteen. He *could* have—— If he saw that squad car pull up so soon—— Hell. I'm beginning to think we're jinxed on this one, boys. Or he could have slipped by, giving a false name and address, of course. That was a risk, but—*¡por Dios!*—our best chance was a quick search right then, and if we'd kept all that mob milling around—— Here's these lists of people who left the building. We'll have to check it out anyway." God, and how long would that take?

"And if he left a fake name, what help is that going to be? Tell us how he got out, is all! And I'll tell you something else, Goddamn the luck," said Higgins ferociously. "Now, after he saw how we reacted to this caper, and being such a cute boy, he knows *we* know their M.O., and he'll know if they try another one that way, we'll get the place covered even faster and the chances are we'd nab him. So they're going to lay low and keep quiet. They're not going to be pulling another one. So it's another dead end, damn it!"

And that was at eight-fifteen on Friday morning.

The uniformed men who had covered the building's exits had all been told to leave their notes at Homicide. Mendoza had picked them up from Sergeant Lake when he came in ten minutes ago and was just now settling down to glance over them: the lists of the people who had left the building while the search was going on.

"And damnation," said Palliser, "this reversible-jacket bit—I had a thought there, could it be that as soon as he actually gets out of the bank he—— I mean, if Lamarr was right and it *was*——"

"*¡Santa María!*" exclaimed Mendoza loudly. "*¡Diez millón demonios desde infierno!* For the love of Christ, what cretinous imbecilic son of——" He reversed the sheet he was looking at and grabbed at the phone. "Get me Traffic, *pronto!* . . . Mendoza, Homicide. You've got a"—he swallowed convulsively—"*patrolman* down there named Harvey Schultz. I want him. In my office in ten minutes, or even sooner! He has—some information I need. Right now . . . All right." He slammed the phone down. "*¡Vaya por Dios!* What kind of Goddamned stupid rookies——"

"What's up?" asked Palliser. "You've found——"

Mendoza shoved the sheet at him. Piggott got up and glanced over Palliser's shoulder. He looked puzzled. "So what's wrong? Just a lot of names."

"For the *love* of—— What year were you born, Matt?"

Piggott looked even more puzzled. "Nineteen thirty-five, why?"

Mendoza laughed sharply. There was no humor in his eyes at all. Higgins took the sheet from Piggott and looked at it. Suddenly he said, "For God's sake! What idiot couldn't spot——"

"Apparently Patrolman Harvey Schultz," said Mendoza in a hard tone.

Patrolman Harvey Schultz, peacefully cruising down Wilshire Boulevard in his squad car, was yanked back to Headquarters in a hurry. Fifteen minutes later, panting slightly and wondering what the hell this was all about, he stood in front of Mendoza's desk, cap in hand, and said, "Yes, sir?" He'd heard a little about Mendoza's reputation, and he felt slightly awed and ill at ease with Mendoza and all these other big Homicide detectives staring at him, but he tried to sound efficient.

"Yesterday afternoon," said Mendoza, "you were on duty at the Pico

Boulevard entrance of that bank, among other things taking down the names and addresses of everybody who left the building."

"Why, yes, sir. I'm sure nobody slipped through," said Schultz earnestly. "We all knew how important it was, a cop killer——"

"How long have you been on the force?" asked Mendoza.

"T-two years, sir. I——"

"All right. All right," said Mendoza. "Christ. We are sure as hell jinxed on this one. I needn't lose my temper about it. How old are you, Schultz?"

"I'm—twenty-three, sir. I—did I do something wrong? I thought I——"

"Oh, God. Not exactly," said Mendoza. "It's just the damn luck put you at that door. It's not your fault. Look, here's your list of everybody who left the building by your door."

"Y-yes, sir? Did I——"

"Didn't," asked Mendoza gently, "the name of Nelson Eddy ring a tiny little bell, Schultz?"

"N-no, sir, why? It was just another name. I mean, I don't recall the particular guy but a little bit, but I do remember him sort of because his job was a little unusual. He said he was a singing teacher——"

"God," said Higgins. "It had to be a rookie not dry behind the ears!"

"Blame the luck," said Mendoza wearily. "For your information, Schultz, Nelson Eddy is a singer. Back in the thirties he was a very popular movie star. I am reasonably certain that he was not in that building yesterday afternoon. But I shouldn't really have expected a man who hadn't been born when Mr. Eddy was at the height of his popularity to have recognized the obviously fake name."

"Oh, gee," said Schultz in dismay. "Oh, Jesus, Lieutenant, is that—? Well, my God, I sure never recognized—— That guy was *him?* The robber? My God——"

"What do you remember about him, anything at all?"

"Jesus, let me try to think—I passed about eighteen or twenty altogether, I couldn't—— He had on a plaid jacket," said Schultz suddenly. "Corduroy. I thought it was funny, in all this heat."

"Oh, my good Christ, I'll cut my throat," said Higgins passionately as everybody else groaned. "You *had* him—you had him right there, you could have—— God, if you'd been ten years older——"

"Well, Jesus, I'm sorry—how should I—— But, Lieutenant," said Schultz. "Look, Lieutenant." He swallowed nervously. "I mean, you know, how it got out in the papers, some of what you've got on this guy, and it seems he's bald. So how could it be that guy I saw? Because one thing I *do* remember definitely about this Nelson Eddy, he's got hair. Quite a lot of hair. He didn't have a hat on."

They all stared at him. And then Mendoza said, "*Caray*. Now I do wonder——"

And maybe God, urgently reminded by both Mrs. MacTaggart and Piggott—or St. Joseph—had a little something to do with it after all. Because at three-ten that afternoon Sergeant Lake came in and laid a long yellow teletype on Mendoza's desk. "The Feds at last," he said. "What they dug up from their records on Walter Leigh."

"*¡Por fin!*" said Mendoza, and started to read rapidly. Palliser and Higgins drifted in from the sergeants' office.

Walter William Leigh was his right name. He'd last been picked up in New Orleans in 1957, on a petty theft charge. He had formerly served a year's term in a county jail in Pennsylvania for extortion. Before that he had done time in New York for petty theft, extortion, and bookmaking. A very smalltime pro, and a drifter; he had little records in New Jersey and Massachusetts and in Michigan and New Mexico. A drifter. Not quite a bum. His record, in fact, went all the way back to 1920. And that charge——

In May 1920 Leigh charged with corrupting morals minor probation no sentence. At that time age 16 was residing with——

Mendoza looked at it. He didn't believe it. Then he did believe it, and he was filled with a cold, incredulous fury, and he snatched up the outside phone and dialed and said, "I want Wolf! Be damned if he's on a tail or what, I want him! He's there? *Bueno*. Tell him to make tracks—we'll give it a try—over to Seventh and Grand." God, God, the very place where Bert—— "Tell him to snap into it, fifteen minutes!"

"What is it?" asked Palliser. "You've got——"

"Come on," said Mendoza. He got up. "We don't know whether he's got his gun on him, and one cop is one too many to lose." He was getting out his own gun. "Yes, we've got him. I don't believe it, but we've got him. We'd have had him last week if the Feds hadn't been so damned slow about looking up records." He picked up his hat.

"But what the hell——"

"Who——"

"Come on!" said Mendoza savagely.

"You got a lead?" asked Wolf eagerly. He had been waiting for them in the lobby—the lobby where Bert Dwyer had died, gun in hand.

"We've got X, period," said Mendoza. They were in the elevator; he had pressed the button for eight.

"Something in the F.B.I. report on Leigh, he won't say," said Palliser.

They got out of the elevator and walked down the hall. Mendoza turned at the door whose frosted-glass panel said 812. It was unlocked. They went in.

A man and a woman were in the room, bent over an old scarred desk. They both looked up. Higgins said in naked astonishment, "But that's——"

"Why, Lieutenant. Is there something I can do for you?"

Mendoza went to the man and took hold of him, not tenderly. He pulled him violently around so that he stood in profile to Wolf, and he looked at Wolf and asked, "What about it?"

"Oh, my God. Yes. Yes, that's him. That's the one. *But*——"

"Lieutenant——"

"What the *hell*," said Palliser. "You don't mean——"

The woman said breathlessly, "What's the meaning of—— Who are these men? You can't——"

And Mendoza let go of the man and reached to the man's untidy shock of dark hair and tugged at it, and it came away in his hands, and the man had a shiny domed bald head.

"And that," said Mendoza in a grim remote tone, "was what Bert started to say. Tried to say. A *toupee*. Not two men. A toupee. He saw you putting it on. *Didn't he, Mr. Warbeck?*"

Eugene Warbeck shrank back from him, but his expression didn't change for a moment.

"Who are these——"

"It's—it's all right, Miss Corsa," said Mr. Warbeck in his gentle voice. "At least, it's not, but—— Yes. Yes, that's so. But it was for the children, you see." He looked unhappy. He said softly, "I'm sorry about the police officer. I didn't know who he was, of course, and he'd have stopped me getting the money—for the children."

—was residing with mother and younger step brother Mrs. May and Eugene Warbeck 1312 Walbrook St., Auburn, N.Y.

TWENTY

And they had been savage to get this one, for vengeance on the one who had killed one of their own, and secretly all of them had been hoping that when they caught up, perhaps he'd run, or fight—so they needn't bring him in all docile, like the gentlemanly cops they were. But now, they still couldn't quite believe they'd got him, and of all of them standing around him there in an interrogation room, nobody had any impulse to raise a hand to soft-spoken Eugene Warbeck.

Because Eugene Warbeck probably wouldn't see the inside of the gas chamber. He wasn't realizing the enormity of what he had done at all. He was explaining—sadly he was explaining. Now that he'd been stopped, all he wanted was the chance to explain.

"It was the children, you see—so many poor, deprived children needing so much! The appeals we send out never seem to bring in much. People give to the big, organized charities, not small groups like ours—but we think we really accomplish more, at the—the personal level, as it were. Things like the Holderby girl's teeth—I was feeling quite desperate about that, we simply didn't have the money, and it's *so* important—— The poor helpless children . . . Yes, sir? Oh, Walter. Poor Walter. Yes, sir, I'll tell you. I'd always looked after Walter, because I promised Mother on her deathbed I would. He was—weak. He never meant any harm, but there's no denying he was *weak*. Yes. But he knew he could always count on me, the little I could afford to send him—because of Mother, you see—and so I usually knew where he *was*. I think it was Marion Holderby's teeth that really decided me, you know." Mr. Warbeck looked up at Mendoza and Higgins standing closest over him and uttered a pleased little giggle. "I've always been quite a detective-novel fan, and I'd often thought *I* could devise quite good plots, and I was right, wasn't I? Wasn't I?"

"You certainly did, Mr. Warbeck. Where did——"

"Banks—all those banks full of money—not like taking it from a—a *person*. *People*. My goodness, my wife would have been surprised—I was a little surprised myself, to find I had the—the courage and boldness to do such a thing. But once I had made up my mind, I meant to *do* it. Do it *right*. Because then I could help the children." He looked earnestly at Mendoza; he said, "Grownups aren't helpless, they can—can change things for themselves, if they really want to. But children—— And you see, I—I lied a little, before, when I said I had enough money to get along. It's only just enough, with what I had to send Walter. When they fired me from the department store—really, I always did resent that. It was most unfair!

"But when I *did* decide to do it, I worked out a plan very carefully. Of course I thought of my toupee at once, because I look quite different without it." He flushed a little. "*I'd* never have bothered with such a thing, but in my job—my job as it was then, floorwalker, you know, you have to —to keep up appearances, and Emily said I should, it made me look so much younger, and I've got into the habit of wearing it. And I thought, and I read about a lot of real-life bank robberies, and it seemed to me that the basic mistake all those men made was in running away, at once I mean. They'd have elaborate plans for changing their—er—getaway cars and so on, but they were always caught. It seemed to me that if I should just quietly go upstairs in the same building and wait awhile in a—a public lavatory, you know, and with my toupee back on, too, nobody would look twice at me coming out——"

"It was just a dandy plan, Mr. Warbeck," said Higgins grimly. "Now, where'd you get the gun? And where is it now?"

"Oh, it's at home. In the room I rent, sir. With everything else," said Mr. Warbeck sadly. "I was especially pleased to find that reversible jacket. I thought that should really make it work. The only little difficulty might be if there should be anyone in the lobbies when I came in from the bank, but that only happened to me once, and I simply walked quietly past and up the stairs and stopped on the landing to put on my toupee and reverse the jacket. You see, what I'd *do*," and he was quite proud, explaining his cleverness, "I'd put the bag of money in my *outside* pocket and then just a few moments later, when I'd reversed the jacket, the money would be *inside* and I'd be taking my toupee out of the outside pocket that was inside before. It really worked very well. And I was surprised at myself, how I didn't hesitate about firing the gun at all. I was quite cool. Those people would have stopped me and taken the money away, and the money was for the children. That's—that's what Walter didn't understand." He suddenly looked very unhappy indeed.

"So you had to—put him out of the way?" asked Mendoza. He was curiously fascinated by Mr. Warbeck; glancing at Higgins, Palliser, Galeano, he saw the same expressions mirrored in their faces.

"Well, you see—I told you I read a lot of detective stories, and I knew the banks would likely have records of the money, and I'd read about these men who—who buy—ah—hot money, it's called, and I thought—it would be so much safer if—— And of course I hadn't the slightest notion of where to find such a man, but I thought Walter might. He—he wasn't a real *criminal*, you know, but he—well, he was rather on the fringes, you might say. I never had much personal contact with him of late years—he—he followed me out here, you know, it was an easy life for *him*, with me sending him money like that—but of course I'd promised Mother—— But when I had the plan all made I did telephone him and met him—down in Pershing Square actually—and asked if he could find such a man. Well, naturally he was curious, and I had to tell him a bit about it before he'd promise to look. And then it turned out no use after all," said Mr. Warbeck dejectedly.

"He didn't find one?" asked Palliser.

"Oh, yes, he did. Somebody he knew—I think he said a bartender—told him a name. I had thought, you see, Walter could exchange the money, so I'd never be—— But it seems men like that don't—don't deal in the sums I had to sell. Only really big money. I've got nearly nine thousand dollars," said Mr. Warbeck, sounding awed, "which seems like a great deal of money to me—just *think* what I can do for all these poor children with so much money! And so then I didn't see how I *could* use the money and not —not be caught, you know. And then Walter got difficult. He was such a weak, selfish fellow—exactly like his father, Mother used to say. He wanted to use the money for *ourselves!* It was wicked—that was what he couldn't see—it was money exactly like the money we might have in our little Good Samaritan treasury, it was for the *children*, it didn't belong to me! Really, you know, Lieutenant, I'd never have dreamed of stealing for *myself!* But Walter got very difficult, and he said there might be a reward for telling, and then, too, he—he sometimes drank too much, and I knew he was apt to say anything when he was—like that. So I decided it was really the only way—— You know, I was really—er—getting quite a kick out of it all, as they say, by then. Did you know, Lieutenant—I'd never known that before myself—that having a gun in your hand makes you feel very,

very important? Because of what you can *do*—if you want to. Just if you want to."

"I have heard that, Mr. Warbeck," said Mendoza very gently, and even to himself his tone sounded sad.

"I'd thought about that very carefully, too, you see. It seemed to me that the first object was to make people realize you were *serious*, and I thought, the bigger and more dangerous-looking the gun was, the better. So that was the kind of gun I wanted——"

"You got it," said Higgins. "Where?"

"Oh, Walter helped me with that too. He said he knew a pawnshop where I could buy one with no questions asked, so we went there, but all the man had were quite small guns and I didn't want any of them, so I went to a real gunshop where they sell new guns, but they were all too expensive, and besides, the man said I'd have to wait three days and then get a policeman to sign something for me or show them a permit, and—— So a few days later I went back to the pawnshop, and then he had a really big gun in, and I bought that. And really, the first time it all went off so beautifully, without any hitch at all—and there I was with all that lovely money—Marion Holderby's teeth, and the operation Jamie needed, and—— But that was when I had the trouble with Walter. He was the second one I shot," said Mr. Warbeck thoughtfully, "and you know, it was really quite exciting in a way. You have no idea of the surge of power—just like an electric current through you. That bank guard, the first one—I'd never owned a gun before, but with a big gun like that, at practically point-blank range, I could hardly miss. It was exhilarating, in a funny kind of way. *Adults* have a *choice*. Those people *needn't* have tried to stop me— then I wouldn't have shot them. It's the poor children who are so helpless, at the mercy of society—cultural patterns—ignorant or cruel or negligent parents—you don't *understand* what a great need there is——" Mr. Warbeck brought his clenched fists to his temples. " 'And whosoever shall offend one of these little ones that believe in Me, it is better for him that a millstone were hanged about his neck, and he were cast into the sea!' They *needn't* have come after me—it was their own choice, their own choice!" Suddenly he looked up, a little wildly. "How—how did you guess I stayed in the buildings? Yesterday when I came out of the lavatory up on the third floor and saw all those policemen——"

"We are sometimes pretty good guessers," said Mendoza. "Why Nelson Eddy, Mr. Warbeck?"

"Oh, did you guess about that?" He was suddenly docile again; he smiled. "That was really very funny. I was startled, I don't deny it. But I had been noticed, you see—coming out—and in any case I could see they were searching the building. I just quietly walked down the stairs and then when I saw there was a policeman taking down names, why, my mind went quite blank. I only saw that I mustn't give my own, because I hadn't any real reason to be in that building. And it was queer—the very first thing that came into my head was Emily—my late wife—and how she was always saying that I wasn't resourceful, hadn't any imagination at all. My, Emily *would* be surprised! And then I remembered for some reason how she'd enjoyed all those old pictures—we used to go quite often, before her arthritis came on—all those old Jeannette MacDonald pictures with Nelson Eddy—*Sweethearts* and so on. So did I—they were very nice pictures. And so——"

"Yes," said Mendoza. "Will you tell us why you picked banks downtown, Mr. Warbeck? In the most crowded section?"

"And the only address I could remember offhand was the place my landlady takes her cat for doctoring—I helped her once—so I gave that. Oh, about that? I had thought that out very carefully too. For one thing, I had a legitimate reason to be downtown several days a week—our little group, you know—and then, more important, I thought where the streets *are* usually very crowded it would seem natural that the bank robber had just mingled with the crowd and vanished. And you did think that, didn't you?"

"For a while," said Mendoza. "And then—you shot a third man, and you found he'd been a cop."

"Fourth—he was the fourth," said Warbeck almost petulantly. "You forgot Walter. That was a really most peculiar thing, you know, and it almost makes me believe in the doctrine of predestination. As I told you, Lieutenant, I'd never owned a gun before. Those other people, they were quite close to me—the guard had his hand on my left arm, and the teller was right up against me—all I had to do was pull the trigger. It was a—a most unusual feeling of—of *power*, but I wasn't *surprised* at having shot them. I couldn't have helped hitting them. But that police officer—I wonder now if it *is* so, that each of us has just a certain allotted time here? Because he would have been familiar with guns, wouldn't he? And he must have been twenty feet away from me. When I came out of that bank, you see, there was no one in the lobby at all, and so I went up to the foot of the stairs where there's a little shadow, and very quickly I turned my jacket inside out and I was just fitting on my toupee—I'd got very quick at putting it on, I'd practiced at home—when he—er—challenged me, and when I turned around he had his gun already out. He fired before I did, when I took *my* gun out, but he missed me—and I just fired blindly, aiming as best I could, but I didn't really know how. I *was* surprised when he fell down. But he *needn't* have got out his gun! It was *his* choice! In another thirty seconds I'd have been on the second floor and taking the elevator up to our little office—I really was expecting Miss Corsa, as I told you——"

"And when you heard it was a police sergeant you'd shot, you got a little nervous, and you thought you'd play very clever by telling me a pretty little fairy tale," said Mendoza.

"Well, I knew, of course—from all my reading—that you'd be all the more anxious to—er—*get* someone who had—— Yes, I'm afraid so, Lieutenant. I thought if you were convinced that the bank robber was injured, it would——"

"Send us off in the wrong direction. So it did. You made some nice plans, Mr. Warbeck," said Mendoza.

"Well, I thought so," said Mr. Warbeck simply, pleased. "Except when it came to the actual money, that was being difficult." Piggott and Scarne were up at the Laurel Canyon house where Mr. Warbeck rented a room, going through that. "Your men will have found it by now, I expect," and on that he sounded depressed again. "Such a *waste*—all I could have done with it! But I knew at least some of the bills would be recognized eventually. Actually I was going to start spending some of it next week. The first payment on Marion Holderby's braces is due, and I thought I would give some of the money to Dr. Gold, the dentist. By the time it was identified, he couldn't possibly say who had given it to him, and he's a busy man with a large practice. I'd hoped——" He sighed. He looked from one to the other of them, standing there staring at him. "You do understand? It was for the *children*——"

They didn't talk much about Mr. Warbeck. They got all of that down in a formal statement, and he signed it quite meekly. Piggott and Scarne came in, looking incredulous and bulging with money—the whole sum of the loot, which had been neatly stacked in paper bags in Mr. Warbeck's closet. They also had the gun and a box of shells.

"I doubt very much," said Mendoza, after they'd got Mr. Warbeck formally charged and booked into the new jail, "that he'll ever see the inside of San Quentin. I think they'll find he's legally insane."

Palliser agreed. "God, what a thing. A regular obsession?"

Higgins said, "What he said about his wife—and I gathered the mother was another strong character. Maybe a whole big bunch of aggression piling up in him all his life, until something had to give."

"*Caray,* you going all psychological, George? That could be. I think the head doctors are going to be interested in him. And at least we've got him locked in tight, boys, and he isn't going to be shooting any more cops—or anybody else—and also without much doubt something new will come along very shortly to plague us all over again, so let's for God's sake go home now." Mendoza yawned. They were standing on the steps of the new jail. Hopefully tonight's ten o'clock temperature felt just slightly cooler than last night's.

Higgins yawned in sympathy. "That high-school kid. Karen Flagg, with all the H in her. I got a vague sort of lead on that today. I guess you're right. See you in the morning." He strode off toward his car.

Mendoza lit a cigarette. "You ever wish you'd decided to go in for plumbing or journalism or something, John?"

Palliser hesitated and laughed. "Not really, I guess. At least it's what you might call varied work—you see a lot of types and run into a lot of different things."

"Now there's the understatement of the month," said Mendoza dryly. "*¡Solo Dios sabe qué pasará,* how true, how true! Go home. I'll see you tomorrow."

"It's my day off."

"So it is. Monday then. I have every faith," said Mendoza, "that something else will come up to keep our noses to the grindstone by then. It nearly always does. See you." He walked away toward the Ferrari.

Alison kept interrupting him with little shocked exclamations, but Mrs. MacTaggart listened in grave silence, her lips compressed.

"—so without much doubt they'll tuck him away at Atascadero, and that's that."

Mrs. MacTaggart said slowly, "I wouldna have believed it. I wouldna have *believed* it. It just doesna seem possible. And all for nought, when you come down to it—all for just nought. Four people deid. It does seem, times, God isna just so very orderly. A body's just got to have faith it's all arranged for some good reason we'll maybe understand in good time."

She went out quietly. They had heard the single pronouncement Máiri would make on Mr. Warbeck.

"Such an awful—— I can hardly believe it either, he seemed like such a mild little man!"

"That's how that kind looks, a lot of times. I wonder if it's too late to call Art. He'll be interested." Mendoza looked at his watch. "Probably not. If I know Art, after all that hospital regime where they firmly turn out the

lights about eight-thirty, he's sitting up watching the Late Show." He
went out to the phone and dialed. Alison trailed after him.

"No, I was still up," said Hackett. "What——"

"Still feeling better?"

"Well, the only thing, damn it," said Hackett, sounding indignant,
"after all that damned bland hospital food, *now* Angel feeds me her nice
exotic French gourmet stuff and I get indigestion!"

Mendoza laughed. "This is not a perfect world, *compadre.* Very possibly it never will be. I thought you'd be interested—we've got him . . ." He
told Hackett the story, and Hackett asked excited questions and said several times he'd be damned.

"One like that. God, so they won't even——"

"No, they won't even."

"*¡Cuidado!*" said Alison, and Mendoza braced himself; Sheba landed
midway up his back and clawed up to sit on his shoulder.

"*Where* she learned such a——" said Alison.

"Just one of the cats," said Mendoza. "You'd better go to bed. I'll drop
over soon, unless something else urgent comes up." He put down the
phone, lifted Sheba to the floor, and said, "At least, the main thing, we
got him. I ought to write to Mary Dwyer."

"Mmh," said Alison. She smoothed his mustache. "So, can you stay
home awhile for a change? Most of the night?"

"*Tal vez.* It's to be seen." He put his arms around her lightly and then
harder. He laughed. "I wonder now. I do just wonder."

"*¿Como?*"

"About George. Higgins. Well, she's a damn good-looking woman.
Bert's wife. When she came in that day, he did look—smitten."

"Oh, really," said Alison. "Sergeant Higgins? He's quite the confirmed
bachelor, isn't he?"

Mendoza absently rolled a lock of her red hair round his forefinger.
"Mmh. Ask me, preconceived idea that no respectable pretty female'd look
twice at him. Well, he's no movie star. But when you get to know him,
George is quite a guy. Only—would she? Even after a while?"

"You mean because——"

"Mmh. Suppose I got shot up tomorrow——"

"Knock on wood, fingers crossed."

"*¡Supersticioso!* Would you be thinking seriously about marrying another cop, a year from now?"

"I would not," said Alison. "You need a shave. I didn't marry a cop. I
married Luis Rodolfo Vicente Mendoza."

"Lady," said Mendoza sadly, "sometimes I think there's no separating the two. Why would any sensible woman want to marry a cop, anyway?"

"Well, there are cops," said Alison, "and then there are cops . . . There go the twins. Isn't it *heavenly* to have somebody *else* to look after them? Didn't you know, I married you for your money, *naturalmente.*"

"*¡Naturalmente!*" said Mendoza. "So come and earn your bank account and your charge accounts."

"You know I don't believe in charge acc——"

But cops are technically on duty twenty-four hours a day.

At three minutes after one Mendoza was just drifting off to sleep, drowsily and comfortably aware of the familiar carnation scent that said *Alison* snuggled close, when the phone rang.

He stirred. Alison murmured something.

The phone rang again, insistently. Mendoza sat up. He said into the darkness, "Damn." He groped for the bedside lamp on his side of the bed. The phone rang again.

Alison said sleepily, "Well, at least——"

"Mendoza here."

"I'm sorry as hell to disturb you, Lieutenant," said Sergeant Thoms, "but we've got this thing. Might be quite a thing. See, the squad-car men called in about five minutes ago. Disturbance at a bar down on Flower. What it is, this guy apparently went berserk. In the bar. He shot up a lot of people—three ambulances on the way, by what the squad-car boys say, four-five people hurt, maybe bad. And he was talking wild about shooting his wife and kids, and he ran out before the squad car got there, and the bartender says he knows him, a regular customer, but he doesn't know his name or where he lives, and—— Well, it could turn into quite a thing, you can see. I thought I'd better—— I sent two other cars over, and Schenke's on his way, but——"

"Yes. O.K. See what you mean. I'm on my way too." Mendoza got out of bed.

"A *cop*," said Alison indistinctly.

"*Desafortunado,*" said Mendoza. He dressed rapidly. He checked his pockets—billfold, badge, keys, cigarettes. He went quietly out the back door to the garage and backed out the Ferrari.

The situation at Headquarters Homicide was very seldom static.

And always it had to do with death. Random death, stalking the streets of the city at random.

COFFIN CORNER

"Man is but man, unconstant still, and various;
There's no tomorrow in him, like today."

—Dryden, *Cleomenes*

ONE

"I don't know which is worst," said Hackett through a yawn: "the times everything happens at once or the times nothing happens at all."

"Knock on wood," said Higgins. "You start complaining and right off you get some real toughie dropped into your lap."

Hackett yawned again. "I don't know that I'd mind, George. I'm bored."

A couple of desks away in the big communal sergeants' room at Headquarters Homicide, Detective Jason Grace had pulled up to his typewriter and was tapping out a report with his usual efficiency. He looked up and said with a grin, "You're just inviting trouble, you know."

"Oh, don't be superstitious," said Hackett.

"Who dat you say dat to, white man?" said Detective Grace, his teeth widely white against his coffee-colored skin.

Hackett picked out the last cigarette, balled up the empty pack and threw it at him. Grace fielded deftly. "So you had to leave college before you got your M.A.," said Hackett. "God, when I think what a narrow escape the American public had." He lit the cigarette. "If you didn't happen to be on the side of the angels, Jase, what a hell of a con man you'd have made."

It was, oddly enough, all too true. There was just something about Jason Grace: in spite of his rather terrifying efficiency, everybody liked him on sight, and Mendoza was known to have said that Grace could persuade the truth out of Ananias if he had the chance.

"Let's be thankful for a little boredom, Sergeant," Jason said philosophically. "The rat race'll get under way again soon enough. Always does." He went back to his report: the suicide turned up yesterday in the Seventh Street hotel.

Hackett smothered another yawn. It was the third of March, a nice spring day, and things were going slow in the office, an unusual state of affairs for Headquarters Homicide of L.A. Possibly the weather had something to do with it: sunny but not too warm. People felt happier, tempers weren't so easily stirred up or accidents likely to happen to harried citizens. The result was a spell of the very-much-routine, the boring routine which always constituted so much of police work anyway: there'd been the suicide, a couple of traffic accidents, a couple of muggings. Landers was doing some legwork on the latter. Grace's report would close out the suicide. Glasser and Piggott had gone out a while ago to clean up another traffic fatality. Sergeant Palliser's mother had died suddenly a couple of days ago and he was taking some time off to cope with all that had to be done in consequence.

"What are you cogitating about, George?" Hackett asked lazily.

"Ohh," said Higgins a little guiltily, "a summer camp for Stevie, maybe." He didn't need to expand on that; and maybe he wouldn't have said it at all, if anybody else had been there.

"Mmm," said Hackett. He felt academically sorry for Higgins, who had several counts against him in his humble pursuit of Bert Dwyer's widow. It wasn't very likely that Mary Dwyer, having had one cop husband killed, would want to acquire a second cop husband. But Higgins liked her kids; he built up little schemes to give them things without Mary's knowing.

"I thought maybe I could tell her," he said now, "that I know one of the managers of the place, or there's a plan to let kids without fathers in at half price—you know, something like that, Art. You think she'd suspect anything? I mean, he does want to go, and she can't afford it, and I just thought—"

Hackett started to say he thought it'd have to be more subtle than that, when Lieutenant Mendoza came in.

"All you hard-working detectives," he said, surveying them. He looked sharp as usual, the narrow mustache trimmed, newish charcoal Dacron suit, discreet tie and the new gold cuff links Alison had given him for his birthday four days ago. "You finished that Wells report, Art?"

"Couple of hours ago. What are we supposed to be working at? Nothing new in so far as I know. I'm *damn* bored."

"I keep warning him," said Grace. "Just inviting trouble." He ripped the triplicate report from the typewriter and neatly aligned all the edges. "So that's that. Poor little girl." He shook his head over the suicide, now just a few typed records to gather dust in the files. "When are we going to get some sensible narcotics laws on the books? If she couldn't have got hold of the stuff so easy—"

"I could argue that one," said Mendoza seriously, hoisting one hip onto the corner of Hackett's desk. "Like the weapon-possessions bit. Doesn't matter what stiff laws you've got, anybody wants anything enough can always get it."

"*And* there's the bit about free will," said Grace thoughtfully. "I guess. I think I'm catching spring fever from the rest of you—I won't argue." He slipped the report into a manila envelope and lit a cigarette.

There hadn't been anything at all except the deadly routine since they'd finally cleared up that Fearing business about ten days ago. A funny one, in a mild way: in spite of all the motives and all the suspects in the killing, it had turned out to be the casual break-in after all. Of course, Homicide seldom got a real mystery to solve: police work is mostly deadly routine. But on the average they got something a little more interesting than they'd had lately—something that made them feel a bit more like the upstanding protectors of law and order instead of a bunch of glorified clerks.

For a space there was silence. These first warm days of spring, no denying, were enervating. Mendoza lit a cigarette and stared at the calendar on the wall. Hackett yawned again. Higgins frowned over his problem of how to get Stevie Dwyer to summer camp without letting Mary know he was paying for it. Jason Grace ruminated somewhat sleepily on what to get his wife for her birthday.

They were just four men who knew each other very well and felt comfortable together, in spite of the fact that Jason Grace had been with them only a few months. It might have been any kind of office at all, the big, rather bare, efficiently laid out room with its desks and swivel chairs and typewriters.

The next minute Sergeant Farrell, who was minding the desk while Sergeant Lake recuperated from an emergency appendectomy, burst into the room. And quite suddenly there were four alert police officers looking at him expectantly.

"D.O.A. at Seventh and Broadway," he announced tersely. "Squad car just called in. A hit-and-run. Probably a lot of witnesses, thank God."

Hackett and Higgins got up resignedly. And Mendoza said without moving, "Not usually so emotional, Rory. Who got it?" His voice was soft.

Farrell looked at him. "You really have got a crystal ball, haven't you, Lieutenant? It's the patrolman on that corner—the traffic man. Harry Cohen. And it looks, by what the squad-car man said, as if it was—done on purpose."

"Oh my God," said Hackett. "Come on, George."

The phone rang shrilly in the anteroom and Farrell plunged to answer it. "Headquarters Homicide, Sergeant Farrell."

"You coming, Luis?" Hackett snatched his hat.

"I don't—"

"Lieutenant!" Farrell was back. "Another one. 'Nother squad-car man. D.O.A. in a store of some kind over on Los Angeles. A woman."

"¡Paso!" said Mendoza sardonically. "Did somebody say something about nothing happening? All right, Jase and I'll take that." He stood up.

Hackett and Higgins went out in a hurry. Mendoza took his hat off the rack, the usual wide-brimmed dark Homburg, and Grace opened the door to the corridor, neatly tucking away the slip of paper with the address scribbled on it in his breast pocket. Piggott and Glasser were just outside, with a woman between them. She was a nice-looking middle-aged woman, well dressed in a neat tan gabardine suit, crisp white blouse; her well-bred little felt hat was just a trifle crooked and her white-gloved hands, clasped together, were shaking, but otherwise she was quite tidy and ordinary. Except that she was talking rapidly, compulsively, breathlessly.

"He stepped right off the curb in front of me, I couldn't have stopped in time, I tried, I did, but right in front of me as if he came out of *nowhere*—I've never had even a parking ticket in my life and I've been driving for twenty years—stepped right off the curb in *front* of me and I couldn't—"

"Yes, we know, Mrs. Madden," said Piggott gently, and to Mendoza, "Accident pure and simple. Damn fool was drunk . . . Rory, call up one of our females, hah? Get this poor woman calmed down to make a statement . . . You just come and sit down quiet, ma'am, we understand how it happened."

Mendoza went out after Grace. "You get the address?"

"Over in the one hundred block on Los Angeles," said Detective Grace. "Secondhand store. Doesn't sound like anything much. Heart attack or something. Just more routine."

They were all to remember that little remark later as something of an understatement.

When Hackett and Higgins got to Seventh and Broadway they found a kind of organized chaos awaiting them. That is normally a very busy intersection in the middle of downtown L.A. anyway, and a sudden and shocking traffic fatality had glued the passing crowds to the pavement on both sides of the street. The chaos, in that rather narrow (for modern traffic) street, was not helped along by the fact that a few alert squad-car men had roped off a large section in the middle of the intersection (for the lab technicians' examination) and a couple of other uniformed men were directing impatient traffic around it one car at a time. The ambulance had gone. Hackett parked the Barracuda alongside a red-painted section of curb and he and Higgins walked out to where several men in uniform stood about the intersection center. "Which of you called in?" asked Hackett.

"Me, sir—Steiner. I got here first—my partner's got the fellow who called, guy named Smith—and we called up reinforcements soon as we saw what it was—my God, I knew Harry Cohen since I've been on the force! Nicest guy you'd want to meet—" Steiner was shaken. "And, my God, you'll have to sort out the witnesses, about a hundred people all rushed up and wanted to say what they saw, you know how it'd be—crowded streets and—"

"Any I.D. on the car at all?" asked Higgins.

"Oh, for God's sake," said Steiner. "For *God's* sake. Do I need to tell you? Just by what I've heard from about twenty people I've talked to—and the rest of the boys are trying to round up everybody who saw anything at all—it could've been anything from a Rolls-Royce to a VW. You know how people are."

Neither Hackett nor Higgins said anything. They knew how people were.

"In general, what most of 'em do say is that this car all of a sudden just speeded up and went straight for him: he was standing right here in the middle, naturally, directing traffic both ways." Steiner gestured. The streets were not all that narrow: plenty of safe margin for the experienced traffic officer in his navy uniform and white gloves to stand there, whistle in hand, expediting the heavy downtown traffic. "My God—Harry. A nice guy. I can't believe it, but that's what everybody says. Car went straight at him—deliberate. Could've been out of control some way—that's easiest to think—maybe a drunk—but, anyway, it knocked him flat and went right over him and screeched around onto Seventh and—my God!" said Steiner. He wore a sick expression; he was a youngish man. "Somebody'd already called an ambulance before I radioed in, but we got here before. Thank God he was dead then—even I knew he was dead. His face—right over his— My God, I've seen my share of accidents, but—" He passed a hand across his mouth. "Harry," he said. "Not maybe the ambitious type, you know, Sergeant? But the hell of a good guy. Been on the force twenty years or so."

"Well, the lab boys are coming," said Hackett. "Any tire marks, you think?"

"I don't know—it's hard to say. All these streets need repaving, mostly—the surface—"

"Could be some on his clothes, Art," said Higgins.

"Um. Lab boys'll look there too. I suppose we'd better start to talk to people," said Hackett.

Four men in uniform were riding herd, over there on the sidewalk, on a bunch of people between two illegally-parked squad cars. They were looking a little desperate, and all the people were talking at the tops of their voices, not listening to each other. Hackett and Higgins moved resignedly toward them.

"I saw it, I got a good look at it, 'twas an old black car like maybe a Dodge or a Buick and about ten years old—"

"Run right *over* the p'liceman, it did, I couldn't *look*, just awful—"

"It was a Mercury, I know cars and it was a—"

"Dark green it was, Officer, I'd know it in a minute if I saw it again—"

"I got the *license* number! I got the *license*—"

The citizenry. Well, often they could be a big help. As well as a headache. Hackett made for the horn-rimmed young man who was waving a slip of paper in the air and insisting he had the license number. Maybe he had and they could clean this one up in a hurry.

Which would be nice. The men at Headquarters Homicide didn't like death any better than the next man, but most of all they disliked the death—the death by violence—of a cop.

Los Angeles Street was, along here, a shabby and depressed city thoroughfare. The buildings lining it were old and grimy, long in need of paint. The address Mendoza and Grace wanted was in the middle of the block, a two-story frame building which comprised nearly the whole block. There were shop-fronts on the ground floor, and here a pair of narrow display windows, long unwashed, dimly revealed a heterogeneous collection of old-fashioned lamps, end tables, framed pictures, and stacks of chipped chinaware. A nearly illegible legend on both windows read *Furniture and Household Goods*. Down from the shop door to the right was another door, which apparently led to the upper regions of the building.

An ambulance was parked in front, and a small knot of curious pedestrians had gathered. A man in uniform was at the door, the squad car parked in a loading zone nearby.

"The interns say it looks like maybe a heart attack," the uniformed man said when Mendoza introduced himself. "Customer went in and found her, called in."

But of course they had to look at it and make a report. They went in. "Hell!" said Mendoza, barking his shin on some unidentifiable object inside the door. "Aren't there any lights in the place?" After the bright sunshine outside, it was very dim in the shop. It was a good-sized place, and as their eyes accommodated to the darkness it appeared to be jam-packed with as motley a collection of dilapidated odds and ends as Mendoza had ever seen. Ancient furniture, everything from floor lamps to beds to dining tables to chairs to bureaus—and piled on and around the furniture were framed pictures, china, glasses, cheap vases, toys—a baby carriage minus a wheel, a grandfather clock with no hands, books, musty dusty stacks of old phonograph records: it was a jungle, threaded by two narrow aisles. At the rear of the store stood a small crowd of people. Two white jackets—the interns. A uniform—the other squad-car man. A couple of other people.

Avoiding the merchandise, Mendoza and Grace joined them.

The center of the little group, and the focal point, was the terrible, still body of the woman. At the rear of the shop, here, was a partition with a doorless opening giving onto, probably, some sort of private office, at the end of one cleared aisle. The woman had fallen some fifteen feet from the opening, and she lay on her back, one arm upflung over her head, mouth gaping horridly, eyes half open, legs twisted. She had not been an attractive woman in life, and in death she was obscene.

She was perhaps sixty and too fat. Her gray hair made a kind of wild halo about her head on the dusty floor. She had on a faded blue-and-white cotton housedress, thick tan stockings and a pair of Cuban-heeled tan oxfords.

"Reckon it must've been a heart attack." The soft southern accent brought Mendoza's eyes to the young slim Negro. "You another officer, sir? I'm Lee Rainey—I come in and found her, poor soul. Just a while ago. Called you people di-reckly." He smiled. "Nice woman she was, if she could be sort of sharp, times. Me and Martha's picked up this 'n' that here a lot. I just come in lookin' for a little table to go beside the bed."

"We've got an I.D., then? You know her name, Mr. Rainey?"

"I got it all down, sir," said the uniformed man. "She was the proprietor here. A Mrs. McCann. Eliza McCann."

"Nice enough woman, if she could be a bit sharp like," said Lee Rainey mildly. He looked at Detective Grace with interest.

"What's it look like?" Mendoza asked the interns. One of them was small and blond, the other hulking and sandy.

That one shrugged. "Suppose you'll want an autopsy. Could be a lot of things. Stroke, cardiac failure. Looks like heart, most likely—no signs of purging. She's been dead somewhere around an hour, I'd say. Can we take her?"

And of course it looked, so far, like the very routine thing. The natural sudden death. Not a young woman. Just another technical homicide, sudden death alone, with the routine investigation to be made and the reports typed up for filing.

Mendoza said, "Take her. Does anybody know where she lived? Is there any family?"

The portly Semitic-looking man standing beside the patrolman spoke up. "Yes, sir, yes, sir, I do—a terrible thing, to die all alone like that, so *sudden*—makes you think, you know. Makes you stop and think. I knew her more than thirty years—beg pardon, my name's Wolf, Max Wolf, I run the pawnshop down the block—thirty-five years next July it's been— Just a terrible thing! Lee, he knows me too and he came up to use my phone—no phone in her store, you know—and I came right back with him to see the poor woman laying there like that—"

"You know where she lived?"

"Yes, sir, I do. A terrible shock it'll be to her family—over on Old High Street, sir, just down from North Broadway—I know she had a couple of brothers, and I think there's a sister too—it's a hotel, called the Celtic Hotel, I guess it is—"

All very routine it was. Probably the sudden heart attack, something like that. And one of the little unpleasant jobs police officers had to do was break the bad news.

Which on this occasion would postpone their lunch hour.

"Where the hell is Old High Street?" asked Mendoza. "I thought I knew this town."

Grace consulted a County Guide. "I never heard of it either. Here—just up from the old plaza, only a couple of blocks long."

That was, of course, the very oldest part of L.A. When they got there, it was a very narrow, ancient blacktop street with a number of derelict-looking frame buildings along both sides of it and, interspersed with those, a few ramshackle old houses. None of them, at first glance, had been built after 1900. A couple of them were authentic General Grant in style, complete with gingerbread eaves and deep front porches, and the Celtic Hotel was one of those.

It was a four-story building whose original tan paint had faded and cracked to uniform grime-color. The word *subfusc* went through Mendoza's mind. The sign sagged dispiritedly over the porch eaves and was barely legible—a much-faded shamrock and turn-of-the-century fancy lettering. There was no sign of life about the building at all.

Immediately next to it stood a one-story building of a scarcely later period and likewise long unpainted. It might have started life as a single house but evidently in more recent years had become a shop of some sort. A small fat man was standing on the sidewalk in front of it—the inevitable widening of old streets had put the sidewalks right up to the buildings—carefully touching up the gilt lettering on the shopwindow. The lettering said in bold Gothic: *McLaughlin the Friendly Undertaker.*

Mendoza and Grace left the Ferrari at the curb and went up to the porch of the hotel. The small unpleasant duty—breaking news of death—did not appeal to either of them.

The front door was locked, and there wasn't a sign of a doorbell.

"¡*Caray!*" said Mendoza, annoyed.

"Seems funny, if it *is* a hotel," said Grace.

"I beg your pardon." The little fat man had left his sign painting and came trotting up the old wooden steps. "What was it you wanted? This is a private hotel, you know. Or perhaps you're looking for an undertaker?" He had moist, eager brown eyes and a rosebud-pink little mouth; he had no hair at all and astonishingly long eyelashes. He was wearing neat tan chino work pants and a white shirt without a tie. "I own the hotel—at least, *we* own it, my family—but if you *should* be happening to want an undertaker, I have my business right next door as you can see—"

"Mr.—"

"Oscar McLaughlin, sir. If you *should* be wanting—"

"Mr. McLaughlin, I understand a Mrs. Eliza McCann lives at this address—" And, as he had too many times over the years, Mendoza broke the news of death.

He was not prepared for the reaction he got. Reactions, of course, varied—people being people.

Oscar McLaughlin just stared at him and said, "Ellie *dead?* You don't mean to tell me Ellie's gone and died, just like that, *away from home?*" He began to look outraged and indignant. "Now that is just too thoughtless of her! I really thought she'd have managed better than that!"

TWO

Mendoza stared back at him. Grace coughed gently and said, "Well, Mr. McLaughlin, it seems to have been very sudden. A heart attack or a stroke. You see—"

"Yes, yes, I daresay," said McLaughlin. He pulled thoughtfully at his pouting lower lip. "But how very vexatious. You don't know what it was? That seems strange, Ellie's always been very robust. Very. In fact, of course, I saw her when she left this morning and she was quite as usual. Dear me, this *is* awkward. I think—yes, you had better come in." He fished in his pocket and produced a key, unlocked the massive old front door, which creaked as it swung open. "We keep it locked because of the monkey," he added. "Henry! Henry, are you here?"

The door let them into a large, very bare room which it took a moment to identify as the original lobby. A counter still ran alongside the right-hand wall with a small section of pigeonholes behind it; both were absolutely bare. The old pine floor was uncarpeted and dusty. A rickety-looking staircase led up at the left rear of the lobby, and a pair of carved double doors at the left were closed. "Henry?" shouted Oscar McLaughlin, and tapped at the double doors.

They slid halfway open. "I'm not yet deaf, Oscar," said a rather fretful voice. "What *is* it? I'm at a *rather* crucial place—the lilies of the valley." Another fat little man appeared in the doorway; his resemblance to Oscar marked them at once as brothers.

"Ellie is dead, Henry. Apparently she had a heart attack or something of that nature and died actually *in* the store. These gentlemen are police. I do call it very awkward."

"Really!" said Henry McLaughlin. "Dead? Well, I must certainly agree with you—who would have expected such a thing? Why, she was only sixty-five. And in the *store*—" He shook his head. "Most unfortunate.

None of our family has ever had heart trouble of any sort." He looked at Mendoza and Grace disapprovingly.

"*Dead?*" It was an anguished feminine wail from the stairs. Mendoza and Grace whirled. The woman halfway down the stairs was easily six feet tall and thin to emaciation. She might have been seventy-five. She was wearing an ancient black chiffon evening gown which had been roughly hemmed to street length or what had been street length some years ago; it hit her at mid-calf. Around her bare shoulders were draped layers of scarves and shawls, pink, blue, crimson, purple. *Solomon in all his glory*, thought Mendoza, awed. She was wearing black silk stockings fancily clocked up the calf and a pair of low-heeled black velvet slippers; she carried over one scrawny arm a large fish-net shopping bag and clutched in her other hand a very large much-buckled-and-strapped black leather handbag. Her hair was dyed henna-purple and hung loose about a face so raddled with heavy make-up that it was difficult to assess her features at all. "*Dead?*" she wailed again. "Ellie? What are you saying, Oscar? And I've been coming along so well with my cooking lessons! *Now* who's to teach me?" She came down the stairs to the lobby and began to cry gently. "I know it sounds selfish, Oscar, and I *loved* Ellie really—how can she be *dead?* She was perfectly all right when she left this morning—But I can't help thinking of Albert coming for me at last, and having our own little home, and me not able to so much as scramble *eggs* for him—I wasn't brought up to it, but I do mean to be a good little wife to him—and I've been *learning*, you know I have, even the eggs—when I remember to add the mustard."

"Yes, yes, Miss Manning," said Oscar. "It's all very awkward all round."

"Mind the monkey," said Henry conversationally. Grace let out an involuntary yell as fingers grasped his ankle; the monkey, a small brown capuchin wearing a bright red collar, swarmed up him rapidly, sat on his shoulder and began busily parting his hair.

"Hey," said Grace nervously.

"Friendly cuss, ain't he? But not everybody likes 'em." The newcomer was a very tall thin old man who appeared from some back regions behind the lobby. He was wearing torn overalls and a blue shirt. "Don't reckon you do. Did I hear somebody say as Eliza's dead?" He plucked the monkey off Grace, who stepped back thankfully and resettled his collar. "Now that *is* a downright shock, ain't it? I don't reckon as old Karl'll be gettin' any more sauerkraut, hey, lessen he fixes it hisself."

"*I'm* not going to do it for him," said Miss Manning disdainfully. "Nasty German stuff. Albert never liked the Germans."

Something brushed by Mendoza's ankles and he glanced down to discover a large and aggressively-jowled black tomcat staring back at him. "Beelzebub," said Henry McLaughlin. "Kindly do not touch him. He bites everyone except me. I daresay you're quite right, Ben. This *is* awkward."

"Mr. McLaughlin," said Mendoza, "we'll want a formal identification. If you or your brother could come now and make that— And we'll want to have an autopsy, unless Mrs. McCann had been under a doctor's care. Excuse me, what relationship was—"

"A doctor? Dear me, no, Ellie was strong as a horse, she never went to doctors. She's my sister, sir—and Henry's, of course. Henry, I expect you had better go up and tell Jane about this. How *extremely* awkward indeed. An identification? At the *morgue*, you mean? Oh, of course, and I had best do that—of course, of course, I'll come with you at once. If you will just wait until I change my clothes—proper respect—I won't be a moment." Oscar bustled off.

"I don't really like to *break* eggs," said Miss Manning mournfully. "Such messy things until they're cooked, aren't they? Dear Ellie—she was so patient with me, I hardly know what I shall do now. And, Henry!" She clutched her throat. "I just *thought*—who is going to take care of Gertrude now? You know she kicks everybody but Ellie."

"I know, I know," said Henry impatiently. "It is *very* awkward indeed."

"You s'pose," said the man called Ben, "Percy or somebody'd want to take over the store? Lease's got a while to run, I guess, and it brings in a little."

"Certainly not Jane," said Henry. "*Or* myself. We shall ask Percy. I have My Own Work." His tone capitalized that. "This has *upset* me. I really don't feel I can do any more today, and I was so hoping to have the peace and quiet to get the lilies done. It's been coming quite well."

"That special order?" said Ben. The monkey sat on his shoulder, picking through his sparse gray hair.

"I don't know that I feel like going out to shop," said Miss Manning mournfully.

"But there's not much in the place that I know of," said Henry. "Our part of the house, that is. Ellie left you the usual shopping list, my dear? I should really like something besides lukewarm mushroom soup tonight. Good heavens, I suppose we shall have to have a funeral."

"I think there's some cold ham," said Miss Manning.

"I never knew as Ellie had a bad heart," said Ben. "Seems funny to me

—big healthy female like that. Right as rain when she went off this morning."

"We don't know what it was, Mr.—"

"Kelly. Ben Kelly. Goin' to cut her up to find out, hey?"

"That's right, sir," said Grace. "When she hadn't been under a doctor's care, the law is that—"

"Just as well," said Ben. "Poor Eliza. Kind of a tough life that poor woman had, all's said and done."

Oscar McLaughlin came bustling back. He had changed into a very tight black suit, a starched white shirt and a spreading black silk Ascot tie; his plump little feet were encased in shiny black patent shoes, and the tip of a white silk handkerchief showed in his breast pocket.

"I'm quite ready, gentlemen," he announced. "Of course I understand it's necessary, *and* the autopsy, though one doesn't like to think of a relative being— But then of course we must remember it is only the dead clay, not the *person*. As an undertaker myself I take a slightly different view of these matters, naturally. Really, I haven't taken it in yet—poor Ellie!"

"Where is she, Oscar?" asked Henry. "Will you be anywhere near Woolworth's?"

Oscar looked at him in slight disapproval. "It is a *sad* errand," he said. "I could stop on the way back."

"I don't know, perhaps it would settle my nerves to work," said Henry. "Such an upset. But one must be practical, after all, and it *is* a special order. And you know very well you are the only one in the house whose eye for color I can trust. Just a moment." He vanished beyond the double doors, to reappear with several short wisps of embroidery silk held carefully between thumb and forefinger. "Please put them away carefully where you won't lose them. I shall need at least three more skeins of the pearl-white and three of the champagne. One of the jade. Here is the money. Oscar, has it occurred to you that there will have to be a funeral?"

"Indeed, indeed," said Oscar, putting away the change in an old-fashioned snap-top purse. "Do you think we could *ask* Dr. Parsifal?"

"But the *cost*," said Henry. "The expense, Oscar!"

"I know, I know. Quite unavoidable, I'm afraid, as matters stand. There it is. Never ill a day in her life, and then this has to happen. But don't fuss, Henry—we shall get over it, we shall get over it. Gentlemen, if you're ready—"

"Jane will want a salad, of course," said Miss Manning. "Fresh lettuce. And the Italian dressing, I *think* Ellie said. What we're to do without her I really don't know— Oh, Ben, do hang onto Robespierre, you know I can't bear him pulling my scarves. And, Ben, I forgot to take the garbage out to Gertrude."

"I'll see to it, ma'am," said Ben.

"I really think perhaps it would *settle* me to work," said Henry, and firmly shut himself behind the double doors.

Oscar viewed the body, then more decently straightened out on the morgue refrigerator slab, and identified it formally. "Really, such an upset," he murmured. "I hardly know how we'll get on without her. Such an efficient person, Ellie. I should certainly have expected her to arrange matters more suitably."

Mendoza looked at him. "That almost sounds as if you were hinting that your sister committed suicide, Mr. McLaughlin. Do you have any reason to suspect—"

Oscar looked shocked. "Oh, dear me, no, sir. No, no. The last thing in the world Ellie would have done. No, no. But it is awkward—there'll be the shop, and all that— Well, I suppose you'll let us know when we can, er, have the body? Just so."

"They do say it takes all sorts," commented Grace after Oscar had identified the body and, clucking, had gone on his way.

"¡Como no!" said Mendoza. "That Manning woman—and Henry—" He started to laugh. "Henry and his embroidery. My God. One thing about being a cop, Jase, you do acquire some stories to tell. And they say all this pernicious conformity is growing, the rugged individualists getting fewer and farther between. Tell it to any cop!"

"That monkey—I tell you the truth, I never have liked monkeys much. In the zoo, O.K.—but not loose."

"I think I agree with you. Well, duty done, we can now have lunch. I might even stand you a drink with it. After Oscar I rather feel I need one."

"Um." Grace brightened. "Came across a new one the other day." Any book Jason Grace got hold of would inevitably receive intensive study; his wife had thoughtlessly given him a paperback copy of the bartenders' encyclopedia a while ago. "Thing called a Serpent's Tooth. Irish whisky, sweet vermouth, lemon juice, kümmel and bitters."

"¡Ay de mi!" said Mendoza. "Antidote for Oscar. I wonder what Art and George got on that hit-and-run . . ."

What they got on the hit-and-run was, of course, too much. The plate number the horn-rimmed young man gave them was JGN-790, and they started checking that out right away. But as for the rest of it—

They took statements from over fifty witnesses, and from those it emerged that the car which had run down Patrolman Harry Cohen had been black, dark green, dark blue, brown, black and white, jade green, royal blue, and dark red. It was a Dodge, a Mercury, a Buick, an Olds, a Ford Galaxie, a Chrysler Newport, a Chevrolet. It was ten years old, five years old; it was brand new. It was a four-door sedan, a two-door sedan, a coupé, a convertible. It had, after running down Patrolman Cohen, turned left on Seventh, gone straight up Broadway, and turned right on Seventh.

The only facts they had, actually, came from the autopsy surgeon and the lab. Patrolman Cohen had been run over by a car, his head and torso crushed; death had been virtually instantaneous. The lab had gone over his clothes. There were tire marks but no identifiable tread marks.

And that—unless the plate number checked out—was all they had.

They were naturally thinking a little harder about Patrolman Cohen than about Eliza McCann then. But that Wednesday afternoon, just before the shift changed, they got the D.M.V. report on that plate number, JGN-790, and it turned out to belong to one Dr. William Haverham, who lived up in Redding and drove a 1959 Pontiac. So that looked as if the horn rimmed young man had copied it down wrong; though of course they'd check out Dr. Haverham. You never did know.

Mendoza went home to Alison, the blessedly-asleep twins, the four cats and the soothing ministrations of Mrs. MacTaggart's cooking. He told Alison about Oscar, Henry, and Miss Manning—and the monkey. "Honestly, people," said Alison. "And the Communists think they can *ever* squash them all into one mass mold?"

Mendoza laughed. "There's the proverb: everyone is as God made him, and very often worse. *Así, así.* People indeed."

Higgins and Landers, both bachelors, went to dinner together at a modest restaurant downtown, and Higgins brought out his notebook over second cups of coffee. "All right, what looks like JGN? T, to start with. TGN." He put that down. "Could anybody mistake an O for a G? Possible. JON. TON. The N could be an M."

"Look," said Landers, "figuring every possible mistake, you'd end up with about a million possible plate numbers to check."

"So all right," said Higgins stubbornly, "you want to get him, don't you? 790. Could be 990? 700? 900?"

"We want to get him," said Landers. "All right." His boyish face wore a deceptively lazy expression. "What sticks in my mind, by what you and Art got, a lot of people said it looked deliberate. As if whoever was driving that car really aimed it at Cohen—took advantage of a little break in traffic, maybe, where he could do it and get away quick. So I say, why? Why did somebody have it in for Cohen?"

"Well, that sounds way out to me, Tom. An ordinary traffic cop, quiet family man. Witnesses—you know what most of 'em are worth. And a car out of control could give that impression, all too likely."

"Maybe. I just think we ought to check that aspect of it," said Landers.

"It's way out. JGN. Could have been JQN? Or TQN?" Higgins went on scribbling.

On Thursday morning another suicide turned up. For pretty sure a suicide. A girl about twenty, found dead in a second-rate hotel on Olive Avenue. Dead in bed. Registered the day before as Mary Brown. One cheap suitcase, a few clothes. Glass from bathroom used, left on the night table. In all probability some kind of sleeping pills. But no suicide note. Of course they didn't always leave one.

Piggott and Landers went out on that. Mendoza listened to Hackett's and Higgins' ideas about Cohen, and Higgins resignedly passed on what Tom Landers had said. Resignedly, because he knew the boss: a tortuous mind, said Hackett, and he *liked* it to be complicated. Higgins wasn't surprised when Mendoza said thoughtfully, "That's an angle. It just could be, you know. No harm to sniff around a little: had Cohen got across anybody lately? Personally or on the job?"

"Look, he was just standing there directing traffic," said Higgins patiently. "I'm inclined to think it was a drunk—or a J.D. in a hot heap. Who lost his head and just kept going."

"And I go along with that," said Hackett. "We'll probably hear from Redding today and find out this Dr. Haverham hasn't been out of town the last year."

"It'll do no harm to look," said Mendoza mildly.

Hackett exchanged a look with Higgins; they went on out. Mendoza called Palliser at home. Palliser was feeling low, understandably. As he sympathized, Mendoza thought of Oscar (very awkward indeed); well, people came all sorts. He supposed he ought to go to Mrs. Palliser's funeral and found the thought depressing.

At ten-thirty there was a teletype in from Redding. Dr. Haverham was, it appeared, a local Methodist minister; and neither he nor his car had been out of the county in the last six months. The car was a white four-door Pontiac.

Well, they hadn't really expected it to be that easy.

At twelve-fifteen, just as Mendoza was thinking of going out for lunch, he had a call from Dr. Bainbridge.

"This McCann woman," said Bainbridge, sounding annoyed. "I've finished the autopsy. And I'll be damned if I know what killed her, Luis."

"What? It wasn't a—"

"Well, I do know in a vague way. You could say. It was a narcotic of some kind—not a barbiturate. Affected the nervous system. But—"

"She was poisoned, for God's sake? What the hell, I thought—"

"Never mind what you thought," said Bainbridge irritably. "I can't make it out. Got curious, you know—I don't like to be stumped—I've been running tests. Got a lot more to run. It wasn't hyoscine or nicotine or atropine. But something along that line, I think. She was a perfectly healthy woman—heart sound as mine."

"¡Porvida!" said Mendoza. "I took it for granted—"

"Which is always a mistake, *as* any detective should know," said Bainbridge. "I'll continue investigations. I suppose it could have been suicide. Didn't it even cross your mind to look for a bottle or glass standing around?"

"For God's sake—" Well, of course they weren't quite as careless as all that. Mendoza thought back to yesterday morning. They had had a look round the shop, of course. Into that back room. Which was half an office, half an impromptu kitchen. Old electric hot plate on a rickety small table, some cheese wrapped in foil, half a loaf of bread on the table, instant coffee. A small sink in one corner, but he hadn't seen any used plates or glasses. And so it hadn't been a natural death after all. Poisoned, for God's sake. Suicide? He thought about Oscar and Henry and Miss Manning.

"You don't know what—"

"Oh, I'll find out," said Bainbridge. "I don't like to be stumped. Run all the damn tests. I just thought you'd like to know you've got a mysterious death on your hands and maybe start doing something about it." He hung up.

Mendoza stared at the phone, absently stroking his mustache. A poisoning. Suicide?

That hotel. Oscar the undertaker. Oh, really?

Landers said he didn't like the suicide. Because there wasn't any note.

"They don't always," said Mendoza.

"No, I know. But the clerk said she was acting all happy and keyed-up when she registered. Happy as a lark, he said. I—"

"What makes larks particularly happy, I wonder. All right, she got a phone call or a letter."

"Neither. She registered, she had dinner at a restaurant down the street, she went back to her room and that's it. They've always got quite a few salesmen in the place, lot of coming and going, so who knows whether anybody went to her room? We don't know she didn't make a phone call somewhere, tell somebody which room. Somebody could have been there. With the sleeping pills. The autopsy report isn't in yet, but that's what it looked like. Dissolved in a drink of some kind."

Mendoza sighed. "So let's find out who she really was."

"I've just been down to Missing Persons. There's a couple of possibles we're going to check out."

The routine. The deadly routine. But just occasionally something a little offbeat.

Eliza McCann. Well, it had looked so ordinary; and just what could they do on it until they knew for certain what *had* killed the woman?

It wasn't until Friday afternoon that Bainbridge called him back. "This," said Bainbridge, "is one for the books, Luis. But very damn really. I've got it. God knows how many tests I ran—I lost count. But what it was was the primitive form of digitalis. The—"

"That's heart medication. You said—"

"No," said Bainbridge. "No. I said the primitive form. I *will* be damned —first time I ever came across such a thing. What killed the woman was an infusion of the common foxglove—*Digitalis purpurea*. Stuff grows wild, very easy, almost anywhere, I understand. You steep the leaves and flowers in a little alcohol, or even plain water, and you get a damn virulent poison. Acts on the nerve centers. That's what killed the McCann woman, and offhand I'd say you've got a kind of mysterious murder to solve. Doubt whether anybody'd pick that for suicide, you know."

"¡Santa María!" said Mendoza. "Come to Papa, I want to hear more about this!"

THREE

"It is," said Bainbridge, "a biennial herb. Has dark red flowers on it, sometimes white ones. Seems to grow anywhere. Almost any part of it is poisonous, but the leaves especially. Here's a picture of it." He produced a small book bound in dark green, titled *Herbs of Healing*. "Got it at the library."

Mendoza looked at a photograph of a rather untidy-looking tall plant and passed the book on to Hackett. Grace was sitting in on this too; he craned over Hackett's shoulder.

"All right," said Mendoza, "give. Is it very hard to extract the poison?"

"Not at all, damn it. They used to think it'd cure epilepsy. Daresay they killed off a few people before they found out it doesn't. Actually the usefulness of the pure extract—digitalin—wasn't discovered until the nineteenth century. You boil up any part of it into a good strong brew, you've got a lethal dose." Dr. Bainbridge clasped his hands over his paunch and sniffed. "Goddamnedest thing I ever ran across. This day and age. In a city. Of course, this I'll say right off—a fatal dose—God, how melodramatic *that* sounds—a fatal dose would be the hell of a lot bigger than if it had been the concentrated stuff. Pure digitalis."

"How big?"

Bainbridge shrugged. "Call it at least half a cup. I suppose you want to know the symptoms and so on. Well, as I said, it acts on the nerve centers, in lay language. There'd have been much-increased heart action, pulse action, gradual numbness of the extremities, symptoms of excitation or even hysteria, and then death. Plain and simple. And don't ask me within what period. There aren't many actual case histories to read up on this one. The best I can do is to say she'd have died anywhere from one to four hours after taking the stuff. Depends on individual reactions, too."

"How nice," said Mendoza. "That seems to take in some of the time before she left home on Wednesday morning? When approximately did she die?"

"Report said she was found at a few minutes after eleven. She hadn't been dead long then, I wouldn't say. Less than an hour. Of course, digestion rates vary too, but around three hours before she died she'd eaten some scrambled eggs, whole-wheat toast, and coffee."

"Breakfast. Yes. Have you any idea what form this stuff was in?"

"Oh, liquid of some kind . . . No, I've no idea what it tastes like, damn it, and I'm not about to make up any to find out," said Bainbridge irritably. "Whatever it tastes like, anybody could add some Sucaryl or vanilla or peppermint or something to disguise it—or add it to something already flavored, like a soft drink. All I will say is I strongly doubt that anybody'd go to the bother of hunting up a patch of foxglove and boiling it up to extract the poison to commit suicide with. Not when so many other things are available so much easier."

"Yes," said Mendoza. "This is a funny one, all right. I'll keep this book. Nothing else occurs to you?"

"Yes, it does damn well occur to me that the book's checked out on my library card, and if you lose it you can pay for it. And I wish you boys fun with your offbeat homicide," said Bainbridge, grinning sardonically.

"Fun and games," said Mendoza. "*Eso sí que está bueno.* What a thing. So let's go take a look at Oscar and company. You like to come along, Art? I've got the feeling we'll need all the brains we've got on this one."

"I can't say I look forward to meeting that monkey again," said Grace gloomily. "One thing, Lieutenant, we noticed at the time that nobody we saw seemed to be much broken up over Eliza."

"Except Miss Manning. Who is obviously missing some marbles. Yes, *indeed,*" said Mendoza suddenly, "and all that talk about cooking: it could turn out to be very simple, if Miss Manning was cooking up tasty little dishes for Eliza."

"Old High Street," said Hackett. "Off North Broadway, you said? Many pretty flowering shrubs decorating back yards in that neck of the woods?"

Probably not, of course. But it was a more interesting something than had come their way for a while, and Hackett went along for the ride. The routine had been set in motion on the hit-and-run. There were fliers out on the car—no make on it, of course, but the consensus was that the car must have sustained some damage too, and all garages in the county were asked to keep an eye out (a futile gesture, very likely, but one that had to be done). The lab was still working on Cohen's clothes, in the hope of getting a paint smear. Higgins had come up with about thirty possible plate numbers that could have been hastily read as JGN-790, and the D.M.V. was checking those out.

Landers and Piggott were out running down the two missing reports which might tie up with Mary Brown, the suicide who maybe wasn't a suicide.

"That seems," said Hackett on the way over, "a funny place for a private hotel."

"Wasn't once," said Mendoza. "Sixty or seventy years ago when it was built. And, damn it, we don't know who's actually living there." He was remembering something else. Old High Street, in this day and age, wasn't by any stretch of the imagination a very classy part of town: the oldest part of town, now in the middle of a slum section—call it that. But the McLaughlins, whatever their eccentricities, had both spoken educated English; so had the more-than-eccentric Manning woman.

Of course they hadn't been quite so careless, taken so much for granted, as Bainbridge had implied: by ordinary police routine they had put a seal on the secondhand shop on Los Angeles Street where the woman had died until the inquest had been held. But, by what Bainbridge said, it was entirely possible that Eliza had been somehow fed the poison before she left home Wednesday morning. And in that case—

Mendoza parked the Ferrari, of necessity, four doors up from the ramshackle Celtic Hotel. On this narrow old street few legitimate parking places were indicated. Toward this end of the block there were half-a-dozen single residences, old frame houses, one-story, then the old house with Oscar McLaughlin's sign on its window.

As they came past the house next to that, the man sitting on the front porch stared at them. There were no lawns or trees here, the sidewalks abutting directly on the buildings, and he wasn't more than six feet away; he leaned forward in his old rocking chair and said, "Hey! Hey, you fellas. I seen you"—he pointed at Mendoza—"come the other day when the sister died. The Eliza. You a police officer—and the black fella too? Hey?"

They stopped. "Yes?" said Mendoza.

The man hopped up and came down the steps of the house. He was a middle-aged man running to paunch, with curly black hair rapidly receding and a drooping black mustache and a heavy Italian accent. He looked at Mendoza. *"Lei é Italiano?"*

"My name's Mendoza. What—"

"Oh. *Scusi.* Caradoccio, me. Luigi. You goin' to see Oscar and them again, some reason? So you tell Oscar from me, Luigi, I get along with the people at the hotel, all my life I get along with people, I don't go askin' trouble, I believe live and let live like they say, *capisce?* But enough is too much, and the opera singer I cannot take her." He waved his hands. "Funny people at the hotel, they come and go, these McLaughlins, they're good enough people if they're funny—they don't look down the nose, you know what I mean—and the goat I don't mind it, but this woman thinks she sings opera, *Corpo di Bacco, miserére!*" Mr. Caradoccio clapped a hand to his forehead. "Night after night she's screeching, and the windows open—it's nice with spring coming on—*a pieni polmoni, capisce?*— loud, loud! I should for my sins have to listen to such a screeching! So you please tell Oscar, who is not a bad man, no more! I lay a complaint."

"You've lived here a long while, Mr. Caradoccio? You know the McLaughlins?"

"Know? Sure I know. My papa bought this house I'm about nine, ten years old. I bring my wife to this house. The McLaughlins live here then, a long time. Thirty years—more, thirty-five. Something's wrong there?"

"Yes," said Mendoza. "I'd like to hear everything you know about the people at the hotel, Mr. Caradoccio."

"Everything? *Dio,* mister, we stand here a long time. Something wrong—police-wrong—at the McLaughlins'? But they're not bad people, mister." He looked puzzled. "Only funny. And now this female screeching. Sure, I tell you—some I hear from my papa, some I know myself. This female, I lay a complaint O.K., sure, she don't stop, but I talk to Oscar first, don't wanta make trouble for neighbors. Not bad people. Been here long as me, maybe. It was back when I was a kid, in the depression, *capisce?* Nobody had any money, times bad. These McLaughlins, lotsa lotsa money they had before depression—I heard. Their folks. Fancy schools they went to, England, I don't know. And then all the money got lost, depression come. Only little piece property they had left, the old hotel there, some grandfather built way back, I heard. When it was nice part of town here. And near the railroad station too. Useta be a fancy hotel, I guess, old days. And the little place beside. Where Oscar still keeps the sign. Oscar was youngest one—not much older 'n me, maybe nineteen, twenny, when they all hadda come live here. It was maybe about thirty-one, thirty-two, when depression was."

"How many McLaughlins are there?"

"Oh, have to remember. Big family. Sister Eliza that died the other day. Another one, Jane, she don't go out no more, what with the rheumatism.

and Stephen. And Earl he useta play the guitar before he went away. Henry. And Willie. And the oldest oldest sister name Dora—Dora—something like. They come to live here because it's the only place left, *capisce?* In bad times. To live how they can. I was only a kid but I remember. They been here ever since, except a couple of older brothers, the oldest sister, go away. Maybe find jobs someplace else, I don't know."

"And Oscar opened his undertaking business when?"

"Oh, mister, that! He tells me once, always he wanted be an undertaker. Not natural this kind of job for a man to want. Me, *grazie,* no! Me, I'm a barber. But there's got to be undertakers. Only Oscar's papa says is not nice for man of their family. Only when the money's gone, then Oscar he goes to a school, learns be an undertaker. Only the business don't do good, no customers, *capisce?* I don't think ever he got a single customer. He keeps the sign painted but he don't get no business."

"I wouldn't think," said Hackett interestedly, "it'd be the kind of business anybody *could* go bankrupt in."

Caradoccio's white teeth flashed in a wide smile. "Maybe he's not such a good undertaker, mister. I dunno. Anyway, they all been here long, a long time. Like I say. And the other people in the hotel, friends of theirs with not so much money too, some funny people—different ones, different times. Percy, a cousin some kind from England, and he talks you know all fancy but don't hold a job. And the poor lady wrong in the head, Oscar says a long time back her boy friend is killed in the war but she still thinks he come—you know—but she don't mean no harm. And that Karl in his wheel chair used to be acrobat in the circus. And the woman reads the stars like the priest says is no good. And that funny Miss Allenby goes through all the trash cans. And old Ben he was forty years in jail for murder, but he acts O.K. now—keeps all their plumbin' fixed. And Bobby he sells newspapers at Second and Grand but he's harmless too. You say something wrong there? What's wrong? I don't wanta put anybody in trouble with cops, it's only this female screechin' at me I complain to Oscar about—"

Mr. Caradoccio had halfway prepared them, but it was a chaotic interview, to say the least.

To start with, the intimation that Eliza had been poisoned set Oscar yelping like a hound-puppy for Henry, who was testily annoyed until the news penetrated his mind and he exclaimed loftily, "Quite impossible!"

"Mr. McLaughlin, we'd like the names of everyone living here at the present, and we'd like to see—"

"Quite preposterous. There is no poison on the premises. Beelzebub keeps down the vermin."

"But, Henry, the *autopsy*—"

"Mr. McLaughlin, please, we must—"

The monkey appeared and made a beeline for Hackett.

"—a list of everyone living here, and—"

"Ben! Ben, are you here? Henry, they would *know*. As a qualified undertaker myself—"

"I resent this intrusion," said Henry. "I am At Work. On a Special Order."

"But, *Henry*—"

Eventually, of course, experience prevailed and everyone in the building was assembled, to Henry's annoyance, in his domain beyond the double doors: originally, Mendoza could guess, the restaurant-bar of the hotel some sixty years ago, a room at least forty feet long. At the rear were an immense four-poster bed, an armchair and a floor lamp; a long table stood before the tall windows on the outside wall, with several straight chairs; another long table on the front wall bore several neatly-wrapped parcels addressed to a local department store. On the first long table was spread out Henry's current work: a banquet cloth of heavy linen, most exquisitely embroidered with a Chinese motif in pale colors. Glancing at it in surprise, Mendoza reflected that eccentric Henry might be, but nonetheless an artist.

"A very Special Order," said Henry, hurrying up to protect his art from possibly prying fingers. "From Bullocks'. A special customer. Not that they pay anything near what it is worth—"

"I don't know if Jane will come, gentlemen—her arthritis—I'll see just who *is* here, I'm not sure—"

In the end Mendoza looked at the assembled residents with disfavor. What sense was to be made out of this crew, God only knew. Karl Svenson, in his wheel chair: a bad-tempered-looking elderly man who, in the midst of all the exclaiming and disclaiming, hadn't spoken a word, just sat there. Miss Manning in her scarves, today layered on over an electric-blue silk gown hanging in tatters over the clocked stockings. Percy Cantwell, distinguished in shabby clothes, with a vacuous smile and an Oxford accent almost too good to be true. A Mrs. Rialto was absent at her job— that was the astrologist. Fortuneteller? Oh, no, said Oscar, sounding shocked; that was merely a *hobby*: Mrs. Rialto was a saleslady at a store on Grand Avenue. Miss Allenby, an elderly unkempt woman looking like a poor relation of the witch of Endor. The woman who fancied herself as an opera singer, a Mrs. Lightfoot, was also out. Liked to take long walks, Ben said laconically; retired lady; walked uptown and hung around Pershing Square mostly. And there was, of course, Ben himself. (Forty years in for murder?) Bobby, who sold newspapers, was missing too. Out selling newspapers.

"—a few questions," said Mendoza unhopefully.

"Oh, anything you want to ask, sir, of course!" said Oscar. "Really, I cannot understand—poison—what *was* it you said?—it must have been an accident, Ellie would never—"

"Wednesday morning. Does any of you know what time she had breakfast, when she left?"

"Oh, Ellie went by the clock, sir. Seven o'clock she was up, and down for breakfast at seven-fifteen. I should explain, sir," said Oscar, all helpfulness, "we have our own little arrangements here. It's such a big place, you see, we *don't* run it as a hotel, but certain of our friends who want a quiet place to live inexpensively—and friends *of* friends—let me see, that's how you came, wasn't it, Karl, that nice Mrs. O'Riordan who lived here back in forty-nine or was it fifty gave you our name—and you see, sir, most of us who live here have our own interests, we like our privacy and solitude, if you understand me. We—myself, Henry, Ellie and Miss Manning —use the original kitchen of the hotel. And one refrigerator. The Kelvinator. I—er—should perhaps explain that dear Miss Manning's sister pays us a small sum to look after the lady and see that she doesn't—er—get into any trouble—"

"I should never dream of getting into trouble," said Miss Manning vaguely. "I wasn't brought up to it."

"—and Ellie or Miss Manning fixes most of Jane's meals there. She has trays mostly, her arthritis—" Jane had not appeared. "Then Karl has his own small refrigerator in his room, that's a small room in back on the ground floor— And Ben and Mrs. Rialto and Percy and Mrs. Lightfoot pay a small charge for one shelf apiece in the *other* refrigerator in the kitchen, the Servel—"

"Wednesday morning," said Mendoza rather loudly. "Did any of you see Mrs. McCann before she left for her shop?"

"Oh, yes, I did." Miss Manning pulled at her multi-colored scarves. "We had breakfast together. I only had coffee because I do have to think of my figure. I think Ellie had an egg. You couldn't put poison in an *egg*, could you? And then she went out to milk Gertrude."

"Now, now," said Oscar fussily, agitatedly, "please, I do know it's technically against the law, sir, but *none* of the neighbors have objected and I do hope—"

"Gertrude," said Hackett. Miss Manning turned her large pale-blue eyes on him.

"Gertrude is the goat. Quite a horrid creature but good with the garbage. Jane says the milk's very healthy. I can't abide it myself, but now I think I must remember to ask Albert if he does, when I write."

"My God," murmured Detective Grace *sotto voce.*

"Did anyone else see Mrs. McCann that morning?" asked Mendoza.

"Well, I did, of course," said Oscar. "I usually did. I came down while she was having breakfast, and I got my own breakfast—that is our arrangement—and then I went out and cleaned up Gertrude's pen and then I went up to the store to get the paint. I wanted to touch up the sign, you see. On my undertaking establishment. So I didn't see her leave, but she always left at ten minutes to eight precisely—or around there."

Karl Svenson laughed hoarsely. "Your establishment! Nobody will bring you even dead bodies!"

Oscar flushed indignantly. *"But,"* he went on loudly, "she was always gone by at least eight o'clock. She always walked to the store, rain or shine, she said it was one reason she kept so well—proper exercise. She didn't hold with doctors at all, never went to one. She thought Jane was foolish for taking even aspirin. At one time she was quite interested in Christian Science, but our dear father was a lifelong agnostic and she could not bring herself to believe in— So you see, sir, it is quite impossible that Ellie would have taken anything. Even—even not knowing what it was. She never took pills of any kind—"

"One thing *I'll* tell you," said Svenson. "She didn't commit suicide, that one." He rubbed his fingers together suggestively. "Too interested in the money, the material of life."

Ben Kelly just slouched against the wall, the monkey on his shoulder, and watched proceedings carefully.

"Did you see Mrs. McCann make the coffee that morning, Miss Manning?"

"Oh, yes, I did. Just like always. And I had a cup of it myself, so you see that was all right. I even counted the spoonfuls with her because Albert likes nice strong coffee and you must always remember *one* heaping tablespoon to a cup."

Mendoza glanced at Hackett. "Nobody else saw Mrs. McCann that morning?"

"I said good-by to her," said Henry. He leaned against his long worktable, drumming his fingers impatiently on it, waiting for them all to finish this nonsense and go away. "I just opened my door as she was going out. I take nothing in the morning at all, only a little hot water, and I have my own hot plate here. She looked quite as usual. This must all be some stupid mistake."

"I'm afraid not, Mr. McLaughlin. No one else?"

Percy Cantwell uttered a harrumph. "Meantersay, you *don't* meantersay gel was murdered? Here? Don't see it. Nobody had any reason. Nice gel. Efficient."

"*Murdered?*" said Oscar. "Oh, dear me, that's simply fantastic—indeed I assure you—"

"Police all a pack of fools," said Henry.

Miss Manning smiled witlessly into the middle distance. The unkempt Miss Allenby went on staring vaguely at the floor. Ben scratched the monkey behind one ear. Nobody said another word. "Well," said Mendoza, "we'd like to see the rest of the property, please. Do you have any kind of garden here—in back of the hotel?"

"A *garden?*" said Oscar in surprise. "Oh, my goodness, sir, we're all much too busy—and, besides, a *garden,* with *Gertrude?* She has to be let out for exercise—"

"Talk about a curious crew," said Detective Grace.

"And try to get any sense out of them!" said Mendoza. "My God. That Manning woman could have added anything from vanilla extract to this damn foxglove concoction to that coffee—just how lunatic is she? Though I suppose the McCann woman was used to watching her, if she's given to—"

"Check 'em all out," said Hackett. "Have to talk to the ones weren't there." He yawned. "A very funny damn bunch all right, could be a couple of 'em besides Ben have pedigrees."

"And she could just as easy have got the stuff after she was in the store," Grace pointed out. "We all know we don't have to show a nice plausible motive by how the law reads, but there's usually *some* kind of motive in a premeditated homicide. So we ask around—what sort of woman she was, whether she'd made any enemies and so on. Around the store."

"Of all the offbeat things," said Hackett. "Yes, sure. Find out who'd been in that morning, who'd seen her."

"Turn the lab boys loose there," said Mendoza. "What a bunch indeed. I wonder if that Manning woman should be tucked away."

"Oscar seems cooperative enough," said Grace.

"Seems," said Mendoza. "And I think Jase was right, Art. You called this one down on us, claiming you were bored. Teach you a lesson."

Hackett laughed. "Could be. But how often do we get the really subtle things like in all the paperbacks, Luis? Probably turn out, with a little closer look, the Manning woman was mixing up some homemade face cream or something and it got into the scrambled eggs by accident."

"Anything could be," said Mendoza, "in that household."

Landers was still out, presumably chasing up missing reports. Higgins was sitting at his desk poring over some notes, still figuring plate numbers and possible errors and transpositions.

Mendoza called the lab and asked for the full treatment on that second-hand shop. Thinking of the collection of odds and ends, he mentally wished the lab boys joy of it.

Funny people, he thought. *Vide* Mr. Caradoccio. With a vengeance. The McLaughlins, brought up with money, not trained to earn livings—but an eccentric family to start with, and finding their own level in this backwater slum. Staying on of inertia, living hand to mouth. Inevitably attracting others of their own kind, the flotsam and jetsam. Living on the proceeds of the secondhand store, the minutely-paying roomers, Henry's embroidery? And what did Oscar the friendly undertaker contribute?

Yes, and Ben. Look up Ben's pedigree.

And, of course, find out more about Eliza McCann. A widow? Evidently. About enemies and friends.

Mendoza yawned and looked at his watch. Five-thirty. He didn't care one hell of a lot who had given Eliza McCann homemade poison, or how, or why. No denying, this nice spring weather was enervating. Conducive to goofing off. He thought a little sleepily that it'd be nice to take off with Alison, say up to Lake Elsinore or somewhere for the weekend, and the hell with the job. The hell with Eliza McCann (yes, a husband—who, where, and when?) and the suicide, and even Patrolman Harry Cohen.

Higgins and his plate numbers.

"You asleep?" asked Sergeant Farrell.

Mendoza started. "No. What's up?"

"George's gone home. I got a note for him. The D.M.V. checked out some of those substitute plate numbers he dreamed up. He's got a Roman Catholic priest in Oxnard, the president of an oil company in Oakland, and a local gynecologist. Well, I suppose anything's *possible*."

Mendoza got up. "I," he said, "am going home too. *Anything's* possible, Rory."

FOUR

At about the same time, Landers was standing in the lobby of the Stewart Hotel on Olive, talking to the desk clerk. The Stewart Hotel was where Mary Brown had or had not committed suicide, and Landers was back there because he wanted to talk to the second-floor maid, who might have talked with Mary Brown and who'd been off duty yesterday.

"Happy as a lark," the desk clerk was saying. "It never crossed my mind —not that you go around expecting guests to commit suicide. This ain't the Beverly Hilton, but it's a respectable hotel, and this girl looks ordinary as could be. Nice smile. Paid in cash, says isn't it a nice day and all, and I— There she is now, just coming in. Oh, Agnes!"

The maid was enlightening. Some. Agnes Rombin, a rather handsome young Negro girl. She had talked with Mary Brown. (Why didn't people use some imagination when they gave false names?) She'd been passing the door of 209 about six o'clock on Wednesday evening when Mary Brown came out and asked her if she knew of a good cheap place to eat nearby.

"She was a nice girl, you could tell," said Agnes. "Just doesn't seem possible she went and did such a thing. Friendly, she was. I thought at the time, it was like she was just sort of bubbling over, kind of, all happy and excited because she was going to be married. Next day, she told me. D'you figure maybe the boy backed out at the last minute and that was the reason?" She shook her head. "An awful thing."

"Oh, really?" said Landers. "That could be. Did she tell you anything else, Miss Rombin? His name?"

"No, it was just a minute or two we talked. I told her Daniels' down the block was nice and clean and not very expensive, and she thanked me, and— Oh, now, there was *that*, yes, sir. She said it was the first time she'd been in L.A., didn't know her way around the city."

"Oh," said Landers. Not a local? So Mary Brown wouldn't be either of the girls reported missing who vaguely matched the description.

That was helpful in a way. But then he went back to the office before quitting for the day, to see whether the autopsy report had come in; it had, and Piggott was reading it. He listened to what Landers had to say about the maid, and said, "So here's the other half of the story," and passed over the report. "You needn't wade through all the six-dollar words. Two things. It was prescriptive sleeping pills, and she was four months' gone."

"Oh, hell," said Landers. "So we know." He hadn't liked the lack of a note; in his admittedly limited experience, pretty young girls who killed themselves left notes—often long ones—saying why. But with this—

"So the father backed out at the last minute and she couldn't face it and bingo," said Piggott.

"Yes," said Landers, and had a second thought. "But, you know, Matt, I still don't like it. Not just on the fact of no note. Because, where'd the pills come from? Prescriptive pills? There wasn't any container in the room. She couldn't have been much over twenty, and coming to the big city to get married, all happy and excited, not very likely she brought anything like that with her—was in the habit of taking it. She couldn't have bought them over the counter. I still think there's something fishy about it."

Piggott scratched his jaw and said when you put it like that he guessed maybe so did he. "And, anyway, we've still got to find out who she was. If just to notify any relatives. And her real name might tell us, *via* the relatives, who the father was apt to be."

"Yes," said Landers. "And maybe we're being too cynical, Matt. Big-city cops. It could be that Mary Brown *is* her real name."

"And so," said Mendoza, "we sealed the door of her bedroom—belatedly, but we'll go over it for prints and so on just in case—and came away." He held out his cup for more coffee.

"You do run into characters," said Alison, pouring from the pot that had been sitting on its warmer. "I like Gertrude. I suppose you'll have to tell the, um, relevant authorities about her? Livestock in the city—"

"I should," said Mendoza; and Sheba landed on his shoulder from behind and he spilled half the coffee over his empty plate. "*¡Vaya por Dios! ¡Monstruo!* Talk about livestock—"

"No, Sheba! Monster is about right, she's doing it to everybody—"

Mendoza plucked her off and dropped her on the floor; Sheba complained loudly. "And I've got to go back there tonight, see those two that were out. Oh, and I suppose Bobby the newsboy. The hell of it is there's no way of knowing just when McCann got it, it could have been after she got to the store—"

"Back down there?" Alison cocked her auburn head at him. "Look, you be careful, *amante*. That's not such a good part of town, and the way these muggings and senseless violence are on the increase— I suppose you wouldn't consider packing the gun?"

Mendoza laughed impatiently. "*¡Ni qué niña muerta!* The more I think about it, the more inclined I am to think that it must have been accidental in some way—though of course— Well, we have to look at it anyway." He shoved his chair back into Nefertiti, crouched just behind it, and Nefertiti yelled and had to be apologized to. Mrs. MacTaggart came in, surveyed Mendoza benignly, and asked if he'd like his rum pudding. "Later, Máiri, couldn't do it now." He got up and stepped on Bast's tail; she yelled. "*¡Porvida!* And the city outlaws one harmless nanny goat! There is too much livestock in this house! And El Señor stealing my rye—"

"Listen," said Alison, linking one arm in his as they went down the hall, "I really don't like it, Luis. That neighborhood—and the ones you'll be driving through. At least, for heaven's sake, lock the car doors."

"You starting to act the nervous wife at this late date?"

Alison made a face at him. "I know, I know! Experienced cop can take care of himself. And that's your stamping ground, you know it. Night *and* day. Just be careful. Some of these J.D.'s—"

"I'll be careful. Don't fuss," said Mendoza inattentively, and reached for his hat.

The ramshackle big building looked different by night, true; the whole street did. Narrow ancient street tucked away in this oldest part of town, now part of the jungle and big city sprouts, any time and anywhere, the jungle of Skid Row, of poor people, of the border line of pro crime, of the wanton violence. Old High Street was a backwater, but a backwater surrounded by the jungle.

He left the Ferrari outside the Caradoccio house, where lights showed and voices sounded, and walked back to the looming old hotel.

Oscar let him in. And he wanted a little talk with Oscar too, and now was as good a time as any to have it. Standing there in the bare dusty lobby, he prodded Oscar with questions. How long had they lived here? Who exactly did live here? Occupations? And so on. He knew the general answers from Caradoccio; he wanted to get Oscar talking, and it wasn't difficult.

"The depression—" Oscar rambled on about that. Money, this the only property left—built by his grandfather, a very fine hotel once— "Well, we managed, we live very simply, as you see, we *had* to at first and I suppose we got in the habit of it . . . Oh, well, yes, my older sister Dottie, yes, well, she finally found a very nice job as companion to an old lady—they travel a good deal. My other brothers, well, really, I don't know why you should be interested; they don't live with us now. I'm afraid we're none of us great letter writers, I seem to recall the last time we heard from Stephen he was in Rome . . . What? Oh, well, Miss Manning—the poor dear's quite harmless, I expect she'll stay on even when Ellie—she's used to our ways now *and* vice versa, as it were—"

"Was your sister a widow?"

"Well, now that I'm afraid we don't know," said Oscar with a small titter. There had been no sound from beyond the double doors, from the rest of the building. "She—ah—married just before we—you know—before all the money went. My father hadn't liked the young man—of course Ellie wasn't exactly young then—thirty, I think—and her husband left her. After the money went. Quite soon. I'm afraid it did rather embitter her. We've never laid eyes on him since . . . Oh, well, I helped her in the shop sometimes, and so did Percy—moving things and so on— And, of course, Percy's family makes him a small monthly allowance." Remittance man, thought Mendoza. He'd thought it was an extinct breed. "It brings in quite a steady little profit—the shop, that is. I suppose I should try to keep it up, but Ellie knew just how to manage—really she was quite sharp at *dickering* with people—"

Oscar was nervous, thought Mendoza. He wondered why. He seemed to be all there, if eccentric; possibly he'd been mulling over the facts. "We'll be looking over your sister's room, of course," he said casually. "Very probably we'll want to search the whole building. She could have had the poison before she left that morning, and if it—"

"The *building!*" squeaked Oscar. "The *hotel?*" He uttered a high titter. "My dear good *sir,* you've no idea—the things one *accumulates* in thirty-five years! And the size of the place—we don't use the top floor at all, not for years and *years*—that's all tiny little servants' quarters and so on—*poison*—you haven't said *what,* and I still think it must have been quite accidental, though that's not *like* Ellie—still, you can't be serious about—my *dear* good sir, there are over eighty rooms here! And I cannot see—"

"Quite serious, Mr. McLaughlin. And I'd like to see Mrs. Rialto now. And the others I didn't see this afternoon."

"Oh dear, oh dear," said Oscar, agitated. "Yes, of course, I'll take you up—I don't think Bobby's home yet—all hours as a rule—but he's only a bit retarded, you know, a simple young fellow. Mrs. Rialto—"

It was an impossible old rabbit warren of a place, and Mendoza wondered if the fire department ever got round to taking a look at some of these old buildings for hazards. Feeling his way up the creaking front staircase after Oscar, he reckoned up mentally: ten people living in an eighty-room building. Scattered around, probably. Liking privacy, you could say. And what a place. By all appearances, the building—old then— had been wired for electricity some time in the twenties: there were obviously converted gas jets at the landing and along the walls in the corridor, and at most they might now be holding forty-watt bulbs; not all of them were switched on. Four stories, top-floor servants' quarters: about twenty rooms to a floor, some on the ground floor besides the offices and lobby.

Oscar was knocking at a door halfway down the corridor. "I'm sorry to disturb you, Myra, but it's this police officer wanting to talk to you—you know the one I mentioned—about Ellie. He—"

"Quite all right, Oscar." The door opened suddenly and Myra Rialto gave them a wide smile. "If this shocking thing is true, we must all cooperate with the authorities to the fullest extent. How do you do? Yes, indeed, I see a dark aura all about you, young man—not your own, but indicating that you deal with dark, dark forces. Come in. What do you want of little Myra?"

She was a plump little woman, about sixty, with pepper-and-salt hair crisply curling and agelessly beautiful immense dark eyes. She'd evidently just washed her face, towel still in one hand, and she wore no make-up; she looked her age but was quite unself-conscious about it. She had on a crisply clean and starched cotton housecoat, zipped up the front, and altogether was the most respectable-looking resident he'd met in the place. He went in. The room was a large one, possibly once one of the best in the hotel, at least twenty feet square. It was pleasantly if shabbily furnished with a double bed neatly made up with a blue cotton spread, a tall walnut chiffonier, a good-sized bookcase full of paperbacks, an old-fashioned standing wardrobe. There was a floor lamp between two shabby old overstuffed chairs, a small table.

Myra Rialto shut the door on Oscar firmly. "Poor little man," she said. "Now, my good police officer, you really must not think that because I live among these delightfully uninhibited people I am myself at all eccentric. To be quite frank, it's very cheap, and I have very little money. A part-time job in a rather vulgar little dress shop. The one thing I will *not* do is take money for the exercise of my psychic gifts—quite fatal, the spirits frown on it absolutely. Now *you* are terribly psychic yourself, you know—I don't know your name. Do sit down."

"Lieutenant Mendoza. What I—"

"Ah, yes. If I could have just a teeny-weeny guess, I'd say you are Pisces. When is your birthday, Lieutenant?"

Mendoza felt small surprise. Once in a long while, he thought, there might be a very little something to— "Yes, February twenty-eighth. Now what I—"

"Of *course*. And what's all this about Ellie being poisoned? I'm sure Oscar had it all wrong . . . No? But, dear me, what a fantastic thing. A very managing person, she was, but after all in this household—I mean the McLaughlins themselves—someone had to be, you know. Of course Henry is a law unto himself. But *poisoned?* With what, may I ask?"

It might start a hare or two to let that out; Mendoza told her. "Oh, really?" she said. "How extremely unusual." She opened the carved wooden box on the coffee table between the chairs and took out a cigarette; he leaned to light it for her. "Do smoke if you like. How very odd. You know, if it had been on a Sunday, I should have said at once, *Tabitha Thirkettle.*" She turned her beautiful dark eyes on him solemnly.

"Tabitha— And why would you say that, Mrs. Rialto?" asked Mendoza equably.

She smiled at him. "Because Eliza was not a churchgoer, you see—a free soul if sadly unbelieving—I don't press belief on anyone, Lieutenant, but my own deep experience and knowledge only lead me to *certainty* of God's great goodness—but Eliza, no. On Sundays Eliza enjoyed her only recreation, one might—" Mrs. Rialto started violently and dropped her cigarette.

From somewhere close at hand a shrill female voice was upraised in what was meant for song. Like a drunken power drill it soared to siren heights and fell to buzz-saw depths.

> "There is bee-yooty in the bellow of the buh-last,
> There is guh-randeur in the guh-rowling of the gale—
> There is elo-quent out-pouring
> When the li-yun is a-roaring
> And the ti-yi-ger is a-lashing of his ta-yul!"

The musical Mrs. Lightfoot tonight had switched to Gilbert and Sullivan. Mendoza repressed a forceful exclamation; he had an ear of sorts, and he liked *The Mikado*.

Mrs. Rialto got up and opened the door. She knocked loudly on the door across the hall.

> "Yay-ess, I like to see a ti-yiger
> From the Congo or the Niger
> And es-peshully when—"

"Dear? Dear Florence—"

> "—a-lash-hashing—"

"Florence!"

> "—of his tay-yail—"

"Oh, Myra. Something, dear?"

"If you wouldn't mind, dear. I've this nice police officer, all about Eliza, and I was just telling him about Tabitha Thirkettle."

"Ooh, of course! The moment Oscar told me, I had the same thought! Not that I've ever laid eyes on the woman, and of course it wasn't a Sunday, was it? Does he want to see me too?"

"Perhaps later, dear. I'll ask him. But if you'd just postpone your practicing?"

"Yes, of course, dear. I'll be only too glad to tell him whatever I can, but I don't know anything at all. I never saw Eliza on Wednesday."

"That's right, dear." Myra came back in and shut the door. "Silly woman, but no harm in her, dear man. No voice, of course. Husband left her practically nothing, and she lives in her dreams. As we all do, as we all do. But I was talking about this Thirkettle woman. On Sundays Eliza always went to a little luncheon party. These four women, old friends—for years these rather dreary little luncheons, the innocuous gossip—I say that because nothing ever happened to any of them, you know, that was important—I believe they did generally meet at the Thirkettle woman's apartment, wherever it is, you could ask Oscar—and I'm afraid that's the only name I know. Of any of the rest of them. Because Eliza had spoken of her. Mmm—scornfully. Eliza had no patience with aches and pains, as someone may have told you. Never even took aspirin. And the Thirkettle woman—yes, it is an odd name, isn't it?" said Myra, uncannily echoing his thought. "The Thirkettle woman has a hobby. She brews simples."

"Simples? I don't—"

"Simples. A charming old word for it. The old-fashioned country remedies. Inner bark of barberry taken in white wine as a purgative—and infusion of poppy seeds for pleurisy—and so on. Quite legendary, most of it, but—interesting. She doses herself, I understand—the Thirkettle woman—cough sirups of horehound and all that sort of thing. And Eliza thought it was utter nonsense. As perhaps it may be, but *then*—you do see what I mean?" The dark eyes widened on him. "I'm afraid I didn't pay all that much attention—Eliza was a rather uncharitable person at the best of times—a young soul who could not grasp the wider reality. Whatever sad experiences we meet, they must be made a maturing influence—but that Eliza did not realize. A *critical* woman, dear man. One should not be. We have all somewhat to give and to receive. But what I was about to say— from the little I heard from Eliza about the Thirkettle woman, I would suppose that wherever she lives, she has some means to grow her little innocent herbs and weeds. And now you are telling us that poor Eliza died of this—concoction. Very peculiar, but if it *had* been on a Sunday, I should at once have blamed the accident on the Thirkettle woman and her simples. Quite without intention, of course. But if she had been experimenting—"

"*¡Pues sí!*" said Mendoza interestedly. "And it could be. You don't know where she lives?"

"No idea, but I expect Oscar would—or Jane. I only thought—"

"This could be very helpful, yes, thanks. Did you see Mrs. McCann that day—Wednesday?"

"No, I didn't. Little Myra was up and away by seven-thirty, and I have a hot plate here for coffee, I stopped at a Mannings' uptown for a real breakfast. And of course it was a shock when Oscar told us all— But now you tell me what it *was*, I did at once think of the Thirkettle woman."

Repeated knocks and calls at all the closed doors on the ground floor failed to raise Oscar or anybody else. There was one feeble overhead light burning in the vast lobby and apparently no other lights anywhere; even now the old doors fitted tightly. The double doors were locked. Mendoza felt his way back down a narrow hall at the rear of the lobby, into another vast room he guessed was the kitchen by the faint odor, but gropings failed to find a switch. He was annoyed; he felt constitutionally incapable of taking any more of the McLaughlins or the Celtic Hotel tonight. This business. Simples—my God. Tabitha Thirkettle. Tomorrow would do; it was after ten.

He groped back to the lobby and let himself out into a thick, black, soft spring night. Little smog; what stars showed were clear and bright. The door clicked solidly shut after him, locking itself. He went down the steps to the sidewalk.

Few street lights along here, and the one in the middle of the block was out: kids throwing rocks, probably. The sidewalk was cracked and uneven; he walked carefully.

The attack was incredibly sudden and savage. A rush of steps behind him, the heavy blow at the back of his neck— As he started to fall, Alison's warning sounded clear inside his head: senseless violence—muggings— With violent effort he twisted as he fell, braced himself to kick up at any continued attack. Vague dark form bending over him—something struck viciously at the side of his head out of the darkness, and that time he went out.

They thought it could cure epilepsy, said Bainbridge.

Simples. My dear good man.

Thirkettle. If it had been a Sunday.

Mendoza uttered a strangled groan and moved. He opened his eyes. He had a terrific headache; odd—he never had headaches. He was staring up at a night sky, city night sky that is never wholly black, and a lot of stars.

Mugger. Hit on the head with something. This part of town. A damned fool; he ought to know better—been on guard—experienced cop taking care of himself—

"*¡Un millón de demonios!*" he muttered. He sat up shakily. Investigated his pockets. He was muzzily surprised to find billfold intact, keys, change.

Alison. Alison saying—

Damn fool. Let some lout of a J.D.—

Painfully he dragged himself to his knees, his feet. He'd been on the way back to the car— He staggered into the darkened lamppost, grazed one hand on its rough surface. The Ferrari—somewhere here—the mugger—

He fell against the car. The shape of the hood under his hands said the Ferrari. He fumbled with the keys, managed to get the door unlocked. He hoisted himself inside, the wrong side—not under the wheel. He shut the door and locked it.

A really terrific headache. He'd never hear the last of it from Alison. *Told you to be careful.* But better not try to drive.

He groped for the telephone installed in the dashboard and dialed the office unsteadily.

"She is," said Angel Hackett, "a perfectly normal baby. Most of them are saying 'gah' at three months and sucking their big toes. Talk about men going idiotic over daughters—"

"She's a very bright little girl, she is," said Hackett fatuously. "She's my own Sheila girl, isn't she? She's Daddy's own—"

"Men!" said Angel. The phone rang.

"Gah," said Daddy's own Sheila brilliantly.

"There, you hear that? I told you—"

"It's the office."

Hackett abruptly made the transition from Daddy to sergeant. "Hackett. What's up? . . . Oh my God! Now what's the damn fool been— All right, all right, I'm on my way! Has anybody called Alison? Better let me—"

FIVE

Slight concussion, said the nurse in First Aid professionally; nothing much, but he'd better spend a day or two in bed. "Be damned if I will," said Mendoza. "If you'll give me something for this headache, I'll be O.K. Why in God's name did they rout you out?" he added to Hackett.

"Break the news to the widow, but seems I'm not due to get your desk so soon. What the hell were you doing down there alone?"

"A quarter block back to the car, for God's sake, I'm grown up. And letting some mugger—"

"Oh, yes?" said Hackett. "When you didn't get rolled? It could have been one of those jokers from the hotel. I don't see why, but that bunch—"

"¡Qué disparate! No reason. The little glimpse I had, it could have been a teen-ager. Inclined to think maybe one who hasn't graduated from the kid stuff and panicked when I showed fight. I couldn't have been out thirty seconds."

"I still think—"

"Now, really, you see Henry stealing out to lay an ambush?" Mendoza sat up, clutching his temple, and the nurse said the pill should work soon.

"There's Ben. Dark horse, that one, if you ask me. He's not in our records, by the way—Jase looked. Come on, I'll get you home. You stay in bed tomorrow."

"Don't be a fool, I'm all right. Thank God that pill *is* taking hold. Listen, what I picked up tonight—" Mendoza told him about Tabitha Thirkettle as they started out. "And I know Alison, if I don't get in at the usual time—"

"Which you won't. I know her too."

"You start to follow that up. It's very likely this female and her little concoctions are mixed up in this somehow."

"Yes, I see that," said Hackett. "I'll get on it."

He drove Mendoza home, to be greeted by an Alison saying, "I *told* you to be careful. Just lucky you weren't killed. Of *all* the idiotic things to do—" He left Mendoza still being lectured and protesting he was all right and went home to tell Angel about it.

Hackett got to the office a few minutes late on Saturday morning and found Landers and Piggott looking glumly at a lab report. "Some garage over in South Pasadena called in," said Landers. "Car left for repairs looked as if it might have been in an accident. Higgins went over to look with a lab man. Look, I'll put it up to you. This Brown thing. No billfold, no identity cards. Well, all right, not all women carry billfolds—a lot do, but a lot don't. And not all women have driver's licenses either, or library cards, or even Social Security cards. Just because there wasn't anything like that there doesn't necessarily say all her identification was taken away. She needn't have had any. There was one of those double-pocket snap-purses in her handbag, with nineteen forty-three in it, bills one side, change the other; a lot of women prefer those to a billfold. There's a suitcase full of clothes, and the only labels are Sears, Roebuck and Lerner's; that says nothing. A girl without much money, maybe no job—that's perfectly natural. Sears is national and Lerner's covers most of California, I think. It doesn't look as if anything was taken, even though the room door wasn't locked. Her prints on the glass—I sent them to Washington, but they're not on record. The hotel maid says the girl told her she'd never been in L.A. before. Came expecting to be married. Didn't say from where. Came expecting to meet the boy friend? Nothing to say where or who."

"Mmm-hmm," said Hackett. "And we would like to find out, wouldn't we? Whether she's a suicide or not. What time did she register at the hotel, and did she come in a cab?"

Landers and Piggott exchanged a mournful glance. "No cab," said Piggott. "Came walking in, lugging the suitcase, and if there'd been a cab the hackie'd have carried it in for her. Not a fancy hotel, no bellhops. She registered about four o'clock Wednesday afternoon."

"So," said Hackett, "it's nice weather for all the legwork. Be thankful it's not September. You cover all the bus companies and railroad stations and, just for kicks, the airports and find out what got in from where between, say, two-thirty and three-thirty, and then you locate all the bus drivers and conductors and stewardesses and show 'em a pretty picture of Mary Brown and ask if she traveled with them."

Landers uttered a groan. "I was hoping we were both wrong about that or you'd be smart enough to figure a short cut. I know, I know. And I suppose the sooner we get started—" The pair of them went out looking resigned, passing Grace on his way in.

Hackett told him about Mendoza's misadventure and what he'd dredged up from the Rialto woman. Grace said thoughtfully, "Bound to say he's probably right—no reason for any of those people to go for him. Though that Ben— So I guess the first move is to locate this Thirkettle woman. With her double-double-toil-and-trouble brews."

"The Rialto woman said the sister might know if Oscar didn't."

"Come to think, we haven't met the sister. I wonder what her peculiarities are—bound to have some."

"By the rest of the family. The lab boys'll be covering Eliza's store today. And unless George gets something hot on the Cohen car—which I doubt—he may as well do a little work on that." Hackett scribbled a note for Higgins and took up his hat.

It was abundantly clear what Jane McLaughlin's peculiarities were the minute they got into her room. It was Miss Manning who let them into the lobby downstairs: no sign of Oscar or Henry. How these people must rattle around in this place, thought Hackett, unwittingly echoing Mendoza's reflections of the night before as they followed the fluttering scarves up the rickety stairs. And a wonder they didn't all have asthma or something, the dust and cobwebs: evidently the rooms in use were kept clean after a fashion, by their occupants, but the vast spaces not in use were just ignored. Dust lay thick in the bare corridors save for a traveled path down the center.

Jane's room was at the very end of the second floor, at the rear of the building. A small window at the end of the corridor there looked down on the rear of the property—as they were aware now, the minute rear yard all black-topped, not a bush or a weed anywhere and, so far as they had seen, not even a potted plant in the hotel, much less anything resembling that straggly foxglove bush.

Miss Manning's murmur at the door was answered by an irascible voice within, and she opened the door with a vague smile past Hackett's shoulder.

The McLaughlins seemed to run to fat. Jane was fatter than Oscar or Henry, white-haired, with an unhealthily-jowled face with a bad-tempered mouth and little dark eyes peering at them suspiciously. Her hands were gnarled with arthritis. One glance and sniff round the room told she was a collector of medicines. Patent medicine mostly. On every free space stood bottles and jars and boxes of medicine. The room, much crowded with very old and shabby furniture, smelled like a pharmacy.

"For heaven's sake, come or go, girl," said Jane testily to Miss Manning. "Don't stand there like an idiot. So the police finally condescend to talk to me?" She stared at Grace with hot brown eyes. "Henry's quite right. A pack of idiots, saying Eliza was poisoned. Ridiculous. And with sarsaparilla or weeping willow or whatever it was Myra was talking about. A silly woman, with her spirits and auras." She was ensconced in an armchair beside the window; half the stuffing from the chair was trailing about the floor from several long rents in the upholstery. "Well, if you've got anything to say, speak up!"

"Just a few questions, Miss McLaughlin," said Hackett. "Your sister had a habit of meeting some friends for lunch every Sunday. Could you tell us their names and addresses?"

Jane uttered a loud snort. "Friends! Riffraff—that's all. Old biddies who came into that shop of hers. Low class. *Shop.* Oscar can talk all he wants about it being our mainstay—I can hear what Father would have said! And filling this place up"—an overstatement, thought Hackett—"with more riffraff!" Suddenly she threw up the window with a crash and leaned to shout down at the rear yard. "Ben! Ben! You there! Where's Oscar? You tell Oscar I want him!" She slammed the window. "*That* one, if you please, is a murderer. Spent thirty or forty years in Sing Sing—I forget which. Oscar must be mad. And that Italian woman who walked away owing fifteen dollars—*fifteen dollars*—room rent and left that wretched monkey behind. I might be murdered in my bed any night. But who cares for *me?* Why, it's all I can do to get Oscar to fill out the forms for me!" She cast off a tattered plaid shawl lying across her lap, to reveal a pile of equally tattered magazines. "Free samples." She waved a hand at all the bottles and jars. "That old witch Miss Allenby—she goes picking over all the trash cans for blocks around, I get her to fetch back all the magazines. Free samples, you see. But Oscar complains about the postage. He's a fool. As I ask him—doesn't he *want* me to get well?"

"Miss McLaughlin," said Grace in his softest voice, "these friends of Mrs. McCann's—you know their names?"

"Oh, one of them was an Ida. I couldn't be bothered. Eliza was coarsened by this impossible environment, she was only a girl when we came, of course. Ida Glidden, I believe. Now Mrs. *Thirkettle*," said Jane grudgingly, "I will admit, while not a lady, is a trifle more genteel. She's the only one I ever met—*or* cared to meet. Brought me some embrocation for my bad knee once. Sensible sort of woman, knows a lot about medicine."

"Do you happen to know where she lives, ma'am?" asked Grace.

"I wouldn't ordinarily have bothered to take note," said Jane loftily, "but as it happens I do. Turner Street. I just recall her mentioning that she was lucky to have a small yard to grow her herbs. Look at that—it's nine o'clock already and Oscar hasn't been near me. That idiotic woman brought my breakfast. Lucky if she doesn't poison me, I daresay. What Ellie is thinking of—"

She scarcely noticed when they left; she was leaning out the window shouting at Ben again.

"By what we can sort out," said Grace as they felt their way down the dark stairs, "it seems Eliza was about the only one with a little common sense. At least she started that secondhand shop, all practical. Rest of 'em seemed to sit back and expect the Lord to provide."

"Well, Oscar had his undertaking parlor."

"In this backwater. I suppose he put the sign up and never did any more advertising at all."

"At least we know where Ben did his time, if she's got that right. Ask Ossining and see."

"Um," said Grace. "You laying any bets on the Thirkettle's brews giving us the answer?"

"Lord knows. By all we've got, Eliza wasn't much for taking pills and such."

At least some progress had been made. When Higgins got back from South Pasadena—they'd towed the suspect car in to Headquarters for a thorough examination—he found that Glasser had just brought in that mugger they'd been looking for. A pal of his had tipped them off, being momentarily on the outs with him over a girl, and he'd come apart as soon as they'd asked him a few questions.

As expectable, a little pedigree. Twenty-one now; three juvenile counts of assault and robbery, one of attempted assault after he was eighteen, and on that—God, these judges—he'd got off with probation. So now he'd killed one old man, put a woman in the hospital, and injured another man, for a total take of around thirty bucks, and God alone knew what the next judge would hand him—a slap on the wrist and a weekend in jail, maybe.

But it wasn't up to the boys in blue to hand down the judgments. Their job was to catch the offenders, and despite the unrealistic judges they went on doggedly and efficiently catching the predators and hoping someday the bench would begin cooperating.

Higgins read the note Hackett had left for him; and about then Hackett called and relayed the news about Ben Kelly and Sing Sing. "O.K., I'll send a teletype," said Higgins.

"And you might do a little work for a change and chase over to that store. Start asking around. Anybody who might have been there on Wednesday morning. Because Bainbridge said one symptom would have been excitement, hysteria, and if anybody found her acting funny, we might pin down the time closer."

"Yes, O.K.," said Higgins. He was feeling dispirited. Nothing at all on the hit-run, and it could be they'd never get anything. He didn't really think this car they'd brought in would tie up; it was an old heap, sort of thing the high-school kids ran, and it was a kid who'd brought it in to the garage for an estimate on repairs. See what the lab came up with, if there were bloodstains. And, damn it, he couldn't for the life of him think of any halfway plausible story to tell Mary Dwyer to get Stevie to summer camp . . . Bert had been dead for not quite six months. The hell of a good guy, Bert. Higgins had settled it in his mind that he couldn't ask her even to go to dinner with him until it had been at least six months.

He sighed, passing a hand over his craggy, unhandsome features. Probably she wouldn't want to marry anybody, much less George Higgins, another cop. Well, he could do what he could for the kids—good kids, nice kids.

He went down the hall and sent off a teletype to Ossining, New York. Then he went over to the secondhand store on Los Angeles Street and started asking around. All the other places in that block, and about any known customers of the McCann woman, whether anybody had visited her shop that morning. And so on.

The lab boys were busy in the store, and that would be quite a job.

Turner Street was a little dead-end street, also a backwater, also part of the jungle, just below the Southern Pacific railroad yards. A street of old, old little houses, frame houses of four, five, six rooms, and unlike a lot of streets down here—but there were a lot like Turner Street too, this being Los Angeles, California, and not New York—the houses were bordered by patches of brown lawn, patches of back and side yards with grass, shrubs, even an occasional tree.

Hackett and Grace had found Mrs. Thirkettle rather easily by asking the clerk in the drugstore at the corner of Alameda; and they'd got this and that about the woman from him, too. Mrs. Thirkettle's house was the sixth down the block, much neater than most of its neighbors, a small white house with a greener little patch of lawn in front. Mrs. Thirkettle herself was a little bird of a woman in her sixties, chipper and alert and brisk, and pathetically pleased for any company come upon any business. But she hadn't known Eliza McCann was dead, and they had to give her a little time to exclaim and eulogize over that. It didn't look like acting, but then good acting wouldn't.

"In the midst of life, that's certainly true, and who would have thought —such a strong woman, and only sixty-five—I might have expected no one would let me know, her family— Well, I always thought she was a little bit ashamed of them, I don't know much at all about the rest of them, she never talked about them. I can't get over it—so sudden!" And so on. Not, thought Hackett, really grieved—as if the McCann woman had been a truly beloved friend—but interested, conventionally sorry, and inevitably a bit uneasy, for her own age— And then, of course, "But you're *police* officers, you said? I don't understand—"

Grace told her, gently and easily. Another spate of talk. "But that's *fantastic!* You can't think—*Eliza?* I don't understand how—"

She was a neat, normally cheerful little woman, her shabby old house neat and clean, a little woman who'd never had much, had made do as she could, you could guess. This and that they had from the clerk, and more had emerged in her flow of words. The husband a railroad man, only in the last few years of his life in on the higher wages, the benefits—no family —this little house paid for by scrimping and saving. The narrow life—a few friends, maybe distant relatives somewhere, her little hobby the one strong interest to her life.

Hackett looked at Grace. A nice little woman. Very ordinary. (Which maybe Eliza had found refreshing, after the Celtic Hotel's inmates.) If somehow Mrs. Tabitha Thirkettle's hobby of brewing old-fashioned simples from herbs had resulted in the death of Eliza McCann, it would have been entirely accidental. Hackett started to ask questions. She was a bright old lady; the sense of the questions penetrated her mind at once, and she stared at him in openmouthed horror.

"Did Eliza ever— What *do* you mean? Are you telling me—it wasn't— wasn't *accidental?* That—"

Hackett told her about the infusion of foxgloves. When she had this hobby, as they'd been told, maybe she'd know about that. *Digitalis purpurea.* And did she—

"Yes," she said mechanically. "Of course. It was—*that?*" Her work-worn, strong little hands tightened on the arms of the old high-backed chair. Everything in this little, very tidy living room was old and worn and proudly maintained. Antimacassars on all the chairs, the couch. Shades drawn halfway to protect the rugs. The Woolworth china figurines on the mantel, the old-fashioned mantel clock, the framed photograph of the late husband—all meticulously dusted. "But—you're not *imagining*—I don't!" she said. "Nothing like that—nothing that could be dangerous—I never have any of those things! *Atropa belladonna* or any of those! I'm very careful about— Only the quite harmless things, fennel and barberry and milkwort and things like— Some of them are hard to grow in this climate, like the marsh plants, any of those that need so much water—but I— Why, I *never* use any of those that could be—"

"We'd just like to know, Mrs. Thirkettle," said Hackett, "whether Mrs. McCann ever asked you for any of your—er—remedies? Took any of them?"

She stared at him, her lips working. "I never use any of the dangerous ones. I've read a lot about it, at the library. I know about the ones can be dangerous. Why, you can look, out back. My little garden. There aren't *any* of those. I never— And, besides, I hadn't seen Eliza since—since last Sunday. When we all met here as usual—for lunch and a little talk. Not since then. She had the store, you know, she had to be there."

"She'd never asked for any of your remedies?"

Mrs. Thirkettle was still staring at him, maybe at the mere size of him in her small living room—the big sandy homicide cop in *her* room. She was shocked, frightened, horrified; she shot a rapid glance from him to Detective Grace, and she swallowed once and said in a firm voice, "No. Never. If you—if you've been asking around about Eliza, you'll have found out that she—she didn't believe in medicine of any sort, she never took anything, even aspirin, or went to doctors. She thought I was—very foolish, believing the old—old cures and herbs and all— Of *course* she never asked me for anything. She talked so much about not believing in it, she wouldn't have even if she'd suddenly wanted to! No. And you can look—I *never* use anything that could be dangerous—"

They looked. Her neat square little back yard was divided into plots and beds of greenery. Hackett had foresightedly brought along the book Dr. Bainbridge had checked out of the library; they looked and peered and saw nothing resembling the leggy green plant labeled *Digitalis purpurea*.

"But we're neither of us botanists," said Grace. "I wouldn't like to swear."

"A nice woman," said Hackett. "Ordinary honest woman. I don't know,

Jase. Look, it says the thing gets about five feet tall. Nothing here that big except the hibiscus against the house—hibiscus I do know."

"Ask the lab boys to take a look? They do seem to know everything."

"Oh, hell," said Hackett. "Let's go see what they've got at the store. And what, if anything, George has turned up."

Mrs. Thirkettle watched them leave. One corner of the cotton-lace curtain at the living-room window was slightly twitched back as they walked down the drive to the red Barracuda.

Alison had done her best, very likely, but Mendoza had showed up at ten o'clock, dapper as always. Hackett and Grace found him outside the secondhand store with Higgins and a scrawny aged woman and the portly Mr. Max Wolf from the pawnshop down the block.

Mendoza was saying, "Mrs. Stepp, if you saw Mrs. McCann that morning—"

"Didn't. Not at all. Swear on the Bible. Times I did, times I didn't, living upstairs like I do. She was a bitch anyways." She gave him an evil smile.

"Now, Mrs. Stepp," said Wolf placatingly.

Mendoza eyed them exasperatedly and beckoned Hackett aside. "So what've you got?"

SIX

Hackett told him. "A great big nothing. Thirkettle says she hadn't seen McCann since last Sunday. And we couldn't spot anything around the place that looked like this foxglove. How'd you get away from Alison?"

"I'm all right," said Mendoza irritably. "Just the remnants of a headache. I said I ought to go to Mrs. Palliser's funeral, and she thought so too. I think marriage is turning me conventional."

"Nothing could. Suppose I ought to too. When is it?"

"One o'clock, Church of the Recessional."

"And who's your girl friend?"

Mendoza grinned. "Lives in the apartment over the store. Gladys, so help me, Stepp. A character."

"We seem to be meeting some."

"Er—Lieutenant—" Wolf took a hesitant step toward them, Mrs. Stepp behind him, still wearing her sinister smile. "There's maybe something I should—I mean, I don't take it in yet, you saying Mrs. McCann got poisoned—it wasn't natural—never crossed my mind—but if that's so—"

"She was a bitch and a miser," said Mrs. Stepp emphatically. Mrs. Stepp was a little scrawny old woman, easily in the seventies and maybe older, stooped and hook-nosed and remarkably reminiscent of a conventional portrayal of any of the witches in *Macbeth*. Her ancient, much-mended cotton house dress needed renewed mending, and she wore over it a man's old sweater; her shoes were grimy tennis sneakers, worn without stockings. "God hates a miser," she remarked. "Says right in the Bible—lay not up thy treasure where moth and rust doth corrupt. She was a hard, selfish woman. And a hypocrite too."

"Were you at home Wednesday morning, Mrs. Stepp?" asked Mendoza.

"I was at home early, minding my own business. I've lived in this apartment for over twenty years. I didn't see the woman that day and nobody can prove I did. Then I went out and I didn't come back till along in the afternoon, and Mr. Wolf's standing in the door of his place and he tells me she's dead. Heart attack or something, he says. And I said good riddance and that's all I can tell you. Except her soul's gone straight to hell."

Hackett and Higgins exchanged a glance. Higgins sighed. Mendoza opened his mouth to ask another question, and one of the lab men stuck his head out the door of the secondhand store and said, "Oh, Lieutenant. Something you'll be interested in."

"Excuse us, Mr. Wolf. I'll talk with you later," said Mendoza. They all went into the store.

The lab man was Duke, and he was looking mildly amused. "Sorry to disappoint you," he said. "So far no poison. Exotic or otherwise." The mobile lab unit was standing at the curb outside; they could conduct on-the-spot tests. "God, what a collection of junk! Take us a month of Sundays to do a thorough job, but we're concentrating on that back room, all this" —he waved a hand at the piled-up secondhand goods—"is just merchandise; not much hope there's anything relevant. And there's not much out of the ordinary back there. Seems she kept the wherewithal to fix herself a little lunch there, and judging by the half loaf of bread and the cheese she brought that fresh every day or two. Maybe from home or stopped somewhere on her way to open up. There's a glass standing on the shelf over the sink—used, but just for water. We tested that. Nothing in it. Her prints on it and nobody else's. No milk or anything else to drink but water from the tap. We've had the furniture apart—old armchair, old Army cot, desk, and that's about it. A ledger of sorts in the desk, she wasn't very businesslike"—he grinned—"it looks like. Just notes of what she sold for what. And then a while ago Scarne happened to notice that one of the floor boards looked a little loose and—well, I think you'll be interested." He was leading them up the gloomy store to the small partitioned-off room where Eliza McCann had spent so many hours of her life. He bent and indicated a dark line in the rear corner of the little place, behind the desk. "Here." He raised it up with his pocket knife and a whole section of the wide old pine planking lifted readily, a piece about ten by four inches: lifted right out. Duke held it out, undermost side toward Mendoza. "Just for fun I put it back the way it was. It's all been printed—just hers on everything."

"¿Qué es esto?" said Mendoza, and took the board. Carefully taped to the underside of it was a plastic bag of the waterproof type in which frozen food was packaged; it was fastened to the board with Scotch tape, and when that was pulled off the bag was carefully folded around several little booklets. Bankbooks.

Dumbly Mendoza looked at the first one. Security-First National Bank, Seventh and Broadway. Savings account: $6,400. Eliza Ann McCann. He handed it to Hackett and opened the next. Fidelity Federal Savings. Eliza A. McCann: $4,300.

"For God's sake!" said Hackett in naked astonishment.

The third one was from the Bank of America. A little over $3,000. Coast Federal Savings: slightly more than $2,000. The California Bank: just over $8,000. The last item was a thick manila envelope. Mendoza slid the flap open and drew out some legal-looking papers folded together. He unfolded them.

"¡Santa María! For God's sake—no cabe duda, isn't it the truth, the female of the species! George, go get Wolf, pronto. Who would have—" He thrust the papers at Hackett.

They were the legal deeds to this entire block of business and rental property—one whole block of Los Angeles Street. Nine ground-floor shop rentals and apartments above. The legal owner was Eliza A. McCann.

"For the love of—" said Hackett.

"Well, well," said Grace amusedly. "I did say she seemed to be the practical one of the family. Who would have expected that, though? And not even a mortgage. Just fancy that."

Higgins came back with Wolf, who was looking uneasy. "And did you know anything about this?" asked Mendoza, displaying the deed.

"If you mean did I know she owned this whole block, well, naturally, I did," said Wolf, looking more uneasy. "I was just going to tell you, sir, just now. Because when everybody thought she'd died of a heart attack or a stroke or something, well, what difference did it make? But then you come around asking questions again and saying she was poisoned, my God, like Dragnet or something, Mrs. McCann, and I get thinking and I don't know what business arrangements she had but I do know she's a damn sharp businesswoman and money, it can cause a lotta trouble. My God, yes. Some people, they'll do anything for money. And I don't know that you know—I mean I do know she was a secretive old lady. It's a funny thing," said Wolf, "but women like her, do I know why, are like that. Well, sure I knew about it. My God, she was my landlady, rent I paid her—for my store and for the apartment upstairs where we live. Me and my wife."

"But, my God," said Higgins, looking at the bankbooks, "how could she? The way we got it, they came back here in the depression without any money, or none to count. Lived hand to mouth ever since. I don't—"

"I don't guess you'd remember much about the depression," said Wolf sadly. "Me, I never had enough ahead to invest, but anybody knows investments'll tell you, real estate. It's always the first thing to drop, depression times, and first to come back, good times. And, brother, did it drop in the thirties. Brother. I don't *know*, but I'd have a little guess maybe she picked up this whole block for around five thousand, not over seventy-five hundred anyways. Payments about twenty a month and everything figured in. I *do* know old man Reed, he owned it then, he didn't own it clear, and he was sickenin' along about then, needed money bad—died o' cancer, he did, thirty-four or thirty-five—and he was likely glad to get the cash, hand the papers over to a bank."

"Seventy-five hundred?" said Higgins. "Why, my God, even down here it'd be worth—there are what?—nine stores and—"

"Nine apartments over," said Wolf sadly. "Yeah, I know. I don't know what anybody else's paying, on accounta some of the apartments are smaller'n mine and some of the stores bigger—hers, and the appliance store, and the drugstore on the corner—but I'm payin' now fifty for the store and forty for the apartment. Acourse it's a five-room apartment."

Mendoza started to laugh. "Talk about the female of the species! But she had thirty-five years to do it in, of course. Paid off the mortgage twenty and thirty bucks a crack—and living hand to mouth to do it. And I'll take a bet that nobody else knew about it—in the family. And sitting on the take all these years—"

"Still living hand to mouth," Hackett pointed out. "Why? Good Lord, Luis, at the least calculation she was taking in—now the property's clear—something like nine hundred a month—and they don't even have a telephone in that hotel!"

"Is that so?" said Wolf. "Well, I didn't know one thing about her family, or not much—only the little she let out—thirty-five years, imagine—but some people are like that. I can't say I'm surprised. Guess that old witch's right, calling her a miser. They do get like that."

"Sitting on it, yes," said Mendoza thoughtfully. "For various reasons. To start with, still scrimping and saving to make the payments. And when there started to be profits, still squirreling it away in case of a rainy day and also not letting the family know a damn thing about it because, as she'd know, that bunch would start to throw her hard-earned money around. And one thing that emerges is that any little generosity seems to have been left out of Eliza. Mmh, yes. And then—" He fell silent.

"Well, when you come to think," said Grace. "Somebody in the family

—great-grandfather, maybe—had to make the money they lost originally. Our Eliza seems to have been the one to inherit the touch."

Mendoza said, "Thanks very much, Mr. Wolf—if that's all you can tell us—"

Wolf shrugged. "I didn't know her good. All business, she was, the whole thirty-five years. Good morning, Mr. Wolf, maybe, when I'm standing at the door when she comes past. Thank you, and the receipt, when I pay the rent. And that's it. For that woman I felt sorry, gentlemen." His long sad face suddenly warmed with a smile. "Such things some people still think about us Jews. Moneygrubbers. They should read the Talmud maybe, where it says *He that maketh haste to be rich shall not be innocent.* I don't get rich but we get along. I got a good wife, we got two good children, thanks to God, and now their kids coming. For this woman McCann I feel pity—she got nothing. Nothing but that." And he nodded at the books and papers in Mendoza's hands. "In a bankbook there's no love, gentlemen. Nothing you get to keep for good, all your life for sure, and it don't leave you when you die either. Nobody can put that in the bank." He walked away down to the front door and out.

Mendoza looked at the bankbooks. *"Desnudo nací, desnudo hallo—ni pierdo, ni gano.* Naked we come and go, so the proverb says. I think I feel sorry for Eliza too. But—"

"Yes, I thought of that too," said Hackett. "Depending on when exactly she got the mortgage paid off, does that represent all the profits? Was she putting money somewhere else? Stock? And I'm with you, I don't think the family knows one blessed thing about this. *And* had she made a will?"

"And," said Higgins, "had some of the family just maybe found out?"

"And," said Grace dreamily, "figured Eliza was being damn selfish with her fortune and maybe deserved whatever she got?"

"All points to think about," said Mendoza. "And giving us places to look. Duke, you go over this place with the proverbial fine-tooth comb. If she had other caches, maybe for a safety-deposit key or investment papers, I want to know. Art, you chase down to this escrow office and find out chapter and verse about the real-estate deal, whether a lawyer was involved. And let's ask at all the banks—most of those have investment counselors, though I think our Eliza relied on her native common sense—see what they know about her, anyway. And we're going to look at everybody in that damned hotel very close—check back on them as we can—and, Duke!"

"Aye, aye, sir?"

"You're going over her room there with another fine-tooth comb. I don't think you'll find anything, I think she took great care not to leave anything revealing around there where anybody in her loving family—or anybody else—might find it. But, look." Mendoza glanced at his watch. "I'll run back to the office, see if anything's in from Ossining, and then if I want to make that funeral—O.K., I'll see you. You know the routine."

Outside, he started down the block to where he'd left the Ferrari. Our Eliza, he thought. Another one like his grandfather, the old ogre on the hearth. Far back as he could remember, screaming about the four-dollar gas bill, grudging the fifty cents for resoling the school shoes: and then, after he died, all those safety-deposit boxes turning up, the gilt-edged stock, the real estate. A gambler, the old man: not like cautious, canny Eliza that way—but another miser.

In a bankbook there's no love, gentlemen. No. That he had found out too: maybe late, but he had found it out. And, money or no, he was safe: unlocking the Ferrari, he had that sudden odd thought. He was safe forever, because there were Alison and the twins at home in the house on Rayo Grande Avenue.

"You mark my words." He looked up from the car door. Mrs. Stepp stood there beside him, wearing her crooked grin. "God hates a miser. She was a wicked woman, not sparing of the poor and the orphan, and her soul went straight to hell-fire and brimstone."

"Possibly so," said Mendoza diplomatically, and slid under the wheel.

Ossining had been commendably prompt in replying to the request for information.

Benjamin Joseph Kelly had been convicted on a homicide charge when he was nineteen, back in 1914. He and another kid had attempted to hold up a saloon—back in 1914 they were still saloons—and the bartender had showed fight. A cop had dropped in by chance during the fight—one Robert Emmet Muldoon—and a shot had been fired—by Kelly, the one with the gun—which had unfortunately killed Muldoon. Place of occurrence: The Bowery, New York. Both Kelly and his pal had been handed life sentences. Even in 1914 cops hadn't liked cops' getting killed. Apparently they'd thrown the key away on Ben; he hadn't got paroled until 1954. It could be guessed, from the terse teletype, on account of his early prison record: obstreperous, a troublemaker, a fighter. Later he seemed to have settled down. And they finally let him out. He'd got official permission to come to California on the plea that he had a brother here. Kelly was now off parole.

Well. That really said nothing at all. And while no brief was to be held for cop-killers, apparently it had been a little scuffle started with no murderous intentions—a couple of wrongheaded kids—and to steal away forty years of a man's life—

But between that and mixing up a lethal dose of homemade poison a great gulf was fixed.

Farrell told him there'd been another D.O.A.—traffic accident. Another drunk walking off the curb against the light. "No loss," said Mendoza absently, and went on to get an early lunch and attend Sergeant Palliser's mother's funeral.

Landers and Piggott had split up all the places they had to cover. About now Landers had got to the Union Station and Piggott to the Continental Bus Lines office in Inglewood.

The first place Landers had checked, of course, was the Greyhound office on Spring Street. They were very helpful. Several buses had arrived at that station, the official L.A. terminus, between two and three-thirty P.M. on March third. There had been an interstate bus starting from Portland, Oregon; a bus from San Francisco; a bus from Sacramento; a cross-country bus from Chicago; and of course every single one of them had made many stops en route—small towns, big towns.

Now at the Union Station he was offered five trains that had arrived within those times—from Chicago, San Francisco (coast route), Seattle, San Diego and San Francisco (inland route). As to checking up on which conductors had been on duty—a little chore, said the official, and in any case the conductors didn't have occasion to notice *everybody* in the train.

God only knew, thought Landers, what Piggott was getting.

It would be one hell of a lot easier to write it off as suicide. Obvious suicide. Wait until some worried relative reported Mary Brown missing and the routine inquiries were set in motion, when L.A. Homicide could teletype back to wherever: Here's what happened to her.

Only, of course, L.A. Homicide didn't operate that way. The L.A.P.D. liked to keep up its reputation of being the smartest force there was: a thing looked fishy, they kept working it until it came apart and the truth showed.

He thanked the official, said he'd check back with him for the names, and started for the airport.

Hackett, Higgins and Grace descended on the Celtic Hotel at eleven-thirty. Not everybody was at home, but to those that were they started to give the full treatment. One by one, they conducted the questioning in depth.

They wanted to know backgrounds, and how long all of them had lived there, and how well had they known Mrs. McCann, and had they ever heard her mention a will—investments—property? And so on and so on.

Detective Grace—even Detective Grace—reduced Miss Manning to tears within half an hour, and Karl Svenson snarled at them ill-temperedly, and Ben stolidly and patiently answered all the questions. They invaded the domain of an irritated Henry, and were nervously fawned on by Oscar, and denounced as a pack of fools by Jane.

But they got some answers; and when they came to sort them out, something might emerge.

They broke for lunch and came back and asked more questions.

Among the questions, of course—the largely futile questions—had been one about "Have you ever seen such a plant as this, et cetera," and Hackett had passed the little book, *Herbs of Healing*, to Higgins at one point.

It was all rather hectic—the McLaughlins and their roomers being what they were—and at some time past three o'clock, when they called a halt and headed back for base, they went tiredly down to Hackett's blinding-scarlet Barracuda and climbed in and Hackett started the engine. And he said, "Oh, you got that book, George? I seem to remember—"

"I haven't got it," said Higgins. "I had—let's see, we were in Henry's room a while ago—I think I put it down on the table there, meant to give it back to you but—"

"Oh, hell," said Hackett.

"I'll go and fetch it," said Grace. "Won't be a minute." He got out of the car. When he came back with the book he reported that there was a big row going on between Henry and Oscar. "Going at it hammer and tongs, and the monkey climbing up the curtains and chattering at them and the Manning woman wringing her hands in the middle of the lobby and wishing Albert would come and take her away."

"*What* a crowd," said Hackett, and let in the clutch.

SEVEN

They found Mendoza leaning back in his desk chair talking to Glasser, who was perched on a corner of the—as usual—inhumanly tidy desk. "So there's no blood or anything on the car, we chase down the kid who brought it in and he's a seventeen-year-old going to Pasadena High School and he hasn't been driving long and rammed it into a tree, that's all. I don't know, Lieutenant, I kind of go along with Higgins, the only hope we've got of getting the car that killed Cohen is to come up with the right plate number. The car needn't have been damaged much, human body's not such a hard object. So our hit-run joker runs home and cleans the car himself in the privacy of his garage—that's that."

"You do any looking on the idea that it was deliberate?" asked Mendoza. "Hello, boys. Come in and join us."

Glasser looked derisive. "That's silly. I looked around. Cohen had a good rep, both personally and with us. Family man. Two grown-up kids. He'd had no trouble of any kind with anybody lately that anybody knew about. I tell you this plate-number thing's the one to follow up. The young fellow gave us that number looks fairly sharp—L.A.C.C. student, third year. He does wear glasses, and he was looking at the plate from the curb, not a direct view. I still think if we figure all the possible mistakes he could have made— Anyway, I thought up a few more the D.M.V.'s checking out."

"And what have you happy gents brought in?" asked Mendoza of Hackett, who had sunk into the chair beside the desk.

"Well, a lot of facts and figures and times," said Hackett, taking out his notebook. "If it's worth anything."

Higgins dragged up another chair and Grace fetched a third from the anteroom. "Thanks for the kind words, Henry, I don't see any other way to come up with that driver either," said Higgins. "The D.M.V. come through with any more makes yet?"

"Hadn't a while ago. I'll see if anything's come in." Glasser drifted out.

"*¡Attención!* This McCann thing. What'd you get?"

"I'll open the ball," said Hackett. "We divided 'em up. Oscar. He saw her on Wednesday morning, but just for a minute—she'd already finished breakfast. Manning—her first name is Vera, by the way—agrees, if that's worth anything. Though she seems competent enough some ways—does all the marketing for them—McCann used to make out the lists. We did find out a good deal about the household and various arrangements. All kind of funny. By all that emerges, the McLaughlins have been happily puttering around their backwater for the last thirty-five years or so without the vaguest realization that the depression's over or times changed. If you'll believe me, they charge the Rialto woman four dollars a week for her room. Karl Svenson pays three—it's a smaller room—and fifty cents a month for the electricity. The Lightfoot female—Florence Lightfoot—pays three-fifty. The Allenby creature, who's another one not all there, pays two bucks for a cubbyhole off a sort of pantry beside the kitchen. Mrs. Rialto and Mrs. Lightfoot pay fifty cents a month for the use of one of the refrigerators in the kitchen and the stove. Svenson has his own refrigerator and a hot plate in his room. Nobody seems to know how Allenby feeds herself, she doesn't use the kitchen except to get water."

"There's one bathroom on every floor," put in Grace. "You should see them. Circa nineteen ten. These seven-foot bathtubs—you could drown in one—all encased in the finest quality black walnut. And fancy chains on the toilets."

"I can imagine," said Mendoza.

"Talk about arrangements," said Hackett. "Well, they're all queer people—I suppose it's only natural. They had a regular time schedule set up. Mrs. Rialto and Mrs. Lightfoot can't use the kitchen in the morning until after nine o'clock, so they don't generally at all; both have hot plates in their rooms. The McLaughlins, which includes Manning, always had dinner between six and seven, so Rialto and Lightfoot can't use the kitchen till after seven-thirty. There's a big table, the McLaughlins eat here. Separately. Svenson keeps pretty much to himself. He—"

"Backgrounds?" said Mendoza plaintively.

"Oh, we got this and that. Svenson was a wire walker and aerialist for forty years, worked circuses mostly. Big time, so he says. Was with the Flying Adriennes, Ringling Brothers, awhile. About ten years ago he took a bad fall, broke his back. Spent most of his savings on medical bills. He lives on the pension now. He can get around on crutches, take care of himself after a fashion. He tells us he was in his room all day on Wednesday, didn't lay eyes on any of the McLaughlins. What was he doing all day? Working on his book: he's writing his memoirs."

"No corroboration?"

"What do you think? He's an unsociable cuss and, anyway, what Oscar told you about all of them liking their privacy was the understatement of the month. Mrs. Rialto and Mrs. Lightfoot have rooms across the hall from each other, but the rest of 'em seem to have got as far away from each other as possible, and in that old barracks of a place that's far enough. Henry lives in his big room off the lobby; the ground-floor bathroom adjoins that, and he's very touchy about anybody using it but him. Svenson is in a room at the back on the ground floor. Rialto and Lightfoot a dozen rooms down the hall on the second floor. Oscar sleeps way up on the fourth floor—tittered and said the air's better up there. Jane is at the very back of the third floor. Manning has a room over at the opposite side of the ground floor from Henry, which I'd guess used to be the manager's office. Ben sleeps out in what used to be the stable, it runs back of the hotel and also back of the little place beside it where Oscar the friendly undertaker still hopes for business. Ben pays two dollars a week, gets it cheaper because he takes care of Gertrude. They're having trouble milking her," added Hackett. "Ellie always did that."

"*Vaya historia.* What's Ben living on? He didn't get a pension from Sing Sing."

"No, but the state of California's not so choosey. I don't know how he managed before he established residency, but he's now on the pension. So is Mrs. Lightfoot. So is Miss Allenby. Mrs. Rialto isn't old enough to qualify, she has a job of sorts but only works part time because she also is writing a book—about astrology. You can gather they all drifted to that place because they're all living on practically nothing. Somebody told somebody else about the McLaughlins and their cheap rooms, and the roomers drifted in. They've had—Oscar says—a lot of people at various times. Some pensioners. He says vaguely, oh, some of them died or went to the hospital and so on. They usually have a few more than they do now."

"I told you," said Grace. "Only one of the family with her head screwed on the right way was our Eliza. And why she let Oscar go on charging those low rents—"

"Well, the hotel belongs jointly to Oscar and Henry. I sort of figure," said Higgins, "when, as we know now, she was sitting on a small fortune all her own, it gave her some private laughs to see Oscar and Henry taking in peanuts when they could have been getting more."

"That sounds like what we know of Eliza," agreed Mendoza. "Who did see her Wednesday morning?"

"Nobody but Oscar, Henry and Manning—according to them. Eliza did fix breakfast for Jane—who doesn't often come downstairs, though she can, she's not all that crippled. Manning says vaguely that 'Jane snoops around all the rooms up there,' which could mean she prowls that floor at least. Anyway, Manning carried the tray up to Jane while Eliza was getting her own breakfast. Then Eliza went out to milk the goat—which was in a pen in the stableyard. But Ben says he didn't see her—hadn't got up yet."

"Oh," said Mendoza. "By the way, according to Sing Sing, he came out here to live with a brother. Where's the brother?"

"Dead. That's how he landed at the Celtic Hotel," said Grace. "Brother was living there. Mrs. Lightfoot, who's a giddy old girl all simpering giggles, heard about the hotel from a woman she got talking to in Pershing Square. She's lived there only about three months. Mrs. Rialto's been there three, four years, heard about it from Miss Manning's sister, who evidently shoved the old lady off on Eliza and glad to be rid of her. Well, I can see she'd be a little embarrassing to have around. Sister paid Eliza forty a month for her. Nobody remembers how long Allenby's been there or how she happened to come."

"Oh," said Mendoza. "Relationships with Eliza?"

"They all talked, but nothing much emerged," said Higgins. "That is a bunch of zanies. It did come out that Eliza kept pretty much to herself, even more than the rest of them—which figures. Duke and Scarne just came in as we were leaving—started looking at her room. Which was on the third floor—where Percy sleeps too, but about as far away as he can get. We just had a look: mainly what's in her room is books. Books and books. A lot of paperbacks, a lot of old books half falling apart. Looks as if she brought home every book that ever came into the store. By what they all said, she wasn't very sociable either. Usually had breakfast alone or with Manning, milked the goat, went off to the store. Came home at six o'clock, fixed her own dinner and Manning's with Manning's help. Sometimes Oscar or Henry would be in the kitchen then too, getting their dinners—which they did separately. Zany," said Higgins. "My God. Living on cheese sandwiches and soup. She gave Manning fifteen bucks a week to do the marketing—made out lists. Woman can go shopping at least."

"Fifteen—"

"I'm telling you. Fifteen per. That's for Eliza and Manning. Sometimes, says Manning, she'd run out before the end of the week, so Eliza would give her another four or five. Oscar and Henry split the room rent, which comes to eighty-two-fifty a month; Percy pays three bucks a week too. The remittance man. They do their own marketing. Henry makes some extra off his embroidery."

"*Caray,*" said Mendoza, thinking of the normal grocery bills Alison reported. "It wouldn't run to much more than cheese sandwiches. You'd think they'd have realized, with today's prices—"

"I'm *telling* you. They don't know what year it is. Crazy. Anyway, they say that after Eliza finished her dinner and washed the dishes, she went straight up to her room. And on Sundays, down to have breakfast, upstairs again until she left at twelve o'clock sharp for this little lunch party with her old friends. Home about five, dinner at six, and that was that. And Henry seems to spend most of his time in his room. How Oscar occupies himself all day is anybody's guess—waiting for customers, maybe. Anyway, there wasn't much fraternizing."

"What it comes down to," said Grace, "in that place anybody could have seen her that morning, privately, and nobody else know about it. As long as they knew where her room was—and everybody did, naturally, except Lightfoot, who hasn't been there long. There's back stairs as well as front. Somebody who knew her regular hours could have been up there before she came down that morning. Ben could also have seen her when she went to milk Gertrude."

"I really should tell the Board of Health about Gertrude," said Mendoza absently. "Yes. But look—it's all very well for Bainbridge to say this foxglove concoction could have been flavored or mixed with a soft drink of some kind. It wouldn't be the easiest thing in the world to approach our Eliza with an ingratiating smile and offer her a Coke at seven o'clock in the morning. Either while she was getting dressed or while she was milking Gertrude. For anybody. Not natural."

"There is that," said Hackett. "So is it more likely she had it in the store? Later? Bainbridge said either time was possible. We'll ask some more—find out about any regular customers who might know—and these women she had her Sunday lunches with, who might also know if she was in the habit of drinking a Coke or something in the middle of the morning. There's that drugstore down the street. But—"

"So she kept herself to herself," said Mendoza. "Yes. I get the impression she didn't think much of the rest of her family. Mmh—feckless as they are. I'm wondering hard whether she made a will. And, if she did, what's in it."

"Duke said they didn't turn up anything else at the store."

"And I'm now wondering something else," said Mendoza suddenly. "*Nothing* else? *¡Quiá!* What about Uncle? Greedy Uncle in Washington? By the deed, she got that property clear of encumbrances in nineteen fifty-two. O.K. At the least, she's cleared a profit of around eleven thousand a year since then, and that's not counting in whatever net she made from the store. I'll just bet you that our canny Eliza never paid a dime of income tax on it. She might just get away with it, you know. They spot-check, but they don't as a rule bother with the little fish—what look like the very little fish from places like Los Angeles Street. The only actual record there'd be would be the rents reported by her tenants on their tax returns—and the bank records, of course. She couldn't get out of the property tax—deed in her name—but I'll just bet she never filed an income-tax return."

"Which says what?" asked Hackett.

"Nothing really. Except that if she didn't make a will, and her loving family comes in for the small fortune, and the whole business has to go through escrow and all the other legal bit to get it transferred, *Dios*, these happy-go-lucky McLaughlins are going to be in trouble with Uncle!" said Mendoza amusedly.

"Oh, brother, are you right," said Higgins, and started to laugh.

"And if I read Eliza right"—Grace grinned—"could be she just planned it that way."

"Which doesn't get us any farther toward finding out who handed her the homemade poison," said Hackett. "For what reason."

"Well, you know," said Grace, "these McLaughlins. All of 'em—Oscar and Henry and Jane. *And* we don't want to overlook the ones that aren't here any more. Moved away. Somewhere. What'd the little barber say? Older sister Dorothy—Stephen—William—Earl. She dies without a will, they come in for the whole bit. If the rest of 'em are anything like those we've met, a seven-way split in twenty or thirty G's might look like Fort Knox to them."

"What's left in Fort Knox?" asked Mendoza sardonically. "So?"

"So, say one of 'em had found out about it—we know both Oscar and Percy helped her at the store sometimes, and they could have got it from Wolf or one of the other tenants—is it likely that one of that bunch would think maybe she'd made a will leaving it all to the Red Cross—*or* have any notion about Uncle and his tax spirals or even inheritance tax? Just doin' what comes naturally—the happy thought, if Ellie should die, we'd all inherit. I suppose they would know that much?" added Grace doubtfully.

"Which is also a thought," agreed Mendoza. "But I can't get over the difficulty. She was very far from a fool, Jase, if she was only elementarily shrewd. It wouldn't have been natural for any of that crowd to offer her any kind of drink at that hour in the morning—" He stopped.

"Mmh-hmm," said Hackett dryly. "He's got there. We talked this over before. So just maybe little Oscar bustled into the store around nine A.M., on his way back from getting the paint, and said, My, it's turned warm, hasn't it, I just thought you'd enjoy a Coke, or some nice orangeade just off the ice—and produced the bottles. Hers spiked beforehand. Or Henry. Or even Percy Cantwell, who I understand is a cousin."

"Yes," said Mendoza thoughtfully, "yes. It's possible. And helpfully rinsed out the glasses afterward. There was a second, unused glass in the cupboard there."

"We gathered sometimes Manning came down to the store with her for a while or dropped in on the way from market."

"Both Percy and Oscar," said Hackett, "are familiar with the store. She acquired stock in a couple of ways—bought it piecemeal from people coming in, took it on consignment at a twenty-per-cent cut, and sometimes she'd dicker for a whole houseful of furniture. Some old person dying and no family, or family selling off the bits and pieces. And both Oscar and Percy had helped her move merchandise—Percy's the only one of the bunch with a driver's license, and a few times he'd rented a pickup truck—Eliza providing the money—and carted stuff to the store. It'd be fairly natural for either of 'em to drop in that way. Or for Manning."

"*Conforme.* But not so easy for either of them to concoct the homemade poison? I gather you need a stove at least—and where, boys, just where—which is the ultimate question—down here in the middle of the neon jungle did anybody locate a nice healthy patch of the common foxglove?"

Hackett shrugged. That was a question all right.

"And knew how to brew the fatal dose?" added Grace.

Which was another question.

"What are Percy's household arrangements?" asked Mendoza.

"He doesn't seem to have any," said Higgins gloomily. "He gets sent a hundred bucks a month by some third cousin or somebody in England. We got that out of him finally. He pays the McLaughlins twelve bucks a month for his room. He eats all his meal out—I'd have a guess, hamburgers and so on—and spends most of his time, he says, in 'the local pub,' which turns out to be Sam's Bar and Grill on North Spring."

"¡Vaya!"

"But, Lieutenant," said Grace softly, "well, I read a lot and a little something sort of came to me about Percy. For whatever it's worth. This and that we got out of him. And he was raised in England. In the country. Place called Wroxton, in the county of Oxfordshire. And you know England—well, it's easy to say backward people, the country people there— it's not that exactly—they don't take to changing ideas to any extent. And in a place like that I'd take a small bet you'd find a few old people who know something about the old-time remedies, same like Tabitha Thirkettle—and what she calls the ones that can be dangerous, too."

Mendoza looked at him. "You do think, don't you? What a business. Up in the air you can say. That *is* a thought, Jase."

Glasser came back into the office. "Report in from the D.M.V.," he said to Higgins. "Your latest brain wave turned up a Baptist preacher in San Diego, a chiropractor in Eureka, and one that could just be—fellow called Alfred Clark in Pasadena. At least he's local. Car's a nineteen-fifty-nine Mercury."

Higgins got up. "So let's go check him out. I can't say I care a tinker's dam who mixed up the brew for Eliza. Nothing to choose among that bunch." He charged out with Glasser in tow.

Tom Landers, at five-thirty that Saturday afternoon, was busy on the phone, checking back with all the helpful officials for all the checked-out names of the bus drivers, conductors, and stewardesses. Piggott hadn't come back yet.

The officials fired names at him and information. This bus driver was on his way to Chicago, wouldn't be back until Tuesday. That one lived in Chatsworth. This one was starting a run from San Diego, due in at midnight. This conductor was on the Portland run, not due back until Monday. This stewardess was in New York, due in at the airport at one-fifteen Sunday but scheduled to staff the four-fifteen to Miami. And so on.

Landers swore. And ten to one the whole damn thing was a mare's nest. Honest-to-God suicide. On the other hand, by the autopsy report there'd been a very small amount of alcohol in the stomach. So had the sleeping pills been in a little drink, maybe, so she hadn't known what she was drinking? Put in the drink by the boy friend or whoever? And she'd been found dead in bed, dressed—or vice versa—in a cheap lace-trimmed blue nightgown. So—

But they had to work it. If only to find out who she'd been and notify any relatives.

Landers swore some more. The deadly routine. There was one bus driver who was off duty until Monday; the address was in Hollywood. Landers started to dial the phone number. Go see him tonight, maybe, show him the picture (post-mortem) of Mary Brown, and ask—

At ten minutes to six Scarne sauntered into Mendoza's office and tossed a legal-sized envelope onto the desk. "We are thorough," he said. "Try to be. About five thousand books in that damned room, but we riffled through every one. Thorough—that's the L.A.P.D. lab. This dropped out of the four thousandth nine hundredth and ninetieth—copy of *Bartlett's Quotations*."

"*¿De veras?*" Mendoza picked it up. Opened the long manila envelope. "*¡Qué mono!*" The long legal-sized folded single sheet, with its blue covering sheet, was headed *Last Will and Testament*.

He skimmed through it rapidly. It had been drawn up—a very simple will—by one Adam Carson, attorney-at-law, and signed by Eliza A. McCann and witnessed by two names strange to the case—lawyer's clerks probably.

It bequeathed all Eliza McCann's property to be evenly divided among three persons: Tabitha Thirkettle, Ida Mae Glidden, and Marcia Hunt. Addresses were appended.

"How extremely interesting indeed," said Mendoza, his long nose twitching.

EIGHT

Alfred Clark, when Higgins and Glasser located him, turned out to be most depressingly unlikely to have driven the hit-and-run car which had killed Patrolman Harry Cohen.

They found Alfred Clark at home, which was a nicely kept frame bungalow in a nice middle-class section of Pasadena. On this mild spring Saturday afternoon, he was out in the back yard playing ball with his two kids, Roy, aged eleven, and Ruth, aged nine. Mrs. Clark led them there looking puzzled; she was a pretty young woman, neatly dressed.

"Wednesday morning?" said Alfred Clark. "Well, I'd have to— The car? You say you're *police*? What on earth have I done?" He was a man about thirty-five, his dark hair receding; he had a pleasantly open and friendly face if he wasn't exactly handsome. The kids came up, interested, and Higgins for once was discouraged by kids who liked cops—the boy saying earnestly *he'd* like to be a cop when he grew up, the girl just staring with wondering big eyes. Rather obviously, a man who raised his kids to admire cops wouldn't be a man who'd inadvertently run down a traffic officer and then speed away.

They looked at the car, whose plate number was JQN-700 and which was utterly undamaged. "Well, it was just a try," said Glasser.

"Wednesday morning," Clark was saying. "Where was I— Oh, yes, of course." And his face cleared. "I was with Mr. Dowd in his office. About eleven o'clock. You see, I've got my own business—hardware—but I'm rather active in our Y.M.C.A. activities here, and Mr. Dowd was interested in our summer-camp plans, he's an executive with a local department store, and we hoped he might want to contribute something, and I took all the papers up to show him. I was with him until about noon. What on earth—what's this all about, gentlemen?"

"Nothing," said Higgins. "A wild-goose chase. We go on a lot of them,

Mr. Clark. Thanks very much, sorry to have bothered you." He grinned at the kids; he and Glasser walked down the drive.

"Well, we have to look," said Glasser with a sigh.

They had to look. It was getting on for six then; Higgins dropped Glasser back at Headquarters and drove up to his old apartment on Bronson Avenue. About now, he thought, Mary Dwyer would be getting home from work and having to fix dinner. A woman ought to be home with her kids. But the pension didn't start to cover everything; she had to work. They were good kids, Steve and Laura, but these days kids could get in trouble so easy, just a couple of wrong friends—and Steve not eleven yet; he needed a man—

But it was really beyond the realm of possibility that Mary Dwyer, who was a very damn good-looking woman, would look twice at George Allen Higgins, with his ugly puss.

He looked in the refrigerator, sighed, made himself a highball, and then went out to a restaurant nearby. And over his steak he suddenly took in the sense of what Mr. Alfred Clark had said, and he thought: Y.M.C.A. summer camp. Could he possibly enter into some deal with Mr. Clark, to build a ruse Mary wouldn't suspect, to get Stevie to camp? Mr. Clark had seemed like a nice guy.

Slightly cheered and trying to think up plausible ideas to put across to Mary, Higgins went home. Providence, he thought. Stevie talking about going to camp this summer ever since Christmas. After all, thought Higgins, he'd managed about Laura's piano lessons, and Mary hadn't any suspicion he was paying half the cost. Somehow he'd get Stevie to summer camp.

Undoubtedly Providence had led him to Alfred Clark. On a wild-goose chase.

Landers called Mr. John Brady and explained what he wanted—all official. Mr. Brady drove buses for the Continental Bus Company: We Cover the Continent. He had driven a bus from Seattle down the coast to L.A. last Tuesday and Wednesday and pulled into L.A. at three-fifteen Wednesday afternoon. Mary Brown could have been on his bus.

"What say your name is?" asked Mr. Brady.

"Landers, sir, Detective Landers, Headquarters. Would it be convenient for you if I dropped by at, say, eight o'clock, if you'll be home, and—"

"Any time," said Brady largely. "Why not now? I'm just sittin' here feelin' sorry for myself, all alone. Glad to have some company, friend."

"Well—" The address was on Detroit Avenue, not so far from where Landers lived; he might as well see Brady and get it over.

The night shift was just coming on. Landers said good night to Farrell, sought his car in the lot and drove up to Hollywood, not without delays at that traffic-ridden hour. He found the address, an old duplex with a velvet-green lawn and manicured flower beds round it; he found Brady in one side of the duplex, a big bald middle-aged man with friendly eyes who opened the door wide, told him to come in and sit down. "What'll you drink—bourbon or Scotch?"

"Well, nothing, really, I—"

"Cops gettin' puritanical?" said Brady. "You look like you could use a drink. Suppose you ran into some bottlenecks on the freeway, up here from downtown. You should try it with a bus full of people yet. Besides, it's seven o'clock, ain't you off duty?"

"Well, yes," said Landers. "Scotch."

"That's better," said Brady. "Might's well be comfortable." When they were settled with their drinks (this hypnotically mild spring weather enervating, you could say: the drink was welcome and warm in Landers' empty stomach) Brady looked at the photograph Landers handed him. "Want to know if she rode with me? That Seattle run, you said? Yeah. This ain't such a hot picture."

"Girl was dead," said Landers.

"That so? Yeah, yeah, I guess I can see that. Poor kid—she don't look over twenty. That's a damn shame. Somebody knocked her off?"

Landers shrugged. "Looks like suicide, but we want to find out who she was if we can. And just maybe somebody did take her off."

Brady shook his head and took a pull at his drink. "Damn shame. Now I'll tell you the truth, boy. She could've rode with me, but I ain't sure. You got things to concentrate on, you're drivin' a bus full of people. I tell you how it is, when you take the bus out from here, or Seattle, or Chicago or wherever, the passengers already in you don't notice. They've handed over the tickets and got settled. O.K. But now take this Seattle run, f'r instance. There's stops in Auburn and Sumner and Tacoma and Olympia and Aberdeen and Raymond and Kelso and Kalama and Woodland and, my God, all the way down the coast I wouldn't like to count the stops—all those are before you get across the border into Oregon even—and then there's Portland and Oregon City and Newberg and McMinnville and Dallas and—well, look, anybody can get on the bus at any of those places. See? And a lot do—maybe just for a forty-mile ride, sometimes all the way."

"Yes," said Landers.

"And the faces I see every week—who could remember 'em all? But the people get on like that you are apt to notice just a little bit more."

"And you think you remember this girl?" For God's sake, thought Landers, had he hit the jackpot the first time round? It could happen.

"Now I ain't goin' so far as to say that," said Brady. "No. This ain't such a hot picture and I couldn't anyways be sure—for one thing, it's black and white, no color. But on the other hand"—he grinned comfortably at Landers—"for all I'm risin' fifty and ain't got no hair, well, you can't help noticin' a pretty girl, you see one."

"Yes," said Landers, grinning back.

"So it just could've been this girl I remember gettin' on, and I can't tell you just exactly what stop it was but someplace after Eureka, on the way down. Up there. Could've been Rio Dell, but I kinda got the feeling it was further down, like Willits or Ukiah. Anyways, she got on and she was goin' all the way to L.A., she had two suitcases with her."

"Remember anything about those?"

"Not a blessed thing. Just there was two of 'em. I helped her get 'em aboard. A damn pretty girl, about twenty. Brown hair—I guess blue eyes. Medium tall and—you know—quite a figger. Nice girl, you could tell," said Brady. Which was exactly what that hotel maid had said about Mary Brown.

Maybe he had hit the jackpot. He asked Brady what she'd been wearing; Brady didn't remember. Just remembered the pretty girl getting on and helping her with her suitcases. But this was something: it might be just exactly what they wanted to know.

"Thanks very much, Mr. Brady," said Landers. He finished his drink and stood up. This had taken a while and he was starving to death, but he ought to call in and get the routine started. "We'll start looking in all those places and see what—"

"Oh, what's the rush?" said Brady. "You want to call your office, there's the phone, boy. You look hungry to me, and I do hate to eat alone, I got a couple nice thick steaks back in the kitchen, suppose we have another little drink while they're fixin', and then you can tell me all about bein' a cop on this force while we eat. O.K.? I got a boy on the force up in Bakersfield."

"Oh," said Landers, "that so?"

Brady took his empty glass. "You call in, you want. I'll start the steaks. That's right."

Landers reached for the phone.

Mendoza didn't often bring cases home with him: the average deadly dull routine of homicide does not make for interesting conversation over the dinner table; but the offbeat ones and the ones that turned out to be tough came home with him because Mendoza had the single-track mind and couldn't stop worrying at a thing until he knew the answer.

"So there you are," he said. "It's wide open. Any of them could have done it. Given the knowledge about the foxglove. And anybody could have found that out by going to the library. And I do wonder whether, in all her collection of books, there happens to be one like that one Bainbridge handed us. And whether anybody in that place was in the habit of borrowing books from her. But even so, and even granting that there's any common foxglove to be found somewhere down there, vacant lots, *I* don't know where—even so, it's such a damned roundabout way of—"

"Well, you might think so," said Alison, considering. "All sorts of other lethal things rather easily available—weed killer and rat poison and so on— *And* of course the first implication that leaps to the eye about that is—"

"Tabitha Thirkettle," said Mendoza. "*De veras.*" They were both comfortably full of dinner; Mendoza had taken off jacket and tie and was stretched out in the largest armchair with Bast purring on his lap. Alison was wearing her most fetching topaz housecoat, and her red head gleamed in the soft lamplight; she had Nefertiti. From a distance there came noises indicative that the twins were resisting bed as usual. El Señor, the miniature lion, lay stretched on the carpet between their chairs. "With her little hobby," said Alison lazily. "The simples."

"But Eliza never took medicine of any kind. I know—that says nothing. Could have been put in a drink of some kind. Oh, I want to know the hell of a lot more about those three old biddies indeed. For all we know they could have been in it together—"

"Jumping to conclusions, *amado.*"

"We'll join them at their regular Sunday get-together tomorrow and ask some pointed questions. Whether any or all of them knew about the will. And where they were last Wednesday and what doing. And I think, just to be thorough, we'll get a warrant and look through the Thirkettle house. And—¡Santa María!" Mendoza exclaimed violently as Sheba landed on him from behind, digging all claws into his shoulder. "Little monster!"

"But, Luis—"

Sheba walked down him onto her mother and started to chew Bast's right ear. Bast remonstrated mildly. "There's not room for two of you," said Mendoza. Offended, Bast left him and began to wash El Señor. Sheba settled down, purring. "Livestock," said Mendoza.

"But, Luis, that could be the reason. For the foxglove. To point so obviously to the Thirkettle woman and her simples."

"I don't somehow feel that anybody we've met in this case so far has quite that subtle a mind, my love."

"But you don't *know*," said Alison. "Not really. It *is* a funny case, all right. And something else occurs to me . . . I ran into that obnoxious Holloway woman in at Bullocks' this afternoon. I hadn't seen her in years. No, you don't know her. We were in school together once. In Hollywood. One of the brief occasions I was in an American school. Age," said Alison, "is a funny thing too. I hardly ever think of it, but some people— Anyway, she's rather a cat. Sorry, I don't mean that, cats are at least honest. If egotists. Anyway, first she asked was I married yet and then if I had any children. *Hers* are eleven and thirteen—paragons, of course. And when I said—"

"What brought this up?" asked Mendoza.

"In a minute. When I said the twins—"

Master John Luis erupted into the living room at full speed. At eighteen months his speed was impressive. After him, at a slightly more dignified pace, came Mrs. MacTaggart, announcing firmly that it was time for all good little boys to be in bed.

"Johnny!" said Alison.

"No!" announced Master John as firmly, and dived under the credenza, leaving his pajamas behind on the floor.

"Now, Johnny—" Mrs. MacTaggart and Alison crouched to haul him out.

"*Bed*," said Alison. "You know you always go to bed now, *come* on."

"No," said Johnny, unwillingly succumbing to superior physical strength.

"Now, *mo croidhe*," said Mrs. MacTaggart, "you be a good boy now, and we'll just hop into beddies and Máiri'll sing you a nice song to send you off to sleep. 'Flow Gently, Sweet Afton'—now that's a nice song to be going off to sleep with—"

"*No me gusta*," said Johnny emphatically. Suddenly restored to amiability, he reached up one hand and patted Alison's cheek. "*Mo croidhe?*" he said doubtfully.

Mendoza burst out laughing. "I swear to God, if these kids are getting nothing else it's a democratic raising. But sooner or later they're going to have to learn to distinguish one language from another."

"Off we go!" said Mrs. MacTaggart. "Well, will you look at that now!" Miss Teresa had appeared in the hall doorway. Her small person was stark naked except for a pair of woolly slippers. "*No afton*," she said. "Bonnie. *Sí. Bueno.*"

"Well, now. 'Tis 'The Banks and Braes o' Bonnie Doon' the lass wants? And will Johnny like that too?"

"O.K.," said Johnny. Mrs. MacTaggart bore him out, shepherding Terry before her.

"Darlings," said Alison fondly.

"Incipient diplomats, God forbid. All the languages. What were you talking about?"

"Well, it only just occurred to me, Luis. This awful Holloway woman. When I said the twins were eighteen months, she said, Goodness, I was lucky to have any, starting so *late*. As if I'd been middle-aged or something, when I was only— But, anyway, you've been talking about the McLaughlins and I just suddenly thought: what about the rest of them?"

"Well, what about them?"

"The older brothers and sister. Dorothy? Well, I don't know, I just wondered. You said Oscar was at least fifty-five and probably older—the McCann woman was sixty-five—Henry somewhere around there and Jane older. And the others were older yet—three brothers and a sister. Oscar told you the sister had a job as companion to an old lady. Well, even if they'd been born quite close together, the older sister would have to be seventy or so at least by now? It just struck me as a little funny. These other McLaughlins—the younger ones—apparently settled into their backwater and just stayed put. Not keeping up with the times. While the older ones evidently found jobs for themselves and got out. Not the way round you'd expect it."

Mendoza considered that. "Well, possibly, but there it is. They're not— mmh—expectable people. I think I need a drink." He got up, putting Sheba down, and she nattered at him.

"I just wondered," said Alison. "And as long as you are, I think I'll have just a little of that peppermint liqueur."

"Female drinks," said Mendoza. He went out to the kitchen, hotly pursued by El Señor. Down the hall came the crooning soft voice of Mrs. MacTaggart in song.

He poured half an ounce of rye into a saucer for El Señor, filled a jigger glass for himself, and half of another with the peppermint liqueur. He went back to the living room. "Anybody," he said, "could have dropped into Eliza's secondhand store that morning without much chance of being noticed particularly. It's a business block. Comings and goings. Drugstore, appliance store, hardware, the pawnshop—and on the other side of the street other small businesses. I wouldn't guess that any of those proprietors hire any help—alone in their shops. Who'd notice who went into the secondhand store? We'll be asking, of course."

"But if the will was the reason," said Alison, "I mean for wanting Eliza out of the way, how did anybody know about it? She had it hidden pretty well. In fact, it was a ridiculous place to put it, it might easily never have been found at all. I don't think she was so clever—just shrewd in a primitive sort of way. And if it *was* any of the family who'd just found out she owned all that—and that I *can* see happening the way you said, Oscar or Percy hearing it from one of the tenants—surely, even as eccentric as they all are, it would have occurred to any of them that she might have made a will? That it wouldn't necessarily come to them just automatically on her death? And besides— But, *Luis!*" She moved excitedly to face him. "*¡No sirve!* It *wouldn't* even if— We have been stupid! She was married! *¿Comprende? ¡Cómo no!*"

Mendoza stared at her. "Now for the love of— *Se me pasó, por alto.* For God's sake—and it never crossed my mind till this minute— Stupid you can say—"

"She was a California resident. No matter what sort of will she made, one-third of whatever she left had to go by law to the living spouse. I remember *that* from what the lawyer said after we were married and you insisted on making that settlement—"

"*¡Un millón de demonios desde el infierno!*" said Mendoza. He stared at the glass in his hand, finished the rye. "True. But is the husband living? Oscar says they don't know—he left her thirty years ago. Oh, yes? And if he is living, where is he? For God's sake, could *he* come into this? How wild can you get?"

"He *could* be. People change in thirty years. And what would that property be worth? Even down there? Twenty, thirty thousand? More? To some people—"

"And, for God's sake, try to trace him, on what vague information we get from Oscar?"

"And another thing," said Alison suddenly. "Would Oscar or Henry—"

"Yes," said Mendoza. "I know. Would they realize that a living husband, under the law, would prevent their inheriting the whole shooting match?"

NINE

Sunday or no, they got out and about the next day. The first thing Mendoza did was apply for a search warrant on the Thirkettle house and, on second thought, also for the hotel property. He and Hackett intended to descend on the three lunchers at Mrs. Thirkettle's house, doubtless interrupting some pleasurable gossip, but there was time to fill before that.

Jason Grace caught him as he came into the office. "There's one thing, Lieutenant. I had to take a summer course back in fifth grade to get caught up on simple arithmetic—Virginia figures all the tax forms for us—but I can add a column, you give me time. I was interested enough to go back yesterday afternoon and check all those other tenants."

"Oh, yes?" said Mendoza. A good man, Grace.

Grace followed him into his office. "You wouldn't stop to think—that shabby old block of run-down stores. On that street. Very small time, you'd think. But when you look at the actual figures, brother, a gold mine. A real gold mine after she got it paid off." He took out his notebook. "It sounds piddling, compared to what rents are even in middle-class districts now. There were four apartments rented at fifty per, one—the one Mrs. Stepp has, three rooms—at thirty, and four at forty. Which adds up to three-ninety a month—right?"

"According to Hoyle."

"And the stores on the ground floor—four at fifty apiece, four at forty-five, which adds up to three-eighty. That's leaving out her own, of course. O.K.?"

"On the nose."

"Well"—Grace scratched one ear lobe reflectively—"you slice it any way, that adds up to nine grand two hundred and forty bucks a year."

"I'll take your word for it. A nice little piece of change." Mendoza scribbled figures. "Yes, indeed."

"All right," said Grace. "Even take some off for times not all of 'em are rented—and I had a talk with Wolf, who's been there longest of any tenant, he says none of the stores has been empty for at least ten years, and it isn't often one of the apartments is vacant. Mrs. Stepp is the next oldest tenant, but the rest of 'em have been there quite some time—five, six years up to ten and fifteen. And Mrs. McCann had owned the property clear for just over thirteen years. So you do a little more adding and multiplying—" He watched Mendoza do just that.

"*Caray*, a gold mine you can call it. Picayune little sums, but they do add up, don't they?"

"I make it a hundred and twenty thousand-odd she's taken out of it in that thirteen years. And even discounting the taxes, which'll be pretty low in that area, and any little repairs she's had to make in the time she's owned it, and the times stores or apartments have been empty and so on, she's got to have cleared somewhere around ninety grand at least, possibly more."

"I should think so," said Mendoza, sounding a little surprised; he stared at the figures. "It does add up. And there's what she took in at her own store, Jase. It wouldn't sound like much, I suppose, but—look, by what we get from Manning, cheeseparing isn't the word. They were apparently living, the two of them, on a thousand a year or less. Fifteen bucks a week for groceries, I ask you. And there was the forty a month Manning's sister gave McCann for baby-sitting with the woman. That's—ah—four-eighty a year. My God, if she cleared a thousand a year from her own store, she could have socked away that entire net profit from the business block."

"Um-hum," said Grace. "Only, where is it? Those bankbooks—they all add up to nearly twenty-four grand. There ought to be more, at any reckoning. We've seen her personal effects—nothing there, cheap clothes and not many, no jewelry."

"Yes," said Mendoza. "Yes. We can't get hold of the lawyer who drew up the will until tomorrow, probably. Or check the banks either. And you know something, Jase? We do occasionally act stupid around here, despite our reputation. It took my wife to remind us that the woman was married and if the husband's still alive and hasn't divorced her that will isn't worth a damn in this state."

"Well, call us dumb. So it isn't. I'm bound to say that never came into my mind."

"Or mine," said Hackett, appearing in the office door with Higgins. "For God's sake! Could the husband come into this?"

"Try to find out," said Mendoza. "It's possible, I suppose. I know Sunday's a bad day to chase people down, but we haven't talked to everybody in that block yet—missed most of the tenants upstairs yesterday. Suppose you and George go over there, Jase, and Art and I'll spring the big surprise on the McLaughlins." He got up.

Landers had started the routine on what Brady had given him overnight: the various police forces in Willits, Rio Dell, and Ukiah would be taking a look in their territories for a girl matching the description of Mary Brown who had left town recently.

But he couldn't count on that; the girl Brady remembered didn't have to be Mary Brown. There were two others he could see today: an off-duty S.P. conductor who'd been in charge of one of the trains from Sacramento that day and the airline stewardess due in at International at one-fifteen. He thought it was a very long chance that Mary Brown had arrived in L.A. by air, but you never did know, you had to check everything.

Piggott came in a few minutes late and said plaintively he had hoped to go to church today. Landers gave him the stewardess to check; there wasn't any more they could do on Mary Brown today, personally, and Piggott might as well take an hour or so off to go to church before seeing the stewardess. "But I understand from Rory the lieutenant's got a couple of search warrants coming through, we may be wanted on that."

"Oh, shoot," said Piggott. Piggot was not a swearing man. "If there's one thing I hate, it's pawing through other people's belongings. Makes me feel like a Russian spy or something."

Which just went to show that cops are only human.

Landers went out to see the S.P. conductor, one Joseph Fritz. He turned out to be a bad-tempered old man, possibly suffering from ulcers or at least acid indigestion, who glanced at the photograph of Mary Brown and snapped, "I can't be expected to notice every last passenger on the train every single run. No, I don't think I ever saw this girl—ordinary girl, why'd I notice?" He thrust the photograph back at Landers ungraciously.

"If you'd take another look to be sure, sir—"

"I already did. If she was on my train I didn't notice her. Expect a little peace and quiet, my day off, and the lousy cops got to come botherin'—"

Well, the citizenry did come all sorts. Landers thanked him very politely and headed back for the office.

"Her *husband?*" said Oscar blankly. "My goodness, I'm afraid I wouldn't know anything about him. Now. She was only married to the man a little while, you know—Henry always said he'd only married Ellie for Father's money—Father was still alive then, he died in, let me see, nineteen thirty—and *then* it came out that all the money was gone—it was all in securities, you know, stocks and bonds and things—I'm afraid I'm rather vague about that, but somehow it was all gone. Henry! Henry, can you come out here a moment?" He tapped at the double doors. "And I expect Henry was quite right, because it was then the man left her. Ellie. I seem to remember they were living in San Francisco—and Ellie came to Stephen—that was our eldest brother—and—Henry!"

"Well, what is it *now?*" asked Henry, opening one of the double doors. "Oh, for heaven's sake, *you* again." He looked at Mendoza, annoyed.

"Henry, they want to know about that young man Ellie married. I don't even remember his first name, do you? So long ago—I was at the wedding, of course, we all were—"

"St. Mark's Episcopal Church in San Francisco. I don't precisely recall the year, but it would have been nineteen twenty-eight or twenty-nine. I must say I do not see why such irrelevant information— His name? Theodore Roosevelt McCann. I considered myself that Father disapproved of him because he was named for a Republican, but I was not so irrational. I saw at once he was only after the money. He had a mustache and hay fever," said Henry disapprovingly. "Sneezed several times during the ceremony, I remember."

"When did he leave your sister?"

"Really, why all this— Oh, a year or two later, I suppose. When the money went."

"Did your sister ever divorce him?"

"She wouldn't do that," said Oscar, "no. It would have cost something, wouldn't it—lawyers and all—and it wasn't as if anybody *else* wanted to marry her."

"I see," said Mendoza. "Well, now, Mr. McLaughlin—" He brushed his own mustache, eying the pair of them, and began telling them about Mrs. McCann's small fortune. The bankbooks, the deed, the accumulated profits. Both McLaughlins stared at him blankly.

"The *building?*" said Oscar. "You mean where the store is? Ellie leased that, I'm—"

"No, Mr. McLaughlin. That may have been what she told you, but she owned it. That whole block of business. She began buying it in nineteen thirty-one, and she paid off the mortgage clear in nineteen fifty-two. At the least calculation she'd realized somewhere around ninety thousand dollars from it in the last thirteen years. We have found the record of a little under twenty-four thousand in savings accounts in various banks. Do—"

"Twenty—" Oscar was stricken speechless.

"Well, I must say," said Henry angrily, "if that isn't exactly like Grand-father Elias! Father always said she was very like him. Behind our backs like that, and never a *word* when I was so bad with flu last year—all that money, I could have gone to a proper doctor— And my eyes, you can say what you like, Oscar, but these magnifying glasses from Woolworth's are *not* as satisfactory as a proper prescription would be, and there Ellie sat lis-tening to me complain and never a *word* when she could have— I must say I always thought her a *very selfish* woman and this only goes to show how right I was! All that money—"

"Ill of the dead, Henry. But it *does* seem as if she could have— I've been badly in need of a new suit for quite some time, and it wouldn't have hurt her to— *Henry!* Do you suppose we shall inherit some of it? We're her only relatives, after all—"

"That just occurred to you, Mr. McLaughlin?" asked Hackett. "You didn't know anything about this before?"

"Know about it? Why, none of us had the *least* suspicion—and I still don't understand how she can have acquired all that— Do you suppose we *will?*" Oscar looked eager and excited: a happy fat child. "I've sometimes thought if I could afford to set up my business in a better neighborhood, a proper business neighborhood—"

"Well, you see, that's why we'd like to know about Mrs. McCann's husband," said Mendoza gently. "Under California law, if he's still living and still legally married to her at the time of her death, he's entitled to one-third of the estate."

The brothers looked momentarily stunned at this intelligence. "That— fortune hunter?" said Henry. "After all this time? Well, I should call that a most monstrous miscarriage of justice, sir. That young whippersnapper!"

"I suppose he could be still alive somewhere," said Oscar, looking ready to cry. "Really, this does surprise me. Ellie was so good at managing things, I should have thought she'd have made better arrangements. I re-ally would. Dying so suddenly, and in the store—but I suppose she couldn't help that, if it's as you say, but still—" He shook his head mourn-fully.

Mendoza went on to tell them about the will. "Of course, if her hus-band is still living and hadn't divorced her, he'll be due his share—but the court does generally take into consideration the deceased's intentions," he said deliberately. "I should doubt that you'll get any of it."

"Oh, dear," said Oscar. "All that money—who would have *dreamed*—"

"Very like Eliza," said Henry acidly. "I've no doubt she planned it that way. Very much like Grandfather Elias. Grasping and selfish. And that being so, Oscar, it appears I had best get on with My Work if we are not actually to starve." He glared at them and retreated behind the double doors, closing the open one with a little crash which raised a fine cloud of dust from the bare floor of the lobby.

"I really don't know what we'd have done," said Oscar, "if we hadn't still owned the hotel. Imagine Ellie saving all that money. You'd have thought she'd have left us *something,* but while one doesn't like to speak ill of the dead, I'm bound to say it *was* like her. She was embittered, I'm afraid. That young man leaving her, and losing all Father's money." He sighed.

"And I had better warn you, Mr. McLaughlin," said Mendoza smoothly, "that we'll be coming back with a search warrant some time today. As some of your sister's—mmh—property does seem to be unaccounted for—and for various other reasons—we'll be making a thorough search of the premises."

"Oh, dear, oh, *dear,*" said Oscar agitatedly. "My good sir, *eighty* rooms! You can't possibly—and I really cannot see what good—"

"We'll be seeing you later," said Hackett. "We just like to be thorough, Mr. McLaughlin."

"Oh, *dear*—"

They left Oscar twittering distractedly. "What do you think?" asked Mendoza.

Hackett shrugged. "Anybody's guess. But I guess I think if Oscar or Henry knew about Eliza's nest egg before, they're both a damn sight better actors than I thought they were."

Mendoza rattled the car keys in his hand meditatively. "I guess I think so too. But that's not to say there wasn't some other reason."

"Oh, granted," said Hackett. "Granted. With this crowd. Lightfoot could have poisoned Ellie because Ellie criticized her singing. But my mind does keep going back to the Thirkettle woman."

"The so-obvious answer. Yes. Well, we'll see what the three legatees seem to add up to." Mendoza unlocked the Ferrari; they got in.

They were, he thought, the three most ordinary old biddies he'd ever laid eyes on. For this part of L.A., for this part of any big city in this nation.

They were types. You could call it poor but honest. Little people. All women in their sixties, women who had lived drab lives with little money and nothing interesting happening to them ever, so that the little things that happened to them were exciting. Uninteresting women, except that every human entity, of immense interest and importance to itself, was interesting.

Tabitha Thirkettle. The little birdlike widow of a railroad man who'd never had any children, lived a routine of saving to pay for the little house, for furniture: whose largest interest was her little hobby of brewing old-fashioned simples. It could be guessed, maybe pressing them on everyone she knew: "Just try it, my dear, you might be surprised, it can't do any harm—"

Ida Mae Glidden. Mrs. Another type. A hearty overblown-looking woman, hair firmly kept brass-blonde, a little too much make-up. Another widow: "Grass," she told them cheerfully. One of those people described as the salt of the earth: not overeducated, very down-to-earth, the kind nothing got down for long. Generous, unimaginative, a little bossy, kind, good-natured—all that she'd be, thought Mendoza: but also she'd lived close to the bone and might have an eye out for the main chance.

Marcia Hunt. A self-effacing woman. Colorless. Medium-sized, medium-complexioned, mouse-brown hair going gray, unnoticeable clothes, no make-up, medium every way. Thin little voice. Also a widow. She was on pension and did baby-sitting on the side sometimes, she said primly. There wouldn't be much of that down here, where parents couldn't afford paid attendants. Her husband had worked for the railroad too: that was where the pension came from and how she happened to know Tabitha Thirkettle.

A funny foursome it had been, thought Mendoza. He looked at Mrs. Glidden, the odd one out in a way. Dyed hair, make-up, the different type from the others: but under the surface, he suspected, a simple soul. "How'd you meet Mrs. McCann?" he asked her conversationally.

"Oh, I was looking for an armchair. Didn't matter for looks, I live alone. *And* haven't much money. It was years ago, I dropped in at her place just looking—but I can't get over it—Ellie *poisoned*—even by accident— Well, my God, you gotta be careful, never know what's in anything these days—some of the tints I use say on the directions—" Mrs. Glidden was a beauty operator. Employed at some two-bit shop on lower Broadway, probably at something like sixty a week.

"Of course it must have been an accident of some kind," said Mrs. Hunt nervously. "I mean, really, it can't have been anything *else*—" She kept darting uneasy little glances at Tabitha; and both she and Mrs. Thirkettle were looking at Mendoza and Hackett like rabbits transfixed by a pair of cobras. But a lot of utterly innocent people, inadvertently mixed up in a homicide, might look at cops that way.

"That's just what I said," said Mrs. Thirkettle faintly.

"How did you meet Mrs. McCann and when?" asked Hackett.

"Oh—well—it was a long time ago—fifteen or sixteen years—I was looking for a—for a *lamp*," said Mrs. Thirkettle, "and somebody'd told me this place on Los Angeles Street had nice things sometimes, and I— And we got to talking, and— She was an educated woman, and we just took to each other—and I felt sorry for her—" She pressed her hands together nervously; they were shaking.

"Now, for goodness' sake, don't take on, Tabby," said Mrs. Glidden. "Accident or whatever—and it don't seem likely to me that Ellie of all people should get, well, my goodness, *murdered*, for heaven's sake—that's senseless, I guess it was some kind accident all right—but nobody could think *you* had anything to do with it!" She was the one not at all disturbed by police on the premises. She uttered a fat comfortable laugh. "I guess we all felt kinda sorry for Ellie—did you say you're a lieutenant?—on accounta, well, leastways all the rest of us, we'd had a few good times, you know? *And* good husbands. Like with my second, Joe, we had some real good times, only he would get to gambling. I mean, we all hadda work hard and all, but we had something, know what I mean, outta life. Look back on. Only Ellie, she never."

"I tried to *tell* them," said Mrs. Thirkettle painfully. "Ida, they think— but it's *not* so! I never—you know I never—use any of the dangerous things—"

"Don't take *on*," said Mrs. Glidden. "That's just foolish, they couldn't think you had anything to do with it, Tabby. What I mean is"—she turned rather protuberant china-blue eyes on Mendoza—"that husband walkin' out on her, not married a year—she was born to a lotta money, I guess you know, and I guess he was just after that, and that kind of sours a woman, you know. She never really had anything, I guess you could sort of forgive and forget, like they say, about her being kind of how she *was*. Sarcastic and all. She hadn't had much of a life. Like me, I had some good times, and I got my married daughter and grandchildren up in Fresno, she's by my first husband, he was a drummer in this band and we—"

"Mr. Hunt and I always went to all the musical shows," said Mrs. Hunt thinly. "I know exactly what you mean, Ida, she had her faults, but haven't we all? Mr. Hunt used to say—"

"But I never do use any of the things that could be dangerous," said

Mrs. Thirkettle. "I *don't*— It just couldn't be—" She put a hand to her mouth.

Three very ordinary women. One of them a killer? Mendoza had met a lot of killers. Like everybody else, they came all sorts.

There was, he thought, one little thing. A very human thing. If you were magnanimous enough to make a will leaving somebody all your worldly wealth, it was a human impulse to let that somebody know about it, to bask in the fulsome gratitude before you shuffled off.

And even these three ordinary women— Well, money was a safeguard. An insurance. An assurance. These women living pretty close to the bone. Always aware (as people in their sixties always would be aware) of what could happen to them. The long painful illness, money cushioning it, the disability. The temptation, knowing— Because if Eliza had told them about the will, she'd have told them what she had to leave too. Wouldn't she? Or would she?

And quite evidently none of them had really been terribly fond of Eliza McCann. Proximity, familiarity had kept these four friends. Eliza McCann was not a woman, by what they knew of her, anybody had been really fond of.

He looked at Hackett, looming impressively beside him in Mrs. Thirkettle's neat and clean little living room, and very gently he said, "Did any of you know that Mrs. McCann was a wealthy woman? That she owned that entire block on Los Angeles Street?"

"*Owned*— What d'you mean? why, for goodness' sake," said Mrs. Glidden, "she—"

"And that she'd made a will leaving her entire estate to be divided among you three?"

"*What?*" said Mrs. Hunt loudly. "Tabitha, you *didn't*—"

"Oh, my God!" said Mrs. Thirkettle, and toppled from her chair in a dead faint.

TEN

"Well, that was a little exercise in futility," said Hackett some forty minutes later as they came back to the car. Mendoza agreed morosely.

On being revived, Mrs. Thirkettle had burst into tears, which had taken the effect of turning Mrs. Glidden indignant at the brutal cops. Whatever had happened to Ellie, it was an accident; and Tabby wouldn't harm a fly, and talking about poison like some horrible true-police thing, and if they hadn't anything better to do than come and bully three innocent women, and last Wednesday she'd been at work all day like the honest woman she was from eight to five, and if they thought—

Mrs. Hunt had nervously admitted to being home all morning on Wednesday and going to the movies in the afternoon. She lived alone.

And a tearful Mrs. Thirkettle had said in a frightened whisper she hadn't gone out all day: worked in her garden. And she *never*—

"Ask the neighbors if anybody saw her?" asked Hackett now. "You can see into the yard from both sides."

He tried one house and Mendoza tried the other, but nobody was home at either place. "Sunday," said Mendoza tersely, starting the engine. "Damnation. So somebody noticed her out in the yard at ten A.M., that doesn't say she couldn't have been out visiting Ellie at nine."

"*De veras.* Where are we heading?"

"Over to the store, see if George and Jase picked up anything new."

On Los Angeles Street they found Higgins outside the closed pawnshop chatting with Wolf. Grace, he said, was upstairs in the next apartment questioning that tenant. "Not an awful lot shows, Luis. Mr. Wolf here saw two women go into the store that morning, but he doesn't know either of 'em, and nobody else we've talked to noticed anybody going in."

"Just two women," said Wolf. "Ordinary. One at a time, I mean. The best I can do it'd be about nine, nine-thirty for one and later for the other.

Business slow and it's nice spring weather, I'm sometimes standing in the door . . . Oh, middle-aged, say, both of 'em."

Mendoza thought about Mrs. Lightfoot, Mrs. Rialto, Miss Manning. "Did you see either of their faces?"

"No, sir, they'd been past my place and was facing up the block when I noticed."

So. Any of those women, seen half a block away from the back, might be described as middle-aged. It might be an idea to have Wolf take a look at them. But—

Grace came out of the door up from the shop door; he was wearing a little smile. He sauntered up to them. "Mrs. McCann tell you she was planning to raise the rents, Mr. Wolf?"

"No, she did not," said Wolf. "My God, was she? It's all I can do, make that ninety now. Did she tell the Rasmussens?"

"Uh-huh. Seems Mrs. Rasmussen was in the store on Tuesday and Mrs. McCann mentioned it. They're paying forty and she was going to raise it by five."

Wolf looked worried. "First time I think of it—who does it go to, you know? Her family? I don't know any of them. Sure, it's a cheap rent, but these are cheap stores, you see for yourself. I don't know—"

"I wouldn't worry," said Mendoza. "I have an idea there may be a little hassle over who inherits, Mr. Wolf. May be some time before the new owner has the leisure to think about raising rents."

"I hope to God," said Wolf. "Well, gentlemen, I don't bother you." He walked off toward the drugstore.

"Somebody's home at all the apartments," said Higgins. "But nobody noticed anybody going into the place on Wednesday. Of course there're the people on the other side of the street. In the apartments. We caught all the proprietors downstairs yesterday, and nobody did."

"She was going to raise the Rasmussens' rent," said Mendoza meditatively. "All of the rents maybe?"

"Mrs. Rasmussen sort of gathered that. Naturally she didn't like it. Nobody around here with much money," said Grace. "That say something to you?"

"Not really," said Mendoza, "no." He sighed. "So let's start asking the people across the street."

They split up and began knocking on doors. The street doors leading to the apartments gave on very narrow, rickety old stairs: upstairs, small square landings fronted single doors. It would be much the same arrangement as in the business block Eliza McCann had owned. The two apart-

ments Mendoza visited were alike except for the furniture: three smallish
rooms with narrow windows looking out on the old street. Neither the
bent-over deaf old woman nor the harassed couple with a sick baby remembered seeing anyone enter the secondhand shop across the street last
Wednesday morning.

He came out to the street again and met Higgins just emerging from
the next door down. "Very small jackpot," said Higgins. "There's usually
one to every couple of blocks or so. The snoopy old maid with nothing
better to do than look out the window most of the day. But—"

"*Claro está*. What did she see?"

"Nothing of much use to us. In fact, just the opposite. She wasn't looking out every minute, but she did see the two women Wolf saw—strangers
to her—and she says the second one went in before the first one came out.
One came out with a big parcel, the other with nothing. She noticed all
the excitement, with the squad cars and ambulance, after Lee Rainey
called in, and I gather she sat there glued to the window even after everybody'd gone away."

"So?"

"So nothing," said Higgins. "She wasn't sitting glued to the window
until then. She did say—backing up what that funny old harridan told us
—that earlier that morning she'd seen Mrs. Stepp come out the door there
and start up the street."

"Mmh," said Mendoza. "And I do just wonder whether Eliza *had*
meant to raise all the rents. She didn't say so outright to the Rasmussens
. . . Mrs. Stepp? That old witch— Well, nice to know somebody's out of
it. Yes, let's see if Eliza'd said anything to her."

They walked across the street, found the street door beside the secondhand shop unlocked, went in, and climbed dusty stairs in a thick fusty
odor compounded of long-ago cabbage, old dust, and some seventy-five
years of humanity living with the windows shut. Mendoza knocked at the
apartment door. After an interval he knocked again.

A shuffling step, and Gladys Stepp peered out at them round the half-
open door. "And what do you want?"

"Just a few questions, Mrs. Stepp, if we may come in—"

"No, you can't come in. I was just takin' my nap. I'm an old woman, I
need my sleep."

"Sorry to bother you, ma'am," said Higgins genially, "but we'd like to
know if you'd talked to Mrs. McCann lately."

"No, I never—"

"She hadn't told you she was going to raise the rent?"

She stared up at him; for a moment there Mendoza had the absurd fleeting thought that it was impossible the two of them could belong to the same species—hunched little ancient witchlike female in her dirty ragged clothes and towering broad-shouldered homicide sergeant in the casual-tailored gray suit and clean white shirt, still looking new-shaven. What meeting of minds? The old woman—slow, tenacious, rapacious mind—blinked and worked her sunken lips together.

"That one, she was a miser and a hypocrite and her soul went straight to hell," she muttered.

"I couldn't say about that," said Higgins, "but had she told you—"

"Can't get blood outta a stone. No, I dunno nothing about that."

She'd brought a filthy rag of handkerchief out of her pocket to wipe her nose; she peered at him over it. "I coulden've paid no more. She'd 'a' knowed that, old bitch. She wouldn't dare. No, mister. Can't get blood out of a stone—that's right in the Bible. I'm a poor old woman with no kin or kith call my own, an' I've lived here twenty years since back I was able work an' earn, but no more. I got the pension and it ain't easy to get along. But God helps them as helps themselves and got faith and prays regular." And she added suddenly and conversationally, "I got to fix my dinner," and shut the door on them.

They looked at each other and started downstairs again. "God, what a place to live," said Higgins.

"Untactful, George. I grew up in much the same kind of neighborhood not so far away."

"Well, having to live down here doesn't mean you've got to live like that."

"And a surprising number of people don't," said Mendoza. He looked at his watch and said come to think of it he and Art had missed lunch. And those search warrants ought to be coming through pretty soon.

They walked up to Higgins' car and found Hackett and Grace sitting in it. "I had thought," Grace was saying, "of just paying off the note on the bedroom set—it's only another thirty dollars—as a kind of practical birthday present. But maybe a little too practical. Pretty woman likes to get something nice for her birthday. Jewelry or something."

"I tell you," said Hackett, "there's this new fad. Costume watches. I wouldn't know, but Angel was mentioning it the other night, there was an ad in the paper. Bullocks', I think. Lapel watches and necklaces and so on. From ten ninety-five up."

"Well, that's a thought," said Grace. "Thanks very much. I might go and look at them."

Mendoza leaned in the car window. "You get anything?"

"*Nada*," said Hackett. He yawned. "Let's knock off and go home, Luis. I've still got spring fever."

"Don't you wish we could. I just realized we missed lunch."

"Well, so we did."

"Neither of us had much either," said Higgins. "Only the drugstore along here—packaged sandwiches."

"Meet you at Federico's in ten minutes," said Mendoza.

Grace brightened. "Sure. Maybe one I came across last night'd sharpen our wits some, Lieutenant. It's called a Bloodhound. Appropriate."

"What's in it?" asked Mendoza fearfully.

"Oh, not much. Half gin, a quarter dry vermouth, a quarter sweet vermouth, and you slice some nice fresh strawberries into it."

"My God!" said the other three in unison.

The search warrants came through by the time they got back to the office, and Mendoza dispatched Piggott and Landers to Mrs. Thirkettle's house. The hotel, of course, would be quite a job. But despite Oscar's chatter about accumulations, when he came to think of it, it was likely that the accumulations were in the actual living quarters. The great majority of the rooms would simply be empty; doubtless the McLaughlins had sold off all the unneeded furniture in their early straits, or it could be that had formed the first stock for Eliza's secondhand store so long ago.

"And you know," he said to Hackett, "how ideal for somebody wanting a little privacy to mix up the homemade poison. That barracks of a place. Quietly slip up to one of the empty rooms miles away from any occupied one, with a hot plate and a basin of water and your pockets stuffed with the common foxglove."

"And I'd still like to know where that came from," said Hackett.

Everyone was at home but the furtive Miss Allenby. Oscar let them in, looking frightened for a moment at their numbers—Mendoza, Hackett, Higgins, Grace and Glasser—and Mendoza apologized. "Really just a formality, Mr. McLaughlin. Here's the warrant."

"Oh, dear," said Oscar. "Such an upset. The last few days have been simply hell, and I'm not a man to swear, but that's what it has been. Ellie *managed* things so well. Gertrude— And shopping lists, you know, though Henry and I were *most* scrupulous about paying for our own things—but she *managed*. And I'm afraid I do tend to be absent-minded, and the milk went sour, and then I quite forgot about bread, and that poor dear Miss Manning got Swiss cheese instead of American, and Henry has a *thing*

about Swiss cheese, on account of the holes, and—I really don't understand what you hope to find— And you haven't said when I can have the
body. You haven't—*already* done anything?"

"The inquest is tomorrow morning, Mr. McLaughlin," said Mendoza.
"Didn't you get a notice to attend?"

"Oh, yes, there was something—we never do get any mail, so I did take
note— And after that I can have the body?"

"That's right." Mendoza looked at him curiously. Was Oscar actually
planning to embalm his sister's body personally?

"And why *must* I be disturbed day and night?" demanded Henry, opening the double doors suddenly and raising a cloud of dust from the floor.

"It's the warrant—I told you about it, Henry. I *told* you."

"Tosh," said Henry.

"Sorry to disturb you, Mr. McLaughlin," said Higgins. "We might as
well start here, I guess." He moved toward Henry, who commenced to
swell like a bullfrog.

"You propose to *search my room*? To *disturb my things*? This is an
outrage! I demand to know—"

"We have a search warrant," said Mendoza patiently. Higgins could be
trusted to deal with Henry; there were, in fact, few things George Higgins
and his seventy-five tough inches could not deal with. He simply stepped
past Henry into the long room, and Henry, put on the defensive, slammed
the door and began to protest incoherently.

"You," said Mendoza to Grace and Glasser, "start with the top floor.
Most of the rooms are probably empty, and it won't take long, but look for
any signs of—well, you know what to look for. Mr. McLaughlin, is there a
safe in the hotel?"

"A *safe*? Oh, you mean—when it was a real hotel in the old days, for
guests' valuables? Oh, yes, there was, but we sold it a long time ago."

Maybe yes and maybe no, thought Mendoza. He went behind the old
counter and Oscar hopped after him. "It was there, sir." A little cupboard
built flush into the wall and fastened once with a hasp and padlock: 1900,
thought Mendoza; what a safe time, and how trusting people had been.
The cupboard was quite empty. He drummed his fingers on the counter.
Well, thorough they tried to be. The deadly routine. "Art," he said absently, "just to get that out of the way, suppose you get Mr. McLaughlin
to let you into his place next door and look that over. I think—"

"*My* place? But I thought—really, there's nothing there, just my—my
equipment, you know—really, I didn't think—"

"Now I hope you'll be cooperative." And Mendoza gave Oscar his suavest smile. "The warrant covers both."

"Oh, well," said Oscar weakly, "oh, well—"

"And I know the lab men covered it, but I think I'll just have another look around her room," added Mendoza to Hackett. "If you don't mind, Mr. McLaughlin?"

"—don't believe in all these fancy new terms," Oscar was chattering nervously as he unlocked the door of the little building next door. "An undertaker is an undertaker, and calling himself a mortician really doesn't change the fact. *As* you can see, there's nothing here, sir, nothing but—but the tools of my work. I've often thought if I could afford to advertise—fix the place up—"

The first room furnished shabbily as an office. And what good all this would do, thought Hackett— Whoever had been elementarily smart enough to get Eliza to swallow the fatal dose would be smart enough not to leave any evidence around, and he or she had had five days to get rid of the evidence. But—

He looked distastefully around at the inner room: long table with grooves in it, just like the one they used for autopsies. The jars, the hypodermic needles, the boxes of cotton wadding—the equipment for dealing with the dead. He agreed with Mr. Caradoccio: not a natural job for a man to *want* to do. Slightly better light in here than in the front room, but still not good: sixty-watt bulbs.

"I—I'm not here really very often," said Oscar, "as a matter of fact." He sounded wistful. "Just to keep it all clean and dusted. And I do try to keep up my—my stock, you know, to have everything on hand in case I *do* get a client."

Hackett went into the little hall. Two doors. He opened the one to the rear room. Trestles stacked together. Folding chairs. An old portable organ with a couple of keys missing.

"That came into the store once. If I had a really proper place to have a *nice* little chapel—"

Hackett tried the other door; it was locked. "What's in here?"

"Just more—more equipment," said Oscar. "That's all. Do you want to—?" Resignedly he sorted out keys, unlocked the door. Hackett went in, as far as he could, which wasn't far. It was a small room, and it was filled with coffins, all spread out over the floor space. Nothing else. The shade was pulled nearly down on the one window, but the westering sun poked light under it to strike gleams here and there.

And in any case this was probably a wild-goose chase. If Oscar had been the one who'd somehow introduced the homemade brew into sister Eliza, he had one dandy place to mix it up. Hackett went back to the room with the long table in the middle. He pried into every drawer and looked into every jar and bottle with grim thoroughness, and he didn't find anything remotely suspicious or suggestive. Of anything except that Oscar was, as they'd already known, a funny one. Funny-peculiar. An undertaker with no customers ever, keeping all his embalming equipment fresh and handy, his long table polished. The coffins spread out for grieving mourners to make a selection.

"Thanks very much," he said on the sidewalk outside.

Oscar locked the front door in unaccustomed silence.

Hackett climbed stairs and hunted down long dusty halls in search of Mendoza and found him still in Eliza's room. He found him unprecedentedly—the fastidious Mendoza, wearing a newish silver-gray Dacron suit—flat on his stomach on a very dusty and old Oriental carpet, worn paper-thin, in front of the narrow little fireplace on the left-hand wall of the room. Originally one of the better rooms of the hotel: about twenty feet square, the fireplace, a very high old double bed, a couple of chairs, a tall chiffonier, and the walls lined with books. Only about a quarter of them on shelves, the rest stacked more or less neatly with spines outward.

"What the hell—" said Hackett.

"¡Válgame Dios!" Mendoza wriggled farther into the opening. "It's coming—if I could just— That you, Art?"

"In person. What in hell are you doing?"

Mendoza wriggled backward and stood up, brushing himself down. "I don't suppose there's a vacuum cleaner in this damn place. My God. How anybody could live in all this filth— I know the lab boys are supposed to be thorough, but sometimes they do lack imagination. You have a try at it. Big he-man, maybe you can shift it. There's an iron plate for coal or whatever, I want to see what's under it."

"For God's sake, thorough," said Hackett. He prudently took off his jacket and lay down prone, worked his head and shoulders into the long-dead grate. He got hold of the plate and yanked. It lifted toward him quite readily; it was, he found, backing out with it, perforated with long slots to let the ashes fall through into a trap below. "You weren't far enough in. It comes out easy enough if you—"

"I have not your inches," said Mendoza. "Yes, and it ought not to, you know. I doubt if there's been a fire built there, or that grate cleaned out, these forty years. See what's there."

"I can't afford a new suit every time I turn around," complained Hackett, and flattened himself again. God, the way some people lived— Dust thick in his nostrils, he sneezed. The trap below, for the ashes, was not very deep: perhaps a foot. He thought irrelevantly, 1900, and servant girls three bucks a week—clean out the damn grate after every evening's fire— His groping fingers met metal, and he pulled it: flat sharp corners. A box. He lifted it out and wriggled back out of the grate.

"Something?" asked Mendoza eagerly.

"Something." Hackett stood up. "You and your crystal ball." He dusted his trousers. They looked at the box.

"Pure logical deduction, Arturo," said Mendoza. "No safety-deposit keys among her personal effects. No other secret caches at the store. And that fairly large sum unaccounted for—call it in round terms sixty grand. I just thought—like the idiot boy and the horse, you know—whatever she put it into or whether she kept it in cash, she might want it close under her eye. Well hidden. Bet you"—he was struggling with the clasp—"she kept her room locked when she was out."

It was a dark-green metal box about ten by eight, six inches deep. Fireproof. A nice safe-deposit box in a very secret place. The catch yielded to pressure and the lid lifted, and they looked at the contents.

"Oh, yes," said Mendoza. "I might have known. I really might have known." Tightly-wound rolls of pale flannel, tied neatly with ribbons. "Like my sainted grandmother, anybody who's lived close to the bone, experienced the overnight crash. Sure, sure, the portable value." He untied the top roll and began to unwind it. The first item, the diamond brooch, winked at them demurely, and Mendoza said, "About fifteen hundred retail. Diamonds hold their value pretty well, even in a depression . . . So here's the missing sixty grand, probably, and now we know."

"I will be damned!" said Hackett.

ELEVEN

"So," said Hackett, "Luis impounded all the crown jewels as evidence. I don't suppose Oscar'd know what to do with 'em. My God, that place. You wouldn't believe half the queer things we found—"

"After what you told me about Oscar and the coffins," said Angel, "I would too. What sort of queer things?"

Hackett regarded her with somnolent affection, his Angel with her brown head bent over a piece of sewing. He was full of dinner, and miraculously for once not-quite-three-year-old Mark had submitted to bed without a murmur: the baby was asleep, and the cat was curled up on Hackett's lap asleep. "Well, for one thing, there was a room on the fourth floor, good-sized room, that was all weather-stripped. The door—an inside door, naturally—and the window. And the walls had big zinc sheets nailed onto them. Funniest setup you ever saw. We asked about it, but nobody knew anything, Oscar said it'd been that way when they came and it wasn't a room in use, they just left it. I ask you."

"How odd," said Angel. "Maybe somebody who lived there years ago—oh, kept tame birds or—a funny pet of some sort—"

Hackett shook his head. "I don't know. And do you know the sister—Jane—kept all her mother's clothes? In a trunk in her room. You wouldn't believe it—stuff dating back to the eighties—most of it in rags. No moth balls. And, my God, I'll never again sneer at astrologists, the Rialto woman was doing something she called erecting a horoscope, and it looked four times as complicated as an income-tax form."

"Nothing could be, Art," said Angel. "Oh, damn," she added as she stabbed herself with the needle and sucked the wound.

"And there were dozens of books in Oscar's room too and every single one of them something to do with undertaking. And a lot of back numbers of a national magazine put out for morticians. With advertisements for embalming fluid and cosmetics and so on. He *is* a funny one. And—you know," said Hackett suddenly, "I can't for the life of me put a finger on it, but something about that other place—Oscar's place—bothers me. Something I noticed there, some little thing—no, it's gone." He shook his head.

"It'll come back to you. Is that the baby?" Angel listened. "False alarm, thank heaven."

"And the Lightfoot woman—my God, these people—she's the one that sings, you know—she's got all sorts of costumes, for all the musical parts, *Carmen* and *Lucia di Lammermoor* and all of Gilbert and Sullivan and—homemade stuff she's put together herself—and the only thing she brought with her, says Oscar, besides her clothes is this great big mirror—what do I mean: a pier glass?—on its own legs. We gathered she puts on the costumes and watches herself sing. People," said Hackett.

"I call that rather pathetic."

"I suppose you can think of it that way. And then that Allenby creature —she wasn't there. Nobody seems to know much about her. But what we found in *her* room was, you might say, sort of suggestive, and Luis called in for a uniformed man to post there till she gets home."

"Oh?"

"Four wrist watches," said Hackett, "and a transistor radio, and half-a-dozen cigarette lighters and a camera and various such stuff—all brand new."

"For heaven's sake!" said Angel amusedly. "You don't mean—"

"Well, it looks sort of suggestive, doesn't it? We had quite a day," said Hackett. At eight-thirty, relaxing at home, he wasn't as yet aware that they were to have quite a night too.

"A shoplifter?" said Angel.

"A snatcher it looks like indeed. Small time. As I say, we left a man to wait for her. I tell you that place attracts the nuts. Or maybe the McLaughlins attract 'em—I don't know. The Manning woman was writing love letters to her Albert. Mrs. Rialto said she finds *that* pathetic. Fellow was killed at Belleau Wood."

"What does she do with them when she's written them?" asked Angel, and put down her sewing to get up and adjust the lamp at her side more advantageously. Hackett had just taken out his lighter, and as the lamp was shifted it struck a gleam of reflective light from the metal. "Actually mail them? I suppose they'd wind up in the dead-letter—"

"By *damn!*" said Hackett. "That was it—it came to me just now—in Oscar's place. The light—" He looked at her, unlighted cigarette in one hand, lighter in the other, with an expression of doubt, speculation, and incredulity. "That was it. Just a little funny thing—room was dark, but what light there was just glinted off it. There was a name plate on one of those coffins. A metal plate. Listen, that's silly. They don't put name plates on empty coffins, do they?"

Angel stared at him. "It must have been a metal part of some kind."

"It was a wooden coffin. I think. No, no, I noticed it at the time, the whole picture's in my mind—" Hackett shut his eyes. "It was the one nearest the door. The sun just hit the plate, it was screwed onto the top of the coffin, nearer one end than the other. Plate about four inches long—I *saw* it and it went right out of my mind, because I was looking for evidence of somebody mixing up that— My God, they *don't*, do they?"

"Oh, don't be silly," said Angel. "You don't mean you think there was—anything—in it?"

"I don't know," said Hackett. "Of course not, there couldn't have been a *body* in it, for God's sake. I don't think Oscar's ever had a client, as he calls it, well, he hasn't even got a hearse—how could he— And he'd have said, and it wouldn't have been just lying there with all the others—" He got up. "I think I'll call Luis. It's nothing, of course, but—" He deposited the cat on the couch.

When Alison answered the phone, she said, "You just caught him. *Luis!* He was going out the door. Your small-time shoplifter just came home and he's going down to see her—they took her over to—it's Art—Headquarters and—"

"And," said Mendoza's deep voice, "she had the day's loot still on her. Inside the bloomers. The old gag."

"Well, well," said Hackett. That was indeed an old trick: the low-necked unbelted dress, the voluminous bloomers, the loot dropped down the décolletage to be held in the bloomers. "I'll be damned. Look, I just thought of something. It's nothing—I don't know *what* it is—but I'll pass it on. There was—I just remembered it—something sort of bothered me about that place of Oscar's, but I couldn't think what it was, and then all of a sudden it came to me, and it's wild, but—there was a name plate on one of those coffins."

"A—"

"A name plate. And, look, they don't put them on until, well, there's a corpse chosen for the coffin. Do they? Or vice versa. But there it was. I saw it without *really* seeing it, and it wasn't until just a minute ago I—"

"A name plate," said Mendoza. "A *name plate*. On one of the—" There was a profound silence at the other end of the line.

"You there?" said Hackett after a minute.

"A—are you sure?"

"I said so. I can see it in my—"

Another silence. "You there?" said Hackett.

"I am," said Mendoza, "adding two and two. I think. *No creo en semejante cosa.* I don't believe it. No. I do not—" And then he uttered a little gasp and said, *"Excepto—la cámara!* But it's not— And I do wonder whether, considering—" Another silence. Hackett was about to speak when Mendoza said, "Listen, Art! You there?"

"I'm right here."

"Yes, and Oscar being Oscar— Listen. Meet me down there. Now. Don't drive into Old High Street. Leave the car a block away and come on foot. I'll meet you and George—I'll call him now—in front of the Caradoccio house as soon as you can get there. And don't come strolling up the center of the sidewalk whistling the latest hit." Mendoza sounded obscurely excited.

"Now what in God's name— Why? Look, I was—"

"Relaxed. *Sé.* If you will have these afterthoughts—I *don't* know—it's fantastic—but I just think we ought to look into it, Arturo. Damn it, I must be seeing visions in the crystal ball this time, but—I'll see you, make it snappy!"

Hackett put the phone down with a groan. "Why did I have to get a boss with built-in radar? I've got to go out again. I don't know why, my Angel. Luis is seeing ghosts."

He left the Barracuda parked around the corner on Bellevue and walked quietly into Old High Street. It was nine-fifty. Old High Street was very dark indeed: not many street lights down here and the one midway of the block was still out. He only hoped none of them would get knocked on the head by the roving J.D.'s again. The old buildings along here were mostly converted to use as shops and stores, and all of those were closed now. A few houses at this end of the block were still in use as residences, but all were mostly dark and silent: everybody home was inside watching TV, thought Hackett sardonically; even people down here behind on the rent had TV.

No grass at the sidewalk's edge, but he walked quietly, wondering what on earth was in Mendoza's mind. Just this side of the Caradoccio house something touched his shoulder out of the dark and he nearly jumped back.

"Art?" A whisper. "What the hell's he got up his sleeve now?"

"I don't know," Hackett hissed back. "Is he here? All I did was mention—and, damn it, how could that have anything—"

"What?" hissed Higgins. "He said to make like a cat burglar, just in case."

"In case of what?" They were leaning against the picket fence round Mr. Caradoccio's property, and they both leaped like startled fawns in the blackness when a hand gripped each of them by an arm.

"You sound like a pair of steam presses," said Mendoza, just audible. "*Dios.* I've been here fifteen minutes. Listen. Single-file, behind me—up to this side of Oscar's place. Thank God there's no moon. Take cover at the side of the building. I think you may be a little entertained if the show lives up to the first act. Now, quiet!"

Hackett crept obediently after Higgins, close along the front of the building; this was about midway of the block, where the blacked-out street light was, and he couldn't see three feet ahead of him in the blackness. They were past the Caradoccio house, almost up to Oscar's little building, when a hand seized his arm and steered him in from the sidewalk to hug the side of that building. Long ago it had been a residence, and this side was the driveway—probably, when a family had lived there, the carriageway. Never-paved, packed earth under his feet.

"Twenty paces up," said Mendoza almost soundlessly in his ear.

Hackett moved, feeling the other two men ahead, counting paces. As he took the twentieth his left foot hit a small stone and it struck the side of the building a glancing slight blow.

Instantly, from just over his head it seemed, a nervous voice said, low, "What was that?"

"A cat, a cat. Wandering." Impatient voice. Henry. "Really, I see no reason why we must do this *now*. They're well enough here."

"No, guess Oscar's right." Ben Kelly. "Night them Eyetalians allus go to the movies, nobody home. And no moon. New one tomorrow night. Might's well get 'em shifted back home. Long as the fuzz already searched. 'Specially considerin' old man Brown."

"Such an upset." Oscar. A heavy dragging sound. "Hold the light steady, Henry, please! There. Have you got her, Ben?"

"I got her. Up we go."

A thin wavering pencil of light outlined a window directly above them: these old places built high off the ground. The window, Hackett figured out, was the window of the room where all those coffins had been.

There was heavy breathing, panting sounds of effort, slow heavy steps. The light moved. The sounds lessened.

"Back door," breathed Mendoza. Hackett moved with him farther up the drive, cautiously, his right hand against the house wall. It fell away as he reached the back wall. A door creaked.

"Do be careful with the light, Henry. I know just where I left the dolly. There. More to the left—more—we must get the weight distributed, Ben. There!" More pants and straining breaths.

"Damn fuzz." Ben. "All this work. All I say is it's a damn shame that whole back yard's blacktopped. If you'd—"

"I know, I know," said Oscar fretfully. "But it would have looked odd if I'd dug it up. And at the *time* we all thought— Well, let's get on. I shan't feel really happy until we've got them all home again, we'll have the rest of the night to get them upstairs— And such a waste of effort when they *did* look at my place after all. But that big one just glanced in. Of course they looked more natural there."

Creaking and puffing. "Hold it, for goodness' sake, don't let it tilt too far—just so the wheels—there."

"Who's this?" grunted Ben. "Must be Brown, too heavy for one of the old ones."

"Well, they're all encased in lead, of course. I didn't notice, we were in such an upset and hurry I didn't put them in order. I *shall* be glad to have them all back decently placed with some respect—" Oscar's low voice was fading away.

The hairs on Hackett's neck began to rise. He heard Higgins breathing rather heavily somewhere near.

The creakings, a subdued rattle of rusty wheels, the soft voices died away. It was a mild spring night, but Hackett felt cold.

They were gone. With—

He felt for Mendoza. "Luis? What in hell—"

"O.K.," said Mendoza. "They'll be ten minutes or so getting that one in the back door of the hotel. You have very timely afterthoughts, Art. Once I leaped to the incredible conclusion, I thought it might be just possible— Oscar being Oscar—that something might be due to happen tonight. I got here just in time to see them—or hear them—start off with the first load. Come on, let's have a look." He produced a flashlight but didn't switch it on. "They'll have left the back door open."

They had. The three of them slipped quietly in, but the door creaked nonetheless, and Hackett nearly jumped again. "Luis, you don't *mean—*" he said.

The flashlight played briefly on ancient kitchen fixtures, the black gaping rectangular hole of an open inner door to the hall.

"I'm reminded," said Mendoza bodilessly out of the dark, "of a funny story—you know the one—"

"My God, jokes at a time like—"

"—about Sullivan coming to console Mrs. O'Neill, with O'Neill on his deathbed. Tells her the doctors know so much nowadays, her husband's going to get well in no time, be just as good as he ever was, soon be back at work and a fine upstanding healthy fellow again—" The flashlight swung down the tiny dark hall. "And then just as he's leaving he looks at the narrow front staircase and says, 'Christ, what a place to get a coffin out of!' Here we are."

Another gaping rectangular blackness. The flashlight pointed at it. The room with the coffins. Spread out on the floor. Only—

"There were more than that—this afternoon." Hackett heard his own whisper.

"Two more," said Mendoza. "Our friends have just carted the second one back home. Let's see." The light played around. "Six left." He walked into the room and bent over the first coffin, a great dark ominous black shape there. "Mmh." The light steadied, pinned to the coffin top. "*Dorothy Esther McLaughlin, 1891-1949* . . . And who's this? Well, well, stranger to us. *Robert Talbot, d. 1941* . . . And here's brother William. *William McLaughlin, 1883-1954.* I wonder if Stephen's somewhere here too. My God, Alison said that—about the older ones—*Pues sí.* And—"

"For the love of Christ!" said Higgins. "Are you saying—" He took an involuntary step backward.

"When you told me about that name plate, Art, I suddenly thought about that room on the fourth floor, and also what little Oscar said that morning we broke the news to— Quiet. Here they come. Let's give them a little surprise party."

Reluctantly Hackett and Higgins joined him in the room, on either side of the door.

Faint voices. "—an *upset.* All because of Ellie. Bringing the *police* down on us. When that Mexican one said that about a search warrant, I really thought I should be sick—"

"And if you'da told me about it then—" Ben. "I coulda told you—silly damn idea go knock him on the head. Wouldn't stop the rest of 'em."

"I will be glad when this is all over. Just like Ellie—making trouble. Though I don't suppose she meant to, poor woman."

Pencil-thin beam of light, pausing in the doorway. Vague dark outlines of the three of them there. One figure bending, tugging. "I *rather* think this must be Earl, it's lighter. Poor Earl—so young to—"

Hackett felt the hair was standing straight up on his head.

A second figure was just bending over the first when Mendoza switched on his own powerful flashlight.

"Have you got a client at last, Mr. McLaughlin?" he asked suavely, and from pinpointing Oscar rapidly swung the light around to show Hackett and Higgins. "We would be so interested to hear all about it."

Oscar uttered a high-pitched scream and fainted across the coffin before him.

But in the end it was Oscar who was most voluble. They carted the three of them off to Headquarters, where Ben Kelly just glowered at them and refused to answer any questions at all; and Henry's burden was "I said much better to leave them there—if Oscar hadn't *insisted*—now look what he's got me into!"

But, revived, Oscar was almost pathetically eager to talk. His hot little brown eyes pleaded for understanding; he gestured emotionally.

"You don't understand how it was! Of *course* I know what the law says about bodies, but doesn't any of you remember how it *was*—the depression— You've got to see how it happened! Earl—poor Earl—he was only thirty-four—that was back in nineteen thirty-two—and it's just terrible to have to tell you—we were brought up strictly, but the times—and living down here—such awful people some of them were, and I'm afraid he got into bad company—just a *tiny* bit drunk and fell down the front stairs and I saw at once his neck was—I was just qualified then. And, my goodness, don't you see, a funeral would have cost—well, there simply wasn't any money for it! I had actually been reduced to selling newspapers at one point—we had put *every* spare penny into my schooling, because we thought a regular business—but I hadn't had any clients at all. And there were the taxes on the hotel—not *much*, and Ellie usually managed to help with her store—we had to keep the taxes up or we wouldn't have had a *roof* over our heads! You see *that*. And the cost of a *funeral*—even then, those times— Well, we talked it all over, you see—the family, I mean—and we didn't see any reason why *not*— The whole problem solved so easily and the money saved for the taxes— Quite practical really, except of course for the body, but I thought of the top story—and I do assure you everything was *always* done according to law, except for actual burial. Absolutely hygienic. I'm a good undertaker, I know my job, the coffins were lined with lead, and just in *case* I lined that room with—and *everything* done with respect, quite proper, and we simply told people Earl had gone— You see how it *was*—"

"And you just went on the same way?" asked Mendoza, unwillingly fascinated.

Oh, well, Ellie hadn't believed in doctors, said Oscar vaguely. Jane was different, but they couldn't ever afford— And Dorothy hadn't been going to a doctor either; that had looked very much like a heart attack to him. "We do have to know some medicine, you know." And, *besides*, Stephen and William were both gone by then: Stephen had liver trouble and Willie, Oscar thought, had had a stroke, and each time it had all gone off without any trouble. "Of course I had everything to *hand*, and really, I assure you, we held a nice little service for all of them—not that we were raised in any sect—Father was a lifelong agnostic—but the proper respect due the poor dead clay was—"

"Who," asked Mendoza curiously, "was Mr. Brown?"

"Oh, well—" Oscar floundered into long-winded explanations. First there had been an old woman, Amanda Tucker, who'd lived at the hotel, gone out cleaning for her living, found dead in bed one day when no one had seen her for a while and someone looked—and she hadn't had any money and— "Well, yes, I did know that the authorities would take care of it if I—but, after all, I *am* an undertaker, and really it seemed easier, and besides one likes to keep one's hand in, and so I just—"

Mendoza looked at Hackett. The routine Oscar had fallen into. In lieu of legitimate clients.

Mr. Brown, it emerged, had been another roomer—died only three months ago. And now Oscar was chattering about Ben's brother. "If I can make you *understand*—all done with respect and taste— But of course I did know how the law reads, but so *narrow*, and after all it seemed so much more practical to— Well, I was so *upset* when I heard you say about searching, and I only thought—"

"You attacked me that night, Mr. McLaughlin?"

"I'm very, very sorry," said Oscar earnestly. "I see now it was a foolish thing to do. Henry said so. And I'm not a violent man, I felt quite sick. But—"

Hackett looked at Mendoza. He still felt that his hair was trying to stand up on end.

Zanies, Higgins said.

My God.

Henry knowing. Ben knowing. Jane—Eliza—who else? Probably not the rest of them. Oscar, the frustrated undertaker, without clients—taking what came to hand. The labor of love. The poor old ones, no family, drifting to the Celtic Hotel. Unknowingly, into Oscar's tender hands. And, come to think, Oscar living up there on the fourth floor with his clients. God. Oscar a little bit more than funny-peculiar?

And—that day Mendoza and Grace had come, routine duty, to break the sad news: Oscar so taken aback, so indignant. Ellie dying away from home, in her secondhand store. If Ellie had delayed dying until she got home—

Of course eventually it would have come to light. The will, the deed to the business block, the—

Or would it?

The coffins—and their contents—had been duly delivered to the morgue. Hackett could hear what Bainbridge would say.

"If I could just make you *understand*—" said Oscar. He looked ready to cry.

People, people. Coming all sorts forever.

You really never could figure what you'd run into next.

TWELVE

Mendoza got home at four-thirty Monday morning and woke Alison to tell her all about it. She sat up in bed hugging her knees, looking alternately horrified, incredulous, and amused.

"—and when we finally got Ben to say anything, well, it seemed his brother died, and there wasn't any money for a funeral, and besides he'd been paroled to the brother and he was afraid if the parole board knew—and Oscar offered his little labor of love and he said it seemed the best thing to do. Said he supposed now we'd stick him back in, and he sure was going to miss that monkey—cute little cuss." Mendoza yawned. "So—"

"Honestly!" said Alison. "You're not serious."

"Oh, you haven't heard it all yet." Mendoza was buttoning his pajamas. "I didn't really think it was urgent to charge Jane, who undoubtedly knew all about it too—I had to look up the statute, it comes under the Board of Health—but we had to dispatch a couple of ambulances after the coffins and a couple of squad cars for extra manpower in getting them aboard. So just as we're thinking of going home, about one-thirty, one of the squad cars called in, so we all chased over to the hotel again—"

"Why?"

"Jane," said Mendoza. He sat down on the edge of the bed and lit a cigarette. "Violently ill. All the women fluttering around—the Rialto woman the only one kept her head, of course. It looked like touch and go, one of the interns said, and they rushed her over to the General, of course it was all very sudden and mysterious—we did get out of Manning that all she'd had for supper was tea and toast—and I suddenly got it into my head, did somebody have it in for all the McLaughlins? Vendetta or something? So I wanted to know what had happened to Jane. I sent Art and George home, but I hung around to see— This is *the* damnedest thing I ever sat in on, which is about all we've been doing. Foxglove, for God's sake. And now— ¡Vaya por Dios!"

"¿Qué occure?" asked Alison impatiently. "For heaven's sake don't tell me Jane was poisoned too?"

"Oh, but, yes, she was. They didn't know whether they'd bring her through for an hour or so—not a young woman. And of course they wanted to know the cause too, on account of antidotes and so on, and rushed the stuff down to the lab, and I really do ask you!" said Mendoza, between exasperation and amusement. "This time it was oleander."

"Oleander! The—"

"Nerium oleander. Grows everywhere. Big tall shrub."

"I know. I had the gardener put in several of them along the back— Is it poisonous? Good heavens, and the twins chasing around out there—" Alison looked alarmed. "They put everything in their mouths—"

Mendoza also looked alarmed. "We've got the damn things here? You'll call the gardener and have him dig them out tomorrow. Today."

"I most certainly will," said Alison. Sheba, Bast and Nefertiti, who were curled in a complicated pile at the foot of the king-sized bed, had not stirred; but El Señor, who had picked the comfortably padded slipper chair in the corner, was muttering profanities at being disturbed. "But how on earth had—"

"No idea," said Mendoza, shrugging. "Manning just looked vague and said she'd washed the dishes. God knows—it could have been put in some of the patent medicine she was dosing herself with, or the tea. Or anything. But what it says to me, obviously, is that our X is somebody in that hotel."

"With a grudge against the McLaughlins," said Alison. "Um, yes. Lord, the McLaughlins. You can't believe such a—"

"And I hope I remember," said Mendoza through another yawn, "first thing I must do tomorrow—today—is tell the Humane Society about Gertrude. And the monkey. Yes. Well, if that is so, at least Oscar and Henry are safely stashed away in jail. And that means—hell, I'll have to see the coroner first thing and explain about that, we'll make it a purely formal inquest, skip the family. Short and sweet."

"You'll be dead on your feet if you don't get some sleep. What a thing."

Mendoza reached for the lamp switch. "Don't let me sleep past eight. The damn coroner—"

By nine he had had an interview with the coroner; he had called the Humane Society and been assured that someone would go round at once to rescue Gertrude and the monkey. Hackett drifted in at nine-thirty, and Mendoza suggested that he look up that lawyer, Adam Carson, who'd drawn up Eliza's will. Hackett agreed it would be a good idea.

"*What* a night. I can hardly believe all that yet. You and my wife have a peculiar sense of humor, she thought it was funny too. My God."

"I always do appreciate Charles Addams," said Mendoza. "Where's George?"

"Not in yet. Farrell's got some more plate numbers for him. He and Glasser are figuring out all the possible combinations that fellow might have misread as JGN-790. This time they've come up with an actors' agent in Beverly Hills, some woman up in Oakland, and a doctor in Costa Mesa."

"That's wild," said Mendoza. He'd like to get the hit-run joker who'd accounted for Patrolman Harry Cohen too, but the chances looked slim; and, what with one thing and another, the McLaughlins had been occupying his mind to the exclusion of anything else. "I've got to be at that inquest. You go find the lawyer."

"He won't tell us much," said Hackett unprophetically, and drifted out.

The coroner had agreed to a curtailed session, just formal identification and medical testimony, so Bainbridge was the chief witness. And what he had to say—somewhat studiously avoiding Mendoza's eye—brought Mendoza to the edge of his chair.

It seemed that Dr. Bainbridge, interested in this off-beat homicide, had been doing a little homework. "There are very few case histories of anything like recent date, but I've looked at all I could find and examined the —er—properties of the raw plant, and the evidence seems quite conclusive that in order to cause actual death the infusion must be—er—cumulative."

"You mean it must be administered over a period of time, Doctor?"

"Well, yes. It's accumulative in the system. Either continued doses of it or a sudden withdrawal will be accompanied by symptoms of poisoning, and of course if more and more is taken, death will eventually result."

"Have you formed any opinion as to how long a period and how massive a dosage might be required to bring about this result?"

"Well, to a certain extent. It's difficult to say with any preciseness, and the individual reaction— But I should say she'd been having doses of it for at least a month and possibly longer. I couldn't offer any suggestion as to quantity beyond a very general guess. Approximately, I'd say, a quarter-cupful of the infusion daily. At least."

"I see." The coroner made a note. Mendoza was staring at the surgeon incredulously.

As he'd expected, the open verdict: short and sweet. He caught Bainbridge in the corridor outside. "Listen, are you telling me now—"

"I *said* nobody knows much about it," said Bainbridge defensively. "How would I know offhand? But I like to be accurate, after I'd finally identified it and told you, I looked up all the authorities I could find, and the consensus . . ."

"You're telling me the woman had to have *repeated* doses of this stuff— maybe even daily—"

"That's what it looks like. And I'm not the detective, but it does occur to me that the vast majority of poisonings—deliberate, that is—are domestic. Somebody who had access to her possessions or spiked some medicine she was taking regularly or—"

"She didn't take any medicines, damn it."

"Well, was she in the habit of drinking coffee or tea with her meals? Or Coke or something in between? *I'm* not the detective," said Bainbridge with a shrug. "All I can give you is the medical evidence."

"Oh, hell and damnation," said Mendoza. He looked at the tubby little surgeon without affection. "My only comfort is that you've got a very pretty little job waiting for you at the morgue."

"Another one? What is it this time?" asked Bainbridge ironically.

"My good God, man, go and see," said Mendoza . . . But this did in a way reinforce his ideas about malice domestic. By all they had, Eliza had not been in the habit of drinking anything in her store except water from the tap; even if she'd habitually gone up to the drugstore in midmorning for coffee or a Coke, it would have been impossible to spike that. So it looked as if she must have got the doses at home, somehow. And just happened to be in the store when it caught up to her.

Manning? He thought about Vera Manning. Just how lunatic was she? She looked harmless enough, but she had apparently been closest to Eliza at home. In the hotel.

God, he thought, I wish I'd never heard of the Celtic Hotel and the McLaughlins.

The various police forces Landers had sent requests to were now coming through with some answers—on Monday morning—and one answer looked rather promising. Brady, the bus driver, had said Rio Dell, Willits or Ukiah; and here was a sergeant on the Willits force reporting that last Tuesday evening a girl named Alice May Cooke, a resident of Willits, had left by bus for Los Angeles intending to look for work there. Relatives in Willits, her parents, address appended. The parents had received a postcard from her postmarked Wednesday, March third, announcing her safe arrival.

Landers tossed the teletype over to Piggott. "Could be Mary Brown all right. She wouldn't have told her parents about being pregnant—sounds like a nice girl from a small town—typical—and if she thought she was going to get the guy to marry her—"

"Yeah," said Piggott.

"Less scandal—do it down here. Stay here until after the baby comes. Or," said Landers suddenly, "I just thought—how about this? That hotel gets a lot of salesmen in and out. Sure, I know, it's corny—the old gag about the traveling salesman—but I can see that, can't you, Matt? The nice innocent small-town girl, and the good-looking fellow just passing through, making up to her—and maybe he's mentioned this hotel here—"

"Yeah," said Piggott again. "But before we begin building any stories about it, let's find out whether this girl was Mary Brown. Didn't you read the tail end of this? Says this Alice Cooke has an aunt living here—over on Silver Lake Boulevard. If this is or isn't Mary Brown, wouldn't she have contacted the aunt when she got in? Called her at least. Maybe not if she figured on meeting this guy. But if this is Mary Brown and she did call, maybe she told the aunt a few things we'd like to know."

"It doesn't say the aunt knew she was coming," Landers pointed out. "But I suppose— And *besides*, of course, the aunt would know from the picture—"

"You're really operating on all two cylinders this morning, aren't you?" said Piggott. "So come on, let's go see if she's home."

But on the ride up to Hollywood Landers was preoccupied. Silver Lake Boulevard reminded him of Mary Dwyer and the kids, because they lived there too. It had been Bert Dwyer—one hell of a nice guy—who'd persuaded Tom Landers to try for rank. And who knew how Mary'd feel— probably, if she ever married again, it'd be anybody but another cop—but Landers was sort of bucking for George Higgins, who was also a hell of a nice guy, to make it. It'd be good for the kids, and Higgins had a heart as big as he was, if well hidden under the very tough exterior. Only Mary—

So they found the aunt's address—a Mrs. Wilfred Roberts she was—and she was home, and also home was Alice May Cooke, a nice small-town girl who was terribly thrilled the *police* had come to see her, thinking she'd been *murdered*, but she hadn't been really, and she'd meant to go to a hotel but Aunt May had insisted she stay with her, and just why on earth the *police* thought—

"False alarm," said Piggott. "So Brady didn't have Mary Brown as a passenger."

"We've still," said Landers, "got bus drivers and conductors to see." Privately he still liked his small idea about the hotel. The traveling salesmen. He thought about it. Not a very big hotel—not like the Biltmore or some place like that. Ask the desk clerk about regulars, men who frequently stayed there? And then try to trace them back? God, what a job. Just a little more difficult and complicated than this deadly routine they were at now.

"Say," Piggott was saying, "did you hear about that funny business last night—that McLaughlin case? Farrell was telling me—"

"Oh, yes," said Adam Carson. "I do remember. Though I only saw her twice." He was interested. "Police? What's your interest?"

Hackett explained economically, suppressing yawns. (God, what a night.) There hadn't been much in the papers about Eliza—they hadn't given the press much—but after the inquest this morning (probably some bored junior newsman there) interest might erupt: the offbeat case.

"Oh, *really?*" said Carson. "Well, what can I tell you—did you say Sergeant?"

"That's right. She came to your office to have a will drawn up. It's dated August of last year."

"That's right," said Carson. His office was on Spring Street; the office, and Carson himself, said he was doing all right in a modest kind of way. Small office, small man: little dapper fellow about five-five, with friendly eyes, who looked with enormous interest at the big beefy homicide sergeant sitting opposite. "I only saw her twice," he repeated, "but I felt sorry for the woman. People—little people." He gestured. "I never asked her how she happened to come to me. Could very well be she picked my name at random out of the phone book." He shrugged. "Anyway, she made an appointment, and all she wanted was the will drawn up. Simple will. I assume you've seen it, what's in it."

"Yes. You remember any details of what she said and so on? Anything you remember, please, Mr. Carson."

Carson smiled. "I remember Mrs. McCann, Sergeant. We do get all sorts of clients, but some of them—stand out. For this or that reason. There she sat, you know—such an ordinary-looking woman, dowdy clothes, cheap, no make-up, and one of those harsh voices—polite word's 'forthright,' about her whole manner—you know what I mean."

"I know what you mean. Yes, she'd have been like that," said Hackett, thinking over Eliza's history.

"Looked as if she wouldn't have five dollars to leave anybody, but you never know, do you? She told me what she wanted to go in the will. I had to ask her specifically about the estate—what it consisted of. She was very reluctant to part with any information at all, but—"

"She would have been. But you got it out of her?"

Carson said musingly, "I don't know. She was easy to read as a very secretive woman—kept saying she couldn't see why I had to know all that, couldn't I just put down 'everything of which I die possessed,' something like that—but she did say one or two things that—"

"There wasn't any mention of jewelry in the will. Did she mention any to you?"

"Jewelry? Certainly not, and she was the last woman I'd have connected— Well, what I remember chiefly are two—er—things," said Carson. "When she gave me the names and addresses of the legatees, she said—this harsh, plain way of talking, you know—that she didn't know who else to leave it to, and it wasn't that she was so fond of these friends, but she wasn't going to see any of it go to her family. I tried to persuade her to let me put in the old business—you know—one dollar to each member of her family, to obviate the possibility of their contesting—but she wouldn't have it at any price. They weren't to have a penny of it. She said one of her brothers was a ghoul and the other one was a fool. I remember *that* all right. And her sister was another fool, mucking up her system with medicines. Was she—the McCann woman—one of these health-food addicts? I just wondered. She went on at some length about how healthy she was because she took a positive attitude and got proper exercise and never took any medicine—that sort of thing."

"Did she mention her husband, Mr. Carson?"

"Oh, yes. I asked, of course, what her marital status was, because if he was living and still legally married to her it would affect the— Just so. She showed me a letter from him saying he'd divorced her—I took down the details, of course—in Reno in nineteen thirty-something. I checked the Reno records to be sure. Which," said Carson, smiling, "upped the fee a trifle, and she complained about that. But we do like to be sure of these things."

"They were definitely divorced? Legally?"

"Oh, yes."

Well, thought Hackett, that was one question answered at least. "And what was the other thing you remembered about her, Mr. Carson?"

"Well, it was rather odd—" Carson hesitated. "But she was an odd woman. Let me think now and try to remember it all exactly. I asked her if she had a safety-deposit box to keep the will in with other important papers, and she said she had 'a good place' to put it. Well, I didn't much like the sound of that, you know—a secretive old lady like that. In my experience there's no knowing where they'll hide important documents—"

"It was in a copy of Bartlett's Quotations," said Hackett dryly.

Carson shut his eyes and said, "God give me strength. Pure luck anyone came across it, I suppose. Well, I told her I'd be happy to keep it for her here, and she said there wasn't any need. Just like that. She was standing at the door, about to leave—it was just after she'd signed the will, you understand—and she said, in that flat nasal voice, 'I'm a strong woman, Mr. Carson, healthy and well, and I mean to live a long time. But I'll know when my time's coming—I'll know because I've never been sick a day, and when I start to sicken I'll know, and then I'll see my will's given into the proper hands and my friends told where to find things. And told if I don't come to my store or see my friends any more, no matter what anybody tells them, they're to tell certain people'—she emphasized that—'certain things.' I remember that because it was so odd. And because of how she looked when she said it—like—like an avenging goddess," said Carson, half laughing. "And I could swear to the actual words."

By God, thought Hackett, she'd meant to blow the thing open—Oscar and his collection of coffins. But she'd left it too late: didn't realize, of course, that she was going to be poisoned. Didn't realize she was "sickening." Meant to give one of those women the will when she thought it was time . . . In a bankbook there's no love, gentlemen. Eliza. The three casual friends casually acquired—didn't know who else to leave it to, away from the family.

The McLaughlins.

"That's all very interesting, Mr. Carson," Hackett said thoughtfully.

Higgins didn't get into the office until after Mendoza had left for the inquest, and technically he hadn't any orders to carry out. He looked at the new plate numbers the D.M.V. had come up with and didn't think much of any of them. It didn't look as if they'd get the joker who had run down Cohen. At this late date. Deliberate or not—and that idea was just wild.

He thought he might use a little time today to contact Alfred Clark. The Y.M.C.A. thing. Clark had seemed like a nice guy.

He found Alfred Clark's hardware store in Pasadena, reintroduced himself, and said he had a little favor to ask and could he buy Clark a cup of coffee, maybe?

"A favor?" said Clark. "Did you say Sergeant? Well, sure, anything I can do for you—I guess I can take fifteen minutes off, down the street at Nick's—" There was a clerk at the other side of the store.

The very funny damn part of it was, Higgins thought gloomily, that God knew he'd never been backward with females. Him, George Allen Higgins, scared to death to ask her to go out to dinner with him for fear she'd say no, and then he'd never dare ask her again. But Mary, of course, wasn't just another female. She was, well, Mary.

She was also Bert Dwyer's widow.

And Bert had been a pal of his. One very good guy.

But, aside from that, Higgins liked kids. He liked Bert's kids. And Stevie wanted to go to summer camp, and Mary couldn't afford it.

He gave an expurgated version to Alfred Clark, leaving Mary out of it mostly and emphasizing Bert and the kids, and Clark was interested and amused.

"I see. You don't want her to know you're—"

"Well, she's a very independent woman," said Higgins. Which she was. "She'd never let me—well, naturally, you see that. But Steve's father was a good friend of mine—he got shot by a bank robber six months back—and I've got no responsibilities myself and I'd like to— I just thought if we could work out a deal—you know? Like making it up there was a fund for fatherless boys, or— The only thing is they live in Hollywood and you're with the Pasadena—"

"Let me think about it," said Clark. He grinned at Higgins. "Good Samaritan, you."

"That's me," said Higgins, thinking about Mary's clear silver-gray eyes and how they smiled sometimes—not often enough—and her trim figure and black curly hair and her voice with the funny little break in it and how desperately much he loved her and wanted to look *after* them all, Mary and Steve and Laura and Brucie, the little Scotty, and the old comfortable house that was always needing new washers in its faucets and electrical repairs—

"World always needs good Samaritans," said Clark in a friendly tone. "I know Bud Wilson over at the Hollywood Y. You let me talk to him,

Sergeant." His expression was sympathetic. "We'll come up with something, I'll bet. Something to get the boy to camp."

Higgins started to thank him. Providence, undoubtedly, had led him to Alfred Clark.

THIRTEEN

When Mendoza came into Federico's at twelve-thirty he found Grace, Landers and Piggott hanging enthralled on Hackett's words, on a graphic description of the goings on at the Celtic Hotel last night. He sat down across from Grace, grinning.

"Why didn't you call me, Lieutenant? I'd have given a year of my life to have been in on it. How right you are, cops might not get rich, but they do acquire stories to tell."

"Well, knowing how all you cullud folks feel about corpses—" said Mendoza.

"Get along, suh, I got so's I can pass a graveyahd in broad daylight and nevah turn a hayuh," said Grace in broad Dixie. He shook his head. "I'll never think of that place by its right name. Coffin Corner. My God, the things we do run into."

A waiter came up with pencil and pad poised and Hackett said, "There's prestige. We've been sitting here ten minutes, but as soon as the lieutenant walks in—"

"Sorry, sir, we're busy like you can see. Drinks, gentlemen?"

Mendoza shook his head, ordered a small steak; Landers said he'd have a scotch and soda, Hackett shared that, Piggott looked disapproving and ordered a steak sandwich, and Grace debated. "Trying to think of something appropriate," he said. "In view of Oscar. There's one called a Great Secret, but I kind of think—yes, you can tell Joe to fix me a Leave It To Me."

"A—yes, sir."

"Joe's pretty good, I haven't stumped him yet," said Grace blandly. "What's in it? Oh, English gin, dry vermouth, apricot brandy, lemon juice and a dash of grenadine."

"Christ," said Higgins, coming up and taking the chair next to him.

"You do find them. Anything new? Bring me a bourbon and water," he added to the waiter.

Hackett brought them up to date with what Carson had to say. "Interesting," said Mendoza. "So she meant Oscar's little labors of love to get found out. And I've got news too." And he told them about Dr. Bainbridge's homework.

"For God's sake," said Hackett, "you mean regular doses of the stuff? It's not enough we've got to find out how somebody got her to take it once?"

"That's right. You have any ideas?"

"I have not," said Hackett. "This is the damnedest—but I'll say this, Luis, that definitely makes it look as if it's got to be somebody at the hotel, and if you want a wild guess, I'll say Manning."

"I don't know," said Grace; "she's the one seemed to like the woman best. Look at how she reacted when we broke the news. And she hasn't got all her buttons, could she act a part?"

"Hell, I don't know either," said Hackett. "I'm just looking at the facts. The way they'd arranged things in that crazy household, if you'd call it that, Eliza and the Manning female ate their meals together—fixed them together. Which says that Manning had the greatest opportunity to add something to the coffee or whatever. On the other hand, I suppose that also says that they mostly had the same meals. We can ask Oscar and Henry."

"Who might or might not know," said Mendoza. "We can. I intend to. We might also ask Manning's sister and get some more background on her. And there's also Jane. Getting poisoned last night. That I'm sure of. I asked the doctor at the General, and about this oleander they seem to know, he said they had cases rather often of kids chewing the leaves and having to have their stomachs pumped out. It's a one-shot deal and acts fairly rapidly. He did say that she'd had a large dose of it, more than would be the case if she'd just chewed a few leaves. I asked him about making up an infusion of it—concentrate, as it were—and he said sure, that would be possible and would make the effect—mmh—more virulent. But he also said death from it is very rare except in the cases of very small children and she'd had nowhere enough to kill her."

They digested that; the drinks came, and Grace looked at the Leave It To Me thoughtfully. "Whoever had it in for Eliza seems to have been more efficient than that."

"We all have off days," said Mendoza. "Are you getting anywhere on Mary Brown, Tom?"

"Don't mention the name to me," said Landers. "We've still got all these bus drivers and conductors to see, and the longer the time lapse the less likely it is anybody'll remember her on the bus or the train . . . Oh, I suppose the routine'll get us there in the end. On this McCann thing, the way I told you yesterday, that Thirkettle house was absolutely clean, and I can't figure the woman in on it. As Matt can say—we poked everywhere—"

"One of those persnickety housekeepers," agreed Piggott. "What my mother calls nasty-nice. She mixes up brews, all right—a lot of bottles in the kitchen, all labeled, and she had some stuff boiling on the stove. Don't think we didn't ask—even took samples for the lab—and I can hear what the boys are saying about that. One of 'em was boiled-up poppy seeds, for instance, painkiller, said Thirkettle. And something called common fumitory for acid indigestion."

"The one I liked," said Landers, swallowing Scotch, "was the purple loosestrife. You ever hear of it? Neither had I, but I'm not a gardener. There's just something sort of exotic-sounding about purple loosestrife."

"What's it supposed to be good for?" asked Grace curiously.

"Eye trouble, she said."

"You ask me," said Piggott, "it's going roundabout. I wouldn't say there isn't something in those old cures, but any of 'em that are worth anything the researchers know about, and why go to the bother of all that fussing with poppy seeds and so on when you can go buy a bottle of aspirin?"

"It's a hobby, I suppose you'd call it," said Landers. "Anybody can have a funny hobby. But the woman didn't strike me as a likely killer, did she you, Matt?"

"Well, you never know. She is one of the legatees under the will."

"Yes," said Mendoza, looking at the steak just set before him, "and some of what you got from Carson, Art— Our Eliza felt pretty confident of herself, didn't she? Confident she'd 'know' when her time was near, when she'd hand the will over to those three. She seems to have been an efficient sort of woman in a way, but that says to me that she was getting— mmh—delusions of omniscience, shall we put it? Hiding that will in a book—where, as Alison so rightly said, it might easily never have been found. The diamonds under the grating in the hearth—¡Caray! Even my grandmother knew better than that! And if she'd been thinking straight, she'd have known that anybody—never sick a day or not—can have a heart attack."

"Well, she was a McLaughlin too," said Hackett. "Maybe a trifle more sense than the others, but still a McLaughlin."

"Coffin Corner," said Grace. "My God."

"Well, it just struck me," said Mendoza, "that, by all that, Eliza was a little overconfident. With reason, maybe, according to how she'd feel. She'd accumulated the small fortune by her own unaided efforts, while the rest of them were living on practically nothing—aimless, hardly planning ahead a day. Feckless. And even more of a triumph, maybe, for Eliza was that she'd kept it a great secret. What a laugh she'd have on them, even from beyond the grave—or the fourth floor of the hotel!—when they found out, and found out they wouldn't come in for a cent of it. What I'm getting at is just possibly Eliza was so confident that she was the hell of a lot smarter than anybody around her that it was all that much easier to trick her in some way. She might not have suspected that anybody would try to pull something on her."

"One little thing," said Grace, finishing the Leave It To Me. "She must have felt *some* symptoms, taking the stuff over a period. Why didn't she suspect something—even just that her natural time was approaching, say— and see the will made open, tell one of those three about the crown jewels?"

Mendoza said, "They do say 'none so blind'— And then you've got to consider human nature, Jase."

"That you've always got to remember, all right. What particular aspect of it you mean?"

"These obnoxious *mens sana in corpore sano* fiends. One of them," said Mendoza, "sprains his ankle, he'll go on denying there *could* be anything wrong."

"Oh," said Hackett. "I get you. That could be."

Landers sighed and said he'd better get on with all the bus drivers and conductors.

Alison called Angel to tell her about the oleander. "Heavens," said Angel, "we've got an enormous one against the rear fence—a young tree. And Mark puts *everything* in his mouth—do you mean to say—? I'll get Art to dig it out on his day off. Just lucky nothing's happened before we found out . . . Isn't this the craziest one they've had yet? Talk about Charles Addams."

Alison said some of it was rather pathetic but the bodies in the attic was really something. "Honestly, people . . . But what fascinates me is the foxglove. I've no idea what it looks like, there could be a bed of it in the back yard and I wouldn't— Well, apparently that has to be prepared, boiled in water or something, isn't dangerous in the raw state, so to speak —but, Angel, down there? Oh, some people in the little old residential streets have a patch of garden, but so much of it is all business, and there's the freight yards, and—"

"Oh, I had a lovely thought about that," said Angel. "I wondered— *No, Mark! Leave the pussy alone!*—about it too, of course, and I was curious enough to look at the County Guide, and you know, Alison, aside from the hypothetical back yards, the only— *Mark, did you hear what I said?*—there's really only one place down there where there might be—"

"Oh," said Alison. "Oh, for heaven's sake! I can *see* Luis' face." She uttered a little scream as Sheba landed on her from behind. "Little monster. Of course. Elysian Park. Where—"

"Where," said Angel, "the Police Academy is. Spang in the middle. I can *hear* what Art would say. X strolling past the Academy, where all those earnest young rookies are studying police science, and gathering the foxglove—"

They both burst out laughing.

Mendoza went over to the new facility on Alameda, where Oscar and Henry were incarcerated, and started to question Oscar about all of Eliza's habits. Before he got down to business, he had to answer a lot of questions from Oscar—about what sort of sentence he might get and would the court get him a lawyer—and when he finally got Oscar to pay attention he didn't get much.

All the McLaughlins seemed to be essential egotists, completely wrapped up in themselves and half blind to other people. Oscar didn't really know much about Eliza's habits at meals or any other time. Coffee, he said vaguely, yes, she drank coffee, but she had one pot she and Miss Manning used and he and Henry had their own. Well, he couldn't say whether she and Miss Manning always had the same thing at meals, but he thought not always because he did remember that Eliza didn't like chicken and at least once that he could recall he was in the kitchen when they were eating and Miss Manning was having creamed chicken. But he really couldn't say— Oh, he didn't *think* Eliza ever had soft drinks in the store. Things like Coca-Cola. It was so expensive, and then the bottles were a nuisance. Sometimes in the summer she'd made lemonade, but she hadn't liked fizzy things. He didn't himself. "It gives me heartburn. Not that that was Ellie's reason, of course, she was *never* sick and always boasting about it. I'm subject to heartburn myself—so is Henry. Jane had some capsules once that seemed to help—one of her samples—but we never came across another sample offer and they were a dollar and a half a box—outrageous. I said to Henry at the time—"

Mendoza prodded at him for an hour and went away with incipient heartburn himself. And despite his remarks about the annoyingly healthy people like Eliza—or perhaps he was the exception to prove the rule—he was another one like that but did no boasting about it. He was annoyed. These damn McLaughlins, he thought.

Coffin Corner, indeed.

A report came in from Glendale about three o'clock that a car had been picked up, not on the hot list anywhere in the county, with what looked like bloodstains on it. Higgins went out there to check it, though after five days he rather doubted that the hit-run car which had killed Cohen would still have blood on it. If it hadn't been abandoned until now. But you never knew, and even in Glendale there were outlying little streets where it could have been sitting for several days without being noticed.

But it hadn't been that sort of street. Quite a busy residential street, and a resident had called in to report the car had been sitting in front of his house for four days. The bloodstains, however, turned out to be inside the car, which was no use to Higgins on the Cohen case. The Glendale boys had a little problem of their own.

And, well, they had these things going to be worked, but he didn't see one blessed thing to do on the McLaughlin business except ask a lot more questions, which he privately thought wouldn't give them anything much at all, and Mendoza and Hackett and Grace would be doing that. Landers and Piggott were doggedly at the routine on Mary Brown. Galeano and Schenke were on night tour, and Glasser would probably be helping out Landers and Piggott. Palliser would probably come back some time this week: upset for him, thought Higgins, losing his mother so sudden; they'd been close, he knew. Probably Palliser and his girl Roberta would get married pretty soon now. And so maybe it was goofing off (the nice spring weather), but Higgins drove back into Hollywood by Silver Lake Boulevard and stopped at Mary Dwyer's house, and the kids had just got home from school, so he played ball awhile with Stevie while Laura practiced her piano lesson.

Good kids. Laura wanted to play him a piece she'd just learned. At least he'd got the kids calling him George. "Gee, I'm awf'lly glad I didn't have to stop piano like Mother said I would because we can't afford it. Wasn't it lucky, George? How you found Miss Jeanie that doesn't cost as much?"

"Don't say gee," said Higgins. "It sounds vulgar. It was lucky, all right. You're getting better all the time, Laurie."

Nice kids. But he ought to be out earning his pay. To, among other things, go on mostly paying for Laura's piano lessons—and if Mary ever found out—!

He went back downtown.

"Yeah, I think it coulda been," said Mike Sullivan. He held the post-mortem picture of Mary Brown at arm's length and studied it. "She's dead, hah? Poor little girl. It just coulda been her. I wouldn't like to swear."

"We have to check on everything, Mr. Sullivan," said Landers. "You think she could have been on your bus on that run?"

"I wouldn't swear," said Sullivan. "Most of the passengers you don't hardly notice—only the ones make some complaint or like that. And one run's pretty much like another. Only, well, the pretty girls a man kind of notices, don't he? Even if he don't intend to do anything about it." He grinned. "Me, I got a pretty wife and three kids, but the girls I notice. Just to notice. Now you say it'd've been that Tuesday or Wednesday, depends where she got on the bus."

"That's right, Mr. Sullivan."

"Well, I took the bus outta Sacramento that Tuesday night at eleven-fifty. Figure it five hunnerd and twenty miles, coming over to the coast route, and I was due in the Greyhound station in L.A. at eight-forty A.M. Only I had engine trouble." Sullivan looked disgusted. Landers had found him, at getting on to five o'clock, by his wife's directions, in a neighborhood bar sitting over a beer. Sullivan had two days off before taking a bus out for Chicago tomorrow. "They keep 'em up, that don't often happen, but there it was. I hadda lay over in San Luis. So I didn't get to L.A. until about two-thirty that Wednesday afternoon, and I won't say there wasn't a lot of complaints, but I couldn't help it—"

"I see," said Landers. "You think this girl could have been on this bus?"

"I don't know if it was her. There was *a* girl about that age on that run—all I can say. I couldn't tell you her name, naturally. A pretty girl. Coulda been that one. All I can say is she was one of 'em that acted reasonable—saw it wasn't my fault."

"Do you remember if she got on at Sacramento or somewhere along the way?"

"Oh, mister, I'm not an encyclopedia. Or one o' these computers. I made four runs since, and passengers, you don't notice 'em much unless they make the complaint, raise a fuss of some kind. I just remember there was a good-lookin' young girl on that run, *which* I only remember on accountta the engine trouble, if you get me. It can be," said Sullivan, "a tough job, but I guess so can yours, hah?"

"Brother," said Landers, "you have said it. Well, thanks very much."

"Welcome," said Sullivan. "Gotta be a good citizen."

Landers left him thirstily swallowing beer, went back to the office and sent off a teletype to the Sacramento boys. Had any young woman been reported missing who matched this description, or had such a young woman been known to have left town for L.A. or anywhere else? He got out a state map, looked at it and sighed. At a conservative guess, about forty places between Sacramento and here where she could have boarded that bus.

He wondered what a bus driver's life was like. In any job, he reflected, difficulties. Into each life some rain—

"Poisoned!" said Jane McLaughlin dramatically. "I was poisoned! Just like Eliza. I thought you were talking nonsense, young man, but it seems you were quite right. There is a *plot*."

Mendoza had called General Hospital: the patient, he was told, was practically recovered and could be seen. She was, in fact, sitting up in the hospital bed, the loose hospital gown slipping dangerously and revealing unhealthy bulges of soft white flesh, supremely unconscious of the other patients in the ward beyond the prim white screens round the bed.

"What I wanted to ask you, Miss McLaughlin," said Mendoza, "was what you had to eat and drink last evening. From, say, six o'clock on to when you were taken ill."

"That Manning woman," said Jane, nodding violently. "That is the answer undoubtedly. Ellie was quite mad, taking her in, and *now* she has her reward. The creature's a complete lunatic. It was in the tea. That I am positive of."

"The tea? You had tea and what else, Miss McLaughlin? When?"

"Of course you want all the *details*," said Jane. "Trying to poison *me!* Of all the outrageous—it was undoubtedly the tea. The Thirkettle woman brought it. What? No, no, young man, not yesterday—some while ago, last month sometime. A herbal tea—maté, I believe she called it—a green tea—Paraguayan—supposed to be very beneficial to the kidneys. Not one of her own making, no, she had actually *bought* it as a present for Eliza, but Eliza did not care for it and gave it to me. Quite unprecedented, *that!* But then Ellie was not one to waste anything. I can't say I cared much for the flavor, but there it was to be used up, and I've been having it with my supper. I *thought* there was something peculiar about the flavor of it last night, and I said so—and that Manning lunatic saying she'd put in a pinch of clove to make it taste better! Never suspected a *thing* until I began to feel sick— Have you arrested her yet, young man?"

Mendoza felt irrelevantly he should thank her for the "young man." After all, he'd been twenty-odd years on the force. "Not yet, Miss McLaughlin. If you could tell me—" Thirkettle? Thirkettle's tea? But what motive on earth could Tabitha Thirkettle have had against Jane? And she couldn't know Jane would wind up with the tea. And in any case if Jane had been drinking the tea with no ill effects up to last night—

"And why *not*, pray? Trying to *poison* me— I told Ellie she was a fool, but all she could see was the money for taking care of the woman—a lunatic like that—"

Thirkettle, Manning? The tea. Try to make sense of it, thought Mendoza. Try to collect the evidence!

In the corridor outside the room he caught an intern and asked when Jane could be released. Any time: she was all but fully recovered and they always needed the space.

And he shuddered to think what her reaction would be to then being charged and arrested—accessory to the charge facing Oscar and Henry.

The bodies in the attic.

Coffin Corner, he thought.

FOURTEEN

He went back to the hotel with Grace. Glasser had taken the warrant on Jane over to the hospital.

They found Vera Manning in her room, engaged in writing her love letters. "The tea?" she said. "What tea?"

"The tea you made for Miss McLaughlin's supper last night," said Grace softly. "We'd like to see the rest of it, ma'am."

"It's in the kitchen. I'm afraid I'm *not* very good at cooking, even though Ellie's tried to teach me. But when I have my own little home and have to cook for Albert—"

"If you'd just come and show us, Miss Manning," said Mendoza.

She drifted out to the kitchen ahead of them. An impossibly big room, originally the restaurant kitchen, a good thirty feet square, and everything in it very old. The flooring was wide-planked, warped old pine boards, and it hadn't been scrubbed in a long time. An ancient Kelvinator stood against one wall, an equally aged Servel against another. A long unpainted wooden table down the center, a few straight chairs. And open shelves round all four sides of the room, littered with a miscellany of items: boxes of crackers and cookies and packaged bakery cakes, cans, instant coffee and tea, breakfast food, half-empty jars of mustard, little wedges of waxed paper refolded to use over again, a topless box with lengths of string filling it higgledy-piggledy (that was Eliza, Mendoza decided), a man's sweater casually tossed down, a crumpled felt hat; and ranged along one shelf the crockery and flatware, unmatched chipped plates and saucers and cups, old cheap-restaurant tinware, much of it bent; and in the center of the rear wall an enormous black iron range that must, he thought, be all of fifty years old and possibly more. Nothing looked very clean.

"There's the tea," said Miss Manning helpfully. "I always read the directions over."

Paraguayan green tea: maté, as Jane had said. In a commercial package with cellophane round it: "59¢" read the stamp on the top of the box. "What did you put in Jane's tea last night, Miss Manning?" asked Mendoza.

"Why, she said she didn't like the taste of it, so I put a little clove in. I think it was clove. Maybe peppermint. She's very annoying, interrupting me so often, she doesn't *realize* how important it is to our brave soldiers to get letters from home. Did you know Gertrude's gone? And Robespierre. Two men came in a truck. They had an awful time catching Robespierre, they had to get a ladder—"

"Yes, we know. What about the oleander, Miss Manning?"

Her large pale eyes turned to Grace with vague speculation. "I don't know, what about it?"

"The oleander leaves you picked and put—"

"I didn't know there were any black men in the police force, it's very interesting. I'm afraid I don't know what that is—what you said. I would *like* to finish my letter," said Miss Manning. She looked oddly pathetic in the full light from the window, the over-tall gawky old woman in her torn dress and layers of bright-colored scarves, her ravaged face covered with heavy make-up. Suddenly she gave Mendoza a wide smile, revealing stained yellowed teeth. "*Such* a festive day when Albert comes home at last!" she said brightly. "He's been gone a long time—I can't even remember how long it is now—but the last letter I had, he said he hoped to be home for Christmas. It's—it's going to be Christmas soon, isn't it?"

"In a little while," said Mendoza. He shrugged at Grace.

"Miss Manning," said Grace persuasively, "when you were fixing Miss McLaughlin's tray last night, did anybody else come into the kitchen? You remember?"

She looked vague. "Oscar was there, I think. Maybe Henry. I didn't know what to fix for *myself*—Ellie always decided. I do try, and Ellie was good to me, but I wasn't brought up to housework and I'm not very good at it. Jane said the water hadn't been boiling. It's so hard to tell when it *is*, you know." She giggled. "I really must finish my letter—"

They looked at each other. "You do that," said Mendoza, and she drifted out. "We'd never get anything out of her. But I continue to wonder just how lunatic she is."

"Me too. Do we know where her sister lives?"

"Mmh. There was a check in Eliza's purse she hadn't cashed yet. A Mrs.

John Binny, up in Hollywood. We might get some more background from her. But let's have a look around here."

It was Grace who spotted the little twig with several leaves still on it under the stove—old-fashioned stove on raised legs—nearly invisible against the grimy old floor. "Oleander. I do know that one—long thin leaf."

"And what does it say? Several people use this stove every day. Could have been Oscar or Henry."

"Well, after all," said Grace, grinning, "they had a program mapped out for last night. And a full night's work too. You think either of them, even if they'd decided Jane was better out of the way, would have planned it for last night—causing a certain amount of upset, Oscar's favorite word, right while they were busy bringing all the coffins back home?"

Mendoza laughed. "There is that. Hell, it's all up in the air. And in a place this size, my God, that Rialto woman could have slipped down in the dead of night to mix up the brew. Or Percy. Or even Ben. Or—my God, Jase, d'you know we've never so much as laid eyes on that Bobby? The newsboy. Just because he hasn't been around when we have—"

"So we haven't. Spring fever," said Grace. "But, then, the McLaughlins do tend to keep our attention focused on them. I suppose we ought to. And find out also just exactly who *did* know about the bodies in the attic. I wonder if Percy did."

"I don't think so. The remittance man, sitting around Sam's bar and grill. Too likely he'd let it out, and Oscar may be eccentric—or even more than that—but he'd know that danger. Yes," said Mendoza thoughtfully, "so where next? Damn it, on this one we can't even fall back on the routine!"

Mrs. John Binny lived on Cahuenga Avenue in Hollywood, in a dignified middle-class apartment, and it dawned belatedly on Mendoza and Grace that Miss Vera Manning, like the McLaughlins, was not native to Old High Street and environs—and also that Mrs. Binny, in paying Eliza McCann forty dollars a month to baby-sit with the erratic Miss Manning, had been getting one hell of a bargain.

If Mrs. Binny had stashed her unsteady-witted sister away at a rest home, about the only other alternative, it couldn't have cost her any less than two hundred a month at prevailing rates. And Mrs. Binny was looking extremely alarmed at the prospect of having to find new accommodations.

She hadn't known that Eliza was dead.

"Of course," she said thinly, "I couldn't leave her there with only the men. Quite unsuitable. Dear me, how annoying—coming so suddenly, too." She was almost as tall as her sister, a thin pale woman with a Roman nose and the same china-blue eyes. She didn't like police in her neat and clean living room, especially when they brought bad news. And, adding insult to injury, her expression said, one of them Mexican and the other Negro, of all things.

They asked patient questions and got some answers which didn't tell them much. Vera Manning had been—"afflicted," said Mrs. Binny delicately—since her poor fiancé had been killed in the First World War. She had then been twenty-six. "Always delicate, of course." She had been living with Mrs. McCann at the Celtic Hotel for nearly twenty years. Mrs. Binny's parents had known the older McLaughlins. "I *knew* the family, of course—such a dreadful thing to lose all they had like that, and it was really an excellent arrangement. Vera seemed quite contented, and it had become impossible to have her in my—" Nice normal home: they could finish that. "Of course I paid her board and paid Mrs. McCann a sum for—"

"Had you been paying Mrs. McCann the same amount all that time, Mrs. Binny?" asked Mendoza.

A little spasm contracted the woman's mouth. "Well, no, of course it was far less at first—but when prices began to go up so drastically, Mrs. McCann did mention that it didn't quite cover—and we finally agreed on —I beg your pardon? Oh, that was about seven years ago, I—"

Eliza good at dickering. Everything grist that came to her mill. She seemed to have been good enough to the Manning woman in her own way. And just how "afflicted" was Manning, anyway? Competent enough to do the simple marketing, left on her own most of the day usually—writing her letters? Occasionally walking down to join Eliza at the store, a good fifteen blocks, without getting lost.

"I beg your pardon? A *psychiatrist?* Oh, dear me, no, we never— When she first showed signs of—ah—her affliction, well, it was obvious—we didn't wish to—I *beg* your pardon?" She recoiled from Mendoza's question fastidiously. "*Violent?* Good heavens, of course not—nothing like that! Really, you can't be thinking that Vera was responsible for whatever happened to Mrs. McCann—why, that's quite outrageous! Of *course* she's never been—"

But never given any treatment. How much of that, wondered Mendoza, was a half-unconscious reversion to childish make-believe, the irresponsibility? The real Vera Manning, if you pinned her down, might just find life easier and more comfortable by pretending to inhabit her unreal little world while a part of her remained fully conscious of what was going on around her.

But one thing they could be sure of. Of everybody who knew Eliza, Vera's sister was at least one they could mark off as having no reason to want her dead.

"I suppose," said Grace on the sidewalk outside, "we could have her looked at by a head doctor."

"And get a lot of double talk," said Mendoza irritably. "Which would tell us exactly nothing. She's an impossible subject for a lie-detector test, of course. I just don't know, Jase."

So, also belatedly, they went down to Second and Grand and hauled in Bobby the newsboy. Who turned out to be a stout forty-year-old with a mental age of around eight, perfectly amiable and cooperative to the best of his ability. Patiently they asked him questions—or, rather, Grace did. Bobby, like so many people, responded to something in easygoing, tender-voiced Detective Grace.

"Oscar, sure," he said. "It's Oscar I give the money to. For my room. He tells me day to pay money."

He knew, he demonstrated eagerly, about money: dimes and pennies and nickels and quarters and half dollars. He could make change good. He knew where to go, get the papers to sell first thing in the morning, and a man brought more papers later.

"Mmh-hmm," said Grace. "And you live at the Celtic Hotel, Bobby?"

Bobby looked blank and said again he paid Oscar for his room. He knew how to find the room. You went up the first stairs and counted the doors and it was number eight you came to. He looked blank again when Grace asked how long he'd lived there. "You didn't always live at that place, did you, Bobby?" asked Grace gently.

After painful thought, Bobby said, "No. Ma—Ma and me—it was before Ma went away. She told me all how to do, before, and I do just like she allus told me." He looked earnestly at Grace. "About selling the papers and everything. And allus be polite to people. And a bath ever' Satidday night. And remember walk straight down Broadway, till two blocks pas' the Mission Church, an' then it's on'y a block down to home. Where our room is. I remember most things good."

Grace straightened up from where he'd been bending over Bobby, sitting in a straight chair. That told the story. The mother settling them there, God knew how long ago; the amiable Bobby learning as best he could to live by rote: and, aside from his amiability, one like Bobby would hardly have been the one to brew the homemade poison for Eliza—or for Jane.

He looked even blanker at mention of both names, and they realized he might very well seldom have set eyes on Eliza and never on Jane. Jane always upstairs, in her room mostly, and Eliza at her store or in her room. And Bobby probably out selling papers on Sundays too.

He was vague about the names of the days, but he enlarged on that for them obligingly. "Sell the papers until all gone. But I like all the pretty lights, night comes—walk up the street, see all the pretty lights. And people."

Oscar had said something about Bobby's being out at all hours.

He looked at Grace anxiously now. "But I don't know *this* place. I be lost, you don't take me back to my place." His place in life, thought Mendoza. His safe, routine, innocent life. Whoever she'd been, Bobby's mother had done her best for him in her way. "You take me back?"

"We'll take you back, Bobby," said Grace. "Where do you eat, Bobby? Breakfast and lunch and dinner?"

Parrotlike, Bobby told him. "The corner up next from where I sell papers. Old man there—his name's Joe—nice old man. He knows Ma. They was men come took her away on a flat thing all white and she never come back." Momentarily his cherubic face crumpled. "But Joe, he gives me breakfast, lunch, dinner. Other folks too. Fixes for everybody come in. I know the money. Three dimes and a nickel—breakfast. Two quarters —lunch. A half dollar and a dime and two nickels—dinner. Good. Joe's nice to me. Most people awful nice. Ma said. You be nice to people, they nice to you. And about pray to God, only I sometimes don't remember all the words she said. I *try* remember. Please, pretty soon you take me back, I got a lot more papers to sell."

"O.K., I'll take you back now, Bobby," said Grace. "You just wait a few minutes." He and Mendoza went out of the interrogation room to the corridor. "So that's that."

"The flotsam and jetsam," said Mendoza, "you find in the jungle—God. That kind. I suppose if any of the social workers knew about him they'd stash him away somewhere. Wonder he hasn't been knocked on the head some night for the few bucks on him."

Detective Grace said, "I don't know, Lieutenant. Maybe Bobby's got a charmed life. Short on brains, but maybe—I sometimes think—the loving heart's a little more important. Bobby seems to get along O.K., doing just like Mama taught him. Just maybe, Lieutenant, Bobby knows a little bit more about what this is supposed to be all about than you or me or the Chief."

Mendoza looked at him. Grace smiled and added, "Not that I'd go preaching at you. Just a thought. I'll take him back to his newspapers and take twenty minutes to stop in at Bullocks' to look at those watches the sergeant was mentioning. For Virginia's birthday."

And another little puzzle: who was going to arrange Eliza's funeral with all her relatives sitting in jail? Well, that was their problem, Mendoza reflected.

At three o'clock that afternoon Hackett came into the office with the information that Eliza had not, after all, flouted Uncle. Inquiries at the local I.R.S. office had turned up the information that she had filed tax returns through a tax accountant. "Fellow named Stein over on Third Street, hole-in-the-wall office. I saw him just now. She was strictly business, he says—furnished him all the facts and figures, and acting as if she hated to do that—"

"Which figures."

"—and that was that. But it was a revelation to *me*," said Hackett, "and I'm seriously thinking about a down-payment on some rental property. He says, what with the value depreciation allowed, and necessary repairs and so on, she got out of practically all the income tax. Can you tie that? Stein seems to know his job. Grinned when I was surprised and said that was one reason smart people bought low-income real estate. I'll be damned."

"And that tells us nothing," said Mendoza rather regretfully, "except that she didn't want to go to jail. Was that smart anyway. At least up to the last little while. I keep thinking of all Carson said, which says to me that Eliza was getting overconfident, not quite as shrewd as she'd been."

"And I keep thinking," said Hackett, "of Tabitha Thirkettle. God, what a name. The obvious answer. And how we'd ever prove it, for God's sake—"

"A little too obvious?"

"You just like it complicated. Not that this one isn't complicated enough."

"*Tal vez*," said Mendoza. He lit a new cigarette and stared at it. "But—"

Sergeant Farrell came in and said they had, probably, another suicide. Corpse just found in an alley off First Street. Suicide note in breast pocket. An old man.

"Oh, hell," said Hackett. "More routine. I know, don't say it, what we're mostly here to do. Glorified clerks." He got up.

At about the same time the desk clerk at that hotel on Olive Avenue was sitting with his feet propped up on a stool, behind the counter, and trying to lose himself again in the current issue of *Startling Detective*.

Only he couldn't quite forget that girl. Hell, it wasn't any of *his* business. If she knew anything about that poor girl killed herself last Wednesday night, she'd probably go to the cops her own self and spill it anyways.

Hell of a thing, he thought. First suicide they'd had since he'd worked here. Damn pretty little girl, looking happy as could be when she registered. Mary Brown.

The other girl not so pretty. Not so young.

That cop around asking—hell, a plain-clothes man, and he didn't look over twenty-one. (The clerk didn't know that that fact was the bane of Tom Landers' life.) Well, he hadn't seen any more in the papers about it; probably they'd found out all they wanted and that was that.

No business of *his*—just because some dame comes in asking for the suicide— He'd thought honest to God she was going to faint away when he told her. Just said *"No!"* and turned white as a sheet. And looked like she was going to faint. And then asking all the questions.

The clerk shifted position and turned a page. *Murder and the Rodeo Star*. That ought to be a good one. He started to read the story, but his mind kept going back to that girl. To both girls.

Just walking out like that, fast, when he asked what her name was. And why the hell he'd done that—

The desk clerk had quit school in the tenth grade, and he didn't especially like hard work; he'd drifted around some; he didn't go to any church since leaving home, and he liked a bet on the ponies now and then, and he'd been known to take up with a few females with somewhat tarnished reputations, and occasionally he tied one on, and all in all he wasn't exactly the most upright and respectable citizen in L.A. County. But he'd been raised in a small town by God-fearing parents, and inevitably some of that had stuck by him: among other things, his father's emphatic strictures about cooperating with the law-enforcement authorities.

For some thirty minutes, *Startling Detective* fought a losing battle with what has been termed *the agen-byte of Ynwit*—at the end of which time the clerk sighed impatiently, reached for the phone book, looked up the number, dialed Headquarters and asked for Homicide. He didn't remember the detective's name; he said, "It's about that Mary Brown. This is—"

"This is," said the phone loudly, "Bainbridge, who the hell did you think— Listen—"

"Oh, yes," said Mendoza. "Are you having fun with all the old and new embalmed corpses?"

"You can go straight to hell," said Bainbridge. "My good God almighty, landing me with— But that's not what I'm calling about, damn it. Listen, I *told* you that book was checked out on my library card! I told you to be— And now I take the damn book back—this morning—and they call me just now and claim it's been defaced—one of the plates torn out—and demand four goddamn bucks because the damn thing's out of print, and what the hell you highhanded cops think you're doing, taking—"

"Oh, really?" said Mendoza. Hackett was still sitting opposite him. "Just a minute," he said. "Art, did you lift a plate out of that book on herbs?"

"Lift a— Of course not. Why? Bainbridge said—"

"Yes . . . We'll look into it, Doctor. Don't fuss about the four bucks. I can run to that if—"

"Fuss!" said Bainbridge. "Cops! Why I ever got myself involved with *cops*—"

FIFTEEN

Landers was out when the desk clerk's call came in, but he came into the office about half an hour later and Sergeant Farrell told him about it. Feeling hopeful, Landers went right out again and chased over to the hotel on Olive. *Something?* he wondered. You slogged your heart out at the deadly routine, day in and day out, and then by pure chance or coincidence something turned up to point a short cut.

Somebody asking for Mary Brown at that hotel . . . "What exactly did she say?" he asked the desk clerk. "Did she give any name?"

"No, she didn't. I thought about it awhile before callin', but I figured I'd better. I never saw her before. She was maybe twenty-six, twenty-seven, not so pretty as the girl killed herself, but nice-enough lookin'. Dark hair, medium-tall, blue eyes, I guess . . . I don't remember what she had on. She just asked for this Mary Brown and I said she wasn't here and then I asked was she a friend of hers, and I sort of broke it to her what happened and, honest to God, I thought she was going to pass out. She turned white as a sheet and says *No!* just like that, and I got up and asked her did she want a glass of water or somethin' and she said, kind of faint, no, and asked when it happened and what you people'd done and all and I told her all I knew. And I said," said the clerk virtuously, "maybe she ought to go see you, but she was on the way out then. She still looked awful—like she was going to pass out . . . I got no idea who she was or where she went. I just thought—"

He said it all over again, but that was it. Landers thanked him for calling in, went out to the sidewalk and stood a minute while he lit a cigarette. That certainly seemed to be that. No way to trace the girl. But—

He'd listened to Mendoza often enough on his somewhat unorthodox ideas about detection. What it came down to, said Mendoza, was very simple first principles. Like the story about the idiot boy and the lost horse. If you were a horse—

Landers looked up and down the street, debating. Girl looked ready to pass out, the clerk said. Friend of Mary Brown? And that was a good hour and a half ago. Still—having just heard that her friend was dead, a presumed suicide—would she just have got on a bus or walked away somewhere—looking ready to pass out?

This was an old part of town along here too, the buildings shabby. Up from the hotel, which stood alone, was a block of stores running up toward Twenty-First Street: shoe repairs, a hole-in-the-wall jewelry shop, Sam's Eatery, a dry cleaner's, a shabby dress shop, and a drugstore on the corner.

Landers tried Sam's Eatery first and drew blank. Nobody remembered such a girl there. Well, he thought philosophically, it wasn't a very inviting-looking place and maybe— He could always come back to the other places, ask if someone had seen her pass. The idea in his mind— He asked at the drugstore and drew blank again. He started back the other way, down toward Twentieth Street. A hand laundry—nothing seen of her there; a shabby music store—ditto; and on that corner a little newsstand with a counter where they also sold cigarettes, cigars, candy, a few sundries. There was a stout, cheerful-looking elderly man behind the counter, and at Landers' question he looked concerned.

"Didn't she get home O.K.? Who are you?"

Jackpot, thought Landers, and asked more questions. Yes, the old man said, that girl had come walking along about two-thirty this afternoon. Stopped and leaned on the counter, looked like she was about to faint away. "So I quick go out and give her an arm, set her down here on my chair, an' shove her head down on her knees, and bring her a glass o' water from the back. And pretty soon she looks some better—nice-lookin' girl, and I got daughters round her age, I was sorry—she thanks me, says she just heard some awful bad news, but she never did such a thing as nearly faint in public, she apologizes. Nice girl. And then she asks can she call a cab, accountta she don't feel well enough to go home on a bus, so I say let me look at the stand down the street, and Eddy was there, just pulled in from a run, so I—"

Jackpot again, thought Landers. Was this thing going to come unstuck all at once? The cabby was Eddy Dale; the old fellow knew him. Landers went down to the cabstand, found it empty, used the direct phone to call the company office, identified himself and requested that Eddy Dale be dispatched from wherever he was to answer some questions.

And twenty minutes later Eddy Dale turned up in his cab. "Oh, that one," he said. "Sure I remember, and anyways I got it down on the record. For the comp'ny. I felt kinda sorry for her—in the cab she starts cryin', quiet-like but all broke up over something—and it's a little trip and comes to quite a fare and she don't look like ordinarily she'd be ridin' in cabs—"

"What was the address?" asked Landers eagerly.

"Martel Street in Hollywood, just north of Fountain—it come to six eighty-three, and she was still cryin', she give me seven singles and a quarter, but I still felt sorry for her—" He looked at the record and added the exact address.

Feeling a little excited, Landers sought the nearest public phone and called the office. "I've got a witness, I think. Who's there?"

"Nobody here but George," said Farrell. "The boss got a call from Bainbridge, and in about five minutes he and Art came tearing out yelling where's Jase, and about then he walked in, so the boss tells me they'll all be at that hotel again—you know—"

"Coffin Corner," said Landers. "Yeah. Well, ask Higgins—hell, no sense using two cars, what time is it—four-thirty. I'll come back and pick him up —we can take my car. I think we've got a real ident on Mary Brown."

"Well, well, progress. I'll tell him."

It was a court, an old one but neat enough and recently painted: a row of three each side, of small stucco duplex apartments, cement walk down the middle, neat strips of lawn.

Higgins had been congratulatory, and Landers felt smug. Of course they didn't know which of the twelve apartments it was, but that was a small stumbling block; they found the manageress in one of the front ones and gave her a description.

She stared at them, a fat middle-aged woman, at cops on her doorstep, and said, "Why, that sounds like Cecilia Dawson, but why on earth the police—well, it's number four this side, but what on earth—"

They thanked her and walked down to number four. And after an interval the door was answered by a pretty, but not strikingly pretty, young brunette. She'd been crying, her eyes still looked puffy, and she'd just washed her face and hadn't put any new make-up on; and she was wearing a neat blue cotton housecoat zipped up the front, and she looked at them dully and said she didn't want to buy anything.

Higgins showed her his badge and said, "You were in the Stewart Hotel this afternoon, Miss Dawson, asking for Miss Mary Brown. We'd like to hear anything you can tell us about Miss Brown. You did know her?"

She stared at them, and then abruptly swung the door wide. "Yes, I knew her," she said. "Come in. I'll tell you whatever I can. I've just been —I can't take it in. Mary. H-how did she do it? That clerk just s-said she killed herself, he didn't seem to— How'd you know where I live?"

They went in. It was a small living room, with old and tired furniture in it, but everything neat and dusted. "Please sit down," she said. She sat in an armchair beside the couch; they saw that there was an open Bible on the table between, and a silver rosary. "I'll tell you anything I can, but the clerk said—last Wednesday—"

"Well, we've had a little trouble finding out who she was," said Landers. "Was Mary Brown her real name, Miss Dawson?"

"Who she was? Her—well, for heaven's sake, of course it was! I don't— And all over that no-good man! I'd been worried about it," said Cecilia Dawson miserably. "Because Mary didn't have any judgment about people, she was—she was just as open and friendly as a—as a puppy. Believe anything anybody told her, and I'd written her—"

"If we can just have it from the beginning, Miss Dawson," said Higgins gently.

When they heard it all, it amounted to quite a lot. Cecilia and Mary had first met nearly five years back, and even though Cecilia was four years older they'd taken to each other right away, for one reason because they'd both been orphans, brought up in orphanages. Cecilia in the Holy Name Home back in Illinois and Mary in a state place here, but— They'd both been working at the same place in Sacramento then, waiting on table at this restaurant. Mary's first job it was; she was only seventeen, just out of the home. "And I tried to help her, give her little tips how to get along, and all—a nice kid, but she didn't have any caution—"

And then a year ago Cecilia had come down here; she'd been going to night school to learn stenography and thought there'd be more openings down here, and she'd got a better job. "But we wrote a lot back and forth, I guess you could say I was Mary's best friend, she made friends easy but not so—not so close like we'd been, we shared a room for four years—" And about six months back Mary had started to write about this fellow. A Harvey Fletcher. "He gave her a big play and she fell for him hard, but she didn't have any *sense* about men," said Cecilia wretchedly. "I've got to try to explain it to you, Mary was a good girl—you mustn't think she wasn't, I'd know that—but she wanted to get married and have a family—well, most girls do, and I guess any of us raised like that in homes, well, we want it even more, make good homes for our kids, you know. The place she grew up, they didn't seem to teach the kids much religion, and I'm not one for trying to press my religion on anybody, but Mary was so sort of lost—that way—we'd done some talking about it, and she came to church with me sometimes. And that's another thing I just can't—because we'd talked about that too, and I remember her saying she couldn't imagine wanting to kill yourself, but—" Cecilia groped for her handkerchief. "But she wrote me *everything*, and some of what she said about this fellow I didn't like the sound of, and I wrote her back and told her to be careful, but about three months ago—" She stopped, looking ashamed and embarrassed.

"Miss Dawson," said Higgins, "we know she was pregnant."

"Oh, it was *awful*. She wrote me," whispered Cecilia. "But you mustn't think she— She was good. She was just such an innocent, even when she'd worked around a little, like me. She—she was the kind that'd have been just innocent and *sweet* if she'd lived to be ninety!" A sob shook her and she groped for the rosary beside her. "*Innocent*—saying of course when he knew they'd get married— I'd believe that when I saw it! And then she wrote—"

"Excuse me, this man—Fletcher—did he work in Sacramento?"

Cecilia shook her head, found her handkerchief again and blew her nose. "No, he's a salesman, he works for Sanborn Manufacturing, they make a lot of farm equipment and he travels all over the state, Mary said. And he's older than Mary—about thirty-five, she said, which I didn't like the sound of—well, you know. And—"

Landers' pulse jumped a little. A traveling man. "You're sure of that?"

Cecilia nodded. "And I didn't believe it when she wrote and said they were going to be married. It sounded as if he'd been stringing her along. And she didn't know his home address, just that he lives in L.A., she asked me to look in the phone book so she could write him. She didn't know when he'd be in Sacramento again, this was j-just after Christmas, and I looked, but he isn't listed. I even called the company, but they wouldn't tell me anything. And so I thought maybe he'd even given her a wrong name—no caution at all, Mary's so friendly and innocent—and then out of the blue I got this letter about ten days ago, and she said they're going to be married! He didn't get up to Sacramento until just the day before she wrote me, so she could tell him, and right away he said, Why, sure they'd be married. And she was so excited and happy about it—even if—you know—the baby'd come only about five months after— And I thought then, well, maybe it was all right and the fellow was all right. Mary so sweet and—"

"Do you know what the arrangements were?" asked Landers.

She nodded, blowing her nose again. "Mary was coming down on the Tuesday-night bus, and he told her to go to that hotel. And he'd come pick her up, and they'd drive over to Vegas that night and be married, so there wouldn't be a waiting period. Well, she called me on Wednesday afternoon where I work—just a couple of minutes, to say she'd got in. The bus had engine trouble, it was late. And she'd called him at a number he gave her and he'd said he'd come get her that evening. She sounded so *happy*— And naturally I didn't try to contact her afterward because she'd said they'd stay over in Vegas the weekend and then come back to that hotel because this Fletcher'd just had a room somewhere here and gave that up and they'd stay at the hotel until they found a place of their own. So I knew she'd be back there today, and probably he'd be at work, and I did want to see her, hear all about it and make sure it *was* all right, and I asked the boss for an hour off—I guess I was still a little worried. And when that clerk s-said—! Just can't take it in. *Mary*. It must be he backed out at the last minute and she just— She must have felt so scared and alone, but I can understand it, she knew *I'd* have stood by her and helped her through it!" Cecilia looked at them piteously. "Please, h-how did she d-do it? She didn't *hang—*"

"She'd taken a lot of sleeping pills, Miss Dawson," said Landers. "An overdose. Was she in the habit of using them? You'd know?"

"Sleeping pills— Well, of course not! *Mary?* Of course not— How'd she *get* them?"

Higgins looked at Landers. "You may have hit a bigger jackpot than you think."

"I thought all along there was something fishy about it," said Landers. "Now we know she'd been working a regular job, where's her Social Security card? She probably had a little savings account too, and— Miss Dawson?"

"Do you mean she d-didn't— That—that man—! Oh! Oh, you've got to— Oh, Mary darling!—" And Cecilia dissolved into tears again.

A block away from the court Landers slammed on the brakes and swerved into a section of red-painted curb. "Suddenly occurs to me, if we get on this fast— It's a quarter of six. Time to get hold of some information where he works, if we're lucky."

He dived into the drugstore on the corner, scrabbling for change in his pocket, and leafed over the phone book, found Sanborn Manufacturing out in Whittier. It was evidently a big outfit, and he got shunted around some even in the personnel office, but finally at just on six o'clock he got hold of a Mr. Forester, who was cooperative. Puzzled, but cooperative.

When he came back to the car and slid under the wheel he asked, "You feel like doing a little overtime on this?"

"After hearing about Mary, I guess I do," said Higgins. "What did you get on Fletcher?"

"The rest of the story, probably," said Landers, shoving the "drive" button and glancing over his shoulder at the oncoming traffic. "The old sad story, but then there's nothing new about human nature either. Fletcher's worked for them for thirteen years—clean record with the company. Makes a good salary, call it twelve, thirteen thousand a year. He's married, has two kids, ten and seven."

"Oh, yes," said Higgins. "So he goes around playing on the side, only this girl knows his right name and where he works—probably different from the usual girls he played with, according to Cecilia—and he's afraid she'll come and make a stink around his nice clean record. And with his wife. Little innocent Mary. So he cons her into coming down here—"

"It's easy to read," said Landers wryly. "But not much evidence. She didn't have access to sleeping pills, we can probably show that. Does his wife take them maybe? Or does he? Lab can tell us the brand or maker. But all her identification taken—that's clear, he could figure, such an ordinary name, we'd never trace her back. Figured maybe we wouldn't try very hard—obvious suicide."

"He doesn't know us," said Higgins.

"No. He gives her a number to call—Cecilia said that—let him know her room number. Comes up with a bottle of wine or something, must celebrate their elopement over to Vegas, and she's all starry-eyed—dear Harvey making an honest woman of her—"

"And then when she passes out he undresses her, washes out the glass with the traces of wine or whatever, dissolves a little more sleeping stuff in it in plain water, gets her prints on the glass, takes the second glass away with him—or maybe, all romantic, they were just using one. Not too bad an effort, Tom. Quite slick, in fact. And we can say that, but how about pinning it on him?"

"Why and how did he take her identification," said Landers, "if she was alive and well when he left? How'll he explain that?"

"He'll say he never was there. Called her on the phone—or—no—he told her when she called him there was nothing doing, after all. So she—"

"And all the coming and going in that hotel—but we might get a break, somebody might remember seeing him. And I kind of think," said Landers in grim satisfaction, "that Miss Cecilia Dawson is going to be our Harvey's nemesis. And Mary's letters, which she'd kept." He patted his pocket; Cecilia had parted with them reluctantly. "Such nice chatty long letters." Suddenly he laughed without much humor. "Harvey didn't know about Cecilia, the bosom friend right in his own home town, and we can guess why. Little Mary, faithfully believing in the old advice to the lovelorn—listen to the boy friend, don't monopolize the conversation—so Harvey never heard about best-friend Cecilia."

Higgins smiled. "Could be. So we're heading?"

"For Harvey. He's at home now—not on the road, that is. South Pasadena."

Even in the absence of the McLaughlins, the Celtic Hotel seemed to generate crises. Mendoza, Hackett and Grace had walked into the middle of one. Evidently Mrs. Binny had come right down like a conscientious relative, unlikable though the task was, to take her sister away. Well, the afternoon editions had had some headlines about the McLaughlins and the bodies in the attic, which she'd probably seen after Mendoza and Grace had seen her. And Miss Manning was being obdurate.

They walked in on a king-size argument between the two of them, with Mrs. Rialto vainly trying to act as peacemaker.

"I'm quite comfortable here now, Eve."

"But it's impossible, you can't stay here alone—this place—don't be silly, Vera, you're coming with me at—"

"Now, my dears, let's all be sensible and discuss it quietly—"

Matters were not helped toward sensible discussion by the invisible presence of Mrs. Lightfoot upstairs, who suddenly and cacophonically burst into hideous song, unfortunately all too audible:

"Away, awa-hay! My heart's on fi-hire;
I burn this ba-hase decep-shun to repay!
This very ni-hight my vengeance di-i-i-ire
Shall guh-lut itself in GORE—"

"Er—Mrs. Rialto," said Mendoza. She cast him a helplessly humorous glance and betook herself upstairs. Presently the cacophony died an abrupt death.

But for a while they didn't get anywhere. "You took a photograph out of that book, Miss Manning. Did—"

"Book? I'm afraid I don't know what you mean." She was demure, adjusting her scarves. "All you tiresome people interrupting my letter writing."

"Listen, Miss Manning. Both Sergeant Higgins and Detective Grace can swear that there were only the three of you in Henry's room when the book was laid on that table. I doubt very much whether either Oscar or Henry tampered with it. You wanted the picture of the foxglove plant, to be able to identify it. Wasn't that it?" She'd been in the lobby when Grace had gone back for the book, but she'd had plenty of opportunity to extract the plate, Grace had said—Oscar and Henry arguing, taking no notice. "You'd heard me say what poison Eliza had had, and so—"

"For goodness' sake!" said Mrs. Binny faintly. "You aren't saying—she's *poisoned* somebody? She's never been—Vera? Oh, no, it isn't—"

"It's so important," murmured Miss Manning with a faraway look, "our poor boys at the front. *Somewhere in France.* They do so look forward to letters from home."

"Miss Manning, if you—"

"We've still got a search warrant, Lieutenant," said Grace mildly.

And so they had. And the very hell of it was, reflected Mendoza, if this hunch was so—and when he considered it, he really couldn't see Oscar or Henry planning to slip Jane the poison (however unlethal) on the same night they had a good many hours' work ahead of them getting all the coffins back home in their peaceful little fourth-floor mausoleum—the hell of it was that this said something rather discouraging. It said that Vera Manning, if she'd been the one to slip the oleander concoction into Jane's tea, had most definitely *not* been the X who had somehow induced Eliza McCann to swallow the very-much-lethal foxglove concentrate. For if she had, she'd scarcely have had any need for the photograph of the foxglove, to hunt more of it.

Miss Manning giggled and simpered at them. Mendoza nodded at Grace and Hackett, who departed to search her room. "Really, Eve, why you have to come bothering me now—I expect Oscar or someone will be home soon, and—"

"Really, my dear Vera, I am *responsible* and you—"

Presently Grace and Hackett came back with the photograph lifted out of the book Dr. Bainbridge had got at the library. Untidily torn out. Probably in her large buckled bag when they had searched the place on Sunday . . . Come to remember, she'd been out somewhere then.

Mrs. Binny said, "Oh, my God. You don't mean—"

"So what about it, Miss Manning?" said Mendoza. She gave him an unexpectedly shrewd look; she giggled again and smoothed her scarves with a long-clawed, veined old hand.

"Someone giving Ellie poison," she said. "Very queer. I can't think who would want to do that. She was patient with me. About the cooking. I wasn't brought up to it, but I *tried*. And you did say—well, Jane was so tiresome. Especially after Ellie was gone. Always interrupting me. And I just thought how much more restful if she wasn't there. To interrupt me." She looked at Mendoza with uncanny directness. "I don't suppose, if I tell you, Eve could take me away somewhere? You'd take me somewhere else. You think I'm crazy. But I suppose they'd be kind. Wherever. And everyone's gone away here. Even Gertrude." Suddenly she looked bewildered and lost. "And Eve isn't really kind, you know. She thinks I'm crazy too. Perhaps I am—I don't really know. It seems such a long time I've had to wait for Albert. To have our own little home and—and babies of our own."

"Miss Manning—" She should have been a ludicrous, nearly obscene figure there, the old scrawny hennaed woman in her tattered clothes; she was only pathetic.

"*My God!*" said Mrs. Binny in a thin scream. "No—the *disgrace*—the newspapers—"

"And Ellie's gone, she always told me what to do. But Jane was *so* tiresome, always calling for something, and I just thought— But I couldn't find any. Anything that looked like the picture. So I looked in Ellie's room —that was on Sunday, I think—she had a lot of books—no, it was Saturday night—"

No seal on that door, of course.

"—and I found one about gardening, and it said that oleander is poisonous, and I did know that when I saw it—such pretty flowers, you know."

"Where did you get it, Miss Manning?" asked Mendoza.

Her pale eyes moved to him. "Oh, that nice park. About the only place nearby. Mr. Caradoccio has an oleander bush in his back yard—a nice man—but I was afraid he'd think it was *rather* queer if he saw me— And I'm quite accustomed to walking, of course. As Ellie did. Miles, sometimes. But that nice park's only about sixteen blocks away—"

My God. Elysian Park, of course. Where the Police Academy was.

"*Vera!*" Mrs. Binny leaned against the wall and shut her eyes.

Miss Manning looked around the empty, bare, dusty lobby. Suddenly she shivered a little. "Everything's changed here. Since Ellie's gone.

Hasn't it? I'll have to go somewhere else. But *not* where *Eve* wants to send me. She's not kind. And I don't *feel* as if I'm crazy, the way Eve says, but it's been such a long time to wait for Albert, and I'm tired." Her gaze came back to Mendoza. "They're all gone. Jane too. She was so annoying, but I suppose I shouldn't have poisoned her. Only I'm very tired now."

SIXTEEN

"We seem," said Detective Grace, "to be kind of decimating the population of this hotel." He looked at its dark ramshackle bulk looming over them.

Mendoza said he had noticed it. There had, of course, been quite a little scene, what with Mrs. Binny moaning about the disgrace and Miss Manning suddenly agitated to hysterics at being expected to leave without every last piece of her belongings—they hadn't a warrant, of course—and Mrs. Rialto had been invaluable, soothing her down, offering to help pack a case: "They'll send all the rest of your things on, I'll see to it personally, dear Miss Manning."

"But all my stationery—my *pen*—my—*where are they taking me?*"

"Now, dear, just a few minutes ago you were quite ready to go with the nice policemen—"

They sent for a squad car and a couple of policewomen in the end, and Mrs. Binny, apparently washing her hands of the whole situation, got into a newish Buick down the block and drove away. Mendoza and Grace were awaiting the policewomen; Hackett was keeping an eye on the bag-packing. Mendoza flicked ash from his cigarette, looking after the Buick. "So, a little money," he said. "She's been getting by very cheap on dear Vera all these years. Camarillo'll come down on her for a bit more."

"I expect," agreed Grace, "that's where Vera'll end up all right."

"Stash her in the psychiatric ward of the General tonight, ship her up there for examination tomorrow. Have to be an indictment and a hearing, but that's where she'll spend the rest of her days, probably. And probably settle down happily enough, as long as they let her go on writing letters to Albert. But you know, Jase—"

"Oh, yes, I had seen that too," said Grace. "She wasn't the one who got the poison into Eliza. Not when she wanted the picture of the foxglove. That just put it in her mind. This is a kind of confused case, isn't it?"

"Understatement. The damnedest thing I've come across—or almost—since I've been in Homicide," said Mendoza.

The policewomen arrived. The squad car arrived with two men. Among them they got Miss Manning, with her little bag, soothed down and into the squad car. Mrs. Rialto was going along. "Just to see her safely tucked in," she said to Mendoza breezily. "Poor thing. Dear me, who would have dreamed all this would happen? These coffins. Well, one never does know about people, does one? Oh, I can't say it really troubles me—the idea of it —but then I'm not at all superstitious. And, after all, they're gone now."

"You'll all have to leave now," said Mendoza, regarding her a little curiously.

"Oh, I don't know. It's been a haven, my dear man, a positive haven for all these little people. Dear Mrs. Lightfoot, living on such a pittance—and poor dear Bobby—and Percy, of course, though he's only here to sleep. *And* little Myra. Where should we all go, to live as cheaply? I could manage the place for Oscar, you know. I've been thinking I should go to see him and offer the proposition. Collect the rents for him. Well, we shall see. But this poor creature—I must reassure her as best as I can until she's—" She gave Mendoza a cheery smile and popped her plump person into the squad car beside Miss Manning and one of the policewomen. "Now, dear, you just relax and let us take care of you—"

"I'd rather go with you than Eve, Myra."

"That's right, dear." The door slammed and the squad car took off.

"Well, just fancy that," murmured Grace. "Collection of zanies still in residence, and what'd you want to bet attracting more of the same kind? I don't suppose Oscar and Henry'll draw much, it's only a misdemeanor, funnily enough."

"Six to nine months, I'd guess," said Hackett, coming up. "And I also guess we don't get dinner for a while."

There was, of course, a lot of paper work to do and routine to get busy at. They put in a request for a warrant and typed up the reports for the justice to sign.

By that time Sergeant Farrell had gone home and Sergeant Thoms had taken his place and Galeano and Schenke, the night-duty men, had come in. At ten minutes past seven Mendoza was just walking out of the office, leaving the last of the reports to Hackett—Grace had already gone home— when Landers and Higgins came in with a man between them. He was a medium-sized, good-looking man about thirty-five, well dressed, and he looked very nervous and frightened.

"Something?" said Mendoza.

"Something." Landers let Higgins take the man into an interrogation room and told Mendoza all about Harvey Fletcher. "I think we've figured it out pretty well. It was murder, all right—put it all together. For one thing, why bring her down here just to tell her it was no go? And I don't think we'll have to lean on him much, the way he's reacted. We walked in just as they were sitting down to dinner." Landers grimaced. "Pretty wife, two nice kids. They were just bewildered. His record says good husband and father. But he never thought anybody could connect him to Mary Brown, and now that we have he can probably see for himself we can connect him up tight."

"Yes, and you know," said Mendoza, "that was a slick little job, Tom. Near as nothing we put it down as suicide. It makes me wonder if it's the first time Mr. Fletcher's stepped off the straight and narrow."

"Well, I hadn't got that far. Could be, I suppose—somewhere," said Landers, "where they don't keep quite such smart bloodhounds." And he smiled.

Mendoza stayed to sit in on the questioning of Fletcher—who just shook his head when punctiliously told he could have an attorney present. For a little while Fletcher attempted to bluster: never knew the girl, didn't know anything about all this, ask his company what a good record he had, ask his wife, and so on. "And how many pretty girls along your sales route, Mr. Fletcher?" asked Higgins.

"Did you ever get a girl in trouble before, Mr. Fletcher?" asked Landers.

"When did you decide to get rid of Mary permanently, Mr. Fletcher?"

"Where'd you get the sleeping pills? Were they your wife's? Your own?"

"You've got this all wrong! I never *knew*—I don't know anything—"

"Mr. Fletcher," said Landers coldly, "you didn't know it, but Mary had a girl friend down here. A Miss Cecilia Dawson. And Mary wrote her all about everything, Mr. Fletcher. What you promised her about going over to Vegas and so on. About coming down here and going to that hotel. You know that hotel, don't you, Mr. Fletcher? You know a lot of other traveling men, and know that there's always coming and going in that hotel, and at least two public entrances. Pick the nice quiet time, say after nine in the evening, you could slip in there without anybody noticing you— which is just what you did. Why should you lure Mary all the way down here just to tell her you were going to back out of the deal? Just, even, to explain that you already had a wife and family, couldn't marry her? You could have told her that in Sacramento, Mr. Fletcher. You had a reason for it. Why did you take away all her identification? She must have had a Social Security card at least."

"I—"

"You had a dandy reason, Mr. Fletcher. We've got all Mary's letters to Cecilia, from about six months ago—all she wrote about you. It was just your little mistake to get mixed up with a nice girl for a change. A girl like Mary—who couldn't be bought off. She could have made trouble for you, ruined that nice clean reputation you've got—at home. Blackmail wouldn't have occurred to her, but she could have gone to your company, to your wife—a nice honest girl, Mary. An innocent. So you had to get rid of her permanently."

"I—look, I don't know—" But Fletcher was curiously gray. He seemed to decrease in size as they watched him, as if he was shrinking inside his clothes. It was an effect the older of them had seen before: the confident, successful man, with the good life made, suddenly caught up with and exposed. He didn't believe it yet, but he was starting to. He blinked up at Landers, and there was a funny little sick smile on his mouth, and he said, "Letters—"

"You're tied in but very tight, Mr. Fletcher," said Higgins. "What'd you take up to her room to celebrate your elopement with? Champagne?"

"Where'd you get the sleeping pills?"

"Tell your wife you were going out on business that night—last Wednesday night?"

"What did you do with her identification? Such a common name—you didn't think we'd ever trace her back. We had a fluke piece of luck there, but in time we would have, you know."

"How long did she take to pass out, Mr. Fletcher? Innocent, friendly little Mary who loved you and wanted a home and a family."

Fletcher looked up at them all and wet his lips. No light glaring in his face, not a finger laid on him, and they'd offered him cigarettes, water. He shook his head dumbly. It wasn't happening to him. Good citizen Fletcher, on the surface—good job, nice house and family, successful man. Like most of that kind, he didn't know much about cops, hadn't had much contact with cops. He looked at them standing around him in a loose circle—the roughhewn, hefty Higgins, the only one you might pick out at a glance as a cop; Mendoza, dapper, slender, mustached, cold-eyed; youthful Landers with his open boyish face and slim gangling height;

stocky, dark Galeano, blue-chinned; sandy little Schenke, who'd just slipped in at five-nine—and he just shook his head. He'd got in a bind, after the years of his furtive playing around away from home; and in a little panic at the threat of being exposed, of losing all of what, probably, he genuinely valued, he'd done a sly sneaking little crime, and thus inevitably showed himself a sly sneaking little man.

"Did you kiss her before you spiked the drink, Mr. Fletcher? She'd have been happy to see you—called you darling, didn't she? Where'd you get the pills, Mr. Fletcher? Did—"

"Stop it," he said. "Stop it." There was nothing in his voice; his voice was dead. "I had an old prescription. It was ordinary stuff. A lot of it around. Yes, she called me darling. She was happy. She didn't even know what was happening. But I knew. She just said she felt—sleepy—and she'd sleep in the car—going over to Vegas—because she wanted to be awake for her own wedding. I never thought there'd be anything—anything at all—to connect to me. How could there be? How many Mary Browns are there? I—"

"Do you want to make a statement, Mr. Fletcher? You have the right to have an attorney present before you do so or answer questions under oath," said Mendoza formally.

Fletcher didn't seem to hear him. "How should I know about this—this other girl? Mary never mentioned her. Women. Women," he said tiredly. "Innocent, all right. I should have steered clear of *that*. One like that. For God's sake. *Me*. I didn't see any way anybody could ever connect—"

"Mr. Fletcher. Do you want to call an attorney?" All the new laws, the damned laws hamstringing them at every turn: a signed confession wouldn't be usable unless Fletcher's lawyer was there at the time.

"I didn't know—how could I know? *Women*," said Fletcher. He sounded very tired. All of a sudden he looked ten years older.

Harvey Fletcher wouldn't, reflected Mendoza, have to do any more worrying about women from here on in.

With persuasion he gave them a lawyer's name. They called him. Mendoza, Higgins and Hackett went home, leaving the rest of the routine to the legitimate night men and Landers. They'd have a busy time, listening to the confession, possibly arguing with the lawyer, getting the confession typed and signed and witnessed.

At least that was one tied up and in the bag.

Over a belated dinner Mendoza told Alison about it. "And I couldn't count how many times I've met Fletcher before. And Mary. What the hell am I doing down there dealing with all the dirt and violence and evil?"

Alison surveyed him benignly, and when she'd married Luis Rodolfo Vicente Mendoza a little over three years ago she'd thought she knew him pretty well, but she knew him even better now, and she said, "I only know what John Lockhart says, sheep dog with the built-in herding instinct. Any good cop. You wouldn't know what to do with yourself. ¡Por supuesto que no!"

"Por de pronto," said Mendoza, holding out his cup for more coffee, "we're still stymied on the McCann woman. What a business." He brought her up to date on that. "You can see, obvio, it wasn't Manning who accounted for Eliza. But who did, and how, and why?"

"Mmh," said Alison. "Where'd she find the oleander—Manning?"

Mendoza looked annoyed. "Up in Elysian Park. Where—" He grunted and swore as Sheba landed on his shoulder without warning.

"She did it to the Helms Bakery driver this morning. He dropped two loaves of bread and a box of coffeecake and said she was a public menace," said Alison. "Where the Police Academy is. Yes. About the only area where there's much greenery down there. Had you thought, Luis, that maybe the foxglove came from there too?"

Mendoza looked at her. Sheba walked down him, stepped onto the table and stuck her black nose into the cream pitcher. After finding it empty, she uttered a low curse and investigated the sugar bowl. "Some people," said Alison, "would be horrified, I suppose. Unhygienic. I just thought, you know—"

"¡Bastante!" said Mendoza. "So do I, belatedly. It just could be. Send somebody to poke around and see if there is any growing there. But it doesn't tell us who. Or why. Or how."

"It was just a thought," said Alison.

At nine o'clock on Tuesday morning Sergeant Farrell thrust his head in the door of the sergeants' room and said somebody wanted to talk to Higgins. Higgins picked up the outside phone, still reading over the confession they'd got out of Fletcher last night, and said, "Sergeant Higgins."

"Oh, Sergeant, this is Clark. Alfred Clark. About the Y-camp business. Look, I saw Bud Wilson last night, and I told him what you said, and we talked it over. We do have a program to get kids to camp at a fairly low rate, you know. Do you think your—uh—friend's widow could afford twenty a week?"

"Well, I don't know," said Higgins doubtfully. "That's—I do appreciate your trying to help me out, Mr. Clark. But—"

"Not at all. Well, I suppose you could tell her it was less. If you—"

Higgins liked Mr. Alfred Clark because he didn't sound amused. He recognized it as a real problem. "Yes, if she didn't investigate herself," he said thoughtfully. "But, look, Mr. Clark. I could tell her I'd run into this Mr. Wilson casually. He'd be the man she'd see about it? He's attached to the Hollywood Y, you said? And if she did, he could tell her—say about a special rate for fatherless boys? That sounds sort of reasonable, I mean I know the Y does a lot of good work with—"

"Sure," said Clark. "I'll give you his number, you can call him."

"I think she'd go for ten bucks a week—about as low as would sound plausible," said Higgins. "And, of course, it'll be a while yet, we can encourage him to save up his own money for it too. He cuts the neighbors' lawns for them."

"We've got a very nice place over on Catalina Island. Transportation included. The boys have to furnish their own bedding and specified clothing—sneakers and jeans and a certain number of shirts and so on—and there's a dollar laundry charge. Open July first through August twentieth."

"Well, I think that'd be fine," said Higgins. "Let me have Wilson's number . . . Thanks. I do appreciate this, Mr. Clark."

"Not at all," said Clark in a friendly tone. "Good Samaritan, you."

"That's me," said Higgins. "Thanks a lot." He put the phone down and sighed. He really didn't know why this had to happen to him. Plodding bachelor George Higgins, doing O.K. with the females now and then, and also interested in the kids, with the Big Brother clubs and so on. Mary Dwyer. And Bert's kids. But mostly Mary, and an independent woman she certainly was, and if she ever found out—!

Well, anyway, he'd talk to Wilson. Get Stevie to summer camp. Tell Mary, all casual, he'd just happened to run into this fellow and they'd got talking and he'd heard about the special rate for fatherless boys and—

He just hoped it would work. After the piano-teacher bit—so dangerously similar. But a detective did run into all sorts of people in the daily routine, after all.

He sighed again and went back to the paper work on Fletcher.

They had by then checked out, through the D.M.V., some forty plate numbers, which Higgins and Glasser had dreamed up, that might have been hastily misread JGN-790. Hunting (needle in a haystack, with the deadly-efficient routine) the car that had killed Patrolman Harry Cohen at Seventh and Broadway last Wednesday. All those cars, located, had been checked on: none of them could have been the one driven by the hit-run driver. The D.M.V. was now checking out some twenty more plate numbers, but the chances were looking slim.

The wild idea that it had been a deliberate kill looked very unlikely too; they had looked at Patrolman Harry Cohen and his record, and there just wasn't anything to suggest that. Quiet family man: forty-nine, been on the force twenty-three years, one married son, one married daughter. Took a drink occasionally but usually at home, usually only one. Happily married. Attended Temple Zion regularly. Not an ambitious man—never got beyond patrolman—but a good man, a reliable man. Seldom off sick. And in the couple of weeks preceding his death he hadn't been known to have had any disagreements with anybody, any quarrels, any trouble. Wife all broken up. Son and daughter ditto. Big attendance at the funeral.

That idea was wild, all right. A hit-run car—driver drunk or hopped up or just a careless, bad driver—out of control; it might look deliberate. In that fairly narrow street. That was all.

But the D.M.V. was still checking. Something might turn up.

Higgins was looking over what the D.M.V. had sent in most recently when Detective Grace wandered in about ten o'clock, sat down at the next desk and lit a cigarette. "At least," he said, "I've got Virginia's birthday present. Nice?" He took a little box out of a paper bag, opened it and showed it to Higgins. It was a lapel watch, a stylized gold cat with its tail arched and wound neatly round a small gold watch. "She likes cats. Think she'll like it."

"Nice," said Higgins, and thought about his modest bank account and how he'd like to buy presents for Mary. "She'll like it."

"I just cannot figure any leads," said Grace, putting the watch away in its box. "That crazy McCann thing. I've been back asking questions around the store. It adds up to nothing. Nobody knew much about her—even the oldest tenants. She had told a couple more of them she was going to raise the rent in April—people living in the apartments upstairs, and the druggist at the corner. But—"

Sergeant Farrell looked in. "Call in from the sheriff's boys, George."

"Oh," said Higgins, and picked up the outside phone. "Sergeant Higgins."

"Deputy Webster speaking," said a crisp no-nonsense voice. "We're holding a man here—one Carlos García—sheriff's station in West Hollywood. Picked up at four A.M., with two other men, attempting to break in private property on the Strip." That was county territory and under the sheriff's jurisdiction. "García has volunteered some information you might be interested in, Sergeant. About that hit-and-run accident where a patrol-man was killed downtown."

"Oh, *yes?*" said Higgins. "What does he say? Any definite—"

"He says he knows who did it," said the deputy. "One Pedro Hernandez. An erstwhile pal of his, only they had a little argument over a game of Spanish monte and García's feeling mean about getting picked up." The deputy's tone was dry.

"They will do it," said Higgins. "Interesting." He scribbled notes. "Thanks very much. You got an address?"

"He says you'll find him in your records. Armed assault and rape. Hernandez isn't long out of Chino. And he says," said the deputy even more dryly, "Hernandez planned on doing it. Getting that patrolman of yours. He told García he was going to do it. Going to get the sonovabitch. He's got an old car about ready to be junked."

"For God's sake," said Higgins. "For—why? I don't—"

"For a reason," said Deputy Webster. He sounded a little tired. "Your patrolman down there had given him a couple of tickets just in the last week or so. Speeding and an illegal left turn. Just coincidence it was the same patrolman, but evidently Hernandez didn't think so. García was with him one of the times."

"For God's *sake!*" said Higgins.

SEVENTEEN

The sheriff's deputy brought García down while Higgins and Grace went out to Hernandez' address on Kohler to see if he was home. He was: he had a hang-over and was feeling mean, but even one like Hernandez knew better than to tangle with Higgins, and he just turned sullen. They brought him back to Headquarters after he told them, with persuasion, where to find the car.

Which, it turned out, they'd have caught up to eventually: its plate number was ION-770, which was one of those Higgins had sent to the D.M.V. as a possible; they hadn't got round to it yet. The car was registered to Rafael Hernandez, who turned out to be Pedro's uncle—who also had a pedigree.

They questioned García and Hernandez separately, with the sheriff's man looking on. They got a statement from García right away; how he'd heard Hernandez saying he was "going to get that cop" and boasting about it afterward. He'd been with Hernandez in the car when Cohen gave him the illegal-turn ticket. So they went to work on Hernandez, and it was uphill work. He was the typical punk—the smart-aleck answers, the childish sullen evasions—the kind any cop's fist ached for; but you couldn't do things that way, great as the temptation was. This worthless punk, no good to anybody including himself, still had the rights as a citizen.

It was a little exercise in futility, because—they hoped—the lab would come up with something on the car. Especially since they did get it out of Hernandez that the car hadn't been driven since last Wednesday, chiefly because neither he nor his uncle had had any spare money for gas.

"Come on, punk," prodded Higgins, "you know we've got you dead to rights. You drove that car that killed Cohen. There'll be traces on it. You might as well—"

"Ah, go t' hell," said Hernandez.

"Where were you last Wednesday morning at eleven o'clock, Pedro?" asked Hackett.

"No business o' yours. Where were you, bloodhound?"

"¡Hombrate!" said Mendoza coldly. "Have you ever heard the old proverb, punk—¿Palabra suelta no tiene vuelta? Careless talk you can't take back. You said this and that to your pal Carlos García."

Hernandez told them what García was.

The car had been towed into the garage, and the lab boys had got busy with it right away. It was lucky the Hernandezes had been using their money for *vino* instead of gas; the lab boys picked up some blood traces from the front bumper and the right front tire and a tiny bit of brain tissue from the bottom of the radiator pan. They sent an informal report up about noon, and Mendoza showed it to Hernandez.

"Have you got the brains to understand that, Pedro? They'll type the blood and it'll match Cohen's."

"Go t' hell," said Hernandez sullenly.

And God knew they'd all met the Hernandezes before: there were too many of them around in any big city, wearing a lot of different names and faces, but once in a while it was brought home, even to the old-pro cops, just how dirty the dirt at the bottom of things was. Patrolman Harry Cohen, the good reliable man, just because he'd written a couple of traffic tickets for the punk. The no-good punk who couldn't think five minutes ahead, who wasn't remotely capable of any emphatic feeling for any other human being—or he wouldn't be a punk.

"All right, up," said Hackett. "Take him down to the jail, Tom, hah? We'll see you later, Pedro."

"You can' hold me! I done nothin'—goddamn cops—"

"We can hold you until the warrant comes through," said Hackett, "to make it nice and legal." They watched Landers tow him out.

"That kind," said Higgins, unconsciously balling his fists. "That kind. God."

"*Lo que no se puede remediar, se ha de aguantar,*" said Mendoza. "What can't be cured." He looked at his watch. "Let's go have lunch."

But he was silent on the way out of the room. Farrell caught them at the door and said Glasser had just finished the paper work on that latest suicide when a new call had come in: old woman found apparently beaten to death in an apartment over an Alpine. Her niece had walked in and found her. Glasser and Piggott had gone out on it. Probably another break-in: thief hopped up or just plain mean.

"Yes," said Mendoza. "Another one. All right, Rory, I'll see them when they come in." He took his hat off the rack and looked at it pensively. "Jungle gets a little more dangerous every day. And the damn laws blunting the edges of our machetes . . . I might even buy us all drinks to celebrate picking up Pedro." But his smile was wry.

And, settled at a table at Federico's, the four of them, Grace said to the waiter, "You tell Joe to mix me a Gloom Chaser. Appropriate. Any of you like to try one with me?"

"What's in it?" asked Hackett apprehensively.

"Grand Marnier, curaçao, lemon juice and grenadine."

"No, thanks," said Hackett. "Fattening, for one thing. I was up two pounds this morning. Scotch and water."

Higgins ordered absently. "But what the hell *is* the answer?" he asked suddenly. "That kind? Just because people are poor, live in what we call slums—and it's all damn relative, most people down here are living a hell of a lot better than the average Czech or Pole or—they aren't criminals. Majority of them law-abiding citizens. Hell, Luis, you grew up down here. But the punks—the damn smart-aleck, worthless punks—"

"There was a time," said Grace thoughtfully, "when I did believe, all idealistic, that the answer was education. But after I got past my twenty-first birthday—I was in college then—it sort of came to me that some people you just can't educate. The ones without many brains."

"But then there's Bobby," said Mendoza. "The newsboy."

"Oh, yes," said Grace, "that does enter in too, doesn't it? Maybe brains haven't really got much to do with the whole thing. Maybe you can have the highest I.Q. there could be and still be the biggest bastard walking on two legs—if you don't have what they call empathy for other people. And I don't think that's a thing anybody can ever learn out of a book."

"There are answers," said Hackett, "if you want to swallow them. The bad homes, the bad parents, the poverty, the— What the hell does it add up to? *Nada.* According to all the psychiatric theories, going by that, Luis here ought to've ended up a fag—brought up tied to a woman's apron strings—and earning his living as a pro cardsharp."

Mendoza grinned. "What it adds up to, my Arturo, is something the head-doctors and the earnest social workers never in this God's world will admit, and that is that people come all sorts. Forever. And you just can't generalize about any of them."

The drinks came. Grace sampled the Gloom Chaser and grimaced. "I don't know that that's a good name for it. A bit sweet. You are so right, Lieutenant. Why, I can think of a lot of colored folk *I* wouldn't want to live next door to. But human nature's been with us a good long time, why're we sitting around moaning about it?"

"Cohen," said Higgins, snapping his lighter. "I guess." He sighed, thinking back to that hot day last September and Bert Dwyer dead in a pool of blood on the marble floor of that bank lobby.

"Well, we've got the punk," said Mendoza more briskly, sipping rye. "Let's forget him, for God's sake, and concentrate on what we haven't got. This McCann thing—let's kick it around a little. Anybody have any ideas?"

"I had what I thought was an idea last night," said Hackett, "but on second thought I don't think it's worth much. The main problem is she had to have repeated doses of this stuff over a period of time—right? Well, after all, nobody seemed to know much about her habits in the store—and she was there a lot of the time. Call it eight-thirty to five six days a week. And, for all we know, she could have been a lone drinker. No, wait, I don't mean a lush. *That* would have shown up right away, sure. But she was sixty-five, she'd never had much of a life, and it could be she'd found the little glass or two of cheap wine gave her a lift—you know. And, likely enough, with her ideas on health and all that, she'd have died before letting anybody know. But somebody could have found out—by coincidence seen her buying a bottle at some market or somewhere out of her usual territory—and—"

"It's a little far out," said Mendoza, "but I suppose it *could* be."

"You can build it up. Take it for granted she'd have been ashamed of it, hidden it. So all right—she'd have kept the bottle stashed away in that back room somewhere—in a cupboard, likeliest. Maybe gone back once or twice a day for a little nip. And somebody—"

"I don't think so much of your brain storm, Art," said Mendoza. "For several reasons, but one irrefutable. She was a miser. She'd have grudged the money. Even for cheap *vino*. And we've got absolutely nothing that says she'd ever tasted anything alcoholic, for God's sake. I don't see it."

"Well, I said I didn't think it was such a hot idea," admitted Hackett. "But how the hell *did* anybody—over a period of time? I suppose it couldn't have been suicide after all? No, I know that's out."

"I'll go along with that," said Grace, finishing the Gloom Chaser. "Any real miser—even some necessities they grudge the money for, let alone the luxuries like strong drink. Um. *Stay me with flagons*, I don't think. And we know from the druggist on the corner she wasn't in the habit of buying Cokes or anything even in summer. More luxuries. So how *did*—"

Higgins said, "My God! My God, Luis, this one's really wild, but it just came to me. Don't anybody laugh. It *has* happened. Could the money have been poisoned—in the cash register? Paper money? If she had the habit of licking her finger when she counted it—a lot of people have. And—"

"*Caray*, George, you should be careful what you read. Are you growing an imagination?"

"Look, do any of you remember that case—somewhere in Europe—where the girl got poisoned with radium?" asked Higgins. "Rejected suitor had put it on the keys of her typewriter, she was a stenographer. The wild ones don't come along once in a blue moon, but they do now and *then*. You know as well as I do. And we know the McCann woman wasn't in the habit of eating or drinking between meals—which she had at the hotel except for lunch—and there she drank tap water—and—"

"Which inclines me to say," said Grace, "that whoever it was, she was getting it at the hotel. And I keep wondering just how lunatic that Manning female really is."

"Oh, yes," said Mendoza. "Oh, yes, there is that. I'm no expert, but she looks pretty genuine to me, just what she is on the surface. I really don't think she's enough on the beam to have figured out that double play—stealing the photograph out of the book to make it obvious that she didn't know what foxglove looks like. But we'll see what the head-doctors say."

"Well, aside from that, I've got no ideas," said Higgins. "It's the damnedest thing—"

"You gentlemen like to order now?" murmured the waiter.

When they got back to the office, Glasser and Piggott had just come in. They were looking unhappy. They had a lot of reports with them.

"Thing is it looked like a pro job," said Piggott. "Old apartment, flimsy lock, easy to open with the cardboard strip—you know—and so we went down to Robbery and Theft and saw Lieutenant Goldberg. See if he spotted something about the M.O. Because—"

"And did he?"

"Oh, brother," said Glasser gloomily. "They've had a regular crime wave down there—about a dozen-square-block area—the last three months. And it's pretty obviously the same guy. Fourteen break-ins altogether. Always women living alone—always between midnight and four A.M. Always a back door used. They got footprints at three places." It had been an unusually wet winter for a change, which Southern California had needed. "Nights it was raining enough so his shoes were wet. And the prints match. They've got pictures, now it's our little problem. Unusual shoe, looks like—narrow, size nine-triple-A, left heel run over toward the inside. So last night he kills somebody, so now we get it laid in our lap."

"Any violence before?" Mendoza sat down in his swivel chair and emptied the ash tray, brushed ashes off the desk.

"Four places the women woke up and he threatened them—one with a knife, the other three he slapped around a little. One of them—a young woman—he threatened to rape."

"Just threatened? So how do we know it *is* this same joker? Who got killed, by the way?"

"A Mrs. Dorothea Friend, widow, sixty-four, on pension, lived alone," said Piggott. "Well, it's kind of cut and dried. It wasn't raining last night, but she'd spilled some flour on the kitchen floor and we've got a partial print where he stepped in it. The same heelprint."

"Oh, really," said Mendoza. "He's got only one pair of shoes maybe? Needle in a haystack. But there are places to look."

"Well, the hell of *that* is," said Glasser, "that Lieutenant Goldberg's already looked. Just this one area, it says ten to one he lives somewhere close by. So all the shoe stores and shoe-repair places have been covered and nothing's showed. And there's no kind of a description of him—"

"Three of them, by the statements," said Piggott, "said he was a Negro, they were pretty sure. But of course it was dark. Who can say?"

"One of the tough ones," said Mendoza. Only the cops, the professionals, knew just how tough that anonymous kind could be: the kind you slogged out day by day, routine check by routine check, by sheer doggedness.

But eventually the footprint should lead somewhere.

"Let me look over the statements," he said. "I'll see if I can spot something."

Piggott handed over the sheaf. "Tune in the built-in radar, Lieutenant. We could use a hunch on this."

But, reading the statements, Mendoza had no hunch. A tiresome business, he thought. Another punk. Whatever his color or name or race, another no-good punk. The elementary cunning, picking out women living alone. The elementary brutality. And probably pulling the break-ins for peanuts in this part of the jungle.

He had no hunch about this punk. A little joke in Homicide—Mendoza and his crystal ball. Well, he got the nuances. He thought of what Hackett had said, smiling slightly. Raised by a woman and—what Hackett hadn't said, but knew—actively hating and fearing the only so-called father figure in his life: the old ogre on the hearth, his grandfather. Well, no pat answers to stock questions: people came all sorts. Given another inherited set of genes, maybe Luis Mendoza would have turned out a punk. Or, instead of joining the force at twenty-one, turned into a pro cardsharp.

He wondered if there was Anything managing things. Just now and then something happened that—

What he would like very damn well to have a hunch on, he thought, was this fantastic McCann thing. Of *all* the offbeat ones—

Foxglove, he thought.

Tabitha Thirkettle and her simples. But an ordinary, unshrewd, simple woman herself. And the way she'd passed out on hearing the news, she hadn't known about that will.

One of the others? Ida Mae Glidden? More of an eye to the main chance, that one. But Eliza, intending to hand over the will when— ¡*Válgame Dios!*—she felt herself sickening and knew her time was near (which reported statement certainly said the woman wasn't thinking logically)—and the will hidden in *Bartlett's Quotations*—

Caray, the McLaughlins. Well, Celts, he thought. The rugged individualists. Insofar as you could generalize at all—which, of course, you couldn't.

Coffin Corner. Oscar and Henry. My God—and the embalmed bodies. All the McLaughlins queer in some way. Obsessive?

Mendoza swiveled around and contemplated the contours of the Hollywood Hills eight miles away, clear in the unsmogged distance, and he had a sudden feeling that he'd just thought something important.

Obsessions.

What about them? Well, an obsession was a—a weakness of some sort. A blind spot? Or the obsession itself creating blindness to all else—

Oscar the undertaker and his labors of love.

Henry and his artistic embroidery.

Jane and her preoccupation with medicine.

Which Eliza had found so foolish. Had no patience with.

What had Eliza's obsession been? Money, *naturalmente*. But—

He stared at the line of hills without seeing them. Faint echoes of this and that came back to him. —*Even if she'd suddenly wanted to. Walked to the store, rain or shine—proper exercise— Even aspirin—* And even his own voice: *these "mens sana in corpore sano" fiends—*

And, a little more distinctly, Art today at lunch: *Take it for granted she'd have been ashamed of it—*

"¡*Vaya por Dios—media vuelta!*" he said to himself softly. "¿*Tal vez?* Now I wonder. I do just wonder."

The hunch. The funny little hunch—but if it was so, it fell into place. In a way. People. And God knew they did come all sorts; but there were types, and you could read them.

Only, even if it was so, what did it say?

What could it say?

The people around the store—*not* the Celtic Hotel. Who, for God's sake, and why? Wolf—

But it would be a step further on. A wider possibility.

And, he thought, he really should have been more on the ball and thought about this some time ago.

Especially considering what Marcia Hunt had said to Tabitha Thirkettle just before Tabitha fainted.

He stood up, put out his cigarette carefully, went out to the anteroom and took down his hat. He said absently to Sergeant Farrell, "Don't think I'll be gone long, Rory."

He went down to the lot and got into the Ferrari. And if it *was* so—the belated hunch (considering Eliza's character)—it was most likely, of course, that X was Tabitha Thirkettle—or, a bit less likely, Marcia Hunt or Ida Mae Glidden. The legatees. Only they hadn't (for pretty sure) known that.

It would have been a small joke. None of those three had really been fond of Eliza—or she of them. She just didn't know who else to leave it to. Away from the feckless family. He could see the small joke being shared. In secret.

But, funnily enough, he couldn't see Tabitha as X.

If this was so, it gave them a very probable M.O., at the least. And more questions to ask.

Talk about hunches, he thought. ¡*Que disparate!* As with any hunch, you examined it with the objective eye; it was just cold logic. Pure deduction. After twenty-odd years of dealing with human nature, you learned this and that.

He braked the Ferrari gently in front of Mrs. Thirkettle's neat little house on Turner Street. He pocketed the keys, went up the short walk to the porch, rang the bell. In thirty seconds the door opened and Mrs. Thirkettle fell back at the sight of him, one veined old hand to her mouth.

"*Oh—*"

"May I come in, Mrs. Thirkettle?" Mendoza smiled at her, taking off his hat. "Just a few more questions, if you don't mind."

She retreated before him into the neat clean little living room. And the other two were there—Ida Mae Glidden, brassy blonde, forthright, nononsense; Marcia Hunt, prim, self-effacing, dowdy.

"What do you—" Mrs. Thirkettle's voice was high and frightened.

"So you're back," said Mrs. Glidden flatly. "And I expect you're wondering what I'm doing here on a working day. Well, long as you're here, I don't see any reason to beat about the bush. Tabby, for goodness' sake, don't be silly. We ought to have told them right off. I said so all along. And the way you two've been carrying on— You've got nothing on your conscience—we know *that*, for heaven's sake, you couldn't any more poison anybody than fly—and what *I* say is we've got to tell them. Because if Eliza *was* poisoned some way, though the good Lord knows that don't sound possible—but if so, well, they've got to find out how. Tell the truth and shame the devil, like my grandmother used—"

"But they'll think—"

Marcia Hunt sniffed. *"I* said—"

"Mrs. Thirkettle," said Mendoza. "Just one question. It should really have occurred to me before. Mrs. McCann *had* asked you for one of your little remedies, hadn't she? In strict secrecy? Feeling as she did about any medication—and having said so much to everyone who knew her—she'd have been very reluctant about it, and a little ashamed—but she did ask you. For one of your—mmh—simples. Very much in secret. And you gave it to her—whatever it was—very much in secret. Only it was a little joke, wasn't it—the never-sick-a-day Eliza, the way she boasted about that, about never taking medicine—and you told Mrs. Hunt and Mrs. Glidden—privately—just as the little joke. Isn't that so?"

"There, you see," said Marcia thinly. "He knows—and if you *did* put anything in it, Tabitha—"

Mrs. Thirkettle burst into tears, fumbling blindly for her handkerchief. "I *never!* I—how could you *think* such a thing, Marcia? I *didn't*—Cinquefoil—that was all I prepared for her—*Potentilla reptans*—so good for the—for the—for the *bowels*." She brought that out with desperate primness even in the midst of tears. "The roots boiled in milk—that was *all*. I swear as I believe in God—I *never*—and you know it *was* just a little joke, Eliza asking, but I made you both swear never to tell— I was *sorry*, I only wanted to *help* her, and I *never*— Cinquefoil—that was all—I swear it—*potentilla reptans,* boiled in milk—"

The little hunch valid. Hunch be damned. One like Eliza—prey to all the flesh is heir to, like everybody else— Pure logical deduction.

EIGHTEEN

Mendoza brought all three of them back to Headquarters to make statements. It took some while to calm Mrs. Thirkettle down; in the end Hackett left Mendoza and Higgins working on it and went out and found Detective Grace, who accomplished it in a few minutes of soft-voiced reassurance.

"What a con man he'd have made," murmured Hackett.

"Now, ma'am, we aren't thinking anything wrong about you at all, we'd just like to have all the help you can give us. It could have been an accident of some sort, and you could help us find out—" Mrs. Thirkettle began to sit up and look less agitated. The other two were eager to talk; the difficulty was to shut them up temporarily. Mrs. Thirkettle was, so to speak, the horse's mouth.

"Accident—it must have been, of course, I'd *never*—"

"That's right, and we'd just like all the help you can give us," said Grace comfortably.

They started questioning her gently, and they got some illuminating—but not unexpected—facts.

"She just hated to ask me, you could tell—of course you could see why, she always boasted so much about her health and about never taking anything. But she wouldn't go and buy anything, she asked me— For one thing, she'd heard me say often enough how much less *expensive*—the prices they ask, when I can make up something just as good for— And, well, I *was* a tiny bit amused, but I didn't let her see it—you just didn't with Eliza—and I said I'd be glad to—

"What? Oh, well, she didn't want to *discuss* it in any way—I think she was ashamed, of course she paid me the *very small amount* it actually cost to prepare—twenty cents—the bottle. That was the arrangement." Mrs.

Thirkettle was almost recovered; she sent a tight-lipped look in Mrs. Hunt's direction. "And how anyone could think—"

"I never *said*, Tabitha—"

"Yes, well, what was the arrangement, Mrs. Thirkettle? Did she come to your house to pick it up?"

"Oh, dear me, no! She wouldn't— No, she said the best way would be for me to bring it to the store— You're going to think it was *queer*. And it was, but—but Eliza was terribly secretive, you know, and especially about this. The—the—well, she just *indicated* to me what she wanted, and I—the cinquefoil— Well, I brought it to the store every Monday, a week's supply, and she *was* so secretive, and in case there was a customer or her brother or someone was there she didn't want me to be seen *leaving* it even, you see, and the arrangement was she'd leave the back door open— on the little alley behind, you know—between ten and eleven every Monday, and I'd just slip in that way and leave the bottle on the shelf. And she'd leave the change for it—just what it cost me to prepare—ready there. I know it sounds queer, but—"

"Not particularly," said Mendoza, "considering her character." Sergeant Farrell was taking it all down in shorthand, to type up later. "In fact, quite in character."

"Well, that's what *I* thought, and I was sorry for her, but I'm afraid I had a little private laugh over it—all of us did—only I told Marcia and Ida she mustn't ever know I *told*— Never have forgiven me, and maybe I shouldn't have— What? Oh, it was all of two months ago—just after New Year's. And—what? Oh, no, I was always *most* careful no one ever saw me going in. I went up the entire alley from the other end of the block, and I'd only be there a minute, you know—the old bottle, the one she'd had the week before, and the money right there on the shelf, and I'd just pop the bottle into my shopping basket and leave the new one—I'm sure no one ever saw me. And do you know, even if she was alone in the store at the time, and heard me just drop in, she'd never come back to— Well, poor Eliza *was* a little queer. It was as if she was sort of trying to pretend it wasn't happening at all. I know it sounds funny, but—what? Oh, well, you take a fairly good bit of it at each dose. I told her half a cup a day. It was quart bottles. Just the roots boiled in milk—*nothing* else, it couldn't possibly have harmed her—"

"She kept the bottle in the store, didn't take it home with her?"

"Well, I imagine so. She wouldn't take the risk of anybody seeing it, I should—"

Yes, thought Mendoza, and here was their *modus operandi* all right.

Somebody had known about that besides—he thought—these three. Or was it the simple answer after all—Tabitha or one of the other two?

"And anybody who thinks one of *us* would have done such a wicked thing," burst out Ida Mae Glidden indignantly. "It's crazy! I'd never heard of that—what was it you called it?—fox something—until— Just crazy. And her leaving all that to us—I can't credit her *having* all that— Innocent as babes unborn, and you can't prove—"

The hell of it was, of course, they couldn't.

And why hadn't they found the current bottle in the store?

Mendoza and Grace asked the questions, heard it all over again, and Farrell typed it up and the three women signed three statements. Grace shepherded them tenderly down to the squad car summoned to take them home, thanking them effusively for their help, and came back to sit in on the discussion.

"—see there's no evidence," Hackett was saying as he came into the office, "but it's obvious. I'm surprised she came apart and admitted that much. Tabitha. She must have known about the will and jumped at the chance when Eliza asked—"

"The easy thing to think. There are points I don't like," said Mendoza. "If so, why *did* she come apart right away? And why in hell did she ever tell the other two? No point in that."

"She could have told them, just passing on the little joke," said Hackett, "and then afterwards decided to spike Eliza's medicine."

"All right. No foxglove in her yard or any place where anything had been dug up recently, and it doesn't seem to be a thing you can grow in a pot. Too big. And, you know, no bottle of cinquefoil or anything else found in that back room. According to Bainbridge, it was a cumulative thing—Tabitha or anybody else couldn't have known exactly when it would finally kill the woman—might have been almost any day, I suppose, after a certain duration—and how could she figure on getting the bottle back? With the evidence intact?"

"And if she didn't," said Grace, "she'd know—she knows enough for that—that an analysis of the stuff would point straight to her."

"*Pues sí.*"

"All right," said Higgins, "who? One of the other two? They knew the arrangements too. My God, people. Talk about queer. But you're right, of course, it was in character for Eliza. Since two months back she's been taking the homemade laxative—I gather that's what it was intended for—and, Bainbridge says, getting dosed with the foxglove at least five weeks." He rubbed his jaw. "Funny she didn't complain to Tabitha her simple wasn't any good, if—"

Mendoza grinned. "She mightn't have noticed the difference. These things so largely psychological sometimes. And I suppose she wouldn't have mentioned any change in taste to her either. Didn't want to discuss it —period, ashamed of taking any medicine at all—"

"Oscar was in the store sometimes, and Percy. And Miss Manning," said Grace thoughtfully.

"I doubt very much," said Mendoza, "that Eliza would have measured out her dosage where or when anybody could have seen her—or even suspected it . . . as far as *she* knew. Yes."

"Yes," said Hackett. "A very funny setup, but natural enough, Eliza being Eliza. I see that. So if you won't buy Tabitha, I still say it's got to be one of the other two—who got told the little joke in strict secrecy, knew about the arrangements—the very funny little arrangements—and waited, and took the chance every Monday morning, to substitute her own bottle of foxglove concoction."

"While the back door was still unlocked," said Higgins. "I'm willing to bet that was the only time it ever was unlocked, too."

"*Conforme*," said Mendoza absently. "So why, Art? How did any of them know about the will? We know pretty definitely what Eliza's intentions were about that. As announced to Carson, the lawyer. Foolish intentions, but that's beside the point. There the will was, still hidden—"

"We don't know she hadn't told one of them. Or all of them," said Grace even more thoughtfully. "I'll just put this in for what it's worth. You've got a nice little nest egg to leave, you make a magnanimous will— it's only human nature for you to want the legatees to know how kind you've been while you can still appreciate the grateful words."

"True," said Mendoza. He'd had that thought himself. "And if that's so, we'll never know for certain. But it strikes me—" He was silent and then said, "Just a bit too much of a coincidence, Jase?"

Grace shrugged and lit a cigarette.

"But this has got to be the M.O.," said Higgins. "Tabitha's brew. It's got to be, either direct from Tabitha or with a substitute bottle, because that was the only thing we now know Eliza was taking habitually in anything like the quantity Bainbridge said—"

"*Conforme*," said Mendoza again mechanically. He was staring unseeingly at the gold desk lighter. "That, I think, is the really valuable part of what Tabitha tells us. The *modus operandi*. I don't go for Tabitha. Or for either of the other two."

"You and your tortuous mind," said Hackett. "The obvious thing it mustn't be. I don't see why not. None of them is exactly the brainiest woman in the world. That Glidden woman—she's got the guts to do it, more than the other two, and she knew—"

"But how did any of them know about the will? I know, I know, we don't have to show motive, but there's got to *be* a motive, however slight, and there'd be no reason apart from the will for any of them to want to— I'll tell you what it says to me," said Mendoza suddenly. "If Jase is right and she had magnanimously told them about the will, then all three of them were in it together. They must have been. Only I don't think any of them is that good an actress, the way they've reacted all along the line. I really don't."

"But you've got to agree that the M.O.," began Higgins, when Mendoza stood up abruptly.

"*¡Pues vámonos va!* Come on, I want to take another look at that store. Shows how observant even a trained detective is, I don't remember whether that back door onto the alley has a pane of glass in it. We didn't pay much attention to it—just the back door, and locked when we looked around. Among us we may dredge up an idea."

Hackett refused to squeeze his bulk into the cramped confines of the Ferrari; he and Higgins drove over in the Barracuda. When they walked up the quarter-block from where he'd parked they found Mendoza and Grace just unlocking the front door of the secondhand store.

And what would happen to all this stuff, Hackett wondered, following them in and immediately barking his shins on a footstool in the dimness. All this junk. Not that: he stumbled over another stool, involuntarily clutched at the nearest piece of furniture to save himself, and came up with an old-fashioned plush-covered photograph album. Odds and ends finding their way down here, waiting to be pawed over by bargain seekers. Suddenly, threading his way up the aisle after the others, he saw this place—any secondhand shop—in a different light. Everything here had been a little piece of home to somebody sometime. Now just waiting here to, maybe, sometime and somewhere be part of home to somebody again.

"Damn forty-watt bulbs," said Mendoza ahead of him. A light came on. They crowded past the partition and looked at the little back room.

Shabby, rather dirty little room: half office, half kitchen. Single sink against the left-hand wall. Shelf above. Cupboards above and below to the right of that. Old desk in the corner. Straight chair: old Army cot with a cotton spread on it. The floor bare.

"She would, of course," said Mendoza, "have rinsed out the glass she took her dose in after drinking it. Possibly, if she hadn't liked the taste of Tabitha's brew, she'd have rinsed it out carefully and had a glass of water to wash it down. Which explains why the lab didn't pick up anything from the glass. And the door is solid." They looked at the back door onto the narrow little alley. Mendoza went over, unlocked it and opened it. Just an unpaved alley: a couple of trash cans.

"But," said Grace, "there's a window over the sink. If what's in your mind was somebody seeing her by chance from outside."

"It was," said Mendoza sadly. "But he'd have had to be about eight feet high, wouldn't he? The height of the window. And who in God's name along here would be enough interested—" He fell silent; his eyes roved around the room, up the walls, absently. With deliberation he got out a cigarette.

"I think you're reaching," said Hackett. "We've got the obvious answer, Luis. Who do we know *did* know about the medicine? Those three—"

"But what the hell happened to the bottle, Art?" asked Higgins plaintively. "You just said a while ago nobody could know even the exact day she'd die and be hanging around to—"

Mendoza uttered a loud yelp. "The bottle—¿y qué es esto? The bottle, for God's sake, the—" He dropped his unlighted cigarette.

They all turned to look at him, and he was staring up at the ceiling— the old-fashioned high ceiling, a good six feet above their heads. "What—" said Higgins.

"¡Donde menos se piensa salta la liebre!" said Mendoza softly, and wheeled and charged out. They went after him.

"What the hell—Luis, what—"

Mendoza went out the front door and turned left, down ten feet to the door leading up to the apartment above the store. It opened to his hand; they climbed after him, up dirty stairs in a mingled odor of old cabbage and dust and humanity, to the little square landing. The four of them crowded close there; Mendoza rapped sharply on the door.

A wait; he knocked again; a shuffle inside. The door creaked open a two-inch crack. "What d'you want? I'm busy fixin' my dinner—"

Mendoza shoved the door open and stepped across the threshold. "I just want to know, I'm just curious, Mrs. Stepp," he said politely. "Why did you want to poison Mrs. McCann?"

"For the love of—" said Higgins *sotto voce*.

She stared up at him, the little hunched scrawny old witchlike woman, without emotion of any sort on her face. And by this room she was living close to the bone: a sagging old couch with half its stuffing out, a straight chair, no rug, a glimpse into a slice of drab kitchenette with something redolent of onions on an unseen stove, another glimpse in the other direction of a cubbyhole bedroom with the foot of a cot visible.

"Why?" asked Mendoza. "I'd just like to know, to have the whole story, Mrs. Stepp." He smiled at her. "I know you did. It's the only answer that fits all the facts. You spied on her, didn't you? I didn't quite catch up to that until just a few minutes ago. You called her a hypocrite—and we knew this and that about her but nothing to suggest that, exactly, until we found out about the medicine she was taking in secret while she boasted about never taking any. You knew about that. That little hole in her ceiling and your floor—the way these old places were built—came in handy, didn't it?"

She worked her mouth a little without saying anything. "A miser," she said in her thin cracked old voice. "I seen her counting her money—*my* money, some of it—after she'd been round collectin' rents. Countin' it like a real woman'd number the hairs on the heads of her children. Children I had once, but they all went off. Ungrateful. Serpent's teeth, like the Bible says, I useta watch her, all right. Miser and evil she was."

"I'd say that convenient hole is somewhere in your kitchen," said Mendoza pleasantly. "In the ceiling of the little back room in the store. Yes. You saw—"

"Tellin' me if I'd take more exercise an' eat proper I wouldn't have no rheumatism. What's *she* know about livin' hard an' old? I lived here more 'n twenty years. Since my husband died. I could still go out an' work some then—cleanin' for people an' such. Not now I can't. I dunno what you mean."

"You saw her," said Mendoza, "taking the medicine out of the bottle. Pretty obviously medicine, when she'd be measuring it with a tablespoon or—and you were curious enough to keep watch and see the other woman bring the bottle—on Monday mornings—and see that the back door was unlocked. And so it was easy enough for you—when you made up your mind to do it—to wait until the woman had gone and whip down with your own prepared bottle of the foxglove infusion and substitute it. While the back door was still unlocked. I see that, Mrs. Stepp. In fact, you're the only one who could have done it, on all the facts. Because that morning Mrs. McCann died, you'd gone off somewhere early, but you'd come back, hadn't you? Without being noticed by anyone. And you saw all the excitement, you guessed what had happened—you'd been waiting for it to happen—and you seized the chance, all very canny, to come down and slip into the store and take the bottle back, didn't you? And I'd guess before the police arrived, when you saw Mr. Wolf hurry up and knew what had happened. That store's damn dark, and you would have crouched down between the stacks of furniture. Lee Rainey and Wolf likely either examining the body or backed off from it waiting for the police. And you got the bottle, knowing where to look for it, and hid it under your clothes. And once you'd got out to the front of the store again, it didn't matter if they saw you, you'd just come in to see what was going on. Was that how it was? But why, Mrs. Stepp? Why did you go to all the trouble?" His tone was merely curious.

She gave him her evil little smile. "You think you're plenty smart. I can say I never."

"We can probably find traces of the foxglove here. In your kitchen. We'll certainly look. I don't think it'll be hard to find evidence. Where'd you get the foxglove? Will we, maybe, find you grew up in the country and knew about that just casually?" Mendoza was smiling at her, hands in pockets, his voice soft.

Suddenly she laughed, a high broken cackle, and Hackett nearly jumped. "I'm eighty-four years old, mister," she said. "I'm a poor old woman and I ain't so much time left to me. You're a smart young fella. I guess nobody'd go to hang me, poor old woman. I talked to some folks around, times, they feed you pretty good in jail, I hear. I ain't got much time anyways, I been feelin' lately." She pulled her tattered old sweater closer around her thin shoulders. "And, anyways, I did for that bitch. I did. Miser and hypocrite and cruel to the old and the orphans. Layin' up treasure—I saw her countin' all the money. I don't mind tellin' you, young man, you askin' polite. Twenty years I been here, an' it's hard enough, anybody oughta know—nothin' but the pension an' prices like they are— twenty cents the day-old bread— And that bitch was gonna raise my rent! Again she was gonna raise it—went up to thirty in nineteen fifty-two— That bitch of a miser she was! Come tellin' me, when I paid her January's rent—April, she says, April it goes up five dollars— Five dollars—"

Of course, of course, the fiscal tax year. Canny Eliza.

"Thought, serve her right, comin' down on a poor old woman like me— got nothin' an' nobody left— And I'd seen her all right, her medicine! Thought at first as she was tipplin' like, private, the other woman fetchin' it for her—but the face she made drinkin' it I seen 'twas medicine some kind— And let me tell you, young man, us old folks know a thing or two as a lot of young folks don't! So we do. The foxglove—I knew 'bout that since I was a little girl." She cackled again. "They knocked some houses down over on San Pedro a while back—dunno what for—just left the lots empty—an' I happened to notice a pretty crop o' foxglove seeded itself there. Pretty flowers. It served that bitch right. Didn't know exactly when it'd do for her, but I watched her pretty steady through my spyhole, so I did. An' I see her that morning staggerin' round after she drunk it, and I figure to myself, be pretty soon. An' a while atter she went outta the back room, so's I couldn't see her through the hole no more, an' I was lookin' out my front window, I see that colored fella go in the store and right away come hurryin' out again, so I thinks maybe old bitch's got it at last. So I just slipped down to see for myself—didn't do no crawlin' around the place like you said! No, sir, I see she's dead, so I just got my bottle back an' out I slip again 'fore that colored fella come back with Mr. Wolf at all." She rocked back and forth a little, clutching the sweater around her, and moved her nearly toothless mouth. "Only I'm sorry now—"

"Sorry you killed her, Mrs. Stepp?"

"No," she said stolidly. "No, I ain't sorry for that. Gonna raise my *rent*. So I'd hafta move someplace cheaper—an' there just *ain't* no place cheaper. Takin' the food out o' my mouth. No place for a poor old woman to go. No. And I ain't like her—hard an' unfeelin'! I went down an' took that bottle back on account I didn't see no reason that other woman get blamed for nothin'. No. I ain't sorry. I see as how that stuff the other woman brung was whitey-like, so's I put in a little skim milk in what I made— color it—but I put in some Dago Red too—I keep a little for myself just now an' then—and I'm right sorry about that now. Waste o' good wine."

Grace uttered a little involuntary chuckle, and Mendoza said, "We'd like you to come with us now, Mrs. Stepp, and make a statement about this. Will you—"

"I'd best turn off the gas under the soup," she said unemotionally. She looked up at him. "They feed you pretty good in jail, don't they?"

"So I've heard."

She nodded. "I been gettin' kinda tired o' doin' for myself. Just let me turn off the gas."

"The built-in radar," said Hackett. "My God, who would have guessed—"

"Once I spotted the hole in the ceiling it was obvious," said Mendoza. "The only one right on the premises to take that bottle away."

He got derisive laughter. "My good God," said Higgins. "Going to raise the rent. That was the answer, after all the suggestive hijinks with Oscar and Henry and—"

"They'll find her incompetent, I suppose," said Grace. "She'll wind up at Camarillo."

"With Miss Manning," said Mendoza. He leaned back in his desk chair. There was still a lot of routine to do on the McCann case, but at least no more detecting. They'd be concentrating on this break-in artist and that footprint. He mentioned that. "Needle in a haystack. So we start all the routine. Art, suppose you—"

"It's after six now," said Hackett, "and tomorrow's my day off."

The very hell of a funny case, thought Higgins; but once in a while they came along, and at least they'd come up with the answer—which, despite their reputation, they didn't always do.

But at the moment he wasn't thinking about the McLaughlins or Eliza McCann or Gladys Stepp. He'd broiled himself a steak, and now, having tidily washed his dishes, he'd built himself a highball and was getting up courage to call Mary. Now as good a time as any. Try to put it over on her —the little scheme to get Stevie to summer camp.

He pulled the phone toward him. He wondered if he'd ever (him, George Higgins) get up the nerve to ask her to go out to dinner with him. To maybe call him by his first name.

His hand was sweaty on the phone. He dialed carefully.

At least he could do what he could for the kids.

"Hello?" she said in her warm sweet voice.

"Oh, Mrs. Dwyer," said Higgins, "this is Serg—uh, George Higgins. I just called to tell you—"

And Grace had a nebulous little idea about that break-in artist's footprint, having heard something about that new one from Piggott.

One like that they wanted to catch up with. Fast.

Business seemed to be picking up a little at Headquarters Homicide, he thought, absently winding his watch.

See Piggott first thing tomorrow and pass on the idea. . . .

"People, people," said Angel. "Sometimes you do wonder just how far we have progressed. By the way, it's your day off tomorrow, isn't it, and you've got to dig out that oleander, Art. I hadn't any *idea* it was poisonous, and you know how Mark—"

"Well," said Hackett, with a mental picture of the oleander, at least fifteen feet high and the roots probably going halfway to China, "we've got this new thing, kind of tough, and I might just want to drop down to the office a couple of—"

"*And* the baby," said Angel. "Everything in her mouth, and—"

"I'll dig it out, I'll dig it out," said Hackett hastily.

"Honestly, people," said Alison. "You wonder— *¡Cuidado!*"

Mendoza braced himself for Sheba's arrival on his shoulder and reached up to pluck her off. "So very ordinary—if slightly lunatic—when you know," he said, rubbing his shoulder where claws had dug in. "Of course the whole business—" Sitting on the bed, half undressed, he started to laugh. "God, those coffins. That night I'll never forget. Stories we do get to tell, *absolutamente.* Oscar—such an *upset*—" He rocked with mirth.

"I have the most awful feeling," said Alison, "that the rest of our lives, whenever we're invited out somewhere, I'll be saying, please don't tell the story about the embalmed corpses over the dinner table. Not everybody has such a macabre sense of humor as homicide cops."

"Don't be silly, *amada.* But what a business—" Mendoza took off his shirt, yawning. "Oh, well, at least we've cleaned it up. And now this damn break-in boy— I did have a stray thought about that footprint." He took off one shoe and stared at it thoughtfully.

"Shoptalk over dinner I will *just* stand," said Alison severely. "But *not* in bed, *amante.*"

"*Así, así,*" said Mendoza, and after quickly shedding the rest of his clothes, he slid in beside her.